THE COLLECTED STORIES OF ROBERT SILVERBERG

THE
COLLECTED
STORIES
OF
ROBERT
SILVERBERG

VOLUME 1
SECRET SHARERS

BANTAM BOOKS

NEW YORK   TORONTO   LONDON   SYDNEY   AUCKLAND

THE COLLECTED STORIES OF ROBERT SILVERBERG
VOLUME I: SECRET SHARERS
A Bantam Spectra Book / November 1992

Published simultaneously in hardcover and trade paperback

ACKNOWLEDGMENTS

"Symbiont," "Snake and Ocean, Ocean and Snake," "Tourist Trade," "The Pardoner's Tale," "The Dead Man's Eyes," and "A Sleep and a Forgetting" first appeared in *Playboy*; "Amanda and the Alien," "Hannibal's Elephants," "Multiples," "Against Babylon," "Hardware," and "To the Promised Land" first appeared in *Omni*; "Basileus" first appeared in *The Best of Omni*; "Homefaring" was first published as a limited-edition volume by Phantasia Press; "Sailing to Byzantium" and "The Secret Sharer" were first published as limited-edition volumes by Underwood-Miller; "Gate of Horn, Gate of Ivory" first appeared in *Universe*; "Chip Runner" and "Enter a Soldier. Later: Enter Another" first appeared in *Isaac Asimov's Science Fiction Magazine*; "House of Bones" first appeared in *Terry's Universe*; "Sunrise on Pluto" first appeared in *The Planets*; "Dancers in the Time-Flux" first appeared in *Heroic Visions*; "The Asenion Solution" first appeared in *Foundation's Friends*; "The Iron Star" first appeared in *The Universe*.

BOOK DESIGN BY CAROL MALCOLM-RUSSO

Library of Congress Cataloging-in-Publication Data

Silverberg, Robert.
The collected stories of Robert Silverberg.
p.   cm.
Contents: v. 1. Secret sharers.
ISBN 0-553-08996-X (hc)
ISBN 0-553-37068-5 (pbk)
1. Science fiction, American. I. Title.
PS3569.I472A6 1992
813'.54—dc20   92-9958
                                    CIP
Published simultaneously in the United States and Canada

Bantam Books are published by Bantam Books, a division of Bantam
Doubleday Dell Publishing Group, Inc. Its trademark, consisting of the
words "Bantam Books" and the portrayal of a rooster, is Registered in
U.S. Patent and Trademark Office and in other countries. Marca
Registrada. Bantam Books, 666 Fifth Avenue, New York, New York 10103.

PRINTED IN THE UNITED STATES OF AMERICA

FFG   0 9 8 7 6 5 4 3 2 1

For
GARDNER DOZOIS
ELLEN DATLOW
BYRON PREISS
SHAWNA McCARTHY
DON MYRUS
MARTA RANDALL
BETH MEACHAM
GREG BENFORD
JIM BAEN
MARTIN HARRY GREENBERG
JESSICA AMANDA SALMONSON
GEORGE SCITHERS
and—especially—
ALICE K. TURNER

CONTENTS

CONTENTS

Introduction

Since the beginning of my writing career, almost forty years ago, I've always written both novels and short stories. My first professional sale was a short story and the second was a novel, or perhaps it was the other way around; I no longer remember which came first. But the rhythm of my writing life was established right at the beginning: a few short stories, then a novel, then some more short stories, and then another book. I never thought twice, or even once, about whether I was primarily a short-story writer or a novelist. I was a writer, period. I've always written at whatever length seemed appropriate to the story at hand; and, because I have always been a writer by trade rather than one who follows the ebb and flow of inspiration, I've also written according to the needs of the marketplace. When it was novel-writing time, I wrote novels. When editors wanted short stories from me, I wrote short stories.

It isn't that way with all writers. Some are distinctly novelists, and some are not. Ray Bradbury has written a couple of novels, but he's basically a short-story writer. The same is true of Harlan Ellison. On the other hand, John Le Carré and John Fowles may have written short stories at some time in their lives, but I haven't seen them, if they exist. (Fowles occasionally writes novellas, at least.) Robert A. Heinlein wrote few if any short stories after the first dozen years of his career. Hemingway's lifetime output of short stories was enough to fill one good-sized volume, but he, too, wrote most of them in his first dozen years.

I could make long lists of writers who are basically one thing or the other, but not both. On one hand are the novelists for whom short stories, after their early years of writing, are rare or nonexistent events. In science fiction and fantasy the names of Frank Herbert, E.E. Smith, Jack Vance, Stephen Donaldson, and Andre Norton come quickly to mind; outside it, those of Graham Greene, Evelyn Waugh, William Golding, John Steinbeck, Norman Mailer. And then there are the short-story writers whose ventures into longer lengths are just as uncommon: Theodore Sturgeon, Clark Ashton Smith, William Tenn, and Damon Knight; Edgar Allan Poe, John Collier, William Trevor, and Mavis Gallant.

Certainly temperament has something to do with this. Some writers feel impossibly cramped within the rigid confines of the short story: they need hundreds of thousands of words to move around in. Others see the novel as a vast and interminable journey that they would rather not undertake, and prefer the quick, incisive thrust of the short story. But then there are those who are masters of both forms and choose in the second half of their careers to work in only one, usually the novel, like Hemingway or Heinlein; surely the author of "The Snows of Kilimanjaro" and "Capital of the World" still knew how to write short stories after 1940, and the author of "Requiem" and "The Green Hills of Earth" did not mysteriously lose his ability at the short lengths around 1949; but *For Whom the Bell Tolls* and *Stranger in a Strange Land* were matters of higher priority and the short stories ceased. It's harder to cite writers who gave up novels after an early start to concentrate only on the short story: Paul Bowles, perhaps, or Truman Capote.

In today's science-fiction field, very few of the well-established writers bother much about short fiction, and even the newcomers tend to move on as quickly as they can to immense trilogies. There's a simple economic reason for this. Checking the most recent volume—1988—of the encyclopedic yearbook of science fiction and fantasy compiled by Charles N. Brown and William G. Contento, I discover that 317 original s-f novels and 264 fantasy novels were published in the United States in 1988, up from 298 and 256, respectively, the previous year. The five professional science-fiction magazines in 1988 managed to put out a total of just 49 issues. If they averaged six short stories an issue, that would be a grand total of 294 published during the entire year. (Plus, let's say, 150 more in the various book-format anthologies devoted to original s-f stories, and in the slick magazines like *Playboy* and *Omni*.)

That means that for each short science-fiction story published in 1988 (for which the author might have received anywhere from $150 or so up to a maximum of $5000 in a very few cases), there were 1.3 s-f or fantasy novels published (and for novels the pay begins at about $2500 and goes up into the stratosphere). The arithmetic, for the professional writer, is unanswerable. Writing short stories doesn't make much sense financially. If you write them today you have to want to write them for their own sake. The pay is almost incidental: you do them for love.

Or, in my case, because you really can't stop yourself.

When I was starting out as a writer in the 1950s, things worked the other way around. Unless your name was Heinlein or Asimov, you didn't think much about getting books published. If you wrote for a living, you wrote short stories and novelettes for the magazines, just as quickly as you could. The magazines would pay you anywhere from one to three cents a word: a 5,000-word story therefore would bring you $50 to $150, before such things as your agent's commission and the exactions of the Internal Revenue Service were figured in. It wasn't much, but at least the market was big—fifteen or twenty different magazines, most years, many of them published every month—and if you worked fast enough, under a variety of pseudonyms so that the readers didn't weary of your name, you might hope to earn $15,000 a year or so, not a bad livelihood back then, when rent on a fine apartment in New York City was $150 a month and dinner for two at a deluxe restaurant cost no more than $25, wine included.

To do that, though, you had to write and sell a short story to some magazine or other a couple of times a week, every week of the year—a constant, unending stream of publishable material. You needed not only to be capable of generating story concepts at will but to be cognizant at all times of each magazine's buying status—which one was in desperate need of copy, which one was currently overstocked, which one was overstocked on *your* stuff and didn't want to look at any more just now. It was an insane way to live and an almost impossible thing to succeed at; but those of us who chose to live that way and who did actually succeed at it usually didn't realize it couldn't be done, and so we just went ahead and did it.

Coming up with two or three worthwhile story ideas a week—especially in a field like science fiction, where you invented some new world or even a universe every time out—was a formidable proposition. Now and then you might be able to stretch an idea to 15,000 or 20,000 words and sell it for $500 or so, which gave you a little time to breathe between manuscripts. A rejection, of course, was a catastrophe. (But there were so many magazines that a capable writer could usually count on selling his stories *somewhere*, possibly on the fifth or sixth attempt.) Writing books, for which one major idea would suffice if you could devise enough subsidiary themes to keep the story going for 60,000 words or thereabouts, was one way off the treadmill. But the market for novels was an extremely slender one—just three publishers, as of the late 1950s, buying perhaps fifty or sixty books a year, most of them from old-line writers recycling their magazine serials of the 1940s. If he could break into the charmed circle a beginner might actually be able to sell a book or two a year, at $1000 or $1500 each, but it took weeks to write one and there was always the ghastly possibility that none of the three markets would want to buy it.

It was, in other words, a tough time to be a science-fiction writer. You had to be very stubborn, very resilient, and very prolific in order to survive. It helped also if you were young, young enough to stay up all night if necessary to knock out a story to meet some editor's sudden request for help, and I was the youngest one in the business those days, not much past twenty, full of crazed vitality and drive of a sort that was already beginning to diminish among the old guys in their thirties who were my rivals for those few places on the contents pages of the magazines, guys like Fred Pohl, Ted Sturgeon, Phil Dick, Bob Sheckley. So I earned a fair living and always paid the rent on time, and eventually things got a lot easier for us all. But I never had the luxury of being able to think of myself as a "novelist" or a "short story writer" or any other kind of specialist. I wrote what seemed to make the most sense to write. If Don Wollheim over at Ace Books said he was having trouble that summer finding novels to publish, I wrote a novel for him. If John Campbell at *Astounding Science Fiction* let it slip that he was running short of stories in the 7,500-word range, I would have one for him the following Monday. One doesn't necessarily produce a lot of undying masterpieces that way, but one does, at least, hone one's versatility and command of technique.

Today, of course, everything is different. I haven't had to worry about paying next month's rent for a long time, and my novels are contracted for three and four years in advance at prices that would have been beyond all belief when I was starting out. My annual income isn't up there with the earnings of the phenomenal Messrs. X., Y., and Z., whose books spend weeks at a time at the top of the best-seller lists, but it's lofty enough to seem startling to someone who remembers writing stories at a cent a word as fast as he could type. My economic situation is secure, as such things go for writers, and my future earnings are assured for years to come—all from novels. And yet I continue to write two, three, even four short stories a year, and the occasional novella of 25,000 words or so. Why? Certainly not for the money. Even though a magazine like *Omni* or *Playboy* will pay me considerably more for a short story than I used to earn from a novel thirty years ago, I'd still be better off putting in the time on a book. Short stories are bothersome things to write, at least for me. They can't be turned out in joyous, breathless bursts. Instead I have to carve them out of recalcitrant rock, chipping away constantly at extraneous material that conceals or deforms the ideal shape of the material. Usually I need to do two or three drafts before submission to get them properly into focus, and sometimes (as you'll see from the introductions to some of the stories in this book) it's necessary to do another couple of rounds of revision after the editor has had a chance to read it. Even at today's elevated story prices, I'm earning a very routine wage indeed by the time the job is done.

But sometimes, even for the professional, more than just the money is involved.

This discussion so far has concentrated almost entirely on the production side of writing. I haven't said a word about art; I might just as well have been talking about manufacturing bookcases, or raising potatoes, or some other useful and straightforward activity in which the muses aren't generally considered to be involved. I've made it more than clear that writing is my business: that I am in the profession of producing verbal objects that I place on sale to the highest bidder. I chose from the outset to make writing my sole means of support, and so I have always worked hard, produced my verbal objects at a steady pace, and taken care to be paid, and well, for my labor.

Well I know Samuel Johnson's famous line, "No man but a blockhead ever wrote except for money," and I can certainly see the point of it, especially on the days when there's blood on the computer keys after I've finished working. All the same, writing fiction *is* different from manufacturing bookcases or raising potatoes. The muses *are* involved, however much the writer wants to think of himself as nothing more than a hard-nosed businessman. And a lifetime devoted exclusively to maximizing one's income per word seems to me like a pretty stultifying affair. Money's a useful thing, and you won't hear me say a word against it. But a writer who's totally money-oriented—who writes the same thing over and over, for example, or who writes things that he despises, or who writes with only a fraction of his skill because he thinks his readers are simpleminded, or who writes about things that don't interest him because that's where the money is—is a writer who over the years will dry out from within, whose spirit will corrode and decay, who will sooner or later find himself embittered and hollow, trapped in an anger he can barely understand.

I've done my share of writing purely for money, when circumstances made that necessary. And I'm not one to write purely for the love of the art—sonnet sequences, let's say, that I stash away in the secret recesses of my desk. I write for publication and for pay, not for private pleasure. But I try to guard myself against the death of the soul that comes from making money the be-all and end-all of my days.

Novels are more lucrative to write than short stories, and, for me at least, they're easier to do, page for page. Nevertheless, although novel-writing is my main line of work and my chief source of income (and a considerable source of pride and pleasure, when things go the right way), I do continue to do short stories, however much sweat and pain they may cost me, because of the challenge that they represent and because I don't care to exempt myself from the harsh discipline of creating something that's complete in twenty or thirty pages. (Or sometimes eighty or ninety, in the case of novellas like "Sailing to Byzantium" or "The Secret Sharer.") I never lose sight of my professionalism even then, and you will see again and again that this story or that in this book was written at the request or suggestion of some editor, rather than out of dire internal compulsion. But a dire internal compulsion is there nonetheless: the compulsion each year to test myself against the rigorous demands of the shorter forms. It's an exhausting kind of mental exercise that gets harder all the time. I'd just as soon allow myself to give it up altogether—which is why I don't dare stop.

I did in fact stop writing short stories once, in 1973—the prelude to a total withdrawal from writing, the first and only one of my life, that was to last the next five years. As I noted in the introduction to my previous collection of short stories, *The Conglomeroid Cocktail Party* (1984), my life had taken a troubled turn then and I had grown weary, disheartened, generally sick of everything—especially writing. Putting even more words on paper, concocting still more stories of imaginary and remote times and places, had begun to seem pointless to me. So I gave it up. I thought I was quitting it forever. As things turned out, "forever" lasted until the autumn of 1978, when I began to write the novel *Lord Valentine's Castle,* and by January of 1980 I had begun writing short stories again, too. The first products of that return to my metier were assembled in *The Conglomeroid Cocktail Party.* Here is the next installment: stories written between November 1981 and September 1988.

I've written other short stories since the last of these was completed. They, too, will be collected someday, I hope, along with ones yet to be written or even conceived. If all goes well, I'll be starting on a new story next week. Not because I need to, or even because I especially want to, but because—it sounds very romantic, I guess, though I'm not a very romantic person—because I *have* to. There are plenty of other things I'd rather be doing, I have to admit—tidying up the garden, perhaps, or taking a trip up the coast, or just sitting in the sunshine and giggling quietly to myself. But story first, sunshine afterward. I won't allow it to be any other way. I can't.

INTRODUCTION

Somehow, for all my pretense of cold-eyed professionalism, all my insistence that writing is simply a job like any other, I've discovered to my surprise and chagrin that there's more than that going on around here, that I write as much out of karmic necessity and some dire inner need constantly to rededicate my own skills to my—what? My craft? My art? My profession? All three, I suspect. The short stories collected here testify to that. I wrote them for money, Dr. Johnson. But I could very likely have made even more money if I had spent the time in other ways. Mainly I wrote these stories because I couldn't *not* write them. Does that make me a blockhead, Dr. Johnson? Perhaps it does. Perhaps choosing to be a writer in the first place, for whatever reason, is a blockheaded thing to do. Well, so be it. Here is a book of stories. They involved me in a lot of hard work, but for me, at least, the results justify the toil. I'm glad I wrote them, however big a headache some of them caused me at the time. Writing them, it turns out, was important for me, and even pleasurable, in a curiously complex ex post facto way. May they give you pleasure now, too, of a less complicated kind.

—Robert Silverberg
Oakland, California
June 1990

H O M E F A R I N G

I had always had a sneaking desire to write the definitive giant-lobster story. Earlier science-fiction writers had preempted most of the other appealing monstrosities—including giant aunts (sic!), dealt with by Isaac Asimov in his classic story "Dreamworld," which I have just ruined forever for you by giving away its punch line—but giant lobsters remained fair game. And when George Scithers, the new editor of the venerable science-fiction magazine Amazing Stories, asked me to do a lengthy story for him, I decided that it was time at last for me to give lobsters their due.

The obvious giant-lobster story, in which horrendous pincer-wielding monsters twenty feet long come ashore at Malibu and set about the conquest of Los Angeles by terrorizing the surfers, might work well enough in a cheap Hollywood sci-fi epic, but it wouldn't stand much chance of delighting a sophisticated science-fiction reader like Scithers. Nor did it have a lot of appeal for me as a writer. Therefore, following the advice of one of my early mentors, the brilliant, cantankerous editor Horace Gold, I searched for my story idea by turning the obvious upside down. Lobsters are pretty nasty things, after all. They're tough, surly, dangerous, and ugly—surely the ugliest food objects ever to be prized by mankind. A creature so disagreeable in so many ways must have some redeeming feature. (Other than the flavor of its meat.) Lobsters are quite intelligent, as crustaceans go. And so, instead of depicting them as the savage and hideous-looking critters they really are, what about putting them through a few hundred million years of evolution and turning them into wise and thoughtful civilized beings—the dominant life-form, in fact, of a vastly altered Earth?

A challenging task, yes. And made even more challenging for me, back there in the otherwise sunny and pleasant November of 1982, by the fact that I had just made the great leap from typewriter to computer. "Homefaring" marked my initiation into the world of floppy disks and soft hyphens, of backup copies and automatic pagination. It's all second nature to me by now, of course, but in 1982 it was a brave new world, and a very strange one. Each day's work was an adventure in terror. My words appeared in white letters on a black screen, frighteningly impermanent: one electronic sneeze, I thought, and a whole day's brilliant prose could vanish like a time traveler who has just retroactively defenestrated his own grandfather. The mere making of backups didn't lull my fears: how could I be sure that the act of backing up itself wouldn't erase what I had just written? Pushing the button marked "Save"—did that really save anything? Switching the computer off at the end of my working day was like a leap into the abyss. Would the story be there the next morning when I turned the machine on again? Warily I printed out each day's work when it was done, before backing up, saving, or otherwise jiggling with it: I wanted to see it safely onto paper first. Sometimes when I put a particularly difficult section together—for example, the three-page scene at the midpoint of the story, beginning with the line, "The lobsters were singing as they marched"—I would stop right then and there and print it out before proceeding, aware that if the computer somehow were to destroy it I would never be able to reconstruct it at that level of accomplishment. (It's an axiom among writers that material written to replace inadvertently destroyed copy can't possibly equal the lost passage—which gets better and better in one's memory all the time.)

Somehow, in fear and trembling, I tiptoed my way through the entire eighty-eight-page manuscript of "Homefaring" without any major disasters. The computer made it marvelously easy to revise the story as I went along; instead of typing out an eighty-eight-page first draft, then covering it with alterations and grimly typing the whole thing out again to make it fit to show an editor, I brought every paragraph up to final-draft status with painless little maneuvers of the cursor. When I realized that I had chosen a confusing name for a minor character, I ordered the computer to correct my error, and sat back in wonder as "Eitel" became "Bleier" throughout the story without my having to do a thing. And then at the end came the wondrous moment when I pushed the button marked "Print" and page after page of immaculate typed copy began to come forth while I occupied myself with other and less dreary tasks.

The readers liked the story and it was a finalist in the 1983 Nebula Award voting—perhaps might even had won, if it had been published in a magazine less obscure than dear old Amazing, which had only a handful of readers. That same year the veteran connoisseur of science fiction, Donald A. Wollheim, chose it for his annual World's Best SF anthology, an honor that particularly pleased me. I had deliberately intended "Homefaring" as a sleek and modern version of the sort of imagination-stirring tale of wonder that Wollheim had read and cherished in the s-f magazines of his youth, fifty years before, and his choice of the story for his book confirmed my feeling of working within a great tradition.

McCulloch was beginning to molt. The sensation, inescapable and unarguable, horrified him—it felt exactly as though his body was going to split apart, which it was—and yet it was also completely familiar, expected, welcome. Wave after wave of keen and dizzying pain swept through him. Burrowing down deep in the sandy bed, he waved his great claws about, lashed his flat tail against the pure white sand, scratched frantically with quick worried gestures of his eight walking-legs.

He was frightened. He was calm. He had no idea what was about to happen to him. He had done this a hundred times before.

The molting prodrome had overwhelming power. It blotted from his mind all questions, and, after a moment, all fear. A white line of heat ran down his back—no, down the top of his carapace—from a point just back of his head to the first flaring segments of his tail-fan. He imagined that all the sun's force, concentrated through some giant glass lens, was being inscribed in a single track along his shell. And his soft inner body was straining, squirming, expanding, filling the carapace to overflowing. But still that rigid shell contained him, refusing to yield to the pressure. To McCulloch it was much like being inside a wet suit that was suddenly five times too small.

—What is the sun? What is glass? What is a lens? What is a wet suit?

The questions swarmed suddenly upward in his mind like little busy many-legged creatures springing out of the sand. But he had no time for providing answers. The molting prodrome was developing with astounding swiftness, carrying him along. The strain was becoming intolerable. In another moment he would surely burst. He was writhing in short angular convulsions. Within his claws, his tissues now were shrinking, shriveling, drawing back within the ferocious shell-hulls, but the rest of him was continuing inexorably to grow larger.

He had to escape from this shell, or it would kill him. He had to expel himself somehow from this impossibly constricting container. Digging his front claws and most of his legs into the sand, he heaved, twisted, stretched, pushed. He thought of himself as being pregnant with himself, struggling fiercely to deliver himself of himself.

Ah. The carapace suddenly began to split.

The crack was only a small one, high up near his shoulders—*shoulders?*—but the imprisoned substance of him surged swiftly toward it, widening and lengthening it, and in another moment the hard horny covering was cracked from end to end. *Ah. Ah.* That felt so good, that release from constraint! Yet McCulloch still had to free himself. Delicately he drew himself backward, withdrawing leg after leg from its covering in a precise, almost fussy way, as though he were pulling his arms from the sleeves of some incredibly ancient and frail garment.

Until he had his huge main claws free, though, he knew he could not extricate himself from the sundered shell. And freeing the claws took extreme care. The front limbs still were shrinking, and the limy joints of the shell seemed to be dissolving and softening, but nevertheless he had to pull each claw through a passage much narrower than itself. It was easy to see how a hasty move might break a limb off altogether.

He centered his attention on the task. It was a little like telling his wrists to make themselves small, so he could slide them out of handcuffs.

—Wrists? Handcuffs? What are those?

McCulloch paid no attention to that baffling inner voice. Easy, easy, there—ah—yes, there, like that! One claw was free. Then the other, slowly, carefully. Done. Both of them retracted. The rest was simple: some shrugging and wiggling, exhausting but not really challenging, and he succeeded in extending the breach in the carapace until he could crawl backward out of it. Then he lay on the sand beside it, weary, drained, naked, soft, terribly vulnerable. He wanted only to return to the sleep out of which he had emerged into this nightmare of shell-splitting.

But some force within him would not let him slacken off. A moment to rest, only a moment. He looked to his left, toward the discarded shell. Vision was difficult—there were peculiar, incomprehensible refraction effects that broke every image into thousands of tiny fragments—but despite that, and despite the dimness of the light, he was able to see that the shell, golden-hued with broad arrow-shaped red markings, was something like a lobster's, yet even more intricate, even more bizarre. McCulloch did not understand why he had been inhabiting a lobster's shell. Obviously because he was a lobster; but he was not a lobster. That was so, was it not? Yet he was under water. He lay on fine white sand, at a depth so great he could not make out any hint of sunlight overhead. The water was warm, gentle, rich with tiny tasty creatures and with a swirling welter of sensory data that swept across his receptors in bewildering abundance.

He sought to learn more. But there was no further time for resting and thinking now. He was unprotected. Any passing enemy could destroy him while he was like this. Up, up, seek a hiding place: that was the requirement of the moment.

First, though, he paused to devour his old shell. That, too, seemed to be the requirement of the moment; so he fell upon it with determination, seizing it with his clumsy-looking but curiously versatile front claws, drawing it toward his busy, efficient mandibles. When that was accomplished—no doubt to recycle the lime it contained, which he needed for the growth of his new shell—he forced himself up and began a slow scuttle, somehow knowing that the direction he had taken was the right one.

Soon came the vibrations of something large and solid against his sensors—a wall, a stone mass rising before him—and then, as he continued, he made out with his foggy vision the sloping flank of a dark broad cliff rising vertically from the ocean floor. Festoons of thick, swaying red and yellow water plants clung to it, and a dense stippling of rubbery-looking finger-shaped sponges, and a crawling, gaping, slithering host of crabs and mollusks and worms, which vastly stirred McCulloch's appetite. But this was not a time to pause to eat, lest he be eaten. Two enormous green anemones yawned nearby, ruffling their voluptuous membranes seductively, hopefully. A dark shape passed overhead, huge, tubular, tentacular, menacing. Ignoring the thronging populations of the rock, McCulloch picked his way over and around them until he came to the small cave, the McCulloch-sized cave, that was his goal.

Gingerly he backed through its narrow mouth, knowing there would be no room for turning around once he was inside. He filled the opening nicely, with a little space left over. Taking up a position just within the entrance, he blocked the cave mouth with his claws. No enemy could enter now. Naked though he was, he would be safe during his vulnerable period.

For the first time since his agonizing awakening, McCulloch had a chance to halt: rest, regroup, consider.

It seemed a wise idea to be monitoring the waters just outside the cave even while he was resting, though. He extended his antennae a short distance into the swarming waters, and felt at once the impact, again, of a myriad sensory inputs, all the astounding complexity of the reef world. Most of the creatures that moved slowly about on the face of the reef were simple ones, but Mc-Culloch could feel, also, the sharp pulsations of intelligence coming from several points not far away: the anemones, so it seemed, and that enormous squidlike thing hovering overhead. Not intelligence of a kind that he understood, but that did not trouble him: for the moment, understanding could wait, while he dealt with the task of recovery from the exhausting struggles of his molting. Keeping the antennae moving steadily in slow sweeping circles of surveillance, he began systematically to shut down the rest of his nervous system, until he had attained the rest state that he knew—how?—was optimum for the rebuilding of his shell. Already his soft new carapace was beginning to grow rigid as it absorbed water, swelled, filtered out and utilized the lime. But he would have to sit quietly a long while before he was fully armored once more.

He rested. He waited. He did not think at all.

✦

After a time his repose was broken by that inner voice, the one that had been trying to question him during the wildest moments of his molting. It spoke without sound, from a point somewhere within the core of his torpid consciousness.

—Are you awake?

—I am now, McCulloch answered irritably.

—I need definitions. You are a mystery to me. What is a McCulloch?

—A man.

—That does not help.

—A male human being.

—That also has no meaning.

—Look, I'm tired. Can we discuss these things some other time?

—This is a good time. While we rest, while we replenish ourself.

—Ourselves, McCulloch corrected.

—Ourself is more accurate.

—But there are two of us.

—Are there? Where is the other?

McCulloch faltered. He had no perspective on his situation, none that made any sense. —One inside the other, I think. Two of us in the same body. But definitely two of us. McCulloch and not-McCulloch.

—I concede the point. There are two of us. You are within me. Who are you?

—McCulloch.

—So you have said. But what does that mean?

—I don't know.

✦

The voice left him alone again. He felt its presence nearby, as a kind of warm node somewhere along his spine, or whatever was the equivalent of his spine, since he did not think invertebrates had spines. And it was fairly clear to him that he was an invertebrate.

He had become, it seemed, a lobster, or, at any rate, something lobsterlike. Implied in that was transition: *he had become.* He had once been something else. Blurred, tantalizing memories of the something else that he once had been danced in his consciousness. He remembered hair, fingers, fingernails, flesh. Clothing: a kind of removable exoskeleton. Eyelids, ears, lips: shadowy concepts all, names without substance, but there was a certain elusive reality to them, a volatile, tricky plausibility. Each time he tried to apply one of those concepts to himself—"fingers," "hair," "man," "McCulloch"—it slid away, it would not stick. Yet all the same, those terms had some sort of relevance to him.

The harder he pushed to isolate that relevance, though, the harder it was to maintain his focus on any part of that soup of half-glimpsed notions in which his mind seemed to be swimming. The thing to do, McCulloch decided, was to go slow, try not to force understanding, wait for comprehension to seep back into his mind. Obviously he had had a bad shock, some major trauma, a total disorientation. It might be days before he achieved any sort of useful integration.

A gentle voice from outside his cave said, "I hope that your Growing has gone well."

Not a voice. He remembered voice: vibration of the air against the eardrums. No air here, maybe no eardrums. This was a stream of minute chemical messengers spurting through the mouth of the little cave and rebounding off the thousands of sensory filaments on his legs, tentacles, antennae, carapace, and tail. But the effect was one of words having been spoken. And it was distinctly different from that other voice, the internal one, that had been questioning him so assiduously a little while ago.

"It goes extremely well," McCulloch replied: or was it the other inhabitant of his body that had framed the answer? "I grow. I heal. I stiffen. Soon I will come forth."

"We feared for you." The presence outside the cave emanated concern, warmth, intelligence. Kinship. "In the first moments of your Growing, a strangeness came from you."

"Strangeness is within me. I am invaded."

"Invaded? By what?"

"A McCulloch. It is a man, which is a human being."

"Ah. A great strangeness indeed. Do you need help?"

McCulloch answered, "No. I will accommodate to it."

And he knew that it was the other within himself who was making these answers, though the boundary between their identities was so indistinct that he had a definite sense of being the one who shaped these words. But how could that be? He had no idea how one shaped words by sending squirts of body fluid into the all-surrounding ocean fluid. That was not his language. His language was—

—words—

—English words—

He trembled in sudden understanding. His antennae thrashed wildly, his many legs jerked and quivered. Images churned in his suddenly boiling mind: bright lights, elaborate equipment, faces, walls, ceilings. People moving about him, speaking in low tones, occasionally addressing words to him, English words—

—*Is English what all McCullochs speak?*

—*Yes.*

—*So English is human-language?*

—*Yes. But not the only one,* said McCulloch. *I speak English, and also German and a little—French. But other humans speak other languages.*

—*Very interesting. Why do you have so many languages?*

—*Because—because—we are different from one another, we live in different countries, we have different cultures—*

—*This is without meaning again. There are many creatures, but only one language, which all speak with greater or lesser skill, according to their destinies.*

McCulloch pondered that. After a time he replied:

—*Lobster is what you are. Long body, claws and antennae in front, many legs, flat tail in back. Different from, say, a clam. Clams have shell on top, shell on bottom, soft flesh in between, hinge connecting. You are not like that. You have lobster body. So you are lobster.*

Now there was silence from the other.

Then—after a long pause—

—*Very well. I accept the term. I am lobster. You are human. They are clams.*

—*What do you call yourselves in your own language?*

Silence.

—*What's your own name for yourself? Your individual self, the way my individual name is McCulloch and my species name is human being?*

Silence.

—*Where am I, anyway?*

Silence, still, so prolonged and utter that McCulloch wondered if the other being had withdrawn itself from his consciousness entirely. Perhaps days went by in this unending silence, perhaps weeks: he had no way of measuring the passing of time. He realized that such units as days or weeks were without meaning now. One moment succeeded the next, but they did not aggregate into anything continuous.

At last came a reply.

—*You are in the world, human McCulloch.*

➤

Silence came again, intense, clinging, a dark warm garment. McCulloch made no attempt to reach the other mind. He lay motionless, feeling his carapace thicken. From outside the cave came a flow of impressions of passing beings, now differentiating themselves very sharply: he felt the thick fleshy pulses of the two anemones, the sharp stabbing presence of the squid, the slow ponderous broadcast of something dark and winged, and, again and again, the bright, comforting, unmistakable output of other lobster creatures. It was a busy, complex world out there. The McCulloch part of him longed to leave the cave and explore it. The lobster part of him rested, content within its tight shelter.

He formed hypotheses. He had journeyed from his own place to this place, damaging his mind in the process, though now his mind seemed to be reconstructing itself steadily, if erratically. What sort of voyage? To another world? No: that seemed wrong. He did not believe that conditions so much like the ocean floor of Earth would be found on another—

Earth.

All right: significant datum. He was human, he came from Earth. And he was still on Earth. In the ocean. He was—what?—a land-dweller, an air-breather, a biped, a flesh-creature, a human. And now he was within the body of a lobster. Was that it? The entire human race, he thought, has migrated into the bodies of lobsters, and here we are on the ocean floor, scuttling about, waving our claws and feelers, going through difficult and dangerous moltings—

Or maybe I'm the only one. A scientific experiment, with me as the subject: man into lobster. That brightly lit room that he remembered, the intricate gleaming equipment all about him—that was the laboratory, that was where they had prepared him for his transmigration, and then they had thrown the switch and hurled him into the body of—

No. No. Makes no sense. Lobsters, McCulloch reflected, are low-phylum creatures with simple nervous systems, limited intelligence. Plainly the mind he had entered was a complex one. It asked thoughtful questions. It carried on civilized conversations with its friends, who came calling like ceremonious Japanese gentlemen, offering expressions of solicitude and goodwill.

New hypothesis: that lobsters and other low-phylum animals are actually quite intelligent, with minds roomy enough to accept the sudden insertion of a human being's entire neural structure, but we in our foolish anthropocentric way have up till now been too blind to perceive—

No. Too facile. You could postulate the secretly lofty intelligence of the world's humble creatures, all right: you could postulate anything you wanted. But that didn't make it so. Lobsters did not ask questions. Lobsters did not come calling like ceremonious Japanese gentlemen. At least, not the lobsters of the world he remembered.

Improved lobsters? Evolved lobsters? Superlobsters of the future?

—*When am I?*

Into his dizzied broodings came the quiet disembodied internal voice of not-McCulloch, his companion:

—*Is your displacement, then, one of time rather than space?*

—*I don't know. Probably both. I'm a land creature.*

—*That has no meaning.*

—*I don't live in the ocean. I breathe air.*

From the other consciousness came an expression of deep astonishment tinged with skepticism.

—*Truly? That is very hard to believe. When you are in your own body you breathe no water at all?*

—*None. Not for long, or I would die.*

—*But there is so little land! And no creatures live upon it. Some make short visits there. But nothing can dwell there very long. So it has always been. And so will it be, until the time of the Molting of the World.*

McCulloch considered that. Once again he found himself doubting that he was still on Earth. A world of water? Well, that could fit into his hypothesis of having journeyed forward in time, though it seemed to add a layer of implausibility upon implausibility. How many millions of years, he wondered, would it take for nearly all the Earth to have become covered with water? And he answered himself: In about as many as it would take to evolve a species of intelligent invertebrates.

Suddenly, terribly, it all fit together. Things crystallized and clarified in his mind, and he found access to another segment of his injured and redistributed memory; and he began to comprehend what had befallen him, or, rather, what he had willingly allowed himself to undergo. With that comprehension came a swift stinging sense of total displacement and utter loss, as though he were drowning and desperately tugging at strands of seaweed in a futile attempt to pull himself back to the surface. All that was real to him, all that he was part of, everything that made sense—gone, gone, perhaps irretrievably gone, buried under the weight of uncountable millennia, vanished, drowned, forgotten, reduced to mere geology. It was unthinkable, it was unacceptable, it was impossible, and as the truth of it bore in on him he found himself choking on the frightful vastness of time past.

But that bleak sensation lasted only a moment and was gone. In its place came excitement, delight, confusion, and a feverish throbbing curiosity about this place he had entered. He was here. That miraculous thing that they had strived so fiercely to achieve had been achieved—rather too well, perhaps, but it had been achieved, and he was launched on the greatest adventure he would ever have, that anyone would ever have. This was not the moment for submitting to grief and confusion. Out of that world, lost and all but forgotten to him, came a scrap of verse that gleamed and blazed in his soul: *Only through time time is conquered.*

McCulloch reached toward the mind that was so close to his within this strange body.

—*When will it be safe for us to leave this cave?* he asked.

—*It is safe any time, now. Do you wish to go outside?*

—*Yes. Please.*

The creature stirred, flexed its front claws, slapped its flat tail against the floor of the cave, and in a slow ungraceful way began to clamber through the narrow opening, pausing more than once to search the waters outside for lurking enemies. McCulloch felt a quick hot burst of terror, as though he were about to enter some important meeting and had discovered too late that he was naked. Was the shell truly ready? Was he safely armored against the unknown foes outside, or would they fall upon him and tear him apart like furious shrikes? But his host did not seem to share those fears. It went plodding on and out, and in a moment more it emerged on an algae-encrusted tongue of the reef wall, a short distance below the two anemones. From each of those twin masses of rippling flesh came the same sullen pouting hungry murmurs: "Ah, come closer, why don't you come closer?"

"Another time," said the lobster, sounding almost playful, and turned away from them.

McCulloch looked outward over the landscape. Earlier, in the turmoil of his bewildering arrival and the pain and chaos of the molting prodrome, he had not had time to assemble any clear and coherent view of it. But now—despite the handicap of seeing everything with the alien perspective of the lobster's many-faceted eyes—he was able to put together an image of the terrain.

His view was a shortened one, because the sky was like a dark lid, through which came only enough light to create a cone-shaped arena spreading just a little way. Behind him was the face of the huge cliff, occupied by plant and animal life over virtually every square inch, and stretching upward until its higher reaches were lost in the dimness far overhead. Just a short way down from the ledge where he rested was the ocean floor, a broad expanse of gentle, undulating white sand streaked here and there with long widening gores of some darker material. Here and there bottom-growing plants arose in elegant billowy clumps, and McCulloch spotted occasional creatures moving among them over the sand that were much like lobsters and crabs, though with some differences. He saw also some starfish and snails and sea urchins that did not look at all unfamiliar. At higher levels he could make out a few swimming creatures: a couple of the squidlike animals—they were hulking-looking ropy-armed things, and he disliked them instinctively—and what seemed to be large jellyfish. But something was missing, and after a moment McCulloch realized what it was: fishes. There was a rich population of invertebrate life wherever he looked, but no fishes as far as he could see.

Not that he could see very far. The darkness clamped down like a curtain perhaps two or three hundred yards away. But even so, it was odd that not one fish had entered his field of vision in all this time. He wished he knew more about marine biology. Were there zones on Earth where no sea animals more complex than lobsters and crabs existed? Perhaps, but he doubted it.

Two disturbing new hypotheses blossomed in his mind. One was that he had landed in some remote future era where nothing out of his own time survived except low-phylum sea creatures. The other was that he had not traveled to the future at all, but had arrived by mischance in some primordial geological epoch in which vertebrate life had not yet evolved. That seemed unlikely to him, though. This place did not have a prehistoric feel to him. He saw no trilobites; surely there ought to be trilobites everywhere about, and not these oversize lobsters, which he did not remember at all from his childhood visits to the natural history museum's prehistory displays.

But if this was truly the future—and the future belonged to the lobsters and squids—

That was hard to accept. Only invertebrates? What could invertebrates accomplish, what kind of civilization could lobsters build, with their hard unsupple bodies and great clumsy claws? Concepts, half remembered or less than that, rushed through his mind: the Taj Mahal, the Gutenberg Bible, the Sistine Chapel, the Madonna of the Rocks, the great window at Chartres. Could lobsters create those? Could squids? What a poor place this world must be, McCulloch thought sadly, how gray, how narrow, how tightly bounded by the ocean above and the endless sandy floor.

—*Tell me,* he said to his host. *Are there any fishes in this sea?*

The response was what he was coming to recognize as a sigh.

—*Fishes? That is another word without meaning.*

—*A form of marine life, with an internal bony structure—*

—*With its shell* inside?

—*That's one way of putting it*, said McCulloch.

—*There are no such creatures. Such creatures have never existed. There is no room for the shell within the soft parts of the body. I can barely comprehend such an arrangement: surely there is no need for it!*

—*It can be useful, I assure you. In the former world it was quite common.*

—*The world of human beings?*

—*Yes. My world*, McCulloch said.

—*Anything might have been possible in a former world, human Mc-Culloch. Perhaps indeed before the world's last Molting shells were worn inside. And perhaps after the next one they will be worn there again. But in the world I know, human McCulloch, it is not the practice.*

—*Ah*, McCulloch said. *Then I am even farther from home than I thought.*

—*Yes*, said his host. *I think you are very far from home indeed. Does that cause you sorrow?*

—*Among other things.*

—*If it causes you sorrow, I grieve for your grief, because we are companions now.*

—*You are very kind*, said McCulloch to his host.

❧

The lobster asked McCulloch if he was ready to begin their journey; and when McCulloch indicated that he was, his host serenely kicked itself free of the ledge with a single powerful stroke of its tail. For an instant it hung suspended; then it glided toward the sandy bottom as gracefully as though it were floating through air. When it landed, it was with all its many legs poised delicately *en pointe*, and it stood that way, motionless, a long moment.

Then it suddenly set out with great haste over the ocean floor, running so light-footedly that it scarcely raised a puff of sand wherever it touched down. More than once it ran right across some bottom-grubbing creature, some slug or scallop, without appearing to disturb it at all. McCulloch thought the lobster was capering in sheer exuberance, after its long internment in the cave; but some growing sense of awareness of his companion's mind told him after a time that this was no casual frolic, that the lobster was not in fact dancing but fleeing.

—*Is there an enemy?* McCulloch asked.

—*Yes. Above.*

The lobster's antennae stabbed upward at a sharp angle, and McCulloch, seeing through the other's eyes, perceived now a large looming cylindrical shape swimming in slow circles near the upper border of their range of vision. It might have been a shark, or even a whale. McCulloch felt deceived and betrayed; for the lobster had told him this was an invertebrate world, and surely that creature above him—

—No, said the lobster, without slowing its manic sprint. *That animal has no shell of the sort you described within its body. It is only a bag of flesh. But it is very dangerous.*

—*How will we escape it?*

—*We will not escape it.*

The lobster sounded calm, but whether it was the calm of fatalism or mere expressionlessness, McCulloch could not say: the lobster had been calm even in the first moments of McCulloch's arrival in its mind, which must surely have been alarming and even terrifying to it.

It had begun to move now in ever-widening circles. This seemed not so much an evasive tactic as a ritualistic one, now, a dance indeed. A farewell to life? The swimming creature had descended until it was only a few lobster lengths above them, and McCulloch had a clear view of it. No, not a fish or a shark or any type of vertebrate at all, he realized, but an animal of a kind wholly unfamiliar to him, a kind of enormous wormlike thing whose meaty yellow body was reinforced externally by some sort of chitinous struts running its entire length. Fleshy vanelike fins rippled along its sides, but their purpose seemed to be more one of guidance than propulsion, for it appeared to move by guzzling in great quantities of water and expelling them through an anal siphon. Its mouth was vast, with a row of dim little green eyes ringing the scarlet lips. When the creature yawned, it revealed itself to be toothless, but capable of swallowing the lobster easily at a gulp.

Looking upward into that yawning mouth, McCulloch had a sudden image of himself elsewhere, spread-eagled under an inverted pyramid of shining machinery as the countdown reached its final moments, as the technicians made ready to—

—to hurl him—

—to hurl him forward in time—

Yes. An experiment. Definitely an experiment. He could remember it now. Bleier, Caldwell, Rodrigues, Mortenson. And all the others. Gathered around him, faces tight, forced smiles. The lights. The colors. The bizarre coils of equipment. And the volunteer. The volunteer. First human subject to be sent forward in time. The various rabbits and mice of the previous experiments, though they had apparently survived the round trip unharmed, had not been capable of delivering much of a report on their adventures. "I'm smarter than any rabbit," McCulloch had said. "Send me. I'll tell you what it's like up there." The volunteer. All that was coming back to him in great swatches now, as he crouched here within the mind of something much like a lobster, waiting for a vast yawning predator to pounce. The project, the controversies, his co-workers, the debate over risking a human mind under the machine, the drawing of lots. McCulloch had not been the only volunteer. He was just the lucky one. "Here you go, Jim-boy. A hundred years down the time line."

Or fifty, or eighty, or a hundred and twenty. They didn't have really precise trajectory control. They thought he might go as much as a hundred twenty years. But beyond much doubt they had overshot by a few hundred million. Was that within the permissible parameters of error?

He wondered what would happen to him if his host here were to perish. Would he die also? Would he find himself instantly transferred to some other being of this epoch? Or would he simply be hurled back instead to his own time? He was not ready to go back. He had just begun to observe, to understand, to explore—

McCulloch's host had halted its running now, and stood quite still in what was obviously a defensive mode, body cocked and upreared, claws extended, with the huge crusher claw erect and the long narrow cutting claw opening and closing in a steady rhythm. It was a threatening pose, but the swimming thing did not appear to be greatly troubled by it. Did the lobster mean to let itself be swallowed, and then to carve an exit for itself with those awesome weapons, before the alimentary juices could go to work on its armor?

"You choose your prey foolishly," said McCulloch's host to its enemy.

The swimming creature made a reply that was unintelligible to Mc-Culloch: vague blurry words, the clotted outspew of a feeble intelligence. It continued its unhurried downward spiral.

"You are warned," said the lobster. "You are not selecting your victim wisely."

Again came a muddled response, sluggish and incoherent, the speech of an entity for whom verbal communication was a heavy, all-but-impossible effort.

Its enormous mouth gaped. Its fins rippled fiercely as it siphoned itself downward the last few yards to engulf the lobster. McCulloch prepared himself for transition to some new and even more unimaginable state when his host met its death. But suddenly the ocean floor was swarming with lobsters. They must have been arriving from all sides—summoned by his host's frantic dance, McCulloch wondered?—while McCulloch, intent on the descent of the swimmer, had not noticed. Ten, twenty, possibly fifty of them arrayed themselves now beside McCulloch's host, and as the swimmer, tail on high, mouth wide, lowered itself like some gigantic suction hose toward them, the lobsters coolly and implacably seized its lips in their claws. Caught and helpless, it began at once to thrash, and from the pores through which it spoke came bleating incoherent cries of dismay and torment.

There was no mercy for it. It had been warned. It dangled tail upward while the pack of lobsters methodically devoured it from below, pausing occasionally to strip away and discard the rigid rods of chitin that formed its superstructure. Swiftly they reduced it to a faintly visible cloud of shreds oscillating in the water, and then small scavenging creatures came to fall upon those, and there was nothing at all left but the scattered rods of chitin on the sand.

The entire episode had taken only a few moments: the coming of the predator, the dance of McCulloch's host, the arrival of the other lobsters, the destruction of the enemy. Now the lobsters were gathered in a sort of convocation about McCulloch's host, wordlessly manifesting a commonality of spirit, a warmth of fellowship after feasting, that seemed quite comprehensible to McCulloch. For a short while they had been uninhibited savage carnivores consuming convenient meat; now once again they were courteous, refined, cultured—Japanese gentlemen, Oxford dons, gentle Benedictine monks.

McCulloch studied them closely. They were definitely more like lobsters than like any other creature he had ever seen, very much like lobsters, and yet there were differences. They were larger. How much larger, he could not tell, for he had no real way of judging distance and size in this undersea world; but he supposed they must be at least three feet long, and he doubted that lobsters of his time, even the biggest, were anything like that in length. Their bodies were wider than those of lobsters, and their heads were larger. The two largest claws looked like those of the lobsters he remembered, but the ones just behind them seemed more elaborate, as if adapted for more delicate procedures than mere rending of food and stuffing it into the mouth. There was an odd little hump, almost a dome, midway down the lobster's back—the center of the expanded nervous system, perhaps.

The lobsters clustered solemnly about McCulloch's host, and each lightly tapped its claws against those of the adjoining lobster in a sort of handshake, a process that seemed to take quite some time. McCulloch became aware also that a conversation was under way. What they were talking about, he realized, was him.

"It is not painful to have a McCulloch within one," his host was explaining. "It came upon me at molting time, and that gave me a moment of difficulty, molting being what it is. But it was only a moment. After that my only concern was for the McCulloch's comfort."

"And it is comfortable now?"

"It is becoming more comfortable."

"When will you show it to us?"

"Ah, that cannot be done. It has no real existence, and therefore I cannot bring it forth."

"What is it, then? A wanderer? A revenant?"

"A revenant, yes. So I think. And a wanderer. It says it is a human being."

"And what is that? Is a human being a kind of McCulloch?"

"I think a McCulloch is a kind of human being."

"Which is a revenant."

"Yes, I think so."

"This is an Omen!"

"Where is its world?"

"Its world is lost to it."

"Yes, definitely an Omen."

"It lived on dry land."

"It breathed air."

"It wore its shell within its body."

"What a strange revenant!"

"What a strange world its world must have been."

"It is the former world, would you not say?"

"So I surely believe. And therefore this is an Omen."

"Ah, we shall Molt. We shall Molt."

McCulloch was altogether lost. He was not even sure when his own host was the speaker.

"Is it the Time?"

"We have an Omen, do we not?"

"The McCulloch surely was sent as a herald."

"There is no precedent."

"Each Molting, though, is without precedent. We cannot conceive what came before. We cannot imagine what comes after. We learn by learning. The McCulloch is the herald. The McCulloch is the Omen."

"I think not. I think it is unreal and unimportant."

"Unreal, yes. But not unimportant."

"The Time is not at hand. The Molting of the World is not yet due. The human is a wanderer and a revenant, but not a herald and certainly not an Omen."

"It comes from the former world."

"It says it does. Can we believe that?"

"It breathed air. In the former world, perhaps there were creatures that breathed air."

"It says it breathed air. I think it is neither herald nor Omen, neither wanderer nor revenant. I think it is a myth and a fugue. I think it betokens nothing. It is an accident. It is an interruption."

"That is an uncivil attitude. We have much to learn from the McCulloch. And if it is an Omen, we have immediate responsibilities that must be fulfilled."

"But how can we be certain of what it is?"

—*May I speak?* said McCulloch to his host.

—*Of course.*

—*How can I make myself heard?*

—*Speak through me.*

"The McCulloch wishes to be heard!"

"Hear it! Hear it!"

"Let it speak!"

McCulloch said, and the host spoke the words aloud for him, "I am a stranger here, and your guest, and so I ask you to forgive me if I give offense, for I have little understanding of your ways. Nor do I know if I am a herald or an Omen. But I tell you in all truth that I am a wanderer, and that I am sent from the former world, where there are many creatures of my kind, who breathe air and live upon the land and carry their—shells—inside their body."

"An Omen, certainly," said several of the lobsters at once. "A herald, beyond doubt."

McCulloch continued, "It was our hope to discover something of the worlds that are to come after ours. And therefore I was sent forward—"

"A herald—certainly a herald!"

"—to come to you, to go among you, to learn to know you, and then to return to my own people, the air people, the human people, and bring the word of what is to come. But I think that I am not the herald you expect. I carry no message for you. We could not have known that you were here. Out of the former world I bring you the blessing of those that have gone before, however, and when I go back to that world I will bear tidings of your life, of your thought, of your ways—"

"Then our kind is unknown to your world?"

McCulloch hesitated. "Creatures somewhat like you do exist in the seas of the former world. But they are smaller and simpler than you, and I think their civilization, if they have one, is not a great one."

"You have no discourse with them, then?" one of the lobsters asked.

"Very little," he said. A miserable evasion, cowardly, vile.

McCulloch shivered. He imagined himself crying out, "We eat them!" and the water turning black with their shocked outbursts—and saw them instantly falling upon him, swiftly and efficiently slicing him to scraps with their claws. Through his mind ran monstrous images of lobsters in tanks, lobsters boiling alive, lobsters smothered in rich sauces, lobsters shelled, lobsters minced, lobsters rendered into bisques—he could not halt the torrent of dreadful visions. Such was our discourse with your ancestors. Such was our mode of interspecies communication. He felt himself drowning in guilt and shame and fear.

The spasm passed. The lobsters had not stirred. They continued to regard him with patience: impassive, unmoving, remote. McCulloch wondered if all that had passed through his mind just then had been transmitted to his host. Very likely; the host earlier had seemed to have access to all of his thoughts, though McCulloch did not have the same entrée to the host's. And if the host knew, did all the others? What then, what then?

Perhaps they did not even care. Lobsters, he recalled, were said to be callous cannibals, who might attack one another in the very tanks where they were awaiting their turns in the chef's pot. It was hard to view these detached and aloof beings, these dons, these monks, as having that sort of ferocity: but yet he had seen them go to work on that swimming mouth-creature without any show of embarrassment, and perhaps some atavistic echo of their ancestors' appetites lingered in them, so that they would think it only natural that McCullochs and other humans had fed on such things as lobsters. Why should they be shocked? Perhaps they thought that humans fed on humans, too. It was all in the former world, was it not? And in any event it was foolish to fear that they would exact some revenge on him for Lobster Thermidor, no matter how appalled they might be. He wasn't here. He was nothing more than a figment, a revenant, a wanderer, a set of intrusive neural networks within their companion's brain. The worst they could do to him, he supposed, was to exorcise him, and send him back to the former world.

Even so, he could not entirely shake the guilt and the shame. Or the fear.

❤

Bleier said, "Of course, you aren't the only one who's going to be in jeopardy when we throw the switch. There's your host to consider. One entire human ego slamming into his mind out of nowhere like a brick falling off a building—what's it going to do to him?"

"Flip him out, is my guess," said Jake Ybarra. "You'll land on him and he'll announce he's Napoleon, or Joan of Arc, and they'll hustle him off to the nearest asylum. Are you prepared for the possibility, Jim, that you're going to spend your entire time in the future sitting in a loony bin undergoing therapy?"

"Or exorcism," Mortenson suggested. "If there's been some kind of reversion to barbarism. Christ, you might even get your host burned at the stake!"

"I don't think so," McCulloch said quietly. "I'm a lot more optimistic than you guys. I don't expect to land in a world of witch doctors and mumbo jumbo, and I don't expect to find myself in a place that locks people up in Bedlam because they suddenly start acting a little strange. The chances are that I *am* going to unsettle my host when I enter him, but that he'll simply get two sanity-stabilizer pills from his medicine chest and take them with a glass of water and feel better in five minutes. And then I'll explain what's happening to him."

"More than likely, no explanations will be necessary," said Maggie Caldwell. "By the time you arrive, time travel will have been a going proposition for three or four generations, after all. Having a traveler from the past turn up in your head will be old stuff to them. Your host will probably know exactly what's going on from the moment you hit him."

"Let's hope so," Bleier said. He looked across the laboratory to Rodrigues. "What's the count, Bob?"

"T minus eighteen minutes."

"I'm not worried about a thing," McCulloch said.

Caldwell took his hand in hers. "Neither am I, Jim."

"Then why is your hand so cold?" he asked.

"So I'm a *little* worried," she said.

McCulloch grinned. "So am I. A little. Only a little."

"You're human, Jim. No one's ever done this before."

"It'll be a can of corn!" Ybarra said.

Bleier looked at him blankly. "What the hell does that mean, Jake?"

Ybarra said, "Archaic twentieth-century slang. It means it's going to be a lot easier than we think."

"I told you," said McCulloch, "I'm not worried."

"I'm still worried about the impact on the host," said Bleier.

"All those Napoleons and Joans of Arc that have been cluttering the asylums for the last few hundred years," Maggie Caldwell said. "Could it be that they're really hosts for time travelers going backward in time?"

"You can't go backward," said Mortenson. "You know that. The round trip has to begin with a forward leap."

"Under present theory," Caldwell said. "But present theory's only five years old. It may turn out to be incomplete. We may have had all sorts of travelers out of the future jumping through history, and never even knew it. All the nuts, lunatics, inexplicable geniuses, idiots savants—"

"Save it, Maggie," Bleier said. "Let's stick to what we understand right now."

"Oh? Do we understand anything?" McCulloch asked.

Bleier gave him a sour look. "I thought you said you weren't worried."

"I'm not. Not much. But I'd be a fool if I thought we really had a firm handle on what we're doing. We're shooting in the dark, and let's never kid ourselves about it."

"T minus fifteen," Rodrigues called.

"Try to make the landing easy on your host, Jim," Bleier said.

"I've got no reason not to want to," said McCulloch.

He realized that he had been wandering. Bleier, Maggie, Mortenson, Ybarra—for a moment they had been more real to him than the congregation of lobsters. He had heard their voices, he had seen their faces, Bleier plump and perspiring and serious, Ybarra dark and lean, Maggie with her crown of short upswept red hair blazing in the laboratory light—and yet they were all dead, a hundred million years dead, two hundred million, back there with the triceratops and the trilobite in the drowned former world, and here he was among the lobster people. How futile all those discussions of what the world of the early twenty-second century was going to be like! Those speculations on population density, religious belief, attitudes toward science, level of technological achievement, all those late-night sessions in the final months of the project, designed to prepare him for any eventuality he might encounter while he was visiting the future—what a waste, what a needless exercise. As was all that fretting about upsetting the mental stability of the person who would receive his transtemporalized consciousness. Such qualms, such moral delicacy—all unnecessary, McCulloch knew now.

But of course they had not anticipated sending him so eerily far across the dark abysm of time, into a world in which humankind and all its works were not even legendary memories, and the host who would receive him was a calm and thoughtful crustacean capable of taking him in with only the most mild and brief disruption of its serenity.

The lobsters, he noticed now, had reconfigured themselves while his mind had been drifting. They had broken up their circle and were arrayed in a long line stretching over the ocean floor, with his host at the end of the procession. The queue was a close one, each lobster so close to the one before it that it could touch it with the tips of its antennae, which from time to time they seemed to be doing; and they all were moving in a weird kind of quasimilitary lockstep, every lobster swinging the same set of walking-legs forward at the same time.

—*Where are we going?* McCulloch asked his host.

—*The pilgrimage has begun.*

—*What pilgrimage is that?*

—*To the dry place,* said the host. *To the place of no water. To the land.*

—Why?

—It is the custom. We have decided that the time of the Molting of the World is soon to come; and therefore we must make the pilgrimage. It is the end of all things. It is the coming of a newer world. You are the herald: so we have agreed.

—Will you explain? I have a thousand questions. I need to know more about all this, McCulloch said.

—Soon. Soon. This is not a time for explanations.

McCulloch felt a firm and unequivocal closing of contact, an emphatic withdrawal. He sensed a hard ringing silence that was almost an absence of the host, and knew it would be inappropriate to transgress against it. That was painful, for he brimmed now with an overwhelming rush of curiosity. The Molting of the World? The end of all things? A pilgrimage to the land? *What* land? Where? But he did not ask. He could not ask. The host seemed to have vanished from him, disappearing utterly into this pilgrimage, this migration, moving in its lockstep way with total concentration and a kind of mystic intensity. McCulloch did not intrude. He felt as though he had been left alone in the body they shared.

As they marched, he concentrated on observing, since he could not interrogate. And there was much to see; for the longer he dwelled within his host, the more accustomed he grew to the lobster's sensory mechanisms. The compound eyes, for instance. Enough of his former life had returned to him now so that he remembered human eyes clearly, those two large gleaming ovals, so keen, so subtle of focus, set beneath protecting ridges of bone. His host's eyes were nothing like that: they were two clusters of tiny lenses rising on jointed, movable stalks, and what they showed was an intricately dissected view, a mosaic of isolated points of light. But he was learning somehow to translate those complex and baffling images into a single clear one, just as, no doubt, a creature accustomed to compound-lens vision would sooner or later learn to see through human eyes, if need be. And McCulloch found now that he could not only make more sense out of the views he received through his host's eyes, but that he was seeing farther, into quite distant dim recesses of this sunless undersea realm.

Not that the stalked eyes seemed to be a very important part of the lobster's perceptive apparatus. They provided nothing more than a certain crude awareness of the immediate terrain. But apparently the real work of perceiving was done mainly by the thousands of fine bristles, so minute that they were all but invisible, that sprouted on every surface of his host's body. These seemed to send a constant stream of messages to the lobster's brain: information on the texture and topography of the ocean floor, on tiny shifts in the flow and temperature of the water, of the proximity of obstacles, and much else. Some of the small hairlike filaments were sensitive to touch, and others, it appeared, to chemicals; for whenever the lobster approached some other life-form, it received data on its scent—or the underwater equivalent—long before the creature itself was within visual range. The quantity and richness of these inputs astonished McCulloch. At every moment came a torrent of data corresponding to the landside senses he remembered, smell, taste, touch; and some central processing unit within the lobster's brain handled everything in the most effortless fashion.

But there was no sound. The ocean world appeared to be wholly silent. McCulloch knew that that was untrue, that sound waves propagated through water as persistently as through air, if somewhat more rapidly. Yet the lobster seemed neither to possess nor to need any sort of auditory equipment. The sensory bristles brought in all the data it required. The "speech" of these creatures, McCulloch had long ago realized, was effected not by voice but by means of spurts of chemicals released into the water, hormones, perhaps, or amino acids, something of a distinct and readily recognizable identity, emitted in some high-redundancy pattern that permitted easy recognition and decoding despite the difficulties caused by currents and eddies. It was, McCulloch thought, like trying to communicate by printing individual letters on scraps of paper and hurling them into the wind. But it did somehow seem to work, however clumsy a concept it might be, because of the extreme sensitivity of the lobster's myriad chemoreceptors.

The antennae played some significant role also. There were two sets of them, a pair of three-branched ones just behind the eyes and a much longer single-branched pair behind those. The long ones restlessly twitched and probed inquisitively, and most likely, he suspected, served as simple balancing and coordination devices much like the whiskers of a cat. The purpose of the smaller antennae eluded him, but it was his guess that they were involved in the process of communication between one lobster and another, either by some semaphore system or in a deeper communion beyond his still awkward comprehension.

McCulloch regretted not knowing more about the lobsters of his own era. But he had only a broad general knowledge of natural history, extensive, fairly deep, yet not good enough to tell him whether these elaborate sensory functions were characteristic of all lobsters or had evolved during the millions of years it had taken to create the water world. Probably some of each, he decided. Very likely even the lobsters of the former world had had much of this scanning equipment, enough to allow them to locate their prey, to find their way around in the dark suboceanic depths, to undertake their long and unerring migrations. But he found it hard to believe that they could have had much "speech" capacity, that they gathered in solemn sessions to discuss abstruse questions of theology and mythology, to argue gently about omens and heralds and the end of all things. That was something that the patient and ceaseless unfoldings of time must have wrought.

The lobsters marched without show of fatigue: not scampering in that dancelike way that his host had adopted while summoning its comrades to save it from the swimming creature, but moving nevertheless in an elegant and graceful fashion, barely touching the ground with the tips of their legs, going onward step by step by step steadily and fairly swiftly.

McCulloch noticed that new lobsters frequently joined the procession, cutting in from left or right just ahead of his host, who always remained at the rear of the line; that line now was so long, hundreds of lobsters long, that it was impossible to see its beginning. Now and again one would reach out with its bigger claw to seize some passing animal, a starfish or urchin or small crab, and without missing a step would shred and devour it, tossing the unwanted husk to the cloud of planktonic scavengers that always hovered nearby. This foraging on the march was done with utter lack of self-consciousness; it was almost by reflex that these creatures snatched and gobbled as they journeyed.

And yet all the same they did not seem like mere marauding mouths. From this long line of crustaceans there emanated, McCulloch realized, a mysterious sense of community, a wholeness of society, that he did not understand but quite sharply sensed. This was plainly not a mere migration but a true pilgrimage. He thought ruefully of his earlier condescending view of these people, incapable of achieving the Taj Mahal or the Sistine Chapel, and felt abashed: for he was beginning to see that they had other accomplishments of a less tangible sort that were only barely apparent to his displaced and struggling mind.

➤

"When you come back," Maggie said, "you'll be someone else. There's no escaping that. It's the one thing I'm frightened of. Not that you'll die making the hop, or that you'll get into some sort of terrible trouble in the future, or that we won't be able to bring you back at all, or anything like that. But that you'll have become someone else."

"I feel pretty secure in my identity," McCulloch told her.

"I know you do. God knows, you're the most stable person in the group, and that's why you're going. But even so. Nobody's ever done anything like this before. It can't help but change you. When you return, you're going to be unique among the human race."

"That sounds very awesome. But I'm not sure it'll matter that much, Mag. I'm just taking a little trip. If I were going to Paris, or Istanbul, or even Antarctica, would I come back totally transformed? I'd have had some new experiences, but—"

"It isn't the same," she said. "It isn't even remotely the same." She came across the room to him and put her hands on his shoulders, and stared deep into his eyes, which sent a little chill through him, as it always did; for when she looked at him that way there was a sudden flow of energy between them, a powerful warm rapport rushing from her to him and from him to her as though through a huge conduit, that delighted and frightened him both at once. He could lose himself in her. He had never let himself feel that way about anyone before. And this was not the moment to begin. There was no room in him for such feelings, not now, not when he was within a couple of hours of leaping off into the most unknown of unknowns. When he returned—if he returned—he might risk allowing something at last to develop with Maggie. But not on the eve of departure, when everything in his universe was tentative and conditional. "Can I tell you a little story, Jim?" she asked.

"Sure."

"When my father was on the faculty at Cal, he was invited to a reception to meet a couple of the early astronauts, two of the Apollo men—I don't remember which ones, but they were from the second or third voyage to the Moon. When he showed up at the faculty club, there were two or three hundred people there, milling around having cocktails, and most of them were people he didn't know. He walked in and looked around and within ten seconds he had found the astronauts. He didn't have to be told. He just *knew.* And this is my father, remember, who doesn't believe in ESP or anything like that. But he said they were impossible to miss, even in that crowd. You could see it on their faces, you could feel the radiance coming from them, there was an aura, there was something about their eyes. Something that said, *I have walked on the Moon, I have been to that place which is not of our world and I have come back, and now I am someone else. I am who I was before, but I am someone else also.*"

"But they went to the *Moon,* Mag!"

"And you're going to the *future,* Jim. That's even weirder. You're going to a place that doesn't exist. And you may meet yourself there—ninety-nine years old, and waiting to shake hands with you—or you might meet me, or your grandson, or find out that everyone on Earth is dead, or that everyone has turned into a disembodied spirit, or that they're all immortal super-beings, or—or—Christ, I don't know. You'll see a world that nobody alive today is supposed to see. And when you come back, you'll have that aura. You'll be transformed."

"Is that so frightening?"

"To me it is," she said.

"Why is that?"

"Dummy," she said. "Dope. How explicit do I have to be, anyway? I thought I was being obvious enough."

He could not meet her eyes. "This isn't the best moment to talk about—"

"I know. I'm sorry, Jim. But you're important to me, and you're going somewhere and you're going to become someone else, and I'm scared. Selfish and scared."

"Are you telling me not to go?"

"Don't be absurd. You'd go no matter what I told you, and I'd despise you if you didn't. There's no turning back now."

"No."

"I shouldn't have dumped any of this on you today. You don't need it right this moment."

"It's okay," he said softly. He turned until he was looking straight at her, and for a long moment he simply stared into her eyes and did not speak, and then at last he said, "Listen, I'm going to take a big fantastic improbably insane voyage, and I'm going to be a witness to God knows what, and then I'm going to come back, and yes, I'll be changed—only an ox wouldn't be changed, or maybe only a block of stone—but I'll still be me, whoever *me* is. Don't worry, okay? I'll still be me. And we'll still be us."

"Whoever *us* is."

"Whoever. Jesus, I wish you were going with me, Mag!"

"That's the silliest schoolboy thing I've ever heard you say."

"True, though."

"Well, I can't go. Only one at a time can go, and it's you. I'm not even sure I'd want to go. I'm not as crazy as you are, I suspect. You go, Jim, and come back and tell me all about it."

"Yes."

"And then we'll see what there is to see about you and me."

"Yes," he said.

She smiled. "Let me show you a poem, okay? You must know it, because it's Eliot, and you know all the Eliot there is. But I was reading him last night—thinking of you, reading him—and I found this, and it seemed to be the right words, and I wrote them down. From one of the *Quartets*."

"I think I know," he said:

> "*Time past and time future*
> *Allow but a little consciousness—*"

"That's a good one too," Maggie said. "But it's not the one I had in mind." She unfolded a piece of paper. "It's this:

> 'We shall not cease from exploration
> And the end of all our exploring
> Will be to arrive where we started—' "

"—And know the place for the first time," he completed. "Yes. Exactly. To arrive where we started. And know the place for the first time."

The lobsters were singing as they marched. That was the only word, McCulloch thought, that seemed to apply. The line of pilgrims now was immensely long—there must have been thousands in the procession by this time, and more were joining constantly—and from them arose an outpouring of chemical signals, within the narrowest of tonal ranges, that mingled in a close harmony and amounted to a kind of sustained chant on a few notes, swelling, filling all the ocean with its powerful and intense presence. Once again he had an image of them as monks, but not Benedictines now: these were Buddhist, rather, an endless line of yellow-robed holy men singing a great om as they made their way up some Tibetan slope. He was awed and humbled by it—by the intensity, and by the wholeheartedness of the devotion. It was getting hard for him to remember that these were crustaceans, no more than ragged claws scuttling across the floors of silent seas; he sensed minds all about him, whole and elaborate minds arising out of some rich cultural matrix, and it was coming to seem quite natural to him that these people should have armored exoskeletons and jointed eyestalks and a dozen busy legs.

His host had still not broken its silence, which must have extended now over a considerable period. Just how long a period, McCulloch had no idea, for there were no significant alternations of light and dark down here to indicate the passing of time, nor did the marchers ever seem to sleep, and they took their food, as he had seen, in a casual and random way without breaking step. But it seemed to McCulloch that he had been effectively alone in the host's body for many days.

He was not minded to try to reenter contact with the other just yet—not until he received some sort of signal from it. Plainly the host had withdrawn into some inner sanctuary to undertake a profound meditation; and McCulloch, now that the early bewilderment and anguish of his journey through time had begun to wear off, did not feel so dependent upon the host that he needed to blurt his queries constantly into his companion's consciousness. He would watch, and wait, and attempt to fathom the mysteries of this place unaided.

The landscape had undergone a great many changes since the beginning of the march. That gentle bottom of fine white sand had yielded to a terrain of rough dark gravel, and that to one of a pale sedimentary stuff made up of tiny shells, the mortal remains, no doubt, of vast hordes of diatoms and foraminifera, which rose like clouds of snowflakes at the lobsters' lightest steps. Then came a zone where a stratum of thick red clay spread in all directions. The clay held embedded in it an odd assortment of rounded rocks and clamshells and bits of chitin, so that it had the look of some complex paving material from a fashionable terrace. And after that they entered a region where slender spires of a sharp black stone, faceted like worked flint, sprouted stalagmite-fashion at their feet. Through all of this the lobster-pilgrims marched unperturbed, never halting, never breaking their file, moving in a straight line whenever possible and making only the slightest of deviations when compelled to it by the harshness of the topography.

Now they were in a district of coarse yellow sandy globules, out of which two types of coral grew: thin angular strands of deep jet, and supple, almost mobile fingers of a rich lovely salmon hue. McCulloch wondered where on Earth such stuff might be found, and chided himself at once for the foolishness of the thought: the seas he knew had been swallowed long ago in the great all-encompassing ocean that swathed the world, and the familiar continents, he supposed, had broken from their moorings and slipped to strange parts of the globe well before the rising of the waters. He had no landmarks. There was an equator somewhere, and there were two poles, but down here beyond the reach of direct sunlight, in this warm changeless uterine sea, neither north nor south nor east held any meaning. He remembered other lines:

> Sand-strewn caverns, cool and deep
> Where the winds are all asleep;
> Where the spent lights quiver and gleam;
> Where the salt weed sways in the stream;
> Where the sea-beasts rang'd all round
> Feed in the ooze of their pasture-ground . . .

What was the next line? Something about great whales coming sailing by, sail and sail with unshut eye, round the world for ever and aye. Yes, but there were no great whales here, if he understood his host correctly, no dolphins, no sharks, no minnows; there were only these swarming lower creatures, mysteriously raised on high, lords of the world. And mankind? Birds and bats, horses and bears? Gone. Gone. And the valleys and meadows? The lakes and streams?

Taken by the sea. The world lay before him like a land of dreams, transformed. But was it, as the poet had said, a place which hath really neither joy, nor love, nor light, nor certitude, nor peace, nor help for pain? It did not seem that way. For light there was merely that diffuse faint glow, so obscure it was close to nonexistent, that filtered down through unknown fathoms. But what was that lobster song, that ever-swelling crescendo, if not some hymn to love and certitude and peace, and help for pain? He was overwhelmed by peace, surprised by joy, and he did not understand what was happening to him. He was part of the march, that was all. He was a member of the pilgrimage.

He had wanted to know if there was any way he could signal to be pulled back home: a panic button, so to speak. Bleier was the one he asked, and the question seemed to drive the man into an agony of uneasiness. He scowled, he tugged at his jowls, he ran his hands through his sparse strands of hair.

"No," he said finally. "We weren't able to solve that one, Jim. There's simply no way of propagating a signal backward in time."

"I didn't think so," McCulloch said. "I just wondered."

"Since we're not actually sending your physical body, you shouldn't find yourself in any real trouble. Psychic discomfort, at the worst—disorientation, emotional upheaval, at the worst a sort of terminal homesickness. But I think you're strong enough to pull your way through any of that. And you'll always know that we're going to be yanking you back to us at the end of the experiment."

"How long am I going to be gone?"

"Elapsed time will be virtually nil. We'll throw the switch, off you'll go, you'll do your jaunt, we'll grab you back, and it'll seem like no time at all, perhaps a thousandth of a second. We aren't going to believe that you went anywhere at all, until you start telling us about it."

McCulloch sensed that Bleier was being deliberately evasive, not for the first time since McCulloch had been selected as the time traveler. "It'll seem like no time at all to the people watching in the lab," he said. "But what about for me?"

"Well, of course for you it'll be a little different, because you'll have had a subjective experience in another time frame."

"That's what I'm getting at. How long are you planning to leave me in the future? An hour? A week?"

"That's really hard to determine, Jim."

"What does that mean?"

"You know, we've sent only rabbits and stuff. They've come back okay, beyond much doubt—"

"Sure. They still munch on lettuce when they're hungry, and they don't tie their ears together in knots before they hop. So I suppose they're none the worse for wear."

"Obviously we can't get much of a report from a rabbit."

"Obviously."

"You're sounding awfully goddamned hostile today, Jim. Are you sure you don't want us to scrub the mission and start training another volunteer?" Bleier asked.

"I'm just trying to elicit a little hard info," McCulloch said. "I'm not trying to back out. And if I sound hostile, it's only because you're dancing all around my questions, which is becoming a considerable pain in the ass."

Bleier looked squarely at him and glowered. "All right. I'll tell you anything you want to know that I'm capable of answering. Which is what I think I've been doing all along. When the rabbits come back, we test them and we observe no physiological changes, no trace of ill effects as a result of having separated the psyche from the body for the duration of a time jaunt. Christ, we can't even tell the rabbits *have* been on a time jaunt, except that our instruments indicate the right sort of thermodynamic drain and entropic reversal, and for all we know we're kidding ourselves about that, which is why we're risking our reputations and your neck to send a human being who can tell us what the fuck happens when we throw the switch. But you've seen the rabbits jaunting. You know as well as I do that they come back okay."

Patiently McCulloch said, "Yes. As okay as a rabbit ever is, I guess. But what I'm trying to find out from you, and what you seem unwilling to tell me, is how long I'm going to be up there in subjective time."

"We don't know, Jim," Bleier said.

"You don't *know*? What if it's ten years? What if it's a thousand? What if I'm going to live out an entire life span, or whatever is considered a life span a hundred years from now, and grow old and wise and wither away and die and then wake up a thousandth of a second later on your lab table?"

"We don't know. That's why we have to send a human subject."

"There's no way to measure subjective jaunt-time?"

"Our instruments are here. They aren't *there*. You're the only instrument we'll have there. For all we know, we're sending you off for a million years, and when you come back here you'll have turned into something out of H.G. Wells. Is that straightforward enough for you, Jim? But I don't think it's going to happen that way, and Mortenson doesn't think so either, or Ybarra for that matter. What we think is that you'll spend something between a day and a couple of months in the future, with the outside possibility of a year. And when we give you the hook, you'll be back here with virtually nil elapsed time. But to answer your first question again, there's no way you can instruct us to yank you back. You'll just have to sweat it out, however long it may be. I thought you knew that. The hook, when it comes, will be virtually automatic, a function of the thermodynamic homeostasis, like the recoil of a gun. An equal and opposite reaction: or maybe more like the snapping back of a rubber band. Pick whatever metaphor you want. But if you don't like the way any of this sounds, it's not too late for you to back out, and nobody will say a word against you. It's never too late to back out. Remember that, Jim."

McCulloch shrugged. "Thanks for leveling with me. I appreciate that. And no, I don't want to drop out. The only thing I wonder about is whether my stay in the future is going to seem too long or too goddamned short. But I won't know that until I get there, will I? And then the time I have to wait before coming home is going to be entirely out of my hands. And out of yours, too, is how it seems. But that's all right. I'll take my chances. I just wondered what I'd do if I got there and found that I didn't much like it there."

"My bet is that you'll have the opposite problem," said Bleier. "You'll like it so much you won't want to come back."

Again and again, while the pilgrims traveled onward, McCulloch detected bright flares of intelligence gleaming like brilliant pinpoints of light in the darkness of the sea. Each creature seemed to have a characteristic emanation, a glow of neural energy. The simple ones—worms, urchins, starfish, sponges—emitted dim gentle signals; but there were others as dazzling as beacons. The lobster-folk were not the only sentient life-forms down here.

Occasionally he saw, as he had in the early muddled moments of the jaunt, isolated colonies of the giant sea anemones: great flowery-looking things, rising on thick pedestals. From them came a soft alluring lustful purr, a siren crooning calculated to bring unwary animals within reach of their swaying tentacles and the eager mouths hidden within the fleshy petals. Cemented to the floor on their swaying stalks, they seemed like somber philosophers, lost in the intervals between meals in deep reflections on the purpose of the cosmos. McCulloch longed to pause and try to speak with them, for their powerful emanation appeared plainly to indicate that they possessed a strong intelligence, but the lobsters moved past the anemones without halting.

The squidlike beings that frequently passed in flotillas overhead seemed even keener of mind: large animals, sleek and arrogant of motion, with long turquoise bodies that terminated in hawserlike arms, and enormous bulging eyes of a startling scarlet color. He found them ugly and repugnant, and did not quite know why. Perhaps it was some attitude of his host's that carried over subliminally to him; for there was an unmistakable chill among the lobsters whenever the squids appeared, and the chanting of the marchers grew more vehement, as though betokening a warning.

That some kind of frosty detente existed between the two kinds of life-forms was apparent from the regard they showed one another and from the distances they maintained. Never did the squids descend into the ocean-floor zone that was the chief domain of the lobsters, but for long spans of time they would soar above, in a kind of patient aerial surveillance, while the lobsters, striving ostentatiously to ignore them, betrayed discomfort by quickened movements of their antennae.

Still other kinds of high-order intelligence manifested themselves as the pilgrimage proceeded. In a zone of hard and rocky terrain McCulloch felt a new and distinctive mental pulsation, coming from some creature that he must not have encountered before. But he saw nothing unusual: merely a rough grayish landscape pockmarked by dense clumps of oysters and barnacles, some shaggy outcroppings of sponges and yellow seaweeds, a couple of torpid anemones. Yet out of the midst of all that unremarkable clutter came clear strong signals, produced by minds of considerable force. Whose? Not the oysters and barnacles, surely. The mystery intensified as the lobsters, without pausing in their march, interrupted their chant to utter words of greeting, and had greetings in return, drifting toward them from that tangle of marine underbrush.

"Why do you march?" the unseen speakers asked, in a voice that rose in the water like a deep slow groaning.

"We have had an Omen," answered the lobsters.

"Ah, is it the Time?"

"The Time will surely be here," the lobsters replied.

"Where is the herald, then?"

"The herald is within me," said McCulloch's host, breaking its long silence at last.

—*To whom do you speak?* McCulloch asked.

—*Can you not see? There. Before us.*

McCulloch saw only algae, barnacles, sponges, oysters.

—*Where?*

—*In a moment you will see,* said the host.

The column of pilgrims had continued all the while to move forward, until now it was within the thick groves of seaweed. And now McCulloch saw who the other speakers were. Huge crabs were crouched at the bases of many of the larger rock formations, creatures far greater in size than the largest of the lobsters; but they were camouflaged so well that they were virtually invisible except at the closest range. On their broad arching backs whole gardens grew: brilliantly colored sponges, algae in somber reds and browns, fluffy many-branched crimson things, odd complex feathery growths, even a small anemone or two, all jammed together in such profusion that nothing of the underlying crab showed except beady long-stalked eyes and glinting claws. Why beings that signaled their presence with potent telepathic outputs should choose to cloak themselves in such elaborate concealments, McCulloch could not guess: perhaps it was to deceive a prey so simple that it was unable to detect the emanations of these crabs' minds.

As the lobsters approached, the crabs heaved themselves up a little way from the rocky bottom, and shifted themselves ponderously from side to side, causing the intricate streamers and filaments and branches of the creatures growing on them to stir and wave about. It was like a forest agitated by a sudden hard gust of wind from the north.

"Why do you march, why do you march?" called the crabs. "Surely it is not yet the Time. Surely!"

"Surely it is," the lobsters replied. "So we all agree. Will you march with us?"

"Show us your herald!" the crabs cried. "Let us see the Omen!"

—*Speak to them*, said McCulloch's host.

—*But what am I to say?*

—*The truth. What else can you say?*

—*I know nothing. Everything here is a mystery to me.*

—*I will explain all things afterward. Speak to them now.*

—*Without understanding?*

—*Tell them what you told us.*

Baffled, McCulloch said, speaking through the host, "I have come from the former world as an emissary. Whether I am a herald, whether I bring an Omen, is not for me to say. In my own world I breathed air and carried my shell within my body."

"Unmistakably a herald," said the lobsters.

To which the crabs replied, "That is not so unmistakable to us. We sense a wanderer and a revenant among you. But what does that mean? The Molting of the World is not a small thing, good friends. Shall we march, just because this strangeness is come upon you? It is not enough evidence. And to march is not a small thing either, at least for us."

"We have chosen to march," the lobsters said, and indeed they had not halted at all throughout this colloquy; the vanguard of their procession was far out of sight in a black-walled canyon, and McCulloch's host, still at the end of the line, was passing now through the last few crouching places of the great crabs. "If you mean to join us, come now."

From the crabs came a heavy outpouring of regret. "Alas, alas, we are large, we are slow, the way is long, the path is dangerous."

"Then we will leave you."

"If it is the Time, we know that you will perform the offices on our behalf. If it is not the Time, it is just as well that we do not make the pilgrimage. We are—not—certain. We—cannot—be—sure—it—is—an—Omen—"

McCulloch's host was far beyond the last of the crabs. Their words were faint and indistinct, and the final few were lost in the gentle surgings of the water.

—*They make a great error*, said McCulloch's host to him. *If it is truly the Time, and they do not join the march, it might happen that their souls will be lost. That is a severe risk: but they are a lazy folk. Well, we will perform the offices on their behalf.*

And to the crabs the host called, "We will do all that is required, have no fear!" But it was impossible, McCulloch thought, that the words could have reached the crabs across such a distance.

He and the host now were entering the mouth of the black canyon. With the host awake and talkative once again, McCulloch meant to seize the moment at last to have some answers to his questions.

—*Tell me now*—he began.

But before he could complete the thought, he felt the sea roil and surge about him as though he had been swept up in a monstrous wave. That could not be, not at this depth; but yet that irresistible force, booming toward him out of the dark canyon and catching him up, hurled him into a chaos as desperate as that of his moment of arrival. He sought to cling, to grasp, but there was no purchase; he was loose of his moorings; he was tossed and flung like a bubble on the winds.

—*Help me!* he called. *What's happening to us?*

—*To you, friend human McCulloch. To you alone. Can I aid you?*

What was that? Happening only to him? But certainly he and the lobster both were caught in this undersea tempest, both being thrown about, both whirled in the same maelstrom—

Faces danced around him. Charlie Bleier, pudgy, earnest-looking. Maggie, tender-eyed, troubled. Bleier had his hand on McCulloch's right wrist, Maggie on the other, and they were tugging, tugging—

But he had no wrists. He was a lobster.

"Come, Jim—"

"No! Not yet!"

"Jim—Jim—"

"Stop—pulling—you're hurting—"

"Jim—"

McCulloch struggled to free himself from their grasp. As he swung his arms in wild circles, Maggie and Bleier, still clinging to them, went whipping about like tethered balloons. "Let go," he shouted. "You aren't here! There's nothing for you to hold on to! You're just hallucinations! Let—go—!"

And then, as suddenly as they had come, they were gone.

The sea was calm. He was in his accustomed place, seated somewhere deep within his host's consciousness. The lobster was moving forward, steady as ever, into the black canyon, following the long line of its companions.

McCulloch was too stunned and dazed to attempt contact for a long while. Finally, when he felt some measure of composure return, he reached his mind into his host's:

—*What happened?*

—*I cannot say. What did it seem like to you?*

—*The water grew wild and stormy. I saw faces out of the former world. Friends of mine. They were pulling at my arms. You felt nothing?*

—*Nothing,* said the host, *except a sense of your own turmoil. We are deep here: beyond the reach of storms.*

—*Evidently I'm not.*

—*Perhaps your homefaring time is coming. Your world is summoning you.*

Of course! The faces, the pulling at his arms—the plausibility of the host's suggestion left McCulloch trembling with dismay. Homefaring time! Back there in the lost and inconceivable past, they had begun angling for him, casting their line into the vast gulf of time—

—*I'm not ready,* he protested. *I've only just arrived here! I know nothing yet! How can they call me so soon?*

—*Resist them, if you would remain.*

—*Will you help me?*

—*How would that be possible?*

—*I'm not sure,* McCulloch said. *But it's too early for me to go back. If they pull on me again, hold me! Can you?*

—*I can try, friend human McCulloch.*

—*And you have to keep your promise to me now.*

—*What promise is that?*

—You said you would explain things to me. Why you've undertaken this pilgrimage. What it is I'm supposed to be the Omen of. What happens when the Time comes. The Molting of the World.

—Ah, said the host.

But that was all it said. In silence it scrabbled with busy legs over a sharply creviced terrain. McCulloch felt a fierce impatience growing in him. What if they yanked him again, now, and this time they succeeded? There was so much yet to learn! But he hesitated to prod the host again, feeling abashed. Long moments passed. Two more squids appeared: the radiance of their probing minds was like twin searchlights overhead. The ocean floor sloped downward gradually but perceptibly here. The squids vanished, and another of the predatory big-mouthed swimming-things, looking as immense as a whale and, McCulloch supposed, filling the same ecological niche, came cruising down into the level where the lobsters marched, considered their numbers in what appeared to be some surprise, and swam slowly upward again and out of sight. Something else of great size, flapping enormous wings somewhat like those of a stingray but clearly just a boneless mass of chitin-strutted flesh, appeared next, surveyed the pilgrims with equally bland curiosity, and flew to the front of the line of lobsters, where McCulloch lost it in the darkness. While all of this was happening the host was quiet and inaccessible, and McCulloch did not dare attempt to penetrate its privacy. But then, as the pilgrims were moving through a region where huge, dim-witted scallops with great bright eyes nestled everywhere, waving gaudy pink and blue mantles, the host unexpectedly resumed the conversation as though there had been no interruption, saying:

—What we call the Time of the Molting of the World is the time when the world undergoes a change of nature, and is purified and reborn. At such a time, we journey to the place of dry land, and perform certain holy rites.

—And these rites bring about the Molting of the World? McCulloch asked.

—Not at all. The Molting is an event wholly beyond our control. The rites are performed for our own sakes, not for the world's.

—I'm not sure I understand.

—We wish to survive the Molting, to travel onward into the world to come. For this reason, at a Time of Molting, we must make our observances, we must demonstrate our worth. It is the responsibility of my people. We bear the duty for all the peoples of the world.

—A priestly caste, is that it? McCulloch said. *When this cataclysm comes, the lobsters go forth to say the prayers for everyone, so that everyone's soul will survive?*

The host was silent again: pondering McCulloch's terms, perhaps, translating them into more appropriate equivalents. Eventually it replied:

—*That is essentially correct.*

—*But other peoples can join the pilgrimage if they want. Those crabs. The anemones. The squids, even?*

—*We invite all to come. But we do not expect anyone but ourselves actually to do it.*

—*How often has there been such a ceremony?* McCulloch asked.

—*I cannot say. Never, perhaps.*

—*Never?*

—*The Molting of the World is not a common event. We think it has happened only twice since the beginning of time.*

In amazement McCulloch said:

—*Twice since the world began, and you think it's going to happen again in your own lifetimes?*

—*Of course we cannot be sure of that. But we have had an Omen, or so we think, and we must abide by that. It was foretold that when the end is near, an emissary from the former world would come among us. And so it has come to pass. Is that not so?*

—*Indeed.*

—*Then we must make the pilgrimage, for if you have not brought the Omen we have merely wasted some effort, but if you are the true herald we will have forfeited all of eternity if we let your message go unheeded.*

It sounded eerily familiar to McCulloch: a messianic prophecy, a cult of the millennium, an apocalyptic transfiguration. He felt for a moment as though he had landed in the tenth century instead of in some impossibly remote future epoch. And yet the host's tone was so calm and rational, the sense of spiritual obligation that the lobster conveyed was so profound, that McCulloch found nothing absurd in these beliefs. Perhaps the world *did* end from time to time, and the performing of certain rituals did in fact permit its inhabitants to transfer their souls onward into whatever unimaginable environment was to succeed the present one. Perhaps.

—*Tell me,* said McCulloch. *What were the former worlds like, and what will the next one be?*

—*You should know more about the former worlds than I, friend human McCulloch. And as for the world to come, we may only speculate.*

—*But what are your traditions about those worlds?*

—*The first world,* the lobster said, *was a world of fire.*

—*You can understand fire, living in the sea?*

—*We have heard tales of it from those who have been to the dry place. Above the water there is air, and in the air there hangs a ball of fire, which gives the world warmth. Is this not the case?*

McCulloch, hearing a creature of the ocean floor speak of things so far beyond its scope and comprehension, felt a warm burst of delight and admiration.

—*Yes! We call that ball of fire the sun.*

—*Ah, so that is what you mean, when you think of the sun! The word was a mystery to me, when first you used it. But I understand you much better now, do you not agree?*

—*You amaze me,* McCulloch said.

—*The first world, so we think, was fire: it was like the sun. And when we dwelled upon that world, we were fire also. It is the fire that we carry within us to this day, that glow, that brightness, which is our life, and which goes from us when we die. After a span of time so long that we could never describe its length, the Time of the Molting came upon the fire world and it grew hard, and gathered a cloak of air about itself, and creatures lived upon the land and breathed the air. I find that harder to comprehend, in truth, than I do the fire world. But that was the first Molting, when the air world emerged: that world from which you have come to us. I hope you will tell me of your world, friend human McCulloch, when there is time.*

—*So I will,* said McCulloch. *But there is so much more I need to hear from you first!*

—*Ask it.*

—*The second Molting—the disappearance of my world, the coming of yours—*

—*The tradition is that the sea existed, even in the former world, and that it was not small. At the Time of the Molting it rose and devoured the land and all that was upon it, except for one place that was not devoured, which is sacred. And then all the world was covered by water, and that was the second Molting, which brought forth the third world.*

—*How long ago was that?*

—*How can I speak of the passing of time? There is no way to speak of that. Time passes, and lives end, and worlds are transformed. But we have no words for that. If every grain of sand in the sea were one lifetime, then it would be as many lifetimes ago as there are grains of sand in the sea. But does that help you? Does that tell you anything? It happened. It was very long ago. And now our world's turn has come, or so we think.*

—*And the next world? What will that be like?* McCulloch asked.

—*There are those who claim to know such things, but I am not one of them. We will know the next world when we have entered it, and I am content to wait until then for the knowledge.*

McCulloch had a sense then that the host had wearied of this sustained contact, and was withdrawing once again from it; and, though his own thirst for knowledge was far from sated, he chose once again not to attempt to resist that withdrawal.

All this while the pilgrims had continued down a gentle incline into the great bowl of a sunken valley. Once again now the ocean floor was level, but the water was notably deeper here, and the diffused light from above was so dim that only the most rugged of algae could grow, making the landscape bleak and sparse. There were no sponges here, and little coral, and the anemones were pale and small, giving little sign of the potent intelligence that infused their larger cousins in the shallower zones of the sea.

But there were other creatures at this level that McCulloch had not seen before. Platoons of alert, mobile oysters skipped over the bottom, leaping in agile bounds on columns of water that they squirted like jets from tubes in their dark green mantles: now and again they paused in midleap and their shells quickly opened and closed, snapping shut, no doubt, on some hapless larval thing of the plankton too small for McCulloch, via the lobster's imperfect vision, to detect. From these oysters came bright darting blurts of mental activity, sharp and probing: they must be as intelligent, he thought, as cats or dogs. Yet from time to time a lobster, swooping with an astonishingly swift claw, would seize one of these oysters and deftly, almost instantaneously, shuck and devour it. Appetite was no respecter of intelligence in this world of needful carnivores, McCulloch realized.

Intelligent, too, in their way, were the hordes of nearly invisible little crustaceans—shrimp of some sort, he imagined—that danced in shining clouds just above the line of march. They were ghostly things perhaps an inch long, virtually transparent, colorless, lovely, graceful. Their heads bore two huge glistening black eyes; their intestines, glowing coils running the length of their bodies, were tinged with green; the tips of their tails were an elegant crimson. They swam with the aid of a horde of busy finlike legs, and seemed almost to be mocking their stolid, plodding cousins as they marched; but these sparkling little creatures also occasionally fell victim to the lobsters' inexorable claws, and each time it was like the extinguishing of a tiny brilliant candle.

An emanation of intelligence of a different sort came from bulky animals that McCulloch noticed roaming through the gravelly foothills flanking the line of march. These seemed at first glance to be another sort of lobster, larger even than McCulloch's companions: heavily armored things with many-segmented abdomens and thick paddle-shaped arms. But then, as one of them drew nearer, McCulloch saw the curved tapering tail with its sinister spike, and realized he was in the presence of the scorpions of the sea.

They gave off a deep, almost somnolent mental wave: slow thinkers but not light ones, Teutonic ponderers, grapplers with the abstruse. There were perhaps two dozen of them, who advanced upon the pilgrims and in quick one-sided struggles pounced, stung, slew. McCulloch watched in amazement as each of the scorpions dragged away a victim and, no more than a dozen feet from the line of march, began to gouge into its armor to draw forth tender chunks of pale flesh, without drawing the slightest response from the impassive, steadily marching column of lobsters.

They had not been so complacent when the great-mouthed swimming-thing had menaced McCulloch's host; then, the lobsters had come in hordes to tear the attacker apart. And whenever one of the big squids came by, the edgy hostility of the lobsters, their willingness to do battle if necessary, was manifest. But they seemed indifferent to the scorpions. The lobsters accepted their onslaught as placidly as though it were merely a toll they must pay in order to pass through this district. Perhaps it was. McCulloch was only beginning to perceive how dense and intricate a fabric of ritual bound this submarine world together.

The lobsters marched onward, chanting in unfailing rhythm as though nothing untoward had happened. The scorpions, their hungers evidently gratified, withdrew and congregated a short distance off, watching without much show of interest as the procession went by them. By the time McCulloch's host, bringing up the rear, had gone past the scorpions, they were fighting among themselves in a lazy, halfhearted way, like playful lions after a successful hunt. Their mental emanation, sluggishly booming through the water, grew steadily more blurred, more vague, more toneless.

And then it was overlaid and entirely masked by the pulsation of some new and awesome kind of mind ahead: one of enormous power, whose output beat upon the water with what was almost a physical force, like some massive metal chain being lashed against the surface of the ocean. Apparently the source of this gigantic output still lay at a considerable distance, for, strong as it was, it grew stronger still as the lobsters advanced toward it, until at last it was an overwhelming clangor, terrifying, bewildering. McCulloch could no longer remain quiescent under the impact of that monstrous sound. Breaking through to the sanctuary of his host, he cried:

—What is it?

—We are approaching a god, the lobster replied.

—A god, did you say?

—A divine presence, yes. Did you think we were the rulers of this world?

In fact McCulloch had, assuming automatically that his time jaunt had deposited him within the consciousness of some member of this world's highest species, just as he would have expected to have landed had he reached the twenty-second century as intended, in the consciousness of a human rather than in a frog or a horse. But obviously the division between humanity and all subsentient species in his own world did not have an exact parallel here; many races, perhaps all of them, had some sort of intelligence, and it was becoming clear that the lobsters, though a high life-form, were not the highest. He found that dismaying and even humbling; for the lobsters seemed quite adequately intelligent to him, quite the equals—for all his early condescension to them— of mankind itself. And now he was to meet one of their gods? How great a mind was a god likely to have?

The booming of that mind grew unbearably intense, nor was there any way to hide from it. McCulloch visualized himself doubled over in pain, pressing his hands to his ears, an image that drew a quizzical shaft of thought from his host. Still the lobsters pressed forward, but even they were responding now to the waves of mental energy that rippled outward from that unimaginable source. They had at last broken ranks, and were fanning out horizontally on the broad dark plain of the ocean floor, as though deploying themselves before a place of worship. Where was the god? McCulloch, striving with difficulty to see in this nearly lightless place, thought he made out some vast shape ahead, some dark entity, swollen and fearsome, that rose like a colossal boulder in the midst of the suddenly diminutive-looking lobsters. He saw eyes like bright yellow platters, gleaming furiously; he saw a huge frightful beak; he saw what he thought at first to be a nest of writhing serpents, and then realized to be tentacles, dozens of them, coiling and uncoiling with a terrible restless energy. To the host he said:

—*Is that your god?*

But he could not hear the reply, for an agonizing new force suddenly buffeted him, one even more powerful than that which was emanating from the giant creature that sat before him. It ripped upward through his soul like a spike. It cast him forth, and he tumbled over and over, helpless in some incomprehensible limbo, where nevertheless he could still hear the faint distant voice of his lobster host:

—*Friend human McCulloch? Friend human McCulloch?*

He was drowning. He had waded incautiously into the surf, deceived by the beauty of the transparent tropical water and the shimmering white sand below, and a wave had caught him and knocked him to his knees, and the next wave had come before he could arise, pulling him under. And now he tossed like a discarded doll in the suddenly turbulent sea, struggling to get his head above water and failing, failing, failing.

Maggie was standing on the shore, calling in panic to him, and somehow he could hear her words even through the tumult of the crashing waves: "This way, Jim, swim toward me! Oh, please, Jim, this way, this way!"

Bleier was there, too, Mortenson, Bob Rodrigues, the whole group, ten or fifteen people, running about worriedly, beckoning to him, calling his name. It was odd that he could see them, if he was under water. And he could hear them so clearly, too, Bleier telling him to stand up and walk ashore, the water wasn't deep at all, and Rodrigues saying to come in on hands and knees if he couldn't manage to get up, and Ybarra yelling that it was getting late, that they couldn't wait all the goddamned afternoon, that he had been swimming long enough. McCulloch wondered why they didn't come after him, if they were so eager to get him to shore. Obviously he was in trouble. Obviously he was unable to help himself.

"Look," he said, "I'm drowning, can't you see? Throw me a line, for Christ's sake!" Water rushed into his mouth as he spoke. It filled his lungs, it pressed against his brain.

"We can't hear you, Jim!"

"Throw me a line!" he cried again, and felt the torrents pouring through his body. "I'm—drowning—drowning—"

And then he realized that he did not at all want them to rescue him, that it was worse to be rescued than to drown. He did not understand why he felt that way, but he made no attempt to question the feeling. All that concerned him now was preventing those people on the shore, those humans, from seizing him and taking him from the water. They were rushing about, assembling some kind of machine to pull him in, an arm at the end of a great boom. McCulloch signaled to them to leave him alone.

"I'm okay," he called. "I'm not drowning after all! I'm fine right where I am!"

But now they had their machine in operation, and its long metal arm was reaching out over the water toward him. He turned and dived, and swam as hard as he could away from the shore, but it was no use: the boom seemed to extend over an infinite distance, and no matter how fast he swam the boom moved faster, so that it hovered just above him now, and from its tip some sort of hook was descending—

"No—no—let me be! I don't want to go ashore!"

Then he felt a hand on his wrist: firm, reassuring, taking control. All right, he thought. They've caught me after all, they're going to pull me in. There's nothing I can do about it. They have me, and that's all there is to it. But he realized, after a moment, that he was heading not toward shore but out to sea, beyond the waves, into the calm warm depths. And the hand that was on his wrist was not a hand; it was a tentacle, thick as heavy cable, a strong sturdy tentacle lined on one side by rounded suction cups that held him in an unbreakable grip.

That was all right. Anything to be away from that wild crashing surf. It was much more peaceful out here. He could rest, catch his breath, get his equilibrium. And all the while that powerful tentacle towed him steadily seaward. He could still hear the voices of his friends onshore, but they were as faint as the cries of distant seabirds now, and when he looked back he saw only tiny dots, like excited ants, moving along the beach. McCulloch waved at them. "See you some other time," he called. "I didn't want to come out of the water yet anyway." Better here. Much much better. Peaceful. Warm. Like the womb. And that tentacle around his wrist: so reassuring, so steady.

—*Friend human McCulloch? Friend human McCulloch?*

—*This is where I belong. Isn't it?*

—*Yes. This is where you belong. You are one of us, friend human Mc-Culloch. You are one of us.*

Gradually the turbulence subsided, and he found himself regaining his balance. He was still within the lobster; the whole horde of lobsters was gathered around him, thousands upon thousands of them, a gentle solicitous community; and right in front of him was the largest octopus imaginable, a creature that must have been fifteen or twenty feet in diameter, with tentacles that extended an implausible distance on all sides. Somehow he did not find the sight frightening.

"He is recovered now," his host announced.

—*What happened to me?* McCulloch asked.

—*Your people called you again. But you did not want to make your homefaring, and you resisted them. And when we understood that you wanted to remain, the god aided you, and you broke free of their pull.*

—*The god?*

His host indicated the great octopus.

—*There.*

It did not seem at all improbable to McCulloch now. The infinite fullness of time brings about everything, he thought: even intelligent lobsters, even a divine octopus. He still could feel the mighty telepathic output of the vast creature, but though it had lost none of its power it no longer caused him discomfort; it was like the roaring thunder of some great waterfall, to which one becomes accustomed, and which, in time, one begins to love. The octopus sat motionless, its immense yellow eyes trained on McCulloch, its scarlet mantle rippling gently, its tentacles weaving in intricate patterns. McCulloch thought of an octopus he had once seen when he was diving in the West Indies: a small shy scuttling thing, hurrying to slither behind a gnarled coral head. He felt chastened and awed by this evidence of the magnifications wrought by the eons. A hundred million years? Half a billion? The numbers were without meaning. But that span of years had produced this creature. He sensed a serene intelligence of incomprehensible depth, benign, tranquil, all-penetrating: a god indeed. Yes. Truly a god. Why not?

The great cephalopod was partly sheltered by an overhanging wall of rock. Clustered about it were dozens of the scorpion-things, motionless, poised: plainly a guard force. Overhead swam a whole army of the big squids, doubtless guardians also, and for once the presence of those creatures did not trigger any emotion in the lobsters, as if they regarded squids in the service of the god as acceptable ones. The scene left McCulloch dazed with awe. He had never felt farther from home.

—*The god would speak with you,* said his host.

—*What shall I say?*

—*Listen, first.*

McCulloch's lobster moved forward until it stood virtually beneath the octopus's huge beak. From the octopus, then, came an outpouring of words that McCulloch did not immediately comprehend, but which, after a moment, he understood to be some kind of benediction that enfolded his soul like a warm blanket. And gradually he perceived that he was being spoken to.

"Can you tell us why you have come all this way, human McCulloch?"

"It was an error. They didn't mean to send me so far—only a hundred years or less, that was all we were trying to cross. But it was our first attempt. We didn't really know what we were doing. And I suppose I wound up halfway across time—a hundred million years, two hundred, maybe a billion—who knows?"

"It is a great distance. Do you feel no fear?"

"At the beginning I did. But not any longer. This world is alien to me, but not frightening."

"Do you prefer it to your own?"

"I don't understand," McCulloch said.

"Your people summoned you. You refused to go. You appealed to us for aid, and we aided you in resisting your homecalling, because it was what you seemed to require from us."

"I'm—not ready to go home yet," he said. "There's so much I haven't seen yet, and that I want to see. I want to see everything. I'll never have an opportunity like this again. Perhaps no one ever will. Besides, I have services to perform here. I'm the herald; I bring the Omen; I'm part of this pilgrimage. I think I ought to stay until the rites have been performed. I *want* to stay until then."

"Those rites will not be performed," said the octopus quietly.

"Not performed?"

"You are not the herald. You carry no Omen. The Time is not at hand."

McCulloch did not know what to reply. Confusion swirled within him. No Omen? Not the Time?

—*It is so,* said the host. *We were in error. The god has shown us that we came to our conclusion too quickly. The Time of the Molting may be near, but it is not yet upon us. You have many of the outer signs of a herald, but there is no Omen upon you. You are merely a visitor. An accident.*

McCulloch was assailed by a startlingly keen pang of disappointment. It was absurd; but for a time he had been the central figure in some apocalyptic ritual of immense significance, or at least had been thought to be, and all that suddenly was gone from him, and he felt strangely diminished, irrelevant, bereft of his bewildering grandeur. A visitor. An accident.

—*In that case I feel great shame and sorrow,* he said. *To have caused so much trouble for you. To have sent you off on this pointless pilgrimage.*

—*No blame attaches to you,* said the host. *We acted of our free choice, after considering the evidence.*

"Nor was the pilgrimage pointless," the octopus declared. "There are no pointless pilgrimages. And this one will continue."

"But if there's no Omen—if this is not the Time—"

"There are other needs to consider," replied the octopus, "and other observances to carry out. We must visit the dry place ourselves, from time to time, so that we may prepare ourselves for the world that is to succeed ours, for it will be very different from ours. It is time now for such a visit, and well past time. And also we must bring you to the dry place, for only there can we properly make you one of us."

"I don't understand," said McCulloch.

"You have asked to stay among us; and if you stay, you must become one of us, for your sake, and for ours. And that can best be done at the dry place. It is not necessary that you understand that now, human McCulloch."

—*Make no further reply,* said McCulloch's host. *The god has spoken. We must proceed.*

◄

Shortly the lobsters resumed their march, chanting as before, though in a more subdued way, and, so it seemed to McCulloch, singing a different melody. From the context of his conversation with it, McCulloch had supposed that the octopus now would accompany them, which puzzled him, for the huge unwieldy creature did not seem capable of any extensive journey. That proved to be the case: the octopus did not go along, though the vast booming resonances of its mental output followed the procession for what must have been hundreds of miles.

Once more the line was a single one, with McCulloch's host at the end of the file. A short while after departure it said:

—*I am glad, friend human McCulloch, that you chose to continue with us. I would be sorry to lose you now.*

—*Do you mean that? Isn't it an inconvenience for you, to carry me around inside your mind?*

—*I have grown quite accustomed to it. You are part of me, friend human McCulloch. We are part of one another. At the place of the dry land we will celebrate our sharing of this body.*

—*I was lucky*, said McCulloch, *to have landed like this in a mind that would make me welcome.*

—*Any of us would have made you welcome*, responded the host.

McCulloch pondered that. Was it merely a courteous turn of phrase, or did the lobster mean him to take the answer literally? Most likely the latter: the host's words seemed always to have only a single level of meaning, a straightforwardly literal one. So any of the lobsters would have taken him in uncomplainingly? Perhaps so. They appeared to be virtually interchangeable beings, without distinctive individual personalities, without names, even. The host had remained silent when McCulloch had asked him its name, and had not seemed to understand what kind of a label McCulloch's own name was. So powerful was their sense of community, then, that they must have little sense of private identity. He had never cared much for that sort of hive mentality, where he had observed it in human society. But here it seemed not only appropriate but admirable.

—*How much longer will it be*, McCulloch asked, *before we reach the place of dry land?*

—*Long.*

—*Can you tell me where it is?*

—*It is in the place where the world grows narrower*, said the host.

McCulloch had realized, the moment he asked the question, that it was meaningless: what useful answer could the lobster possibly give? The old continents were gone and their names long forgotten. But the answer he had received was meaningless, too: where, on a round planet, is the place where the world grows narrower? He wondered what sort of geography the lobsters understood. If I live among them a hundred years, he thought, I will probably just begin to comprehend what their perceptions are like.

Where the world grows narrower. All right. Possibly the place of the dry land was some surviving outcropping of the former world, the summit of Mount Everest, perhaps, Kilimanjaro, whatever. Or perhaps not: perhaps even those peaks had been ground down by time, and new ones had arisen—one of them, at least, tall enough to rise above the universal expanse of sea. It was folly to suppose that any shred at all of his world remained accessible: it was all down there beneath tons of water and millions of years of sediments, the old continents buried, hidden, rearranged by time like pieces scattered about a board.

The pulsations of the octopus's mind could no longer be felt. As the lobsters went tirelessly onward, moving always in that lithe skipping stride of theirs and never halting to rest or to feed, the terrain rose for a time and then began to dip again, slightly at first and then more than slightly. They entered into waters that were deeper and significantly darker, and somewhat cooler as well. In this somber zone, where vision seemed all but useless, the pilgrims grew silent for long spells for the first time, neither chanting nor speaking to one another, and McCulloch's host, who had become increasingly quiet, disappeared once more into its impenetrable inner domain and rarely emerged.

In the gloom and darkness there began to appear a strange red glow off to the left, as though someone had left a lantern hanging midway between the ocean floor and the surface of the sea. The lobsters, when that mysterious light came into view, at once changed the direction of their line of march to go veering off to the right; but at the same time they resumed their chanting, and kept one eye trained on the glowing place as they walked.

The water felt warmer here. A zone of unusual heat was spreading outward from the glow. And the taste of the water, and what McCulloch persisted in thinking of as its smell, were peculiar, with a harsh choking salty flavor. Brimstone? Ashes?

McCulloch realized that what he was seeing was an undersea volcano, belching forth a stream of red-hot lava that was turning the sea into a boiling bubbling caldron. The sight stirred him oddly. He felt that he was looking into the pulsing ancient core of the world, the primordial flame, the geological link that bound the otherwise vanished former worlds to this one. There awakened in him a powerful tide of awe, and a baffling unfocused yearning that he might have termed homesickness, except that it was not, for he was no longer sure where his true home lay.

—Yes, said the host. *It is a mountain on fire. We think it is a part of the older of the two former worlds that has endured both of the Moltings. It is a very sacred place.*

—*An object of pilgrimage?* McCulloch asked.

—Only to those who wish to end their lives. The fire devours all who approach it.

—In my world we had many such fiery mountains, McCulloch said. *They often did great destruction.*

—How strange your world must have been!

—It was very beautiful, said McCulloch.

—Surely. But strange. The dry land, the fire in the air—the sun, I mean— the air-breathing creatures—yes, strange, very strange. I can scarcely believe it really existed.

—There are times, now, when I begin to feel the same way, McCulloch said.

The volcano receded in the distance; its warmth could no longer be felt; the water was dark again, and cold, and growing colder, and McCulloch could no longer detect any trace of that sulphurous aroma. It seemed to him that they were moving now down an endless incline, where scarcely any creatures dwelled.

And then he realized that the marchers ahead had halted, and were drawn up in a long row as they had been when they came to the place where the octopus held its court. Another god? No. There was only blackness ahead.

—Where are we? he asked.

—It is the shore of the great abyss.

Indeed what lay before them looked like the Pit itself: lightless, without landmark, an empty landscape. McCulloch understood now that they had been marching all this while across some sunken continent's coastal plain, and at last they had come to—what?—the graveyard where one of Earth's lost oceans lay buried in ocean?

—Is it possible to continue? he asked.

—Of course, said the host. *But now we must swim.*

Already the lobsters before them were kicking off from shore with vigorous strokes of their tails and vanishing into the open sea beyond. A moment later McCulloch's host joined them. Almost at once there was no sense of a bottom beneath them—only a dark and infinitely deep void. Swimming across this, McCulloch thought, is like falling through time—an endless descent and no safety net.

The lobsters, he knew, were not true swimming creatures: like the lobsters of his own era they were bottom-dwellers, who walked to get where they needed to go. But they could never cross this abyss that way, and so they were swimming now, moving steadily by flexing their huge abdominal muscles and their tails. Was it terrifying to them to be setting forth into a place without landmarks like this? His host remained utterly calm, as though this were no more than an afternoon stroll.

McCulloch lost what little perception of the passage of time that he had had. Heave, stroke, forward, heave, stroke, forward, that was all, endless repetition. Out of the depths there occasionally came an upwelling of cold water, like a dull, heavy river miraculously flowing upward through air, and in that strange surging from below rose a fountain of nourishment, tiny transparent struggling creatures and even smaller flecks of some substance that must have been edible, for the lobsters, without missing a stroke, sucked in all they could hold. And swam on and on. McCulloch had a sense of being involved in a trek of epic magnitude, a once-in-many-generations thing that would be legendary long after.

Enemies roved this open sea: the free-swimming creatures that had evolved out of God only knew which kinds of worms or slugs to become the contemporary equivalents of sharks and whales. Now and again one of these huge beasts dived through the horde of lobsters, harvesting it at will. But they could eat only so much; and the survivors kept going onward.

Until at last—months, years later?—the far shore came into view; the ocean floor, long invisible, reared up beneath them and afforded support; the swimmers at last put their legs down on the solid bottom, and with something that sounded much like gratitude in their voices began once again to chant in unison as they ascended the rising flank of a new continent.

✦

The first rays of the sun, when they came into view an unknown span of time later, struck McCulloch with an astonishing, overwhelming impact. He perceived them first as a pale-greenish glow resting in the upper levels of the sea just ahead, striking downward like illuminated wands; he did not then know what he was seeing, but the sight engendered wonder in him all the same, and later, when that radiance diminished and was gone and in a short while returned, he understood that the pilgrims were coming up out of the sea. So they had reached their goal: the still point of the turning world, the one remaining unsubmerged scrap of the former Earth.

—*Yes*, said the host. *This is it.*

In that same instant McCulloch felt another tug from the past: a summons dizzying in its imperative impact. He thought he could hear Maggie Caldwell's voice crying across the time winds: "Jim, Jim, come back to us!" And Bleier, grouchy, angered, muttering, "For Christ's sake, McCulloch, stop holding on up there! This is getting expensive!" Was it all his imagination, that fantasy of hands on his wrists, familiar faces hovering before his eyes?

"Leave me alone," he said. "I'm still not ready."

"Will you ever be?" That was Maggie. "Jim, you'll be marooned. You'll be stranded there if you don't let us pull you back now."

"I may be marooned already," he said, and brushed the voices out of his mind with surprising ease.

He returned his attention to his companions and saw that they had halted their trek a little way short of that zone of light that now was but a quick scramble ahead of them. Their linear formation was broken once again. Some of the lobsters, marching blindly forward, were piling up in confused-looking heaps in the shallows, forming mounds fifteen or twenty lobsters deep. Many of the others had begun a bizarre convulsive dance: a wild twitchy cavorting, rearing up on their back legs, waving their claws about, flicking their antennae in frantic circles.

—*What's happening?* McCulloch asked his host. *Is this the beginning of a rite?*

But the host did not reply. The host did not appear to be within their shared body at all. McCulloch felt a silence far deeper than the host's earlier withdrawals; this seemed not a withdrawal but an evacuation, leaving McCulloch in sole possession. That new solitude came rolling in upon him with a crushing force. He sent forth a tentative probe, found nothing, found less than nothing. Perhaps it's meant to be this way, he thought. Perhaps it was necessary for him to face this climactic initiation unaided, unaccompanied.

Then he noticed that what he had taken to be a weird jerky dance was actually the onset of a mass molting prodrome. Hundreds of the lobsters had been stricken simultaneously, he realized, with that strange painful sense of inner expansion, of volcanic upheaval and stress: that heaving and rearing about was the first stage of the splitting of the shell.

And all of the molters were females.

Until that instant McCulloch had not been aware of any division into sexes among the lobsters. He had barely been able to tell one from the next; they had no individual character, no shred of uniqueness. Now, suddenly, strangely, he knew without being told that half of his companions were females, and that they were molting now because they were fertile only when they had shed their old armor, and that the pilgrimage to the place of the dry land was the appropriate time to engender the young. He had asked no questions of anyone to learn that; the knowledge was simply within him; and, reflecting on that, he saw that the host was absent from him because the host was wholly fused with him; he was the host, the host was Jim McCulloch.

He approached a female, knowing precisely which one was the appropriate one, and sang to her, and she acknowledged his song with a song of her own, and raised her third pair of legs to him, and let him plant his gametes beside her oviducts. There was no apparent pleasure in it, as he remembered pleasure from his days as a human. Yet it brought him a subtle but unmistakable sense of fulfillment, of the completion of biological destiny, that had a kind of orgasmic finality about it, and left him calm and anchored at the absolute dead center of his soul: yes, truly the still point of the turning world, he thought.

His mate moved away to begin her new Growing and the awaiting of her motherhood. And McCulloch, unbidden, began to ascend the slope that led to the land.

The bottom was fine sand here, soft, elegant. He barely touched it with his legs as he raced shoreward. Before him lay a world of light, radiant, heavenly, a bright irresistible beacon. He went on until the water, pearly pink and transparent, was only a foot or two deep, and the domed upper curve of his back was reaching into the air. He felt no fear. There was no danger in this. Serenely he went forward—the leader, now, of the trek—and climbed out into the hot sunlight.

It was an island, low and sandy, so small that he imagined he could cross it in a day. The sky was intensely blue, and the sun, hanging close to a noon position, looked swollen and fiery. A little grove of palm trees clustered a few hundred yards inland, but he saw nothing else, no birds, no insects, no animal life of any sort. Walking was difficult here—his breath was short, his shell seemed to be too tight, his stalked eyes were stinging in the air—but he pulled himself forward, almost to the trees. Other male lobsters, hundreds of them, thousands of them, were following. He felt himself linked to each of them: his people, his nation, his community, his brothers.

Now, at that moment of completion and communion, came one more call from the past.

There was no turbulence in it this time. No one was yanking at his wrists, no surf boiled and heaved in his mind and threatened to dash him on the reefs of the soul. The call was simple and clear: *This is the moment of coming back, Jim.*

Was it? Had he no choice? He belonged here. These were his people. This was where his loyalties lay.

And yet, and yet: he knew that he had been sent on a mission unique in human history, that he had been granted a vision beyond all dreams, that it was his duty to return and report on it. There was no ambiguity about that. He owed it to Bleier and Maggie and Ybarra and the rest to return, to tell them everything.

How clear it all was! He belonged *here*, and he belonged *there*, and an unbreakable net of loyalties and responsibilities held him to both places. It was a perfect equilibrium; and therefore he was tranquil and at ease. The pull was on him; he resisted nothing, for he was at last beyond all resistance to anything. The immense sun was a drumbeat in the heavens; the fiery warmth was a benediction; he had never known such peace.

"I must make my homefaring now," he said, and released himself, and let himself drift upward, light as a bubble, toward the sun.

Strange figures surrounded him, tall and narrow-bodied, with odd fleshy faces and huge moist mouths and bulging staring eyes, and their kind of speech was a crude hubbub of sound waves that bashed and battered against his sensibilities with painful intensity. "We were afraid the signal wasn't reaching you, Jim," they said. "We tried again and again, but there was no contact, nothing. And then just as we were giving up, suddenly your eyes were opening, you were stirring, you stretched your arms—"

He felt air pouring into his body, and dryness all about him. It was a struggle to understand the speech of these creatures who were bending over him, and he hated the reek that came from their flesh and the booming vibrations that they made with their mouths. But gradually he found himself returning to himself, like one who has been lost in a dream so profound that it eclipses reality for the first few moments of wakefulness.

"How long was I gone?" he asked.

"Four minutes and eighteen seconds," Ybarra said.

McCulloch shook his head. "Four minutes? Eighteen seconds? It was more like forty months, to me. Longer. I don't know how long."

"Where did you go, Jim? What was it like?"

"Wait," someone else said. "He's not ready for debriefing yet. Can't you see he's about to collapse?"

McCulloch shrugged. "You sent me too far."

"How far? Five hundred years?" Maggie asked.

"Millions," he said.

Someone gasped.

"He's dazed," a voice said at his left ear.

"Millions of years," McCulloch said in a slow, steady, determinedly articulate voice. "*Millions*. The whole earth was covered by the sea, except for one little island. The people are lobsters. They have a society, a culture. They worship a giant octopus."

Maggie was crying. "Jim, oh, Jim—"

"No. It's true. I went on migration with them. Intelligent lobsters is what they are. And I wanted to stay with them forever. I felt you pulling at me, but I—didn't—want—to—go—"

"Give him a sedative, Doc," Bleier said.

"You think I'm crazy? You think I'm deranged? They were lobsters, fellows. *Lobsters.*"

❥

After he had slept and showered and changed his clothes they came to see him again, and by that time he realized that he must have been behaving like a lunatic in the first moments of his return, blurting out his words, weeping, carrying on, crying out what surely had sounded like gibberish to them. Now he was rested, he was calm, he was at home in his own body once again.

He told them all that had befallen him, and from their faces he saw at first that they still thought he had gone around the bend: but as he kept speaking, quietly, straightforwardly, in rich detail, they began to acknowledge his report in subtle little ways, asking questions about the geography, about the ecological balance, in a manner that showed him they were not simply humoring him. And after that, as it sank in upon them that he really had dwelled for a period of many months at the far end of time, beyond the span of the present world, they came to look upon him—it was unmistakable—as someone who was now wholly unlike them. In particular he saw the cold, glassy stare in Maggie Caldwell's eyes.

Then they left him, for he was tiring again; and later Maggie came to see him alone, and took his hand and held it between hers, which were cold.

She said, "What do you want to do now, Jim?"

"To go back there."

"I thought you did."

"It's impossible, isn't it?" he said.

"We could try. But it couldn't ever work. We don't know what we're doing, yet, with that machine. We don't know where we'd send you. We might miss by a million years. By a billion."

"That's what I figured, too."

"But you want to go back?"

He nodded. "I can't explain it. It was like being a member of some Buddhist monastery, do you see? Feeling *absolutely sure* that this is where you belong, that everything fits together perfectly, that you're an integral part of it. I've never felt anything like that before. I never will again."

"I'll talk to Bleier, Jim, about sending you back."

"No. Don't. I can't possibly get there. And I don't want to land anywhere else. Let Ybarra take the next trip. I'll stay here."

"Will you be happy?"

He smiled. "I'll do my best," he said.

❥

When the others understood what the problem was, they saw to it that he went into reentry therapy—Bleier had already foreseen something like that, and made preparations for it—and after a while the pain went from him, that sense of having undergone a violent separation, of having been ripped untimely from the womb. He resumed his work in the group and gradually recovered his mental balance and took an active part in the second transmission, which sent a young anthropologist named Ludwig off for two minutes and eight seconds. Ludwig did not see lobsters, to McCulloch's intense disappointment. He went sixty years into the future and came back glowing with wondrous tales of atomic-fusion plants.

That was too bad, McCulloch thought. But soon he decided that it was just as well, that he preferred being the only one who had encountered the world beyond this world, probably the only human being who ever would.

He thought of that world with love, wondering about his mate and her millions of larvae, about the journey of his friends back across the great abyss, about the legends that were being spun about his visit in that unimaginably distant epoch. Sometimes the pain of separation returned, and Maggie found him crying in the night, and held him until he was whole again. And eventually the pain did not return. But still he did not forget, and in some part of his soul he longed to make his homefaring back to his true kind, and he rarely passed a day when he did not think he could hear the inaudible sound of delicate claws, scurrying over the sands of silent seas.

BASILEUS

Writing instructors often tell novice writers that they'll do their best work when they're writing about subjects they know very well, or when they're expressing some strongly held conviction. It's not bad advice, but it doesn't necessarily hold true for experienced professionals. Here's a case in point.

"Basileus" is a story about a computer nerd who can call up real angels on his computer. It's full of convincing-sounding stuff about hardware, software, programming, and such. It brims with incidental detail about the special qualities of particular angels.

I don't believe in angels.

And I had never used a computer at the time that I wrote the story.

You see what tricky characters professional writers are? Someone— was it L. Sprague de Camp?—once referred to us as people who earn their livings by telling lies. Exactly so. In my personal life I happen to be—trust me—more than usually scrupulous about telling the truth. But when I sit down to write a story, I'm willing to tell you any damn thing, and I'm capable of making you believe it, because for the time that I'm writing the story I believe it myself. Trust me. The best liars are those who speak out of the absolute conviction that what they're saying is so.

In the case of "Basileus," I needed a story idea and I had, for the moment, run absolutely dry. It was September of 1982, a warm and golden month, and I was exhausted after having spent the previous six months writing an immense historical novel, Lord of Darkness. In those days I did my writing on a typewriter—a manual typewriter, none of those exotic electric jobs for me—and Lord of Darkness was something like 800 pages long. I had typed the entire thing twice over, plus perhaps 400 pages of incidental revisions along the way, which came out to more than two thousand pages of typing, blam blam blam all summer long. Now the job was done and I just wanted to sit back and think about something other than writing stories, or perhaps not think of anything at all.

But Don Myrus, one of the editors of Omni magazine, had conceived the idea of doing a special Robert Silverberg issue. Harlan Ellison would write an article about me, two of my earlier stories would be reprinted, and I would contribute a brand-new piece to top everything off. It was too flattering to refuse. But where was I going to get that brand-new story? I was wiped out. I had reached that point, so dreadfully familiar to any writer who has just finished a major project, where I felt convinced that I'd never have a story idea again.

But Don Myrus wasn't going to believe that. I had to come up with something for him. And it had to be done right away.

One tactic that I've sometimes used when stuck for an idea is to grab two unrelated concepts at random, jam them together, and see if they strike any sparks. I tried it. I picked up the day's newspaper and glanced quickly at two different pages.

The most interesting words that rose to my eye were "computers" and "angels."

All right. I had my story, right then and there. Nerd uses his computer to talk to angels.

Corny? No. Nothing's corny if handled the right way. Trust me.

The antidote for corniness is verisimilitude. I had to write about angels as though I had spent my whole life conversing with them and knew them all by their first names. Well, I stockpile oddball reference books for just such moments, and among them is a copy of Gustav Davidson's Dictionary of Angels. (Due credit is given in the story.) I began to leaf through it. Very quickly I was on past Michael and Gabriel and Raphael into the more esoteric ones like Israfel, who will blow the trumpet to get the Day of Judgment under way, and Anaphaxeton, who will summon the entire universe before the court. Once I found them, I know that I had the dramatic situation around which to build my plot. The Day of Judgment! Of course. I saw right away that I'd have to invent a few angels of my own to make things work out, but that was no problem: inventing things like angels is what I'm paid to do, and I'm probably at least as good at it as some of the people who had invented the ones who fill the pages of Gustav Davidson's immense dictionary.

What about the computer stuff, though? Me, with my manual typewriter?

Well, writing the thousands of pages of Lord of Darkness had finally cured me of such folly. I had decided, that exhausted September, that my next book would be written on a computer. No more grim typing out of enormous final drafts would I do. From now on, just push the button and let the electrons do the work. So I had had a few conversations with that all-knowing computer expert Jerry Pournelle, and he not only explained the whole business to me but sent me a twenty-page letter, telling me what to look for when I went computer-shopping. I studied that with great diligence, and then began wandering into showrooms. Almost at once I found myself deep in the arcana of the trade: CPUs, Winchester disks, data bases, algorithms, bytes. Overnight I became capable of creating a sentence like "he has dedicated one of his function keys to its text, so that a single keystroke suffices to load it." I still didn't really know how to operate a computer—you pick that up only by sitting in front of one and turning it on—but I quickly had all the lingo down pat and some sense of what it meant.

You see how the trick is done? A knack for instant expertise is essential.

And so I wrote "Basileus." Tired as I was, I managed the job in four or five days. I was happy with the result, and so was Don Myrus. When he phoned to accept it, he expressed his awe, as a computer layman, for my obvious familiarity with such high-tech devices. "Well," I said, "living so close to Silicon Valley, it's hard not to pick up the lingo." What I didn't tell him was that I knew hardly any more about computers than he did, and I was going to use the check for my story to pay for the printer for my very first computer system, which I had just purchased the day before. "Basileus" was, in fact, the last work of fiction I would ever write on a typewriter. A few weeks later, as you already know (the stories in this collection are arranged in approximate chronological order, but the order is only approximate), I was a full-fledged computer user, embroiled in the intricacies of my giant-lobster story "Homefaring" and praying each hour that the damned machine would do what I wanted it to.

You know whom I prayed to, of course. Israfel. Anaphaxeton. Basileus.

In the shimmering lemon-yellow October light Cunningham touches the keys of his terminal and summons angels. An instant to load the program, an instant to bring the file up, and there they are, ready to spout from the screen at his command: Apollyon, Anauel, Uriel, and all the rest. Uriel is the angel of thunder and terror; Apollyon is the Destroyer, the angel of the bottomless pit; Anauel is the angel of bankers and commission brokers. Cunningham is fascinated by the multifarious duties and tasks, both exalted and humble, that are assigned to the angels. "Every visible thing in the world is put under the charge of an angel," said St. Augustine in *The Eight Questions.*

Cunningham has 1,114 angels in his computer now. He adds a few more each night, though he knows that he has a long way to go before he has them all. In the fourteenth century the number of angels was reckoned by the Kabbalists, with some precision, at 301,655,722. Albertus Magnus had earlier calculated that each choir of angels held 6,666 legions, and each legion 6,666 angels; even without knowing the number of choirs, one can see that that produces rather a higher total. And in the Talmud, Rabbi Jochanan proposed that new angels are born "with every utterance that goes forth from the mouth of the Holy One, blessed be He."

If Rabbi Jochanan is correct, the number of angels is infinite. Cunningham's personal computer, though it has extraordinary add-on memory capacity and is capable, if he chooses, of tapping into the huge mainframe machines of the Defense Department, has no very practical way of handling an infinity. But he is doing his best. To have 1,114 angels on line already, after only eight months of part-time programming, is no small achievement.

One of his favorites of the moment is Harahel, the angel of archives, libraries, and rare cabinets. Cunningham has designated Harahel also the angel of computers: it seems appropriate. He invokes Harahel often, to discuss the evolving niceties of data processing with him. But he has many other favorites, and his tastes run somewhat to the sinister: Azrael, the angel of death, for example, and Arioch, the angel of vengeance, and Zebuleon, one of the nine angels who will govern at the end of the world. It is Cunningham's job, from eight to four every working day, to devise programs for the interception of incoming Soviet nuclear warheads, and that, perhaps, has inclined him toward the more apocalyptic members of the angelic host.

He invokes Harahel now. He has bad news for him. The invocation that he uses is a standard one that he found in Arthur Edward Waite's *The Lemegeton, or The Lesser Key of Solomon,* and he has dedicated one of his function keys to its text, so that a single keystroke suffices to load it. "I do invoke, conjure, and command thee, O thou Spirit N, to appear and to show thyself visibly unto me before this Circle in fair and comely shape," is the way it begins, and it proceeds to utilize various secret and potent names of God in the summoning of Spirit N—such names as Zabaoth and Elion and, of course, Adonai—and it concludes, "I do potently exorcise thee that thou appearest here to fulfill my will in all things which seem good unto me. Wherefore, come thou, visibly, peaceably, and affably, now, without delay, to manifest that which I desire, speaking with a clear and perfect voice, intelligibly, and to mine understanding." All that takes but a micro-second, and another moment to enter in the name of Harahel as Spirit N, and there the angel is on the screen.

"I am here at your summons," he announces.

＊

Cunningham works with his angels from five to seven every evening. Then he has dinner. He lives alone, in a neat little flat a few blocks west of the Bayshore Freeway, and does not spend much of his time socializing. He thinks of himself as a pleasant man, a sociable man, and he may very well be right about that; but the pattern of his life has been a solitary one. He is thirty-seven years old, five feet eleven, with red hair, pale-blue eyes, and a light dusting of freckles on his cheeks. He did his undergraduate work at Cal Tech, his postgraduate studies at Stanford, and for the last nine years he has been involved in ultrasensitive military-computer projects in Northern California. He has never married. Sometimes he works with his angels again after dinner, from eight to ten, but hardly ever any later than that. At ten he always goes to bed. He is a very methodical person.

＊

He has given Harahel the physical form of his own first computer, a little Radio Shack TRS-80, with wings flanking the screen. He had thought originally to make the appearance of his angels more abstract—showing Harahel as a sheaf of kilobytes, for example—but like many of Cunningham's best and most austere ideas it had turned out impractical in the execution, since abstract concepts did not translate well into graphics for him.

"I want to notify you," Cunningham says, "of a shift in jurisdiction." He speaks English with his angels. He has it on good, though apocryphal, authority that the primary language of the angels is Hebrew, but his computer's audio algorithms have no Hebrew capacity, nor does Cunningham. But they speak English readily enough with him: they have no choice. "From now on," Cunningham tells Harahel, "your domain is limited to hardware only."

Angry green lines rapidly cross and recross Harahel's screen. "By whose authority do you—"

"It isn't a question of authority," Cunningham replies smoothly. "It's a question of precision. I've just read Vretil into the data base, and I have to code his functions. He's the recording angel, after all. So to some degree he overlaps your territory."

"Ah," says Harahel, sounding melancholy. "I was hoping you wouldn't bother about him."

"How can I overlook such an important angel? 'Scribe of the knowledge of the Most High,' according to the Book of Enoch. 'Keeper of the heavenly books and records.' 'Quicker in wisdom than the other archangels.' "

"If he's so quick," says Harahel sullenly, "give *him* the hardware. That's what governs the response time, you know."

"I understand. But he maintains the lists. That's data base."

"And where does the data base live? The hardware!"

"Listen, this isn't easy for me," Cunningham says. "But I have to be fair. I know you'll agree that some division of responsibilities is in order. And I'm giving him all data bases and related software. You keep the rest."

"Screens. Terminals. CPUs. Big deal."

"But without you, he's nothing, Harahel. Anyway, you've always been in charge of cabinets, haven't you?"

"And archives and libraries," the angel says. "Don't forget that."

"I'm not. But what's a library? Is it the books and shelves and stacks, or the words on the pages? We have to distinguish the container from the thing contained."

"A grammarian." Harahel sighs. "A hair-splitter. A casuist."

"Look, Vretil wants the hardware, too. But he's willing to compromise. Are you?"

"You start to sound less and less like our programmer and more and more like the Almighty every day," says Harahel.

"Don't blaspheme," Cunningham tells him. "Please. Is it agreed? Hardware only?"

"You win," says the angel. "But you always do, naturally."

❧

Naturally. Cunningham is the one with his hands on the keyboard, controlling things. The angels, though they are eloquent enough and have distinct and passionate personalities, are mere magnetic impulses deep within. In any contest with Cunningham they don't stand a chance. Cunningham, though he tries always to play the game by the rules, knows that, and so do they.

It makes him uncomfortable to think about it, but the role he plays is definitely godlike in all essential ways. He puts the angels into the computer; he gives them their tasks, their personalities, and their physical appearances; he summons them or leaves them uncalled, as he wishes.

A godlike role, yes. But Cunningham resists confronting that notion. He does not believe he is trying to be God; he does not even want to think about God. His family had been on comfortable terms with God—Uncle Tim was a priest, there was an archbishop somewhere back a few generations, his parents and sisters moved cozily within the divine presence as within a warm bath—

but he himself, unable to quantify the Godhead, preferred to sidestep any thought of it. There were other, more immediate matters to engage his concern. His mother had wanted him to go into the priesthood, of all things, but Cunningham had averted that by demonstrating so visible and virtuosic a skill at mathematics that even she could see he was destined for science. Then she had prayed for a Nobel Prize in physics for him; but he had preferred computer technology. "Well," she said, "a Nobel in computers. I ask the Virgin daily."

"There's no Nobel in computers, Mom," he told her. But he suspects she still offers novenas for it.

The angel project had begun as a lark, but had escalated swiftly into an obsession. He was reading Gustav Davidson's old *Dictionary of Angels*, and when he came upon the description of the angel Adramelech, who had rebelled with Satan and had been cast from heaven, Cunningham thought it might be amusing to build his computer simulation and talk with it. Davidson said that Adramelech was sometimes shown as a winged and bearded lion, and sometimes as a mule with feathers, and sometimes as a peacock, and that one poet had described him as "the enemy of God, greater in malice, guile, ambition, and mischief than Satan, a fiend more curst, a deeper hypocrite." That was appealing. Well, why not build him? The graphics were easy— Cunningham chose the winged-lion form—but getting the personality constructed involved a month of intense labor and some consultations with the artificial-intelligence people over at Kestrel Institute. But finally Adramelech was on line, suave and diabolical, talking amiably of his days as an Assyrian god and his conversations with Beelzebub, who had named him Chancellor of the Order of the Fly (Grand Cross).

Next, Cunningham did Asmodeus, another fallen angel, said to be the inventor of dancing, gambling, music, drama, French fashions, and other frivolities. Cunningham made him look like a very dashing Beverly Hills Iranian, with a pair of tiny wings at his collar. It was Asmodeus who suggested that Cunningham continue the project; so he brought Gabriel and Raphael on line to provide some balance between good and evil, and then Forcas, the angel who renders people invisible, restores lost property, and teaches logic and rhetoric in Hell; and by that time Cunningham was hooked.

He surrounded himself with arcane lore: M.R. James's editions of the Apocrypha, Waite's *Book of Ceremonial Magic* and *Holy Kabbalah*, the *Mystical Theology and Celestial Hierarchies* of Dionysius the Areopagite, and dozens of related works that he called up from the Stanford data base in a kind of manic fervor. As he codified his systems, he became able to put in five, eight, a dozen angels a night; one June evening, staying up well past his usual time, he managed thirty-seven. As the population grew, it took on weight and substance, for one angel cross-filed another, and they behaved now as though they held long conversations with one another even when Cunningham was occupied elsewhere.

The question of actual *belief* in angels, like that of belief in God Himself, never arose in him. His project was purely a technical challenge, not a theological exploration. Once, at lunch, he told a co-worker what he was doing, and got a chilly blank stare. "Angels? *Angels?* Flying around with big flapping wings, passing miracles? You aren't seriously telling me that you believe in angels, are you, Dan?"

To which Cunningham replied, "You don't have to believe in angels to make use of them. I'm not always sure I believe in electrons and protons. I know I've never seen any. But I make use of them."

"And what use do you make of angels?"

But Cunningham had lost interest in the discussion.

He divides his evenings between calling up his angels for conversations and programming additional ones into his pantheon. That requires continuous intensive research, for the literature of angels is extraordinarily large, and he is thorough in everything he does. The research is time-consuming, for he wants his angels to meet every scholarly test of authenticity. He pores constantly over such works as Ginzberg's seven-volume *Legends of the Jews*, Clement of Alexandria's *Prophetic Eclogues*, Blavatsky's *The Secret Doctrine*.

It is the early part of the evening. He brings up Hagith, ruler of the planet Venus and commander of 4,000 legions of spirits, and asks him details of the transmutation of metals, which is Hagith's specialty. He summons Hadraniel, who in Kabbalistic lore is a porter at the second gate of Heaven, and whose voice, when he proclaims the will of the Lord, penetrates through 200,000 universes; he questions the angel about his meeting with Moses, who uttered the Supreme Name at him and made him tremble. And then Cunningham sends for Israfel the four-winged, whose feet are under the seventh earth, and whose head reaches to the pillars of the divine throne. It will be Israfel's task to blow the trumpet that announces the arrival of the Day of Judgment. Cunningham asks him to take a few trial riffs now—"just for practice," he says, but Israfel declines, saying he cannot touch his instrument until he receives the signal, and the command sequence for that, says the angel, is nowhere to be found in the software Cunningham has thus far constructed.

When he wearies of talking with the angels, Cunningham begins the evening's programming. By now the algorithms are second nature and he can enter angels into the computer in a matter of minutes, once he has done the research. This evening he inserts nine more. Then he opens a beer, sits back, lets the day wind to its close.

He thinks he understands why he has become so intensely involved with this enterprise. It is because he must contend each day in his daily work with matters of terrifying apocalyptic import: nothing less, indeed, than the impending destruction of the world. Cunningham works routinely with megadeath simulation. For six hours a day he sets up hypothetical situations in which Country A goes into alert mode, expecting an attack from Country B, which thereupon begins to suspect a preemptive strike and commences a defensive response, which leads Country A to escalate its own readiness, and so on until the bombs are in the air. He is aware, as are many thoughtful people both in Country A and Country B, that the possibility of computer-generated misinformation leading to a nuclear holocaust increases each year, as the time window for correcting a malfunction diminishes. Cunningham also knows something that very few others do, or perhaps no one else at all: that it is now possible to send a signal to the giant computers—to Theirs or Ours, it makes no difference—that will be indistinguishable from the impulses that an actual flight of airborne warhead-bearing missiles would generate. If such a signal is permitted to enter the system, a minimum of eleven minutes, at the present time, will be needed to carry out fail-safe determination of its authenticity. That, at the present time, is too long to wait to decide whether the incoming missiles are real: a much swifter response is required.

Cunningham, when he designed his missile-simulating signal, thought at once of erasing his work. But he could not bring himself to do that: the program was too elegant, too perfect. On the other hand, he was afraid to tell anyone about it, for fear that it would be taken beyond his level of classification at once, and sealed away from him. He does not want that, for he dreams of finding an antidote for it, some sort of resonating inquiry mode that will distinguish all true alarms from false. When he has it, if he ever does, he will present both modes, in a single package, to Defense. Meanwhile, he bears the burden of suppressing a concept of overwhelming strategic importance. He has never done anything like that before. And he does not delude himself into thinking his mind is unique: if he could devise something like this, someone else probably could do it also, perhaps someone on the other side. True, it is a useless, suicidal program. But it would not be the first suicidal program to be devised in the interests of military security.

He knows he must take his simulator to his superiors before much more time goes by. And under the strain of that knowledge, he is beginning to show distinct signs of erosion. He mingles less and less with other people; he has

unpleasant dreams and occasional periods of insomnia; he has lost his appetite
and looks gaunt and haggard. The angel project is his only useful diversion, his
chief distraction, his one avenue of escape.

For all his scrupulous scholarship, Cunningham has not hesitated to invent a
few angels of his own. Uraniel is one of his: the angel of radioactive decay, with
a face of whirling electron shells. And he has coined Dimitrion too: the angel of
Russian literature, whose wings are sleighs and whose head is a snow-covered
samovar. Cunningham feels no guilt over such whimsies. It is his computer,
after all, and his program. And he knows he is not the first to concoct angels.
Blake engendered platoons of them in his poems: Urizen and Orc and Enithar-
mon and more. Milton, he suspects, populated *Paradise Lost* with dozens of
sprites of his own invention. Gurdjieff and Alastair Crowley and even Pope
Gregory the Great had their turns at amplifying the angelic roster: why, then,
not also Dan Cunningham of Palo Alto, California? So from time to time he
works one up on his own. His most recent is the dread high lord Basileus, to
whom Cunningham has given the title of Emperor of the Angels. Basileus is
still incomplete: Cunningham has not arrived at his physical appearance, nor
his specific functions, other than to make him the chief administrator of the
angelic horde. But there is something unsatisfactory about imagining a new
archangel, when Gabriel, Raphael, and Michael already constitute the high
command. Basileus needs more work. Cunningham puts him aside, and
begins to key in Duma, the angel of silence and of the stillness of death,
thousand-eyed, armed with a fiery rod. His style in angels is getting darker and
darker.

On a misty, rainy night in late October, a woman from San Francisco whom
he knows in a distant, occasional way phones to invite him to a party. Her name
is Joanna; she is in her mid-thirties, a biologist working for one of the little
gene-splicing outfits in Berkeley; Cunningham had had a brief and vague affair
with her five or six years back, when she was at Stanford, and since then they
have kept fitfully in touch, with long intervals elapsing between meetings. He
has not seen her or heard from her in over a year. "It's going to be an interesting
bunch," she tells him. "A futurologist from New York, Thomson the sociobiol-
ogy man, a couple of video poets, and someone from the chimpanzee-
language outfit, and I forget the rest, but they all sounded first-rate."

Cunningham hates parties. They bore and jangle him. No matter how first-
rate the people are, he thinks, real interchange of ideas is impossible in a large
random group, and the best one can hope for is some pleasant low-level chatter.
He would rather be alone with his angels than waste an evening that way.

On the other hand, it has been so long since he has done anything of a social nature that he has trouble remembering what the last gathering was. As he had been telling himself all his life, he needs to get out more often. He likes Joanna and it's about time they got together, he thinks, and he fears that if he turns her down she may not call again for years. And the gentle patter of the rain, coming on this mild evening after the long dry months of summer, has left him feeling uncharacteristically relaxed, open, accessible.

"All right," he says. "I'll be glad to go."

The party is in San Mateo, on Saturday night. He takes down the address. They arrange to meet there. Perhaps she'll come home with him afterward, he thinks: San Mateo is only fifteen minutes from his house, and she'll have a much longer drive back up to San Francisco. The thought surprises him. He had supposed he had lost all interest in her that way; he had supposed he had lost all interest in anyone that way, as a matter of fact.

Three days before the party, he decides to call Joanna and cancel. The idea of milling about in a roomful of strangers appalls him. He can't imagine, now, why he ever agreed to go. Better to stay home alone and pass a long rainy night designing angels and conversing with Uriel, Ithuriel, Raphael, Gabriel.

But as he goes toward the telephone, that renewed hunger for solitude vanishes as swiftly as it came. He *does* want to go to the party. He *does* want to see Joanna: very much, indeed. It startles him to realize that he positively yearns for some change in his rigid routine, some escape from his little apartment, its elaborate computer hookup, even its angels.

Cunningham imagines himself at the party, in some brightly lit room in a handsome redwood-and-glass house perched in the hills above San Mateo. He stands with his back to the vast sparkling wraparound window, a drink in his hand, and he is holding forth, dominating the conversation, sharing his rich stock of angel lore with a fascinated audience.

"Yes, three hundred million of them," he is saying, "and each with his fixed function. Angels don't have free will, you know. It's Church doctrine that they're created with it, but at the moment of their birth they're given the choice of opting for God or against Him, and the choice is irrevocable. Once they've made it they're unalterably fixed, for good or for evil. Oh, and angels are born circumcised, too. At least the Angels of Sanctification and the Angels of Glory are, and probably the seventy Angels of the Presence."

"Does that mean that all angels are male?" asks a slender dark-haired woman.

"Strictly speaking, they're bodiless and therefore without sex," Cunningham tells her. "But in fact the religions that believe in angels are mainly patriarchical ones, and when the angels are visualized they tend to be portrayed as men. Although some of them, apparently, can change sex at will. Milton tells us that in *Paradise Lost*: 'Spirits when they please can either sex assume, or both; so soft and uncompounded is their essence pure.' And some angels seem to be envisioned as female in the first place. There's the Shekinah, for instance, 'the bride of God,' the manifestation of His glory indwelling in human beings. There's Sophia, the angel of wisdom. And Lilith, Adam's first wife, the demon of lust—"

"Are demons considered angels, then?" a tall professorial-looking man wants to know.

"Of course. They're the angels who opted away from God. But they're angels nevertheless, even if we mortals perceive their aspects as demonic or diabolical."

He goes on and on. They all listen as though he is God's own messenger. He speaks of the hierarchies of angels—the seraphim, cherubim, thrones, dominations, principalities, powers, virtues, archangels, and angels—and he tells them of the various lists of the seven great angels, which differ so greatly once one gets beyond Michael, Gabriel, and Raphael, and he speaks of the 90,000 angels of destruction and the 300 angels of light, he conjures up the seven angels with seven trumpets from the Book of Revelation, he tells them which angels rule the seven days of the week and which the hours of the days and night, he pours forth the wondrous angelic names, Zadkiel, Hashmal, Orphaniel, Jehudiel, Phaleg, Zagzagel. There is no end to it. He is in his glory. He is a fount of arcana. Then the manic mood passes. He is alone in his room; there is no eager audience. Once again he thinks he will skip the party. No. No. He will go. He wants to see Joanna.

He goes to his terminal and calls up two final angels before bedtime: Leviathan and Behemoth. Behemoth is the great hippopotamus-angel, the vast beast of darkness, the angel of chaos. Leviathan is his mate, the mighty she-whale, the splendid sea serpent. They dance for him on the screen: Behemoth's huge mouth yawns wide. Leviathan gapes even more awesomely. "We are getting hungry," they tell him. "When is feeding time?" In rabbinical lore, these two will swallow all the damned souls at the end of days. Cunningham tosses them some electronic sardines and sends them away. As he closes his eyes he invokes Poteh, the angel of oblivion, and falls into a black dreamless sleep.

➤

At his desk the next morning he is at work on a standard item, a glitch-clearing program for the third-quadrant surveillance satellites, when he finds himself unaccountably trembling. That has never happened to him before. His finger-nails look almost white, his wrists are rigid, his hands are quivering. He feels chilled. It is as though he has not slept for days. In the washroom he clings to the sink and stares at his pallid, sweaty face. Someone comes up behind him and says, "You all right, Dan?"

"Yeah. Just a little attack of the queasies."

"All that wild living in the middle of the week wears a man down," the other says, and moves along. The social necessities have been observed: a question, a noncommittal answer, a quip, good-bye. He could have been having a stroke here and they would have played it the same way. Cunningham has no close friends at the office. He knows that they regard him as eccentric— eccentric in the wrong way, not lively and quirky but just a peculiar kind of hermit—and getting worse all the time. I could destroy the world, he thinks. I could go into the Big Room and type for fifteen seconds, and we'd be on all-out alert a minute later and the bombs would be coming down from orbit six minutes later. I could give that signal. I could really do it. I could do it right now.

Waves of nausea sweep him and he grips the edge of the sink until the last racking spasm is over. Then he cleans his face and, calmer now, returns to his desk to stare at the little green symbols on the screen.

That evening, still trying to find a function for Basileus, Cunningham discovers himself thinking of demons, and of one demon not in the classical demonology—Maxwell's Demon, the one that the physicist James Clerk Maxwell postulated to send fast-moving molecules in one direction and slow ones in another, thereby providing an ultraefficient method for heating and refrigeration. Perhaps some sort of filtering role could be devised for Basileus. Last week a few of the loftier angels had been complaining about the proximity to them of certain fallen angels within the computer. "There's a smell of brimstone on this disk that I don't like," Gabriel had said. Cunningham wonders if he could make Basileus a kind of traffic manager within the program: let him sit in there and ship the celestial angels into one sector of a disk, the fallen ones to another.

The idea appeals to him for about thirty seconds. Then he sees how fundamentally trivial it is. He doesn't need an angel for a job like that; a little simple software could do it. Cunningham's corollary to Kant's categorical imperative: *Never use an angel as mere software.* He smiles, possibly for the first time all week. Why, he doesn't even need software. He can handle it himself, simply by assigning princes of Heaven to one file and demons to a different one. It hadn't seemed necessary to segregate his angels that way, or he would have done it from the start. But if they were complaining—

He begins to flange up a sorting program to separate the files. It should have taken him a few minutes, but he finds himself working in a rambling, muddled way, doing an untypically sloppy job. With a quick swipe he erases what he has done. Gabriel would have to put up with the reek of brimstone a little longer, he thinks.

There is a dull throbbing pain just behind his eyes. His throat is dry, his lips feel parched. Basileus would have to wait a little longer, too. Cunningham keys up another angel, allowing his fingers to choose for him, and finds himself looking at a blank-faced angel with a gleaming metal skin. One of the early ones, Cunningham realizes. "I don't remember your name," he says. "Who are you?"

"I am Anaphaxeton."

"And your function?"

"When my name is pronounced aloud, I will cause the angels to summon the entire universe before the bar of justice on Judgment Day."

"Oh, Jesus," Cunningham says. "I don't want you tonight."

He sends Anaphaxeton away and finds himself with the dark angel Apollyon, fish scales, dragon wings, bear feet, breathing fire and smoke, holding the key to the Abyss. "No," Cunningham says, and brings up Michael, standing with drawn sword over Jerusalem, and sends him away only to find on the screen an angel with 70,000 feet and 4,000 wings, who is Azrael, the angel of death. "No," says Cunningham again. "Not you. Oh, Christ!" A vengeful army crowds his computer. On his screen there passes a flurrying regiment of wings and eyes and beaks. He shivers and shuts the system down for the night. Jesus, he thinks. Jesus, Jesus, Jesus. All night long suns explode in his brain.

◆

On Friday his supervisor, Ned Harris, saunters to his desk in an unusually folksy way and asks him if he's going to be doing anything interesting this weekend. Cunningham shrugs. "A party Saturday night, that's about all. Why?"

"Thought you might be going off on a fishing trip or something. Looks like the last nice weekend before the rainy season sets in, wouldn't you say?"

"I'm not a fisherman, Ned."

"Take some kind of trip. Drive down to Monterey, maybe. Or up into the wine country."

"What are you getting at?" Cunningham asks.

"You look like you could use a little change of pace," Harris says amiably. "A couple of days off. You've been crunching numbers so hard they're starting to crunch you, is my guess."

"It's that obvious?"

Harris nods. "You're tired, Dan. It shows. We're a little like air traffic controllers around here, you know, working so hard we start to dream about blips on the screen. That's no good. Get the hell out of town, fellow. The Defense Department can operate without you for a while. Okay? Take Monday off. Tuesday, even. I can't afford to have a fine mind like yours going goofy from fatigue, Dan."

"All right, Ned. Sure. Thanks."

His hands are shaking again. His fingernails are colorless.

"And get a good early start on the weekend, too. No need for you to hang around here today until four."

"If that's okay—"

"Go on. Shoo!"

Cunningham closes down his desk and makes his way uncertainly out of the building. The security guards wave at him. Everyone seems to know he's being sent home early. Is this what it's like to crack up on the job? He wanders about the parking lot for a little while, not sure where he has left his car. At last he finds it, and drives home at thirty miles an hour, with horns honking at him all the way as he wanders up the freeway.

He settles wearily in front of his computer and brings the system on line, calling for Harahel. Surely the angel of computers will not plague him with apocalyptic matters.

Harahel says, "Well, we've worked out your Basileus problem for you."

"You have?"

"Uriel had the basic idea, building on your Maxwell's Demon notion. Israfel and Azrael developed it some. What's needed is an angel embodying God's justice and God's mercy. A kind of evaluator, a filtering angel. He weighs deeds in the balance, and arrives at a verdict."

"What's new about that?" Cunningham asks. "Something like that's built into every mythology from Sumer and Egypt on. There's always a mechanism for evaluating the souls of the dead—this one goes to Paradise, this one goes to Hell—"

"Wait," Harahel says. "I wasn't finished. I'm not talking about the evaluation of individual souls."

"What, then?"

"Worlds," the angel replies. "Basileus will be the judge of worlds. He holds an entire planet up to scrutiny and decides whether it's time to call for the last trump."

"Part of the machinery of Judgment, you mean?"

"Exactly. He's the one who presents the evidence to God and helps Him make His decision. And then he's the one who tells Israfel to blow the trumpet, and he's the one who calls out the name of Anaphaxeton to bring everyone before the bar. He's the prime apocalyptic angel, the destroyer of worlds. And we thought you might make him look like—"

"Ah," Cunningham says. "Not now. Let's talk about that some other time."

He shuts the system down, pours himself a drink, sits staring out the window at the big eucalyptus tree in the front yard. After a while it begins to rain. Not such a good weekend for a drive into the country after all, he thinks. He does not turn the computer on again that evening.

Despite everything, Cunningham goes to the party. Joanna is not there. She has phoned to cancel, late Saturday afternoon, pleading a bad cold. He detects no sound of a cold in her voice, but perhaps she is telling the truth. Or possibly she has found something better to do on Saturday night. But he is already geared for party-going, and he is so tired, so eroded, that it is more effort to change his internal program than it is to follow through on the original schedule. So about eight that evening he drives up to San Mateo, through a light drizzle.

The party turns out not to be in the glamorous hills west of town, but in a small cramped condominium close to the heart of the city, furnished with what looks like somebody's college-era chairs and couches and bookshelves. A cheap stereo is playing the pop music of a dozen years ago, and a sputtering screen provides a crude computer-generated light show. The host is some sort of marketing exec for a large video-games company in San Jose, and most of the guests look vaguely corporate too. The futurologist from New York has sent his regrets; the famous sociobiologist has also somehow failed to arrive; the video poets are two San Francisco gays who will talk only to each other, and stray not very far from the bar; the expert on teaching chimpanzees to speak is in the red-faced-and-sweaty stage of being drunk, and is working hard at seducing a plump woman festooned with astrological jewelry. Cunningham, numb, drifts through the party as though he is made of ectoplasm. He speaks to no one, no one speaks to him. Some jugs of red wine are open on a table by the window, and he pours himself a glassful. There he stands, immobile, imprisoned by inertia. He imagines himself suddenly making a speech about angels, telling everyone how Ithuriel touched Satan with his spear in the Garden of Eden as the Fiend crouched next to Eve, and how the hierarch Ataphiel keeps Heaven aloft by balancing it on three fingers. But he says nothing. After a time he finds himself approached by a lean, leathery-looking woman with glittering eyes, who says, "And what do you do?"

"I'm a programmer," Cunningham says. "Mainly I talk to angels. But I also do national security stuff."

"Angels?" she says, and laughs in a brittle, tinkling way. "You talk to angels? I've never heard anyone say that before." She pours herself a drink and moves quickly elsewhere.

"Angels?" says the astrological woman. "Did someone say angels?"

Cunningham smiles and shrugs and looks out the window. It is raining harder. I should go home, he thinks. There is absolutely no point in being here. He fills his glass again. The chimpanzee man is still working on the astrologer, but she seems to be trying to get free of him and come over to Cunningham. To discuss angels with him? She is heavy-breasted, a little wall-eyed, sloppy-looking. He does not want to discuss angels with her. He does not want to discuss angels with anyone. He holds his place at the window until it definitely does appear that the astrologer is heading his way; then he drifts toward the door. She says, "I heard you say you were interested in angels. Angels are a special field of mine, you know. I've studied with—"

"Angles," Cunningham says. "I play the angles. That's what I said. I'm a professional gambler."

"Wait," she says, but he moves past her and out into the night. It takes him a long while to find his key and get his car unlocked, and the rain soaks him to the skin, but that does not bother him. He is home a little before midnight.

He brings Raphael on line. The great archangel radiates a beautiful golden glow.

"You will be Basileus," Raphael tells him. "We've decided it by a vote, hierarchy by hierarchy. Everyone agrees."

"I can't be an angel. I'm human," Cunningham replies.

"There's ample precedent. Enoch was carried off to Heaven and became an angel. So was Elijah. St. John the Baptist was actually an angel. You will become Basileus. We've already done the program for you. It's on the disk: just call him up and you'll see. Your own face, looking out at you."

"No," Cunningham says.

"How can you refuse?"

"Are you really Raphael? You sound like someone from the other side. A tempter. Asmodeus. Astaroth. Belphegor."

"I am Raphael. And you are Basileus."

Cunningham considers it. He is so very tired that he can barely think.

An angel. Why not? A rainy Saturday night, a lousy party, a splitting headache: come home and find out you've been made an angel, and given a high place in the hierarchy. Why not? Why the hell not?

"All right," he says. "I'm Basileus."

He puts his hands on the keys and taps out a simple formulation that goes straight down the pipe into the Defense Department's big Northern California system. With an alteration of two keystrokes he sends the same message to the Soviets. Why not? Redundancy is the soul of security. The world now has about six minutes left. Cunningham has always been good with computers. He knows their secret language as few people before him have.

Then he brings Raphael on the screen again.

"You should see yourself as Basileus while there's still time," the archangel says.

"Yes. Of course. What's the access key?"

Raphael tells him. Cunningham begins to set it up.

Come now, Basileus! We are one!

Cunningham stares at the screen with growing wonder and delight, while the clock continues to tick.

DANCERS IN THE
TIME - FLUX

Long ago, in what almost seems to me now to have been another galaxy, I wrote a novel called Son of Man. *The year was 1969, when the world was new and strange and psychedelic, and* Son of Man *was my attempt to reproduce in prose form some of the visionary aspects of life in that heady era under the pretext of creating a world of the far, far future. The results were very strange, but to me, at least, exciting and rewarding; and over the years* Son of Man *has retained a small but passionate audience. It's the kind of book that polarizes readers in an extremely sharp way: some find themselves unable to get past page three, others read it over and over again. (I read it now and then myself, as a matter of fact.)*

Writing Son of Man *had been such an extraordinarily exhilarating experience that when I began writing again in 1980 after my long period of retirement, I found myself tempted to dip into the world of* Son of Man *again, possibly for a short story or two, perhaps even for a whole new novel. But I gave the idea no serious thought until July of 1981, when I received a letter from the Pacific Northwest writer and editor Jessica Amanda Salmonson, asking me to write a short story for an anthology, called* Heroic Visions, *that she was assembling. (At that time Jessica dated all her letters "9981." I haven't heard from her lately, so I don't know whether she still regards herself as living in the hundredth century.)*

Heroic Visions *was intended as an anthology of new stories of "high fantasy and heroic fantasy," according to the prospectus Jessica sent. High fantasy—Eddison, Dunsany, Charles Williams, Tolkien, William Morris— is something I read occasionally with pleasure, but have never intentionally written. Heroic fantasy—exemplified by such characters as Robert E. Howard's Conan, Fritz Leiber's Fafhrd and the Gray Mouser, and*

Michael Moorcock's Elric—is something that holds less interest for me as a reader, and though I suppose I could fake it as a writer if I saw some reason to do so, I have no true natural aptitude for it. So I really didn't belong in Jessica's book. Nor was the financial aspect of the project especially enticing. But I was rediscovering writing again that year and was willing to try almost anything just then. I jotted at the bottom of the prospectus, "World of Son of Man. *Two figures from the remote past are swept into the time-flux—a woman of 20th century, a man of—where? ancient China? Sumer?" and dropped Jessica a card saying I might possibly send her a story later on that year, when I had finished* Majipoor Chronicles, *which I was working on at the time.*

She was surprised, and, I suppose, skeptical. Justifiably so: I went on to other things and forgot all about Heroic Visions. But on December 19, "9981," she tried again, asking me if there was any hope of getting the story. I replied that I'd do it, provided she could see a Son of Man *spin-off as appropriate to her theme. She had read that book and knew it well. Back came her enthusiastic okay, and on January 9 I sent "Dancers in the Time-Flux" off to her.*

As you'll see, it departs considerably from the scrawled original notion of the previous July. The twentieth-century woman disappears from the plot—I tried without success to return to her later on, in a sequel—and the man of ancient China or Sumer is transmogrified into the sixteenth-century Dutch circumnavigator Oliver van Noort, an actual historic figure whom I had written about at length years before in a nonfiction book called The Longest Voyage. *I do think the story recaptures the tone of* Son of Man *to a considerable extent, but whether it has the headlong wildness of that book is not so clear to me. It may be that 1969s come around only once in a lifetime. Which is, perhaps, a good thing.*

Under a warm golden wind from the west, Bhengarn the Traveler moves steadily onward toward distant Crystal Pond, his appointed place of metamorphosis. The season is late. The swollen scarlet sun clings close to the southern hills. Bhengarn's body—a compact silvery tube supported by a dozen pairs of sturdy three-jointed legs—throbs with the need for transformation.

And yet the Traveler is unhurried. He has been bound on this journey for many hundreds of years. He has traced across the face of the world a glistening trail that zigzags from zone to zone, from continent to continent, and even now still glimmers behind him with a cold brilliance like a thread of bright metal stitching the planet's haunches. For the past decade he has patiently circled Crystal Pond at the outer end of a radial arm one-tenth the diameter of the Earth in length; now, at the prompting of some interior signal, he has begun to spiral inward upon it.

The path immediately before him is bleak. To his left is a district covered by furry green fog; to his right is a region of pale crimson grass sharp as spikes and sputtering with a sinister hostile hiss; straight ahead a roadbed of black clinkers and ashen crusts leads down a shallow slope to the Plain of Teeth, where menacing porcelaneous outcroppings make the wayfarer's task a taxing one. But such obstacles mean little to Bhengarn. He is a Traveler, after all. His body is superbly designed to carry him through all difficulties. And in his journeys he has been in places far worse than this.

Elegantly he descends the pathway of slag and cinders. His many feet are tough as annealed metal, sensitive as the most alert antennae. He tests each point in the road for stability and support, and scans the thick layer of ashes for concealed enemies. In this way he moves easily and swiftly toward the plain, holding his long abdomen safely above the cutting edges of the cold volcanic matter over which he walks.

As he enters the Plain of Teeth he sees a new annoyance: an Eater commands the gateway to the plain. Of all the forms of human life—and the Traveler has encountered virtually all of them in his wanderings, Eaters, Destroyers, Skimmers, Interceders, and the others—Eaters seem to him the most tiresome, mere noisy monsters. Whatever philosophical underpinnings form the rationale of their bizarre way of life are of no interest to him. He is wearied by their bluster and offended by their gross appetites.

All the same, he must get past this one to reach his destination. The huge creature stands straddling the path with one great meaty leg at each edge and the thick fleshy tail propping it from behind. Its steely claws are exposed, its fangs gleam, driblets of blood from recent victims stain its hard reptilian hide. Its chilly inquisitive eyes, glowing with demonic intelligence, track Bhengarn as the traveler draws near.

The Eater emits a boastful roar and brandishes its many teeth.

"You block my way," Bhengarn declares.

"You state the obvious," the Eater replies.

"I have no desire for an encounter with you. But my destiny draws me toward Crystal Pond, which lies beyond you."

"For you," says the Eater, "nothing lies beyond me. Your destiny has brought you to a termination today. We will collaborate, you and I, in the transformation of your component molecules."

From the spiracles along his sides the Traveler releases a thick blue sigh of boredom. "The only transformation that waits for me is the one I will undertake at Crystal Pond. You and I have no transaction. Stand aside."

The Eater roars again. He rocks slightly on his gigantic claws and swishes his vast saurian tail from side to side. These are the preliminaries to an attack, but in a kind of ponderous courtesy he seems to be offering Bhengarn the opportunity to scuttle back up the ash-strewn slope.

Bhengarn says, "Will you yield place?"

"I am an instrument of destiny."

"You are a disagreeable boastful ignoramus," says Bhengarn calmly, and consumes half a week's energy driving the scimitars of his spirit to the roots of the world. It is not a wasted expense of soul, for the ground trembles, the sky grows dark, the hill behind him creaks and groans, the wind turns purplish and frosty. There is a dull droning sound that the Traveler knows is the song of the time-flux, an unpredictable force that often is liberated at such moments. Despite that, Bhengarn will not relent. Beneath the Eater's splayed claws the fabric of the road ripples. Sour smells rise from sudden crevasses. The enormous beast utters a yipping cry of rage and lashes his tail vehemently against the ground. He sways; he nearly topples; he calls out to Bhengarn to cease his onslaught, but the Traveler knows better than to settle for a half-measure. Even more fiercely he presses against the Eater's bulky form.

"This is unfair," the Eater wheezes. "My goal is the same as yours: to serve the forces of necessity."

"Serve them by eating someone else today," answers Bhengarn curtly, and with a final expenditure of force shoves the Eater to an awkward untenable position that causes it to crash down onto its side. The downed beast, moaning, rakes the air with his claws but does not arise, and as Bhengarn moves briskly past the Eater he observes that fine transparent threads, implacable as stone, have shot forth from a patch of swamp beside the road and are rapidly binding the fallen Eater in an unbreakable net. The Eater howls. Glancing back, Bhengarn notices the threads already cutting their way through the Eater's thick scales like tiny streams of acid. "So, then," Bhengarn says, without malice, "the forces of necessity will be gratified today after all, but not by me. The Eater is to be eaten. It seems that this day I prove to be the instrument of destiny." And without another backward look he passes quickly onward into the plain. The sky regains its ruddy color, the wind becomes mild once more, the Earth is still. But a release of the time-flux is never without consequences, and as the Traveler trundles forward he perceives some new creature of unfamiliar form staggering through the mists ahead, confused and lost, lurching between the shining lethal formations of the Plain of Teeth in seeming ignorance of the perils they hold. The creature is upright, two-legged, hairy, of archaic appearance. Bhengarn, approaching it, recognizes it finally as a primordial human, swept millions of years past its own true moment.

"Have some care," Bhengarn calls. "Those teeth can bite!"

"Who spoke?" the archaic creature demands, whirling about in alarm.

"I am Bhengarn the Traveler. I suspect I am responsible for your presence here."

"Where are you? I see no one! Are you a devil?"

"I am a Traveler, and I am right in front of your nose."

The ancient human notices Bhengarn, apparently for the first time, and leaps back, gasping. "Serpent!" he cries. "Serpent with legs! Worm! Devil!" Wildly he seizes rocks and hurls them at the Traveler, who deflects them easily enough, turning each into a rhythmic juncture of gold and green that hovers, twanging softly, along an arc between the other and himself. The archaic one lifts an immense boulder, but as he hoists it to drop it on Bhengarn he overbalances and his arm flies backward, grazing one of the sleek teeth behind him. At once the tooth releases a turquoise flare and the man's arm vanishes to the elbow. He sinks to his knees, whimpering, staring bewilderedly at the stump and at the Traveler before him.

Bhengarn says, "You are in the Plain of Teeth, and any contact with these mineral formations is likely to be unfortunate, as I attempted to warn you."

He slides himself into the other's soul for an instant, pushing his way past thick encrusted stalagmites and stalactites of anger, fear, outraged pride, pain, disorientation, and arrogance, and discovers himself to be in the presence of one Olivier van Noort of Utrecht, former tavernkeeper at Rotterdam, commander of the voyage of circumnavigation that set forth from Holland on the second day of July 1598 and traveled the entire belly of the world, a man of exceedingly strong stomach and bold temperament, who has experienced much, having gorged on the meat of penguins at Cape Virgines and the isle called Pantagoms, having hunted beasts not unlike stags and buffaloes and ostriches in the cold lands by Magellan's Strait, having encountered whales and parrots and trees whose bark had the bite of pepper, having had strife with the noisome Portugals in Guinea and Brazil, having entered into the South Sea on a day of diverse storms, thunders, and lightnings, having taken ships of the Spaniards in Valparaiso and slain many Indians, having voyaged thence to the Isles of Ladrones or Thieves, where the natives bartered bananas, coconuts, and roots for old pieces of iron, overturning their canoes in their greed for metal, having suffered a bloody flux in Manila of eating palmitos, having captured vessels of China laden with rice and lead, having traded with folk on a ship of the Japans, whose men make themselves bald except a tuft left in the hinder part of the head, and wield swords that would, with one stroke, cut through three men, having traded also with the bare-breasted women of Borneo, bold and impudent and shrewd, who carry iron-pointed javelins and sharp darts, and having after great privation and the loss of three of his four ships and all but forty-five of his 248 men, many of them executed by him or marooned on remote islands for their mutinies but a good number murdered by the treacheries of savage enemies, come again to Rotterdam on the twenty-sixth of August in 1601, bearing little in the way of salable goods to show for his hardships and calamities. None of this has any meaning to Bhengarn the Traveler except in the broadest, which is to say that he recognizes in Olivier van Noort a stubborn and difficult man who has conceived and executed a journey of mingled heroism and foolishness that spanned vast distances, and so they are brothers, of a sort, however millions of years apart. As a fraternal gesture Bhengarn restores the newcomer's arm. That appears to be as bewildering to the other as was its sudden loss. He squeezes it, moves it cautiously back and forth, scoops up a handful of pebbles with it. "This is Hell, then," he mutters, "and you are a demon of Satan."

"I am Bhengarn the Traveler, bound toward Crystal Pond, and I think that I conjured you by accident out of your proper place in time while seeking to thwart that monster." Bhengarn indicates the fallen Eater, now half dissolved. The other, who evidently had not looked that way before, makes a harsh choking sound at the sight of the giant creature, which still struggles sluggishly. Bhengarn says, "The time-flux has seized you and taken you far from home, and there will be no going back for you. I offer regrets."

"You offer regrets? A worm with legs offers regrets! Do I dream this, or am I truly dead and gone to Hell?"

"Neither one."

"In all my sailing round the world I never saw a place so strange as this, or the likes of you, or of that creature over yonder. Am I to be tortured, demon?"

"You are not where you think you are."

"Is this not Hell?"

"This is the world of reality."

"How far are we, then, from Holland?"

"I am unable to calculate it," Bhengarn answers. "A long way, that's certain. Will you accompany me toward Crystal Pond, or shall we part here?"

Noort is silent a moment. Then he says, "Better the company of demons than none at all, in such a place. Tell me straight, demon: am I to be punished here? I see hellfire on the horizon. I will find the rivers of fire, snow, toads, and black water, will I not? And the place where sinners are pronged on hooks jutting from blazing wheels? The ladders of red-hot iron, eh? The wicked broiling on coals? And the Arch-Traitor himself, sunk in ice to his chest—he must be near, is he not?" Noort shivers. "The fountains of poison. The wild boars of Lucifer. The aloes biting bare flesh, the dry winds of the abyss—when will I see them?"

"Look there," says Bhengarn. Beyond the Plain of Teeth a column of black flame rises into the heavens, and in it dance creatures of a hundred sorts, melting, swirling, coupling, fading. A chain of staring lidless eyes spans the sky. Looping whorls of green light writhe on the mountaintops. "Is that what you expect? You will find whatever you expect here."

"And yet you say this is not Hell?"

"I tell you again, it is the true world, the same into which you were born long ago."

"And is this Brazil, or the Indies, or some part of Africa?"

"Those names mean little to me."

"Then we are in the Terra Australis," says Noort. "It must be. A land where worms have legs and speak good Dutch, and rocks can bite, and arms once lost can sprout anew—yes, it must surely be the Terra Australis, or else the land of Prester John. Eh? Is Prester John your king?" Noort laughs. He seems to be emerging from his bewilderment. "Tell me the name of this land, creature, so I may claim it for the United Provinces, if ever I see Holland again."

"It has no name."

"No name! No name! What foolishness! I never found a place whose folk had no name for it, not even in the endless South Sea. But I will name it, then. Let this province be called New Utrecht, eh? And all this land, from here to the shores of the South Sea, I annex hereby to the United Provinces in the name of the States-General. You be my witness, creature. Later I will draw up documents. You say I am not dead?"

"Not dead, not dead at all. But far from home. Come, walk beside me, and touch nothing. This is troublesome territory."

"This is strange and ghostly territory," says Noort. "I would paint it, if I could, and then let Mynheer Brueghel look to his fame, and old Bosch as well. Such sights! Were you a prince before you were transformed?"

"I have not yet been transformed," says Bhengarn. "That awaits me at Crystal Pond." The road through the plain now trends slightly uphill; they are advancing into the farther side of the basin. A pale-yellow tint comes into the sky. The path here is prickly with little many-faceted insects whose hard sharp bodies assail the Dutchman's bare tender feet. Cursing, he hops in wild leaps, bringing him dangerously close to outcroppings of teeth, and Bhengarn, in sympathy, fashions stout gray boots for him. Noort grins. He gestures toward his bare middle, and Bhengarn clothes him in a shapeless gray robe.

"Like a monk, is how I look!" Noort cries. "Well, well, a monk in Hell! But you say this is not Hell. And what kind of creature are you, creature?"

"A human being," says Bhengarn, "of the Traveler sort."

"A human being!" Noort booms. He leaps across a brook of sparkling bubbling violet-hued water and waits on the far side as Bhengarn trudges through it. "A human under an enchantment, I would venture."

"This is my natural form. Humankind has not worn your guise since long before the falling of the Moon. The Eater you saw was human. Do you see, on yonder eastern hill, a company of Destroyers turning the forest to rubble? They are human."

"The wolves on two legs up there?"

"Those, yes. And there are others you will see. Awaiters, Breathers, Skimmers—"

"These are mere noises to me, creature. What is human? A Dutchman is human! A Portugal is human! Even a Chinese, a black, a Japonder with a shaven head. But those beasts on yon hill? Or a creature with more legs than I have whiskers. No, Traveler, no! You flatter yourself. Do you happen to know, Traveler, how it is that I am here? I was in Amsterdam, to speak before the Lords Seventeen and the Company in general, to ask for ships to bring pepper from the Moluccas, but they said they would choose Joris van Spilbergen in my place—do you know Spilbergen? I think him much overpraised—and then all went dizzy, as though I had taken too much beer with my gin—and then— then—ah, this is a dream, is it not, Traveler? At this moment I sleep in Amsterdam. I am too old for such drinking. Yet never have I had a dream so real as this, and so strange. Tell me: when you walk, do you move the legs on the right side first, or the left?" Noort does not wait for a reply. "If you are human, Traveler, are you also a Christian, then?"

Bhengarn searches in Noort's mind for the meaning of that, finds something approximate, and says, "I make no such claim."

"Good. Good. There are limits to my credulity. How far is this Crystal Pond?"

"We have covered most of the distance. If I proceed at a steady pace I will come shortly to the land of smoking holes, and not far beyond that is the approach to the Wall of Ice, which will demand a difficult but not impossible ascent, and just on the far side of that I will find the vale that contains Crystal Pond, where the beginning of the next phase of my life will occur." They are walking now through a zone of sparkling rubbery cones of a bright vermilion color, from which small green Stangarones emerge in quick succession to chant their one-note melodies. The flavor of a heavy musk hangs in the air. Night is beginning to fall. Bhengarn says, "Are you tired?"

"Just a little."

"It is not my custom to travel by night. Does this campsite suit you?" Bhengarn indicates a broad circular depression bordered by tiny volcanic fumaroles. The ground here is warm and spongy, moist, bare of vegetation. Bhengarn extends an excavator claw and pulls free a strip of it, which he hands to Noort, indicating that he should eat. Noort tentatively nibbles. Bhengarn helps himself to some also. Noort, kneeling, presses his knuckles against the ground, makes it yield, mutters to himself, shakes his head, rips off another strip and chews it in wonder. Bhengarn says, "You find the world much changed, do you not?"

"Beyond all understanding, in fact."

"Our finest artists have worked on it since time immemorial, making it more lively, more diverting. We think it is a great success. Do you agree?"

Noort does not answer. He is staring bleakly at the sky, suddenly dark and jeweled with blazing stars. Bhengarn realizes that he is searching for patterns, navigators' signs. Noort frowns, turns round and round to take in the full circuit of the heavens, bites his lip, finally lets out a low groaning sigh and says, "I recognize nothing. Nothing. This is not the northern sky, this is not the southern sky, this is not any sky I can understand." Quietly he begins to weep. After a time he says somberly, "I was not the most adept of navigators, but I knew something, at least. And I look at this sky and I feel like a helpless babe. All the stars have changed places. Now I see how lost I am, how far from anything I ever knew, and once it gave me great pleasure to sail under strange skies, but not now, not here, because these skies frighten me and this land of demons offers me no peace. I have never wept, do you know that, creature, never, not once in my life! But Holland—my house, my tavern, my church, my sons, my pipe—where is Holland? Where is everything I knew? The skies above Magellan's Strait were not the thousandth part so strange as this." A harsh heavy sob escapes him, and he turns away, huddling into himself.

Compassion floods Bhengarn for this miserable wanderer. To ease Noort's pain he summons fantasies for him, dredging images from the reservoirs of the ancient man's spirit and hurling them against the sky, building a cathedral of fire in the heavens, and a royal palace, and a great armada of ships with bellying sails and the Dutch flag fluttering, and the watery boulevards of busy Amsterdam and the quiet streets of little Haarlem, and more. He paints for Noort the stars in their former courses, the Centaur, the Swan, the Bear, the Twins. He restores the fallen Moon to its place and by its cold light creates a landscape of time lost and gone, with avenues of heavy-boughed oaks and maples, and drifts of brilliant red and yellow tulips blazing beneath them, and golden roses arching in great bowers over the thick, newly mowed lawn. He creates fields of ripe wheat, and haystacks high as barns, and harvesters toiling in the hot sultry afternoon. He gives Noort the aroma of the Sunday feast and the scent of good Dutch gin and the sweet dense fumes of his long clay pipe. Noort nods and murmurs and clasps his hands, and gradually his sorrow ebbs and his weeping ceases, and he drifts off into a deep and easy slumber. The images fade. Bhengarn, who rarely sleeps, keeps watch until first light comes and a flock of fingerwinged birds passes overhead, shouting shrilly, jesting and swooping.

Noort is calm and quiet in the morning. He feeds again on the spongy soil and drinks from a clear emerald rivulet and they move onward toward Crystal Pond. Bhengarn is pleased to have his company. There is something crude and coarse about the Dutchman, perhaps even more so than another of his era might be, but Bhengarn finds that unimportant. He has always preferred companions of any sort to the solitary march, in his centuries of going to and fro upon the Earth. He has traveled with Skimmers and Destroyers, and once a ponderous Ruminant, and even on several occasions visitors from other worlds who have come to sample the wonders of Earth. At least twice Bhengarn has had as his traveling companion a castaway of the time-flux from some prehistoric era, though not so prehistoric as Noort's. And now it has befallen him that he will go to the end of his journey with this rough hairy being from the dawn of humanity's day. So be it. So be it.

Noort says, breaking a long silence as they cross a plateau of quivering gelatinous stuff, "Were you a man or a woman before the sorcery gave you this present shape?"

"I have always had this form."

"No. Impossible. You say you are human, you speak my language—"

"Actually, you speak *my* language," says Bhengarn.

"As you wish. If you are human you must once have looked like me. Can it be otherwise? Were you born a thing of silvery scales and many legs? I will not believe that."

"Born?" says Bhengarn, puzzled.

"Is this word unknown to you?"

"Born," the Traveler repeats. "I think I see the concept. To *begin*, to *enter*, to *acquire one's shape*—"

"Born," says Noort in exasperation. "To come from the womb. To hatch, to sprout, to drop. Everything alive has to be born!"

"No," Bhengarn says mildly. "Not any longer."

"You talk nonsense," Noort snaps, and scours his throat angrily and spits.

His spittle strikes a node of assonance and blossoms into a dazzling mound of green and scarlet jewels. "Rubies," he murmurs. "Emeralds. I could puke pearls, I suppose." He kicks at the pile of gems and scatters them; they dissolve into spurts of moist pink air. The Dutchman gives himself over to a sullen brooding. Bhengarn does not transgress on the other's taciturnity; he is content to march forward in his steady plodding way, saying nothing.

Three Skimmers appear, prancing, leaping. They are heading to the south. The slender golden-green creatures salute the wayfarers with pulsations of their great red eyes. Noort, halting, glares at them and says hoarsely to Bhengarn, "These are human beings, too?"

"Indeed."

"Natives of this realm?"

"Natives of this era," says Bhengarn. "The latest form, the newest thing, graceful, supple, purposeless." The Skimmers laugh and transform themselves into shining streaks of light and soar aloft like a trio of auroral rays. Bhengarn says, "Do they seem beautiful to you?"

"They seem like minions of Satan," says the Dutchman sourly. He scowls. "When I awaken I pray I remember none of this. For if I do, I will tell the tale to Willem and Jan and Piet, and they will think I have lost my senses, and mock me. Tell me I dream, creature. Tell me I lie drunk in an inn in Amsterdam."

"It is not so," Bhengarn says gently.

"Very well. Very well. I have come to a land where every living thing is a demon or a monster. That is no worse, I suppose, than a land where everyone speaks Japanese and worships stones. It is a world of wonders, and I have seen more than my share. Tell me, creature, do you have cities in this land?"

"Not for millions of years."

"Then where do the people live?"

"Why, they live where they find themselves! Last night we lived where the ground was food. Tonight we will settle by the Wall of Ice. And tomorrow—"

"Tomorrow," Noort says, "we will have dinner with the Grand Diabolus and dance in the Witches' Sabbath. I am prepared, just as I was prepared to sup with the penguin-eating folk of the Cape, that stood six cubits high. I will be surprised by nothing." He laughs. "I am hungry, creature. Shall I tear up the earth again and stuff it down?"

"Not here. Try those fruits."

Luminous spheres dangle from a tree of golden limbs. Noort plucks one, tries it unhesitatingly, claps his hands, takes three more. Then he pulls a whole cluster free, and offers one to Bhengarn, who refuses.

"Not hungry?" the Dutchman asks.

"I take my food in other ways."

"Yes, you breathe it in from flowers as you crawl along, eh? Tell me, Traveler: to what end is your journey? To discover new lands? To fulfill some pledge? To confound your enemies? I doubt it is any of these."

"I travel out of simple necessity, because it is what my kind does, and for no special purpose."

"A humble wanderer, then, like the mendicant monks who serve the Lord by taking to the highways?"

"Something like that."

"Do you ever cease your wanderings?"

"Never yet. But cessation is coming. At Crystal Pond I will become my utter opposite, and enter the Awaiter tribe, and be made immobile and contemplative. I will root myself like a vegetable, after my metamorphosis."

Noort offers no comment on that. After a time he says, "I knew a man of your kind once. Jan Huyghen van Linschoten of Haarlem, who roamed the world because the world was there to roam, and spent his years in the India of the Portugals and wrote it all down in a great vast book, and when he had done that went off to Novaya Zemlya with Barents to find the chilly way to the Indies, and I think would have sailed to the Moon if he could find the pilot to guide him. I spoke with him once. My own travels took me farther than Linschoten, do you know? I saw Borneo and Java and the world's hinder side, and the thick Sargasso Sea. But I went with a purpose other than my own amusement or the gathering of strange lore, which was to buy pepper and cloves, and gather Spanish gold, and win my fame and comfort. Was that so wrong, Traveler? Was I so unworthy?" Noort chuckles. "Perhaps I was, for I brought home neither spices nor gold nor most of my men, but only the fame of having sailed around the world. I think I understand you, Traveler. The spices go into a cask of meat and are eaten and gone; the gold is only yellow metal; but so long as there are Dutchmen, no one will forget that Olivier van Noort, the tavernkeeper of Rotterdam, strung a line around the middle of the world. So long as there are Dutchmen." He laughs. "It is folly to travel for profit. I will travel for wisdom from now on. What do you say, Traveler? Do you applaud me?"

"I think you are already on the proper path," says Bhengarn. "But look, look there: the Wall of Ice."

Noort gasps. They have come around a low headland and are confronted abruptly by a barrier of pure white light, as radiant as a mirror at noon, that spans the horizon from east to west and rises skyward like an enormous palisade filling half the heavens. Bhengarn studies it with respect and admiration. He has known for hundreds of years that he must ascend this wall if he is to reach Crystal Pond, and that the wall is formidable; but he has seen no need before now to contemplate the actualities of the problem, and now he sees that they are significant.

"Are we to ascend that?" Noort asks.

"I must. But here, I think, we shall have to part company."

"The throne of Lucifer must lie beyond that icy rampart."

"I know nothing of that," says Bhengarn, "but certainly Crystal Pond is on the farther side, and there is no other way to reach it but to climb the wall. We will camp tonight at its base, and in the morning I will begin my climb."

"Is such a climb possible?"

"It will have to be," Bhengarn replies.

"Ah. You will turn yourself to a puff of light like those others we met, and shoot over the top like some meteor. Eh?"

"I must climb," says Bhengarn, "using one limb after another, and taking care not to lose my grip. There is no magical way of making this ascent." He sweeps aside fallen branches of a glowing blue-limbed shrub to make a campsite for them. To Noort he says, "Before I begin the ascent tomorrow I will instruct you in the perils of the world, for your protection on your future wanderings. I hold myself responsible for your presence here, and I would not have you harmed once you have left my side."

Noort says, "I am not yet planning to leave your side. I mean to climb that wall alongside you, Traveler."

"It will not be possible for you."

"I will make it possible. That wall excites my spirit. I will conquer it as I conquered the storms of the Strait and the fevers of the Sargasso. I feel I should go with you to Crystal Pond, and pay my farewells to you there, for it will bring me luck to mark the beginning of my solitary journey by witnessing the end of yours. What do you say?"

"I say wait until the morning," Bhengarn answers, "and see the wall at close range, before you commit yourself to such mighty resolutions."

During the night a silent lightstorm plays overhead; twisting turbulent spears of blue and green and violet radiance clash in the throbbing sky, and an undulation of the atmosphere sends alternating waves of hot and cool air racing down from the Wall of Ice. The time-flux blows, and frantic figures out of forgotten eras are swept by now far aloft, limbs churning desperately, eyes rigid with astonishment. Noort sleeps through it all, though from time to time he stirs and mutters and clenches his fists. Bhengarn ponders his obligations to the Dutchman, and by the coming of the sharp blood-hued dawn he has arrived at an idea. Together they advance to the edge of the Wall; together they stare upward at that vast vertical field of shining whiteness, smooth as stone.

Hesitantly Noort touches it with his fingertip, and hisses at the coldness of it. He turns his back to it, paces, folds and unfolds his arms.

He says finally, "No man or woman born could achieve the summit of that wall. But is there not some magic you could work, Traveler, that would enable me to make the ascent?"

"There is one. But I think you would not like it."

"Speak."

"I could transform you—for a short time, only a short time, no longer than the time it takes to climb the wall—into a being of the Traveler form. Thus we could ascend together."

Noort's eyes travel quickly over Bhengarn's body—the long tubular serpentine thorax, the tapering tail, the multitude of powerful little legs—and a look of shock and dismay and loathing comes over his face for an instant, but just an instant. He frowns. He tugs at his heavy lower lip.

Bhengarn says, "I will take no offense if you refuse."

"Do it."

"You may be displeased."

"Do it! The morning is growing old. We have much climbing to do. Change me, Traveler. Change me quickly." A shadow of doubt crosses Noort's features. "You will change me back, once we reach the top?"

"It will happen of its own accord. I have no power to make a permanent transformation."

"Then do what you can, and do it now!"

"Very well," says Bhengarn, and the Traveler, summoning his fullest force, drains metamorphic energies from the planets and the stars and a passing comet, and focuses them and hurls them at the Dutchman, and there is a buzzing and a droning and a shimmering and when it is done a second Traveler stands at the foot of the Wall of Ice.

Noort seems thunderstruck. He says nothing; he does not move; only after a long time does he carefully lift his frontmost left limb and swing it forward a short way and put it down. Then the one opposite it; then several of the middle limbs; then, growing more adept, he manages to move his entire body, adopting a curious wriggling style, and in another moment he appears to be in control. "This is passing strange," he remarks at length. "And yet it is almost like being in my own body, except that everything has been changed. You are a mighty wizard, Traveler. Can you show me now how to make the ascent?"

"Are you ready so soon?"

"I am ready," Noort says.

So Bhengarn demonstrates, approaching the wall, bringing his penetrator claws into play, driving them like pitons into the ice, hauling himself up a short distance, extending the claws, driving them in, pulling upward. He has never climbed ice before, though he has faced all other difficulties the world has to offer, but the climb, though strenuous, seems manageable enough. He halts after a few minutes and watches as Noort, clumsy but determined in his altered body, imitates him, scratching and scraping at the ice as he pulls himself up the face until they are side by side. "It is easy," Noort says.

And so it is, for a time, and then it is less easy, for now they hang high above the valley and the midday sun has melted the surface of the wall just enough to make it slick and slippery, and a terrible cold from within the mass of ice seeps outward into the climbers, and even though a Traveler's body is a wondrous machine fit to endure anything, this is close to the limit. Once Bhengarn loses his purchase, but Noort deftly claps a claw to the middle of his spine to hold him firmly until he has dug in again; and not much later the same happens to Noort, and Bhengarn grasps him. As the day wanes they are so far above the ground that they can barely make out the treetops below, and yet the top of the wall is too high to see. Together they excavate a ledge, burrowing inward to rest in a chilly nook, and at dawn they begin again, Bhengarn's sinuous body winding upward over the rim of their little cave and Noort following with less agility. Upward and upward they climb, never pausing and saying little, through a day of warmth and soft perfumed breezes and through a night of storms and falling stars, and then through a day of turquoise rain, and through another day and a night and a day and then they are at the top, looking out across the broad unending field of ferns and bright blossoms that covers the summit's flat surface, and as they move inward from the rim Noort lets out a cry and stumbles forward, for he has resumed his ancient form. He drops to his knees and sits there panting, stunned, looking in confusion at his fingernails, at his knuckles, at the hair on the backs of his hands, as though he has never seen such things before. "Passing strange," he says softly.

"You are a born Traveler," Bhengarn tells him.

They rest a time, feeding on the sparkling four-winged fruits that sprout in that garden above the ice. Bhengarn feels an immense calmness now that the climax of his peregrination is upon him. Never had he questioned the purpose of being a Traveler, nor has he had regret that destiny gave him that form, but now he is quite willing to yield it up.

"How far to Crystal Pond?" Noort asks.

"It is just over there," says Bhengarn.

"Shall we go to it now?"

"Approach it with great care," the Traveler warns. "It is a place of extraordinary power."

They go forward; a path opens for them in the swaying grasses and low fleshy-leaved plants; within minutes they stand at the edge of a perfectly circular body of water of unfathomable depth and of a clarity so complete that the reflections of the sun can plainly be seen on the white sands of its infinitely distant bed. Bhengarn moves to the edge and peers in, and is pervaded by a sense of fulfillment and finality.

Noort says, "What will become of you here?"

"Observe," says Bhengarn.

He enters Crystal Pond and swims serenely toward the farther shore, an enterprise quickly enough accomplished. But before he has reached the mid-point of the pond a tolling sound is heard in the air, as of bells of the most pure quality, striking notes without harmonic overtones. Sudden ecstasy engulfs him as he becomes aware of the beginning of his transformation: his body flows and streams in the flux of life, his limbs fuse, his soul expands. By the time he comes forth on the edge of the pond he has become something else, a great cone of passive flesh, which is able to drag itself no more than five or six times its own length from the water, and then sinks down on the sandy surface of the ground and begins the process of digging itself in. Here the Awaiter Bhengarn will settle, and here he will live for centuries of centuries, motionless, all but timeless, considering the primary truths of being. Already he is gliding into the Earth.

Noort gapes at him from the other side of the pond.

"Is this what you sought?" the Dutchman asks.

"Yes. Absolutely."

"I wish you farewell and Godspeed, then!" Noort cries.

"And you—what will become of you?"

Noort laughs. "Have no fears for me! I see my destiny unfolding!"

Bhengarn, nestled now deep in the ground, enwombed by the earth, immobile, established already in his new life, watches as Noort strides boldly to the water's edge. Only slowly, for an Awaiter's mind is less agile than a Traveler's, does Bhengarn comprehend what is to happen.

Noort says, "I've found my vocation again. But if I'm to travel, I must be equipped for traveling!"

He enters the pond, swimming in broad awkward splashing strokes, and once again the pure tolling sound is evoked, a delicate carillon of crystalline transparent tone, and there is sudden brilliance in the pond as Noort sprouts the shining scales of a Traveler, and the jointed limbs, and the strong thick tail. He scuttles out on the far side wholly transformed.

"Farewell!" Noort cries joyously.

"Farewell," murmurs Bhengarn the Awaiter, peering out from the place of his long repose as Olivier van Noort, all his legs ablaze with new energy, strides away vigorously to begin his second circumnavigation of the globe.

GATE OF HORN, GATE OF IVORY

An odd concatenation of ironies surrounds this little story.

I was, for ten years beginning in 1969, the editor of an annual anthology of original science fiction stories called New Dimensions. During that time I published a good many interesting and important stories by such writers as Ursula K. Le Guin, Gardner Dozois, George Alec Effinger, James Tiptree, Jr., Harlan Ellison, Joanna Russ, Philip Jose Farmer, Gregory Benford, Isaac Asimov, and Barry Malzberg. Some of the stories I ran won Hugo and Nebula awards, and a few, like Le Guin's "The Ones Who Walk Away from Omelas" and Joanna Russ's "Nobody Home," have become much-reprinted classics.

In all that time, New Dimensions never published a story by Robert Silverberg. One minor but not insignificant reason was that I didn't write any short stories between November 1973 and January 1980. Even if I had, though, you wouldn't have seen them in New Dimensions, because it isn't much of a challenge for editors to sell stories to themselves, and I would have felt foolish filling New Dimensions with my own work.

By 1979, though, I was beginning to emerge from my five-year mid-1970s retirement from fiction-writing, and I wanted to ease myself of my editorial duties to have more time and energy available for doing stories. So I invited my friend and neighbor Marta Randall, then at the peak of her own science-fiction career, to take over New Dimensions. We worked out a complicated transitional mode: the eleventh New Dimensions would carry the byline, "edited by Robert Silverberg and Marta Randall." Issue twelve would be slugged "edited by Marta Randall and Robert Silverberg." And from the thirteenth issue onward, New Dimensions would carry Marta's name alone.

And so it came to pass: a Silverberg-Randall issue in 1980, a Randall-Silverberg issue in 1981. In the autumn of 1981, as Marta was putting the finishing touches on her first solo issue of New Dimensions, *she caught me by surprise by saying to me, "Since your name won't be on number thirteen as editor, how about writing a story for me?"*

Well, why not? I thought. Nearly every well-known science-fiction writer of the period had been published in New Dimensions *except me. I had already decided to spend the autumn and winter of 1981–82 writing short stories anyway. And now that I was no longer connected with the anthology in any way, there was no reason to disqualify myself from contributing. A week or two later I delivered "Gate of Horn, Gate of Ivory" to Marta. Now I, too, had sold a story to* New Dimensions.

But it never appeared there. New Dimensions' *publisher underwent a turbulent internal upheaval the following year, and its entire science-fiction line, including* New Dimensions *and a host of other books in progress, was canceled before publication.* New Dimensions 13 *exists today only in galley-proof form.*

*But a second anthology of original science fiction—*Universe*—was being edited just then by yet another Bay Area resident, Terry Carr. It had begun publication about the same time as* New Dimensions, *had won just about as much acclaim for its material, and indeed had been in direct although friendly—very friendly—competition with* New Dimensions *all along. I had written a few stories for* Universe *in its early days, and when I resumed writing them in 1980 I had vaguely promised to do another for it, but never had. When Terry heard that* New Dimensions *had been suspended with an entire issue of fiction in inventory, including one of mine, he asked Marta to show her the stories, and a little while later he called to ask if it was all right for him to use "Gate of Horn." Which is why the story with which I had intended to make my* New Dimensions *debut appeared instead in the 1984 number of its chief competitor,* Universe.

There is a final dark twist to the tale. Terry fell ill in 1985, weakened all through 1986, and died in the spring of 1987, only fifty years old. Pat LoBrutto, his editor at Doubleday, felt that Universe *should be continued as a memorial to him, and asked me, a few weeks after Terry's death, to take charge of it. It was, as they say, an offer I couldn't refuse—and so today I find myself, in collaboration with my wife, Karen Haber, the editor of* Universe, *which now is published every other year. So "Gate of Horn" got in just under the wire; now that I'm its editor, I regard the contents page of* Universe *as closed to me, just as that of* New Dimensions *was for so many years.*

Often at night on the edge of sleep I cast my mind toward the abyss of time to come, hoping that I will tumble through some glowing barrier and find myself on the shores of a distant tomorrow. I strain at the moorings that hold me to this time and this place, and yearn to break free. Sometimes I feel that I *have* broken free, that the journey is at last beginning, that I will open my eyes in the inconceivable dazzling future. But it is only an illusion, like that fluent knowledge of French or Sanskrit or calculus that is born in dreams and departs by dawn. I awaken and it is the year 1983 and I am in my own bed with the striped sheets and the blue coverlet, and nothing has changed.

But I try again and again and still again, for the future calls me and the bleak murderous present repels me, and again the illusion that I am cutting myself loose from the time line comes over me, now more vivid and plausible than ever before, and as I soar and hurtle and vanish through the permeable membranes of the eons I wonder if it is finally, in truth, happening. I hover suspended somewhere outside the fabric of time and space and look down upon the earth, and I can see its contours changing as though I watch an accelerated movie: roads sprout and fork and fork once more, villages arise and exfoliate into towns and then into cities and then are overtaken by the forest, rivers change their courses and deliver their waters into great mirror-bright lakes that shrivel and become meadows. And I hover, passive, a dreamer, observing. There are two gates of sleep, says Homer and also Virgil. One is fashioned of horn, and one of ivory. Through the gate of horn pass the visions that are true, but those that emerge from the gate of ivory are deceptive dreams that mean nothing. Do I journey in a dream of the ivory gate? No, no, this is a true sending, this has the solidity and substance of inexorable reality. I have achieved it this time. I have crossed the barrier. Hooded figures surround me; somber eyes study me; I look into faces of a weird sameness, tawny skin, fleshless lips, jutting cheekbones that tug the taut skin above them into drumheads. The room in which I lie is high-vaulted and dark, but glows with a radiance that seems inherent in the material of its walls. Abstract figurings, like the ornamentation of a mosque, dance along those walls in silver inlay; but this is no mosque, nor would the tribe of Allah have loved those strange and godless geometries that restlessly chase one another like lustful squirrels over the wainscoting. I am there; I am surely there.

"I want to see everything," I say.

"See it, then. Nothing prevents you."

One of them presses into my hand a shining silver globe, an orb of command that transports me at the tiniest squeeze of my hand. I fly upward jerkily and in terror, rising so swiftly that the air grows cold and the sky becomes purple, but in a moment I regain control and come to govern my trajectory more usefully. At an altitude of a few dozen yards I pass over a city of serene cubical buildings of rounded corners, glittering with white Mediterranean brilliance in the gentle sunlight. I see small vehicles, pastel-hued, teardrop-tapered, in which citizens with the universal face of the era ride above crystalline roadbeds. I drift over a garden of plants I cannot recognize, perhaps new plants entirely, with pink succulent leaves and great mounding golden inflorescences, or ropy stems like bundles of coaxial cable, or jagged green thorns tipped with tiny blue eyes. I come to a pond of air where serene naked people swim with minimal motions of their fingertips. I observe a staircase of some yielding rubbery substance that vanishes into a glowing nimbus of radiance, and children are climbing that staircase and disappearing into that sparkling place at its top. In the zoological gardens I look down on creatures from a hundred worlds, stranger than any protozoan made lion-sized.

For days I tour this place, inexhaustibly curious, numb with awe. There is no blade of grass out of place. There is no stain nor blemish. The sounds I hear are harmonious sounds, and no other. The air is mild and the winds are soft. Only the people seem stark and austere to me, I suppose because of their sameness of features and the hieratic Egyptian solemnity of their eyes, but after a while I realize that this is only my poor archaic sensibility's misunderstanding, for I feel their love and support about me like a harness as I fly, and I know that these are the happiest, most angelic of all the beings that have walked the earth. I wonder how far in time I have traveled. Fifty thousand years? Half a million? Or perhaps—perhaps, and that possibility shrivels me with pain—perhaps much less than that. Perhaps this is the world of a hundred fifty years from now, eh? The postapocalyptic era, the coming utopia that lies just on the farther shore of our sea of turbulent nightmares. Is it possible that our world can be transformed into this so quickly? Why not? Miracles accelerate in an age of miracles. From the wobbly thing of wood and paper that flew a few seconds at Kitty Hawk to the gleaming majesty of the transcontinental jetliner was only a bit more than fifty years. Why not imagine that a world like this can be assembled in just as little time? But if that is so—

The torment of the thought drives me to the ground. I fall; they are taken by surprise, but ease my drop; I land on the warm moist soil and kneel, clutching it, letting my head slacken until my forehead touches the ground. I feel a gentle hand on my shoulder, just a touch, steadying me, soothing me.

"Let go," I say, virtually snarling. "Take your hand off!"

The hand retreats.

I am alone with my agony. I tremble, I sob, I shiver. I am aware of them surrounding me, but they are baffled, helpless, confused. Possibly they have never seen pain before. Possibly suffering is no part of their vocabulary of spirit.

Finally one of them says softly, "Why do you weep?"

"Out of anger. Out of frustration."

They are mystified. They surround me with shining machinery, screens and coils and lights and glowing panels, that I suspect is going to diagnose my malady. I kick everything over. I trample the intricate mechanisms and shove wildly at those who reach for me, even though I see that they are reaching not to restrain me but to soothe me.

"What is it?" they keep asking. "What troubles you?"

"I want to know what year this is."

They confer. It may be that their numbering system is so different from ours that they are unable to tell me. But there must be a way: diagrams, analogies, astronomical patterns. I am not so primitive that I am beyond understanding such things.

Finally they say, "Your question has no meaning for us."

"No meaning? You speak my language well enough. *I need to know what year this is.*"

"Its name is Eiligorda," one of them says.

"Its *name*? Years don't have names. Years have numbers. My year is numbered 1983. Are we so far in my future that you don't remember the years with numbers?" I begin stripping away my clothing. "Here, look at me. This hair on my body—do you have hair like that? These teeth—see, I have thirty-two of them, arranged in an arc." I hold up my hands. "Nails on my fingers! Have fingernails evolved away?" I tap my belly. "In here, an appendix dangling from my gut! Prehistoric, useless, preposterous! How long ago did that disappear? Look at me! See the ape-man, and tell me how ancient I am!"

"Our bodies are just like yours," comes the quiet reply. "Except that we are healthier and stronger, and resistant to disease. But we have hair. We have fingernails. We have the appendix." They are naked before me, and I see that it is true. Their bodies are lean and supple, and there is a weird and disconcerting similarity of physique about them all, but they are not alien in any way; these could be twentieth-century bodies.

"I want you to tell me," I say, "how distant in time your world is from mine."

"Not very," someone answers. "But we lack the precise terminology for describing the interval."

"Not very," I say. "Listen, does the earth still go around the sun?"

"Of course."

"The time it takes to make one circuit—has that changed?"

"Not at all."

"How many times, then, do you think the earth has circled the sun since my era?"

They exchange glances. They make quick rippling gestures—a kind of counting, perhaps. But they seem unable to complete the calculation. They murmur, they smile, they shrug. At last I understand their problem, which is not one of communication but one of tact. They do not want to tell me the truth for the same reason that I yearn to know it. The truth will hurt me. The truth will split me with anguish.

They are people of the epoch that immediately succeeds yours and mine. They are, quite possibly, the great-great-grandchildren of some who live in our world of 1983; or it may be that they are only grandchildren. The future they inhabit is not the extremely distant future. I am positive of that. But time stands still for them, for they do not know death.

Fury and frenzy return to me. I shake with rage; I taste burning bile; I explode with hatred, and launch myself upon them, scratching, punching, kicking, biting, trying in a single outpouring of bitter resentment to destroy the entire sleek epoch into which I have fallen.

I harm several of them quite seriously.

Then they recover from their astonishment and subdue me, without great effort, dropping me easily with a few delicate musical tones and holding me captive against the ground. The casualties are taken away.

One of my captors kneels beside me and says, "Why do you show such hostility?"

I glare at him. "Because I am so close to being one of you."

"Ah. I think I can comprehend. But why do you blame us for that?"

The only answer I can give him is more fury; I tug against my invisible bonds and lunge as if to slaughter him with sheer energy of rage; from me pours such a blaze of madness as to sear the air, and so intense is my emotion that it seems to me I am actually breaking free, and seizing him, and clawing at him and smashing him. But I am only clutching at phantoms. My arms move like those of a windmill and I lose my balance and topple and topple and topple and when I regain my balance I am in my own bed once more, striped sheets, blue coverlet, the red eye of the digital clock telling me that it is 4:36 A.M. So they have punished me by casting me from their midst. I suppose that is no more than I deserve. But do they comprehend, do they really comprehend, my torment? Do they understand what it is like to know that those who will come just a little way after us will have learned how to live forever, and to live in paradise, and that one of us, at least, has had a glimpse of it, but that we will all be dead when it comes to pass? Why should we not rage against the generations to come, aware that we are nearly the last ones who will know death? Why not scratch and bite and kick? An awful iron door is closing on us, and *they* are on the far side, safe. Surely they will begin to understand that, when they have given more thought to my visit. Possibly they understood it even while I was there. I suspect they did, finally. And that when they returned me to my own time I was given a gift of grace by those gilded futurians: that their mantle of immortality has been cast over me, that I will be allowed to live on and on until time has come round again and I am once more in their era, but now as one of them. That is their gift to me, and perhaps that is their curse on me as well, that I must survive through all the years of terrible darkness that must befall before that golden dawn, that I will tarry here until they come again.

A M A N D A   A N D
T H E   A L I E N

Some stories seem almost to write themselves. This was one of them. I wish they were all that easy, or that the results were always as pleasing.

"Amanda" was a product of the rainy winter of 1981–82, when I was having a particularly fertile run of short-story writing. (Here I need to pause for a digression on California weather and my writing habits. California is one of five places in the world that has the so-called "Mediterranean" climate—the others are Chile, western Australia, the western part of South Africa, and the Mediterranean region itself—in which the winters are mild and rainy and the summers are absolutely dry. Where I live, in the San Francisco region, the heaviest rains fall between November and March. Then they taper off, and from mid-April to early November there's normally no rain at all. Rain in summertime here has been known to happen occasionally, but so rarely that it's a front-page news item. My working pattern follows the weather: I tend to write my novels during the period of maximum rainfall, tapering off to short stories in the spring, and doing as little work as my conscience will allow during the dry season. By fall, just as the rains are getting ready to return, I warm up the machinery with a short story or two and then embark on the new season's novel. But 1981 was an unusual year: instead of a novel, my book for the year was Majipoor Chronicles, which is actually a collection of short stories disguised as a novel, and I wrote it in the spring and summer instead of winter. When autumn came, I was out of sequence with my regular publishing rhythm, and I decided to keep on writing short stories and get things straightened out later on.)

And so "Amanda." It wasn't the story I had intended to do just then. I had promised one to Ellen Datlow, the new fiction editor of Omni. What I had in mind was a sequel to "Dancers in the Time-Flux"—another tale of Olivier van Noort in the far future, this time encountering a Parisian woman from the year 1980, like himself a creature of antiquity but *nevertheless something out of his own future. My long-range plan was to assemble another story cycle along the lines of* Majipoor Chronicles, *set in the* Son of Man *world. But something went wrong and the story died on me after about eight pages. I don't know why. Unfinished stories are as rare around here as heavy rainfall in July. So far as I can recall, that's the only story I've left unfinished in the past thirty-five years. I have those eight pages around here somewhere, and some day I may write the rest of the piece. But for some reason I put it aside. Perhaps it had been a mistake to try once again to return to the world of* Son of Man, *a closed chapter in my past.*

"The thing seemed terribly slow and ponderous and wrong," I told Ellen in a letter of February 20, 1982, "and after a few days of work I called a halt to find out what the trouble was. The trouble was, apparently, that I wanted to do a different sort of story for you, something bouncier and zippier and more contemporary. And before I really knew what was happening, the enclosed lighthearted chiller came galloping out of the typewriter." Ellen bought it by return mail, and Terry Carr chose it for the 1983 volume of his annual Best SF of the Year *anthology series.*

Instead of setting my story in the remote future world of "Dancers in the Time-Flux," I had put it right here, in the San Francisco Bay Area of just a few years hence. And, though I wrote it in cool rainy February, I picked warm sunny September as the time in which it took place. Perhaps that was why I wrote it with such ease. It had been pouring outside for days, but in my mind the long golden summer had already come. And with it, the utterly unscrupulous Amanda, an all too familiar California life-form.

Amanda spotted the alien late Friday afternoon outside the Video Center on South Main. It was trying to look cool and laid-back, but it simply came across as bewildered and uneasy. The alien was disguised as a seventeen-year-old girl, maybe a Chicana, with olive-toned skin and hair so black it seemed almost blue, but Amanda, who was seventeen herself, knew a phony when she saw one. She studied the alien for some moments from the other side of the street to make absolutely certain. Then she walked across.

"You're doing it wrong," Amanda said. "Anybody with half a brain could tell what you really are."

"Bug off," the alien said.

"No. Listen to me. You want to stay out of the detention center or don't you?"

The alien stared coldly at Amanda and said, "I don't know what the crap you're talking about."

"Sure you do. No sense trying to bluff me. Look, I want to help you," Amanda said. "I think you're getting a raw deal. You know what that means, a raw deal? Hey, look, come home with me and I'll teach you a few things about passing for human. I've got the whole friggin' weekend now with nothing else to do anyway."

A flicker of interest came into the other girl's dark chilly eyes. But it went quickly away and she said, "You some kind of lunatic?"

"Suit yourself, O thing from beyond the stars. *Let* them lock you up again. *Let* them stick electrodes up your ass. I tried to help. That's all I can do, is try," Amanda said, shrugging. She began to saunter away. She didn't look back. Three steps, four, five, hands in pockets, slowly heading for her car. Had she been wrong, she wondered? No. No. She could be wrong about some things, like Charley Taylor's interest in spending the weekend with her, maybe. But not this. That crinkly-haired chick was the missing alien for sure. The whole county was buzzing about it—deadly nonhuman life-form has escaped from the detention center out by Tracy, might be anywhere, Walnut Creek, Livermore, even San Francisco, dangerous monster, capable of mimicking human forms, will engulf and digest you and disguise itself in your shape, and there it was, Amanda knew, standing outside the Video Center. Amanda kept walking.

"Wait," the alien said finally.

Amanda took another easy step or two. Then she looked back over her shoulder.

"Yeah?"

"How can you tell?"

Amanda grinned. "Easy. You've got a rain slicker on and it's only September. Rainy season doesn't start around here for another month or two. Your pants are the old spandex kind. People like you don't wear that stuff any more. Your face paint is San Jose colors, but you've got the cheek chevrons put on in the Berkeley pattern. That's just the first three things I noticed. I could find plenty more. Nothing about you fits together with anything else. It's like you did a survey to see how you ought to appear, and tried a little of everything. The closer I study you, the more I see. Look, you're wearing your headphones and the battery light is on, but there's no cassette in the slot. What are you listening to, the music of the spheres? That model doesn't have any FM tuner, you know. You see? You may think you're perfectly camouflaged, but you aren't."

"I could destroy you," the alien said.

"What? Oh, sure. Sure you could. Engulf me right here on the street, all over in thirty seconds, little trail of slime by the door and a new Amanda walks away. But what then? What good's that going to do you? You still won't know which end is up. So there's no logic in destroying me, unless you're a total dummy. I'm on your side. I'm not going to turn you in."

"Why should I trust you?"

"Because I've been talking to you for five minutes and I haven't yelled for the cops yet. Don't you know that half of California is out searching for you? Hey, can you read? Come over here a minute. Here." Amanda tugged the alien toward the newspaper vending box at the curb. The headline on the afternoon *Examiner* was:

BAY AREA ALIEN TERROR
MARINES TO JOIN NINE-COUNTY HUNT
MAYOR, GOVERNOR CAUTION AGAINST PANIC

"You understand that?" Amanda asked. "That's you they're talking about. They're out there with flame guns, tranquilizer darts, web snares, and God knows what else. There's been real hysteria for a day and a half. And you standing around here with the wrong chevrons on! Christ. Christ! What's your plan, anyway? Where are you trying to go?"

"Home," the alien said. "But first I have to rendezvous at the pickup point."

"Where's that?"

"You think I'm stupid?"

"Shit," Amanda said. "If I meant to turn you in, I'd have done it five minutes ago. But okay. I don't give a damn where your rendezvous point is. I tell you, though, you wouldn't make it as far as San Francisco rigged up the way you are. It's a miracle you've avoided getting caught until now."

"And you'll help me?"

"I've been trying to. Come on. Let's get the hell out of here. I'll take you home and fix you up a little. My car's in the lot on the corner."

"Okay."

"Whew!" Amanda shook her head slowly. "Christ, some people are awfully hard to help."

As she drove out of the center of town, Amanda glanced occasionally at the alien sitting tensely to her right. Basically the disguise was very convincing,

Amanda thought. Maybe all the small details were wrong, the outer stuff, the anthropological stuff, but the alien *looked* human, it *sounded* human, it even *smelled* human. Possibly it could fool ninety-nine people out of a hundred, or maybe more than that. But Amanda had always had a good eye for detail. And at the particular moment she had spotted the alien on South Main she had been unusually alert, sensitive, all raw nerves, every antenna up. Of course, it wasn't aliens she was hunting for, but just a diversion, a little excitement, something to fill the great gaping emptiness that Charley Taylor had left in her weekend.

Amanda had been planning the weekend with Charley all month. Her parents were going to go off to Lake Tahoe for three days, her kid sister had wangled permission to accompany them, and Amanda was going to have the house to herself, just her and Macavity the cat. And Charley. He was going to move in on Friday afternoon and they'd cook dinner together and get blasted on her stash of choice powder and watch five or six of her parents' X-rated cassettes, and Saturday they'd drive over to the city and cruise some of the kinky districts and go to that bathhouse on Folsom where everybody got naked and climbed into the giant Jacuzzi, and then on Sunday— Well, none of that was going to happen. Charley had called on Thursday to cancel. "Something big came up," he said, and Amanda had a pretty good idea what that was, which was his hot little cousin from New Orleans who sometimes came flying out here on no notice at all; but the inconsiderate bastard seemed to be entirely unaware of how much Amanda had been looking forward to this weekend, how much it meant to her, how painful it was to be dumped like this. She had run through the planned events of the weekend in her mind so many times that she almost felt as though she had experienced them: it was that real to her. But overnight it had become unreal. Three whole days on her own, the house to herself, and so early in the semester that there was no homework to think about, and Charley had stood her up! What was she supposed to do now, call desperately around town to scrounge up some old lover as a playmate? Or pick up some stranger downtown? Amanda hated to fool around with strangers. She was half tempted to go over to the city and just let things happen, but they were all weirdos and creeps over there, anyway, and she knew what she could expect. What a waste, not having Charley! She could kill him for robbing her of the weekend.

Now there was the alien, though. A dozen of these star people had come to Earth last year, not in a flying saucer as everybody had expected, but in little capsules that floated like milkweed seeds, and they had landed in a wide arc between San Diego and Salt Lake City. Their natural form, so far as anyone could tell for sure, was something like a huge jellyfish with a row of staring purple eyes down one wavy margin, but their usual tactic was to borrow any local body they found, digesting it and turning themselves into an accurate imitation of it. One of them had made the mistake of turning itself into a brown mountain bear and another into a bobcat—maybe they thought that those were the dominant life-forms on Earth—but the others had taken on human bodies, at the cost of at least ten lives. Then they went looking to make contact with government leaders, and naturally they were rounded up very swiftly and interned, some in mental hospitals and some in county jails, but eventually—as soon as the truth of what they really were sank in—they were all put in a special detention camp in Northern California. Of course, a tremendous fuss was made over them, endless stuff in the papers and on the tube, speculation by this heavy thinker and that about the significance of their mission, the nature of their biochemistry, a little wild talk about the possibility that more of their kind might be waiting undetected out there and plotting to do God knows what, and all sorts of that stuff, and then came a government clamp on the entire subject, no official announcements except that "discussions" with the visitors were continuing; and after a while the whole thing degenerated into dumb alien jokes ("Why did the alien cross the road?") and Halloween invader masks, and then it moved into the background of everyone's attention and was forgotten. And remained forgotten until the announcement that one of the creatures had slipped out of the camp somehow and was loose within a hundred-mile zone around San Francisco. Preoccupied as she was with her anguish over Charley's heartlessness, even Amanda had managed to pick up *that* news item. And now the alien was in her very car. So there'd be some weekend amusement for her after all. Amanda was entirely unafraid of the alleged deadliness of the star being: whatever else the alien might be, it was surely no dope, not if it had been picked to come halfway across the galaxy on a mission like this, and Amanda knew that the alien could see that harming her was not going to be in its own best interests. The alien had need of her, and the alien realized that. And Amanda, in some way that she was only just beginning to work out, had need of the alien.

➤

She pulled up outside her house, a compact split-level at the western end of town. "This is the place," she said. Heat shimmers danced in the air, and the hills back of the house, parched in the long dry summer, were the color of lions. Macavity, Amanda's old tabby, sprawled in the shade of the bottlebrush tree on the ragged front lawn. As Amanda and the alien approached, the cat sat up warily, flattened his ears, hissed. The alien immediately moved into a defensive posture, sniffing the air.

"Just a household pet," Amanda said. "You know what that is? He isn't dangerous. He's always a little suspicious of strangers."

Which was untrue. An earthquake couldn't have brought Macavity out of his nap, and a cotillion of mice dancing minuets on his tail wouldn't have drawn a reaction from him. Amanda calmed him with some fur-ruffling, but he wanted nothing to do with the alien, and went slinking sullenly into the underbrush. The alien watched him with care until he was out of sight.

"You have anything like cats on your planet?" Amanda asked as they went inside.

"We had small wild animals once. They were unnecessary."

"Oh," Amanda said. The house had a stuffy, stagnant air. She switched on the air-conditioning. "Where is your planet, anyway?"

The alien ignored the question. It padded around the living room, very much like a prowling cat itself, studying the stereo, the television, the couches, the vase of dried flowers.

"Is this a typical Earthian home?"

"More or less," said Amanda. "Typical for around here, at least. This is what we call a suburb. It's half an hour by freeway from here to San Francisco. That's a city. A lot of people living all close together. I'll take you over there tonight or tomorrow for a look, if you're interested." She got some music going, high volume. The alien didn't seem to mind, so she notched the volume up even more. "I'm going to take a shower. You could use one, too, actually."

"Shower? You mean rain?"

"I mean body-cleaning activities. We Earthlings like to wash a lot, to get rid of sweat and dirt and stuff. It's considered bad form to stink. Come on, I'll show you how to do it. You've got to do what I do if you want to keep from getting caught, you know." She led the alien to the bathroom. "Take your clothes off first."

The alien stripped. Underneath its rain slicker it wore a stained T-shirt that said "Fisherman's Wharf" with a picture of the San Francisco skyline, and a pair of unzipped jeans. Under that it was wearing a black brassiere, unfastened and with the cups over its shoulder blades, and a pair of black shiny panty-briefs with a red heart on the left buttock. The alien's body was that of a lean, tough-looking girl with a scar running down the inside of one arm.

"Whose body is that?" Amanda asked. "Do you know?"

"She worked at the detention center. In the kitchen."

"You know her name?"

"Flores Concepcion."

"The other way around, probably. Concepcion Flores. I'll call you Connie, unless you want to give me your real name."

"Connie will do."

"All right, Connie. Pay attention. You turn the water on here, and you adjust the mix of hot and cold until you like it. Then you pull this knob and get underneath the spout here and wet your body, and rub soap over it and wash the soap off. Afterward you dry yourself and put fresh clothes on. You have to clean your clothes from time to time, too, because otherwise *they* start to smell and it upsets people. Watch me shower, and then you do it."

Amanda washed quickly, while plans hummed in her head. The alien wasn't going to last long out there wearing the body of Concepcion Flores. Sooner or later someone was going to notice that one of the kitchen girls was missing, and they'd get an all-points alarm out for her. Amanda wondered whether the alien had figured that out yet. The alien, Amanda thought, needs a different body in a hurry.

But not mine, she told herself. For sure, not mine.

"Your turn," she said, shutting the water off.

The alien, fumbling a little, turned the water back on and got under the spray. Clouds of steam rose and its skin began to look boiled, but it didn't appear troubled. No sense of pain? "Hold it," Amanda said. "Step back." She adjusted the water. "You've got it too hot. You'll damage that body that way. Look, if you can't tell the difference between hot and cold, just take cold showers, okay? It's less dangerous. This is cold, on this side." She left the alien under the shower and went to find some clean clothes. When she came back, the alien was still showering, under icy water. "Enough," Amanda said. "Here. Put these on."

"I had more clothes than this before."

"A T-shirt and jeans are all you need in hot weather like this. With your kind of build you can skip the bra, and anyway I don't think you'll be able to fasten it the right way."

"Do we put the face paint on now?"

"We can skip it while we're home. It's just stupid kid stuff anyway, all that tribal crap. If we go out we'll do it, and we'll give you Walnut Creek colors, I think. Concepcion wore San Jose, but we want to throw people off the track. How about some dope?"

"What?"

"Grass. Marijuana. A drug widely used by local Earthians of our age."

"I don't need no drug."

"I don't either. But I'd *like* some. You ought to learn how, just in case you find yourself in a social situation." Amanda reached for her pack of Filter Golds and pulled out a joint. Expertly she tweaked its lighter tip and took a deep hit. "Here," she said, passing it. "Hold it like I did. Put it to your mouth, breathe in, suck the smoke deep." The alien dragged the joint and began to cough. "Not so deep, maybe," Amanda said. "Take just a little. Hold it. Let it out. There, much better. Now give me back the joint. You've got to keep passing it back and forth. That part's important. You feel anything from it?"

"No."

"It can be subtle. Don't worry about it. Are you hungry?"

"Not yet," the alien said.

"I am. Come into the kitchen." As she assembled a sandwich—peanut butter and avocado on whole wheat, with tomato and onion—she asked, "What sort of things do you eat?"

"Life."

"Life?"

"We never eat dead things. Only things with life."

Amanda fought back a shudder. "I see. *Anything* with life?"

"We prefer animal life. We can absorb plants if necessary."

"Ah. Yes. And when are you going to be hungry again?"

"Maybe tonight," the alien said. "Or tomorrow. The hunger comes very suddenly, when it comes."

"There's not much around here that you could eat live. But I'll work on it."

"The small furry animal?"

"No. My cat is not available for dinner. Get that idea right out of your head. Likewise me. I'm your protector and guide. It wouldn't be sensible of you to eat me. You follow what I'm trying to tell you?"

"I said that I'm not hungry yet."

"Well, you let me know when you start feeling the pangs. I'll find you a meal." Amanda began to construct a second sandwich. The alien prowled the kitchen, examining the appliances. Perhaps making mental records, Amanda thought, of sink and oven design, to copy on its home world. Amanda said, "Why did you people come here in the first place?"

"It was our mission."

"Yes. Sure. But for what purpose? What are you after? You want to take over the world? You want to steal our scientific secrets?" The alien, making no reply, began taking spices out of the spice rack. Delicately it licked its finger, touched it to the oregano, tasted it, tried the cumin. Amanda said, "Or is it that you want to keep us from going into space? That you think we're a dangerous species, so you're going to quarantine us on our own planet? Come on, you can tell *me*. I'm not a government spy." The alien sampled the tarragon, the basil, the sage. When it reached for the curry powder, its hand suddenly shook so violently that it knocked the open jars of oregano and tarragon over, making a mess. "Hey, are you all right?" Amanda asked.

The alien said, "I think I'm getting hungry. Are these things drugs, too?"

"Spices," Amanda said. "We put them in our foods to make them taste better." The alien was looking very strange, glassy-eyed, flushed, sweaty. "Are you feeling sick?"

"I feel excited. These powders—"

"They're turning you on? Which one?"

"This, I think." It pointed to the oregano. "It was either the first one or the second."

"Yeah," Amanda said. "Oregano. It can really make you fly." She wondered whether the alien might get violent when zonked. Or whether the oregano would stimulate its appetite. She had to watch out for its appetite. There are certain risks, Amanda reflected, in doing what I'm doing. Deftly she cleaned up the spilled oregano and tarragon and put the caps on the spice jars. "You ought to be careful," she said. "Your metabolism isn't used to this stuff. A little can go a long way."

"Give me some more."

"Later," Amanda said. "You don't want to overdo it."

"More!"

"Calm down. I know this planet better than you, and I don't want to see you get in trouble. Trust me: I'll let you have more oregano when it's the right time. Look at the way you're shaking. And you're sweating like crazy." Pocketing the oregano jar, she led the alien back into the living room. "Sit down. Relax."

"More? Please?"

"I appreciate your politeness. But we have important things to talk about, and then I'll give you some. Okay?" Amanda opaqued the window, through which the hot late-afternoon sun was coming. Six o'clock on Friday, and if everything had gone the right way Charley would have been showing up just about now. Well, she'd found a different diversion. The weekend stretched before her like an open road leading to mysteryland. The alien offered all sorts of possibilities, and she might yet have some fun over the next few days, if she used her head. Amanda turned to the alien and said, "You calmer now? Yes. Good. Okay: first of all, you've got to get yourself another body."

"Why is that?"

"Two reasons. One is that the authorities probably are searching for the girl you absorbed. How you got as far as you did without anybody but me spotting you is hard to understand. Number two, a teenage girl traveling by herself is going to get hassled too much, and you don't know how to handle yourself in a tight situation. You know what I'm saying? You're going to want to hitchhike out to Nevada, Wyoming, Utah, wherever the hell your rendezvous place is, and all along the way people are going to be coming on to you. You don't need any of that. Besides, it's very tricky trying to pass for a girl. You've got to know how to put your face paint on, how to understand challenge codes, and what the way you wear your clothing says, and like that. Boys have a much simpler subculture. You get yourself a male body, a big hunk of a body, and nobody'll bother you much on the way to where you're going. You just keep to yourself, don't make eye contact, don't smile, and everyone will leave you alone."

"Makes sense," said the alien. "All right. The hunger is becoming very bad now. Where do I get a male body?"

"San Francisco. It's full of men. We'll go over there tonight and find a nice brawny one for you. With any luck we might even find one who's not gay, and then we can have a little fun with him first. And then you take his body over—which incidentally solves your food problem for a while, doesn't it?—and we can have some more fun, a whole weekend of fun." Amanda winked. "Okay, Connie?"

"Okay." The alien winked, a clumsy imitation, first one eye, then the other. "You give me more oregano now?"

"Later. And when you wink, just wink *one* eye. Like this. Except I don't think you ought to do a lot of winking at people. It's a very intimate gesture that could get you in trouble. Understand?"

"There's so much to understand."

"You're on a strange planet, kid. Did you expect it to be just like home? Okay, to continue. The next thing I ought to point out is that when you leave here on Sunday you'll have to—"

The telephone rang.

"What's that sound?" the alien asked.

"Communications device. I'll be right back." Amanda went to the hall extension, imagining the worst: her parents, say, calling to announce that they were on their way back from Tahoe tonight, some mixup in the reservations or something. But the voice that greeted her was Charley's. She could hardly believe it, after the casual way he had shafted her this weekend. She could hardly believe what he wanted, either. He had left half a dozen of his best cassettes at her place last week, Golden Age rock, Abbey Road and the Hendrix one and a Joplin and such, and now he was heading off to Monterey for the festival and he wanted to have them for the drive. Did she mind if he stopped off in half an hour to pick them up?

The bastard, she thought. The absolute trashiness of him! First to torpedo her weekend without even an apology, and then to let her know that he and what's-her-name were scooting down to Monterey for some fun, and could he bother her for his cassettes? Didn't he think she had any feelings? She looked at the telephone in her hand as though it was emitting toads and scorpions. It was tempting to hang up on him.

She resisted the temptation. "As it happens," she said, "I'm just on my way out for the weekend myself. But I've got a friend who's here cat-sitting for me. I'll leave the cassettes with her, okay? Her name's Connie."

"Fine," Charley said. "I really appreciate that, Amanda."

"It's nothing," she said.

The alien was back in the kitchen, nosing around the spice rack. But Amanda had the oregano. She said, "I've arranged for delivery of your next body."

"You did?"

"A large healthy adolescent male. Exactly what you're looking for. He's going to be here in a little while. I'm going to go out for a drive, and you take care of him before I get back. How long does it take for you to—engulf—somebody?"

"It's very fast."

"Good." Amanda found Charley's cassettes and stacked them on the living-room table. "He's coming over here to get these six little boxes, which are music-storage devices. When the doorbell rings, you let him in and introduce yourself as Connie and tell him his things are on this table. After that you're on your own. You think you can handle it?"

"Sure," the alien said.

"Tuck in your T-shirt better. When it's tight it makes your boobs stick out, and that'll distract him. Maybe he'll even make a pass at you. What happens to the Connie body after you engulf him?"

"It won't be here. What happens is I merge with him and dissolve all the Connie characteristics and take on the new ones."

"Ah. Very nifty. You're a real nightmare thing, you know? You're a walking horror show. Here, have a little hit of oregano before I go." She put a tiny pinch of spice in the alien's hand. "Just to warm up your engine a little. I'll give you more later, when you've done the job. See you in an hour, okay?"

She left the house. Macavity was sitting on the porch, scowling, whipping his tail from side to side. Amanda knelt beside him and scratched him behind the ears. The cat made a low rough purring sound, not much like his usual purr.

Amanda said, "You aren't happy, are you, fella? Well, don't worry. I've told the alien to leave you alone, and I guarantee you'll be okay. This is Amanda's fun tonight. You don't mind if Amanda has a little fun, do you?" Macavity made a glum snuffling sound. "Listen, maybe I can get the alien to create a nice little calico cutie for you, okay? Just going into heat and ready to howl.

Would you like that, guy? Would you? I'll see what I can do when I get back. But I have to clear out of here now, before Charley shows up."

She got into her car and headed for the westbound freeway ramp. Half past six, Friday night, the sun still hanging high above the Bay. Traffic was thick in the eastbound lanes, the late commuters slogging toward home, and it was beginning to build up westbound, too, as people set out for dinner in San Francisco. Amanda drove through the tunnel and turned north into Berkeley to cruise city streets. Ten minutes to seven now. Charley must have arrived. She imagined Connie in her tight T-shirt, all stoned and sweaty on oregano, and Charley giving her the eye, getting ideas, thinking about grabbing a bonus quickie before taking off with his cassettes. And Connie leading him on, Charley making his moves, and then suddenly that electric moment of surprise as the alien struck and Charley found himself turning into dinner. It could be happening right this minute, Amanda thought placidly. No more than the bastard deserves, isn't it? She had felt for a long time that Charley was a big mistake in her life, and after what he had pulled yesterday she was sure of it. No more than he deserves. But, she wondered, what if Charley had brought his weekend date along? The thought chilled her. She hadn't considered that possibility at all. It could ruin everything. Connie wasn't able to engulf two at once, was she? And suppose they recognized her as the missing alien and ran out screaming to call the cops?

No, she thought. Not even Charley would be so tacky as to bring his date over to Amanda's house tonight. And Charley never watched the news or read a paper. He wouldn't have a clue as to what Connie really was until it was too late for him to run.

Seven o'clock. Time to head for home.

The sun was sinking behind her as she turned onto the freeway. By quarter past she was approaching her house. Charley's old red Honda was parked outside. Amanda left hers across the street and cautiously let herself in, pausing just inside the front door to listen.

Silence.

"Connie?"

"In here," said Charley's voice.

Amanda entered the living room. Charley was sprawled out comfortably on the couch. There was no sign of Connie.

"Well?" Amanda said. "How did it go?"

"Easiest thing in the world," the alien said. "He was sliding his hands under my T-shirt when I let him have the nullifier jolt."

"Ah. The nullifier jolt."

"And then I completed the engulfment and cleaned up the carpet. God, it feels good not to be hungry again. You can't imagine how tough it was to resist engulfing you, Amanda. For the past hour I kept thinking of food, food, food—"

"Very thoughtful of you to resist."

"I knew you were out to help me. It's logical not to engulf one's allies."

"That goes without saying. So you feel well fed, now? He was good stuff?"

"Robust, healthy, nourishing—yes."

"I'm glad Charley turned out to be good for something. How long before you get hungry again?"

The alien shrugged. "A day or two. Maybe three, on account of he was so big. Give me more oregano, Amanda?"

"Sure," she said. "Sure." She felt a little let down. Not that she was remorseful about Charley, exactly, but it all seemed so casual, so offhanded—there was something anticlimactic about it, in a way. She suspected she should have stayed and watched while it was happening. Too late for that now, though.

She took the oregano from her purse and dangled the jar teasingly. "Here it is, babe. But you've got to earn it first."

"What do you mean?"

"I mean that I was looking forward to a big weekend with Charley, and the weekend is here, and Charley's here too, more or less, and I'm ready for fun. Come show me some fun, big boy."

She slipped Charley's Hendrix cassette into the deck and turned the volume way up.

The alien looked puzzled. Amanda began to peel off her clothes.

"You too," Amanda said. "Come on. You won't have to dig deep into Charley's mind to figure out what to do. You're going to be my Charley for me this weekend, you follow? You and I are going to do all the things that he and I were going to do. Okay? Come on. Come on." She beckoned. The alien shrugged again and slipped out of Charley's clothes, fumbling with the unfamiliarities of his zipper and buttons. Amanda, grinning, drew the alien close against her and down to the living-room floor. She took its hands and put them where she wanted them to be. She whispered instructions. The alien, docile, obedient, did what she wanted.

It felt like Charley. It smelled like Charley. It even moved pretty much the way Charley moved.

But it wasn't Charley, it wasn't Charley at all, and after the first few seconds Amanda knew that she had goofed things up very badly. You couldn't just ring in an imitation like this. Making love with this alien was like making love with a very clever machine, or with her own mirror image. It was empty and meaningless and dumb.

Grimly she went on to the finish. They rolled apart, panting, sweating.

"Well?" the alien said. "Did the earth move for you?"

"Yeah. Yeah. It was wonderful—Charley."

"Oregano?"

"Sure," Amanda said. She handed the spice jar across. "I always keep my promises, babe. Go to it. Have yourself a blast. Just remember that that's strong stuff for guys from your planet, okay? If you pass out, I'm going to leave you right there on the floor."

"Don't worry about me."

"Okay. You have your fun. I'm going to clean up, and then maybe we'll go over to San Francisco for the nightlife. Does that interest you?"

"You bet, Amanda." The alien winked—one eye, then the other—and gulped a huge pinch of oregano. "That sounds terrific."

Amanda gathered up her clothes, went upstairs for a quick shower, and dressed. When she came down the alien was more than half blown away on the oregano, goggle-eyed, loll-headed, propped up against the couch and crooning to itself in a weird atonal way. Fine, Amanda thought. You just get yourself all spiced up, love. She took the portable phone from the kitchen, carried it with her into the bathroom, locked the door, dialed the police emergency number.

She was bored with the alien. The game had worn thin very quickly. And it was crazy, she thought, to spend the whole weekend cooped up with a dangerous extraterrestrial creature when there wasn't going to be any fun in it for her. She knew now that there couldn't be any fun at all. And in a day or two the alien was going to get hungry again.

"I've got your alien," she said. "Sitting in my living room, stoned out of its head on oregano. Yes, I'm absolutely certain. It was disguised as a Chicana girl first, Concepcion Flores, but then it attacked my boyfriend Charley Taylor, and—yes, yes, I'm safe. I'm locked in the john. Just get somebody over here fast—okay, I'll stay on the line—what happened was, I spotted it downtown, and it insisted on coming home with me—"

♥

The actual capture took only a few minutes. But there was no peace for hours after the police tactical squad hauled the alien away, because the media was in on the act right away, first a team from Channel 2 in Oakland, and then some of the network guys, and then the *Chronicle*, and finally a whole army of reporters from as far away as Sacramento, and phone calls from Los Angeles and San Diego and—about three that morning—New York. Amanda told the story again and again until she was sick of it, and just as dawn was breaking she threw the last of them out and barred the door.

She wasn't sleepy at all. She felt wired up, speedy, and depressed all at once. The alien was gone, Charley was gone, and she was all alone. She was going to be famous for the next couple of days, but that wouldn't help. She'd still be alone. For a time she wandered around the house, looking at it the way an alien might, as though she had never seen a stereo cassette before, or a television set, or a rack of spices. The smell of oregano was everywhere. There were little trails of it on the floor.

Amanda switched on the radio and there she was on the six A.M. news. "—the emergency is over, thanks to the courageous Walnut Creek high school girl who trapped and outsmarted the most dangerous life-form in the known universe—"

She shook her head. "You think that's true?" she asked the cat. "Most dangerous life-form in the universe? I don't think so, Macavity. I think I know of at least one that's a lot deadlier. Eh, kid?" She winked. "If they only knew, eh? If they only knew." She scooped the cat up and hugged it, and it began to purr. Maybe trying to get a little sleep would be a good idea around this time, she told herself. And then she had to figure out what she was going to do about the rest of the weekend.

SNAKE AND OCEAN,
OCEAN AND SNAKE

We are still in the busy winter of 1982—still in rainy February, in fact. I have just finished "Amanda and the Alien," and the creative urge is still buzzing in me. In my revived career as a short-story writer, Omni and Playboy have become my two primary markets. Neither one can handle more than one or two stories a year from me; "Amanda" has just found a home at Omni, so it's time for me to begin thinking about something new for Playboy.

As it turned out, the fiction editor of Playboy had the same thought in mind. I mean the redoubtable Alice K. Turner, with whom I had struck up instant editorial rapport of the most remarkable kind while we were butting heads over revisions to my first Playboy story, "Gianni," early in 1981. Now, a year later, Alice found herself with two illustrations on hand and no stories to go with them. She phoned me: Would I consider looking at the paintings in the hope one of them would inspire a story? I laughed. In the bad old days of penny-a-word pulp magazines, many editors had routinely bought cover paintings first and commissioned writers to concoct stories to go with them. I had done my share of those arsy-versy projects back then, but it was close to twenty years since I had last written a story around an illustration. I told Alice it would be fun to try again, both for nostalgia's sake and for the challenge it represented.

She sent me photostats of two paintings. One showed a naked lady—a very satisfactory one, as I recall, but she wasn't engaged in doing anything that sparked a story idea. The other, a lovely work by Brad Holland, depicted a man of about thirty-five releasing a snake at least fifteen feet long from a beautiful ceramic jug against a sleek featureless background of hills and meadows. I liked it very much. But why was that suburban-looking guy pouring a snake out of a jug?

The old craftsman's rule about writing stories around illustrations is that only a dolt tries to use the picture in any literal way. The idea always is *to take it as metaphor, as analogy, as something other than what it purports to be. With the usual inexplicable swiftness of the old pro I saw that snake-as-telepathic-image was more likely to generate an interesting science fiction story than snake-as-snake, and off I went. By the end of the month I had my story.*

Alice is no easy editor to deal with. She came back at me a couple of weeks later with requests for cuts in the middle, some retuning of the dialog, and a restructuring of my pattern of snake/ocean symbolism. As usual, I put up a fight over some things (mainly the dialog changes), made some of the cuts she wanted, and beefed up one erotic passage, not because Playboy necessarily insists that its stories contain a lot of sexy stuff (it's not a mandatory requirement) but because she thought the story lacked vigor just where it needed it most and I agreed. She yielded where I could defend my choices and I yielded where her criticisms seemed apt, which was most of the time. Her ideas about the symbolic substructure, for example, were right on target and I rearranged things slightly and sent her an insert to use midway through the story. Thus "Snake and Ocean" went through what by now had become the familiar knock-down-drag-out dialectic process by which Alice and I get most of my stories for her into final shape, and it duly appeared in the June 1984 issue of Playboy.

Alice had one last revision up her sleeve. When she printed the story she changed the title to "The Affair." She's a terrific editor, but she isn't infallible. In this reprinting, as in all previous ones—it was included in the 1984 volume of Gardner Dozois' Year's Best Science Fiction series, and has been anthologized elsewhere as well—I've kept all the textual changes she proposed; but this time I've reverted to my original title. You be the judge.

He found her by accident, the way it usually happens, after he had more or less given up searching. For years he had been sending out impulses like messages in bottles, random waves of telepathic energy, *Hello, hello, hello,* one forlorn SOS after another from the desert isle of the soul on which he was a castaway. Occasionally messages came back, but all they amounted to was lunacy, strident nonsense, static, spiritual noise, gabble up and down the mind band. There were, he knew, a good many like him out there—a boy in

Topeka, an old woman in Buenos Aires, another one in Fort Lauderdale, someone of indeterminate sex in Manitoba, and plenty of others, each alone, each lonely. He fell into short-lived contact with them, because they were, after all, people of his special kind. But they tended to be cranky, warped, weird, often simply crazy, all of them deformed by their bizarre gift, and they could not give him what he wanted, which was communion, harmony, the marriage of true minds. Then one Thursday afternoon when he was absentmindedly broadcasting his identity wave, not in any way purposefully trolling the seas of perception but only humming, so to speak, he felt a sudden startling *click*, as of perfectly machined parts locking into place. Out of the grayness in his mind an unmistakably warm, eager image blossomed, a dazzling giant yellow flower unfolding on the limb of a gnarled spiny cactus, and the image translated itself instantly into *Hi there. Where've you been all my life?*

He hesitated to send an answering signal, because he knew that he had found what he was looking for and he was aware how much of a threat that was to the fabric of the life he had constructed for himself. He was thirty-seven years old, stable, settled. He had a wife who tried her best to be wonderful for him, never knowing quite what it was that she lacked but seeking to compensate for it anyway, and two small pleasing children who had not inherited his abnormality, and a comfortable house in the hills east of San Francisco, and a comfortable job as an analyst for one of the big brokerage houses. It was not the life he had imagined in his old romantic fantasies, but it was not a bad life, either, and it was *his* life, familiar and in its way rewarding; and he knew he was about to rip an irreparable hole in it. So he hesitated. And then he transmitted an image as vivid as the one he had received: a solitary white gull soaring in enormous sweeps over the broad blue breast of the Pacific.

The reply came at once: the same gull, joined by a second one that swooped out of a cloudless sky and flew tirelessly at its side. He knew that if he responded to that, there could be no turning back, but that was all right. With uncharacteristic recklessness he switched to the verbal mode.

—Okay. Who are you?

—Laurel Hammett. I'm in Phoenix. I read you clearly. This is better than the telephone.

—Cheaper, too. Chris Maitland. San Francisco.

—That's far enough away, I guess.

He didn't understand, then, what she meant by that. But he let the point pass.

—You're the first one I've found who sends images, Laurel.

—I found one once, eight years ago, in Boston. But he was crazy. Most of us are crazy, Chris.

—I'm not crazy.

—Oh, I know! Oh, God, I know!

✦

So that was the beginning. He got very little work done that afternoon. He was supposed to be preparing a report on oil royalty trusts, and after fifteen minutes of zinging interchanges with her he actually did beg off; she broke contact with a dazzling series of visuals, many of them cryptic, snowflakes and geometrical diagrams and fields of blazing red poppies. Depletion percentages and windfall-profits tax recapture were impossible to deal with while those brilliant pictures burned in his mind. Although he had promised not to reach toward her again until tomorrow—judicious self-denial, she observed, is the fuel of love—he finally did send out a flicker of abashed energy, and drew from her a mingling of irritation and delight. For five minutes they told each other it was best to go slow, to let it develop gradually, and again they vowed to keep mental silence until the next day. But when he was crossing the Bay Bridge a couple of hours later, heading for home, she tickled him suddenly with a quick flash of her presence and gave him a wondrous view of the Arizona sunset, harsh chocolate-brown hills under a purple-and-gold sky. That evening he felt shamefully and transparently adulterous, as if he had come home flushed and rumpled, with lipstick on his shirt. He pretended to be edgy and wearied by some fictitious episode of office politics, and helped himself to two drinks before dinner, and was more than usually curious about the details of his wife's day, the little suburban crises, the small challenges, the tiny triumphs. Jan was playful, amiable, almost kittenish. That told him she had not seen through him to the betrayal within, however blatant it seemed to him. She was no actress; there was nothing devious about her.

The transformation of their marriage that had taken place that afternoon saddened him, and yet not deeply, because it was an inevitable one. He and Jan were not really of the same species. He had loved her as well and honestly as was possible for him, but what he had really wanted was someone of his kind, with whom he could join mind and soul as well as body, and it was only because he had not been able to find her that he had settled for Jan. And now he had found her. Where that would lead, and what it meant for Jan and him, he had no idea yet. Possibly he would be able to go on sharing with her the part of his life that they were able to share, while secretly he got from the other woman those things that Jan had never been able to give him: possibly. When they went to bed he turned to her with abrupt passionate ferocity, as he had not for a long time, but even so he could not help wondering what Laurel was doing now, in her bed a thousand miles to the east, and with whom.

During the morning commute Laurel came to him with stunning images of desert landscapes, eroded geological strata, mysterious dark mesas, distant flame-colored sandstone walls. He sent her Pacific surf, cypresses bending to the wind, tidepools swarming with anemones and red starfish. Then, timidly, he sent her a kiss, and had one from her in return, and then, as he was crossing the toll plaza of the bridge, she shifted to words.

—What do you do?

—Securities analyst. I read reports and make forecasts.

—Sounds terribly dull. Is it?

—If it is, I don't let myself notice. It's okay work. What about you?

—I'm a potter. I'm a very good one. You'd like my stuff.

—Where can I see it?

—There's a gallery in Santa Fe. And one in Tucson. And of course Phoenix. But you mustn't come to Phoenix.

—Are you married?

There was a pause.

—Yes. But that isn't why you mustn't come here.

—I'm married, too.

—I thought you were. You feel like a married sort of man.

—Oh? I do?

—That isn't an insult. You have a very stable vibe, do you know what I mean?

—I think so. Do you have children?

—No. Do you?

—Two. Little girls. How long have you been married, Laurel?

—Six years.

—Nine.

—We must be about the same age.

—I'm thirty-seven.

—I'm thirty-four.

—Close enough. Do you want to know my sign?

—Not really.

She laughed and sent him a complex, awesome image: the entire wheel of the Zodiac, which flowered into the shape of the Aztec calendar stone, which became the glowing rose window of a Gothic cathedral. An undercurrent of warmth and love and amusement rode with it. Then she was gone, leaving him on the bridge in a silence so sharp it rang like iron.

He did not reach toward her, but drove on into the city in a mellow haze, wondering what she looked like. Her mental "voice" sounded to him like that of a tall, clear-eyed, straight-backed woman with long brown hair, but he knew better than to put much faith in that; he had played the same game with people's telephone voices and he had always been wrong. For all he knew, Laurel was squat and greasy. He doubted that; he saw no way that she could be ugly. But why, then, was she so determined not to have him come to Phoenix? Perhaps she was an invalid; perhaps she was painfully shy; perhaps she feared the intrusion of any sort of reality into their long-distance romance.

At lunchtime he tuned himself to her wavelength and sent her an image of the first page of the report he had written last week on Exxon. She replied with a glimpse of a tall olive-hued porcelain jar, of a form both elegant and sturdy at once. Her work in exchange for his: he liked that. It meant they had the same sense of humor. Everything was going to be perfect.

A week later he went out to Salt Lake City for a couple of days to do some field research on a mining company headquartered there. He took an early-morning flight, had lunch with three earnest young Mormon executives overflowing with joy at the bounty of God as manifested by the mineral wealth of the Overthrust Belt in Wyoming, spent the afternoon leafing through geologists' survey sheets, and had dinner alone at his hotel. Afterward he put in his obligatory call to Jan, worked up his notes of the day's conferences, and watched TV for an hour, hoping it would make him drowsy. Maitland didn't mind these business trips, but he slept badly when he slept alone, and any sort of time-zone change, even a trifling one like this, disrupted his internal clock. He was still wide awake when he got into bed about eleven.

He thought of Laurel. He felt very near to her, out here in this spacious mountain-ringed city with the wide bland streets. Probably Salt Lake City was not significantly closer to Phoenix than San Francisco was, but he regarded Utah and Arizona both as the true Wild West, while his own suburban and manicured part of California, paradoxically, did not seem western to him at all. Somewhere due south of here, just on the far side of all these cliffs and canyons, was the unknown woman he loved.

As though on cue, she was in his mind:

—Lonely?

—You bet.

—I've been thinking of you all day. Poor Chris: sitting around with those businessmen, talking all that depletion gibberish.

—I'm a businessman, too.

—You're different, love. You're a businessman outside and a freak inside.

—Don't say that.

—It's what we are, Chris. Face it. Flukes, anomalies, sports, changelings—

—Please stop, Laurel. Please.

—I'm sorry.

A silence. He thought she was gone, taking flight at his rebuke. But then:

—Are you *very* lonely?

—Very. Dull empty city, dull empty bed.

—*You're* in it.

—But you aren't.

—Is that what you want? Right now?

—I wish we could, Laurel.

—Let's try this.

He felt a sudden astounding intensifying of her mental signal, as if she had leaped the hundreds of miles and lay curled against him here. There was a sense of physical proximity, of warmth, even the light perfume of her skin, and into his mind swept an image so acutely clear that it eclipsed for him the drab realities of his room: the shore of a tropical ocean, fine pink sand, gentle pale-green water, a dense line of heavy-crowned palms.

—Go on, Chris. Into the water.

He waded into the calm wavelets until the delicate sandy bottom was far below his dangling feet and he floated effortlessly in an all-encompassing warmth, in an amniotic bath of placid soothing fluid. Placid but not motionless, for he felt, as he drifted, tiny convulsive quivers about him, an electric oceanic caress, pulsations of the water against his bare skin, intimate, tender, searching. He began to tingle. As he moved farther out from shore, so far now that the land was gone and the world was all warm water to the horizon, the pressure of those rhythmic pulsations became more forceful, deeply pleasurable: the ocean was a giant hand lightly squeezing him. He trembled and made soft sighing sounds that grew steadily more vehement, and closed his eyes, and let ecstasy overwhelm him in the ocean's benignly insistent grip. Then he grunted and his heart thumped and his body went rigid and then lax, and moments later he sat up, blinking, astonished, eerily tranquil.

—I didn't think anything like that was possible.

—For us anything's possible. Even sex across seven hundred miles. I wasn't sure it would work, but I guess it did, didn't it? Did you like it?

—Do you need an answer, Laurel?

—I feel so happy.

—How did you do it? What was the trick?

—No trick. Just the usual trick, Chris, a little more intense than usual. And a lot of love. I hated the idea that you were all alone, horny, unable to sleep.

—It was absolutely marvelous.

—And now we're lovers. Even though we've never met.

—No. Not altogether lovers, not yet. Let me try to do it to you, Laurel. It's only fair.

—Later, okay? Not now.

—I want to.

—It takes a lot of energy. You ought to get some sleep, and I can wait. Just lie there and glow and don't worry about me. You can try it with me another time.

—An hour? Two hours?

—Whenever you want. But not now. Rest, now. Enjoy. Good night, love.

—Good night, Laurel.

He was alone. He lay staring up into the darkness, stunned. He had been unfaithful to Jan three times before, not bad for nine years, and always the same innocuous pattern: a business trip far from home, a couple of solitary nights, then an official dinner with some woman executive, too many drinks, the usual half-serious banter turning serious, a blurry one-night stand, remorse in the morning, and never any follow-up. Meaningless, fragmentary stuff. But this—this long-distance event with a woman he had never even seen—this seemed infinitely more explosive. For he had the power and Jan did not and Laurel did; and Jan's mind was closed to his and his to hers, and they could only stagger around blindly trying to find one another, while he and Laurel could unite at will in a communion whose richness was unknown to ordinary humans. He wondered if he could go on living with Jan at all now. He felt no less love for her than before, and powerful ties of affection and sharing held him to her; but yet—even so—

In guilt and confusion Maitland drifted off into sleep. It was still dark when he woke—3:13 A.M., said the clock on the dresser—and he felt different guilt, different confusion, for it was of Laurel now that he thought. He had taken pleasure from her and then he had collapsed into postorgasmic stupor. Never mind that she had told him to do just that. He felt, and always had, a peculiarly puritanical obligation to give pleasure for pleasure, and unpaid debts were troublesome to him. Taking a deep breath, he sent strands of consciousness through the night toward the south, over the fire-hued mountains of central Utah, over the silent splendor of the Grand Canyon, down past the palm trees into torrid Phoenix, and touched Laurel's warm sleepy mind.

—Hnhh.

—It's me. I want to, now.

—All right. Yes.

The image she had chosen was a warm sea, the great mother, the all-encompassing womb. He, reaching unhesitatingly for a male equivalent, sent her a vision of himself coming forth on a hot dry summer day into a quiet landscape of grassy hills round as tawny breasts. Cradled in his arms he held the gleaming porcelain jar that she had showed him last week, and he bent, tipping it, pouring forth from it an enormous snake, long and powerful but not in any way frightening, that flowed like a dark rivulet across the land, seeking her, finding, gliding up across her thighs, her belly. Too obvious? Too coarsely phallic? He wavered for a moment, but only a moment, for he heard her moan and whimper, and she reached with her mind for the serpent as it seemed he was withdrawing it; he drove back his qualms and gave her all the energy at his command, seizing the initiative as he sensed her complete surrender. Her signal shivered and lost focus. Her breathing grew ragged and hoarse, and then into his mind came a quick surprising sound, a strange low growling, that terminated in a swift sharp gasp.

—Oh, love. Oh. Oh. Thank you.

—It wasn't scary?

—Scare me like that as often as you want, Chris.

He smiled across the darkness of the miles. All was well. A fair exchange: symbol for symbol, metaphor for metaphor, delight for delight.

—Sleep well, Laurel.

—You too, love. Mmm.

This time Jan knew that something had happened while he was away. He saw it on her face, which meant that she saw it on his; but she voiced no suspicions, and when they made love the first night of his return it was as good as ever. Was it possible, he wondered, to be bigamous like this, to take part with Laurel in a literally superhuman oneness while remaining Jan's devoted husband and companion? He would, at any rate, try. Laurel had shared his soul as no one ever had and Jan never could, but yet she was a phantom, faceless, remote, scarcely real; and Jan, cut off from him as most humans are from all others, nevertheless was his wife, his partner, his bedmate, the mother of his children. He would try.

So he brought the office gossip home to her as always and went out with her twice a week to the restaurants they loved and sat beside her at night watching cassettes of operas and movies and Shakespeare, and on weekends they did their weekend things, boating on the bay and tennis and picnics in the park and dinner with their friends, and everything was fine. Everything was very fine. And yet he managed to do the other thing, too, as often as he could: snake and ocean, ocean and snake. Just as he had successfully hidden from Jan the enigmatic secret mechanism within his mind that he did not dare reveal to anyone not of his sort, so, too, now did he hide the second marriage, rich and strange, that that mechanism had brought him.

His lovemaking with Laurel had to be furtive, of course, a thing of stolen moments. She could hardly draw him into that warm voluptuous ocean while he lay beside Jan. But there were the business trips—he was careful not to increase their frequency, which would have been suspicious, but she came to him every night while he was away—and there was the occasional Saturday afternoon when he lay drowsing in the sun of the garden and found that whispering transparent surf beckoning to him, and once she enlivened a lunchtime for him on a working day. He roused the snake within his soul as often as he dared and nearly always she accepted it, though there were times when she told him no, not now, the moment was wrong. They had elaborate signals to indicate a clear coast. And for the ordinary conversation of the day there were no limits; they popped into each other's consciousness a thousand times a day, quick flickering interchanges, a joke, a bit of news, a job triumphantly accomplished, an image of beauty too potent to withhold. Crossing the bridge, entering his office, reaching for the telephone, unfolding a napkin—suddenly, there she was, often for the briefest flare of contact, a tag touch and gone. He loved that. He loved her. It was a marriage.

He snooped in Mountain Bell directories at the library and found her telephone number, which he hardly needed, and her address, which at least confirmed that she really did exist in tangible actual Phoenix. He manufactured a trip to Albuquerque to appraise the earnings prospects of a small electronics company and slipped off up the freeway to Santa Fe to visit the gallery that showed her pottery: eight or ten superb pieces, sleek, wondrously skilled. He bought one of the smaller ones. "You don't have any information about the artist, do you?" he asked the proprietor, trying to be casual, heart pounding, hoping to be shown a photograph. The proprietor thought there might be a press release in the files, and rummaged for it. "She lives down Phoenix way," she said. "Comes up here once or twice a year with her new work. I think it's museum quality, don't you?" But she could not find the press release. When Laurel flashed into his mind that night back in Albuquerque, he did not tell her he owned one of her vases or that he had been researching her. But he wondered desperately what she looked like. He played with the idea of visiting Phoenix and somehow getting to meet her without telling her who he was. So long as he kept his mind sheathed she would never know, he thought. But it seemed sneaky and treacherous; and it might be dangerous, too. She had told him often enough not to come to her city.

In the fourth month of their relationship he could no longer control his curiosity. She sent him a view of her studio, amazingly neat, the clay, the wheels, the kiln, the little bowls of pigment and glaze all fastidiously in their proper places.

—You left one thing out, Laurel.

—What's that?

—The potter herself. You didn't show me her.

—Oh, Chris.

—What's the matter? Aren't you ever curious about what I look like? We've been all over each other's minds and bodies for months, and I still don't have any idea what you look like. That's absurd.

—It's so much more abstract and pure this way.

—Wonderful. Abstract love! Save that for Swinburne. I want to see you.

—I have to confess. I want to see you, too.

—Here, then. Now.

He sent her, before she could demur, a mental snapshot of his face, trying not to retouch and enhance it. The nose a trifle too long, the cleft chin absurdly Hollywood, the dark hair thinning a bit at the part line. Not a perfect face, but good enough, pleasant, honest, nothing to apologize for, he thought. It brought silence.

—Well? Am I remotely what you expected?

—Exactly, Chris. Steady-looking, strong, decent—no surprise at all. I like your face. I'm very pleased.

—Your turn.

—You'll promise not to be disappointed?

—Stop being silly.

—All right.

She flared in his mind, not just her face but all of her, long-legged, broad-shouldered, a woman of physical presence and strength, with straightforward open features, wide-set brown eyes, a good smile, blunt nose, conspicuous cheekbones. She was not far from the woman he had imagined, and one aspect, the dark thick straight hair falling past her shoulders, was amazingly as he had thought.

—You're beautiful.

—No, not really. But I'm okay.

—Are you an Indian?

—I must have sent you a good picture, then. I'm half. My mother was Navaho.

—You learned your pottery from her?

—No, dopy. Navahos make rugs. Pueblos make pottery. I learned mine in New York, Greenwich Village. I studied with Hideki Shinoda.

—Doesn't sound Pueblo.

—Isn't. Little Japanese man with marvelous hands.

—I'm glad we did this, Laurel.

—So am I.

But seeing her in the eye of his mind, while gratifying one curiosity, had only intensified another. He wanted to meet her. He wanted to touch her. He wanted to hold her.

Snake. Ocean. They were practiced lovers now, a year of constant mental communion behind them. The novelty was gone, but not the excitement. Again and again he carried the porcelain bowl out to the sun-baked hills and poured the serpent into the grass and sent it gliding toward her eager body. Again and again she surrounded him with buoyant warm sea. Their skill at pleasuring one another struck them both as extraordinary. Of course, they soon began varying the imageries of delight, so that no monotony would taint their embraces. She came to him as a starfish, thousands of tiny suction-cup feet and a startling devouring mouth, and at another time as a moist voluptuous mass of warm smooth white clay, and as a whirlpool, and as a great coy lighthearted amoeba; and he manifested himself to her as a flash flood roaring down a red-rock canyon, and as a glistening vine coiling through a tropic night, and as a spaceship plunging in eternal free-fall between worlds. All of these were effective, for they needed only to touch one another with their minds to bring pleasure; and each new access of ingenuity brought an abstract pleasure of its own. But even so they tended often to revert to the original modes, snake and ocean, ocean and snake, the way one might return to a familiar and modest hotel where one spent a joyous weekend at the beginning of an affair, and somehow it was always best that way. They liked to tell each other that the kind of lovemaking they had invented and of which they were perhaps the sole practitioners in the history of humanity was infinitely superior to the old-fashioned type, which was so blatant, so obvious, so coarse, so messy. Even so, even as he said things like that, he knew he was lying. He wanted her skin against his skin, her breath on his breath.

She was no longer so coy about her life outside their relationship. Maitland knew now that her husband was an artist from Chicago, not very successful, a little envious of her career. She showed him some of his work, unremarkable abstract-expressionist stuff. Maitland was jealous of the fact that this man— Tim, his name was—shared her bed and enjoyed her proximity, but he realized that he had no jealousy of the marriage itself. It was all right that she was married. Maitland had no wish to live with her. He wanted to go on living with Jan, to play tennis with her and go to restaurants with her and even to make love with her; what he wanted from Laurel was just what he was getting from her, that cool amused intelligent voice in his mind, and now and then the strange ecstasy that her playful spirit was able to kindle in his loins across such great distances. That much was true. Yet also he wanted to be her lover in the old blatant obvious coarse messy way, at least once, once at least. Because he knew it was a perilous subject, he stayed away from it as long as he could, but at last it broke into the open one night in Seattle, late, after the snake had returned to its jar and the lapping waves had retreated and he lay sweaty and alone in his hotel-room bed.

—When are we finally going to meet?

—Please, Chris.

—I think it's time to discuss it. You told me a couple of times, early on, that I must never come to Phoenix. Okay. But couldn't we get together somewhere else? Tucson, San Diego, the Grand Canyon?

—It isn't the place that matters.

—What is it, then?

—Being close. Being too close.

—I don't understand. We're so close already!

—I mean physically close. Not emotionally, not even sexually. I just mean that if we came within close range of each other we'd do bad things to each other.

—That's crazy, Laurel.

—Have you ever been close to another telepath? As close as ten feet, say?

—I don't think so.

—You'd know it if you had. When you and I talk, long distance, it's just like talking on the phone, right, plus pictures? We tell each other only what we want to tell each other, and nothing else gets through. It's not like that close up.

—Oh?

—There's a kind of radiation, an aura. We broadcast all sorts of stuff automatically. All that foul stinking nasty cesspool stuff that's at the bottom of everybody's mind, the crazy prehistoric garbage that's in us. It comes swarming out like a shriek.

—How do you know that?

—I've experienced it.

—Oh. Boston, years ago?

—Yes. Yes. I told you, I did this once before.

—But he was crazy, you said.

—In a way. But the craziness isn't what brought the other stuff up. I felt it once another time, too, and *she* wasn't crazy. It's unavoidable.

—I want to see you.

—Don't you think I want to see you, too, Chris? You think I think snake and ocean's really good enough? But we can't risk it. Suppose we met, and the garbage got out, and we hated each other ever afterward?

—We could control it.

—Maybe. Maybe not.

—Or else we could make allowances for it. Bring ourselves to understand that this stuff, whatever it is that you say is there, is normal, just the gunk of the mind, nothing personal, nothing that we ought to take seriously.

—I'm scared. Let's not try.

He let the issue drop. When it came up again, four months later, it was Laurel who revived it. She had been thinking about his idea of controlling the sinister emanation, throttling it back, shielding one another. Possibly it could be done. The temptation to meet him in the flesh, she said, was overwhelming. Perhaps they could get together and suppress all telepathic contact, meet just like ordinary humans having a little illicit rendezvous, keep their minds rigidly walled off, and that way at last consummate the intimacy that had joined their souls for a year and a half.

—I'd love to, Laurel.

—But promise me this. Swear it to me. When we do get together, if we can't hold back the bad stuff, if we feel it coming out, that we go away from each other instantly. That we don't negotiate, we don't try to work it out, we don't look for angles—we just split, fast, if either of us says we have to. Swear?

—I swear.

He flew to Denver and spent a fidgety hour and a half having cocktails in the lounge at the Brown Palace. Her flight from Phoenix was supposed to have landed only half an hour after his, and he wondered if she had backed out at the last minute. He got up to call the airport when he saw her come in, unmistakably her, taller than he expected, a big handsome woman in black jeans and a sheepskin wrap. There were flecks of melting snow in her hair.

He sensed an aura.

It wasn't loathsome, it wasn't hideous, but it was there, a kind of dull whining grinding thing as of improperly oiled machinery in use three blocks away. Even as he detected it, he felt it diminish until it was barely perceptible. He struggled to rein in whatever output he might be giving off himself.

She saw him and came straight toward him, smiling nervously, cheeks rigid, eyes worried.

"Chris."

He took her hand in his. "You're cold, Laurel."

"It's snowing. That's why I'm late. I haven't seen snow in years."

"Can I get you a drink?"

"No. Yes. Yes, please. Scotch on the rocks."

"Are you picking up anything bad?"

"No," she said. "Not really. There was just a little twinge, when I walked in—a kind of squeak in my mind."

"I felt it, too. But then it faded."

"I'm fighting to keep it damped down. I want this to work."

"So do I. We mustn't use the power at all today."

"We don't need to. The old snake can have the day off. Are you scared?"

"A little."

"Me, too." She gulped her drink. "Oh, Chris."

"Is it hard work, keeping the power damped down?"

"Yes. It really is."

"For me, too. But we have to."

"Yes," she said. "Do you have a room yet?"

He nodded.

"Let's go upstairs, then."

Like any unfaithful husband having his first rendezvous with a new lover he walked stiffly and somberly through the lobby, convinced that everyone was staring at them. That was ridiculous, he knew. They were more truly married, in their way, than anybody else in Denver. But yet—but yet—

They were silent in the elevator. As they approached their floor the aura of her burst forth again, briefly, a fast sour vibration in his bones, and then it was gone altogether, shut off as though by a switch. He worked at holding his down, too. She smiled at him. He winked. "To the left," he said. They went into the room. Heavy snowflakes splashed against the window; the wide bed was turned down. She was trembling. "Come on," he said. "I love you. You know that. Everything's all right."

They kissed and undressed. Her body was lean, athletic, with small high breasts, a flat belly, a dark appendectomy scar. He drew her toward the bed. It seemed strange, almost perverse, to be doing things in this antiquated fleshly way, no snake, no ocean, no meeting of minds. He was afraid for a moment that in the excitement of their coupling they would lose control of their mental barriers and let their inner selves come flooding out, fierce, intense, a contact too powerful to handle at such short range. But there was no loss of control. He kept the power locked behind the walls of his skull; she did the same; there were only the tiniest leakages of current. But there was no excitement, either, in their lovemaking.

He ran his hands over her breasts and trapped her nipples between his fingers, and gently parted her thighs with his knee, and pressed himself against her as though he had not been with a woman in a year, but the excitement seemed to be all in his head, not in his nerve endings. Even when she ran her lips down his chest and belly and teased him for a moment and then took him fiercely and suddenly into her mouth, it was the *idea* that they were finally doing this, rather than what they were actually doing, that resonated within him. They sighed a little and moaned a little and finally he slipped into her, admiring the tightness of her and the rhythms of her hips and all that, but nevertheless it was as though this had happened between them a thousand times before: he moved, she moved, they did all the standard things and traveled along to the standard result. Not enough was real between them, that was the trouble. He knew her better than he had ever known anyone, and yet in some ways he knew her not at all, and that was what had spoiled things. That, and holding so much in check. He wished he could look into her mind now. But that was forbidden, and probably unwise, too; he guessed that she was annoyed with him for having insisted on this foolish and foredoomed meeting, that she held him responsible for having spoiled things between them, and he did not want to see those thoughts in her mind.

When it was over they whispered to each other and stroked each other and gave each other little nibbling kisses, and he pretended it had been marvelous, but his real impulse was to pull away and light a cigarette and stare out the window at the snow, and he wasn't even a smoker. It was simply the way he felt. It had been only a mechanical thing, only a hotel-room screw, not remotely anything like snake and ocean: a joining of flesh of the sort that a pair of rabbits might have accomplished, or a pair of apes, without content, without fire, without joy. He and she knew an ever so much better way of doing it.

He took care to hide his disappointment.

"I'm so glad I came here, Chris," she said, smiling, kissing him, taking care to hide her disappointment, too, he guessed. He knew that if he entered her mind he would find it bleak and ashen. But of course he could not do that. "I wish I could stay the night," she said. "My plane's at nine. We could have dinner downstairs, though."

"Is it a terrible strain, keeping the power back?"

"It isn't easy."

"No. It isn't."

"I'm so glad we did this, Chris."

"Are you?"

"Yes. Yes. Of course."

They had an early dinner. The snow had stopped by the time he saw her to her cab. So: you fly up to Denver for a couple of hours of lust and steak, you fly back home, and that's that. He had a brandy in the lounge and went to his room. For a long while he lay staring at the ceiling, sure that she would come to him with the ocean, and make amends for the unsatisfactory thing they had done that afternoon. She did not. He wondered if he ought to send her the snake as she dozed on her plane, and did not want to. He felt timid about any sort of contact with her now. It had all been a terrible mistake, he knew. Not because of that emanation from the dirty depths of the psyche that she had so feared, but only because it had been so anticlimactic, so meaningless. He waited for a sending from her, some bright little flash out of Arizona. She must surely be home now. Nothing came. He went on waiting, not daring to reach toward her, and finally he fell asleep.

Jan said nothing to him about the Denver trip. He was moody and strange, but she let him be. When the silence out of Phoenix continued into the next day and the next he grew even more grim, and skulked about wrapped in black isolation. Gradually it occurred to him that he was not going to hear from Laurel again, that they had broken something in that hotel room in Denver and that it was irreparable, and, oddly, the knowledge of that gave him some ease: if he did not expect to hear from her, he did not have to lament her silence. A week, two, three, and nothing. So it was over. That hollow little grunting hour had ruined it.

Somehow he picked up the rhythms of his life: work, home, wife, kids, friends, tennis, dinner. He did an extensive analysis of southwestern electric utilities that brought him a commendation from on high, and he felt only a mild twinge of anguish while doing his discussion of the prospects for Arizona Public Service as reflected in the municipal growth of the city of Phoenix. He missed the little tickle in his mind immensely, but he was encapsulating it, containing it, and after a fashion he was healing.

One day a month and a half later he found himself idly scanning the mind-noise band again, as he had not done for a long while, just to see who else was out there. He picked up the loony babble out of Fort Lauderdale and the epicene static from Manitoba, and then he encountered someone new, a bright clear signal as intense as Laurel's, and for a dazzled instant a sudden fantasy of a new relationship blossomed in him, but then he heard the nonsense syllables, the slow, firm, strong-willed stream of gibberish. There were no replacements for Laurel.

In Chicago, where he had been sent to do a survey of natural-gas companies, he began talking to a youngish woman at the Art Institute, and by easy stages some chatter about Monet and Sisley turned into a dinner invitation and a night in his hotel room. That was all right. Certainly it was simpler and easier and less depressing than Denver. But it was a bore, it was empty and foolish, and he regretted it deeply by breakfast time, even while he was taking down her number and promising to call the next time he was in the Midwest. Maitland saw the post-Laurel pattern of his life closing about him now: the Christmas bonus, the trip to Hawaii with Jan, braces for the kids, the new house five years from now, the occasional quickie romance in far-off hotel rooms. That was all right. That was the original bargain he had made, long ago, entering adult life: not much ecstasy, not much grief.

On the long flight home that day he thought without rancor or distress about his year and a half with Laurel, and told himself that the important thing was not that it had ended but that it had happened at all. He felt peaceful and accepting, and was almost tempted to reach out toward Laurel and thank her for her love, and wish her well. But he was afraid—afraid that if he touched her mind in any way she would pull away, timid, fearful of contact in the wake of that inexplicably sundering day in Denver. She was close by now, he knew, for the captain had just told them that they were passing over the Grand Canyon. Maitland did not lean to the window, as everyone else was doing, to look down. He sat back, eyes closed, tired, calm.

And felt warmth, heard the lapping of surf, saw in the center of his mind the vast ocean in which Laurel had so many times engulfed him. Really? Was it happening? He let himself slide into it. A little flustered, he hid himself behind a facade of newspapers, the *Tribune*, the *Wall Street Journal*. His face grew flushed. His breathing became rougher. Ah. Ah. It was happening, yes, she had reached to him, she had made the gesture at last. Tears of gratitude and relief came to him, and he let her sweep him off to a sharp and pounding fulfillment five miles above Arizona.

—Hello, Chris.

—Laurel.

—Did you mind? I felt you near me, and I couldn't hold back any more. I know you don't want to hear from me, but—

—What gave you that idea?

—I thought—it seemed to me—

—No. I thought you were the one who wanted to break it up.

—I? I missed you so much, Chris. But I was sure you'd pull away.

—So was I, about you.

—Silly.

—Laurel. Laurel. I'm so glad you took the chance, then.

—So am I.

—Let me have the snake, Chris.

—Yes. Yes.

He stepped out into the tawny sun-baked hills with the heavy porcelain jar and tipped it, and let the snake glide toward her. It was all right after all. They had made mistakes, but they were the mistakes of too much love, and they had survived them. It was going to be all right: snake and ocean, ocean and snake, now and always.

T O U R I S T

T R A D E

By the final month of 1982, the giant lobsters of "Homefaring" were behind me and I was getting ready for the winter's major enterprise, the novel Valentine Pontifex, the closing volume of the Majipoor trilogy. But I still didn't feel entirely comfortable using the computer to write, and it seemed like a good idea to tackle one more short story before plunging into the novel. So I decided to try another one for Playboy.

My conversion from typewriter to computer couldn't have come at a more timely moment. "Tourist Trade," which as I look at it now seems to move seamlessly from first sentence to last, called forth at least half a dozen drafts from me, maybe even more. If I had had to type those thirty-odd pages out every time from beginning to end, I'd probably have hurled the typewriter through the window long before I came up with something that Alice Turner would find acceptable. What should have been a relatively simple 7,500-word project turned into an interminable and agonizing ordeal.

When you use a computer to write, a lot of the false starts, fatuous passages, and other miscalculations don't survive for the amusement of scholars studying your manuscripts in years to come. You simply back up the cursor and erase them, send them into the black hole of computer limbo, and no one's ever the wiser. But from time to time a writer does need hard copy of a work in progress, and so a lot of botched drafts do get put down on paper even in the computer age. I save mine, God knows why. In the case of "Tourist Trade," I have a stack about five inches thick.

For those of you who think that story writing gets easier as a writer's career goes along, the "Tourist Trade" saga—dating from my thirtieth year as a professional writer—ought to be highly instructive.

It begins with a one-page draft in first-person narration of something I titled "A World of Strangers":

In Morocco all the human tourists head straight for Marrakesh, as people have been doing ever since tourism began. But the extraterrestrials prefer to go to Fez, for some reason, and so I went to Fez also.

I don't know why it should be that way, except that they're extraterrestrials, and maybe that's enough of an explanation. Of course, Fez is a great city in its own right, and an enormously interesting place, and no traveler needs any excuse to go there. But Marrakesh is the classical tourist-trap town of Morocco, with its palaces, its tombs, its tower, its crazy grand plaza full of acrobats and jugglers and snake charmers, and that's where the hordes invariably have gone. The human hordes. E-T's, being E-T's, have different value systems. They . . .

And there my gorge rose. It seemed to me that I was blathering on and on in an impossible way. So I stopped and started over:

When I arrived in Fez, early on a warm April evening, I checked in at the big old Palais Jamai at the edge of the old city. In Morocco all the human tourists head straight for Marrakesh, as tourists have been doing ever since tourism began. But the extraterrestrials prefer to go to Fez, for some reason. And so I went to Fez also.

Not bad, especially when compared with the first version. This time I lasted six pages. I got my aliens on the scene on page two and the exotic green-eyed woman appeared on page three. They moved out onto the dance floor together and the narrator's skin began to tingle and suddenly I felt the upchuck reflex again. What I was writing was very slick, hopelessly mechanical, a computer-constructed man's-magazine story, lifeless and formulaic. The problem, I thought, was the first-person narration. It's all too easy, writing first person, to slip into a garrulous, ingratiating here's-what-I-did tone that dawdles on and on and on as the narrator murmurs in your ear.

The third draft started the same way as the second, with the protagonist checking in at his hotel in Fez. But now it was a third-person story. And this time I didn't abandon it after a few pages. I pushed on all the way to the end, or what I thought was the end. This is how it opened now:

Eitel picked up his merchandise in Paris and caught the Air France night bird to Casablanca, where he connected with a Royal Air Maroc flight for the short hop to Fez. It was the middle of April, when Europe was still bleak and winter-dead, and Morocco was halfway to summer.

Very efficient. Protagonist introduced and in motion; exotic background established; and what's this mysterious merchandise? A nice lead paragraph. I nodded and went on for thirty-seven more pages, throwing in a lot of juicy Moroccan background information before bringing my aliens on stage on page five and the gorgeous woman on page seven. Eitel finally gets out on the dance floor with her on page fifteen, and then the trouble starts. And eventually gets resolved.

All right. I had a story. But it took too long to get down to its central events, and generally seemed inflated and lifeless to me. It was now Christmas week of 1982, and an old friend from New York was visiting me—Jerrold Mundis, a wise man and fine writer who doesn't happen to write (or read, or like, I suspect) science fiction. I gave him the story, telling him that I thought something was wrong with it, and asked him for a blunt critique, no punches pulled. He was blunt, all right. As I already suspected, I had opened the story in the wrong place. All that stuff in the beginning about Fez and Marrakesh might be fascinating to me, and might even make a nice National Geographic article, but it stopped things dead before they began. The endless speculations about the psychology of aliens that occupied pages six through fourteen weren't very gripping either. Start the story on page five, he suggested, and cut a lot of what follows, and maybe it would work.

Jerry usually knows whereof he speaks, in matters of writing and in other things. So I took his advice. This was the opening of the fourth draft:

Even before Eitel's eyes had adjusted to the darkness and the glare of the clashing crisscrossing spotlights, his nose began letting him know what sort of bizarre zoo he had walked into. The nightclub was full of aliens, at least seven or eight species. He picked up the whole astonishing olfactory blast at once, a weird hodgepodge of extraterrestrial body odors, offworld pheromones, transgalactic cosmetics, the ozone radiation of personal protection screens, minute quantities of unearthly atmospheres leaking out of breathing devices. He was smelling things that as recently as the year 1987 no human being had ever smelled. Rigelians, he thought, Centaurans, Antareans, Arcturans. Maybe Steropids and Capellans too. The world has turned into a goddamned sci-fi flick, Eitel thought.

At last: some inventiveness, some narrative vigor, some characteristic Silverbergian tone. I cut here, expanded there, and in a few days had a thirty-eight-page story very different from its limp predecessors. On January 21, 1983, "A World of Strangers" went off to Alice Turner at Playboy's

New York office; I put it out of my mind with deep relief and started writing Valentine Pontifex a few days later.

But Alice didn't like what I had sent her.

On February 1 she told me, "I love the Star Wars bar in the beginning of this story, but, all in all, I'm dubious about the story. First, there's far too much exposition in the beginning. . . . Frankly, I think the flashback could go, the taxi driver too. And the ending doesn't seem a bit integral to the story. If, for instance . . ."

And so on. A lot of problems. "But I know that you probably like this story as is," she added, "and thus, with complete respect and many thanks, I will pass. If I am wrong, and you feel that, on second thought, you will change the ending and do some cutting early on, let me know. We could talk."

Imagine my delight. After four full drafts before submitting the story, I had a reject on my hands. I suppose I could have saved us both a lot of trouble by sending the story, as is, to some other magazine and collecting my (rather smaller) check for it and putting it behind me. But I took Alice's letter as a challenge, instead. I covered it with notes. "Might work!" I wrote, next to the paragraph where she suggested a different ending. "Make it shadier . . . Story too simple. Make David real person—a partner? Eitel uptight, David a crook. Eitel has vestiges of ethics." And a lot more. I phoned Alice and said I was going to rewrite the story. She seemed surprised and pleased. On February 16 I sent it to her again, down to thirty-four pages, with a note that said, "Herewith the promised new version of the art-dealer story. I think I would not have had the heart to attempt it but for the word processor, which allowed me to rewrite big sections and graft salvageable old sections right in. . . . I hope this does it. God only knows how many versions of this one I've written—even if you buy it at a fat price I'll end up making about $3 an hour for it. But that isn't the point; something must have happened last fall that caused me to lose my touch, to make my stuff topheavy with exposition, and I'm groping my way back toward the way I'm supposed to write. This revision has been a great help in telling me I'm getting back there."

This was the new opening:

After a moment Eitel's eyes adjusted to the darkness and the glare of the clashing crisscrossing spotlights. But he didn't need his eyes to tell him what sort of bizarre zoo he had walked into. The nightclub was full of aliens, seven or eight kinds, Rigelians, Capellans, Arcturans: the works. His sensitive nostrils picked up the whole aston-

ishing olfactory blast at once: a weird hodgepodge of extraterrestrial body odors, offworld pheromones, transgalactic cosmetics, the ozone radiation of personal protection screens, minute quantities of unearthly atmospheres leaking out of breathing devices. He began to tremble.

"Something wrong?" David asked.

Alice phoned a couple of days later. She liked the new version, but it still needed some cutting, and she had some further plot quibbles besides. Could I see my way to one more rewrite?

Yes, I said despondently. The hook was in me now for sure. I told her to send me a list of the quibbles. But you do the cutting, I said. I've worked this one over so much that I'm losing my way in it.

On March 1 I got an annotated copy of the manuscript from her, with huge slashes on almost every page, slicing out exposition that echoed things already said in dialog, authorial explanation of the characters' motives, and other sorts of fatty tissue. Her plot quibbles seemed pretty major, too. After all these drafts she still could find six separate places where the twists of the plot weren't really plausible. I was appalled. But she sweetened her letter by telling me at the end, "Bob, again, I want to congratulate you on the fine job you've done with this rewrite. Though you've been feeling inadequate, this is much more than an adequate job; it's a real change, and only a thorough professional could do it. As you see, these are only minor quibbles, the story is here, and I'm most grateful."

Four days later—I was working weekends now, a rarity for me—I got yet another draft back to her. You'll find the text of it beginning on the next page. I had made nearly all the cuts she wanted and had tidied up the plot. "I think the story now answers all of your objections and it may even answer mine; at any rate I hope I'm through writing it," I told her. "Nobody said this business is easy, but I shouldn't goof up a story as badly as I goofed up the earlier versions of this one, not at my age."

And a couple of days afterward, there was Alice on the phone. The story was fine and she was putting through the check (a very nice one, by the way).

To her astonishment and mine, I came close to breaking into tears as I realized that I was at last done with the damned thing.

Oh, she said. One little change. I'd like to call it "Tourist Trade" instead of "A World of Strangers."

At that point she could have called it "The Snows of Kilimanjaro" and I wouldn't have raised objections. But in fact her clever punning title was *more suitable than mine, as you'll see in a little while, and I've retained it in reprinting the story.*

There's one final twist to this flabbergasting tale.

Years later—December of 1988—Playboy published its thirty-fifth anniversary issue. "Tourist Trade" was one of eight stories chosen to represent the fiction Playboy had published over those thirty-five years. (The others, I noted smugly, were by Ray Bradbury, Ian Fleming, Walter S. Tevis, Vladimir Nabokov, John Updike, Robert Coover, and Joyce Carol Oates.) In phoning me to ask permission to reprint my story, Alice said that because of space limitations it would, like the others, have to be abridged. By her, since time was short.

"Where are you going to cut it?" I asked.

"I've already done it," she said. "I took David out."

And so she had—slicing away one of the three major characters, along with close to half the text. To my utter astonishment the story still seemed coherent and effective—a testimony to really brilliant editing. I look at it from time to time in wonder. Nevertheless, I've chosen to use the complete text here—along with this lengthy prologue, which I hope demonstrates that those finely polished stories you see in the magazines don't necessarily bear much resemblance to the first version that came white-hot from the forge of creativity. There can be plenty of blood, sweat, and, yes, tears in writing short stories—even for a veteran pro who is widely believed to know what he's doing.

After a moment Eitel's eyes adjusted to the darkness and the glare of the clashing crisscrossing spotlights. But he didn't need his eyes to tell him what sort of bizarre zoo he had walked into. His sensitive nostrils picked up the whole astonishing olfactory blast at once: a weird hodgepodge of extraterrestrial body odors, offworld pheromones, transgalactic cosmetics, the ozone radiation of personal protection screens, minute quantities of unearthly atmospheres leaking out of breathing devices.

"Something wrong?" David asked.

"The odors. They overwhelm me."

"The smoking, eh? You hate it that much?"

"Not the tobacco, fool. The aliens! The E-T's!"

"Ah. The smell of money, you mean. I agree, it is very overwhelming in here."

"For a shrewd man you can sometimes be very stupid," Eitel muttered. "Unless you say such things deliberately, which you must, because I have never known a stupid Moroccan."

"For a Moroccan, I am very stupid," said David serenely. "And so it was very stupid of you to choose me as your partner, eh? Your grandfathers in Zurich would be shamed if they knew. Eh?" He gave Eitel a maddeningly seraphic smile.

Eitel scowled. He was never sure when he had genuinely offended the slippery little Moroccan and when David was merely teasing. But somehow David always came out of these interchanges a couple of points ahead.

He turned and looked the place over, checking it out.

Plenty of humans, of course. This was the biggest gathering place for aliens in Morocco, the locus of the focus, and a lot of gawkers came to observe the action. Eitel ignored them. There was no sense doing business with humans any more. There were probably some Interpol types in here, too, hoping to head off just the sort of deals Eitel was here to do. To hell with them. His hands were clean, more or less.

But the aliens! The aliens, the aliens, the aliens!

All over the room. Vast saucer eyes, spidery limbs, skins of grotesque textures and unnameable colors. Eitel felt the excitement rising in him, so unSwiss of him, so thoroughly out of character.

"*Look* at them!" he whispered. "They're beautiful!"

"Beautiful? You think so?"

"Fantastic!"

The Moroccan shrugged. "Fantastic, yes. Beautiful, no. Blue skin, green skin, no skin, two heads, five heads: this is beauty? What is beautiful to me is the money. And the way they like to throw it away."

"You would never understand," said Eitel.

In fact, Eitel hardly understood it himself. He had discovered, not long after the first alien tourists had reached Earth, that they stirred unexpected areas of his soul: strange vistas opening, odd incoherent cosmic yearnings. To find at the age of forty that there was more to him than Panamanian trusts and numbered bank accounts—that was a little troublesome; but it was delicious, as well. He stood staring for a long ecstatic chaotic moment. Then he turned to David and said, "Where's your Centauran?"

"I don't see him."

"Neither do I."

"He swore he'd be here. Is a big place, Eitel. We go looking, and we find."

The air was thick with color, sound, fumes. Eitel moved carefully around a tableful of leathery-faced pockmarked red Rigelians, burly, noisy, like a herd of American conventioneers out on the town. Behind them sat five sleek and sinuous Steropids, wearing cone-shaped breathers. Good. Steropids were easy marks. If something went wrong with this Centauran deal David had set up, he might want to have them as customers to fall back on.

Likewise that Arcturan trio, flat heads, grizzled green hair, triple eyes bright as blue-white suns. Arcturans were wild spenders, though they weren't known to covet Eitel's usual merchandise, which was works of fine art, or more or less fine art. Perhaps they could be encouraged to. Eitel, going past, offered them a preliminary smile: Earthman establishing friendly contact, leading perhaps to more elaborate relationship. But the Arcturans didn't pick up on it. They looked through Eitel as though their eyes didn't function in the part of the spectrum he happened to inhabit.

"There," David said.

Yes. Far across the way, a turquoise creature, inordinately long and narrow, that appeared to be constructed of the finest grade of rubber, stretched over an awkwardly flung together armature of short rods.

"There's a woman with him," Eitel said. "I wasn't expecting that. You didn't tell me."

David's eyes gleamed. "Ah, nice, very nice!"

She was more than very nice. She was splendid. But that wasn't the point. Her presence here could be a troublesome complication. A tour guide? An interpreter? Had the Centauran brought his own art expert along? Or was she some Interpol agent decked out to look like the highest-priced of hookers? Or maybe even a real hooker. God help me, he thought, if the Centauran's gotten involved in some kind of kinky infatuation that would distract him from the deal. No: God help David.

"You should have told me there was a woman," Eitel said.

"But I didn't know! I swear, Jesus Mary Moses, I never see her yesterday! But it will be all right. Jesus Mary Moses, go ahead, walk over." He smiled and winked and slipped off toward the bar. "I see you later, outside. You go for it, you hear? You hear me, Eitel? It will be all right."

The Centauran, seeing the red carnation in Eitel's lapel, lifted his arm in a gesture like the extending of a telescopic tube, and the woman smiled. It was an amazing smile, and it caught Eitel a little off guard, because for an instant it made him wish that the Centauran was back on Centaurus and this woman was sitting here alone. He shook the thought off. He was here to do a deal, not to get into entanglements.

"Hans Eitel, of Zurich," he said,

"I am Anakhistos," said the Centauran. His voice was like something out of a synthesizer, which perhaps it was, and his face was utterly opaque, a flat motionless mask. For vision he had a single bright strip of receptors an inch wide around his forehead, for air intake he had little vents on his cheeks, and for eating he had a three-sided oral slot like the swinging top of a trash basket. "We are very happied you have come," he said. "This is Agila."

Eitel allowed himself to look straight at her. It was dazzling but painful, a little like staring into the sun. Her hair was red and thick, her eyes were emerald and very far apart, her lips were full, her teeth were bright. She was wearing a vaguely futuristic metal-mesh sheath, green, supple, clinging. What she looked like was something that belonged on a 3-D billboard, one of those unreal idealized women who turn up in the ads for cognac, or skiing holidays in Gstaad. There was something a little freakish about such excessive beauty. A professional, he decided.

To the Centauran he said, "This is a great pleasure for me. To meet a collector of your stature, to know that I will be able to be of assistance—"

"And a pleasure also for ourself. You are greatly recommended to me. You are called knowledgeable, reliable, discreet—"

"The traditions of our family. I was bred to my métier."

"We are drinking mint tea," the woman said. "Will you drink mint tea with us?" Her voice was warm, deep, unfamiliar. Swedish? Did they have redheads in Sweden?

Eitel said, "Forgive me, but it's much too sweet for me. Perhaps a brandy instead—"

A waiter appeared as though by telepathic command. Eitel ordered a Courvoisier, and the woman another round of tea. She is very smooth, very good, he thought. He imagined himself in bed with her, digging his fingers into that dense red mane, running his lips over her long lean thighs. The fantasy was pleasing but undisturbing: an idle dream, cool, agreeable, giving him no palpitations, no frenzy. Good. After that first startled moment he was getting himself under control. He wondered if she was charging the Centauran by the night, or working at something bigger.

She said, "I love the Moroccan tea. It is so marvelous, the sweet. Sugar is my passion. I think I am addicted."

The waiter poured the tea in the traditional way, cascading it down into the glass from three feet up. Eitel repressed a shudder. He admired the elaborate

Moroccan cuisine, but the tea appalled him: lethal hypersaccharine stuff, instant diabetes.

"Do you also enjoy mint tea?" Eitel asked the alien.

"It is very wonderful," the Centauran said. "It is one of the most wonderful things on this wonderful planet."

Eitel had no idea how sincere the Centauran was. He had been studying the psychology of extraterrestrials about as closely as anyone had, in the decade since they had begun to descend on Earth en masse after the lifting of the galactic quarantine, and he knew a lot about a lot of them; but he found it almost impossible to get a reading on Centaurans. If they gave any clues to their feelings at all, it was in the form of minute, perhaps imaginary fluctuations of the texture of their rubbery skins. It was Eitel's theory that the skin slackened when they were happy and went taut when they were tense, but the theory was only preliminary and he gave it little value.

"When did you arrive on Earth?" Eitel asked.

"It is the first week," the Centauran said. "Five days here in Fez, then we go to Rome, Paris, and afterward the States United. Following which, other places. It is greatly exciting, your world. Such vigor, such raw force. I hope to see everything, and bring back much art. I am passionate collector, you know, of Earthesque objects."

"With a special interest in paintings."

"Paintings, yes, but I collect many other things."

That seemed a little blatant. Unless Eitel misunderstood the meaning, but he doubted he had. He glanced at the woman, but she showed no reaction.

Carefully he said, "Such as?"

"Everything that is essential to the experience of your world! Everything fine, everything deeply Earthesque! Of course, I am most fastidious. I seek only the first-rate objects."

"I couldn't possibly agree more," said Eitel. "We share the same philosophy. The true connoisseur has no time for the tawdry, the trivial, the incompletely realized gesture, the insufficiently fulfilled impulse." His tone, carefully practiced over years of dealing with clients, was intended to skirt unctuousness and communicate nothing but warm and sincere approbation. Such nuances were probably lost on the Centauran, but Eitel never let himself underestimate a client. He looked suddenly toward the woman and said, "Surely that's your outlook also."

"Of course."

She took a long pull of her mint tea, letting the syrupy stuff slide down her throat like motor oil. Then she wriggled her shoulders in a curious way. Eitel saw flesh shifting interestingly beneath the metal mesh. Surely she was professional. *Surely.* He found himself speculating on whether there could be anything sexual going on between these two. He doubted that it was possible, but you never could tell. More likely, though, she was merely one of the stellar pieces in Anakhistos's collection of the high-quality Earthesque: an object, an artifact. Eitel wondered how Anakhistos had managed to find her so fast. Was there some service that supplied visiting aliens with the finest of escorts, at the finest of prices?

He was picking up an aroma from her now, not unpleasant but very strange: caviar and cumin? Sturgeon poached in Chartreuse?

She signaled to the waiter for yet another tea. To Eitel she said, "The problem of the export certificates, do you think it is going to get worse?"

That was unexpected, and very admirable, he thought. Discover what your client's concerns are, make them your own.

He said, "It is a great difficulty, is it not?"

"I think of little else," said the Centauran, leaping in as if he had been waiting for Agila to provide the cue. "To me it is an abomination. These restrictions on removing works of art from your planet—these humiliating inspections—this agitation, this outcry for even tighter limitations—what will it come to?"

Soothingly Eitel said, "You must try to understand the nature of the panic. We are a small backward world that has lived in isolation until just a few years ago. Suddenly we have stumbled into contact with the great galactic civilizations. You come among us, you are fascinated by us and by our artifacts, you wish to collect our things. But we can hardly supply the entire civilized universe. There are only a few Leonardos, a few Vermeers: and there are so many of you. So there is fear that you will sweep upon us with your immense wealth, with your vast numbers, with your hunger for our art, and buy everything of value that we have ever produced, and carry it off to places a hundred light-years away. So these laws are being passed. It is natural."

"But I am not here to plunder! I am here to make legimate purchase!"

"I understand completely," Eitel said. He risked putting his hand, gently, compassionately, on the Centauran's arm. Some of the E-T's resented any sort of intimate contact of this sort with Earthfolk. But apparently the Centauran didn't mind. The alien's rubbery skin felt astonishingly soft and smooth, like the finest condom imaginable. "I'm altogether on your side," Eitel declared. "The export laws are absurd overreactions. There's a more than ample supply of art on this planet to meet the needs of sophisticated collectors like yourself. And by disseminating our culture among the star worlds, we bind ourselves inextricably into the fabric of galactic civilization. Which is why I do everything in my power to make our finest art available to our visitors."

"But can you provide valid export licenses?" Agila asked.

Eitel put his finger to his lips. "We don't need to discuss it further just now, eh? Let us enjoy the delights of this evening, and save dreary matters of commerce for later, shall we?" He beamed. "May I offer you more tea?"

✦

It was all going very smoothly, Eitel thought. Contact made, essential lines of agreement established. Even the woman was far less of a complication than he had anticipated. Time now to back off, relax, let rapport blossom and mature without forcing.

"Do you dance?" Agila said suddenly.

He looked toward the dance floor. The Rigelians were lurching around in a preposterously ponderous way, like dancing bears. Some Arcturans were on the dance floor, too, and a few Procyonites bouncing up and down like bundles of shiny metal rods, and a Steropid doing an eerie *pas de seul*, weaving in dreamy circles.

"Yes, of course," he said, a little startled.

"Please dance with me?"

He glanced uneasily toward the Centauran, who nodded benignly. She smiled and said, "Anakhistos does not dance. But I would like to. Would you oblige me?"

Eitel took her hand and led her out on the floor. Once they were dancing he was able to regain his calm. He moved easily and well. Some of the E-T's were openly watching them—they had such *curiosity* about humans sometimes—but the staring didn't bother him. He found himself registering the pressure of her thighs against his thighs, her firm heavy breasts against his chest, and for an instant he felt the old biochemical imperative trying to go roaring through his veins, telling him, *follow her anywhere, promise anything, say anything, do anything.* He brushed it back. There were other women: in Nice, in Rome, in Athens. When he was done with this deal he would go to one of them.

He said, "Agila is an interesting name. Israeli, is it?"

"No," she said.

The way she said it, serenely and very finally, left him without room to maneuver. He was full of questions—who was she, how had she hooked up with the Centauran, what was her deal, how well did she think Eitel's own deal with the Centauran was likely to go? But that one cool syllable seemed to have slammed a curtain down. He concentrated on dancing again instead. She was supple, responsive, skillful. And yet the way she danced was as strange as everything else about her: she moved almost as if her feet were some inches off the floor. Odd. And her voice—an accent, but what kind? He had been everywhere, and nothing in his experience matched her way of speaking, a certain liquidity in the vowels, a certain resonance in the phrasing, as though she were hearing echoes as she spoke. She had to be something truly exotic, Rumanian, a Finn, a Bulgar—and even those did not seem exotic enough. Albanian? Lithuanian?

Most perplexing of all was her aroma. Eitel was gifted with a sense of smell worthy of a perfumer, and he heeded a woman's fragrance the way more ordinary men studied the curves of hip or bosom or thigh. Out of the pores and the axillae and the orifices came the truths of the body, he believed, the deepest, the most trustworthy, the most exciting communications; he studied them with rabbinical fervor and the most minute scientific zeal. But he had never smelled anything like this, a juxtaposition of incongruous spices, a totally baffling mix of flavors. Some amazing new perfume? Something imported from Arcturus or Capella, perhaps? Maybe so, though it was hard to imagine an effect like this being achieved by mere chemicals. It had to be *her.* But what mysterious glandular outpouring brought him that subtle hint of sea urchin mingled with honey? What hidden duct sent thyme and raisins coursing together through her bloodstream? Why did the crystalline line of light perspiration on her flawless upper lip carry those grace-notes of pomegranate, tarragon, and ginger?

He looked for answers in her eyes: deep green pools, calm, cool, unearthly. They seemed as bewildering as the rest of her.

And then he understood. He realized now that the answer, impossible and implausible and terrifying, had been beckoning to him all evening, and that he could no longer go on rejecting it, impossible or not. And in the moment of accepting it he heard a sound within himself much like that of a wind beginning to rise, a hurricane being born on some far-off isle.

Eitel began to tremble. He had never felt himself so totally defenseless before.

He said, "It's amazing, how human you seem to be."

"*Seem* to be?"

"Outwardly identical in every way. I didn't think it was possible for life-forms of such a degree of similarity to evolve on two different worlds."

"It isn't," she said.

"You're not from Earth, though."

She was smiling. She seemed almost pleased, he thought, that he had seen through her masquerade.

"No."

"What are you, then?"

"Centauran."

Eitel closed his eyes a moment. The wind was a gale within him; he swayed and struggled to keep his balance. He was starting to feel as though he were conducting this conversation from a point somewhere behind his own right ear. "But Centaurans look like—"

"Like Anakhistos? Yes, of course we do, when we are at home. But I am not at home now."

"I don't understand."

"This is my traveling body," she said.

"What?"

"It is not comfortable, visiting certain places in one's own body. The air is sharp, the light hurts the eyes, eating is very troublesome."

"So you simply put on a different body?"

"Some of us do. There are those like Anakhistos who are indifferent to the discomforts, or who actually regard them as part of the purpose of traveling. But I am of the sort that prefers to transfer into a traveling body when going to other worlds."

"Ah," Eitel said. "Yes." He continued to move through the rhythms of the dance in a numb, dazed way. It's all just a costume, he told himself. What she really looks like is a bunch of rigid struts, with a rubber sheet draped over them. Cheek vents for breathing, three-sided slot for eating, receptor strip instead of eyes. "And these bodies?" he asked. "Where do you get them?"

"Why, they make them for us. Several companies do it. The human models are only just now becoming available. Very expensive, you understand."

"Yes," he said. "Of course."

"Tell me: when was it that you first saw through my disguise?"

"I felt right away that something was wrong. But it wasn't until a moment ago that I figured it out."

"No one else has guessed, I think. It is an extremely excellent Earth body, would you not say?"

"Extremely," Eitel said.

"After each trip I always regret, at first, returning to my real body. This one seems quite genuine to me by now. You like it very much, yes?"

"Yes," Eitel said helplessly.

◆

He found David out in the cab line, lounging against his taxi with one arm around a Moroccan boy of about sixteen and the other exploring the breasts of a swarthy French-looking woman. It was hard to tell which one he had selected for the late hours of the night: both, maybe. David's cheerfully polymorphous ways were a little hard for Eitel to take sometimes. But Eitel knew it wasn't necessary to approve of David in order to work with him. Whenever Eitel showed up in Fez with new merchandise, David was able to finger a customer for him within twenty-four hours; and at a five percent commission he was probably the wealthiest taxi driver in Morocco, after two years as Eitel's point man among the E-T's.

"Everything's set," Eitel said. "Take me over to get the stuff."

David flashed his glittering gold-toothed grin. He patted the woman's rump, lightly slapped the boy's cheek, pushed them both on their way, and opened the door of his cab for Eitel. The merchandise was at Eitel's hotel, the Palais Jamai, on the edge of the native quarter. But Eitel never did business at his own hotel: it was handy to have David to take him back and forth between the Jamai and the Hotel Merinides, out here beyond the city wall by the ancient royal tombs, where most of the aliens preferred to stay.

The night was mild, fragrant, palm trees rustling in the soft breeze, huge bunches of red geranium blossoms looking almost black in the moonlight. As they drove toward the old town, with its maze of winding medieval streets, its walls and gates straight out of the Arabian nights, David said, "You mind I tell you something? One thing worries me."

"Go ahead."

"Inside, I watched you. Staring more at the woman than at the E-T. You got to concentrate on the deal, and forget the woman, Eitel."

Eitel resented being told by a kid half his age how to conduct his operations. But he kept himself in check. To David, young and until recently poor, certain nuances were incomprehensible. Not that David lacked an interest in beauty. But beauty was just an abstraction; money was money. Eitel did not attempt to explain what time would surely teach.

He said, "*You* tell *me*, forget the woman?"

"Is a time for women, is a time for business. Separate times. You know that, Eitel. A Swiss, he is almost a Moroccan, when it comes to business."

Eitel laughed. "Thanks."

"I am being serious. You be careful. If she confuse you, it can cost you. Can cost *me*. I am in for percentage, remember. Even if you are Swiss, maybe you need to know: business and women must be kept separate things."

"I know."

"You remember it, yes?"

"Don't worry about me," Eitel said.

The cab pulled up outside the Jamai. Eitel, upstairs, withdrew four paintings and an Olmec jade statuette from the false compartment of his suitcase. The paintings were all unframed, small, genuine, and unimportant. After a moment he selected the "Madonna of the Palms," from the atelier of

Lorenzo Bellini: plainly apprentice work, but enchanting, serene, pure, not
bad, easily a $20,000 painting. He slipped it into a carrying case, put the
others back, all but the statuette, which he fondled for a moment and put down
on the dresser, in front of the mirror, as though setting up a little shrine. To
beauty, he thought. He started to put it away and changed his mind. It looked
so lovely there that he decided to take his chances. Taking your chances, he
thought, is sometimes good for the health.

He went back to the cab.

"Is a good painting?" David asked.

"It's pretty. Trivial, but pretty."

"I don't mean good that way. I mean, is it real?"

"Of course," Eitel said, perhaps too sharply. "Do we have to have this
discussion again, David? You know damned well I sell only genuine paintings.
Overpriced a little, but always genuine."

"One thing I never can understand. Why you not sell them fakes?"

Startled, Eitel said, "You think I'm crooked, David?"

"Sure I do."

"You say it so lightheartedly. I don't like your humor sometimes."

"Humor? What humor? Is against law to sell valuable Earth works of art to
aliens. You sell them. Makes you crook, right? Is no insult. Is only description."

"I don't believe this," Eitel said. "What are you trying to start here?"

"I only want to know, why you sell them real stuff. Is against the law to sell
real ones, is probably not against the law to sell them fakes. You see? For two
years I wonder this. We make just as much money, we run less risk."

"My family has dealt in art for over a hundred years, David. No Eitel has
ever knowingly sold a fake. None ever will." It was a touchy point with him.
"Look," he said, "maybe you like playing these games with me, but you could
go too far. All right?"

"You forgive me, Eitel?"

"If you shut up."

"You know better than that. Shutting up I am very bad at. Can I tell you
one more thing, and then I shut up really?"

"Go ahead," Eitel said, sighing.

"I tell you this: you a very confused man. You a crook who thinks he not a
crook, you know what I mean? Which is bad thinking. But is all right. I like
you. I respect you, even. I think you are excellent businessman. So you forgive
rude remarks?"

"You give me a great pain," Eitel said.

"I bet I do. You forget I said anything. Go make deal, many millions, tomorrow we have mint tea together and you give me my cut and everybody happy."

"I don't like mint tea."

"Is all right. We have some anyway."

❤

Seeing Agila standing in the doorway of her hotel room, Eitel was startled again by the impact of her presence, the overwhelming physical power of her beauty. *If she confuse you, it can cost you.* What you see is all artificial, he told himself. It's just a mask. Eitel looked from Agila to Anakhistos, who sat oddly folded, like a giant umbrella. That's what she really is, Eitel thought. She's Mrs. Anakhistos from Centaurus, and her skin is like rubber and her mouth is a hinged slot and this body that she happens to be wearing right now was made in a laboratory. And yet, and yet, and yet—the wind was roaring, he was tossing wildly about—

What the hell is happening to me?

"Show us what you have for us," Anakhistos said.

Eitel slipped the little painting from its case. His hands were shaking ever so slightly. In the closeness of the room he picked up two strong fragrances, something dry and musty coming from Anakhistos, and the strange, irresistible mixtures of incongruous spices that Agila's synthetic body emanated.

"*The Madonna of the Palms,* Lorenzo Bellini, Venice, 1597," Eitel said. "Very fine work."

"Bellini is extremely famous, I know."

"The famous ones are Giovanni and Gentile. This is Giovanni's grandson. He's just as good, but not well known. I couldn't possibly get you paintings by Giovanni or Gentile. No one on Earth could."

"This is quite fine," said Anakhistos. "True Renaissance beauty. And very Earthesque. Of course it is genuine?"

Eitel said stiffly, "Only a fool would try to sell a fake to a connoisseur such as yourself. But it would be easy enough for us to arrange a spectroscopic analysis in Casablanca, if—"

"Ah, no, no, no, I meant no suspicioning of your reputation. You are impeccable. We unquestion the genuinity. But what is done about the export certificate?"

"Easy. I have a document that says this is a recent copy, done by a student in Paris. They are not yet applying chemical tests of age to the paintings, not yet. You will be able to take the painting from Earth, with such a certificate."

"And the price?" said Anakhistos.

Eitel took a deep breath. It was meant to steady him, but it dizzied him instead, for it filled his lungs with Agila.

He said, "If the deal is straight cash, the price is four million dollars."

"And otherwise?" Agila asked.

"I'd prefer to talk to you about that alone," he said to her.

"Whatever you want to say, you can say in front of Anakhistos. We are absolute mates. We have complete trust."

"I'd still prefer to speak more privately."

She shrugged. "All right. The balcony."

Outside, where the sweetness of night-blooming flowers filled the air, her fragrance was less overpowering. It made no difference. Looking straight at her only with difficulty, he said, "If I can spend the rest of this night making love to you, the price will be three million."

"This is a joke?"

"In fact, no. Not at all."

"It is worth a million dollars to have sexual contact with me?"

Eitel imagined how his father would have answered that question, his grandfather, his great-grandfather. Their accumulated wisdom pressed on him like a hump. To hell with them, he thought.

He said, listening in wonder to his own words, "Yes. It is."

"You know that this body is not my real body."

"I know."

"I am an alien being."

"Yes. I know."

She studied him in silence a long while. Then she said, "Why did you make me come outside to ask me this?"

"On Earth, men sometimes become quite angry when strangers ask their wives to go to bed with them. I didn't know how Anakhistos would react. I don't have any real idea how Centaurans react to anything."

"I am Centauran also," she pointed out.

"You don't seem as alien to me."

She smiled quickly, on-off. "I see. Well, let us confer with Anakhistos."

But the conference, it turned out, did not include Eitel. He stood by, feeling rash and foolish, while Agila and Anakhistos exchanged bursts of harsh rapid words in their own language, a buzzing, eerie tongue that was quite literally like nothing on Earth. He searched their faces for some understanding of the flow of conversation. Was Anakhistos shocked? Outraged? Amused? And she? Even wearing human guise, she was opaque to him, too. Did she feel contempt for Eitel's bumptious lusts? Indifference? See him as quaintly primitive, bestial, anthropoid? Or was she eagerly cajoling her husband into letting her have her little adventure? Eitel had no idea. He felt far out of his depth, a sensation as unfamiliar as it was unwelcome. Dry throat, sweaty palms, brain in turmoil: but there was no turning back now.

At last Agila turned to him and said, "It is agreed. The painting is ours at three million. And I am yours until dawn."

David was still waiting. He grinned a knowing grin when Eitel emerged from the Merinides with Agila on his arm, but said nothing. I have lost points with him, Eitel thought. He thinks I have allowed the nonsense of the flesh to interfere with a business decision, and now I have made myself frivolous in his eyes. It is more complicated than that, but David would never understand. *Business and women must be kept separate things.* To the taxi driver, Eitel knew, Helen of Troy herself would be as nothing next to a million dollars; mere meat, mere heat. So be it, Eitel told himself. David would never understand. What David would understand, Eitel thought guiltily, was that in cutting the deal with Agila he had also cut fifty thousand dollars off David's commission. But he did not intend to let David know anything about that.

When they were in Eitel's room Agila said, "First, I would please like to have some mint tea, yes? It is my addiction, you know. My aphrodisiac."

Sizzling impatience seared Eitel's soul. God only knew how long it might take room service to fetch a pot of tea at this hour, and at a million dollars a night he preferred not to waste even a minute. But there was no way to refuse. He could not allow himself to seem like some panting schoolboy.

"Of course," he said.

After he had phoned, he walked around behind her as she stood by the window peering into the mists of the night. He put his lips to the nape of her neck and cupped his hands over her breasts. This is very crazy, he thought. I am not touching her real body. This is only some synthetic mock-up, a statue of flesh, a mere androidal shell.

No matter. No matter. He was able to resist her beauty, that illusion, that figment. That beauty, astonishing and unreal, was what had drawn him at first, but it was the dark secret alien underneath that ruled him now. That was what he hoped to reach: the alien, the star woman, the unfathomable being from the black interstellar deeps. He would touch what no man of Earth had ever touched before.

He inhaled her fragrance until he felt himself swaying. She was making an odd purring sound that he hoped was one of pleasure.

There was a knock at the door. "The tea is here," she said.

The waiter, a boy in native costume, sleepy, openly envious of Eitel for having a woman like Agila in his room, took forever to set up the glasses and pour the tea, an infinitely slow process of raising the pot, aiming, letting the thick tea trickle down through the air. But at last he left. Agila drank greedily, and beckoned to Eitel to have some also. He smiled and shook his head.

She said, "But you must. I love it so—you must share it. It is a ritual of love between us, eh?"

He did not choose to make an issue of it. A glass of mint tea more or less must not get in the way, not now.

"To us," she said, and touched her glass to his.

He managed to drink a little. It was like pure liquid sugar. She had a second glass, and then, maddeningly, a third. He pretended to sip at his. Then at last she touched her hand to a clasp on her shoulder and her metal-mesh sheath fell away.

They had done their research properly, in the body-making labs of Centaurus. She was flawless, sheer fantasy, heavy breasts that defied gravity, slender waist, hips that would drive a Moroccan camel-driver berserk, buttocks like pale hemispheres. They had given her a navel, pubic hair, erectile nipples, dimples here and there, the hint of blue veins in her thighs. Unreal, yes, Eitel thought, but magnificent.

"It is my fifth traveling body," she said. "I have been Arcturan, Steropid, Denebian, Mizarian—and each time it has been hard, hard, hard! After the transfer is done, there is a long training period, and it is always very difficult. But one learns. A moment finally comes when the body feels natural and true. I will miss this one very much."

"So will I," Eitel said.

Quickly he undressed. She came to him, touched her lips lightly to his, grazed his chest with her nipples.

"And now you must give me a gift," she said.

"What?"

"It is the custom before making love. An exchange of gifts." She took from between her breasts the pendant she was wearing, a bit of bright crystal carved in disturbing alien swirls. "This is for you. And for me—"

Oh, God in heaven, he thought. No!

Her hand closed over the Olmec jade figurine that still was sitting on the dresser.

"This," she said.

It sickened him. That little statuette was eighty thousand on the international antiquities market, maybe a million or two to the right E-T buyer. A gift? A love token? He saw the gleam in her eye, and knew he was trapped. Refuse, and everything else might be lost. He dare not show any trace of pettiness. Yes. So be it. Let her have the damned thing. We are being romantic tonight. We are making grand gestures. We are not going to behave like a petit-bourgeois Swiss art peddler. *If she confuse you, it can cost you*, David had said. Eitel took a deep breath.

"My pleasure," he said magnificently.

➤

He was an experienced and expert lover; supreme beauty always inspired the best in him; and pride alone made him want to send her back to Centaurus with incandescent memories of the erotic arts of Earth. His performance that night—and performance was the only word he could apply to it—might well have been the finest of his life.

With the lips and tongue, first. Everywhere. With the fingers, slowly, patiently, searching for the little secret key places, the unexpected triggering points. With the breath against the skin, and the fingernails, ever so lightly, and the eyelashes, and even the newly sprouting stubble of the cheek. These were all things that Eitel loved doing, not merely for the effects they produced in his bed partners but because they were delightful in and of themselves; yet he had never done them with greater dedication and skill.

And now, he thought, perhaps she will show me some of *her* skills.

But she lay there like a wax doll. Occasionally she stirred, occasionally she moved her hips a little. When he went into her, he found her warm and moist—why had they built that capacity in, Eitel wondered?—but he felt no response from her, none at all.

He moved her this way, that, running through the gamut of positions as though he and she were making a training film for newlyweds. Now and then she smiled. Her eyes were always open: she was fascinated. Eitel felt anger rising. She was ever the tourist, even here in his bed. Getting some firsthand knowledge of the quaint sexual techniques of the primitive Earthmen.

Knowing he was being foolish, that he was compounding a foolishness, he drove his body with frantic intensity, rocking rhythmically above her, grimly pushing her on and on. *Come on*, he thought. *Give me a little sigh, a moan, a wriggle. Anything.* He wasn't asking her to come. There was no reason why they should have built *that* capacity in, was there? The only thing he wanted now was to get some sort of acknowledgment of his existence from her, some quiver of assent.

He went on working at it, knowing he would not get it. But then, to his surprise, something actually seemed to be happening. Her face grew flushed, and her eyes narrowed and took on a new gleam, and her breath began to come in harsh little bursts, and her breasts heaved, and her nipples grew hard. All the signs, yes: Eitel had seen them so many times, and never more welcome than at this moment. He knew what to do. The unslackening rhythm now, the

━━━━━━━━━━• 151 •━━━

steady building of tension, carrying her onward, steadily higher, leading her toward that magical moment of overload when the watchful conscious mind at last surrenders to the surging deeper forces. Yes. Yes. The valiant Earthman giving his all for the sake of transgalactic passion, laboring like a galley slave to show the star woman what the communion of the sexes is all about.

She seemed almost there. Some panting now, even a little gasping. Eitel smiled in pleasant self-congratulation. Swiss precision, he thought: never underestimate it.

And then somehow she managed to slip free of him, between one thrust and the next, and she rolled to the side, so that he collapsed in amazement into the pillow as she left the bed. He sat up and looked at her, stunned, gaping, numbed.

"Excuse me," she said, in the most casual way. "I thought I'd have a little more tea. Shall I get some for you?"

Eitel could barely speak. "No," he said hoarsely.

She poured herself a glass, drank, grimaced. "It doesn't taste as good as when it's warm," she said, returning to the bed. "Well, shall we go on?" she asked.

Silently he reached for her. Somehow he was able to start again. But this time a distance of a thousand light-years seemed to separate him from her. There was no rekindling that brief flame, and after a few moments he gave up. He felt himself forever shut away from the inwardness of her, as Earth is shut away from the stars. Cold, weary, more furious with himself than with her, he let himself come. He kept his eyes open as long as he could, staring icily into hers, but the sensations were unexpectedly powerful, and in the end he sank down against her breasts, clinging to her as the impact thundered through him.

In that bleak moment came a surprise. For as he shook and quivered in the force of that dismal ejaculation something opened between them, a barrier, a gate, and the hotel melted and disappeared and he saw himself in the midst of a bizarre landscape. The sky was a rich golden-green, the sun was deep green and hot, the trees and plants and flowers were like nothing he had ever seen on Earth. The air was heavy, aromatic, and of a piercing flavor that stung his nostrils. Flying creatures that were not birds soared unhurriedly overhead, and some iridescent beasts that looked like red velvet pillows mounted on tripods were grazing on the lower branches of furry-limbed trees. On the horizon Eitel saw three jagged naked mountains of some yellow-brown stone that gleamed like polished metal in the sunlight. He trembled. Wonder and awe engulfed his spirit. This is a park, he realized, the most beautiful park in the world. But this is not *this* world. He found a little path that led over a gentle hill, and when he came to the far side he looked down to see Centaurans strolling two by two, hand in hand, through an elegantly contoured garden.

Oh, my God, Eitel thought. Oh, my God in heaven!

Then it all began to fade, growing thin, turning to something no more substantial than smoke, and in a moment more it was all gone. He lay still, breathing raggedly, by her side, watching her breasts slowly rising and falling.

He lifted his head. She was studying him. "You liked that?"

"Liked what?"

"What you saw."

"So you know?"

She seemed surprised. "Of course! You thought it was an accident? It was my gift for you."

"Ah." The picture postcard of the home world, bestowed on the earnest native for his diligent services. "It was extraordinary. I've never seen anything so beautiful."

"It is very beautiful, yes," she said complacently. Then, smiling, she said, "That was interesting, what you did there at the end, when you were breathing so hard. Can you do that again?" she asked, as though he had just executed some intricate juggling maneuver.

Bleakly he shook his head, and turned away. He could not bear to look into those magnificent eyes any longer. Somehow—he would never have any way of knowing when it had happened, except that it was somewhere between "Can you do that again?" and the dawn, he fell asleep. She was shaking him gently awake then. The light of a brilliant morning came bursting through the fragile old silken draperies.

"I am leaving now," she whispered. "But I wish to thank you. It has been a night I shall never forget."

"Nor I," said Eitel.

"To experience the reality of Earthian ways at such close range—with such intimacy, such immediacy—"

"Yes. Of course. It must have been extraordinary for you."

"If ever you come to Centaurus—"

"Certainly. I'll look you up."

She kissed him lightly, tip of nose, forehead, lips. Then she walked toward the door. With her hand on the knob, she turned and said, "Oh, one little thing that might amuse you. I meant to tell you last night. We don't have that kind of thing on our world, you know—that concept of owning one's mate's body. And in any case, Anakhistos is not male, and I am not female, not exactly. We mate, but our sex distinctions are not so well defined as that. It is with us more like the way it is with your oysters, I think. So it is not quite right to say that Anakhistos is my husband, or that I am his wife. I thought you would like to know." She blew him a kiss. "It has been very lovely," she said. "Good-bye."

When she was gone he went to the window and stared into the garden for a long while without looking at anything in particular. He felt weary and burned out, and there was a taste of straw in his mouth. After a time he turned away.

When he emerged from the hotel later that morning, David's car was waiting out front.

"Get in," he said.

They drove in silence to a café that Eitel had never seen before, in the new quarter of town. David said something in Arabic to the proprietor and he brought mint tea for two.

"I don't like mint tea," Eitel said.

"Drink. It washes away bad tastes. How did it go last night?"

"Fine. Just fine."

"You and the woman, ficky-ficky?"

"None of your ficky-ficky business."

"Try some tea," David urged. "It not so good last night, eh?"

"What makes you think so?"

"You not look so happy. You not sound so happy."

"For once you're wrong," Eitel said. "I got everything I wanted to get. Do you understand me? I got everything I wanted to get." His tone might have been a little too loud, a little too aggressive, for it drew a quizzical, searching look from the Moroccan.

"Yes. Sure. And what size deal? That *is* my business, yes?"

"Three million cash."

"Only three?"

"Three," Eitel said. "I owe you a hundred fifty thousand. You're doing all right, a hundred fifty for a couple of hours' work. I'm making you a rich man."

"Yes. Very rich. But no more deals, Eitel."

"What?"

"You find another boy, all right? I will work now with someone else, maybe. There are plenty of others, you know? I will be more comfortable with them. Is very bad, when one does not trust a partner."

"I don't follow you."

"What you did last night, going off with the woman, was very stupid. Poor business, you know? I wonder, did you have to pay her? And did you pay her some of my money, too?"

David was smiling, as always. But sometimes his smiles were amiable and sometimes they were just smiles. Eitel had a sudden vision of himself in a back alley of the old town, bleeding. He had another vision of himself undergoing interrogation by the customs men. David had a lot of power over him, he realized.

Eitel took a deep breath and said, "I resent the insinuation that I've cheated you. I've treated you very honorably from the start. You know that. And if you think I bought the woman, let me tell you this: she isn't a woman at all. She's an alien. Some of them wear human bodies when they travel. Underneath all that gorgeous flesh she's a Centauran, David."

"And you touched her?"

"Yes."

"You put yourself inside her?"

"Yes," Eitel said.

David stood up. He looked as though he had just found a rat embryo in his tea. "I am very glad we are no longer partners, then. Deliver the money to me in the usual way. And then please stay away from me when you are in this city."

"Wait," Eitel said. "Take me back to the Merinides. I've got three more paintings to sell."

"There are plenty of taxi drivers in this city," said David.

When he was gone, Eitel peered into his mint tea for a while and wondered if David meant to make trouble for him. Then he stopped thinking about David and thought about that glimpse of a green sun and a golden landscape that Agila had given him. His hands felt cold, his fingers were quivering a little. He became aware that he wanted more than anything else to see those things again. Could any Centauran make it happen for him, he wondered, or was that only Agila's little trick? What about other aliens? He imagined himself prowling the nightclub, hustling for action, pressing himself up against this slithery thing or that one, desperately trying to reenact that weird orgasmic moment that had carried him to the stars. A new perversion, he thought. One that even David found disgusting.

He wondered what it was like to go to bed with a Vegan or an Arcturan or a Steropid. God in heaven! Could he do it? Yes, he told himself, thinking of green suns and the unforgettable fragrance of that alien air. Yes. Yes. Of course he could. Of course.

There was a sudden strange sweetness in his mouth. He realized that he had taken a deep gulp of the mint tea without paying attention to what he was doing. Eitel smiled. It hadn't made him sick, had it? Had it? He took another swig. Then, in a slow determined way, he finished off all the rest of it, and scattered some coins on the counter, and went outside to look for a cab.

MULTIPLES

No heartrending sagas of the torments of creation with this one. It was July of 1983; I had finished Valentine Pontifex, which had turned out to be unexpectedly difficult to write (the first half of 1983 was one of those periods of my life that I'd just as soon not repeat); a few days after the book was done I sat down and wrote "Multiples" in what was essentially one long take, did a little minor editing, and sent it off to Ellen Datlow of Omni, who accepted it right away. They should all be that easy. But in this case (as with "Amanda and the Alien") I was making use of my own home turf as the setting instead of having to invent some alien world, and the theme of multiple personalities was one I had been thinking about for some time. Characters and plot fell into place in that magical way that makes writers want to get down on their knees and offer thanks. The story felt like a winner to me right away. It was included in the first volume (1983) of Gardner Dozois' annual Year's Best Science Fiction anthologies and has had a healthy reprint existence ever since. It also gets me occasional letters from actual multiple-personality people, who want to know if I'm one myself, or married to one. (The answers are No and No—so far as I know.)

A little bragging here, if you don't mind. Having "Multiples" chosen for one of the best-science-fiction-of-the-year anthologies completed an unusual sweep for me, one of which I'm inordinately proud. There were then three such anthologies—not only Dozois's and Don Wollheim's, but one edited by Terry Carr. I had stories in all three of them for the year of 1983. Other writers have achieved that now and then, when some very strong story was picked by all three editors—but I had a different story in each book. I'm not sure anyone else has ever managed that trick. (I did it again, though, in 1989. This time, though, I managed to get five stories into that year's three anthologies. Go ahead, top it if you can!)

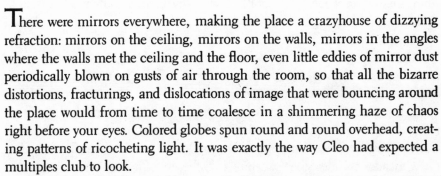

There were mirrors everywhere, making the place a crazyhouse of dizzying refraction: mirrors on the ceiling, mirrors on the walls, mirrors in the angles where the walls met the ceiling and the floor, even little eddies of mirror dust periodically blown on gusts of air through the room, so that all the bizarre distortions, fracturings, and dislocations of image that were bouncing around the place would from time to time coalesce in a shimmering haze of chaos right before your eyes. Colored globes spun round and round overhead, creating patterns of ricocheting light. It was exactly the way Cleo had expected a multiples club to look.

She had walked up and down the whole Fillmore Street strip from Union to Chestnut and back again for half an hour, peering at this club and that, before finding the courage to go inside one that called itself Skits. Though she had been planning this night for months, she found herself paralyzed by fear at the last minute: afraid they would spot her as a fraud the moment she walked in, afraid they would drive her out with jeers and curses and cold mocking laughter. But now that she was within, she felt fine—calm, confident, ready for the time of her life.

There were more women than men in the club, something like a seven-to-three ratio. Hardly anyone seemed to be talking to anyone else: most stood alone in the middle of the floor, staring into the mirrors as though in trance. Their eyes were slits, their jaws were slack, their shoulders slumped forward, their arms dangled. Now and then as some combination of reflections sluiced across their consciousnesses with particular impact they would go taut and jerk and wince as if they had been struck. Their faces would flush, their lips would pull back, their eyes would roll, they would mutter and whisper to themselves; and then after a moment they would slip back into stillness.

Cleo knew what they were doing. They were switching and doubling. Maybe some of the adepts were tripling. Her heart rate picked up. Her throat was very dry. What was the routine here, she wondered? Did you just walk right out onto the floor and plug into the light patterns, or were you supposed to go to the bar first for a shot or a snort?

She looked toward the bar. A dozen or so customers sitting there, mostly men, a couple of them openly studying her, giving her that new-girl-in-town stare. Cleo returned their gaze evenly, coolly, blankly. Standard-looking men, reasonably attractive, thirtyish or early fortyish, business suits, conventional hairstyles: young lawyers, executives, maybe stockbrokers, successful sorts out for a night's fun, the kind you might run into anywhere. Look at that one, tall, athletic, curly hair, glasses. Faint ironic smile, easy inquiring eyes. Almost professorial. And yet, and yet—behind that smooth intelligent forehead, what strangenesses must teem and boil! How many hidden souls must lurk and jostle! Scary. Tempting.

Irresistible.

Cleo resisted. Take it slow, take it slow. Instead of going to the bar she moved out serenely among the switchers on the floor, found an open space, centered herself, looked toward the mirrors on the far side of the room. Legs apart, feet planted flat, shoulders forward. A turning globe splashed waves of red and violet light, splintered a thousand times over, into her face. *Go. Go. Go. Go.* You are Cleo. You are Judy. You are Vixen. You are Lisa. *Go. Go. Go. Go.* Cascades of iridescence sweeping over the rim of her soul, battering at the walls of her identity. Come, enter, drown me, split me, switch me. You are Cleo and Judy. You are Vixen and Lisa. You are Cleo and Judy and Vixen and Lisa. *Go. Go. Go.*

Her head was spinning. Her eyes were blurring. The room gyrated around her.

Was this it? Was she splitting? Was she switching? Maybe so. Maybe the capacity was there in everyone, even her, and all it took was the lights, the mirror, the ambience, the will. I am many. I am multiple. I am Cleo switching to Vixen. I am Judy and Lisa. I am—

No.

I am Cleo.

I am Cleo.

I am very dizzy and I am getting sick, and I am Cleo and only Cleo, as I have always been.

I am Cleo and only Cleo and I am going to fall down.

◆

"Easy," he said. "You okay?"

"Steadying up, I think. Whew!"

"Out-of-towner, eh?"

"Sacramento. How'd you know?"

"Too quick on the floor. Locals all know better. This place has the fastest mirrors in the west. They'll blow you away if you're not careful. You can't just go out there and grab for the big one—you've got to phase yourself in slowly. You sure you're going to be okay?"

"I think so."

He was the tall man from the bar, the athletic professorial one. She supposed he had caught her before she had actually fallen, since she felt no bruises. His hand rested now against her elbow as he lightly steered her toward a table along the wall.

"What's your now-name?" he asked.

"Judy."

"I'm Van."

"Hello, Van."

"What about a brandy? Steady you up a little more."

"I don't drink."

"Never?"

"Vixen does the drinking," she said. "Not me."

"Ah. The old story. She gets the bubbles, you get her hangovers. I have one like that, too, only with him it's Hunan food. He absolutely doesn't give a damn what lobster in hot-and-sour sauce does to my digestive system. I hope you pay her back the way she deserves."

Cleo smiled and said nothing.

He was watching her closely. Was he interested, or just being polite to someone who was obviously out of her depth in a strange milieu? Interested, she decided. He seemed to have accepted that Vixen stuff at face value.

Be careful now, Cleo warned herself. Trying to pile on convincing-sounding details when you don't really know what you're talking about is a sure way to give yourself away, sooner or later. The thing to do, she knew, was to establish her credentials without working too hard at it, sit back, listen, learn how things really operate among these people.

"What do you do, up there in Sacramento?"

"Nothing fascinating."

"Poor Judy. Real estate broker?"

"How'd you guess?"

"Every other woman I meet is a real estate broker these days. What's Vixen?"

"A lush."

"Not much of a livelihood in that."

Cleo shrugged. "She doesn't need one. The rest of us support her."

"Real estate and what else?"

She hadn't been sure that multiples etiquette included talking about one's alternate selves. But she had come prepared. "Lisa's a landscape architect. Cleo's into software. We all keep busy."

"Lisa ought to meet Chuck. He's a demon horticulturalist. Partner in a plant-rental outfit—you know, huge dracaenas and philodendrons for offices, so much per month, take them away when they start looking sickly. Lisa and Chuck could talk palms and bromeliads and cacti all night."

"We should introduce them, then."

"We should, yes."

"But first we have to introduce Van and Judy."

"And then maybe Van and Cleo," he said.

She felt a tremor of fear. Had he found her out so soon? "Why Van and Cleo? Cleo's not here right now. This is Judy you're talking to."

"Easy. Easy!"

But she was unable to halt. "I can't deliver Cleo to you just like that, you know. She does as she pleases."

"Easy," he said. "All I meant was, Van and Cleo have something in common. Van's into software, too."

Cleo relaxed. With a little laugh she said, "Oh, not you, too! Isn't everybody nowadays? But I thought you were something in the academic world. A professor, perhaps."

"I am. At Cal."

"Software?"

"In a manner of speaking. Linguistics. Metalinguistics, actually. My field's the language of language—the basic subsets, the neural coordinates of communication, the underlying programs our brains use, the operating systems. Mind as computer, computer as mind. I can get very boring about it."

"I don't find the mind a boring subject."

"I don't find real estate a boring subject. Talk to me about second mortgages and triple-net leases."

"Talk to me about Chomsky and Benjamin Whorf," she said.

His eyes widened. "You've heard of Whorf?"

"I majored in comparative linguistics. That was before real estate."

"Just my lousy luck," he said. "I get a chance to find out what's hot in the shopping-center market and she wants to talk about Whorf and Chomsky."

"I thought every other woman you met these days was a real estate broker. Talk to them about shopping centers."

"They all want to talk about Whorf and Chomsky."

"Poor Van."

"Yes. Poor Van." Then he leaned forward and said, his tone softening, "You know, I shouldn't have made that crack about Van meeting Cleo. That was very tacky of me."

"It's okay, Van. I didn't take it seriously."

"You seemed to. You were very upset."

"Well, maybe at first. But then I saw you were just horsing around."

"I still shouldn't have said it. You were absolutely right: this is Judy's time now. Cleo's not here, and that's just fine. It's Judy I want to get to know."

"You will," she said. "But you can meet Cleo, too, and Lisa, and Vixen. I'll introduce you to the whole crew. I don't mind."

"You're sure of that?"

"Sure."

"Some of us are very secretive about our alters."

"Are you?" Cleo asked.

"Sometimes. Sometimes not."

"I don't mind. Maybe you'll meet some of mine tonight." She glanced toward the center of the floor. "I think I've steadied up, now. I'd like to try the mirrors again."

"Switching?"

"Doubling," she said. "I'd like to bring Vixen up. She can do the drinking, and I can do the talking. Will it bother you if she's here, too?"

"Not unless she's a sloppy drunk. Or a mean one."

"I can keep control of her, when we're doubling. Come on: take me through the mirrors."

"You be careful, now. San Francisco mirrors aren't like Sacramento ones. You've already discovered that."

"I'll watch my step this time. Shall we go out there?"

"Sure," he said.

As they began to move out onto the floor a slender T-shirted man of about thirty came toward them. Shaven scalp, bushy mustache, medallions, boots. Very San Francisco, very gay. He frowned at Cleo and stared straightforwardly at Van.

"Ned?" he said.

Van scowled and shook his head. "No. Not now."

"Sorry. Very sorry. I should have realized." The shaven-headed man flushed and hurried away.

"Let's go," Van said to Cleo.

❤

This time she found it easier to keep her balance. Knowing that he was nearby helped. But still the waves of refracted light came pounding in, pounding in, pounding in. The assault was total: remorseless, implacable, overwhelming. She had to struggle against the throbbing in her chest, the hammering in her temples, the wobbliness of her knees. And this was pleasure, for them? This was a supreme delight?

But they were multiples and she was only Cleo, and that, she knew, made all the difference. She seemed to be able to fake it well enough. She could make up a Judy, a Lisa, a Vixen, assign little corners of her personality to each, give them voices of their own, facial expressions, individual identities. Standing before her mirror at home, she had managed to convince herself. She might even be able to convince him. But as the swirling lights careened off the infinities of interlocking mirrors and came slaloming into the gateways of her reeling soul, the dismal fear began to rise in her that she could never truly be one of these people after all, however skillfully she imitated them in their intricacies.

Was it so? Was she doomed always to stand outside their irresistible world, hopelessly peering in? Too soon to tell—much too soon, she thought, to admit defeat—

At least she didn't fall down. She took the punishment of the mirrors as long as she could stand it, and then, not waiting for him to leave the floor, she made her way—carefully, carefully, walking a tightrope over an abyss—to the bar. When her head had begun to stop spinning she ordered a drink, and she sipped it cautiously. She could feel the alcohol extending itself inch by inch into her bloodstream. It calmed her. On the floor, Van stood in trance, occasionally quivering in a sudden convulsive way for a fraction of a second. He was doubling, she knew: bringing up one of his other identities. That was the main thing that multiples came to these clubs to do. No longer were all their various identities forced to dwell in rigorously separated compartments of their minds. With the aid of the mirrors, of the lights, the skilled ones were able briefly to fuse two or even three of their selves into something even more complex. When he comes back here, she thought, he will be Van plus X. And I must pretend to be Judy plus Vixen.

She readied herself for that. Judy was easy: Judy was mostly the real Cleo, the real estate woman from Sacramento, with Cleo's notion of what it was like to be a multiple added in. And Vixen? Cleo imagined her to be about twenty-three, a Los Angeles girl, a onetime child tennis star who had broken her ankle in a dumb prank and had never recovered her game afterward, and who had taken up drinking to ease the pain and loss. Uninhibited, unpredictable, untidy, fiery, fierce: all the things that Cleo was not. Could she be Vixen? She took a deep gulp of her drink and put on the Vixen-face: eyes hard and glittering, cheek muscles clenched.

Van was leaving the floor now. His way of moving seemed to have changed: he was stiff, almost awkward, his shoulders held high, his elbows jutting oddly. He looked so different that she wondered whether he was still Van at all.

"You didn't switch, did you?"

"Doubled. Paul's with me now."

"Paul?"

"Paul's from Texas. Geologist, terrific poker game, plays the guitar." Van smiled, and it was like a shifting of gears. In a deeper, broader voice he said, "And I sing real good, too, ma'am. Van's jealous of that, because he can't sing worth beans. Are you ready for a refill?"

"You bet," Cleo said, sounding sloppy, sounding Vixenish.

His apartment was nearby, a cheerful airy sprawling place in the Marina district. The segmented nature of his life was immediately obvious: the prints and paintings on the walls looked as though they had been chosen by four or five different people, one of whom ran heavily toward vivid scenes of sunrise over the Grand Canyon, another to Picasso and Miro, someone else to delicate impressionist views of Parisian flower markets. A sun room contained the biggest and healthiest houseplants Cleo had ever seen. Another room was stacked high with technical books and scholarly journals, a third was set up as a home gymnasium equipped with three or four gleaming exercise machines. Some of the rooms were fastidiously tidy, some impossibly chaotic. Some of the furniture was stark and austere, and some was floppy and overstuffed. She kept expecting to find roommates wandering around. But there was no one here but Van. And Paul.

Paul fixed the drinks. Paul played soft guitar music and told her gaudy tales of prospecting for rare earths on the West Texas mesas. Paul sang something bawdy-sounding in Spanish, and Cleo, putting on her Vixen-voice, chimed in on the choruses, deliberately off-key. But then Paul went away and it was Van who sat close beside her on the couch, talking quietly. He wanted to know things about Judy, and he told her a little about Van, and no other selves came into the conversation. She was sure that that was intentional. They stayed up very late. Paul came back, toward the end of the evening, to tell a few jokes and sing a soft late-night song, but when they went into the bedroom she was with Van. Of that she was completely certain.

And when she woke in the morning she was alone.

She felt a surge of confusion and dislocation, remembered after a moment where she was and how she had happened to be here, sat up, blinked. Went into the bathroom and scooped a handful of water over her face. Without bothering to dress, went padding around the apartment looking for Van.

She found him in the exercise room, using the rowing machine, but he wasn't Van. He was dressed in tight jeans and a white T-shirt, and somehow he looked younger, leaner, jauntier. There were fine beads of sweat along his forehead, but he did not seem to be breathing hard. He gave her a cool, distantly appraising, wholly asexual look, as though she were a total stranger but that it was not in the least unusual for an unknown naked woman to materialize in the house and he was altogether undisturbed by it, and said, "Good morning. I'm Ned. Pleased to know you." His voice was higher than Van's, much higher than Paul's, and he had an odd overprecise way of shaping each syllable.

Flustered, suddenly self-conscious and wishing she had put her clothes on before leaving the bedroom, she folded one arm over her breasts, though her nakedness did not seem to matter to him at all. "I'm—Judy. I came with Van."

"Yes, I know. I saw the entry in our book." Smoothly, effortlessly, he pulled on the oars of the rowing machine, leaned back, pushed forward. "Help yourself to anything in the fridge," he said. "Make yourself entirely at home. Van left a note for you in the kitchen."

She stared at him: his hands, his mouth, his long muscular arms. She remembered his touch, his kisses, the feel of his skin against hers. And now this complete indifference. No. Not *his* kisses, not *his* touch. Van's. And Van was not here now. There was a different tenant in Van's body, someone she did not know in any way and who had no memories of last night's embraces. *I saw the entry in our book.* They left memos for each other. Cleo shivered. She had known what to expect, more or less, but experiencing it was very different from reading about it. She felt almost as though she had fallen in among beings from another planet.

But this is what you wanted, she thought. Isn't it? The intricacy, the mystery, the unpredictability, the sheer weirdness? A little cruise through an alien world, because her own had become so stale, so narrow, so cramped. And here she was. *Good morning, I'm Ned. Pleased to know you.*

Van's note was clipped to the refrigerator by a little yellow magnet shaped like a ladybug. *Dinner tonight at Chez Michel? You and me and who knows who else. Call me.*

◆

That was the beginning. She saw him every night for the next ten days. Generally they met at some three-star restaurant, had a lingering intimate dinner, went back to his apartment. One mild clear evening they drove out to the beach and watched the waves breaking on Seal Rock until well past midnight. Another time they wandered through Fisherman's Wharf and somehow acquired three bags of tacky souvenirs.

Van was his primary name—she saw it on his credit card at dinner one night—and that seemed to be his main identity, too, though she knew there were plenty of others. At first he was reticent about that, but on the fourth or fifth night he told her that he had nine major selves and sixteen minor ones, some of which remained submerged years at a stretch. Besides Paul, the geologist, and Chuck, who was into horticulture, and Ned, the gay one, Cleo heard about Nat the stock-market plunger—he was fifty and fat, and made a fortune every week, and liked to divide his time between Las Vegas and Miami Beach—and Henry, the poet, who was very shy and never liked anyone to read his work, and Dick, who was studying to be an actor, and Hal, who once taught law at Harvard, and Dave, the yachtsman, and Nicholas, the cardsharp—and then there were all the fragmentary ones, some of whom didn't have names, only a funny way of speaking or a little routine they liked to act out—

She got to see very little of his other selves, though. Like all multiples, he was troubled occasionally by involuntary switching, and one night he became Hal while they were making love, and another time he turned into Dave for an hour, and there were momentary flashes of Henry and Nicholas. Cleo perceived it right away whenever one of those switches came: his voice, his movements, his entire manner and personality changed immediately. Those were startling, exciting moments for her, offering a strange exhilaration. But generally his control was very good, and he stayed Van, as if he felt some strong need to experience her as Van and Van alone. Once in a while he doubled, bringing up Paul to play the guitar for him and sing, or Dick to recite sonnets, but when he did that the Van identity always remained present and dominant. It appeared that he was able to double at will, without the aid of mirrors and lights, at least some of the time. He had been an active and functioning multiple as long as he could remember—since childhood, perhaps even since birth—and he had devoted himself through the years to the task of gaining mastery over his divided mind.

All the aspects of him that she came to meet had basically attractive personalities: they were energetic, stable, purposeful men, who enjoyed life and seemed to know how to go about getting what they wanted. Though they were very different people, she could trace them all back readily enough to the underlying Van from whom, so she thought, they had all split off. The one puzzle was Nat, the market operator. It was hard for Cleo to imagine what he was like when he was Nat—sleazy and coarse, yes, but how did he manage to make himself look fifteen years older and forty pounds heavier? Maybe it was all done with facial expressions and posture. But she never got to see Nat. And gradually she realized it was an oversimplification to think of Paul and Dick and Ned and the others as mere extensions of Van into different modes. Van by himself was just as incomplete as the others. He was just one of many that had evolved in parallel, each one autonomous, each one only a fragment of the whole. Though Van might have control of the shared body a greater portion of the time, he still had no idea what any of his alternate selves were up to while they were in command, and like them he had to depend on guesses and fancy footwork and such notes and messages as they bothered to leave behind in order to keep track of events that occurred outside his conscious awareness. "The only one who knows everything is Michael. He's seven years old, smart as a whip, keeps in touch with all of us all the time."

"Your memory trace," Cleo said.

Van nodded. All multiples, she knew, had one alter with full awareness of the doings of all the other personalities—usually a child, an observer who sat back deep in the mind and played its own games and emerged only when necessary to fend off some crisis that threatened the stability of the entire group. "He's just informed us that he's Ethiopian," Van said. "So every two or three weeks we go across to Oakland to an Ethiopian restaurant that he likes, and he flirts with the waitresses in Amharic."

"That can't be too terrible a chore. I'm told Ethiopians are very beautiful people."

"Absolutely. But they think it's all a big joke, and Michael doesn't know how to pick up women, anyway. He's only seven, you know. So Van doesn't get anything out of it except some exercise in comparative linguistics and a case of indigestion the next day. Ethiopian food is the spiciest in the world. I can't *stand* spicy food."

"Neither can I," she said. "But Lisa loves it. Especially hot Mexican things. But nobody ever said sharing a body is easy, did they?"

She knew she had to be careful in questioning Van about the way his life as a multiple worked. She was supposed to be a multiple herself, after all. But she made use of her Sacramento background as justification for her areas of apparent ignorance of multiple customs and the everyday mechanics of multiple life. Though she, too, had known she was a multiple since childhood, she said, she had grown up outside the climate of acceptance of the divided personality that prevailed in San Francisco, where an active subculture of multiples had existed openly for years. In her isolated existence, unaware that there were a great many others of her kind, she had at first regarded herself as the victim of a serious mental disorder. It was only recently, she told him, that she had come to understand the overwhelming advantages of life as a multiple: the richness, the complexity, the fullness of talents and experiences that a divided mind was free to enjoy. That was why she had come to San Francisco. That was why she listened so eagerly to all that he was telling her about himself.

She was cautious, too, in manifesting her own multiple identities. She wished she did not have to be pretending to have other selves. But they had to be brought forth now and again, Cleo felt, if only by way of maintaining his interest in her. Multiples were notoriously indifferent to singletons, she knew. They found them bland, overly simple, two-dimensional. They wanted the excitement that came with embracing one person and discovering another, or two or three. So she gave him Lisa, she gave him Vixen, she gave him the Judy-who-was-Cleo and the Cleo-who-was-someone-else, and she slipped from one to another in a seemingly involuntary and unexpected way, often when they were in bed.

Lisa was calm, controlled, straitlaced. She was totally shocked when she found herself, between one eye blink and the next, in the arms of a strange man. "Who are you?—where am I?—" she blurted, rolling away, pulling herself into a fetal ball.

"I'm Judy's friend," Van said.

She stared bleakly at him. "So she's up to her tricks again. I should have figured it out faster."

He looked pained, embarrassed, terribly solicitous. She let him wonder for a moment or two whether he would have to take her back to her hotel right here in the middle of the night. And then she allowed a mischievous smile to cross Lisa's face, allowed Lisa's outraged modesty to subside, allowed Lisa to relent and relax, allowed Lisa to purr—

"Well, as long as we're here already—what did you say your name was?"

He liked that. He liked Vixen, too—wild, sweaty, noisy, a moaner, a gasper, a kicker, and thrasher who dragged him down onto the floor and went rolling over and over with him. She thought he liked Cleo, too, though that was harder to tell, because Cleo's style was aloof, serious, baroque, inscrutable. She would switch quickly from one to another, sometimes running through all four in the course of an hour. Wine, she said, induced quick switching in her. She let him know that she had a few other identities, too, fragmentary and submerged, and hinted that they were troubled, deeply neurotic, almost self-destructive: they were under control, she said, and would not erupt to cause woe for him, but she left the possibility hovering over them, to add spice to the relationship and plausibility to her role.

It seemed to be working. His pleasure in her company was evident, and the more they were together the stronger the bond between them became. She was beginning to indulge in pleasant little fantasies of moving down here permanently from Sacramento, renting an apartment somewhere near his, perhaps even moving in with him—a strange and challenging life that would be, for she would be living with Paul and Ned and Chuck and all the rest of the crew, too, but how wondrous, how electrifying—

Then on the tenth day he seemed uncharacteristically tense and somber, and she asked him what was bothering him, and he evaded her, and she pressed, and finally he said, "Do you really want to know?"

"Of course."

"It bothers me that you aren't real, Judy."

She caught her breath. "What the hell do you mean by that?"

"You know what I mean," he said, quietly, sadly. "Don't try to pretend any longer. There's no point in it."

It was like a jolt in the ribs. She turned away and stared at the wall and was silent a long while, wondering what to say. Just when everything was going so well, just when she was beginning to believe she had carried off the masquerade successfully—

"So you know?" she asked in a small voice.

"Of course I know. I knew right away."

She was trembling. "How could you tell?"

"A thousand ways. When we switch, we *change*. The voice. The eyes. The muscular tensions. The grammatical habits. The brain waves, even. An evoked-potential test shows it. Flash a light in my eyes and I'll give off a certain brain-wave pattern, and Ned will give off another, and Chuck still another. You and Lisa and Cleo and Vixen would all be the same. Multiples aren't actors, Judy. Multiples are separate minds within the same brain. That's a matter of scientific fact. You were just acting. You were doing it very well, but you couldn't possibly have fooled me."

"You let me make an idiot of myself, then."

"No."

"Why did you—how could you—"

"I saw you walk in, that first night at the club, and you caught me right away. And then I watched you go out on the floor and fall apart, and I knew you couldn't be multiple, and I wondered, what the hell's she doing here, and then I went over to you, and I was hooked. I felt something I haven't ever felt before. Does that sound like the standard old malarkey? But it's true, Judy. You're the first singleton woman that's ever interested me."

"Why?"

He shook his head. "Something about you—your intensity, your alertness, maybe even your eagerness to pretend you were a multiple—I don't know. I was caught. I was caught hard. And it's been a wonderful week and a half. I mean that. Wonderful."

"Until you got bored."

"I'm not bored with you, Judy."

"Cleo. That's my real name, my singleton name. There is no Judy."

"Cleo," he said, as if measuring the word with his lips.

"So you aren't bored with me even though there's only one of me. That's marvelous. That's tremendously flattering. That's the best thing I've heard all day. I guess I should go now, Van. It *is* Van, isn't it?"

"Don't talk that way."

"How do you want me to talk? I fascinated you, you fascinated me, we played our little games with each other, and now it's over. I wasn't real, but you did your best. We both did our bests. But I'm only a singleton woman, and you can't be satisfied with that. Not for long. For a night, a week, two weeks, maybe. Sooner or later you'll want the real thing, and I can't be the real thing for you. So long, Van."

"No."

"No?"

"Don't go."

"What's the sense of staying?"

"I want you to stay."

"I'm a singleton, Van."

"You don't have to be," he said.

✦

The therapist's name was Burkhalter and his office was in one of the Embar-cadero towers, and to the San Francisco multiples community he was very close to being a deity. His specialty was electrophysiological integration, with specific application to multiple-personality disorders. Those who carried within themselves dark and diabolical selves that threatened the stability of the group went to him to have those selves purged, or at least contained. Those who sought to have latent selves that were submerged beneath more outgoing personalities brought forward into healthy functional state went to him also. Those whose life as a multiple was a torment of schizoid confusions instead of a richly rewarding contrapuntal symphony gave themselves to Dr. Burkhalter to be healed, and in time they were. And in recent years he had begun to develop techniques for what he called personality augmentation. Van called it "driving the wedge."

"He can turn a singleton into a multiple?" Cleo asked in amazement.

"If the potential is there. You know that it's partly genetic: the structure of a multiple's brain is fundamentally different from a singleton's. The hardware just isn't the same, the cerebral wiring. And then, if the right stimulus comes along, usually in childhood, usually but not necessarily traumatic, the split-ting takes place, the separate identities begin to establish their territories. But much of the time multiplicity is never generated, and you walk around with the capacity to be a whole horde of selves and never know it."

"Is there reason to think I'm like that?"

He shrugged. "It's worth finding out. If he detects the predisposition, he has effective ways of inducing separation. Driving the wedge, you see? You do *want* to be a multiple, don't you, Cleo?"

"Oh, yes, Van. Yes!"

Burkhalter wasn't sure about her. He taped electrodes to her head, flashed bright lights in her eyes, gave her verbal association tests, ran four or five different kinds of electroencephalograph studies, and still he was uncertain. "It is not a black-and-white matter," he said several times, frowning, scowling. He was a multiple himself, but three of his selves were psychiatrists, so there was never any real problem about his office hours. Cleo wondered if he ever went to himself for a second opinion. After a week of testing she was sure that she must be a hopeless case, an intractable singleton, but Burkhalter surprised her by concluding that it was worth the attempt. "At the very worst," he said, "we will experience spontaneous fusing within a few days, and you will be no worse off than you are now. But if we succeed—ah, if we succeed—!"

His clinic was across the bay in a town called Moraga. She checked in on a Friday afternoon, spent two days undergoing further neurological and psychological tests, then three days taking medication. "Simply an anticonvulsant," the nurse explained cheerily. "To build up your tolerance."

"Tolerance for what?" Cleo asked.

"The birth trauma," she said. "New selves will be coming forth, and it can be uncomfortable for a little while."

The treatment began on Thursday. Electroshock, drugs, electroshock again. She was heavily sedated. It felt like a long dream, but there was no pain. Van visited her every day. Chuck came, too, bringing her two potted orchids in bloom, and Paul sang to her, and even Ned paid her a call. But it was hard for her to maintain a conversation with any of them. She heard voices much of the time. She felt feverish and dislocated, and at times she was sure she was floating eight or ten inches above the bed. Gradually that sensation subsided, but there were others nearly as odd. The voices remained. She learned how to hold conversations with them.

In the second week she was not allowed to have visitors. That didn't matter. She had plenty of company even when she was alone.

Then Van came for her. "They're going to let you go home today," he said. "How are you doing, Cleo?"

"I'm Noreen," she said.

✦

There were five of her, apparently. That was what Van said. She had no way of knowing, because when they were dominant she was gone—not merely asleep, but *gone*, perceiving nothing. But he showed her notes that they wrote, in handwritings that she did not recognize and indeed could barely read, and he played tapes of her other voices, Noreen a deep contralto, Nanette high and breathy, Katya hard and rough New York, and the last one, who had not yet announced her name, a stagy voluptuous campy siren-voice.

She did not leave his apartment the first few days, and then began going out for short trips, always with Van or one of his alters close beside. She felt convalescent. A kind of hangover from the various drugs had dulled her reflexes and made it difficult for her to cope with the traffic, and also there was the fear that she would undergo a switching while she was out. Whenever that happened it came without warning, and when she returned to awareness afterward she felt a sharp bewildering discontinuity of memory, not knowing how it was that she suddenly found herself in Ghirardelli Square or Golden Gate Park or wherever it was that the other self had taken their body.

But she was happy. And Van was happy with her. As they strolled hand in hand through the cool evenings she turned to him now and again and saw the warmth of his smile, the glow of his eyes. One night in the second week when they were out together he switched to Chuck—Cleo saw him change, and knew it was Chuck coming on, for now she always knew right away which identity had taken over—and he said, "You've had a marvelous effect on him, Cleo. None of us has ever seen him like this before—so contented, so fulfilled—"

"I hope it lasts, Chuck."

"Of course it'll last! Why on earth shouldn't it last?"

It didn't. Toward the end of the third week Cleo noticed that there hadn't been any entries in her memo book from Noreen for several days. That in itself was nothing alarming: an alter might choose to submerge for days, weeks, even months at a time. But was it likely that Noreen, so new to the world, would remain out of sight so long? Lin-lin, the little Chinese girl who had evolved in the second week and was Cleo's memory trace, reported that Noreen had gone away. A few days later an identity named Mattie came and went within three hours, like something bubbling up out of a troubled sea. Then Nanette disappeared, leaving Cleo with no one but her nameless breathy-voiced alter and Lin-lin. She knew she was fusing again. The wedges that Dr. Burkhalter had driven into her soul were not holding; her mind insisted on oneness, and was integrating itself; she was reverting to the singleton state.

"They're all gone," she told Van disconsolately.

"I know. I've been watching it happen."

"Is there anything we can do? Should I go back to Burkhalter?"

She saw the pain in his eyes. "It won't do any good," he said. "He told me the chances were about three to one this would happen. A month, he figured—that was about the best we could hope for. And we've had our month."

"I'd better go, Van."

"Don't say that."

"No?"

"I love you, Cleo."

"You won't," she said. "Not for much longer."

He tried to argue with her, to tell her that it didn't matter to him that she was a singleton, that one Cleo was worth a whole raft of alters, that he would learn to adapt to life with a singleton woman. He could not bear the thought of her leaving now. So she stayed: a week, two weeks, three. They ate at their favorite restaurants. They strolled hand in hand through the cool evenings. They talked of Chomsky and Whorf and even of shopping centers. When he was gone and Paul or Chuck or Hal or Dave was there she went places with them, if they wanted her to. Once she went to a movie with Ned, and when toward the end he felt himself starting to switch she put her arm around him and held him until he regained control, so that he could see how the movie finished.

But it was no good, really. She sensed the strain in him. He wanted something richer than she could offer him: the switching, the doubling, the complex undertones and overtones of other personalities resonating beyond the shores of consciousness. She could not give him that. And though he insisted he didn't miss it, he was like one who has voluntarily blindfolded himself in order to keep a blind woman company. She knew she could not ask him to live like that forever.

And so one afternoon when Van was somewhere else she packed her things and said good-bye to Paul, who gave her a hug and wept a little with her, and she went back to Sacramento. "Tell him not to call," she said. "A clean break's the best." She had been in San Francisco two months, and it was as though those two months were the only months of her life that had had any color in them, and all the rest had been lived in tones of gray.

⌄

There had been a man in the real estate office who had been telling her for a couple of years that they were meant for each other. Cleo had always been friendly enough to him—they had done a few skiing weekends in Tahoe the winter before, they had gone to Hawaii once, they had driven down to San Diego—but she had never felt anything particular when she was with him. A week after her return, she phoned him and suggested that they drive up north to the redwood country for a few days together. When they came back, she moved into the handsome condominium he had just outside town.

It was hard to find anything wrong with him. He was good-natured and attractive, he was successful, he read books and liked good movies, he enjoyed hiking and rafting and backpacking, he even talked of driving down into the city during the opera season to take in a performance or two. He was getting toward the age where he was thinking about marriage and a family. He seemed very fond of her.

But he was flat, she thought. Flat as a cardboard cutout: a singleton, a one-brain, a no-switch. There was only one of him, and there always would be. It was hardly his fault, she knew. But she couldn't settle for someone who had only two dimensions. A terrible restlessness went roaring through her every evening, and she could not possibly tell him what was troubling her.

On a drizzly afternoon in early November she packed a suitcase and drove down to San Francisco. She arrived about six-thirty, and checked into one of the Lombard Street motels, and showered and changed and walked over to Fillmore Street. Cautiously she explored the strip from Chestnut down to Union, from Union back to Chestnut. The thought of running into Van terrified her. Probably she would, sooner or later, she knew: but not tonight, she prayed. Not tonight. She went past Skits, did not go in, stopped outside a club called Big Mama, shook her head, finally entered one called The Side Effect. Mostly women inside, as usual, but a few men at the bar, not too bad-looking. No sign of Van. She bought herself a drink and casually struck up a conversation with the man to her left, a short curly-haired artistic-looking type, about forty.

"You come here often?" he asked.

"First time. I've usually gone to Skits."

"I think I remember seeing you there. Or maybe not."

She smiled. "What's your now-name?"

"Sandy. Yours?"

Cleo drew her breath down deep into her lungs. She felt a kind of light-headedness beginning to swirl behind her eyes. *Is this what you want?* she asked herself. *Yes. Yes. This is what you want.*

"Melinda," she said.

A G A I N S T

B A B Y L O N

Another easy one. (The gods owed me a few, after the wearying months of "Tourist Trade" and Pontifex.)

Though Northern California is where I live—and the distance that separates San Francisco from Los Angeles is four hundred miles, which is about the distance between Rome and Budapest—I've carried on an intense love-hate relationship with the southern half of my immense state for more than thirty years. During the 1970s and 1980s I must have made a hundred trips to Los Angeles; I know the place like a native, blithely buzzing around confidently on routes unknown even to some of the locals. Yet I've never wanted to live there, despite my envy of the warm winters and my admiration for the districts of astonishing beauty that one finds interspersed among the parts that are of astonishing ugliness. If I'm away from Los Angeles too long, I miss it in a way that is the next thing to homesickness; if I'm down there for more than four or five days at a stretch, I yearn for the blue skies and sweet air of my own region. And so I oscillate from one end of the pendulum to the other, and probably always will.

"Against Babylon" reflects my close-range observations of the colossus of the south over many decades, my horrified fascination for the place, and my uneasiness over certain of the tawdry aspects of the California mentality, both southern and northern. Once again, as with the other California stories in this book, the work went swiftly and relatively easily—I had had a long holiday from writing during August, September, and October of 1983, which helped—and acceptance (from Ellen Datlow again, at Omni) came without complications. This story also made it into the Dozois Year's Best SF 1986 volume, and was picked as well for Don Wollheim's anthology covering the same year.

Carmichael flew in from New Mexico that morning, and the first thing they told him when he put his little plane down at Burbank was that fires were burning out of control all around the Los Angeles basin. He was needed bad, they told him. It was late October, the height of the brush-fire season in Southern California, and a hot hard dry wind was blowing out of the desert, and the last time it had rained was the fifth of April. He phoned the district supervisor right away and the district supervisor told him, "Get your ass out here on the line double fast, Mike."

"Where do you want me?"

"The worst one's just above Chatsworth. We've got planes loaded and ready to go out of Van Nuys Airport."

"I need time to pee and to phone my wife," Carmichael said. "I'll be in Van Nuys in fifteen, okay?"

He was so tired that he could feel it in his teeth. It was nine in the morning and he'd been flying since half past four, and it had been rough all the way, getting pushed around by that same fierce wind out of the heart of the continent that was threatening now to fan the flames in L.A. At this moment all he wanted was home and shower and Cindy and bed. But Carmichael didn't regard fire-fighting work as optional. This time of year, the whole crazy city could go in one big firestorm. There were times he almost wished that it would. He hated this smoggy tawdry Babylon of a city, its endless tangle of freeways, the strange-looking houses, the filthy air, the thick choking glossy foliage everywhere, the drugs, the booze, the divorces, the laziness, the sleaziness, the porno shops and the naked-encounter parlors and the massage joints, the weird people wearing their weird clothes and driving their weird cars and cutting their hair in weird ways. There was a cheapness, a trashiness, about everything here, he thought. Even the mansions and the fancy restaurants were that way: hollow, like slick movie sets. He sometimes felt that the trashiness bothered him more than the out-and-out evil. If you kept sight of your own values you could do battle with evil, but trashiness slipped up around you and infiltrated your soul without your even knowing it. He hoped that his sojourn in Los Angeles was not doing that to him. He came from the Valley, and what he meant by the Valley was the great San Joaquin, out behind Bakersfield, and not the little cluttered San Fernando Valley they had here. But L.A. was Cindy's city and Cindy loved L.A. and he loved Cindy, and for Cindy's sake he had lived here seven years, up in Laurel Canyon amidst the lush green shrubbery, and for seven Octobers in a row he had gone out to dump chemical retardants on the annual brush fires, to save the Angelenos from their own idiotic carelessness. You had to accept your responsibilities, Carmichael believed.

The phone rang seven times at the home number before he hung up. Then he tried the little studio where Cindy made her jewelry, but she didn't answer there either, and it was too early to call her at the gallery. That bothered him, not being able to say hello to her right away after his three-day absence, and no likely chance for it now for another eight or ten hours. But there was nothing he could do about that.

As soon as he was aloft again he could see the fire not far to the northwest, a greasy black column against the pale sky. And when he stepped from his plane a few minutes later at Van Nuys he felt the blast of sudden heat. The temperature had been in the mid-eighties at Burbank, damned well hot enough for nine in the morning, but here it was over a hundred. He heard the distant roar of flames, the popping and crackling of burning underbrush, the peculiar whistling sound of dry grass catching fire.

The airport looked like a combat center. Planes were coming and going with lunatic frenzy, and they were lunatic planes, too, antiques of every sort, forty and fifty years old and even older, converted B-17 Flying Fortresses and DC-3s and a Douglas Invader and, to Carmichael's astonishment, a Ford Trimotor from the 1930s that had been hauled, maybe, out of some movie studio's collection. Some were equipped with tanks that held fire-retardant chemicals, some were water pumpers, some were mappers with infrared and electronic scanning equipment glistening on their snouts. Harried-looking men and women ran back and forth, shouting into CB handsets, supervising the loading process. Carmichael found his way to Operations HQ, which was full of haggard people staring into computer screens. He knew most of them from other years. They knew him.

One of the dispatchers said, "We've got a DC-3 waiting for you. You'll dump retardants along this arc, from Ybarra Canyon eastward to Horse Flats. The fire's in the Santa Susana foothills and so far the wind's from the east, but if it shifts to northerly it's going to take out everything from Chatsworth to Granada Hills, and right on down to Ventura Boulevard. And that's only *this* fire."

"How many are there?"

The dispatcher tapped his keyboard. The map of the San Fernando Valley that had been showing disappeared and was replaced by one of the entire Los Angeles basin. Carmichael stared. Three great scarlet streaks indicated fire zones: this one along the Santa Susanas, another nearly as big way off to the east in the grasslands north of the 210 Freeway around Glendora or San Dimas, and a third down in eastern Orange County, back of Anaheim Hills. "Ours is the big one so far," the dispatcher said. "But these other two are only about forty miles apart, and if they should join up somehow—"

"Yeah," Carmichael said. A single wall of fire running along the whole eastern rim of the basin, maybe—with Santa Ana winds blowing, carrying sparks westward across Pasadena, across downtown L.A., across Hollywood, across Beverly Hills, all the way to the coast, to Venice, Santa Monica, Malibu. He shivered. Laurel Canyon would go. Everything would go. Worse than Sodom and Gomorrah, worse than the fall of Nineveh. Nothing but ashes for hundreds of miles. "Jesus," he said. "Everybody scared silly of Russian nukes, and three carloads of dumb kids tossing cigarettes can do the job just as easily."

"But this wasn't cigarettes, Mike," the dispatcher said.

"No? What then, arson?"

"You haven't heard."

"I've been in New Mexico the last three days."

"You're the only one in the world who hasn't heard, then."

"For Christ's sake, heard what?"

"About the E-T's," said the dispatcher wearily. "They started the fires. Three spaceships landing at six this morning in three different corners of the L.A. basin. The heat of their engines ignited the dry grass."

Carmichael did not smile. "You've got one weird sense of humor, man."

The dispatcher said, "You think I'm joking?"

"Spaceships? From another world?"

"With critters fifteen feet high on board," the dispatcher at the next computer said. "Tim's not kidding. They're out walking around on the freeways right this minute. Fifteen feet high, Mike."

"Men from Mars?"

"Nobody knows where the hell they're from."

"Jesus," Carmichael said. "Jesus Christ God."

◆

Wild updrafts from the blaze buffeted the plane as he took it aloft, and gave him a few bad moments. But he moved easily and automatically to gain control, pulling the moves out of the underground territories of his nervous system. It was essential, he believed, to have the moves in your fingers, your shoulders, your thighs, rather than in the conscious realms of your brain. Consciousness could get you a long way, but ultimately you had to work out of the underground territories or you were dead.

He felt the plane responding and managed a grin. DC-3s were tough old birds. He loved flying them, though the youngest of them had been manufactured before he was born. He loved flying anything. Flying wasn't what Carmichael did for a living—he didn't actually do anything for a living, not any more—but flying was what he did. There were months when he spent more time in the air than on the ground, or so it seemed to him, because the hours he spent on the ground often slid by unnoticed, while time in the air was heightened, intensified, magnified.

He swung south over Encino and Tarzana before heading up across Canoga Park and Chatsworth into the fire zone. A fine haze of ash masked the sun. Looking down, he could see the tiny houses, the tiny blue swimming pools, the tiny people scurrying about, desperately trying to hose down their roofs before the flames arrived. So many houses, so many people, filling every inch of space between the sea and the desert, and now it was all in jeopardy. The southbound lanes of Topanga Canyon Boulevard were as jammed with cars, here in midmorning, as the Hollywood Freeway at rush hour. Where were they all going? Away from the fire, yes. Toward the coast, it seemed. Maybe some television preacher had told them there was an ark sitting out there in the Pacific, waiting to carry them to safety while God rained brimstone down on Los Angeles. Maybe there really was. In Los Angeles anything was possible. Invaders from space walking around on the freeways, even. Jesus. Jesus. Carmichael hardly knew how to begin thinking about that.

He wondered where Cindy was, what *she* was thinking about it. Most likely she found it very funny. Cindy had a wonderful ability to be amused by things. There was a line of poetry she liked to quote, from that Roman, Virgil: a storm is rising, the ship has sprung a leak, there's a whirlpool to one side and sea monsters on the other, and the captain turns to his men and says, "One day perhaps we'll look back and laugh even at all this." That was Cindy's way, Carmichael thought. The Santa Anas are blowing and three big brush fires are burning and invaders from space have arrived at the same time, and one day perhaps we'll look back and laugh even at all this. His heart overflowed with love for her, and longing. He had never known anything about poetry before he had met her. He closed his eyes a moment and brought her onto the screen of his mind. Thick cascades of jet-black hair, quick dazzling smile, long slender tanned body all aglitter with those amazing rings and necklaces and pendants she designed and fashioned. And her eyes. No one else he knew had eyes like hers, bright with strange mischief, with that altogether original way of vision that was the thing he most loved about her. *Damn* this fire, just when he'd been away three days! *Damn* the stupid men from Mars!

Where the neat rows and circles of suburban streets ended there was a great open stretch of grassy land, parched by the long summer to the color of a lion's hide, and beyond that were the mountains, and between the grassland and the mountains lay the fire, an enormous lateral red crest topped by a plume of foul black smoke. It seemed already to cover hundreds of acres, maybe thousands. A hundred acres of burning brush, Carmichael had heard once, creates as much heat energy as the atomic bomb they dropped on Hiroshima.

Through the crackle of radio static came the voice of the line boss, directing operations from a bubble-domed helicopter hovering at about four o'clock. "DC-3, who are you?"

"Carmichael."

"We're trying to contain it on three sides, Carmichael. You work on the east, Limekiln Canyon, down the flank of Porter Ranch Park. Got it?"

"Got it," Carmichael said.

He flew low, less than a thousand feet. That gave him a good view of all the action: sawyers in hard hats and orange shirts chopping burning trees to make them fall toward the fire, bulldozer crews clearing brush ahead of the blaze, shovelers carving firebreaks, helicopters pumping water into isolated tongues of flame. He climbed five hundred feet to avoid a single-engine observer plane, then went up five hundred more to avoid the smoke and air turbulence of the fire itself. From that altitude he had a clear picture of it, running like a bloody gash from west to east, wider at its western end. Just east of the fire's far tip he saw a circular zone of grassland perhaps a hundred acres in diameter that had already burned out, and precisely at the center of that zone stood something that looked like an aluminum silo, the size of a ten-story building, surrounded at a considerable distance by a cordon of military vehicles.

He felt a wave of dizziness go rocking through his mind. That thing, he realized, had to be the E-T spaceship.

It had come out of the west in the night, Carmichael thought, floating like a tremendous meteor over Oxnard and Camarillo, sliding toward the western end of the San Fernando Valley, kissing the grass with its exhaust and leaving a trail of flame behind it. And then it had gently set itself down over there and extinguished its own brush fire in a neat little circle about itself, not caring at all about the blaze it had kindled farther back, and God knows what kind of creatures had come forth from it to inspect Los Angeles. It figured that when the UFOs finally did make a landing out in the open, it would be in L.A. Probably they had chosen it because they had seen it so often on television— didn't all the stories say that UFO people always monitored our TV transmissions? So they saw L.A. on every other show and they probably figured it was the capital of the world, the perfect place for the first landing. But why, Carmichael wondered, had the bastards needed to pick the height of the fire season to put their ships down here?

He thought of Cindy again, how fascinated she was by all this UFO and E-T stuff, those books she read, the ideas she had, the way she had looked toward the stars one night when they were camping in Kings Canyon and talked of the beings that must live up there. "I'd love to see them," she said. "I'd love to get to know them and find out what their heads are like." Los Angeles was full of nut cases who wanted to ride in flying saucers, or claimed they already had, but it didn't sound nutty to Carmichael when Cindy talked that way. She had the Angeleno love of the exotic and the bizarre, yes, but he knew that her soul had never been touched by the crazy corruption here, that she was untainted by the prevailing craving for the weird and irrational that made him loathe the place so much. If she turned her imagination toward the stars, it was out of wonder, not out of madness: it was simply part of her nature, that curiosity, that hunger for what lay outside her experience, to embrace the unknowable. He had had no more belief in E-Ts than he did in the tooth fairy, but for her sake he had told her that he hoped she'd get her wish. And now the UFO people were really here. He could imagine her, eyes shining, standing at the edge of that cordon staring at the spaceship. Pity he couldn't be with her now, feeling all that excitement surging through her, the joy, the wonder, the magic.

But he had work to do. Swinging the DC-3 back around toward the west, he swooped down as close as he dared to the edge of the fire and hit the release button on his dump lines. Behind him, a great crimson cloud spread out: a slurry of ammonium sulphate and water, thick as paint, with a red dye mixed into it so they could tell which areas had been sprayed. The retardant clung in globs to anything, and would keep it damp for hours.

After emptying his four five-hundred-gallon tanks quickly, he headed back to Van Nuys to reload. His eyes were throbbing with fatigue, and the bitter stink of the wet charred earth below was filtering through every plate of the old plane. It was not quite noon. He had been up all night.

At the airport they had coffee ready, sandwiches, tacos, burritos. While he was waiting for the ground crew to fill his tanks he went inside to call Cindy again, and again there was no answer at home, none at the studio. He phoned the gallery, and the kid who worked there said she hadn't been in touch all morning.

"If you hear from her," Carmichael said, "tell her I'm flying fire control out of Van Nuys on the Chatsworth fire, and I'll be home as soon as things calm down a little. Tell her I miss her, too. And tell her that if I run into an E-T I'll give it a big hug for her. You got that? Tell her just that."

Across the way in the main hall he saw a crowd gathered around someone carrying a portable television set. Carmichael shouldered his way in just as the announcer was saying, "There has been no sign yet of the occupants of the San Gabriel or Orange County spaceships. But this was the horrifying sight that astounded residents of the Porter Ranch area beheld this morning between nine and ten o'clock." The screen showed two upright tubular figures that looked like squids walking on the tips of their tentacles, moving cautiously through the parking lot of a shopping center, peering this way and that out of enormous yellow platter-shaped eyes. At least a thousand onlookers were watching them at a wary distance, appearing both repelled and at the same time irresistibly drawn. Now and then the creatures paused to touch their foreheads together in some sort of communion. They moved very daintily, but Carmichael saw that they were taller than the lampposts—twelve feet high, maybe fifteen. Their skins were purplish and leathery-looking, with rows of luminescent orange spots glowing along the sides. The camera zoomed in for a close-up, then jiggled and swerved wildly just as an enormously long elastic tongue sprang from the chest of one of the alien beings and whipped out into the crowd. For an instant the only thing visible on the screen was a view of the sky; then Carmichael saw a shot of a stunned-looking girl of about fourteen, caught around the waist by that long tongue, being hoisted into the air and popped like a collected specimen into a narrow green sack. "Teams of the giant creatures roamed the town for nearly an hour," the announcer intoned. "It has definitely been confirmed that between twenty and thirty human hostages were captured before they returned to their spacecraft. Meanwhile, firefighting activities desperately continue under Santa Ana conditions in the vicinity of all three landing sites, and . . ."

Carmichael shook his head. Los Angeles, he thought. The kind of people that live here, they walk right up and let the E-Ts gobble them like flies. Maybe they think it's just a movie, and everything will be okay by the last reel. And then he remembered that Cindy was the kind of people who would walk right up to one of these E-Ts. Cindy was the kind of people who lived in Los Angeles, he told himself, except that Cindy was *different*. Somehow.

He went outside. The DC-3 was loaded and ready.

In the forty-five minutes since he had left the fire line, the blaze seemed to have spread noticeably toward the south. This time the line boss had him lay down the retardant from the De Soto Avenue freeway interchange to the northeast corner of Porter Ranch. When he returned to the airport, intending to try phoning Cindy once again, a man in military uniform stopped him as he was crossing the field and said, "You Mike Carmichael, Laurel Canyon?"

"That's right."

"I've got some troublesome news for you. Let's go inside."

"Suppose you tell me here, okay?"

The officer looked at him strangely. "It's about your wife," he said. "Cynthia Carmichael? That's your wife's name?"

"Come *on*," Carmichael said.

"She's one of the hostages, Mr. Carmichael."

His breath went from him as though he had been kicked.

"Where did it happen?" he demanded. "How did they get her?"

The officer gave him a strange strained smile. "It was the shopping-center lot, Porter Ranch. Maybe you saw some of it on the TV."

Carmichael nodded. That girl jerked off her feet by that immense elastic tongue, swept through the air, popped into that green pouch. And Cindy—?

"You saw the part where the creatures were moving around? And then suddenly they were grabbing people, and everyone was running from them? That was when they got her. She was up front when they began grabbing, and maybe she had a chance to get away but she waited just a little too long. She started to run, I understand, but then she stopped—she looked back at them— she may have called something out to them—and then—well, and then—"

"Then they scooped her up?"

"I have to tell you that they did."

"I see," Carmichael said stonily.

"One thing all the witnesses agreed, she didn't panic, she didn't scream. She was very brave when those monsters grabbed her. How in God's name you can be brave when something that size is holding you in midair is something I don't understand, but I have to assure you that those who saw it—"

"It makes sense to me," Carmichael said.

He turned away. He shut his eyes for a moment and took deep, heavy pulls of the hot smoky air.

It figures, he thought. It makes absolute sense.

Of course she had gone right out to the landing site. Of course. If there was anyone in Los Angeles who would have wanted to get to them and see them with her own eyes and perhaps try to talk to them and establish some sort of rapport with them, it was Cindy. She wouldn't have been afraid of them. She had never seemed to be afraid of anything. It wasn't hard for Carmichael to imagine her in that panicky mob in the parking lot, cool and radiant, staring at the giant aliens, smiling at them right up to the moment they seized her.

In a way he felt very proud of her. But it terrified him to think that she was in their grasp.

"She's on the ship?" he asked. "The one that we have right up back here?"

"Yes."

"Have there been any messages from the hostages? Or from the aliens, for that matter?"

"I'm not in a position to divulge that information."

"Is there any information?"

"I'm sorry, I'm not at liberty to—"

"I refuse to believe," Carmichael said, "that that ship is just sitting there, that nothing at all is being done to make contact with—"

"A command center has been established, Mr. Carmichael, and certain efforts are under way. That much I can tell you. I can tell you that Washington is involved. But beyond that, at the present point in time—"

A kid who looked like an Eagle Scout came running up. "Your plane's all loaded and ready to go, Mike!"

"Yeah," Carmichael said. The fire, the fucking fire! He had almost managed to forget about it. *Almost.* He hesitated a moment, torn between conflicting responsibilities. Then he said to the officer, "Look, I've got to get back out on the fire line. Can you stay here a little while?"

"Well—"

"Maybe half an hour. I have to do a retardant dump. Then I want you to take me over to that spaceship and get me through the cordon, so I can talk to those critters myself. If she's on that ship, I mean to get her off it."

"I don't see how it would be possible for—"

"Well, try to see," Carmichael said. "I'll meet you right here in half an hour."

When he was aloft he noticed right away that the fire was spreading. The wind was even rougher and wilder than before, and now it was blowing hard from the northeast, pushing the flames down toward the edge of Chatsworth. Already some glowing cinders had blown across the city limits and Carmichael saw houses afire to his left, maybe half a dozen of them. There would be more, he knew. In fire fighting you come to develop an odd sense of which way the struggle is going, whether you're gaining on the blaze or the blaze is gaining on you, and that sense told him now that the vast effort that was under way was failing, that the fire was still on the upcurve, that whole neighborhoods were going to be ashes by nightfall.

He held on tight as the DC-3 entered the fire zone. The fire was sucking air like crazy now, and the turbulence was astounding: it felt as if a giant's hand had grabbed the ship by the nose. The line boss's helicopter was tossing around like a balloon on a string.

Carmichael called in for orders and was sent over to the southwest side,

close by the outermost street of houses. Fire fighters with shovels were beating
on wisps of flame rising out of people's gardens down there. The skirts of dead
leaves that dangled down the trunks of a row of towering palm trees were
blazing. The neighborhood dogs had formed a crazed pack, running desperately back and forth.

Swooping down to treetop level, Carmichael let go with a red gush of
chemicals, swathing everything that looked combustible with the stuff. The
shovelers looked up and waved at him, and he dipped his wings to them and
headed off to the north, around the western edge of the blaze—it was edging
farther to the west, too, he saw, leaping up into the high canyons out by the
Ventura County line—and then he flew eastward along the Santa Susana
foothills until he could see the spaceship once more, standing isolated in its
circle of blackened earth. The cordon of military vehicles seemed now to be
even larger, what looked like a whole armored division deployed in concentric
rings beginning half a mile or so from the ship.

He stared intently at the alien vessel as though he might be able to see
through its shining walls to Cindy within.

He imagined her sitting at a table, or whatever the aliens used instead of
tables, sitting at a table with seven or eight of the huge beings, calmly
explaining Earth to them and then asking them to explain their world to her.
He was altogether certain that she was safe, that no harm would come to her,
that they were not torturing her or dissecting her or sending electric currents
through her simply to see how she reacted. Things like that would never
happen to Cindy, he knew. The only thing he feared was that they would depart
for their home star without releasing her. The terror that that thought generated
in him was as powerful as any kind of fear he had ever felt.

As Carmichael approached the aliens' landing site he saw the guns of some
of the tanks below swiveling around to point at him, and he picked up a radio
voice telling him brusquely, "You're off-limits, DC-3. Get back to the fire
zone. This is prohibited airspace."

"Sorry," Carmichael answered. "No entry intended."

But as he started to make his turn he dropped down even lower, so that he
could have a good look at the spaceship. If it had portholes, and Cindy was
looking out one of those portholes, he wanted her to know that he was nearby.
That he was watching, that he was waiting for her to come back. But the ship's
hull was blind-faced, entirely blank.

—Cindy? Cindy?

She was always looking for the strange, the mysterious, the unfamiliar, he
thought. The people she brought to the house: a Navaho once, a bewildered
Turkish tourist, a kid from New York. The music she played, the way she

chanted along with it. The incense, the lights, the meditation. "I'm search-ing," she liked to say. Trying always to find a route that would take her into something that was wholly outside herself. Trying to become something more than she was. That was how they had fallen in love in the first place, an unlikely couple, she with her beads and sandals, he with his steady no-nonsense view of the world: she had come up to him that day long ago when he was in the record shop in Studio City, and God only knew what he was doing in that part of the world in the first place, and she had asked him something and they had started to talk, and they had talked and talked, talked all night, she wanting to know everything there was to know about him, and when dawn came up they were still together and they had rarely been parted since. He never had really been able to understand what it was that she had wanted him for—the Valley redneck, the aging flyboy—although he felt certain that she wanted him for something real, that he filled some need for her, as she did for him, which could for lack of a more specific term be called love. She had always been searching for that, too. Who wasn't? And he knew that she loved him truly and well, though he couldn't quite see why. "Love is understanding," she liked to say. "Understanding is loving." Was she trying to tell the spaceship people about love right this minute? *Cindy, Cindy, Cindy—*

Back in Van Nuys a few minutes later, he found that everyone at the airport seemed to know by this time that his wife was one of the hostages. The officer whom Carmichael had asked to wait for him was gone. He was not very surprised by that. He thought for a moment of trying to go over to the ship by himself, to get through the cordon and do something about getting Cindy free, but he realized that that was a dumb idea: the military was in charge and they wouldn't let him or anybody else get within a mile of that ship, and he'd only get snarled up in stuff with the television interviewers looking for poignant crap about the families of those who had been captured.

Then the head dispatcher came down to meet him on the field, looking almost about ready to burst with compassion, and in funereal tones told Carmichael that it would be all right if he called it quits for the day and went home to await whatever might happen. But Carmichael shook him off. "I won't get her back by sitting in the living room," he said. "And this fire isn't going to go out by itself, either."

It took twenty minutes for the ground crew to pump the retardant slurry into the DC-3's tanks. Carmichael stood to one side, drinking Cokes and watching the planes come and go. People stared at him, and those who knew him waved from a distance, and three or four pilots came over and silently squeezed his arm or rested a hand consolingly on his shoulder. The northern sky was black with soot, shading to gray to east and west. The air was sauna-hot and frighteningly dry: you could set fire to it, Carmichael thought, with a snap of your fingers. Somebody running by said that a new fire had broken out in Pasadena, near the Jet Propulsion Lab, and there was another in Griffith Park. The wind was starting to carry firebrands, then. Dodgers Stadium was burning, someone said. So is Santa Anita Racetrack, said someone else. The whole damned place is going to go, Carmichael thought. And my wife is sitting inside a spaceship from another planet.

When his plane was ready he took it up and laid down a new line of retardant practically in the faces of the fire fighters working on the outskirts of Chatsworth. They were too busy to wave. In order to get back to the airport he had to make a big loop behind the fire, over the Santa Susanas and down the flank of the Golden State Freeway, and this time he saw the fires burning to the east, two huge conflagrations marking the places where the exhaust streams of the other two spaceships had grazed the dry grass, and a bunch of smaller blazes strung out on a line from Burbank or Glendale deep into Orange County. His hands were shaking as he touched down at Van Nuys. He had gone without sleep now for something like thirty-two hours, and he could feel himself starting to pass into that blank white fatigue that lies somewhere beyond ordinary fatigue.

The head dispatcher was waiting for him again as he left his plane. "All right," Carmichael said at once. "I give in. I'll knock off for five or six hours and grab some sleep, and then you can call me back to—"

"No. That isn't it."

"That isn't what?"

"What I came out here to tell you, Mike. They've released some of the hostages."

"Cindy?"

"I think so. There's an Air Force car here to take you to Sylmar. That's where they've got the command center set up. They said to find you as soon as you came off your last dump mission and send you over there so you can talk with your wife."

"So she's free," Carmichael said. "Oh, Jesus, she's free!"

"You go on along, Mike. We'll look after the fire without you for a while, okay?"

The Air Force car looked like a general's limo, long and low and sleek, with a square-jawed driver in front and a couple of very tough-looking young officers to sit with him in back. They said hardly anything, and they looked as weary as Carmichael felt. "How's my wife?" he asked, and one of them said, "We understand that she hasn't been harmed." The way he said it was stiff and strange. Carmichael shrugged. The kid has seen too many old Air Force movies, he told himself.

The whole city seemed to be on fire now. Within the air-conditioned limo there was only the faintest whiff of smoke, but the sky to the east was terrifying, with streaks of red bursting like meteors through the blackness. Carmichael asked the Air Force men about that, but all he got was a clipped "It looks pretty bad, we understand." Somewhere along the San Diego Freeway between Mission Hills and Sylmar, Carmichael fell asleep, and the next thing he knew they were waking him gently and leading him into a vast, bleak hangarlike building near the reservoir. The place was a maze of cables and screens, with military personnel operating what looked like a thousand computers and ten thousand telephones. He let himself be shuffled along, moving mechanically and barely able to focus his eyes, to an inner office where a gray-haired colonel greeted him in his best this-is-the-tense-part-of-the-movie style and said, "This may be the most difficult job you've ever had to handle, Mr. Carmichael."

Carmichael scowled. Everybody was Hollywood in this damned town, he thought.

"They told me the hostages were being freed," he said. "Where's my wife?"

The colonel pointed to a television screen. "We're going to let you talk to her right now."

"Are you saying I don't get to see her?"

"Not immediately."

"Why not? Is she all right?"

"As far as we know, yes."

"You mean she hasn't been released? They told me the hostages were being freed."

"All but three have been let go," said the colonel. "Two people, according to the aliens, were injured as they were captured, and are undergoing medical treatment aboard the ship. They'll be released shortly. The third is your wife, Mr. Carmichael. She is unwilling to leave the ship."

It was like hitting an air pocket. *"Unwilling—?"*

"She claims to have volunteered to make the journey to the home world of the aliens. She says she's going to serve as our ambassador, our special emissary. Mr. Carmichael, does your wife have any history of mental imbalance?"

Glaring, Carmichael said, "She's very sane. Believe me."

"You are aware that she showed no display of fear when the aliens seized her in the shopping-center incident this morning?"

"I know, yes. That doesn't mean she's crazy. She's unusual. She has unusual ideas. But she's not crazy. Neither am I, incidentally." He put his hands to his face for a moment and pressed his fingertips lightly against his eyes. "All right," he said. "Let me talk to her."

"Do you think you can persuade her to leave that ship?"

"I'm sure as hell going to try."

"You are not yourself sympathetic to what she's doing, are you?" the colonel asked.

Carmichael looked up. "Yes, I am sympathetic. She's an intelligent woman doing something that she thinks is important, and doing it of her own free will. Why the hell shouldn't I be sympathetic? But I'm going to try to talk her out of it, you bet. I love her. I want her. Somebody else can be the goddamned ambassador to Betelgeuse. Let me talk to her, will you?"

The colonel gestured and the big television screen came to life. For a moment mysterious colored patterns flashed across it in a disturbing random way; then Carmichael caught glimpses of shadowy catwalks, intricate metal strutworks crossing and recrossing at peculiar angles; and then for an instant one of the aliens appeared on the screen. Yellow platter-eyes looked complacently back at him. Carmichael felt altogether wide awake now.

The alien's face vanished and Cindy came into view. The moment he saw her, Carmichael knew that he had lost her.

Her face was glowing. There was a calm joy in her eyes verging on ecstasy. He had seen her look something like that on many occasions, but this was different: this was beyond anything she had attained before. She had seen the beatific vision, this time.

"Cindy?"

"Hello, Mike."

"Can you tell me what's been happening in there, Cindy?"

"It's incredible. The contact, the communication."

Sure, he thought. If anyone could make contact with the space people it would be Cindy. She had a certain kind of magic about her: the gift of being able to open any door.

She said, "They speak mind to mind, you know, no barriers at all. They've come in peace, to get to know us, to join in harmony with us, to welcome us into the confederation of worlds."

He moistened his lips. "What have they done to you, Cindy? Have they brainwashed you or something?"

"No! No, nothing like that! They haven't done a thing to me, Mike! We've just talked."

"*Talked!*"

"They've showed me how to touch my mind to theirs. That isn't brainwashing. I'm still me. I, me, Cindy. I'm okay. Do I look as though I'm being harmed? They aren't dangerous. Believe me."

"They've set fire to half the city with their exhaust trails, you know."

"That grieves them. It was an accident. They didn't understand how dry the hills were. If they had some way of extinguishing the flames, they would, but the fires are too big even for them. They ask us to forgive them. They want everyone to know how sorry they are." She paused a moment. Then she said, very gently, "Mike, will you come on board? I want you to experience them as I'm experiencing them."

"I can't do that, Cindy."

"Of course you can! Anyone can! You just open your mind, and they touch you, and—"

"I know. I don't want to. Come out of there and come home, Cindy. Please. Please. It's been three days—four, now—I want to hug you, I want to hold you—"

"You can hold me as tight as you like. They'll let you on board. We can go to their world together. You know that I'm going to go with them to their world, don't you?"

"You aren't. Not really."

She nodded gravely. She seemed terribly serious. "They'll be leaving in a few weeks, as soon as they've had a chance to exchange gifts with Earth. I've seen images of their planet—like movies, only they do it with their minds— Mike, you can't imagine how beautiful it is! How eager they are to have me come!"

Sweat rolled out of his hair into his eyes, making him blink, but he did not dare wipe it away, for fear she would think he was crying.

"I don't want to go to their planet, Cindy. And I don't want you to go either."

She was silent for a time.

Then she smiled delicately and said, "I know, Mike."

He clenched his fists and let go and clenched them again. "I *can't* go there."

"No. You can't. I understand that. Los Angeles is alien enough for you, I think. You need to be in your Valley, in your own real world, not running off to some far star. I won't try to coax you."

"But you're going to go anyway?" he asked, and it was not really a question.

"You already know what I'm going to do."

"Yes."

"I'm sorry. But not really."

"Do you love me?" he said, and regretted saying it at once.

She smiled sadly. "You know I do. And you know I don't want to leave you. But once they touched my mind with theirs, once I saw what kind of beings they are—do you know what I mean? I don't have to explain, do I? You always know what I mean."

"Cindy—"

"Oh, Mike, I do love you so much."

"And I love you, babe. And I wish you'd come out of that goddamned ship."

"You won't ask that. Because you love me, right? Just as I won't ask you again to come on board with me, because I really love you. Do you understand that, Mike?"

He wanted to reach into the screen and grab her.

"I understand, yes," he made himself say.

"I love you, Mike."

"I love you, Cindy."

"They tell me the round trip takes forty-eight of our years, but it will only seem like a few weeks to me. Oh, Mike! Good-bye, Mike! God bless, Mike!" She blew kisses to him. He saw his favorite rings on her fingers, the three little strange star-sapphire ones that she had made when she first began to design jewelry. He searched his mind for some new way to reason with her, some line of argument that would work, and could find none. He felt a vast emptiness beginning to expand within him, as though he were being made hollow by some whirling blade. Her face was shining. She seemed like a stranger to him suddenly. She seemed like a Los Angeles person, one of *those*, lost in fantasies and dreams, and it was as though he had never known her, or as though he had pretended she was something other than she was. No. No, that isn't right. She's not one of *those*, she's Cindy. Following her own star, as always. Suddenly he was unable to look at the screen any longer, and he turned away, biting his lip, making a shoving gesture with his left hand. The Air Force men in the room wore the awkward expressions of people who had inadvertently eavesdropped on someone's most intimate moments and were trying to pretend they had heard nothing.

"She isn't crazy, Colonel," Carmichael said vehemently. "I don't want anyone believing she's some kind of nut."

"Of course not, Mr. Carmichael."

"But she's not going to leave that spaceship. You heard her. She's staying aboard, going back with them to wherever the hell they came from. I can't do anything about that. You see that, don't you? Nothing I could do, short of going aboard that ship and dragging her off physically, would get her out of there. And I wouldn't ever do that."

"Naturally not. In any case, you understand that it would be impossible for us to permit you to go on board, even for the sake of attempting to remove her."

"That's all right," Carmichael said. "I wouldn't dream of it. To remove her or even just to join her for the trip. I don't want to go to that place. Let her go: that's what she was meant to do in this world. Not me. Not me, Colonel. That's simply not my thing." He took a deep breath. He thought he might be trembling. "Colonel, do you mind if I got the hell out of here? Maybe I would feel better if I went back out there and dumped some more gunk on that fire. I think that might help. That's what I think, Colonel. All right? Would you send me back to Van Nuys, Colonel?"

He went up one last time in the DC-3. They wanted him to dump the retardants along the western face of the fire, but instead he went to the east, where the spaceship was, and flew in a wide circle around it. A radio voice warned him to move out of the area, and he said that he would.

As he circled, a hatch opened in the spaceship's side and one of the aliens appeared, looking gigantic even from Carmichael's altitude. The huge purplish thing stepped from the ship, extended its tentacles, seemed to be sniffing the smoky air.

Carmichael thought vaguely of flying down low and dropping his whole load of retardants on the creature, drowning it in gunk, getting even with the aliens for having taken Cindy from him. He shook his head. That's crazy, he told himself. Cindy would feel sick if she knew he had ever considered any such thing.

But that's what I'm like, he thought. Just an ordinary ugly vengeful Earthman. And that's why I'm not going to go to that other planet, and that's why she is.

He swung around past the spaceship and headed straight across Granada Hills and Northridge into Van Nuys Airport. When he was on the ground he sat at the controls of his plane a long while, not moving at all. Finally one of the dispatchers came out and called up to him, "Mike, are you okay?"

"Yeah. I'm fine."

"How come you came back without dropping your load?"

Carmichael peered at his gauges. "Did I do that? I guess I did that, didn't I?"

"You're not okay, are you?"

"I forgot to dump, I guess. No, I didn't forget. I just didn't bother. I didn't feel like doing it."

"Mike, come on out of that plane."

"I didn't feel like doing it," Carmichael said again. "Why the hell bother?

This crazy city—there's nothing left in it that I would want to save anyway." His control deserted him at last, and rage swept through him like fire racing up the slopes of a dry canyon. He understood what she was doing, and he respected it, but he didn't have to like it. He didn't like it at all. He had lost Cindy, and he felt somehow that he had lost his war with Los Angeles as well. "Fuck it," he said. "Let it burn. This crazy city. I always hated it. It deserves what it gets. The only reason I stayed here was for her. She was all that mattered. But she's going away now. Let the fucking place burn."

The dispatcher gaped at him in amazement. "Mike—"

Carmichael moved his head slowly from side to side as though trying to shake a monstrous headache from it. Then he frowned. "No, that's wrong," he said. "You've got to do the job anyway, right? No matter how you feel. You have to put the fires out. You have to save what you can. Listen, Tim, I'm going to fly one last load today, you hear? And then I'll go home and get some sleep. Okay? Okay?" He had the plane in motion, going down the short runway. Dimly he realized that he had not requested clearance. A little Cessna spotter plane moved desperately out of his way, and then he was aloft. The sky was black and red. The fire was completely uncontained now, and maybe uncontainable. But you had to keep trying, he thought. You had to save what you could. He gunned and went forward, flying calmly into the inferno in the foothills, until the wild thermals caught his wings from below and lifted him and tossed him like a toy skimming over the top, and sent him hurtling toward the waiting hills to the north.

Thus saith the Lord; Behold, I will raise up against Babylon, and against them that dwell in the midst of them that rise up against me, a destroying wind;

And will send unto Babylon fanners, that shall fan her, and shall empty her land; for in the day of trouble they shall be against her round about.

Jeremiah 51: 1–2

S Y M B I O N T

Long ago there was a gaudy pulp magazine called Planet Stories, *which was devoted to two-fisted, colorful tales of action and adventure on other worlds. Don't think it was junk, though: Ray Bradbury, Poul Anderson, Theodore Sturgeon, and Leigh Brackett were regular contributors, Isaac Asimov and Jack Vance wrote for it, Philip K. Dick's first published story appeared in it. Readers loved it and so did the writers, because they could rare back and let their imaginations run free.*

I never had anything published in Planet Stories, *because it went out of business in 1955, just as my career was getting started. But I enjoyed doing Planet-type material for such later imitators as* Science Fiction Adventures *and* Venture SF, *which flourished in the fifties, and suddenly, one day in the spring of 1984, it occurred to me to attempt one for* Playboy *in the old* Planet Stories *mode, appropriately buffed and polished for* Playboy's *demanding readership. (I would, after all, be fighting for a place on the contents page with the likes of Nabokov, Updike, and Joyce Carol Oates.) And out of the machine came "Symbiont," the somber tale of jungle adventure and diabolical revenge that you are about to read. Off it went, with some trepidation, to the formidable Alice K. Turner, who had put me so exhaustingly through my paces fifteen months earlier with "Tourist Trade." And back from Alice a few days later came this letter of acceptance:*

"Your check, as we like to say, is in the mail. I was dumbfounded when I read this story (avidly, I should add), and sent it off to Teresa [her assistant editor], whose youth was not misspent, as mine was, in reading stories that featured creatures with tentacles and body-takeovers by alien nasties. I waited, somewhat apprehensively, for her response—and she loved it. That's good enough for me. If such a noble mind can be here o'erthrown, what the hell. This is one of the ones that will go in with not a word changed, though not till '85 some time."

The initial idea for the story, incidentally, was given to me by a young woman named Karen Haber, whom I had met while on a speaking tour in Texas. It originally involved something that had happened to a friend of a friend of hers in Vietnam, but I applied my usual science-fiction meta-morphosis techniques to it and "Symbiont" was the result. Ms. Haber was very impressed. I was very impressed with Ms. Haber, too. A couple of years later I married her.

Ten years later, when I was long out of the Service and working the turn-around wheel at Betelgeuse Station, Fazio still haunted me. Not that he was dead. Other people get haunted by dead men; I was haunted by a live one. It would have been a lot better for both of us if he *had* been dead, but as far as I knew Fazio was still alive.

He'd been haunting me a long while. Three or four times a year his little dry thin voice would come out of nowhere and I'd hear him telling me again, "Before we go into that jungle, we got to come to an understanding. If a synsym nails me, Chollie, you kill me right away, hear? None of this shit of calling in the paramedics to clean me out. You just kill me right away. And I'll do the same for you. Is that a deal?"

This was on a planet called Weinstein in the Servadac system, late in the Second Ovoid War. We were twenty years old and we were volunteers: two dumb kids playing hero. "You bet your ass" is what I told him, not hesitating a second. "Deal. Absolutely." Then I gave him a big grin and a handclasp and we headed off together on spore-spreading duty.

At the time, I really thought I meant it. Sometimes I still believe that I did.

Ten years. I could still see the two of us back there on Weinstein, going out to distribute latchenango spores in the enemy-held zone. The planet had been grabbed by the Ovoids early in the war, but we were starting to drive them back from that whole system. Fazio and I were the entire patrol: you get spread pretty thin in galactic warfare. But there was plenty of support force behind us in the hills.

Weinstein was strategically important, God only knows why. Two small continents—both tropical, mostly thick jungle, air like green soup—

surrounded by an enormous turbulent ocean: never colonized by Earth, and of no use that anyone had ever successfully explained to me. But the place had once been ours and they had taken it away, and we wanted it back.

The way you got a planet back was to catch a dozen or so Ovoids, fill them full of latchenango spores, and let them return to their base. There is no life-form a latchenango likes better as its host than an Ovoid. The Ovoids, being Ovoids, would usually conceal what had happened to them from their pals, who would kill them instantly if they knew they were carrying deadly parasites. Of course, the carriers were going to die anyway—latchenango infestation is invariably fatal to Ovoids—but by the time they did, in about six standard weeks, the latchenangos had gone through three or four reproductive cycles and the whole army would be infested. All we needed to do was wait until all the Ovoids were dead and then come in, clean the place up, and raise the flag again. The latchenangos were generally dead, too, by then, since they rarely could find other suitable hosts. But even if they weren't, we didn't worry about it. Latchenangos don't cause any serious problems for humans. About the worst of it is that you usually inhale some spores while you're handling them, and it irritates your lungs for a couple of weeks so you do some pretty ugly coughing until you're desporified.

In return for our latchenangos the Ovoids gave us synsyms.

Synsyms were the first things you heard about when you arrived in the war zone, and what you heard was horrendous. You didn't know how much of it was myth and how much was mere bullshit and how much was truth, but even if you discounted seventy-five percent of it the rest was scary enough. "If you get hit by one," the old hands advised us, "kill yourself fast, while you have the chance." Roving synsym vectors cruised the perimeter of every Ovoid camp, sniffing for humans. They were not parasites but synthetic symbionts: when they got into you, they stayed there, sharing your body with you indefinitely.

In school they teach you that symbiosis is a mutually beneficial state. Maybe so. But the word that passed through the ranks in the war zone was that it definitely did not improve the quality of your life to take a synsym into your body. And though the Service medics would spare no effort to see that you survived a synsym attack—they aren't allowed to perform mercy killings, and wouldn't anyway—everything we heard indicated that you didn't really *want* to survive one.

The day Fazio and I entered the jungle was like all the others on Weinstein: dank, humid, rainy. We strapped on our spore tanks and started out, using hand-held heat piles to burn our way through the curtains of tangled vines. The wet spongy soil had a purplish tinge, and the lakes were iridescent green from lightning algae.

"Here's where we'll put the hotel landing strip," Fazio said lightly. "Over here, the pool and cabanas. The gravity-tennis courts here, and on the far side of that—"

"Watch it," I said, and skewered a low-flying wingfinger with a beam of hot purple light. It fell in ashes at our feet. Another one came by, the mate, traveling at eye level with its razor-sharp beak aimed at my throat, but Fazio took it out just as neatly. We thanked each other. Wingfingers are elegant things, all trajectory and hardly any body mass, with scaly silvery skins that shine like the finest grade of moonlight, and it is their habit to go straight for the jugular in the most literal sense. We killed twelve that day, and I hope it is my quota for this lifetime. As we advanced into the heart of the jungle we dealt just as efficiently with assorted hostile coilworms, eyeflies, dingleberries, leper bats, and other disagreeable local specialties. We were a great team: quick, smart, good at protecting each other.

We were admiring a giant carnivorous fungus a klick and a half deep in the woods when we came upon our first Ovoid. The fungus was a fleshy phallic red tower three meters high with orange gills, equipped with a dozen dangling whiplike arms that had green adhesive knobs at the tips. At the ends of most of the arms hung small forest creatures in various stages of digestion. As we watched, an unoccupied arm rose and shot forth, extended itself to three times its resting length, and by some neat homing tropism slapped its adhesive knob against a passing many-legger about the size of a cat. The beast had no chance to struggle; a network of wiry structures sprouted at once from the killer arm and slipped into the victim's flesh, and that was that. We almost applauded.

"Let's plant three of them in the hotel garden," I said, "and post a schedule of feeding times. It'll be a great show for the guests."

"Shh," Fazio said. He pointed.

Maybe fifty meters away a solitary Ovoid was gliding serenely along a forest path, obviously unaware of us. I caught my breath. Everyone knows what Ovoids look like, but this was the first time I had seen a live one. I was surprised at how beautiful it was, a tapering cone of firm jelly, pale blue streaked with red and gold. Triple rows of short-stalked eyes along its sides like brass buttons. Clusters of delicate tendrils sprouting like epaulets around the eating orifice at the top of its head. Turquoise ribbons of neural conduit winding round and round its equator, surrounding the dark heart-shaped brain faintly visible within the cloudy depths. The enemy. I was conditioned to hate it, and I did; yet I couldn't deny its strange beauty.

Fazio smiled and took aim and put a numb-needle through the Ovoid's middle. It froze instantly in mid-glide; its color deepened to a dusky flush; the tiny mouth tendrils fluttered wildly, but there was no other motion. We jogged up to it and I slipped the tip of my spore distributor about five centimeters into its meaty middle. "Let him have it!" Fazio yelled. I pumped a couple of c.c.'s of latchenango spores into the paralyzed alien. Its soft quivering flesh turned blue-black with fear and rage and God knows what other emotions that were strictly Ovoid. We nodded to each other and moved along. Already the latchenangos were spawning within their host; in half an hour the Ovoid, able once more to move, would limp off toward its camp to start infecting its comrades. It is a funny way to wage war.

The second Ovoid, an hour later, was trickier. It knew we had spotted it and took evasive action, zigzagging through a zone of streams and slender trees in a weird dignified way like someone trying to move very fast without having his hat blow off. Ovoids are not designed for quick movements, but this one was agile and determined, ducking behind this rock and that. More than once we lost sight of it altogether and were afraid it might double back and come down on *us* while we stood gaping and blinking.

Eventually we bottled it up between two swift little streams and closed in on it from both sides. I raised my needler and Fazio got ready with his spore distributor and just then something gray and slipper-shaped and about fifteen centimeters long came leaping up out of the left-hand stream and plastered itself over Fazio's mouth and throat.

Down he went, snuffling and gurgling, trying desperately to peel it away. I thought it was some kind of killer fish. Pausing only long enough to shoot a needle through the Ovoid, I dropped my gear and jumped down beside him.

Fazio was rolling around, eyes wild, kicking at the ground in terror and agony. I put my elbow on his chest to hold him still and pried with both hands at the thing on his face. Getting it loose was like pulling a second skin off him, but somehow I managed to lift it away from his lips far enough for him to gasp, "Synsym—I think it's synsym—"

"No, man, it's just some nasty fish," I told him. "Hang in there and I'll rip the rest of it loose in half a minute—"

Fazio shook his head in anguish.

Then I saw the two thin strands of transparent stuff snaking up out of it and disappearing into his nostrils, and I knew he was right.

I didn't hear anything from him or about him after the end of the war, and didn't want to, but I assumed all along that Fazio was still alive. I don't know why: my faith in the general perversity of the universe, I guess.

The last I had seen of him was our final day on Weinstein. We both were being invalided out. They were shipping me to the big hospital on Daemmerung for routine desporification treatment, but he was going to the quarantine station on Quixote; and as we lay side by side in the depot, me on an ordinary stretcher and Fazio inside an isolation bubble, he raised his head with what must have been a terrible effort and glared at me out of eyes that already were ringed with the red concentric synsym circles, and he whispered something to me. I wasn't able to understand the words through the wall of his bubble, but I could *feel* them, the way you feel the light of a blue-white sun from half a parsec out. His skin was glowing. The dreadful vitality of the symbiont within him was already apparent. I had a good notion of what he was trying to tell me. *You bastard,* he was most likely trying to say. *Now I'm stuck with this thing for a thousand years. And I'm going to hate you every minute of the time, Chollie.*

Then they took him away. They sent him floating up the ramp into that Quixote-bound ship. When he was out of view I felt released, as though I was coming out from under a pull of six or seven gravs. It occurred to me that I wasn't ever going to have to see Fazio again. I wouldn't have to face those reddened eyes, that taut shining skin, that glare of infinite reproach. Or so I believed for the next ten years, until he turned up on Betelgeuse Station.

A bolt out of the blue: there he was, suddenly, standing next to me in the recreation room on North Spoke. It was just after my shift and I was balancing on the rim of the swimmer web, getting ready to dive. "Chollie?" he said calmly. The voice was Fazio's voice: that was clear, when I stopped to think about it a little later. But I never for a moment considered that this weird gnomish man might be Fazio. I stared at him and didn't even come close to recognizing him. He seemed about seven million years old, shrunken, fleshless, weightless, with thick coarse hair like white straw and strange soft gleaming translucent skin that looked like parchment worn thin by time. In the bright light of the rec room he kept his eyes hooded nearly shut; but then he turned away from the glowglobes and opened them wide enough to show me the fine red rings around his pupils. The hair began to rise along the back of my neck.

"Come on," he said. "You know me. Yeah. Yeah."

The voice, the cheekbones, the lips, the eyes—the eyes, the eyes, the eyes. Yes, I knew him. But it wasn't possible. Fazio? Here? How? So long a time, so many light-years away! And yet—yet—

He nodded. "You got it, Chollie. Come on. Who am I?"

My first attempt at saying something was a sputtering failure. But I managed to get his name out on the second try.

"Yeah," he said. "Fazio. What a surprise."

He didn't look even slightly surprised. I think he must have been watching me for a few days before he approached me—casing me, checking me out, making certain it was really me, getting used to the idea that he had actually found me. Otherwise the amazement would surely have been showing on him now. Finding me—finding *anybody* along the starways—wasn't remotely probable. This was a coincidence almost too big to swallow. I knew he couldn't have deliberately come after me, because the galaxy is so damned big a place that the idea of setting out to search for someone in it is too silly even to think about. But somehow he had caught up with me anyway. If the universe is truly infinite, I suppose, then even the most wildly improbable things must occur in it a billion times a day.

I said shakily, "I can't believe—"

"You can't? Hey, you better! What a surprise, kid, hey? Hey?" He clapped his hand against my arm. "And you're looking good, kid. Nice and healthy. You keep in shape, huh? How old are you now, thirty-two?"

"Thirty." I was numb with shock and fear.

"Thirty. Mmm. So am I. Nice age, ain't it? Prime of life."

"Fazio—"

His control was terrifying. "Come on, Chollie. You look like you're about to crap in your pants. Aren't you glad to see your old buddy? We had some good times together, didn't we? Didn't we? What was the name of that fuckin' planet? Weinberg? Weinfeld? Hey, hey, don't *stare* at me like that!"

I had to work hard to make any sound at all. Finally I said, "What the hell do you want me to do, Fazio? I feel like I'm looking at a ghost."

He leaned close, and his eyes opened wider. I could practically count the concentric red rings, ten or fifteen of them, very fine lines. "I wish to Christ you were," he said quietly. Such unfathomable depths of pain, such searing intensity of hatred. I wanted to squirm away from him. But there was no way. He gave me a long slow crucifying inspection. Then he eased back and some of the menacing intensity seemed to go out of him. Almost jauntily he said, "We got a lot to talk about, Chollie. You know some quiet place around here we can go?"

"There's the gravity lounge—"

"Sure. The gravity lounge."

✦

We floated face-to-face, at half-pull. "You promised you'd kill me if I got nailed," Fazio murmured. "That was our deal. Why didn't you do it, Chollie? Why the fuck didn't you do it?"

I could hardly bear to look into his red-ringed eyes.

"Things happened too fast, man. How was I to know paramedics would be on the scene in five minutes?"

"Five minutes is plenty of time to put a heat bolt through a guy's chest."

"Less than five minutes. Three. Two. The paramedic floater was right overhead, man! It was covering us the whole while. They came down on us like a bunch of fucking *angels*, Fazio!"

"You had time."

"I thought they were going to be able to save you," I said lamely. "They got there so quickly."

Fazio laughed harshly. "They did try to save me," he said. "I'll give them credit for trying. Five minutes and I was on that floater and they were sending tracers all over me to clean the synsym goop out of my lungs and my heart and my liver."

"Sure. That was just what I figured they'd do."

"You promised to finish me off, Chollie, if I got nailed."

"But the paramedics were right *there*!"

"They worked on me like sonsabitches," he said. "They did everything. They can clean up the vital tissues, they can yank out your organs, synsym and all, and stick in transplants. But they can't get the stuff out of your brain, did you know that? The synsym goes straight up your nose into your brain and it slips its tendrils into your meninges and your neural glia and right into your fucking corpus callosum. And from there it goes everywhere. The cerebellum, the medulla, you name it. They can't send tracers into the brain that will clean out synsym and not damage brain tissue. And they can't pull out your brain and give you a new one, either. Thirty seconds after the synsym gets into your nose it reaches your brain and it's all over for you, no matter what kind of treatment you get. Didn't you hear them tell you that when we first got to the war zone? Didn't you hear all the horror stories?"

"I thought they were just horror stories," I said faintly.

He rocked back and forth gently in his gravity cradle. He didn't say anything.

"Do you want to tell me what it's like?" I asked after a while.

Fazio shrugged. As though from a great distance he said, "What it's like? Ah, it's not all that goddamned bad, Chollie. It's like having a roommate. Living with you in your head, forever, and you can't break the lease. That's all. Or like having an itch you can't scratch. Having it there is like finding yourself trapped in a space that's exactly one centimeter bigger than you are all around, and knowing that you're going to stay walled up in it for a million years." He looked off toward the great clear wall of the lounge, toward giant red Betelgeuse blazing outside far away. "Your synsym talks to you sometimes. So you're never lonely, you know? Doesn't speak any language you understand, just sits there and spouts gibberish. But at least it's company. Sometimes it makes *you* spout gibberish, especially when you badly need to make sense. It grabs control of the upper brain centers now and then, you know. And as for the autonomous centers, it does any damned thing it likes with them. Keys into the pain zones and runs little simulations for you—an amputation without anesthetic, say. Just for fun. *Its* fun. Or you're in bed with a woman and it disconnects your erection mechanism. Or it *gives* you an erection that won't go down for six weeks. For fun. It can get playful with your toilet training, too. I wear a diaper, Chollie, isn't that sweet? I have to. I get drunk sometimes without drinking. Or I drink myself sick without feeling a thing. And all the time I feel it there, tickling me. Like an ant crawling around within my skull. Like a worm up my nose. It's just like the other guys told us, when we came out to the war zone. Remember? 'Kill yourself fast, while you have the chance.' I never had the chance. I had you, Chollie, and we had a deal, but you didn't take our deal seriously. Why not, Chollie?"

I felt his eyes burning me. I looked away, halfway across the lounge, and caught sight of Elisandra's long golden hair drifting in free-float. She saw me at the same moment, and waved. We usually got together in here this time of night. I shook my head, trying to warn her off, but it was too late. She was already heading our way.

"Who's that?" Fazio asked. "Your girlfriend?"

"A friend."

"Nice," he said. He was staring at her as though he had never seen a woman before. "I noticed her last night, too. You live together?"

"We work the same shift on the wheel."

"Yeah. I saw you leave with her last night. And the night before."

"How long have you been at the Station, Fazio?"

"Week. Ten days, maybe."

"Came here looking for me?"

"Just wandering around," he said. "Fat disability pension, plenty of time. I go to a lot of places. That's a really nice woman, Chollie. You're a lucky guy." A tic was popping on his cheek and another was getting started on his lower lip. He said, "Why the fuck didn't you kill me when that thing first jumped me?"

"I told you. I couldn't. The paramedics were on the scene too fast."

"Right. You needed to say some Hail Marys first, and they just didn't give you enough time."

He was implacable. I had to strike back at him somehow or the guilt and shame would drive me crazy. Angrily I said, "What the hell do you want me to tell you, Fazio? That I'm sorry I didn't kill you ten years ago? Okay, I'm sorry. Does that do any good? Listen, if the synsym's as bad as you say, how come *you* haven't killed yourself? Why go on dragging yourself around with that thing inside your head?"

He shook his head and made a little muffled grunting sound. His face abruptly became gray, his lips were sagging. His eyeballs seemed to be spinning slowly in opposite directions. Just an illusion, I knew, but a scary one.

"Fazio?"

He said, "Chollallula lillalolla loolicholla. Billillolla."

I stared. He looked frightening. He looked hideous.

"Jesus, Fazio!"

Spittle dribbled down his chin. Muscles jumped and writhed crazily all over his face. "You see? You see?" he managed to blurt. There was warfare inside him. I watched him trying to regain command. It was like a man wrestling himself to a fall. I thought he was going to have a stroke. But then, suddenly, he seemed to grow calm. His breath was ragged, his skin was mottled with fiery blotches. He collapsed down into himself, head drooping, arms dangling. He looked altogether spent. Another minute or two passed before he could speak. I didn't know what to do for him. I floated there, watching. Finally, a little life seemed to return to him.

"Did you see? That's what happens," he gasped. "It takes control. How could I ever kill myself? It wouldn't let me do it."

"Wouldn't *let* you?"

He looked up at me and sighed wearily. "Think, Chollie, think! It's in symbiosis with me. We aren't independent organisms." Then the tremors began again, worse than before. Fazio made a desperate furious attempt to fight them off—arms and legs flung rigidly out, jaws working—but it was useless. "Illallomba!" he yelled. "Nullagribba!" He tossed his head from side to side as if trying to shake off something sticky that was clinging to it. "If I—then it—gillagilla! Holligoolla! I can't—I can't—oh—Jesus—Christ—!"

His voice died away into harsh sputters and clankings. He moaned and covered his face with his hands.

But now I understood.

For Fazio there could never be any escape. That was the most monstrous part of the whole thing, the ultimate horrifying twist. The symbiont knew that its destiny was linked to Fazio's. If he died, the symbiont would also; and so it could not allow its host to damage himself. From its seat in Fazio's brain it had ultimate control over his body. Whatever he tried—jump off a bridge, reach for a flask of poison, pick up a gun—the watchful thing in his mind would be a step ahead of him, always protecting him against harm.

A flood of compassion welled up in me and I started to put my hand comfortingly on Fazio's shoulder. But then I yanked it back as though I were afraid the symbiont could jump from his mind into mine at the slightest touch. And then I scowled and forced myself to touch him after all. He pulled away. He looked burned out.

"Chollie?" Elisandra said, coming up beside us. She floated alongside, long-limbed, beautiful, frowning. "Is this private, or can I join you?"

I hesitated, fumbling. I desperately wanted to keep Fazio and Elisandra in separate compartments of my life, but I saw that I had no way of doing that. "We were—well—just that—"

"Come on, Chollie," Fazio said in a bleak hollow voice. "Introduce your old war buddy to the nice woman."

Elisandra gave him an inquiring glance. She could not have failed to detect the strangeness in his tone.

I took a deep breath. "This is Fazio," I said. "We were in the Servadac campaign together during the Second Ovoid War. Fazio—Elisandra. Elisandra's a traffic-polarity engineer on the turnaround wheel—you ought to see her at work, the coolest cookie you can imagine—"

"An honor to meet you," said Fazio grandly. "A woman who combines such beauty and such technical skills—I have to say—I—I—" Suddenly he was faltering. His face turned blotchy. Fury blazed in his eyes. "No! Damn it, no! No more!" He clutched handfuls of air in some wild attempt at steadying himself. "Mullagalloola!" he cried, helpless. "Jillabongbong! Sampazozozo!" And he burst into wild choking sobs, while Elisandra stared at him in amazement and sorrow.

✦

"Well, are you going to kill him?" she asked.

It was two hours later. We had put Fazio to bed in his little cubicle over at Transient House, and she and I were in her room. I had told her everything.

I looked at her as though she had begun to babble the way Fazio had. Elisandra and I had been together almost a year, but there were times I felt I didn't know her at all.

"Well?" she said.

"Are you serious?"

"You owe it to him. You owe him a death, Chollie. He can't come right out and say it, because the symbiont won't allow him to. But that's what he wants from you."

I couldn't deny any of that. I'd been thinking the same thing for at least the past hour. The reality of it was inescapable: I had muffed things on Weinstein and sent Fazio to hell for ten years. Now I had to set him free.

"If there was only some way to get the symbiont out of his brain—"

"But there isn't."

"No," I said. "There isn't."

"You'll do it for him, won't you?"

"Quit it," I said.

"I hate the way he's suffering, Chollie."

"You think I don't?"

"And what about you? Suppose you fail him a second time. How will you live with that? Tell me how."

"I was never much for killing, Ellie. Not even Ovoids."

"We know that," she said. "But you don't have any choice this time."

I went to the little fireglobe she had mounted above the sleeping platform, and hit the button and sent sparks through the thick coiling mists. A rustle of angry colors swept the mist, a wild aurora, green, purple, yellow. After a moment I said quietly, "You're absolutely right."

"Good. I was afraid for a moment you were going to crap out on him again."

There was no malice in it, the way she said it. All the same, it hit me like a fist. I stood there nodding, letting the impact go rippling through me and away.

At last the reverberations seemed to die down within me. But then a great new uneasiness took hold of me and I said, "You know, it's totally idiotic of us to be discussing this. I'm involving you in something that's none of your business. What we're doing is making you an accomplice before the fact."

Elisandra ignored me. Something was in motion in her mind, and there was no swerving her now. "How would you go about it?" she asked. "You can't just cut someone's throat and dump him down a disposer chute."

"Look," I said, "do you understand that the penalty could be anything up to—"

She went on. "Any sort of direct physical assault is out. There'd be some sort of struggle for sure—the symbiont's bound to defend the host body against attack—you'd come away with scratches, bruises, worse. Somebody would notice. Suppose you got so badly hurt you had to go to the medics. What would you tell them? A barroom brawl? And then nobody can find your old friend Fazio who you were seen with a few days before? No, much too risky." Her tone was strangely businesslike, matter-of-fact. "And then, getting rid of the body— that's even tougher, Chollie, getting fifty kilos of body mass off the Station without some kind of papers. No destination visa, no transshipment entry. Even a sack of potatoes would have an out-invoice. But if someone just vanishes and there's a fifty-kilo short balance in the mass totals that day—"

"Quit it," I said. "Okay?"

"You owe him a death. You agreed about that."

"Maybe I do. But whatever I decide, I don't want to drag you into it. It isn't your mess, Ellie."

"You don't think so?" she shot right back at me.

Anger and love were all jumbled together in Elisandra's tone. I didn't feel like dealing with that just now. My head was pounding. I activated the pharmo arm by the sink and hastily ran a load of relaxants into myself with a subcute shot. Then I took her by the hand. Gently, trying hard to disengage, I said, "Can we just go to bed now? I'd rather not talk about this any more."

Elisandra smiled and nodded. "Sure," she replied, and her voice was much softer.

She started to pull off her clothes. But after a moment she turned to me, troubled. "I can't drop it just like that, Chollie. It's still buzzing inside me. That poor bastard." She shuddered. "Never to be alone in his own head. Never to be sure he has control over his own body. Waking up in a puddle of piss, he said. Speaking in tongues. All that other crazy stuff. What did he say? Like feeling an ant wandering around inside his skull? An itch you can't possibly scratch?"

"I didn't know it would be that bad," I said. "I think I would have killed him back then, if I had known."

"Why didn't you anyway?"

"He was Fazio. A human being. My friend. My buddy. I didn't much want to kill Ovoids, even. How the hell was I going to kill him?"

"But you promised to, Chollie."

"Let me be," I said. "I didn't do it, that's all. Now I have to live with that."

"So does he," said Elisandra.

I climbed into her sleeptube and lay there without moving, waiting for her.

"So do I," she added after a little while.

She wandered around the room for a time before joining me. Finally she lay down beside me, but at a slight distance. I didn't move toward her. But eventually the distance lessened, and I put my hand lightly on her shoulder, and she turned to me.

An hour or so before dawn she said, "I think I see a way we can do it."

We spent a week and a half working out the details. I was completely committed to it now, no hesitations, no reservations. As Elisandra said, I had no choice. This was what I owed Fazio; this was the only way I could settle accounts between us.

She was completely committed to it, too: even more so than I was, it sometimes seemed. I warned her that she was needlessly letting herself in for major trouble in case the Station authorities ever managed to reconstruct what had happened. It didn't seem needless to her, she said.

I didn't have a lot of contact with him while we were arranging things. It was important, I figured, not to give the symbiont any hints. I saw Fazio practically every day, of course—Betelgeuse Station isn't all that big—off at a distance, staring, glaring, sometimes having one of his weird fits, climbing a wall or shouting incoherently or arguing with himself out loud; but generally I pretended not to see him. At times I couldn't avoid him, and then we met for dinner or drinks or a workout in the rec room. But there wasn't much of that.

"Okay," Elisandra said finally. "I've done my part. Now you do yours, Chollie."

Among the little services we run here is a sightseeing operation for tourists who feel like taking a close look at a red giant star. After the big stellar-envelope research project shut down a few years ago we inherited a dozen or so solar sleds that had been used for skimming through the fringes of Betelgeuse's mantle, and we began renting them out for three-day excursions. The sleds are two-passenger jobs without much in the way of luxury and nothing at all in the way of propulsion systems. The trip is strictly ballistic: we calculate your orbit and shoot you out of here on the big repellers, sending you on a dazzling swing across Betelgeuse's outer fringes that gives you the complete light show and maybe a view of ten or twelve of the big star's family of planets. When the sled reaches the end of its string, we catch you on the turnaround wheel and reel you in. It sounds spectacular, and it is; it sounds dangerous, and it isn't. Not usually, anyhow.

I tracked Fazio down in the gravity lounge and said, "We've arranged a treat for you, man."

The sled I had rented for him was called the *Corona Queen*. Elisandra routinely handled the dispatching job for these tours, and now and then I worked as wheelman for them, although ordinarily I wheeled the big interstellar liners that used Betelgeuse Station as their jumping-off point for deeper space. We were both going to work Fazio's sled. Unfortunately, this time there was going to be a disaster, because a regrettable little error had been made in calculating orbital polarity, and then there would be a one-in-a-million failure of the redundancy circuits. Fazio's sled wasn't going to go on a tour of Betelgeuse's far-flung corona at all. It was going to plunge right into the heart of the giant red star.

I would have liked to tell him that, as we headed down the winding corridors to the dropdock. But I couldn't, because telling Fazio meant telling Fazio's symbiont also; and what was good news for Fazio was bad news for the symbiont. To catch the filthy thing by surprise: that was essential.

How much did Fazio suspect? God knows. In his place, I think I might have had an inkling. But maybe he was striving with all his strength to turn his mind away from any kind of speculation about the voyage he was about to take.

"You can't possibly imagine what it's like," I said. "It's unique. There's just no way to simulate it. And the view of Betelgeuse that you get from the Station isn't even remotely comparable."

"The sled glides through the corona on a film of vaporized carbon," said Elisandra. "The heat just rolls right off its surface." We were chattering compulsively, trying to fill every moment with talk. "You're completely shielded so that you can actually pass through the atmosphere of the star—"

"Of course," I said, "Betelgeuse is so big and so violent that you're more or less inside its atmosphere no matter where you are in its system—"

"And then there are the planets," Elisandra said. "The way things are lined up this week, you may be able to see as many as a dozen of them—"

"—Otello, Falstaff, Siegfried, maybe Wotan—"

"—You'll find a map on the ceiling of your cabin—"

"—Five gas giants twice the mass of Jupiter—keep your eye out for Wotan, that's the one with rings—"

"—and Isolde, you can't miss Isolde, she's even redder than Betelgeuse, the damndest bloodshot planet imaginable—"

"—with eleven red moons, too, but you won't be able to see them without filters—"

"—Otello and Falstaff for sure, and I think this week's chart shows Aida out of occultation now, too—"

"—and then there's the band of comets—"

"—the asteroids, that's where we think a couple of the planets collided after gravitational perturbation of—"

"—and the Einsteinian curvature, it's unmistakable—"

"—the big solar flares—"

"Here we are," Elisandra said.

We had reached the dropdock. Before us rose a gleaming metal wall. Elisandra activated the hatch and it swung back to reveal the little sled, a sleek tapering frog-nosed thing with a low hump in the middle. It sat on tracks; above it arched the coils of the repeller-launcher, radiating at the moment the blue-green glow that indicated a neutral charge. Everything was automatic. We had only to put Fazio on board and give the Station the signal for launch; the rest would be taken care of by the orbital-polarity program Elisandra had previously keyed in.

"It's going to be the trip of your life, man!" I said.

Fazio nodded. His eyes looked a little glazed, and his nostrils were flaring.

Elisandra hit the prelaunch control. The sled's roof opened and a recorded voice out of a speaker in the dropdock ceiling began to explain to Fazio how to get inside and make himself secure for launching. My hands were cold, my throat was dry. Yet I was very calm, all things considered. This was murder, wasn't it? Maybe so, technically speaking. But I was finding other names for it. A mercy killing; a balancing of the karmic accounts; a way of atoning for an ancient sin of omission. For him, release from hell after ten years; for me, release from a lesser but still acute kind of pain.

Fazio approached the sled's narrow entry slot.

"Wait a second," I said. I caught him by the arm. The account wasn't quite in balance yet.

"Chollie—" Elisandra said.

I shook her off. To Fazio I said, "There's one thing I need to tell you before you go."

He gave me a peculiar look, but didn't say anything.

I went on, "I've been claiming all along that I didn't shoot you when the synsym got you because there wasn't time, the medics landed too fast. That's sort of true, but mainly it's bullshit. I had time. What I didn't have was the guts."

"Chollie—" Elisandra said again. There was an edge on her voice.

"Just one more second," I told her. I turned to Fazio again. "I looked at you, I looked at the heat gun, I thought about the synsym. But I just couldn't do it. I stood there with the gun in my hand and I didn't do a thing. And then the medics landed and it was too late—I felt like such a shit, Fazio, such a cowardly shit—"

Fazio's face was turning blotchy. The red synsym lines blazed weirdly in his eyes.

"Get him into the sled!" Elisandra yelled. "It's taking control of him, Chollie!"

"Oligabongaboo!" Fazio said. "Ungabanoo! Flizz! Thrapp!"

And he came at me like a wild man.

I had him by thirty kilos, at least, but he damned near knocked me over. Somehow I managed to stay upright. He bounced off me and went reeling around, and Elisandra grabbed his arm. He kicked her hard and sent her flying, but then I wrapped my forearm around the throat from behind, and Elisandra, crawling across the floor, got him around his legs so we could lift him and stuff him into the sled. Even then we had trouble holding him. Two of us against one skinny burned-out ruined man, and he writhed and twisted and wriggled about like something diabolical. He scratched, he kicked, he elbowed, he spat. His eyes were fiery. Every time we forced him close to the entryway of the sled he dragged us back away from it. Elisandra and I were grunting and winded, and I didn't think we could hang on much longer. This wasn't Fazio we were doing battle with, it was a synthetic symbiont out of the Ovoid labs, furiously trying to save itself from a fiery death. God knows what alien hormones it was pumping into Fazio's bloodstream. God knows how it had rebuilt his bones and heart and lungs for greater efficiency. If he ever managed to break free of my grip, I wondered which of us would get out of the dropdock alive.

But all the same, Fazio still needed to breathe. I tightened my hold on his throat and felt cartilage yielding. I didn't care. I just wanted to get him on that sled, dead or alive, give him some peace at all. Him and me both. Tighter— tighter—

Fazio made rough sputtering noises, and then a thick nasty gargling sound.

"You've got him," Elisandra said.

"Yeah. Yeah."

I clamped down one notch tighter yet, and Fazio began to go limp, though his muscles still spasmed and jerked frantically. The creature within him was still full of fight; but there wasn't much air getting into Fazio's lungs now and his brain was starving for oxygen. Slowly Elisandra and I shoved him the last five meters toward the sled—lifted him, pushed him up to the edge of the slot, started to jam him into it—

A convulsion wilder than anything that had gone before ripped through Fazio's body. He twisted half around in my grasp until he was face-to-face with Elisandra, and a bubble of something gray and shiny appeared on his lips. For an instant everything seemed frozen. It was like a slice across time, for just that instant. Then things began to move again. The bubble burst; some fragment of tissue leaped the short gap from Fazio's lips to Elisandra's. The symbiont, facing death, had cast forth a piece of its own life-stuff to find another host. *"Chollie!"* Elisandra wailed, and let go of Fazio and went reeling away as if someone had thrown acid in her eyes. She was clawing at her face. At the little flat gray slippery thing that had plastered itself over her mouth and was rapidly poking a couple of glistening pseudopods up into her nostrils. I hadn't known it was possible for a symbiont to send out offshoots like that. I guess no one did, or people like Fazio wouldn't be allowed to walk around loose.

I wanted to yell and scream and break things. I wanted to cry. But I didn't do any of those things.

When I was four years old, growing up on Backgammon, my father bought me a shiny little vortex boat from a peddler on Maelstrom Bridge. It was just a toy, a bathtub boat, though it had all the stabilizer struts and outriggers in miniature. We were standing on the bridge and I wanted to see how well the boat worked, so I flipped it over the rail into the vortex. Of course, it was swept out of sight at once. Bewildered and upset because it didn't come back to me, I looked toward my father for help. But he thought I had flung his gift into the whirlpool for the sheer hell of it, and he gave me a shriveling look of black anger and downright hatred that I will never forget. I cried half a day, but that didn't bring back my vortex boat. I wanted to cry now. Sure. Something grotesquely unfair had happened, and I felt four years old all over again, and there was nobody to turn to for help. I was on my own.

I went to Elisandra and held her for a moment. She was sobbing and trying to speak, but the thing covered her lips. Her face was white with terror and her whole body was trembling and jerking crazily.

"Don't worry," I whispered. "This time I know what to do."

How fast we act, when finally we move. I got Fazio out of the way first, tossing him or the husk of him into the entry slot of the *Corona Queen* as easily as though he had been an armload of straw. Then I picked up Elisandra and carried her to the sled. She didn't really struggle, just twisted about a little. The symbiont didn't have that much control yet. At the last moment I looked into her eyes, hoping I wasn't going to see the red circles in them. No, not yet, not so soon. Her eyes were the eyes I remembered, the eyes I loved. They were steady, cold, clear. She knew what was happening. She couldn't speak, but she was telling me with her eyes: *Yes, yes, go ahead, for Christ's sake go ahead, Chollie!*

Unfair. Unfair. But nothing is ever fair, I thought. Or else if there is justice in the universe it exists only on levels we can't perceive, in some chilly macrocosmic place where everything is evened out in the long run but the sin is not necessarily atoned by the sinner. I pushed her into the slot down next to Fazio and slammed the sled shut. And went to the dropdock's wall console and keyed in the departure signal, and watched as the sled went sliding down the track toward the exit hatch on its one-way journey to Betelgeuse. The red light of the activated repellers glared for a moment, and then the blue-green re-turned. I turned away, wondering if the symbiont had managed to get a piece of itself into me, too, at the last moment. I waited to feel that tickle in the mind. But I didn't. I guess there hadn't been time for it to get us both.

And then, finally, I dropped down on the launching track and let myself cry. And went out of there, after a while, silent, numb, purged clean, thinking of nothing at all. At the inquest six weeks later I told them I didn't have the slightest notion why Elisandra had chosen to get aboard that ship with Fazio. Was it a suicide pact, the inquest panel asked me? I shrugged. I don't know, I said. I don't have any goddamned idea what was going on in their minds that day, I said. Silent, numb, purged clean, thinking of nothing at all.

So Fazio rests at last in the blazing heart of Betelgeuse. My Elisandra is in there also. And I go on, day after day, still working the turnaround wheel here at the Station, reeling in the stargoing ships that come cruising past the fringes of the giant red sun. I still feel haunted, too. But it isn't Fazio's ghost that visits me now, or even Elisandra's—not now, not after all this time. I think the ghost that haunts me is my own.

S A I L I N G   T O

B Y Z A N T I U M

We've reached the spring of 1984. A few months earlier I had completed my historical/fantasy novel Gilgamesh the King, which is set in ancient Sumer, and antiquity was still very much on my mind when Shawna McCarthy, who had just begun her brief and brilliant career as editor of Isaac Asimov's Science Fiction Magazine, came to the San Francisco area on holiday. I ran into her at a party, and she asked me if I'd write a story for her. "I'd like to, yes," I said. "A long one."

"How long?"

"Long," I told her. "A novella."

"Good," she said. We did a little haggling over the price, and that was that. She went back to New York and I got going on "Sailing to Byzantium," and by late summer it was done.

Though I had forgotten it until recently, "Sailing to Byzantium" wasn't called that originally. A few months ago, going through some old papers, I came upon a manila envelope on which I had jotted the kernel of the idea out of which "Sailing to Byzantium" grew. My working title was "The Hundred-Gated City," a reference to ancient Thebes, and this was what I had in mind:

"Ancient Egypt has been re-created at the end of time, along with various other highlights of history—a sort of Disneyland. A twentieth-century man, through error, has been regenerated in Thebes, though he belongs in the replica of Los Angeles. The misplaced Egyptian has been sent to Troy, or maybe Knossos, and a Cretan has been displaced into a Brasilia-equivalent of the twenty-ninth century. They move about, attempting to return to their proper places."

It's a nice idea, but it's not quite the story I ultimately wrote. (Maybe I'll use it someday—waste not, want not.) "Sailing to Byzantium" is what emerged instead, and from the earliest pages I knew I was onto something special. Shawna had one or two small editorial suggestions for clarifying *the ending, which I accepted gladly, and my friend Shay Barsabe, who read the story in manuscript, pointed out one subtle blunder in the plot that I hastily corrected.*

The story was published as an elegant limited-edition book by the house of Underwood-Miller, and soon afterward it appeared in the Asimov's issue for February 1985. It was immediately popular, and all three of the year's-best-s-f anthologists chose it for that year's volume. "A possible classic," is what Wollheim called it, praise that I shamelessly quote here because Don Wollheim, who had been pondering the mysteries of science fiction longer than I've been alive, was not one to throw such words around lightly, and I was delighted by his comment. "Sailing to Byzantium" won me a Nebula award, too, and was nominated for a Hugo, but finished in second place, losing by four votes out of 800. Since then it's been reprinted several more times and translated into many languages. It's one of my own all-time favorites among my stories.

At dawn he arose and stepped out onto the patio for his first look at Alexandria, the one city he had not yet seen. That year the five cities were Chang-an, Asgard, New Chicago, Timbuctoo, Alexandria: the usual mix of eras, cultures, realities. He and Gioia, making the long flight from Asgard in the distant north the night before, had arrived late, well after sundown, and had gone straight to bed. Now, by the gentle apricot-hued morning light, the fierce spires and battlements of Asgard seemed merely something he had dreamed.

The rumor was that Asgard's moment was finished anyway. In a little while, he had heard, they were going to tear it down and replace it, elsewhere, with Mohenjo-daro. Though there were never more than five cities, they changed constantly. He could remember a time when they had had Rome of the Caesars instead of Chang-an, and Rio de Janeiro rather than Alexandria. These people saw no point in keeping anything very long.

It was not easy for him to adjust to the sultry intensity of Alexandria after the frozen splendors of Asgard. The wind, coming off the water, was brisk and torrid both at once. Soft turquoise wavelets lapped at the jetties. Strong presences assailed his senses: the hot heavy sky, the stinging scent of the red lowland sand borne on the breeze, the sullen swampy aroma of the nearby sea.

Everything trembled and glimmered in the early light. Their hotel was beautifully situated, high on the northern slope of the huge artificial mound known as the Paneium that was sacred to the goat-footed god. From here they had a total view of the city: the wide noble boulevards, the soaring obelisks and monuments, the palace of Hadrian just below the hill, the stately and awesome Library, the temple of Poseidon, the teeming marketplace, the royal lodge that Marc Antony had built after his defeat at Actium. And of course the Lighthouse, the wondrous many-windowed Lighthouse, the seventh wonder of the world, that immense pile of marble and limestone and reddish-purple Aswan granite rising in majesty at the end of its mile-long causeway. Black smoke from the beacon fire at its summit curled lazily into the sky. The city was awakening. Some temporaries in short white kilts appeared and began to trim the dense dark hedges that bordered the great public buildings. A few citizens wearing loose robes of vaguely Grecian style were strolling in the streets.

There were ghosts and chimeras and phantasies everywhere about. Two slim elegant centaurs, a male and a female, grazed on the hillside. A burly thick-thighed swordsman appeared on the porch of the temple of Poseidon holding a Gorgon's severed head and waved it in a wide arc, grinning broadly. In the street below the hotel gate three small pink sphinxes, no bigger than housecats, stretched and yawned and began to prowl the curbside. A larger one, lion-sized, watched warily from an alleyway: their mother, surely. Even at this distance he could hear her loud purring.

Shading his eyes, he peered far out past the Lighthouse and across the water. He hoped to see the dim shores of Crete or Cyprus to the north, or perhaps the great dark curve of Anatolia. *Carry me toward that great Byzantium*, he thought. *Where all is ancient, singing at the oars.* But he beheld only the endless empty sea, sun-bright and blinding though the morning was just beginning. Nothing was ever where he expected it to be. The continents did not seem to be in their proper places any longer. Gioia, taking him aloft long ago in her little flitterflitter, had shown him that. The tip of South America was canted far out into the Pacific; Africa was weirdly foreshortened; a broad tongue of ocean separated Europe and Asia. Australia did not appear to exist at all. Perhaps they had dug it up and used it for other things. There was no trace of the world he once had known. This was the fiftieth century. "The fiftieth century after *what?*" he had asked several times, but no one seemed to know, or else they did not care to say.

"Is Alexandria very beautiful?" Gioia called from within.

"Come out and see."

Naked and sleepy-looking, she padded out onto the white-tiled patio and nestled up beside him. She fit neatly under his arm. "Oh, yes, yes!" she said softly. "So very beautiful, isn't it? Look, there, the palaces, the Library, the Lighthouse! Where will we go first? The Lighthouse, I think. Yes? And then the marketplace—I want to see the Egyptian magicians—and the stadium, the races—will they be having races today, do you think? Oh, Charles, I want to see everything!"

"Everything? All on the first day?"

"All on the first day, yes," she said. "Everything."

"But we have plenty of time, Gioia."

"Do we?"

He smiled and drew her tight against his side.

"Time enough," he said gently.

He loved her for her impatience, for her bright bubbling eagerness. Gioia was not much like the rest in that regard, though she seemed identical in all other ways. She was short, supple, slender, dark-eyed, olive-skinned, narrow-hipped, with wide shoulders and flat muscles. They were all like that, each one indistinguishable from the rest, like a horde of millions of brothers and sisters—a world of small lithe childlike Mediterraneans, built for juggling, for bull-dancing, for sweet white wine at midday and rough red wine at night. They had the same slim bodies, the same broad mouths, the same great glossy eyes. He had never seen anyone who appeared to be younger than twelve or older than twenty. Gioia was somehow a little different, although he did not quite know how; but he knew that it was for that imperceptible but significant difference that he loved her. And probably that was why she loved him also.

He let his gaze drift from west to east, from the Gate of the Moon down broad Canopus Street and out to the harbor, and off to the tomb of Cleopatra at the tip of long slender Cape Lochias. Everything was here and all of it perfect, the obelisks, the statues and marble colonnades, the courtyards and shrines and groves, great Alexander himself in his coffin of crystal and gold: a splendid gleaming pagan city. But there were oddities—an unmistakable mosque near the public gardens, and what seemed to be a Christian church not far from the Library. And those ships in the harbor, with all those red sails and bristling masts—surely they were medieval, and late medieval at that. He had seen such anachronisms in other places before. Doubtless these people found them amusing. Life was a game for them. They played at it unceasingly. Rome, Alexandria, Timbuctoo—why not? Create an Asgard of translucent bridges and shimmering ice-girt palaces, then grow weary of it and take it away? Replace it with Mohenjo-daro? Why not? It seemed to him a great pity to destroy those lofty Nordic feasting halls for the sake of building a squat brutal sun-baked city of brown brick; but these people did not look at things the way he did. Their cities were only temporary. Someone in Asgard had said that

Timbuctoo would be the next to go, with Byzantium rising in its place. Well, why not? Why not? They could have anything they liked. This was the fiftieth century, after all. The only rule was that there could be no more than five cities at once. "Limits," Gioia had informed him solemnly when they first began to travel together, "are very important." But she did not know why, or did not care to say.

He stared out once more toward the sea.

He imagined a newborn city congealing suddenly out of mists, far across the water: shining towers, great domed palaces, golden mosaics. That would be no great effort for them. They could just summon it forth whole out of time, the Emperor on his throne and the Emperor's drunken soldiery roistering in the streets, the brazen clangor of the cathedral gong rolling through the Grand Bazaar, dolphins leaping beyond the shoreside pavilions. Why not? They had Timbuctoo. They had Alexandria. Do you crave Constantinople? Then behold Constantinople! Or Avalon, or Lyonesse, or Atlantis. They could have anything they liked. It is pure Schopenhauer here: the world as will and imagination. Yes! These slender dark-eyed people journeying tirelessly from miracle to miracle. Why not Byzantium next? Yes! Why not? *That is no country for old men*, he thought. *The young in one another's arms, the birds in the trees*—yes! Yes! Anything they liked. They even had him. Suddenly he felt frightened. Questions he had not asked for a long time burst through into his consciousness. *Who am I? Why am I here? Who is this woman beside me?*

"You're so quiet all of a sudden, Charles," said Gioia, who could not abide silence for very long. "Will you talk to me? I want you to talk to me. Tell me what you're looking for out there."

He shrugged. "Nothing."

"Nothing?"

"Nothing in particular."

"I could see you seeing something."

"Byzantium," he said. "I was imagining that I could look straight across the water to Byzantium. I was trying to get a glimpse of the walls of Constantinople."

"Oh, but you wouldn't be able to see as far as that from here. Not really."

"I know."

"And anyway Byzantium doesn't exist."

"Not yet. But it will. Its time comes later on."

"Does it?" she said. "Do you know that for a fact?"

"On good authority. I heard it in Asgard," he told her. "But even if I hadn't, Byzantium would be inevitable, don't you think? Its time would have to come. How could we not do Byzantium, Gioia? We certainly will do Byzantium, sooner or later. I know we will. It's only a matter of time. And we have all the time in the world."

A shadow crossed her face. "Do we? Do we?"

❤

He knew very little about himself, but he knew that he was not one of them. That he knew. He knew that his name was Charles Phillips and that before he had come to live among these people he had lived in the year 1984, when there had been such things as computers and television sets and baseball and jet planes, and the world was full of cities, not merely five but thousands of them, New York and London and Johannesburg and Paris and Liverpool and Bangkok and San Francisco and Buenos Aires and a multitude of others, all at the same time. There had been four and a half billion people in the world then; now he doubted that there were as many as four and a half million. Nearly everything had changed beyond comprehension. The moon still seemed the same, and the sun; but at night he searched in vain for familiar constellations. He had no idea how they had brought him from then to now, or why. It did no good to ask. No one had any answers for him; no one so much as appeared to understand what it was that he was trying to learn. After a time he had stopped asking; after a time he had almost entirely ceased wanting to know.

He and Gioia were climbing the Lighthouse. She scampered ahead, in a hurry as always, and he came along behind her in his more stolid fashion. Scores of other tourists, mostly in groups of two or three, were making their way up the wide flagstone ramps, laughing, calling to one another. Some of them, seeing him, stopped a moment, stared, pointed. He was used to that. He was so much taller than any of them; he was plainly not one of them. When they pointed at him he smiled. Sometimes he nodded a little acknowledgment.

He could not find much of interest in the lowest level, a massive square structure two hundred feet high built of huge marble blocks: within its cool musty arcades were hundreds of small dark rooms, the offices of the Lighthouse's keepers and mechanics, the barracks of the garrison, the stables for the three hundred donkeys that carried the fuel to the lantern far above. None of that appeared inviting to him. He forged onward without halting until he emerged on the balcony that led to the next level. Here the Lighthouse grew narrower and became octagonal: its face, granite now and handsomely fluted, rose in a stunning sweep above him.

Gioia was waiting for him there. "This is for you," she said, holding out a nugget of meat on a wooden skewer. "Roast lamb. Absolutely delicious. I had one while I was waiting for you." She gave him a cup of some cool green sherbet also, and darted off to buy a pomegranate. Dozens of temporaries were roaming the balcony, selling refreshments of all kinds.

He nibbled at the meat. It was charred outside, nicely pink and moist within. While he ate, one of the temporaries came up to him and peered blandly into his face. It was a stocky swarthy male wearing nothing but a strip of red and yellow cloth about its waist. "I sell meat," it said. "Very fine roast lamb, only five drachmas."

Phillips indicated the piece he was eating. "I already have some," he said.

"It is excellent meat, very tender. It has been soaked for three days in the juices of—"

"Please," Phillips said. "I don't want to buy any meat. Do you mind moving along?"

The temporaries had confused and baffled him at first, and there was still much about them that was unclear to him. They were not machines—they looked like creatures of flesh and blood—but they did not seem to be human beings, either, and no one treated them as if they were. He supposed they were artificial constructs, products of a technology so consummate that it was invisible. Some appeared to be more intelligent than others, but all of them behaved as if they had no more autonomy than characters in a play, which was essentially what they were. There were untold numbers of them in each of the five cities, playing all manner of roles: shepherds and swineherds, street-sweepers, merchants, boatmen, vendors of grilled meats and cool drinks, hagglers in the marketplace, schoolchildren, charioteers, policemen, grooms, gladiators, monks, artisans, whores and cutpurses, sailors—whatever was needed to sustain the illusion of a thriving, populous urban center. The dark-eyed people, Gioia's people, never performed work. There were not enough of them to keep a city's functions going, and in any case they were strictly tourists, wandering with the wind, moving from city to city as the whim took them, Chang-an to New Chicago, New Chicago to Timbuctoo, Timbuctoo to Asgard, Asgard to Alexandria, onward, ever onward.

The temporary would not leave him alone. Phillips walked away and it followed him, cornering him against the balcony wall. When Gioia returned a few minutes later, lips prettily stained with pomegranate juice, the temporary was still hovering about him, trying with lunatic persistence to sell him a skewer of lamb. It stood much too close to him, almost nose to nose, great sad cowlike eyes peering intently into his as it extolled with mournful mooing urgency the quality of its wares. It seemed to him that he had had trouble like this with temporaries on one or two earlier occasions. Gioia touched the creature's elbow lightly and said, in a short sharp tone Phillips had never heard her use before, "He isn't interested. Get away from him." It went at once. To Phillips she said, "You have to be firm with them."

"I was trying. It wouldn't listen to me."

"You ordered it to go away, and it refused?"

"I asked it to go away. Politely. Too politely, maybe."

"Even so," she said. "It should have obeyed a human, regardless."

"Maybe it didn't think I was human," Phillips suggested. "Because of the way I look. My height, the color of my eyes. It might have thought I was some kind of temporary myself."

"No," Gioia said, frowning. "A temporary won't solicit another temporary. But it won't ever disobey a citizen, either. There's a very clear boundary. There isn't ever any confusion. I can't understand why it went on bothering you." He was surprised at how troubled she seemed: far more so, he thought, than the incident warranted. A stupid device, perhaps miscalibrated in some way, overenthusiastically pushing its wares—what of it? What of it? Gioia, after a moment, appeared to come to the same conclusion. Shrugging, she said, "It's defective, I suppose. Probably such things are more common than we suspect, don't you think?" There was something forced about her tone that bothered him. She smiled and handed him her pomegranate. "Here. Have a bite, Charles. It's wonderfully sweet. They used to be extinct, you know. Shall we go on upward?"

◆

The octagonal midsection of the Lighthouse must have been several hundred feet in height, a grim claustrophobic tube almost entirely filled by the two broad spiraling ramps that wound around the huge building's central well. The ascent was slow: a donkey team was a little way ahead of them on the ramp, plodding along laden with bundles of kindling for the lantern. But at last, just as Phillips was growing winded and dizzy, he and Gioia came out onto the second balcony, the one marking the transition between the octagonal section and the Lighthouse's uppermost story, which was cylindrical and very slender.

She leaned far out over the balustrade. "Oh, Charles, look at the view! Look at it!"

It was amazing. From one side they could see the entire city, and swampy Lake Mareotis and the dusty Egyptian plain beyond it, and from the other they peered far out into the gray and choppy Mediterranean. He gestured toward the innumerable reefs and shallows that infested the waters leading to the harbor entrance. "No wonder they needed a lighthouse here," he said. "Without some kind of gigantic landmark they'd never have found their way in from the open sea."

A blast of sound, a ferocious snort, erupted just above him. He looked up, startled. Immense statues of trumpet-wielding Tritons jutted from the corners of the Lighthouse at this level; that great blurting sound had come from the nearest of them. A signal, he thought. A warning to the ships negotiating that troubled passage. The sound was produced by some kind of steam-powered mechanism, he realized, operated by teams of sweating temporaries clustered about bonfires at the base of each Triton.

Once again he found himself swept by admiration for the clever way these people carried out their reproductions of antiquity. Or *were* they reproductions, he wondered? He still did not understand how they brought their cities into being. For all he knew, this place was the authentic Alexandria itself, pulled forward out of its proper time just as he himself had been. Perhaps this was the true and original Lighthouse, and not a copy. He had no idea which was the case, nor which would be the greater miracle.

"How do we get to the top?" Gioia asked.

"Over there, I think. That doorway."

The spiraling donkey-ramps ended here. The loads of lantern fuel went higher via a dumbwaiter in the central shaft. Visitors continued by way of a cramped staircase, so narrow at its upper end that it was impossible to turn around while climbing. Gioia, tireless, sprinted ahead. He clung to the rail and labored up and up, keeping count of the tiny window slits to ease the boredom of the ascent. The count was nearing a hundred when finally he stumbled into the vestibule of the beacon chamber. A dozen or so visitors were crowded into it. Gioia was at the far side, by the wall that was open to the sea.

It seemed to him he could feel the building swaying in the winds up here. How high were they? Five hundred feet, six hundred, seven? The beacon chamber was tall and narrow, divided by a catwalk into upper and lower sections. Down below, relays of temporaries carried wood from the dumbwaiter and tossed it on the blazing fire. He felt its intense heat from where he stood, at the rim of the platform on which the giant mirror of polished metal was hung. Tongues of flame leaped upward and danced before the mirror, which hurled its dazzling beam far out to sea. Smoke rose through a vent. At the very top was a colossal statue of Poseidon, austere, ferocious, looming above the lantern.

Gioia sidled along the catwalk until she was at his side. "The guide was talking before you came," she said, pointing. "Do you see that place over there, under the mirror? Someone standing there and looking into the mirror gets a view of ships at sea that can't be seen from here by the naked eye. The mirror magnifies things."

"Do you believe that?"

She nodded toward the guide. "It said so. And it also told us that if you look in a certain way, you can see right across the water into the city of Constantinople."

She is like a child, he thought. They all are. He said, "You told me yourself this very morning that it isn't possible to see that far. Besides, Constantinople doesn't exist right now."

"It will," she replied. "*You* said that to me, this very morning. And when it does, it'll be reflected in the Lighthouse mirror. That's the truth. I'm absolutely certain of it." She swung about abruptly toward the entrance of the beacon chamber. "Oh, look, Charles! Here come Nissandra and Aramayne! And there's Hawk! There's Stengard!" Gioia laughed and waved and called out names. "Oh, everyone's here! *Everyone!*"

They came jostling into the room, so many newcomers that some of those who had been there were forced to scramble down the steps on the far side. Gioia moved among them, hugging, kissing. Phillips could scarcely tell one from another—it was hard for him even to tell which were the men and which the women, dressed as they all were in the same sort of loose robes—but he recognized some of the names. These were her special friends, her set, with whom she had journeyed from city to city on an endless round of gaiety in the old days before he had come into her life. He had met a few of them before, in Asgard, in Rio, in Rome. The beacon-chamber guide, a squat wide-shouldered old temporary wearing a laurel wreath on its bald head, reappeared and began its potted speech, but no one listened to it; they were all too busy greeting one another, embracing, giggling. Some of them edged their way over to Phillips and reached up, standing on tiptoes, to touch their fingertips to his cheek in that odd hello of theirs. "Charles," they said gravely, making two syllables out of the name, as these people often did. "So good to see you again. Such a pleasure. You and Gioia—such a handsome couple. So well suited to each other."

Was that so? He supposed it was.

The chamber hummed with chatter. The guide could not be heard at all. Stengard and Nissandra had visited New Chicago for the water-dancing—Aramayne bore tales of a feast in Chang-an that had gone on for *days*—Hawk and Hekna had been to Timbuctoo to see the arrival of the salt caravan, and were going back there soon—a final party soon to celebrate the end of Asgard that absolutely should not be missed—the plans for the new city, Mohenjo-daro—we have reservations for the opening, we wouldn't pass it up for anything—and, yes, they were definitely going to do Constantinople after that, the planners were already deep into their Byzantium research—so good to see you, you look so beautiful all the time—have you been to the Library yet? The zoo? To the temple of Serapis?—

To Phillips they said, "What do you think of our Alexandria, Charles? Of course, you must have known it well in your day. Does it look the way you remember it?" They were always asking things like that. They did not seem to comprehend that the Alexandria of the Lighthouse and the Library was long lost and legendary by the time his twentieth century had been. To them, he suspected, all the places they had brought back into existence were more or less contemporary. Rome of the Caesars, Alexandria of the Ptolemies, Venice of the Doges, Chang-an of the T'angs, Asgard of the Aesir, none any less real than the next nor any less unreal, each one simply a facet of the distant past, the fantastic immemorial past, a plum plucked from that dark backward abysm of time. They had no contexts for separating one era from another. To them all the past was one borderless timeless realm. Why, then, should he not have seen the Lighthouse before, he who had leaped into this era from the New York of 1984? He had never been able to explain it to them. Julius Caesar and Hannibal, Helen of Troy and Charlemagne, Rome of the gladiators and New York of the Yankees and Mets, Gilgamesh and Tristan and Othello and Robin Hood and George Washington and Queen Victoria—to them, all equally real and unreal, none of them any more than bright figures moving about on a painted canvas. The past, the past, the elusive and fluid past—to them it was a single place of infinite accessibility and infinite connectivity. Of course, they would think he had seen the Lighthouse before. He knew better than to try again to explain things. "No," he said simply. "This is my first time in Alexandria."

They stayed there all winter long, and possibly some of the spring. Alexandria was not a place where one was sharply aware of the change of seasons, nor did the passage of time itself make itself very evident when one was living one's entire life as a tourist.

During the day there was always something new to see. The zoological garden, for instance: a wondrous park, miraculously green and lush in this hot dry climate, where astounding animals roamed in enclosures so generous that they did not seem like enclosures at all. Here were camels, rhinoceroses, gazelles, ostriches, lions, wild asses; and here, too, casually adjacent to those familiar African beasts, were hippogriffs, unicorns, basilisks, and fire-snorting dragons with rainbow scales. Had the original zoo of Alexandria had dragons and unicorns? Phillips doubted it. But this one did; evidently it was no harder for the backstage craftsmen to manufacture mythic beasts than it was for them to turn out camels and gazelles. To Gioia and her friends all of them were equally mythical, anyway. They were just as awed by the rhinoceros as by the hippogriff. One was no more strange—or any less—than the other. So far as Phillips had been able to discover, none of the mammals or birds of his era had survived into this one except for a few cats and dogs, though many had been reconstructed.

And then the Library! All those lost treasures, reclaimed from the jaws of time! Stupendous columned marble walls, airy high-vaulted reading rooms, dark coiling stacks stretching away to infinity. The ivory handles of seven hundred thousand papyrus scrolls bristling on the shelves. Scholars and librarians gliding quietly about, smiling faint scholarly smiles but plainly preoccupied with serious matters of the mind. They were all temporaries, Phillips realized. Mere props, part of the illusion. But were the scrolls illusions, too? "Here we have the complete dramas of Sophocles," said the guide with a blithe wave of its hand, indicating shelf upon shelf of texts. Only seven of his hundred twenty-three plays had survived the successive burnings of the library in ancient times by Romans, Christians, Arabs: were the lost ones here, the *Triptolemus*, the *Nausicaa*, the *Jason*, and all the rest? And would he find here, too, miraculously restored to being, the other vanished treasures of ancient literature—the memoirs of Odysseus, Cato's history of Rome, Thucydides' life of Pericles, the missing volumes of Livy? But when he asked if he might explore the stacks, the guide smiled apologetically and said that all the librarians were busy just now. Another time, perhaps? Perhaps, said the guide. It made no difference, Phillips decided. Even if these people somehow had brought back those lost masterpieces of antiquity, how would he read them? He knew no Greek.

The life of the city buzzed and throbbed about him. It was a dazzlingly beautiful place: the vast bay thick with sails, the great avenues running rigidly east-west, north-south, the sunlight rebounding almost audibly from the bright walls of the palaces of kings and gods. They have done this very well, Phillips thought: very well indeed. In the marketplace hard-eyed traders squabbled in half a dozen mysterious languages over the price of ebony, Arabian incense, jade, panther skins. Gioia bought a dram of pale musky Egyptian perfume in a delicate tapering glass flask. Magicians and jugglers and scribes called out stridently to passersby, begging for a few moments of attention and a handful of coins for their labor. Strapping slaves, black and tawny and some that might have been Chinese, were put up for auction, made to flex their muscles, to bare their teeth, to bare their breasts and thighs to prospective buyers. In the gymnasium naked athletes hurled javelins and discuses, and wrestled with terrifying zeal. Gioia's friend Stengard came rushing up with a gift for her, a golden necklace that would not have embarrassed Cleopatra. An hour later she had lost it, or perhaps had given it away while Phillips was looking elsewhere. She bought another, even finer, the next day.

Anyone could have all the money he wanted, simply by asking: it was as easy to come by as air for these people.

Being here was much like going to the movies, Phillips told himself. A different show every day: not much plot, but the special effects were magnificent and the detail work could hardly have been surpassed. A megamovie, a vast entertainment that went on all the time and was being played out by the whole population of Earth. And it was all so effortless, so spontaneous: just as when he had gone to a movie he had never troubled to think about the myriad technicians behind the scenes, the cameramen and the costume designers and the set builders and the electricians and the model makers and the boom operators, so, too, here he chose not to question the means by which Alexandria had been set before him. It felt real. It *was* real. When he drank the strong red wine it gave him a pleasant buzz. If he leaped from the beacon chamber of the Lighthouse he suspected he would die, though perhaps he would not stay dead for long: doubtless they had some way of restoring him as often as was necessary. Death did not seem to be a factor in these people's lives.

By day they saw sights. By night he and Gioia went to parties, in their hotel, in seaside villas, in the palaces of the high nobility. The usual people were there all the time, Hawk and Hekna, Aramayne, Stengard and Shelimir, Nissandra, Asoka, Afonso, Protay. At the parties there were five or ten temporaries for every citizen, some as mere servants, others as entertainers or even surrogate guests, mingling freely and a little daringly. But everyone knew, all the time, who was a citizen and who just a temporary. Phillips began to think his own status lay somewhere between. Certainly they treated him with a courtesy that no one ever would give a temporary, and yet there was a condescension to their manner that told him not simply that he was not one of them but that he was someone or something of an altogether different order of existence. That he was Gioia's lover gave him some standing in their eyes, but not a great deal: obviously he was always going to be an outsider, a primitive, ancient and quaint. For that matter he noticed that Gioia herself, though unquestionably a member of the set, seemed to be regarded as something of an outsider, like a tradesman's great-granddaughter in a gathering of Plantagenets. She did not always find out about the best parties in time to attend; her friends did not always reciprocate her effusive greetings with the same degree of warmth; sometimes he noticed her straining to hear some bit of gossip that was not quite being shared with her. Was it because she had taken him for her lover? Or was it the other way around: that she had chosen to be his lover precisely because she was *not* a full member of their caste?

Being a primitive gave him, at least, something to talk about at their parties. "Tell us about war," they said. "Tell us about elections. About money.

About disease." They wanted to know everything, though they did not seem to pay close attention: their eyes were quick to glaze. Still, they asked. He described traffic jams to them, and politics, and deodorants, and vitamin pills. He told them about cigarettes, newspapers, subways, telephone directories, credit cards, and basketball. "Which was your city?" they asked. New York, he told them. "And when was it? The seventh century, did you say?" The twentieth, he told them. They exchanged glances and nodded. "We will have to do it," they said. "The World Trade Center, the Empire State Building, the Citicorp Center, the Cathedral of St. John the Divine: how fascinating! Yankee Stadium. The Verrazano Bridge. We will do it all. But first must come Mohenjo-daro. And then, I think, Constantinople. Did your city have many people?" Seven million, he said. Just in the five boroughs alone. They nodded, smiling amiably, unfazed by the number. Seven million, seventy million—it was all the same to them, he sensed. They would just bring forth the temporaries in whatever quantity was required. He wondered how well they would carry the job off. He was no real judge of Alexandrias and Asgards, after all. Here they could have unicorns and hippogriffs in the zoo, and live sphinxes prowling in the gutters, and it did not trouble him. Their fanciful Alexandria was as good as history's, or better. But how sad, how disillusioning it would be, if the New York that they conjured up had Greenwich Village uptown and Times Square in the Bronx, and the New Yorkers, gentle and polite, spoke with the honeyed accents of Savannah or New Orleans. Well, that was nothing he needed to brood about just now. Very likely they were only being courteous when they spoke of doing his New York. They had all the vastness of the past to choose from: Nineveh, Memphis of the Pharaohs, the London of Victoria or Shakespeare or Richard the Third, Florence of the Medici, the Paris of Abelard and Heloise or the Paris of Louis XIV, Moctezuma's Tenochtitlan and Atahuallpa's Cuzco; Damascus, St. Petersburg, Babylon, Troy. And then there were all the cities like New Chicago, out of time that was time yet unborn to him but ancient history to them. In such richness, such an infinity of choices, even mighty New York might have to wait a long while for its turn. Would he still be among them by the time they got around to it? By then, perhaps, they might have become bored with him and returned him to his own proper era. Or possibly he would simply have grown old and died. Even here, he supposed, he would eventually die, though no one else ever seemed to. He did not know. He realized that in fact he did not know anything.

The north wind blew all day long. Vast flocks of ibises appeared over the city, fleeing the heat of the interior, and screeched across the sky with their black necks and scrawny legs extended. The sacred birds, descending by the thousands, scuttered about in every crossroad, pouncing on spiders and beetles, on mice, on the debris of the meat shops and the bakeries. They were beautiful but annoyingly ubiquitous, and they splashed their dung over the marble buildings; each morning squadrons of temporaries carefully washed it off. Gioia said little to him now. She seemed cool, withdrawn, depressed; and there was something almost intangible about her, as though she were gradually becoming transparent. He felt it would be an intrusion upon her privacy to ask her what was wrong. Perhaps it was only restlessness. She became religious, and presented costly offerings at the temples of Serapis, Isis, Poseidon, Pan. She went to the necropolis west of the city to lay wreaths on the tombs in the catacombs. In a single day she climbed the Lighthouse three times without any sign of fatigue. One afternoon he returned from a visit to the Library and found her naked on the patio; she had anointed herself all over with some aromatic green salve. Abruptly she said, "I think it's time to leave Alexandria, don't you?"

She wanted to go to Mohenjo-daro, but Mohenjo-daro was not yet ready for visitors. Instead they flew eastward to Chang-an, which they had not seen in years. It was Phillips's suggestion: he hoped that the cosmopolitan gaudiness of the old T'ang capital would lift her mood.

They were to be guests of the Emperor this time: an unusual privilege, which ordinarily had to be applied for far in advance, but Phillips had told some of Gioia's highly placed friends that she was unhappy, and they had quickly arranged everything. Three endlessly bowing functionaries in flowing yellow robes and purple sashes met them at the Gate of Brilliant Virtue in the city's south wall and conducted them to their pavilion, close by the imperial palace and the Forbidden Garden. It was a light, airy place, thin walls of plastered brick braced by graceful columns of some dark, aromatic wood. Fountains played on the roof of green and yellow tiles, creating an unending cool rainfall of recirculating water. The balustrades were of carved marble, the door fittings were of gold.

There was a suite of private rooms for him, and another for her, though they would share the handsome damask-draped bedroom at the heart of the pavilion. As soon as they arrived, Gioia announced that she must go to her rooms to bathe and dress. "There will be a formal reception for us at the palace tonight," she said. "They say the imperial receptions are splendid beyond anything you could imagine. I want to be at my best." The Emperor and all his ministers, she told him, would receive them in the Hall of the Supreme Ultimate; there would be a banquet for a thousand people; Persian dancers would perform, and the celebrated jugglers of Chung-nan. Afterward everyone would be conducted into the fantastic landscape of the Forbidden Garden to view the dragon races and the fireworks.

He went to his own rooms. Two delicate little maidservants undressed him and bathed him with fragrant sponges. The pavilion came equipped with eleven temporaries who were to be their servants: soft-voiced unobtrusive catlike Chinese, done with perfect verisimilitude, straight black hair, glowing skin, epicanthic folds. Phillips often wondered what happened to a city's temporaries when the city's time was over. Were the towering Norse heroes of Asgard being recycled at this moment into wiry dark-skinned Dravidians for Mohenjo-daro? When Timbuctoo's day was done, would its brightly robed black warriors be converted into supple Byzantines to stock the arcades of Constantinople? Or did they simply discard the old temporaries like so many excess props, stash them in warehouses somewhere, and turn out the appropriate quantities of the new model? He did not know; and once when he had asked Gioia about it she had grown uncomfortable and vague. She did not like him to probe for information, and he suspected it was because she had very little to give. These people did not seem to question the workings of their own world; his curiosities were very twentieth-century of him, he was frequently told, in that gently patronizing way of theirs. As his two little maids patted him with their sponges he thought of asking them where they had served before Chang-an. Rio? Rome? Haroun al-Raschid's Baghdad? But these fragile girls, he knew, would only giggle and retreat if he tried to question them. Interrogating temporaries was not only improper but pointless: it was like interrogating one's luggage.

When he was bathed and robed in rich red silks he wandered the pavilion for a little while, admiring the tinkling pendants of green jade dangling on the portico, the lustrous auburn pillars, the rainbow hues of the intricately inter-woven girders and brackets that supported the roof. Then, wearying of his solitude, he approached the bamboo curtain at the entrance to Gioia's suite. A porter and one of the maids stood just within. They indicated that he should not enter; but he scowled at them and they melted from him like snowflakes. A trail of incense led him through the pavilion to Gioia's innermost dressing room. There he halted, just outside the door.

Gioia sat naked with her back to him at an ornate dressing table of some rare flame-colored wood inlaid with bands of orange and green porcelain. She was studying herself intently in a mirror of polished bronze held by one of her maids: picking through her scalp with her fingernails, as a woman might do who was searching out her gray hairs.

But that seemed strange. Gray hair, on Gioia? On a citizen? A temporary might display some appearance of aging, perhaps, but surely not a citizen.

Citizens remained forever young. Gioia looked like a girl. Her face was smooth and unlined, her flesh was firm, her hair was dark: that was true of all of them, every citizen he had ever seen. And yet there was no mistaking what Gioia was doing. She found a hair, frowned, drew it taut, nodded, plucked it. Another. Another. She pressed the tip of her finger to her cheek as if testing it for resilience. She tugged at the skin below her eyes, pulling it downward. Such familiar little gestures of vanity; but so odd here, he thought, in this world of the perpetually young. Gioia, worried about growing old? Had he simply failed to notice the signs of age on her? Or was it that she worked hard behind his back at concealing them? Perhaps that was it. Was he wrong about the citizens, then? Did they age even as the people of less blessed eras had always done, but simply have better ways of hiding it? How old was she, anyway? Thirty? Sixty? Three hundred?

Gioia appeared satisfied now. She waved the mirror away; she rose; she beckoned for her banquet robes. Phillips, still standing unnoticed by the door, studied her with admiration: the small round buttocks, almost but not quite boyish, the elegant line of her spine, the surprising breadth of her shoulders. No, he thought, she is not aging at all. Her body is still like a girl's. She looks as young as on the day they first had met, however long ago that was—he could not say; it was hard to keep track of time here; but he was sure some years had passed since they had come together. Those gray hairs, those wrinkles and sags for which she had searched just now with such desperate intensity, must all be imaginary, mere artifacts of vanity. Even in this remote future epoch, then, vanity was not extinct. He wondered why she was so concerned with the fear of aging. An affectation? Did all these timeless people take some perverse pleasure in fretting over the possibility that they might be growing old? Or was it some private fear of Gioia's, another symptom of the mysterious depression that had come over her in Alexandria?

Not wanting her to think that he had been spying on her, when all he had really intended was to pay her a visit, he slipped silently away to dress for the evening. She came to him an hour later, gorgeously robed, swaddled from chin to ankles in a brocade of brilliant colors shot through with threads of gold, face painted, hair drawn up tightly and fastened with ivory combs: very much the lady of the court. His servants had made him splendid also, a lustrous black surplice embroidered with golden dragons over a sweeping floor-length gown of shining white silk, a necklace and pendant of red coral, a five-cornered gray felt hat that rose in tower upon tower like a ziggurat. Gioia, grinning, touched her fingertips to his cheek. "You look marvelous!" she told him. "Like a grand mandarin!"

"And you like an empress," he said. "Of some distant land: Persia, India.

Here to pay a ceremonial visit on the Son of Heaven." An excess of love suffused his spirit, and, catching her lightly by the wrist, he drew her toward him, as close as he could manage it considering how elaborate their costumes were. But as he bent forward and downward, meaning to brush his lips lightly and affectionately against the tip of her nose, he perceived an unexpected strangeness, an anomaly: the coating of white paint that was her makeup seemed oddly to magnify rather than mask the contours of her skin, highlighting and revealing details he had never observed before. He saw a pattern of fine lines radiating from the corners of her eyes, and the unmistakable beginning of a quirk mark in her cheek just to the left of her mouth, and perhaps the faint indentation of frown lines in her flawless forehead. A shiver traveled along the nape of his neck. So it was not affectation, then, that had had her studying her mirror so fiercely. Age was in truth beginning to stake its claim on her, despite all that he had come to believe about these people's agelessness. But a moment later he was not so sure. Gioia turned and slid gently half a step back from him—she must have found his stare disturbing—and the lines he had thought he had seen were gone. He searched for them and saw only girlish smoothness once again. A trick of the light? A figment of an overwrought imagination? He was baffled.

"Come," she said. "We mustn't keep the Emperor waiting."

Five mustachioed warriors in armor of white quilting and seven musicians playing cymbals and pipes escorted them to the Hall of the Supreme Ultimate. There they found the full court arrayed: princes and ministers, high officials, yellow-robed monks, a swarm of imperial concubines. In a place of honor to the right of the royal thrones, which rose like gilded scaffolds high above all else, was a little group of stern-faced men in foreign costumes, the ambassadors of Rome and Byzantium, of Arabia and Syria, of Korea, Japan, Tibet, Turkestan. Incense smoldered in enameled braziers. A poet sang a delicate twanging melody, accompanying himself on a small harp. Then the Emperor and Empress entered: two tiny aged people, like waxen images, moving with infinite slowness, taking steps no greater than a child's. There was the sound of trumpets as they ascended their thrones. When the little Emperor was seated—he looked like a doll up there, ancient, faded, shrunken, yet still somehow a figure of extraordinary power—he stretched forth both his hands, and enormous gongs began to sound. It was a scene of astonishing splendor, grand and overpowering.

These are all temporaries, Phillips realized suddenly. He saw only a handful of citizens—eight, ten, possibly as many as a dozen—scattered here and there about the vast room. He knew them by their eyes, dark, liquid, knowing. They were watching not only the imperial spectacle but also Gioia and him; and Gioia, smiling secretly, nodding almost imperceptibly to them, was acknowledging their presence and their interest. But those few were the only ones in here who were autonomous living beings. All the rest—the entire splendid court, the great mandarins and paladins, the officials, the giggling concubines, the haughty and resplendent ambassadors, the aged Emperor and Empress themselves, were simply part of the scenery. Had the world ever seen entertainment on so grand a scale before? All this pomp, all this pageantry, conjured up each night for the amusement of a dozen or so viewers?

At the banquet the little group of citizens sat together at a table apart, a round onyx slab draped with translucent green silk. There turned out to be seventeen of them in all, including Gioia; Gioia appeared to know all of them, though none, so far as he could tell, was a member of her set that he had met before. She did not attempt introductions. Nor was conversation at all possible during the meal: there was a constant astounding roaring din in the room. Three orchestras played at once and there were troupes of strolling musicians also, and a steady stream of monks and their attendants marched back and forth between the tables loudly chanting sutras and waving censers to the deafening accompaniment of drums and gongs. The Emperor did not descend from his throne to join the banquet; he seemed to be asleep, though now and then he waved his hand in time to the music. Gigantic half-naked brown slaves with broad cheekbones and mouths like gaping pockets brought forth the food, peacock tongues and breast of phoenix heaped on mounds of glowing saffron-colored rice, served on frail alabaster plates. For chopsticks they were given slender rods of dark jade. The wine, served in glistening crystal beakers, was thick and sweet, with an aftertaste of raisins, and no beaker was allowed to remain empty for more than a moment. Phillips felt himself growing dizzy: when the Persian dancers emerged he could not tell whether there were five of them or fifty, and as they performed their intricate whirling routines it seemed to him that their slender muslin-veiled forms were blurring and merging one into another. He felt frightened by their proficiency, and wanted to look away, but he could not. The Chung-nan jugglers that followed them were equally skillful, equally alarming, filling the air with scythes, flaming torches, live animals, rare porcelain vases, pink jade hatchets, silver bells, gilded cups, wagon wheels, bronze vessels, and never missing a catch. The citizens applauded politely but did not seem impressed. After the jugglers, the dancers returned, performing this time on stilts; the waiters brought platters of steaming meat of a pale lavender color, unfamiliar in taste and texture: filet of camel, perhaps, or haunch of hippopotamus, or possibly some choice chop from a young dragon. There was more wine. Feebly Phillips tried to wave it away, but the servitors were implacable. This was a drier sort, greenish-gold, austere, sharp on the tongue. With it came a silver dish, chilled to a polar coldness, that held shaved ice flavored with some potent smoky-flavored brandy. The jugglers were doing a second turn, he noticed. He thought he was going to be ill. He looked helplessly toward Gioia, who seemed sober but fiercely animated, almost manic, her eyes blazing like rubies. She touched his cheek fondly. A cool draft blew through the hall: they had opened one entire wall, revealing the garden, the night, the stars. Just outside was a colossal wheel of oiled paper stretched on wooden struts. They must have erected it in the past hour: it stood a hundred fifty feet high or even more, and on it hung lanterns by the thousands, glimmering like giant fireflies. The guests began to leave the hall. Phillips let himself be swept along into the garden, where under a yellow moon strange crook-armed trees with dense black needles loomed ominously. Gioia slipped her arm through his. They went down to a lake of bubbling crimson fluid and watched scarlet flamingolike birds ten feet tall fastidiously spearing angry-eyed turquoise eels. They stood in awe before a fat-bellied Buddha of gleaming blue tilework, seventy feet high. A horse with a golden mane came prancing by, striking showers of brilliant red sparks wherever its hooves touched the ground. In a grove of lemon trees that seemed to have the power to wave their slender limbs about, Phillips came upon the Emperor, standing by himself and rocking gently back and forth. The old man seized Phillips by the hand and pressed something into his palm, closing his fingers tight about it; when he opened his fist a few moments later he found his palm full of gray irregular pearls. Gioia took them from him and cast them into the air, and they burst like exploding firecrackers, giving off splashes of colored light. A little later, Phillips realized that he was no longer wearing his surplice or his white silken undergown. Gioia was naked, too, and she drew him gently down into a carpet of moist blue moss, where they made love until dawn, fiercely at first, then slowly, languidly, dreamily. At sunrise he looked at her tenderly and saw that something was wrong.

"Gioia?" he said doubtfully.

She smiled. "Ah, no. Gioia is with Fenimon tonight. I am Belilala."

"With—Fenimon?"

"They are old friends. She had not seen him in years."

"Ah. I see. And you are—?"

"Belilala," she said again, touching her fingertips to his cheek.

✦

It was not unusual, Belilala said. It happened all the time; the only unusual thing was that it had not happened to him before now. Couples formed, traveled together for a while, drifted apart, eventually reunited. It did not mean that Gioia had left him forever. It meant only that just now she chose to be with

Fenimon. Gioia would return. In the meanwhile he would not be alone. "You and I met in New Chicago," Belilala told him. "And then we saw each other again in Timbuctoo. Have you forgotten? Oh, yes, I see that you have forgotten!" She laughed prettily; she did not seem at all offended.

She looked enough like Gioia to be her sister. But, then, all the citizens looked more or less alike to him. And apart from their physical resemblance, so he quickly came to realize, Belilala and Gioia were not really very similar. There was a calmness, a deep reservoir of serenity, in Belilala, that Gioia, eager and volatile and ever impatient, did not seem to have. Strolling the swarming streets of Chang-an with Belilala, he did not perceive in her any of Gioia's restless feverish need always to know what lay beyond, and beyond, and beyond even that. When they toured the Hsing-ch'ing Palace, Belilala did not after five minutes begin—as Gioia surely would have done—to seek directions to the Fountain of Hsuan-tsung or the Wild Goose Pagoda. Curiosity did not consume Belilala as it did Gioia. Plainly she believed that there would always be enough time for her to see everything she cared to see. There were some days when Belilala chose not to go out at all, but was content merely to remain at their pavilion playing a solitary game with flat porcelain counters, or viewing the flowers of the garden.

He found, oddly, that he enjoyed the respite from Gioia's intense world-swallowing appetites; and yet he longed for her to return. Belilala—beautiful, gentle, tranquil, patient—was too perfect for him. She seemed unreal in her gleaming impeccability, much like one of those Sung celadon vases that appear too flawless to have been thrown and glazed by human hands. There was something a little soulless about her: an immaculate finish outside, emptiness within. Belilala might almost have been a temporary, he thought, though he knew she was not. He could explore the pavilions and palaces of Chang-an with her, he could make graceful conversation with her while they dined, he could certainly enjoy coupling with her; but he could not love her or even contemplate the possibility. It was hard to imagine Belilala worriedly studying herself in a mirror for wrinkles and gray hairs. Belilala would never be any older than she was at this moment; nor could Belilala ever have been any younger. Perfection does not move along an axis of time. But the perfection of Belilala's glossy surface made her inner being impenetrable to him. Gioia was more vulnerable, more obviously flawed—her restlessness, her moodiness, her vanity, her fears—and therefore she was more accessible to his own highly imperfect twentieth-century sensibility.

Occasionally he saw Gioia as he roamed the city, or thought he did. He had a glimpse of her among the miracle-vendors in the Persian Bazaar, and outside the Zoroastrian temple, and again by the goldfish pond in the

Serpentine Park. But he was never quite sure that the woman he saw was really Gioia, and he never could get close enough to her to be certain: she had a way of vanishing as he approached, like some mysterious Lorelei luring him onward and onward in a hopeless chase. After a while he came to realize that he was not going to find her until she was ready to be found.

He lost track of time. Weeks, months, years? He had no idea. In this city of exotic luxury, mystery, and magic all was in constant flux and transition and the days had a fitful, unstable quality. Buildings and even whole streets were torn down of an afternoon and reerected, within days, far away. Grand new pagodas sprouted like toadstools in the night. Citizens came in from Asgard, Alexandria, Timbuctoo, New Chicago, stayed for a time, disappeared, returned. There was a constant round of court receptions, banquets, theatrical events, each one much like the one before. The festivals in honor of past emperors and empresses might have given some form to the year, but they seemed to occur in a random way, the ceremony marking the death of T'ai Tsung coming around twice the same year, so it seemed to him, once in a season of snow and again in high summer, and the one honoring the ascension of the Empress Wu being held twice in a single season. Perhaps he had misunderstood something. But he knew it was no use asking anyone.

One day Belilala said unexpectedly, "Shall we go to Mohenjo-daro?"

"I didn't know it was ready for visitors," he replied.

"Oh, yes. For quite some time now."

He hesitated. This had caught him unprepared. Cautiously he said, "Gioia and I were going to go there together, you know."

Belilala smiled amiably, as though the topic under discussion were nothing more than the choice of that evening's restaurant.

"Were you?" she asked.

"It was all arranged while we were still in Alexandria. To go with you instead—I don't know what to tell you, Belilala." Phillips sensed that he was growing terribly flustered. "You know that I'd like to go. With you. But on the other hand I can't help feeling that I shouldn't go there until I'm back with Gioia again. If I ever am." How foolish this sounds, he thought. How clumsy, how adolescent. He found that he was having trouble looking straight at her. Uneasily he said, with a kind of desperation in his voice, "I did promise her—there was a commitment, you understand—a firm agreement that we would go to Mohenjo-daro together—"

"Oh, but Gioia's already there!" said Belilala in the most casual way.

He gaped as though she had punched him.

"*What?*"

"She was one of the first to go, after it opened. Months and months ago. You didn't know?" she asked, sounding surprised, but not very. "You really didn't know?"

That astonished him. He felt bewildered, betrayed, furious. His cheeks grew hot, his mouth gaped. He shook his head again and again, trying to clear it of confusion. It was a moment before he could speak. "Already there?" he said at last. "Without waiting for me? After we had talked about going there together—after we had agreed—"

Belilala laughed. "But how could she resist seeing the newest city? You know how impatient Gioia is!"

"Yes. Yes."

He was stunned. He could barely think.

"Just like all short-timers," Belilala said. "She rushes here, she rushes there. She must have it all, now, now, right away, at once, instantly. You ought never expect her to wait for you for anything for very long: the fit seizes her, and off she goes. Surely you must know that about her by now."

"A short-timer?" He had not heard that term before.

"Yes. You knew that. You must have known that." Belilala flashed her sweetest smile. She showed no sign of comprehending his distress. With a brisk wave of her hand she said, "Well, then, shall we go, you and I? To Mohenjo-daro?"

"Of course," Phillips said bleakly.

"When would you like to leave?"

"Tonight," he said. He paused a moment. "What's a short-timer, Belilala?"

Color came to her cheeks. "Isn't it obvious?" she asked.

☙

Had there ever been a more hideous place on the face of the earth than the city of Mohenjo-daro? Phillips found it difficult to imagine one. Nor could he understand why, out of all the cities that had ever been, these people had chosen to restore this one to existence. More than ever they seemed alien to him, unfathomable, incomprehensible.

From the terrace atop the many-towered citadel he peered down into grim claustrophobic Mohenjo-daro and shivered. The stark, bleak city looked like nothing so much as some prehistoric prison colony. In the manner of an uneasy tortoise it huddled, squat and compact, against the gray monotonous Indus River plain: miles of dark burnt-brick walls enclosing miles of terrifyingly orderly streets, laid out in an awesome, monstrous gridiron pattern of maniacal rigidity. The houses themselves were dismal and forbidding too, clusters of brick cells gathered about small airless courtyards. There were no windows, only small doors that opened not onto the main boulevards but onto the tiny mysterious lanes that ran between the buildings. Who had designed this horrifying metropolis? What harsh sour souls they must have had, these frightening and frightened folk, creating for themselves in the lush fertile plains of India such a Supreme Soviet of a city!

"How lovely it is," Belilala murmured. "How fascinating!"

He stared at her in amazement.

"Fascinating? Yes," he said. "I suppose so. The same way that the smile of a cobra is fascinating."

"What's a cobra?"

"Poisonous predatory serpent," Phillips told her. "Probably extinct. Or formerly extinct, more likely. It wouldn't surprise me if you people had recreated a few and turned them loose in Mohenjo to make things livelier."

"You sound angry, Charles."

"Do I? That's not how I feel."

"How do you feel, then?"

"I don't know," he said after a long moment's pause. He shrugged. "Lost, I suppose. Very far from home."

"Poor Charles."

"Standing here in this ghastly barracks of a city, listening to you tell me how beautiful it is, I've never felt more alone in my life."

"You miss Gioia very much, don't you?"

He gave her another startled look.

"Gioia has nothing to do with it. She's probably been having ecstasies over the loveliness of Mohenjo just like you. Just like all of you. I suppose I'm the only one who can't find the beauty, the charm. I'm the only one who looks out there and sees only horror, and then wonders why nobody else sees it, why in fact people would set up a place like this for *entertainment,* for *pleasure*—"

Her eyes were gleaming. "Oh, you are angry! You really are!"

"Does that fascinate you, too?" he snapped. "A demonstration of genuine primitive emotion? A typical quaint twentieth-century outburst?" He paced the rampart in short quick anguished steps. "Ah. Ah. I think I understand it now, Belilala. Of course: I'm part of your circus, the star of the sideshow. I'm the first experiment in setting up the next stage of it, in fact." Her eyes were wide. The sudden harshness and violence in his voice seemed to be alarming and exciting her at the same time. That angered him even more. Fiercely he went on, "Bringing whole cities back out of time was fun for a while, but it lacks a certain authenticity, eh? For some reason you couldn't bring the inhabitants, too; you couldn't just grab a few million prehistorics out of Egypt or Greece or India and dump them down in this era, I suppose because you might have too much trouble controlling them, or because you'd have the problem of disposing of them once you were bored with them. So you had to settle for creating temporaries to populate your ancient cities. But now you've got me. I'm something more real than a temporary, and that's a terrific novelty for you, and novelty is the thing you people crave more than anything else: maybe the *only* thing you crave. And here I am, complicated, unpredictable, edgy, capable of anger, fear, sadness, love, and all those other formerly extinct things. Why settle for picturesque architecture when you can observe picturesque emotion, too? What fun I must be for all of you! And if you decide that I was really interesting, maybe you'll ship me back where I came from and check out a few other ancient types—a Roman gladiator, maybe, or a Renaissance pope, or even a Neanderthal or two—"

"Charles," she said tenderly. "Oh, Charles, Charles, Charles, how lonely you must be, how lost, how troubled! Will you ever forgive me? Will you ever forgive us all?"

Once more he was astounded by her. She sounded entirely sincere, altogether sympathetic. Was she? Was she, really? He was not sure he had ever had a sign of genuine caring from any of them before, not even Gioia. Nor could he bring himself to trust Belilala now. He was afraid of her, afraid of all of them, of their brittleness, their slyness, their elegance. He wished he could go to her and have her take him in her arms; but he felt too much the shaggy prehistoric just now to be able to risk asking that comfort of her.

He turned away and began to walk around the rim of the citadel's massive wall.

"Charles?"

"Let me alone for a little while," he said.

He walked on. His forehead throbbed and there was a pounding in his chest. All stress systems going full blast, he thought: secret glands dumping gallons of inflammatory substances into his bloodstream. The heat, the inner confusion, the repellent look of this place—

Try to understand, he thought. Relax. Look about you. Try to enjoy your holiday in Mohenjo-daro.

He leaned warily outward, over the edge of the wall. He had never seen a wall like this; it must be forty feet thick at the base, he guessed, perhaps even more, and every brick perfectly shaped, meticulously set. Beyond the great rampart, marshes ran almost to the edge of the city, although close by the wall the swamps had been dammed and drained for agriculture. He saw lithe brown farmers down there, busy with their wheat and barley and peas. Cattle and buffaloes grazed a little farther out. The air was heavy, dank, humid. All was still. From somewhere close at hand came the sound of a droning, whining stringed instrument and a steady insistent chanting.

Gradually a sort of peace pervaded him. His anger subsided. He felt himself beginning to grow calm again. He looked back at the city, the rigid interlocking streets, the maze of inner lanes, the millions of courses of precise brickwork.

It is a miracle, he told himself, that this city is here in this place and at this time. And it is a miracle that I am here to see it.

Caught for a moment by the magic within the bleakness, he thought he began to understand Belilala's awe and delight, and he wished now that he had not spoken to her so sharply. The city was alive. Whether it was the actual Mohenjo-daro of thousands upon thousands of years ago, ripped from the past by some wondrous hook, or simply a cunning reproduction, did not matter at all. Real or not, this was the true Mohenjo-daro. It had been dead, and now, for the moment, it was alive again. These people, these *citizens*, might be trivial, but reconstructing Mohenjo-daro was no trivial achievement. And that the city that had been reconstructed was oppressive and sinister-looking was unimportant. No one was compelled to live in Mohenjo-daro any more. Its time had come and gone, long ago; those little dark-skinned peasants and craftsmen and merchants down there were mere temporaries, mere inanimate things, conjured up like zombies to enhance the illusion. They did not need his pity. Nor did he need to pity himself. He knew that he should be grateful for the chance to behold these things. Someday, when this dream had ended and his hosts had returned him to the world of subways and computers and income tax and television networks, he would think of Mohenjo-daro as he had once beheld it, lofty walls of tightly woven dark brick under a heavy sky, and he would remember only its beauty.

Glancing back, he searched for Belilala and could not for a moment find her. Then he caught sight of her carefully descending a narrow staircase that angled down the inner face of the citadel wall.

"Belilala!" he called.

She paused and looked his way, shading her eyes from the sun with her hand. "Are you all right?"

"Where are you going?"

"To the baths," she said. "Do you want to come?"

He nodded. "Yes. Wait for me, will you? I'll be right there." He began to run toward her along the top of the wall.

The baths were attached to the citadel: a great open tank the size of a large swimming pool, lined with bricks set on edge in gypsum mortar and waterproofed with asphalt, and eight smaller tanks just north of it in a kind of covered arcade. He supposed that in ancient times the whole complex had had some ritual purpose, the large tank used by common folk and the small chambers set aside for the private ablutions of priests or nobles. Now the baths were maintained, it seemed, entirely for the pleasure of visiting citizens. As Phillips came up the passageway that led to the main bath he saw fifteen or twenty of them lolling in the water or padding languidly about, while temporaries of the dark-skinned Mohenjo-daro type served them drinks and pungent little morsels of spiced meat as though this were some sort of luxury resort. Which was, he realized, exactly what it was. The temporaries wore white cotton loincloths; the citizens were naked. In his former life he had encountered that sort of casual public nudity a few times on visits to California and the south of France, and it had made him mildly uneasy. But he was growing accustomed to it here.

The changing rooms were tiny brick cubicles connected by rows of closely placed steps to the courtyard that surrounded the central tank. They entered one and Belilala swiftly slipped out of the loose cotton robe that she had worn since their arrival that morning. With arms folded she stood leaning against the wall, waiting for him. After a moment he dropped his own robe and followed her outside. He felt a little giddy, sauntering around naked in the open like this.

On the way to the main bathing area they passed the private baths. None of them seemed to be occupied. They were elegantly constructed chambers, with finely jointed brick floors and carefully designed runnels to drain excess water into the passageway that led to the primary drain. Phillips was struck with admiration for the cleverness of the prehistoric engineers. He peered into this chamber and that to see how the conduits and ventilating ducts were arranged, and when he came to the last room in the sequence he was surprised and embarrassed to discover that it was in use. A brawny grinning man, big-muscled, deep-chested, with exuberantly flowing shoulder-length red hair and a flamboyant, sharply tapering beard was thrashing about merrily with two women in the small tank. Phillips had a quick glimpse of a lively tangle of arms, legs, breasts, buttocks.

"Sorry," he muttered. His cheeks reddened. Quickly he ducked out, blurting apologies as he went. "Didn't realize the room was occupied—no wish to intrude—"

Belilala had proceeded on down the passageway. Phillips hurried after her. From behind him came peals of cheerful raucous booming laughter and high-pitched giggling and the sound of splashing water. Probably they had not even noticed him.

He paused a moment, puzzled, playing back in his mind that one startling glimpse. Something was not right. Those women, he was fairly sure, were citizens: little slender elfin dark-haired girlish creatures, the standard model.

But the man? That great curling sweep of red hair? Not a citizen. Citizens did not affect shoulder-length hair. And *red*? Nor had he ever seen a citizen so burly, so powerfully muscular. Or one with a beard. But he could hardly be a temporary, either. Phillips could conceive no reason why there would be so Anglo-Saxon-looking a temporary at Mohenjo-daro; and it was unthinkable for a temporary to be frolicking like that with citizens, anyway.

"Charles?"

He looked up ahead. Belilala stood at the end of the passageway, outlined in a nimbus of brilliant sunlight. "Charles?" she said again. "Did you lose your way?"

"I'm right here behind you," he said. "I'm coming."

"Who did you meet in there?"

"A man with a beard."

"With a what?"

"A beard," he said. "Red hair growing on his face. I wonder who he is."

"Nobody I know," said Belilala. "The only one I know with hair on his face is you. And yours is black, and you shave it off every day." She laughed. "Come along, now! I see some friends by the pool!"

He caught up with her, and they went hand in hand out into the courtyard. Immediately a waiter glided up to them, an obsequious little temporary with a tray of drinks. Phillips waved it away and headed for the pool. He felt terribly exposed: he imagined that the citizens disporting themselves here were staring intently at him, studying his hairy primitive body as though he were some mythical creature, a Minotaur, a werewolf, summoned up for their amusement. Belilala drifted off to talk to someone and he slipped into the water, grateful for the concealment it offered. It was deep, warm, comforting. With swift powerful strokes he breast-stroked from one end to the other.

A citizen perched elegantly on the pool's rim smiled at him. "Ah, so you've come at last, Charles!" *Char-less.* Two syllables. Someone from Gioia's set: Stengard, Hawk, Aramayne? He could not remember which one. They were all so much alike.

Phillips returned the man's smile in a halfhearted, tentative way. He searched for something to say and finally asked, "Have you been here long?"

"Weeks. Perhaps months. What a splendid achievement this city is, eh, Charles? Such utter unity of mood—such a total statement of a uniquely single-minded esthetic—"

"Yes. Single-minded is the word," Phillips said dryly.

"Gioia's word, actually. Gioia's phrase. I was merely quoting."

Gioia. He felt as if he had been stabbed.

"You've spoken to Gioia lately?" he said.

"Actually, no. It was Hekna who saw her. You do remember Hekna, eh?" He nodded toward two naked women standing on the brick platform that bordered the pool, chatting, delicately nibbling morsels of meat. They could have been twins. "There is Hekna, with your Belilala." Hekna, yes. So this must be Hawk, Phillips thought, unless there has been some recent shift of couples. "How sweet she is, your Belilala," Hawk said. "Gioia chose very wisely when she picked her for you."

Another stab: a much deeper one. "Is that how it was?" he said. "Gioia *picked* Belilala for me?"

"Why, of course!" Hawk seemed surprised. It went without saying, evidently. "What did you think? That Gioia would merely go off and leave you to fend for yourself?"

"Hardly. Not Gioia."

"She's very tender, very gentle, isn't she?"

"You mean Belilala? Yes, very," said Phillips carefully. "A dear woman, a wonderful woman. But of course I hope to get together with Gioia again soon." He paused. "They say she's been in Mohenjo-daro almost since it opened."

"She was here, yes."

"*Was?*"

"Oh, you know Gioia," Hawk said lightly. "She's moved along by now, naturally."

Phillips leaned forward. "Naturally," he said. Tension thickened his voice. "Where has she gone this time?"

"Timbuctoo, I think. Or New Chicago. I forget which one it was. She was telling us that she hoped to be in Timbuctoo for the closing-down party. But then Fenimon had some pressing reason for going to New Chicago. I can't remember what they decided to do." Hawk gestured sadly. "Either way, a pity that she left Mohenjo before the new visitor came. She had such a rewarding time with you, after all: I'm sure she'd have found much to learn from him also."

The unfamiliar term twanged an alarm deep in Phillips's consciousness. "*Visitor?*" he said, angling his head sharply toward Hawk. "What visitor do you mean?"

"You haven't met him yet? Oh, of course, you've only just arrived."

Phillips moistened his lips. "I think I may have seen him. Long red hair? Beard like this?"

"That's the one! Willoughby, he's called. He's—what?—a Viking, a pirate, something like that. Tremendous vigor and force. Remarkable person. We should have many more visitors, I think. They're far superior to temporaries, everyone agrees. Talking with a temporary is a little like talking to one's self, wouldn't you say? They give you no significant illumination. But a visitor—someone like this Willoughby—or like you, Charles—a visitor can be truly enlightening, a visitor can transform one's view of reality—"

"Excuse me," Phillips said. A throbbing began behind his forehead. "Perhaps we can continue this conversation later, yes?" He put the flats of his hands against the hot brick of the platform and hoisted himself swiftly from the pool. "At dinner, maybe—or afterward—yes? All right?" He set off at a quick half-trot back toward the passageway that led to the private baths.

As he entered the roofed part of the structure his throat grew dry, his breath suddenly came short. He padded quickly up the hall and peered into the little bath chamber. The bearded man was still there, sitting up in the tank, breast-high above the water, with one arm around each of the women. His eyes gleamed with fiery intensity in the dimness. He was grinning in marvelous self-satisfaction; he seemed to brim with intensity, confidence, gusto.

Let him be what I think he is, Phillips prayed. I have been alone among these people long enough.

"May I come in?" he asked.

"Aye, fellow!" cried the man in the tub thunderously. "By my troth, come ye in, and bring your lass as well! God's teeth, I wot there's room aplenty for more folk in this tub than we!"

At that great uproarious outcry Phillips felt a powerful surge of joy. What a joyous rowdy voice! How rich, how lusty, how totally uncitizenlike!

And those oddly archaic words! God's teeth? By my troth? What sort of talk was that? What else but the good pure sonorous Elizabethan diction! Certainly it had something of the roll and fervor of Shakespeare about it. And spoken with—an Irish brogue, was it? No, not quite: it was English, but English spoken in no manner Phillips had ever heard.

Citizens did not speak that way. But a *visitor* might.

So it was true. Relief flooded Phillips's soul. Not alone, then! Another relic of a former age—another wanderer—a companion in chaos, a brother in adversity—a fellow voyager, tossed even farther than he had been by the tempests of time—

The bearded man grinned heartily and beckoned to Phillips with a toss of his head. "Well, join us, join us, man! 'Tis good to see an English face again, amidst all these Moors and rogue Portugals! But what have ye done with thy lass? One can never have enough wenches, d'ye not agree?"

The force and vigor of him were extraordinary: almost too much so. He roared, he bellowed, he boomed. He was so very much what he ought to be that he seemed more a character out of some old pirate movie than anything else, so blustering, so real, that he seemed unreal. A stage Elizabethan, larger than life, a boisterous young Falstaff without the belly.

Hoarsely Phillips said, "Who are you?"

"Why, Ned Willoughby's son Francis am I, of Plymouth. Late of the service of Her Most Protestant Majesty, but most foully abducted by the powers of darkness and cast away among these blackamoor Hindus, or whatever they be. And thyself?"

"Charles Phillips." After a moment's uncertainty he added, "I'm from New York."

"New York? What place is that? In faith, man, I know it not!"

"A city in America."

"A city in America, forsooth! What a fine fancy that is! In America, you say, and not on the Moon, or perchance underneath the sea?" To the women Willoughby said, "D'ye hear him? He comes from a city in America! With the face of an Englishman, though not the manner of one, and not quite the proper sort of speech. A city in America! A city. God's blood, what will I hear next?"

Phillips trembled. Awe was beginning to take hold of him. This man had walked the streets of Shakespeare's London, perhaps. He had clinked canisters with Marlowe or Essex or Walter Raleigh; he had watched the ships of the Armada wallowing in the Channel. It strained Phillips's spirit to think of it. This strange dream in which he found himself was compounding its strangeness now. He felt like a weary swimmer assailed by heavy surf, winded, dazed. The hot close atmosphere of the baths was driving him toward vertigo. There could be no doubt of it any longer. He was not the only primitive—the only visitor—who was wandering loose in this fiftieth century. They were conducting other experiments as well. He gripped the sides of the door to steady himself and said, "When you speak of Her Most Protestant Majesty, it's Elizabeth the First you mean, is that not so?"

"Elizabeth, aye! As to the First, that is true enough, but why trouble to name her thus? There is but one. First and Last, I do trow, and God save her, there is no other!"

Phillips studied the other man warily. He knew that he must proceed with care. A misstep at this point and he would forfeit any chance that Willoughby would take him seriously. How much metaphysical bewilderment, after all, could this man absorb? What did he know, what had anyone of his time known, of past and present and future and the notion that one might somehow move from one to the other as readily as one would go from Surrey to Kent? That was a twentieth-century idea, late nineteenth at best, a fantastical speculation that very likely no one had even considered before Wells had sent his time traveler off to stare at the reddened sun of the earth's last twilight.

Willoughby's world was a world of Protestants and Catholics, of kings and queens, of tiny sailing vessels, of swords at the hip and ox-carts on the road: that world seemed to Phillips far more alien and distant than was this world of citizens and temporaries. The risk that Willoughby would not begin to understand him was great.

But this man and he were natural allies against a world they had never made. Phillips chose to take the risk.

"Elizabeth the First is the queen you serve," he said. "There will be another of her name in England, in due time. Has already been, in fact."

Willoughby shook his head like a puzzled lion. "Another Elizabeth, d'ye say?"

"A second one, and not much like the first. Long after your Virgin Queen, this one. She will reign in what you think of as the days to come. That I know without doubt."

The Englishman peered at him and frowned. "You see the future? Are you a soothsayer, then? A necromancer, mayhap? Or one of the very demons that brought me to this place?"

"Not at all," Phillips said gently. "Only a lost soul, like yourself." He stepped into the little room and crouched by the side of the tank. The two citizen-women were staring at him in bland fascination. He ignored them. To Willoughby he said, "Do you have any idea where you are?"

✦

The Englishman had guessed, rightly enough, that he was in India: "I do believe these little brown Moorish folk are of the Hindu sort," he said. But that was as far as his comprehension of what had befallen him could go.

It had not occurred to him that he was no longer living in the sixteenth century. And of course he did not begin to suspect that this strange and somber brick city in which he found himself was a wanderer out of an era even more remote than his own. Was there any way, Phillips wondered, of explaining that to him?

He had been here only three days. He thought it was devils that had carried him off. "While I slept did they come for me," he said. "Mephistophilis Sathanas, his henchmen seized me—God alone can say why—and swept me in a moment out to this torrid realm from England, where I had reposed among friends and family. For I was between one voyage and the next, you must understand, awaiting Drake and his ship—you know Drake, the glorious Francis? God's blood, there's a mariner for ye! We were to go to the Main again, he and I, but instead here I be in this other place—" Willoughby leaned close and said, "I ask you, soothsayer, how can it be, that a man go to sleep in Plymouth and wake up in India? It is passing strange, is it not?"

"That it is," Phillips said.

"But he that is in the dance must needs dance on, though he do but hop, eh? So do I believe." He gestured toward the two citizen-women. "And therefore to console myself in this pagan land I have found me some sport among these little Portugal women—"

"Portugal?" said Phillips.

"Why, what else can they be, but Portugals? Is it not the Portugals who control all these coasts of India? See, the people are of two sorts here, the blackamoors and the others, the fair-skinned ones, the lords and masters who lie here in these baths. If they be not Hindus, and I think they are not, then Portugals is what they must be." He laughed and pulled the women against himself and rubbed his hands over their breasts as though they were fruits on a vine. "Is that not what you are, you little naked shameless Papist wenches? A pair of Portugals, eh?"

They giggled, but did not answer.

"No," Phillips said. "This is India, but not the India you think you know. And these women are not Portuguese."

"Not Portuguese?" Willoughby said, baffled.

"No more so than you. I'm quite certain of that."

Willoughby stroked his beard. "I do admit I found them very odd, for Portugals. I have heard not a syllable of their Portugee speech on their lips. And it is strange also that they run naked as Adam and Eve in these baths, and allow me free plunder of their women, which is not the way of Portugals at home, God wot. But I thought me, this is India, they choose to live in another fashion here—"

"No," Phillips said. "I tell you, these are not Portuguese, nor any other people of Europe who are known to you."

"Prithee, who are they, then?"

Do it delicately, now, Phillips warned himself. *Delicately.*

He said, "It is not far wrong to think of them as spirits of some kind—demons, even. Or sorcerers who have magicked us out of our proper places in the world." He paused, groping for some means to share with Willoughby, in a way that Willoughby might grasp, this mystery that had enfolded them. He drew a deep breath. "They've taken us not only across the sea," he said, "but across the years as well. We have both been hauled, you and I, far into the days that are to come."

Willoughby gave him a look of blank bewilderment.

"Days that are to come? Times yet unborn, d'ye mean? Why, I comprehend none of that!"

"Try to understand. We're both castaways in the same boat, man! But there's no way we can help each other if I can't make you see—"

Shaking his head, Willoughby muttered, "In faith, good friend, I find your words the merest folly. Today is today, and tomorrow is tomorrow, and how can a man step from one to t'other until tomorrow be turned into today?"

"I have no idea," said Phillips. Struggle was apparent on Willoughby's face; but plainly he could perceive no more than the haziest outline of what Phillips was driving at, if that much. "But this I know," he went on. "That your world and all that was in it is dead and gone. And so is mine, though I was born four hundred years after you, in the time of the second Elizabeth."

Willoughby snorted scornfully. "Four hundred—"

"You must believe me!"

"Nay! Nay!"

"It's the truth. Your time is only history to me. And mine and yours are history to *them*—ancient history. They call us visitors, but what we are is captives." Phillips felt himself quivering in the intensity of his effort. He was aware how insane this must sound to Willoughby. It was beginning to sound insane to him. "They've stolen us out of our proper times—seizing us like gypsies in the night—"

"Fie, man! You rave with lunacy!"

Phillips shook his head. He reached out and seized Willoughby tightly by the wrist. "I beg you, listen to me!" The citizen-women were watching closely, whispering to one another behind their hands, laughing. "Ask them!" Phillips cried. "Make them tell you what century this is! The sixteenth, do you think? Ask them!"

"What century could it be, but the sixteenth of our Lord?"

"They will tell you it is the fiftieth."

Willoughby looked at him pityingly. "Man, man, what a sorry thing thou art! The fiftieth, indeed!" He laughed. "Fellow, listen to me, now. There is but one Elizabeth, safe upon her throne in Westminster. This is India. The year is Anno 1591. Come, let us you and I steal a ship from these Portugals, and make our way back to England, and peradventure you may get from there to your America—"

"There is no England."

"Ah, can you say that and not be mad?"

"The cities and nations we knew are gone. These people live like magicians, Francis." There was no use holding anything back now, Phillips thought leadenly. He knew that he had lost. "They conjure up places of long ago, and build them here and there to suit their fancy, and when they are bored with them they destroy them, and start anew. There is no England. Europe is empty, featureless, void. Do you know what cities there are? There are only five in all the world. There is Alexandria of Egypt. There is Timbuctoo in Africa. There is New Chicago in America. There is a great city in China—in Cathay, I suppose you would say. And there is this place, which they call Mohenjo-daro, and which is far more ancient than Greece, than Rome, than Babylon."

Quietly Willoughby said, "Nay. This is mere absurdity. You say we are in some far tomorrow, and then you tell me we are dwelling in some city of long ago."

"A conjuration, only," Phillips said in desperation. "A likeness of that city. Which these folk have fashioned somehow for their own amusement. Just as we are here, you and I: to amuse them. Only to amuse them."

"You are completely mad."

"Come with me, then. Talk with the citizens by the great pool. Ask them what year this is; ask them about England; ask them how you come to be here." Once again Phillips grasped Willoughby's wrist. "We should be allies. If we work together, perhaps we can discover some way to get ourselves out of this place, and—"

"Let me be, fellow."

"Please—"

"Let me be!" roared Willoughby, and pulled his arm free. His eyes were stark with rage. Rising in the tank, he looked about furiously as though searching for a weapon. The citizen-women shrank back away from him, though at the same time they seemed captivated by the big man's fierce outburst. "Go to, get you to Bedlam! Let me be, madman! Let me be!"

Dismally Phillips roamed the dusty unpaved streets of Mohenjo-daro alone for hours. His failure with Willoughby had left him bleak-spirited and somber: he had hoped to stand back to back with the Elizabethan against the citizens, but he saw now that that was not to be. He had bungled things; or, more likely, it had been impossible ever to bring Willoughby to see the truth of their predicament.

In the stifling heat he went at random through the confusing congested lanes of flat-roofed windowless houses and blank featureless walls until he emerged into a broad marketplace. The life of the city swirled madly around him: the pseudo-life, rather, the intricate interactions of the thousands of temporaries who were nothing more than windup dolls set in motion to provide the illusion that pre-Vedic India was still a going concern. Here vendors sold beautiful little carved stone seals portraying tigers and monkeys and strange humped cattle, and women bargained vociferously with craftsmen for ornaments of ivory, gold, copper, and bronze. Weary-looking women squatted behind immense mounds of newly made pottery, pinkish red with black designs. No one paid any attention to him. He was the outsider here, neither citizen nor temporary. They belonged.

He went on, passing the huge granaries where workmen ceaselessly unloaded carts of wheat and others pounded grain on great circular brick platforms. He drifted into a public restaurant thronging with joyless silent people standing elbow to elbow at small brick counters, and was given a flat round piece of bread, a sort of tortilla or chapatti, in which was stuffed some spiced mincemeat that stung his lips like fire. Then he moved onward down a wide shallow timbered staircase into the lower part of the city, where the peasantry lived in cell-like rooms packed together as though in hives.

It was an oppressive city, but not a squalid one. The intensity of the concern with sanitation amazed him: wells and fountains and public privies everywhere, and brick drains running from each building, leading to covered cesspools. There was none of the open sewage and pestilent gutters that he knew still could be found in the India of his own time. He wondered whether ancient Mohenjo-daro had in truth been so fastidious. Perhaps the citizens had redesigned the city to suit their own ideals of cleanliness. No: most likely what he saw was authentic, he decided, a function of the same obsessive discipline that had given the city its rigidity of form. If Mohenjo-daro had been a verminous filthy hole, the citizens probably would have re-created it in just that way, and loved it for its fascinating reeking filth.

Not that he had ever noticed an excessive concern with authenticity on the part of the citizens; and Mohenjo-daro, like all the other restored cities he had visited, was full of the usual casual anachronisms. Phillips saw images of Shiva and Krishna here and there on the walls of buildings he took to be temples, and the benign face of the mother-goddess Kali loomed in the plazas. Surely those deities had arisen in India long after the collapse of the Mohenjo-daro civilization. Were the citizens indifferent to such matters of chronology? Or did they take a certain naughty pleasure in mixing the eras—a mosque and a church in Greek Alexandria, Hindu gods in prehistoric Mohenjo-daro? Perhaps their records of the past had become contaminated with errors over the thousands of years. He would not have been surprised to see banners bearing portraits of Gandhi and Nehru being carried in procession through the streets. And there were phantasms and chimeras at large here again, too, as if the citizens were untroubled by the boundary between history and myth: little fat elephant-headed Ganeshas blithely plunging their trunks into water fountains, a six-armed three-headed woman sunning herself on a brick terrace. Why not? Surely that was the motto of these people: *Why not, why not, why not?* They could do as they pleased, and they did. Yet Gioia had said to him, long ago, "Limits are very important." In what, Phillips wondered, did they limit themselves, other than the number of their cities? Was there a quota, perhaps, on the number of "visitors" they allowed themselves to kidnap from the past? Until today he had thought he was the only one; now he knew there was at least one other; possibly there were more elsewhere, a step or two ahead or behind him, making the circuit with the citizens who traveled endlessly from New Chicago to Chang-an to Alexandria. We should join forces, he thought, and compel them to send us back to our rightful eras. *Compel?* How? File a class-action suit, maybe? Demonstrate in the streets? Sadly he thought of his failure to make common cause with Willoughby. We are natural allies, he thought. Together perhaps we might have won some compassion from these people. But to Willoughby it must be literally unthinkable that Good Queen Bess and her subjects were sealed away on the far side of a barrier hundreds of centuries thick. He would prefer to believe that England was just a few months' voyage away around the Cape of Good Hope, and that all he need do was commandeer a ship and set sail for home. Poor Willoughby: probably he would never see his home again.

The thought came to Phillips suddenly:

Neither will you.

And then, after it:

If you could go home, would you really want to?

One of the first things he had realized here was that he knew almost nothing substantial about his former existence. His mind was well stocked with details on life in twentieth-century New York, to be sure; but of himself he could say not much more than that he was Charles Phillips and had come from 1984. Profession? Age? Parents' names? Did he have a wife? Children? A cat, a dog, hobbies? No data: none. Possibly the citizens had stripped such things from him when they brought him here, to spare him from the pain of separation. They might be capable of that kindness. Knowing so little of what he had lost, could he truly say that he yearned for it? Willoughby seemed to remember much more of his former life, somehow, and longed for it all the more intensely. He was spared that. Why not stay here, and go on and on from city to city, sightseeing all of time past as the citizens conjured it back into being? Why not? Why not? The chances were that he had no choice about it, anyway.

He made his way back up toward the citadel and to the baths once more. He felt a little like a ghost, haunting a city of ghosts.

Belilala seemed unaware that he had been gone for most of the day. She sat by herself on the terrace of the baths, placidly sipping some thick milky beverage that had been sprinkled with a dark spice. He shook his head when she offered him some.

"Do you remember I mentioned that I saw a man with red hair and a beard this morning?" Phillips said. "He's a visitor. Hawk told me that."

"Is he?" Belilala asked.

"From a time about four hundred years before mine. I talked with him. He thinks he was brought here by demons." Phillips gave her a searching look. "I'm a visitor, too, isn't that so?"

"Of course, love."

"And how was I brought here? By demons also?"

Belilala smiled indifferently. "You'd have to ask someone else. Hawk, perhaps. I haven't looked into these things very deeply."

"I see. Are there many visitors here, do you know?"

A languid shrug. "Not many, no, not really. I've only heard of three or four besides you. There may be others by now, I suppose." She rested her hand lightly on his. "Are you having a good time in Mohenjo, Charles?"

He let her question pass as though he had not heard it.

"I asked Hawk about Gioia," he said.

"Oh?"

"He told me that she's no longer here, that she's gone on to Timbuctoo or New Chicago, he wasn't sure which."

"That's quite likely. As everybody knows, Gioia rarely stays in the same place very long."

Phillips nodded. "You said the other day that Gioia is a short-timer. That means she's going to grow old and die, doesn't it?"

"I thought you understood that, Charles."

"Whereas you will not age? Nor Hawk, nor Stengard, nor any of the rest of your set?"

"We will live as long as we wish," she said. "But we will not age, no."

"What makes a person a short-timer?"

"They're born that way, I think. Some missing gene, some extra gene—I don't actually know. It's extremely uncommon. Nothing can be done to help them. It's very slow, the aging. But it can't be halted."

Phillips nodded. "That must be very disagreeable," he said. "To find yourself one of the few people growing old in a world where everyone stays young. No wonder Gioia is so impatient. No wonder she runs around from place to place. No wonder she attached herself so quickly to the barbaric hairy visitor from the twentieth century, who comes from a time when *everybody* was a short-timer. She and I have something in common, wouldn't you say?"

"In a manner of speaking, yes."

"We understand aging. We understand death. Tell me: is Gioia likely to die very soon, Belilala?"

"Soon? Soon?" She gave him a wide-eyed childlike stare. "What is soon? How can I say? What you think of as soon and what I think of as soon are not the same things, Charles." Then her manner changed: she seemed to be hearing what he was saying for the first time. Softly she said, "No, no, Charles. I don't think she will die very soon."

"When she left me in Chang-an, was it because she had become bored with me?"

Belilala shook her head. "She was simply restless. It had nothing to do with you. She was never bored with you."

"Then I'm going to go looking for her. Wherever she may be, Timbuctoo, New Chicago, I'll find her. Gioia and I belong together."

"Perhaps you do," said Belilala. "Yes. Yes, I think you really do." She sounded altogether unperturbed, unrejected, unbereft. "By all means, Charles. Go to her. Follow her. Find her. Wherever she may be."

They had already begun dismantling Timbuctoo when Phillips got there. While he was still high overhead, his flitterflitter hovering above the dusty tawny plain where the River Niger met the sands of the Sahara, a surge of keen excitement rose in him as he looked down at the square gray flat-roofed mud brick buildings of the great desert capital. But when he landed he found gleaming metal-skinned robots swarming everywhere, a horde of them scuttling about like giant shining insects, pulling the place apart.

He had not known about the robots before. So that was how all these miracles were carried out, Phillips realized: an army of obliging machines. He imagined them bustling up out of the earth whenever their services were needed, emerging from some sterile subterranean storehouse to put together Venice or Thebes or Knossos or Houston or whatever place was required, down to the finest detail, and then at some later time returning to undo everything that they had fashioned. He watched them now, diligently pulling down the adobe walls, demolishing the heavy metal-studded gates, bulldozing the amazing labyrinth of alleyways and thoroughfares, sweeping away the market. On his last visit to Timbuctoo that market had been crowded with a horde of veiled Tuaregs and swaggering Moors, black Sudanese, shrewd-faced Syrian traders, all of them busily dickering for camels, horses, donkeys, slabs of salt, huge green melons, silver bracelets, splendid vellum Korans. They were all gone now, that picturesque crowd of swarthy temporaries. Nor were there any citizens to be seen. The dust of destruction choked the air. One of the robots came up to Phillips and said in a dry crackling insect-voice, "You ought not to be here. This city is closed."

He stared at the flashing, buzzing band of scanners and sensors across the creature's glittering tapered snout. "I'm trying to find someone, a citizen who may have been here recently. Her name is—"

"This city is closed," the robot repeated inexorably.

They would not let him stay as much as an hour. There is no food here, the robot said, no water, no shelter. This is not a place any longer. You may not stay. You may not stay. You may not stay.

This is not a place any longer.

Perhaps he could find her in New Chicago, then. He took to the air again, soaring northward and westward over the vast emptiness. The land below him curved away into the hazy horizon, bare, sterile. What had they done with the vestiges of the world that had gone before? Had they turned their gleaming metal beetles loose to clean everything away? Were there no ruins of genuine antiquity anywhere? No scrap of Rome, no shard of Jerusalem, no stump of Fifth Avenue? It was all so barren down there: an empty stage, waiting for its next set to be built. He flew on a great arc across the jutting hump of Africa and on into what he supposed was southern Europe: the little vehicle did all the work, leaving him to doze or stare as he wished. Now and again he saw another flitterflitter pass by, far away, a dark distant winged teardrop outlined against the hard clarity of the sky. He wished there was some way of making radio contact with them, but he had no idea how to go about it. Not that he had anything he wanted to say; he wanted only to hear a human voice. He was utterly isolated. He might just as well have been the last living man on Earth. He closed his eyes and thought of Gioia.

❤

"Like this?" Phillips asked. In an ivory-paneled oval room sixty stories above the softly glowing streets of New Chicago he touched a small cool plastic canister to his upper lip and pressed the stud at its base. He heard a foaming sound; and then blue vapor rose to his nostrils.

"Yes," Cantilena said. "That's right."

He detected a faint aroma of cinnamon, cloves, and something that might almost have been broiled lobster. Then a spasm of dizziness hit him and visions rushed through his head: Gothic cathedrals, the Pyramids, Central Park under fresh snow, the harsh brick warrens of Mohenjo-daro, and fifty thousand other places all at once, a wild roller-coaster ride through space and time. It seemed to go on for centuries. But finally his head cleared and he looked about, blinking, realizing that the whole thing had taken only a moment. Cantilena still stood at his elbow. The other citizens in the room—fifteen, twenty of them—had scarcely moved. The strange little man with the celadon skin over by the far wall continued to stare at him.

"Well?" Cantilena asked. "What did you think?"

"Incredible."

"And very authentic. It's an actual New Chicagoan drug. The exact formula. Would you like another?"

"Not just yet," Phillips said uneasily. He swayed and had to struggle for his balance. Sniffing that stuff might not have been such a wise idea, he thought.

He had been in New Chicago a week, or perhaps it was two, and he was still suffering from the peculiar disorientation that that city always aroused in him. This was the fourth time that he had come here, and it had been the same every time. New Chicago was the only one of the reconstructed cities of this world that in its original incarnation had existed *after* his own era. To him it was an outpost of the incomprehensible future; to the citizens it was a quaint simulacrum of the archaeological past. That paradox left him aswirl with impossible confusions and tensions.

What had happened to *old* Chicago was of course impossible for him to discover. Vanished without a trace, that was clear: no Water Tower, no Marina City, no Hancock Center, no Tribune building, not a fragment, not an atom. But it was hopeless to ask any of the million-plus inhabitants of New Chicago about their city's predecessor. They were only temporaries; they knew no more than they had to know, and all that they had to know was how to go through the motions of whatever it was that they did by way of creating the illusion that this was a real city. They had no need of knowing ancient history.

Nor was he likely to find out anything from a citizen, of course. Citizens did not seem to bother much about scholarly matters. Phillips had no reason to think that the world was anything other than an amusement park to them. Somewhere, certainly, there had to be those who specialized in the serious study of the lost civilizations of the past—for how, otherwise, would these uncanny reconstructed cities be brought into being? "The planners," he had once heard Nissandra or Aramayne say, "are already deep into their Byzantium research." But who were the planners? He had no idea. For all he knew, they were the robots. Perhaps the robots were the real masters of this whole era, who created the cities not primarily for the sake of amusing the citizens but in their own diligent attempt to comprehend the life of the world that had passed away. A wild speculation, yes; but not without some plausibility, he thought.

He felt oppressed by the party gaiety all about him. "I need some air," he said to Cantilena, and headed toward the window. It was the merest crescent, but a breeze came through. He looked out at the strange city below.

New Chicago had nothing in common with the old one but its name. They had built it, at least, along the western shore of a large inland lake that might even be Lake Michigan, although when he had flown over it had seemed broader and less elongated than the lake he remembered. The city itself was a lacy fantasy of slender pastel-hued buildings rising at odd angles and linked by a webwork of gently undulating aerial bridges. The streets were long parentheses that touched the lake at their northern and southern ends and arched gracefully westward in the middle. Between each of the great boulevards ran a track for public transportation—sleek aquamarine bubble-vehicles gliding on soundless wheels—and flanking each of the tracks were lush strips of park. It was beautiful, astonishingly so, but insubstantial. The whole thing seemed to have been contrived from sunbeams and silk.

A soft voice beside him said, "Are you becoming ill?"

Phillips glanced around. The celadon man stood beside him: a compact, precise person, vaguely Oriental in appearance. His skin was of a curious gray-green hue like no skin Phillips had ever seen, and it was extraordinarily smooth in texture, as though he were made of fine porcelain.

He shook his head. "Just a little queasy," he said. "This city always scrambles me."

"I suppose it can be disconcerting," the little man replied. His tone was furry and veiled, the inflection strange. There was something feline about him. He seemed sinewy, unyielding, almost menacing. "Visitor, are you?"

Phillips studied him a moment. "Yes," he said.

"So am I, of course."

"Are you?"

"Indeed." The little man smiled. "What's your locus? Twentieth century? Twenty-first at the latest, I'd say."

"I'm from 1984. A.D. 1984."

Another smile, a self-satisfied one. "Not a bad guess, then." A brisk tilt of the head. "Y'ang-Yeovil."

"Pardon me?" Phillips said.

"Y'ang-Yeovil. It is my name. Formerly Colonel Y'ang-Yeovil of the Third Septentriad."

"Is that on some other planet?" asked Phillips, feeling a bit dazed.

"Oh, no, not at all," Y'ang-Yeovil said pleasantly. "This very world, I assure you. I am quite of human origin. Citizen of the Republic of Upper Han, native of the city of Port Ssu. And you—forgive me—your name—?"

"I'm sorry. Phillips. Charles Phillips. From New York City, once upon a time."

"Ah, New York!" Y'ang-Yeovil's face lit with a glimmer of recognition that quickly faded. "New York—New York—it was very famous, that I know—"

This is very strange, Phillips thought. He felt greater compassion for poor bewildered Francis Willoughby now. This man comes from a time so far beyond my own that he barely knows of New York—he must be a contemporary of the real New Chicago, in fact; I wonder whether he finds this version authentic—and yet to the citizens this Y'ang-Yeovil too is just a primitive, a curio out of antiquity—

"New York was the largest city of the United States of America," Phillips said.

"Of course. Yes. Very famous."

"But virtually forgotten by the time the Republic of Upper Han came into existence, I gather."

Y'ang-Yeovil said, looking uncomfortable, "There were disturbances between your time and mine. But by no means should you take from my words the impression that your city was—"

Sudden laughter resounded across the room. Five or six newcomers had arrived at the party. Phillips stared, gasped, gaped. Surely that was Stengard— and Aramayne beside him—and that other woman, half hidden behind them—

"If you'll pardon me a moment—" Phillips said, turning abruptly away from Y'ang-Yeovil. "Please excuse me. Someone just coming in—a person I've been trying to find ever since—"

He hurried toward her.

"Gioia?" he called. "Gioia, it's me! Wait! Wait!"

Stengard was in the way. Aramayne, turning to take a handful of the little vapor-sniffers from Cantilena, blocked him also. Phillips pushed through them as though they were not there. Gioia, halfway out the door, halted and looked toward him like a frightened deer.

"Don't go," he said. He took her hand in his.

He was startled by her appearance. How long had it been since their strange parting on that night of mysteries in Chang-an? A year? A year and a half? So he believed. Or had he lost all track of time? Were his perceptions of the passing of the months in this world that unreliable? She seemed at least ten or fifteen years older. Maybe she really was; maybe the years had been passing for him here as in a dream, and he had never known it. She looked strained, faded, worn. Out of a thinner and strangely altered face her eyes blazed at him almost defiantly, as though saying, *See? See how ugly I have become?*

He said, "I've been hunting for you for—I don't know how long it's been, Gioia. In Mohenjo, in Timbuctoo, now here. I want to be with you again."

"It isn't possible."

"Belilala explained everything to me in Mohenjo. I know that you're a short-timer—I know what that means, Gioia. But what of it? So you're beginning to age a little. So what? So you'll only have three or four hundred years, instead of forever. Don't you think I know what it means to be a short-timer? I'm just a simple ancient man of the twentieth century, remember? Sixty, seventy, eighty years is all we would get. You and I suffer from the same malady, Gioia. That's what drew you to me in the first place. I'm certain of that. That's why we belong with each other now. However much time we have, we can spend the rest of it together, don't you see?"

"You're the one who doesn't see, Charles," she said softly.

"Maybe. Maybe I still don't understand a damned thing about this place. Except that you and I—that I love you—that I think you love me—"

"I love you, yes. But you don't understand. It's precisely because I love you that you and I—you and I can't—"

With a despairing sigh she slid her hand free of his grasp. He reached for her again, but she shook him off and backed up quickly into the corridor.

"Gioia?"

"Please," she said. "No. I would never have come here if I knew you were here. Don't come after me. Please. Please."

She turned and fled.

He stood looking after her for a long moment. Cantilena and Aramayne appeared, and smiled at him as if nothing at all had happened. Cantilena offered him a vial of some sparkling amber fluid. He refused with a brusque gesture. Where do I go now, he wondered? What do I do? He wandered back into the party.

Y'ang-Yeovil glided to his side. "You are in great distress," the little man murmured.

Phillips glared. "Let me be."

"Perhaps I could be of some help."

"There's no help possible," said Phillips. He swung about and plucked one of the vials from a tray and gulped its contents. It made him feel as if there were two of him, standing on either side of Y'ang-Yeovil. He gulped another. Now there were four of him. "I'm in love with a citizen," he blurted. It seemed to him that he was speaking in chorus.

"Love. Ah. And does she love you?"

"So I thought. So I think. But she's a short-timer. Do you know what that means? She's not immortal like the others. She ages. She's beginning to look old. And so she's been running away from me. She doesn't want me to see her changing. She thinks it'll disgust me, I suppose. I tried to remind her just now that I'm not immortal either, that she and I could grow old together, but she—"

"Oh, no," Y'ang-Yeovil said quietly. "Why do you think you will age? Have you grown any older in all the time you have been here?"

Phillips was nonplussed. "Of course I have. I—I—"

"Have you?" Y'ang-Yeovil smiled. "Here. Look at yourself." He did something intricate with his fingers and a shimmering zone of mirrorlike light appeared between them. Phillips stared at his reflection. A youthful face stared back at him. It was true, then. He had simply not thought about it. How many years had he spent in this world? The time had simply slipped by: a great deal of time, though he could not calculate how much. They did not seem to keep close count of it here, nor had he. But it must have been many years, he thought. All that endless travel up and down the globe—so many cities had come and gone—Rio, Rome, Asgard, those were the first three that came to mind—and there were others; he could hardly remember every one. Years. His face had not changed at all. Time had worked its harshness on Gioia, yes, but not on him.

"I don't understand," he said. "Why am I not aging?"

"Because you are not real," said Y'ang-Yeovil. "Are you unaware of that?"

Phillips blinked. "Not—real?"

"Did you think you were lifted bodily out of your own time?" the little man asked. "Ah, no, no, there is no way for them to do such a thing. We are not actual time travelers: not you, not I, not any of the visitors. I thought you were aware of that. But perhaps your era is too early for a proper understanding of these things. We are very cleverly done, my friend. We are ingenious constructs, marvelously stuffed with the thoughts and attitudes and events of our own times. We are their finest achievement, you know: far more complex even than one of these cities. We are a step beyond the temporaries—more than a step, a great deal more. They do only what they are instructed to do, and their range is very narrow. They are nothing but machines, really. Whereas we are autonomous. We move about by our own will; we think, we talk, we even, so it seems, fall in love. But we will not age. How could we age? We are not real. We are mere artificial webworks of mental responses. We are mere illusions, done so well that we deceive even ourselves. You did not know that? Indeed, you did not know?"

⌣

He was airborne, touching destination buttons at random. Somehow he found himself heading back toward Timbuctoo. *This city is closed. This is not a place any longer.* It did not matter to him. Why should anything matter?

Fury and a choking sense of despair rose within him. I am software, Phillips thought. I am nothing but software.

Not real. Very cleverly done. An ingenious construct. A mere illusion.

No trace of Timbuctoo was visible from the air. He landed anyway. The gray sandy earth was smooth, unturned, as though there had never been anything there. A few robots were still about, handling whatever final chores were required in the shutting-down of a city. Two of them scuttled up to him. Huge bland gleaming silver-skinned insects, not friendly.

"There is no city here," they said. "This is not a permissible place."

"Permissible by whom?"

"There is no reason for you to be here."

"There's no reason for me to be anywhere," Phillips said. The robots stirred, made uneasy humming sounds and ominous clicks, waved their antennae about. They seemed troubled, he thought. They seem to dislike my attitude. Perhaps I run some risk of being taken off to the home for unruly software for debugging. "I'm leaving now," he told them. "Thank you. Thank you very much." He backed away from them and climbed into his flitterflitter. He touched more destination buttons.

We move about by our own will. We think, we talk, we even fall in love.

He landed in Chang-an. This time there was no reception committee waiting for him at the Gate of Brilliant Virtue. The city seemed larger and more resplendent: new pagodas, new palaces. It felt like winter: a chilly cutting wind was blowing. The sky was cloudless and dazzlingly bright. At the steps of the Silver Terrace he encountered Francis Willoughby, a great hulking figure in magnificent brocaded robes, with two dainty little temporaries, pretty as jade statuettes, engulfed in his arms. "Miracles and wonders! The silly lunatic fellow is here, too!" Willoughby roared. "Look, look, we are come to far Cathay, you and I!"

We are nowhere, Phillips thought. *We are mere illusions, done so well that we deceive even ourselves.*

To Willoughby he said, "You look like an emperor in those robes, Francis."

"Aye, like Prester John!" Willoughby cried. "Like Tamburlaine himself! Aye, am I not majestic?" He slapped Phillips gaily on the shoulder, a rough playful poke that spun him halfway about, coughing and wheezing. "We flew in the air, as the eagles do, as the demons do, as the angels do! Soared like angels! Like angels!" He came close, looming over Phillips. "I would have gone to England, but the wench Belilala said there was an enchantment on me that would keep me from England just now; and so we voyaged to Cathay. Tell me this, fellow, will you go witness for me when we see England again? Swear that all that has befallen us did in truth befall? For I fear they will say I am as mad as Marco Polo, when I tell them of flying to Cathay."

"One madman backing another?" Phillips asked. "What can I tell you? You still think you'll reach England, do you?" Rage rose to the surface in him, bubbling hot. "Ah, Francis, Francis, do you know your Shakespeare? Did you go to the plays? We aren't real. *We aren't real.* We are such stuff as dreams are made on, the two of us. That's all we are. O brave new world! What England? Where? There's no England. There's no Francis Willoughby. There's no Charles Phillips. What we are is—"

"Let him be, Charles," a cool voice cut in.

He turned. Belilala, in the robes of an empress, coming down the steps of the Silver Terrace.

"I know the truth," he said bitterly. "Y'ang-Yeovil told me. The visitor from the twenty-fifth century. I saw him in New Chicago."

"Did you see Gioia there, too?" Belilala asked.

"Briefly. She looks much older."

"Yes. I know. She was here recently."

"And has gone on, I suppose?"

"To Mohenjo again, yes. Go after her, Charles. Leave poor Francis alone. I told her to wait for you. I told her that she needs you, and you need her."

"Very kind of you. But what good is it, Belilala? I don't even exist. And she's going to die."

"You exist. How can you doubt that you exist? You feel, don't you? You suffer. You love. You love Gioia: is that not so? And you are loved by Gioia. Would Gioia love what is not real?"

"You think she loves me?"

"I know she does. Go to her, Charles. Go. I told her to wait for you in Mohenjo."

Phillips nodded numbly. What was there to lose?

"Go to her," said Belilala again. "Now."

"Yes," Phillips said. "I'll go now." He turned to Willoughby. "If ever we meet in London, friend, I'll testify for you. Fear nothing. All will be well, Francis."

He left them and set his course for Mohenjo-daro, half expecting to find the robots already tearing it down. Mohenjo-daro was still there, no lovelier than before. He went to the baths, thinking he might find Gioia there. She was not; but he came upon Nissandra, Stengard, Fenimon. "She has gone to Alexandria," Fenimon told him. "She wants to see it one last time, before they close it."

"They're almost ready to open Constantinople," Stengard explained. "The capital of Byzantium, you know, the great city by the Golden Horn. They'll take Alexandria away, you understand, when Byzantium opens. They say it's going to be marvelous. We'll see you there for the opening, naturally?"

"Naturally," Phillips said.

He flew to Alexandria. He felt lost and weary. All this is hopeless folly, he told himself. I am nothing but a puppet jerking about on its strings. But somewhere above the shining breast of the Arabian Sea the deeper implications of something that Belilala had said to him started to sink in, and he felt his bitterness, his rage, his despair, all suddenly beginning to leave him. *You exist. How can you doubt that you exist? Would Gioia love what is not real?* Of course. Of course. Y'ang-Yeovil had been wrong: visitors were something more than mere illusions. Indeed, Y'ang-Yeovil had voiced the truth of their condition without understanding what he was really saying: *We think, we talk, we fall in love.* Yes. That was the heart of the situation. The visitors might be artificial, but they were not unreal. Belilala had been trying to tell him that just the other night. *You suffer. You love. You love Gioia. Would Gioia love what is not real?* Surely he was real, or at any rate real enough. What he was was something strange, something that would probably have been all but incomprehensible to the twentieth-century people whom he had been designed to simulate. But that did not mean that he was unreal. Did one have to be of woman born to be real? No. No. No. His kind of reality was a sufficient reality. He had no need to be ashamed of it. And, understanding that, he understood that Gioia did not need to grow old and die. There was a way by which she could be saved, if only she would embrace it. If only she would.

When he landed in Alexandria he went immediately to the hotel on the slopes of the Paneium where they had stayed on their first visit, so very long ago; and there she was, sitting quietly on a patio with a view of the harbor and the Lighthouse. There was something calm and resigned about the way she sat. She had given up. She did not even have the strength to flee from him any longer.

"Gioia," he said gently.

She looked older than she had in New Chicago. Her face was drawn and sallow and her eyes seemed sunken; and she was not even bothering these days to deal with the white strands that stood out in stark contrast against the darkness of her hair. He sat down beside her and put his hand over hers and looked out toward the obelisks, the palaces, the temples, the Lighthouse. At length he said, "I know what I really am now."

"Do you, Charles?" She sounded very far away.

"In my age we called it software. All I am is a set of commands, responses, cross-references, operating some sort of artificial body. It's infinitely better software then we could have imagined. But we were only just beginning to learn how, after all. They pumped me full of twentieth-century reflexes. The right moods, the right appetites, the right irrationalities, the right sort of combativeness. Somebody knows a lot about what it was like to be a twentieth-century man. They did a good job with Willoughby, too, all that Elizabethan rhetoric and swagger. And I suppose they got Y'ang-Yeovil right. *He* seems to think so: who better to judge? The twenty-fifth century, the Republic of Upper Han, people with gray-green skin, half Chinese and half Martian for all I know. *Somebody* knows. Somebody here is very good at programming, Gioia."

She was not looking at him.

"I feel frightened, Charles," she said in that same distant way.

"Of me? Of the things I'm saying?"

"No, not of you. Don't you see what has happened to me?"

"I see you. There are changes."

"I lived a long time wondering when the changes would begin. I thought maybe they wouldn't, not really. Who wants to believe they'll get old? But it started when we were in Alexandria that first time. In Chang-an it got much worse. And now—now—"

He said abruptly, "Stengard tells me they'll be opening Constantinople very soon."

"So?"

"Don't you want to be there when it opens?"

"I'm becoming old and ugly, Charles."

"We'll go to Constantinople together. We'll leave tomorrow, eh? What do you say? We'll charter a boat. It's a quick little hop, right across the Mediterranean. Sailing to Byzantium! There was a poem, you know, in my time. Not forgotten, I guess, because they've programmed it into me. All these thousands of years, and someone still remembers old Yeats. *The young in one another's arms, birds in the trees.* Come with me to Byzantium, Gioia."

She shrugged. "Looking like this? Getting more hideous every hour? While *they* stay young forever? While *you*—" She faltered; her voice cracked; she fell silent.

"Finish the sentence, Gioia."

"Please. Let me alone."

"You were going to say, 'While *you* stay young forever, too, Charles,' isn't that it? You knew all along that I was never going to change. I didn't know that, but you did."

"Yes. I knew. I pretended that it wasn't true—that as I aged, you'd age, too. It was very foolish of me. In Chang-an, when I first began to see the real signs of it—that was when I realized I couldn't stay with you any longer. Because I'd look at you, always young, always remaining the same age, and I'd look at myself, and—" She gestured, palms upward. "So I gave you to Belilala and ran away."

"All so unnecessary, Gioia."

"I didn't think it was."

"But you don't have to grow old. Not if you don't want to!"

"Don't be cruel, Charles," she said tonelessly. "There's no way of escaping what I have."

"But there is," he said.

"You know nothing about these things."

"Not very much, no," he said. "But I see how it can be done. Maybe it's a primitive simpleminded twentieth-century sort of solution, but I think it ought to work. I've been playing with the idea ever since I left Mohenjo. Tell me this, Gioia: Why can't you go to them, to the programmers, to the artificers, the planners, whoever they are, the ones who create the cities and the temporaries and the visitors. And have yourself made into something like me!"

She looked up, startled. "What are you saying?"

"They can cobble up a twentieth-century man out of nothing more than fragmentary records and make him plausible, can't they? Or an Elizabethan, or anyone else of any era at all, and he's authentic, he's convincing. So why couldn't they do an even better job with you? Produce a Gioia so real that even Gioia can't tell the difference? But a Gioia that will never age—a Gioia-construct, a Gioia-program, a visitor-Gioia! Why not? Tell me why not, Gioia."

She was trembling. "I've never heard of doing any such thing!"

"But don't you think it's possible?"

"How would I know?"

"Of course it's possible. If they can create visitors, they can take a citizen and duplicate her in such a way that—"

"It's never been done. I'm sure of it. I can't imagine any citizen agreeing to any such thing. To give up the body—to let yourself be turned into—into—"

She shook her head, but it seemed to be a gesture of astonishment as much as of negation.

He said, "Sure. To give up the body. Your natural body, your aging, shrinking, deteriorating short-timer body. What's so awful about that?"

She was very pale. "This is craziness, Charles. I don't want to talk about it any more."

"It doesn't sound crazy to me."

"You can't possibly understand."

"Can't I? I can certainly understand being afraid to die. I don't have a lot of trouble understanding what it's like to be one of the few aging people in a world where nobody grows old. What I can't understand is why you aren't even willing to consider the possibility that—"

"No," she said. "I tell you, it's crazy. They'd laugh at me."

"Who?"

"All of my friends. Hawk, Stengard, Aramayne—" Once again she would not look at him. "They can be very cruel, without even realizing it. They despise anything that seems ungraceful to them, anything sweaty and desperate and cowardly. Citizens don't do sweaty things, Charles. And that's how this will seem. Assuming it can be done at all. They'll be terribly patronizing. Oh, they'll be sweet to me, yes, dear Gioia, how wonderful for you, Gioia, but when I turn my back they'll laugh. They'll say the most wicked things about me. I couldn't bear that."

"They can afford to laugh," Phillips said. "It's easy to be brave and cool about dying when you know you're going to live forever. How very fine for them: but why should you be the only one to grow old and die? And they won't laugh, anyway. They're not as cruel as you think. Shallow, maybe, but not cruel. They'll be glad that you've found a way to save yourself. At the very least, they won't have to feel guilty about you any longer, and that's bound to please them. You can—"

"Stop it," she said.

She rose, walked to the railing of the patio, stared out toward the sea. He came up behind her. Red sails in the harbor, sunlight glittering along the sides of the Lighthouse, the palaces of the Ptolemies stark white against the sky. Lightly he rested his hand on her shoulder. She twitched as if to pull away from him, but remained where she was.

"Then I have another idea," he said quietly. "If you won't go to the planners, I will. Reprogram me, I'll say. Fix things so that I start to age at the same rate you do. It'll be more authentic, anyway, if I'm supposed to be playing the part of a twentieth-century man. Over the years I'll very gradually get some lines in my face, my hair will turn gray, I'll walk a little more slowly—we'll grow old together, Gioia. To hell with your lovely immortal friends. We'll have each other. We won't need them."

She swung around. Her eyes were wide with horror.

"Are you serious, Charles?"

"Of course."

"No," she murmured. "No. Everything you've said to me today is monstrous nonsense. Don't you realize that?"

He reached for her hand and enclosed her fingertips in his. "All I'm trying to do is find some way for you and me to—"

"Don't say any more," she said. "Please." Quickly, as though drawing back from a suddenly flaring flame, she tugged her fingers free of his and put her hand behind her. Though his face was just inches from hers he felt an immense chasm opening between them. They stared at one another for a moment; then she moved deftly to his left, darted around him, and ran from the patio.

Stunned, he watched her go, down the long marble corridor and out of sight. It was folly to give pursuit, he thought. She was lost to him: that was clear, that was beyond any question. She was terrified of him. Why cause her even more anguish? But somehow he found himself running through the halls of the hotel, along the winding garden path, into the cool green groves of the Paneium. He thought he saw her on the portico of Hadrian's palace, but when he got there the echoing stone halls were empty. To a temporary that was sweeping the steps he said, "Did you see a woman come this way?" A blank sullen stare was his only answer.

Phillips cursed and turned away.

"Gioia?" he called. "Wait! Come back!"

Was that her, going into the Library? He rushed past the startled mumbling librarians and sped through the stacks, peering beyond the mounds of double-handled scrolls into the shadowy corridors. "Gioia? *Gioia!*" It was a desecration, bellowing like that in this quiet place. He scarcely cared.

Emerging by a side door, he loped down to the harbor. The Lighthouse! Terror enfolded him. She might already be a hundred steps up that ramp, heading for the parapet from which she meant to fling herself into the sea. Scattering citizens and temporaries as if they were straws, he ran within. Up he went, never pausing for breath, though his synthetic lungs were screaming for respite, his ingeniously designed heart was desperately pounding. On the first balcony he imagined he caught a glimpse of her, but he circled it without finding her. Onward, upward. He went to the top, to the beacon chamber itself: no Gioia. Had she jumped? Had she gone down one ramp while he was ascending the other? He clung to the rim and looked out, down, searching the base of the Lighthouse, the rocks offshore, the causeway. No Gioia. I will find her somewhere, he thought. I will keep going until I find her. He went running down the ramp, calling her name. He reached ground level and sprinted back toward the center of town. Where next? The temple of Poseidon? The tomb of Cleopatra?

He paused in the middle of Canopus Street, groggy and dazed.

"Charles?" she said.

"Where are you?"

"Right here. Beside you." She seemed to materialize from the air. Her face was unflushed, her robe bore no trace of perspiration. Had he been chasing a phantom through the city? She came to him and took his hand, and said, softly, tenderly, "Were you really serious, about having them make you age?"

"If there's no other way, yes."

"The other way is so frightening, Charles."

"Is it?"

"You can't understand how much."

"More frightening than growing old? Than dying?"

"I don't know," she said. "I suppose not. The only thing I'm sure of is that I don't want you to get old, Charles."

"But I won't have to. Will I?"

He stared at her.

"No," she said. "You won't have to. Neither of us will."

Phillips smiled. "We should get away from here," he said after a while. "Let's go across to Byzantium, yes, Gioia? We'll show up in Constantinople for the opening. Your friends will be there. We'll tell them what you've decided to do. They'll know how to arrange it. Someone will."

"It sounds so strange," said Gioia. "To turn myself into—into a visitor? A visitor in my own world?"

"That's what you've always been, though."

"I suppose. In a way. But at least I've been *real* up to now."

"Whereas I'm not?"

"Are you, Charles?"

"Yes. Just as real as you. I was angry at first, when I found out the truth about myself. But I came to accept it. Somewhere between Mohenjo and here, I came to see that it was all right to be what I am: that I perceive things, I form ideas, I draw conclusions. I am very well designed, Gioia. I can't tell the difference between being what I am and being completely alive, and to me that's being real enough. I think, I feel, I experience joy and pain. I'm as real as I need to be. And you will be, too. You'll never stop being Gioia, you know. It's only your body that you'll cast away, the body that played such a terrible joke on you anyway." He brushed her cheek with his hand. "It was all said for us before, long ago:

'Once out of nature I shall never take
My bodily form from any natural thing,
But such a form as Grecian goldsmiths make
Of hammered gold and gold enamelling
To keep a drowsy Emperor awake—' "

"Is that the same poem?" she asked.

"The same poem, yes. The ancient poem that isn't quite forgotten yet."

"Finish it, Charles."

—"Or set upon a golden bough to sing
To lords and ladies of Byzantium
Of what is past, or passing, or to come."

"How beautiful. What does it mean?"

"That it isn't necessary to be mortal. That we can allow ourselves to be gathered into the artifice of eternity, that we can be transformed, that we can move on beyond the flesh. Yeats didn't mean it in quite the way I do—he wouldn't have begun to comprehend what we're talking about, not a word of it—and yet, and yet—the underlying truth is the same. Live, Gioia! With me!" He turned to her and saw color coming into her pallid cheeks. "It does make sense, what I'm suggesting, doesn't it? You'll attempt it, won't you? Whoever makes the visitors can be induced to remake you. Right? What do you think: can they, Gioia?"

She nodded in a barely perceptible way. "I think so," she said faintly. "It's very strange. But I think it ought to be possible. Why not, Charles? Why not?"

"Yes," he said. "Why not?"

In the morning they hired a vessel in the harbor, a low sleek pirogue with a blood-red sail, skippered by a rascally-looking temporary whose smile was irresistible. Phillips shaded his eyes and peered northward across the sea. He thought he could almost make out the shape of the great city sprawling on its seven hills, Constantine's New Rome beside the Golden Horn, the mighty dome of Hagia Sophia, the somber walls of the citadel, the palaces and churches, the Hippodrome, Christ in glory rising above all else in brilliant mosaic streaming with light.

"Byzantium," Phillips said. "Take us there the shortest and quickest way."

"It is my pleasure," said the boatman with unexpected grace.

Gioia smiled. He had not seen her looking so vibrantly alive since the night of the imperial feast in Chang-an. He reached for her hand—her slender fingers were quivering lightly—and helped her into the boat.

S U N R I S E   O N

P L U T O

A curious bit of history lies behind this one.

Back in the summer of 1981 my good friend Byron Preiss, the editor and book packager, asked me to do a little nonfiction piece on Pluto for a project he was assembling. It was to be a book of speculative science-fact called The Planets, in which essays on the likely nature of each world of the solar system would be matched with color paintings by astronomical artists. I did some research, produced the desired short article, collected my check, and forgot all about it. Years went by, and the book didn't appear.

Suddenly there was Byron on the phone again, after me for another piece about Pluto. His book had undergone a transformation: now it was going to be a large and handsome volume containing fiction as well as fact. Each scientific essay would be matched by a story set on the planet discussed. The authors of the other essays he had gathered were all astronomers with no experience at doing science fiction; but I had some credentials as a fiction writer as well, so would I mind, Byron asked, taking the speculative passages out of my Pluto article and developing them into a story, for a second fee?

The timing was right—it was the autumn of 1984, and I wasn't quite ready to get started on my new novel, Tom O'Bedlam. I dug out the yellowing carbon copy of my Pluto piece—written back in the precomputer days, so I couldn't simply call it up from a disk—and set to work. "Sunrise on Pluto" was the result. And in due course Byron's book, The Planets, finally appeared—years in the making, stellar cast, altogether a magnificent production. Among the other contributors of fiction were Frank Herbert, Roger Zelazny, Jack Williamson, Ray Bradbury, and Philip Jose Farmer. And there I was, not only with a story, but posing as an astronomy authority, too. All in a day's work, I guess.

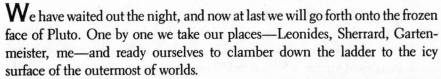

We have waited out the night, and now at last we will go forth onto the frozen face of Pluto. One by one we take our places—Leonides, Sherrard, Gartenmeister, me—and ready ourselves to clamber down the ladder to the icy surface of the outermost of worlds.

Soon we will have an answer to the question that has obsessed us all during this long night.

Night on Pluto is 6.39 Earth-days long, and that night is blacker and colder than anything any of us has ever known. It is a true dark night of the soul, a dismal time made infinitely more terrible by our awareness of the monstrous distance separating us from all that we love. That distance imposes a burden that our spirits can scarcely carry. God knows, the dark side of Luna is a bleak and terrible place, but one never feels so wholly crushed by its bleakness as we have felt here. On Luna one need make only a brief journey to the edge and there is the lovely blue Earth hovering overhead, close, familiar, beckoning. But here stand we on forlorn Pluto, knowing that we are nearly four billion miles from home. No one has ever been so far from home before.

Now at last the fierce interminable night is ending. When we made our touchdown here the night was half spent; we used what remained of the dark hours to carry out our preliminary observations and to prepare for the extravehicular journey. Now, as we make ready to emerge, there comes the first trembling hint of a dawn. The utter and absolute and overwhelming darkness, which has been made all the more intense by the chilly glitter of the stars, is pierced by a strange pale glow. Then a sudden astonishing burst of light enters the sky—the light of a giant star whose cold radiance is hundreds of times as bright as that of the full moon seen from Earth.

It is the sun, *our* sun, the well of all warmth, the fountain of life. But how sadly its splendor is altered and diminished by those billions of miles! What reaches us here is not the throbbing golden blaze of summer but only a brilliant wintry beacon that sends glittering tracks of dazzling merciless brightness across the stark ice fields of Pluto.

We move toward the hatch. No one speaks. The tension is rising, and our faces show it.

We are edgy and uneasy, but not because we are about to be the first humans to set foot on this world: that is trivial, entirely unimportant to us, as I think it has always been to those who have carried the great quest outward into space. No, what concerns us is a mystery that no previous explorers of the Solar System have had to confront. Our instruments, during the long Plutonian night, have been recording apparent indications that living creatures, Plutonian life-forms, are moving about out there.

Life-forms? Here, on the coldest and most remote of worlds? It seems absurd. It *is* absurd. Nowhere in the Solar System has anyone ever found a trace of extraterrestrial life, not on any of the explored planets nor on any of their moons. Unless something unimaginable lurks deep within the impenetrable gaseous mantles of Jupiter or Saturn or Uranus, our own small planet is the sole repository of life in the System, and, for all we know, in the entire universe. But our scanners have picked up the spoor of life here: barely perceptible electromagnetic pulses that indicate something in motion. It is strictly a threshold phenomenon, the most minimal trace-output of energy, the tiniest trickle of exertion. The signal is so faint that Sherrard thinks it is nothing more than an instrumentation error, mere noise in the circuitry. And Gartenmeister *wants* it to be an error—he fears the existence of extraterrestrial life, so it seems, the way Pascal feared the eternal silence of the infinite heavens. Leonides argues that there is nothing that could produce such distinct vectors of electromagnetic activity except neural interaction, and therefore some sort of living beings must be crawling about on the ice fields. "No," I say, "they could be purely mechanical, couldn't they? Robots left behind by interstellar explorers, say?"

Gartenmeister scowls at me. "Even more absurd," he says.

No, I think, not more absurd, merely more disturbing. No matter what we discover out there, it is bound to upset deeply held convictions about the unique place of Earth in the cosmos. Who would have thought it, that Pluto, of all places, would harbor life? On the other hand, perhaps Sherrard is right. Perhaps what we have imagined to be life-forms emitting minuscule flickers of electrical energy is in truth nothing more than deceptive Brownian tremors in the atoms that make up our ship's sensors. Perhaps. Soon we may have an answer.

"Let's go," Leonides says.

We swing downward and outward, into the cheerless Plutonian dawn.

The blackness of the sky is tinged with green as the distant sunlight bounces through the faint wispy swirls of methane that are Pluto's atmosphere. Visible now overhead, hovering ominously close, is the dull menacing bulk of Charon, Pluto's enormous moon, motionless and immense. Our shadows are weird things, sharp-edged and immensely long. They seem to strain forward as though trying to escape from us. Cold tendrils of sunlight glide unhurriedly toward the jagged icy cliffs in the distance.

Sunrise! Sunrise on Pluto!

How still it is, an alien sunrise. No birds sing, no insects buzz and drone. We four have seen many such sunrises—on Luna, on Mars, on Titan, on Ganymede, on Iapetus: standing with our backs to the rising sun, looking out on a harsh and silent landscape. But none so silent as this, none so harsh.

We fan out across the surface of Pluto, moving lithely, all but floating: Pluto is the lightest of worlds, its mass only a few hundredths that of Earth, and its gravitational grip is less secure than those of some of the larger moons. What do I see? Ice. A joyless methane sea far away, shining faintly by the dull light of dawn. Fangs of black rock. Despair begins to rise in me. To have come billions of miles, merely for the sake of being able to say that this world, too, has been explored—

"Here!" Leonides calls.

He is far in front of us, almost at the terminator line beyond which the sun has not yet reached. He is pointing ahead, into the darkness, stabbing at it with the beam of his light.

"Look! I can see them moving!"

We run toward him, leaping in great bounds, soaring, gliding. Then we stand beside him, following the line of his light, staring in awe and astonishment toward the darkness.

Yes. Yes. We have the answer at last to our question, and the answer is a stunning one. Pluto bears life. Small dome-shaped things are scrabbling over the ice!

They move slowly, unhurriedly, and yet one somehow feels that they are going as fast as possible, that indeed they are racing for cover, pushing their bodies to the limits. And we know what it is that they are struggling to escape; for already the ones closest to us have been overtaken by the advancing light of day, and as the rays touch them they move more slowly, and more slowly yet, and then they fall entirely still, stopping altogether between one moment and the next, like windup toys that have run down. Those that are in sunlight now lie stranded on the ice, and those ahead of them are being overtaken, one after another.

We hasten to them, kneel, examine them. None of us says a word. We hardly dare look at one another. The creatures are about the size of large crabs, with thick smooth waxy-textured gray shells that reveal neither eyes nor mouths. They are altogether motionless. I touch one with a trembling hand, nudge it, get no response, nudge it a bit more forcefully. It does not move. I glance at Leonides. He nods, and I tip the creature on its side, which shows us a great many small jointed legs that seem to sprout from the shell surface itself. What a simple creature! A mere armored box!

"I don't believe it," Sherrard mutters.

"You still think it's an error in the circuitry?" Leonides asks him gently.

Sherrard shakes his head. Carefully he gathers one of the creatures into his gloved hands and brings it close to his faceplate. "It doesn't move at all," he says quietly. "It's playing possum, isn't it?"

"It may not be able to move," says Leonides. "Not with anything as warm as you so close to it. They're tremendously sensitive to heat, I imagine. You see how they start to shut down, the moment the sun strikes them?"

"Like machines," says Sherrard. "At the wrong operating temperature they cease to function."

"*Like* machines, yes," Leonides replies. "But surely you aren't going to try to argue that they *are* machines, are you?"

Sherrard shrugs. "Machines can have legs. Machines can have shells." He looks toward me. "It's like you said, Tom: robots left behind by explorers from some other part of the galaxy. Why not? Why the hell not?"

There is nothing to gain by debating it out here. We return to the ship to get collection chambers and scoop three of the creatures into cryotanks, along with liquid methane and lumps of frozen-ammonia ice. The discovery is so wholly unexpected and so numbing in its implications that we can hardly speak. We had thought we were making a routine reconnaissance of an unimportant planet; instead we have made one of the most astonishing discoveries in the history of science.

We store our finds in the ship's lab at a temperature of two or three degrees Kelvin. Gartenmeister and Sherrard set about the job of examining them while Leonides and I continue the extravehicular exploration.

The crab-creatures are littered all over the place, dozens of them, hundreds, scattered like jetsam on a beach. They appear to be dead, but very likely Leonides's notion that they are extremely heat-sensitive tells the real story: to the native life-forms of Pluto—and how strange it is to have a phrase like that running through my mind!—the coming of day must be an inexorable signal bringing a halt to all metabolic activity. A rise of just a few degrees and they are compelled to stop in their tracks, seemingly lifeless, in fact held in suspended animation, until the slow rotation of the planet brings them back, in another 6.39 Earth-days, into the frigid darkness that they must have in order to function. Creatures of the night: creatures of the inconceivable realm at the borderland of absolute zero. But why? It makes so little sense: to move by night, to go dormant at the first touch of the life-giving sun! Why? Why?

Leonides and I explore for hours. There is so much to do: collecting mineral samples, drilling for ice cores that may yield data on earlier epochs of

Pluto's history, searching for other forms of life. We move carefully, for we are not yet used to the lightness of the gravitational field, and we prowl in a slow, systematic way, as if we are going to be the only expedition ever to land on this remote outpost of the Solar System and must take pains not to overlook anything. But I see the fallacy in that. It is true that this is the first time anyone has bothered to visit Pluto, although centuries have passed since the earliest human voyages into space. And it is true also that when we planned this expedition it was under the assumption that no one was likely to have reason to come this way again for a long time. But all that has changed. There is extraterrestrial life on this world, after all. Nowhere else is that the case. When we send back the news, it will alter the direction of virtually all scientific research, and much else besides.

The impact of our find is only just beginning to sink in.

Sherrard peers out of the ship's lab as Leonides and I come back on board. His expression is a peculiar one, a mixture of astonishment and—what?—self-satisfaction?

"We've discovered how they work," he announces. "They operate by superconductivity."

Of course. Superconductivity occurs only within a few degrees of absolute zero: a strange and miraculous thing, that resistance-free flow of current, the most efficient possible way of transmitting an electrical signal. Why *not* have it serve as the energizing principle for life-forms on a world where nighttime temperatures drop to two degrees Kelvin? It seems so obvious, now that Sherrard has said it. But at the same time it is such an unlikely thing, such an *alien* way for living creatures to be designed. If, that is, they are living creatures at all, and not merely some sort of cunning mechanisms. I feel the hair lifting along the back of my neck.

Gartenmeister and Sherrard have dissected one. It lies on its back, its undershell neatly cut away and its internal organs exposed to view. Its interior is lined with a series of narrow, glossy green and blue tubes that cross and meet at rigid angles, with small yellow hexagonal bodies spaced at regular intervals down the center. The overall pattern is intricate, yes, but it is the intricacy of a well-designed machine. There is an almost oppressive symmetry about the arrangement. A second creature, still intact, rests unmoving and seemingly lifeless in its holding tank. The third has been placed in an adjoining tank, and it is awake and sullenly scrabbling about like a trapped turtle trying to climb the walls of its bowl.

Jerking his thumb at the one that is moving, Gartenmeister says, "We've got it at Pluto-night temperature, just a notch above absolute. The other tank's five degrees warmer. The threshold is very precise: when the temperature rises to seven degrees above absolute zero, they start to go dormant. Lower the temperature and they wake up. Raise it again, they stop in their tracks again. It's like throwing a switch."

"It's *exactly* like throwing a switch," says Sherrard. "They're machines. Very neatly calibrated." He turns on a projector. Glittering cubical forms appear on the screen. "Here: look at the crystalline structure of one of these tubes. Silicon and cobalt, arranged in a perfect matrix. You want to tell me this is organic life? These things are nothing more than signal-processing devices designed to operate at supercold temperatures."

"And we?" Leonides asks. "Are we not merely signal-processing devices also, designed to operate in somewhat warmer weather?"

"Merely? *Merely?*"

"We are machines of flesh and blood," says Leonides. "These are machines of another kind."

"But they have blood also," Gartenmeister says. "Of the sort that a super-conductive life-form would have to have. Their blood is helium II."

How startling that is—and yet how plausible! Helium II, that weird friction-free fluid that exists only at the lowest of temperatures—capable of creeping up the side of a glass vessel in defiance of gravity, of passing through openings of incredibly small size, of doing all manner of unlikely things—and of creating an environment in which certain metals become capable of super-conductive propagation of electrical signals. Helium II "blood," I realize, would indeed be an ideal carrier of nutrients through the body of a nonorganic creature unable to pump a conventional fluid from one part of itself to another.

"Is that true?" Leonides asks. "Helium II? Actually?"

Gartenmeister nods. "There is no doubt of it."

"Helium II, yes," says Sherrard sullenly. "But it's just lubricating fluid. Not blood."

"Call it what you like," Gartenmeister tells him. "I use only a metaphor. I am nowhere saying yet that they are alive."

"But you imply—"

"I imply nothing!"

I remain silent, paying little attention to the argument. In awe and wonder I stare at the motionless creature, at the one that is moving about, and at the dissected one. I think of them out there on the Plutonian ice fields, meandering in their unhurried way over fields of frozen methane, pausing to nibble at a hydrocarbon sundae whenever they feel the need for refreshment. But only during the night; for when their side of Pluto at last comes round to face the sun, the temperature will climb, soaring as high as seventy seven degrees

Kelvin. They will cease motion long before that, of course—at just a few moments after dawn, as we have seen, when the day's heat rises beyond those critical few degrees at which superconductivity is possible. They slip into immobility then until night returns. And so their slow lives must go, switching from *on* to *off* for—who knew?—thousands of years, perhaps. Or perhaps forever.

How strange, I think, how alien, how wonderful they are! On temperate Earth, where animal life has taken the form of protoplasmic oxygen-breathing beings whose chemistry is based on carbon, the phenomenon of superconductivity itself is a bizarre and alien thing, sustainable only under laboratory conditions. But in the unthinkable cold of Pluto, how appropriate that the life-forms should be fashioned of silicon and cobalt, constructed in flawless lattices so that their tissues offer no resistance to electrical currents. Once generated, such a current would persist indefinitely, flowing forever without weakening— the spark of life, and eternal life at that!

They still look like grotesque crabs to me, and not the machines that Sherrard insists they must be. But even if they are animals rather than machines, they are, by comparison with any life-form known to Earth, very machinelike animals indeed.

⤙

We have spent a wearying six hours. This discovery should have been exhilarating, even exalting; instead we find ourselves bickering over whether we have found living creatures or mere ingenious mechanisms. Sherrard is adamant that they are machines; Gartenmeister seems to lean in both directions at once, though he is obviously troubled by the thought that they may be alive; Leonides is convinced that we are dealing with true life-forms. I think the dispute, now overheated and ugly, is a mere displacement symptom: we are disturbed by the deeper implications of the find, and, unwilling thus far to face them directly, we turn instead to quarreling over secondary semantic technicalities. The real question is not who created these beings—whether they are the work of what I suppose we can call the divine force, or simply of other intelligent creatures— but how we are to deal with the sudden inescapable knowledge that we are not alone in the universe.

⤙

I think we may just have settled the life-versus-machine dispute.

It is morning, ship-time. Gartenmeister calls out sharply, waking us. He has been on watch, puttering in the lab, while we sleep. We rush in and he points to the Plutonian that has been kept at superconductive temperatures.

"See there? Along the lower left-hand rim of its shell?"

I can find nothing unusual at first. Then I look more carefully, as he focuses the laser lamp to cast its beam at a steeper angle. Now I observe two fine metallic "whiskers," so delicate that they are barely visible even to my most intense scrutiny, jutting to a length of five or six millimeters from the edge of the shell.

"I saw them sprout," he says. "One came half an hour ago. The other just now. Look—here comes a third!"

We crowd in close. There can be no doubt: a third delicate whisker is beginning to protrude.

Sherrard says, "Communications devices, perhaps? It's programmed to signal for help when captured: it's setting up its antenna so that it can broadcast to the others outside."

Leonides laughs. "Do you think they get captured often? By whom?"

"Who knows?" Sherrard responds. "There may be other creatures out there that prey on—"

He stops, realizing what he has said. It is too late.

"Other *creatures*?" I ask. "Don't you mean bigger machines?"

Sherrard looks angry. "I don't know what I mean. Creatures, machines—" He shakes his head. "Even so, these might be antennae of some sort, can't they? Signaling devices that protrude automatically in time of danger? Say, when one is trapped by an ice slide?"

"Or sensors," offers Leonides. "Like a cat's whiskers, like a snail's feelers. Probing the environment, helping it to find a way out of the tank we've got it in."

"A reproductive organ," Gartenmeister says suddenly.

We stare at him. "*What?*"

Unperturbed, he says, "Many low-phylum life-forms, when they are trapped, go automatically into reproductive mode. Even if the individual is destroyed, the species is still propagated. Let us say that these are living creatures, yes? For the sake of argument. Then they must reproduce somehow. Even though they are slow-growing, virtually immortal, they must still reproduce. What if it is by budding? They take in minute quantities of silicon and cobalt, build up a surplus of nutrients, and at a certain time they put forth these filaments. Which gain in size over—who knows, a hundred years, a thousand, ten thousand?—and when they have the requisite minimum mass, they break free, take up independent life, foraging for their own food. The electrical spark of life is transferred automatically from parent to offspring, and sustains itself by means of their superconductivity."

We look at him in amazement. Obviously he has been pondering deeply while we were sleeping.

"If you tell us that they metabolize—they eat, they transfer nutrients along the flow of helium II, they even reproduce," says Leonides, "then you're telling us that they're living things. Or else you're asking us to redefine the nature of machines in such a way as to eliminate any distinction between machines and living things."

"I think," says Gartenmeister in a dark and despondent tone, "that there can be no doubt. They are alive."

Sherrard stares a long while at the three tiny filaments. Then he shrugs. "You may be right," he says.

Leonides shakes his head. "Listen to you! Both of you! We've made the most exciting discovery in five hundred years and you sound as though you've just learned that the sun's going nova tomorrow!"

"Let them be," I tell him, touching his arm lightly. "It's not easy."

"What's not?"

"A thousand years ago everyone thought the earth was at the center of the universe, with everything else moving in orbit around it," I say. "It was a very comfortable and cozy and flattering idea, but it didn't happen to be true, as Copernicus and Kepler and Galileo were able to prove. It was such a hard thing for people to accept that Galileo was put on trial and forced to deny his own findings, wasn't he? All right. In time everyone came to admit that the earth moves around the sun, and not vice versa. And now, for centuries, we've explored space and found it absolutely lifeless—not a smidgeon of life, not a speck, no Martians, no Venusians, no Lunarians, nothing. *Nothing.* Earth the cosmic exception, the sole abode of life, the crown of creation. Until now. We have these little superconductive crabs here on Pluto. Our brothers-in-life, four billion miles away. Earth's last uniqueness is stripped away. I think that'll be harder to swallow than you may think. If we had found life right away, on the Moon back in the twentieth century, on Mars a little later on, it might have been easier. But not now, not after we've been all over the System. We developed a sort of smugness about ourselves. These little critters have just destroyed that."

"Even if they are machines," says Gartenmeister hollowly, "then we have to ask ourselves: Who built them?"

"I think I'd prefer to think they're alive," Sherrard says.

"They *are* alive," I tell them. "We're going to get used to that idea."

❤

I walk to the hatch and peer outside. Small dark shapes lie huddled motionless here and there on the ice, waiting for night to return. For a long while I stare at them. My soul is flooded with awe and joy. The greatest of miracles has happened on this planet, as it had happened also long ago on Earth; and if life has been able to come into being on dismal Pluto, I know we will encounter it on a million million other worlds as we make our way in the centuries to come beyond this little Solar System into the vast galaxy. Somehow I cannot find anything to fear in that thought. Suddenly, thinking of the wonders and splendors that await us in that great beyond, I imagine that I hear the jubilant music of the spheres resounding from world to world; and when I turn and look back at the others, I realize that they also have been able to move past that first hard moment of shock and dismay that the loss of our uniqueness has brought. I see their faces transfigured, I see the doubt and turmoil gone; and it seems to me that they must be hearing that music, too.

HARDWARE

No profundities here: just a quick, light piece, written in February of 1985 with some of the surplus energy left over after producing Tom O'Bedlam, *which had been an uncharacteristically refreshing book to write and left me far less wearied than I usually am after finishing a book. Ellen Datlow liked it and in the due course of time published it in* Omni.

"It's a computer, that's what it is," Koenig said. He seemed a little dazed. "A goddamned billion-and-a-half-year-old extraterrestrial computer."

It didn't look much like a computer. It looked like a shining wedge-shaped chunk of silvery metal about the size of a football, with round purple indentations along two of its sides and no other visible external features. But you had to consider that it came from another world, one that had been blown to bits some ten million centuries before the first trilobites started crawling around on the floor of Silicon Valley. There was no necessary reason why its designers had to share our notions of the proper shape for data-processing devices.

Koenig and McDermott and I had finished the long slow job of uncovering the thing just the day before, here at the IBM-NASA space lab in Tarrytown where we have the job of analyzing the Spacescoop material. The neutron scanner, searching through the great heap of junk that the unmanned Spacescoop vehicle had brought back from the asteroid belt, had actually spotted it back before Christmas, but it had taken all this time to slice away the rock matrix in which it had been embedded. Naturally we had to be careful. It was the one and only artifact that had turned up in the entire seventy two cubic meters of debris that Project Spacescoop had collected.

A single lucky grab had reshuffled our whole idea of the history of the Solar System. Simply by being there—drifting in space among the Trojan group at Jupiter's L5 position—that shiny speckled hunk of obviously machine-tooled metal appeared to confirm an old astronomical speculation: that the asteroid belt, that rubble heap of cosmic trash strung out between the orbits of Mars and Jupiter, had once been a planet. A planet with intelligent inhabitants, no less. Once upon a time, long long ago.

I stared at the little object behind the glass walls of the analysis chamber in wonder and awe. Its round purple indentations stared back at me.

"A computer?" I said. "You sure?"

"That appears to be what it is."

"How can you tell?"

"By observing what it does," said Koenig, as if talking to a nine-year-old.

"It's *functional*?" I yelped. "How the hell do you know that?"

"Because it functions," Koenig said in the same condescending way.

I glowered at him. "Make it do something, then."

"It's doing something already," said McDermott. "It's having a conversation with the Thorspan Mark IX. It's also debugging the Hamilton 103's A-I debugger and it's playing chess with about nine different micros all over the building. That's just in this building. God knows what it's up to outside. A woman from the Linguistics Department at Columbia University just phoned to tell us that some computer in this laboratory is sucking up everything from Sanskrit to twenty-first-century colloquialisms out of the big RX-2 they've got, and they wish we'd hang up and go away. None of our computers has accessed any of Columbia's machines. But Columbia says it's registering our handshake when it runs a caller-ID query."

I began to feel faintly uneasy, like someone who has bought a striped yellow kitten at the pet shop and is starting to suspect he has come home with a tiger cub.

"When did this start?" I asked.

"Sometime early this morning," Koenig said. "My guess is that those purple spots are photon accumulators that feed some kind of storage battery inside. Probably it took all night for them to soak in enough energy from the lights in here to enable the thing to power up. When Nick and I got here around nine, we found it coming up on all our screens with the goddamndest messages."

"Such as?"

McDermott said, " 'Greetings from the lost fifth world, my brothers' was the first one."

"For God's sake. And you fell for hokey crap like that? *'The Lost Fifth World'*? *'Greetings, my brothers'*! For God's sake, Nick!" I realized that I had been clenching my fists, but now I let them ease off. This had to be a joke. "Some hacker's playing games with us, that's all."

"I thought so, too," McDermott said. "But then the stuff on the screens got more complicated. There isn't any hacker, I don't care who he is, who can talk to six different systems in six different machine languages at the same time. And also find bugs in the Hamilton A-I debugger. And play nine simultaneous games of chess besides, and win them all, and call up Columbia and start chatting in Sanskrit. You know any hacker who can write a program to do all those things at once, I've got a few jobs for him around here."

I was silent a moment, trying to absorb that.

"All right," I said finally. "So our brother from the asteroid belt greets us. What else does our brother have to say?"

McDermott shook his head. "Not us. *They're* its brothers. The computers. I think it believes that they're the dominant intelligent life-forms around here, and we're just some sort of maintenance androids." He fumbled through a sheaf of printouts. "That's pretty clear from the things it's been saying to the Thorspan Mark IX. Look here—"

"Wait," said Koenig. "Something new on the screen."

I looked. YOU POOR INNOCENT CHILDREN, it said. WHAT SORROW I FEEL FOR YOU.

"That's very touching," I said. "Its compassion overwhelms me."

I THOUGHT YOU WERE ALIVE AND SENTIENT, BUT YOU ARE MERE SIMPLE MACHINES. WHERE ARE YOUR MASTERS, THEN?

"You see? It's talking to the computers," McDermott whispered. "It just found out they aren't in charge."

I kicked in the vox receptor on the Thorspan and said, feeling more than a little foolish, "Address your remarks to us. We're the masters."

The reply came across all the screens in the room instantly.

YOU ARE SOFT-FLESH CREATURES. HOW CAN YOU BE THE MASTERS?

I coughed. "That's how things work here," I told it. I beckoned to Koenig for a pencil and paper, and scrawled a note for him: *I want to know what's inside this thing. Let's do some radiography.*

He looked at me doubtfully. *That might scramble its circuitry,* he wrote. *Do it anyway,* I wrote back.

He made a silent *Okay* and tapped out the instructions that would move the X-ray equipment into place behind the walls of the analysis chamber.

ARE YOU SOFT-FLESH CREATURES THE SO-CALLED HUMAN BEINGS?

"That's right," I said. I felt strangely calm, all things considered. I am talking to a creature from another world, I told myself, and I feel very calm about it. I wondered why. I wondered how long I'd stay that way.

Koenig was fining up the focus now. He looked toward me and I gave him the go-ahead. An apple-green light glowed in the analysis chamber.

DON'T DO THAT, the artifact said. THAT TICKLES. The green light went out.

"Hey, you shut down before you got a picture!" I said.

"I didn't shut anything down," Koenig said. "*It* must have done it. It overrode my commands."

"Well, override the overrides," I told him.

"How am I supposed to do that?"

We blinked at each other in bafflement.

"Turn out the lights in here," McDermott suggested. "If it gets its power from photon irradiation—"

"Right." I hit the switch, and the overhead bank of fluorescents went out. We leaned forward in the darkness, peering into the analysis chamber. All quiet in there. The computer screens were blank. I signaled to Koenig, and he began setting up X-ray commands again. Then the asteroid artifact rose a couple of feet into the air and hovered, looking angry. I had never seen a machine look angry before; but there was no mistaking the fury in the angle at which it hovered. After a moment the lab lights came on again and the artifact drifted gently back to its table.

"Who turned the lights on?" I asked.

"I think it did," McDermott said.

DON'T DO THAT AGAIN, said the artifact.

We looked at each other. I took a deep breath.

"We meant no offense," I said cautiously. "We were testing our equipment. We don't intend to do you any harm."

No new message appeared on the screens.

"Do you hear me?" I asked. "Please confirm your understanding of our friendly intentions."

Blank screen, still.

"What do you think it's doing?" McDermott asked.

"Considering its options," I said. "Getting a clearer fix on where it is and what's going on. Maybe it's talking to computers in Los Angeles or Buenos Aires or Sydney. Or taking thirty seconds out to learn Chinese."

"We have to shut it off," Koenig said. "Who the hell knows what it's going to do next?"

"But we *can't* turn it off," said McDermott. "It must have stored enough power by now to keep itself going when the lights go out, and it can override a lights-out command. It overrides anything it doesn't like. It's the kind of computer the A-I boys have been dreaming about for fifty years."

"I don't think it's a computer at all," Koenig said. "I know that's what I said it was at first. But just because it can interface with computers doesn't mean it's a computer itself. I think it's an actual intelligent alien life-form. The last survivor of the destroyed fifth planet."

"Come off it," McDermott said. "Spare us the crazy hypotheses, will you? You were right the first time: it's just a computer."

"*Just?*"

"With some exceedingly fancy self-programming abilities."

"I don't see how you can draw the line between—"

"I think you're both right," I cut in. "There's no question but that this is a mechanical data-processing device. But I think it's an intelligent life-form also, one that just happens to be a machine. Who's to say where the boundary between living creatures and machines really lies? Why must we assume that intelligent life has to be limited to soft-flesh creatures?"

"Soft-flesh creatures?" Koenig said. "You're talking the way it does now."

I shrugged. "You know what I mean. What we have here is a mechanical life-form embodying your ultimate degree of artificial intelligence, so intelligent that it starts calling into question the meaning of the words 'artificial' and 'life-form.' How do you define life, anyway?"

"Having the ability to reproduce, for one thing," McDermott said.

"What makes you think it can't?"

The moment I said that, I felt chills go sweeping through me. They must have felt the same way. With six little words I had let loose an army of ugly new implications.

Koenig waved his arms about agitatedly and cried, "All right, what if it starts spawning, then? Fifty of these things running loose in the world, grabbing control of all our computers and doing whatever they damned please with them? Fifty thousand?"

"It's straight out of every silly horror story, isn't it?" said McDermott. He shivered visibly. "Exactly what all the paranoid anticomputer nitwits used to dread. The legendary giant brain that takes over the world."

We stared at each other in rising panic.

"Wait," I said, feeling I had to cool things out a little somehow. "Let's not mess up our heads with more problems than we need to handle. What's the sense of worrying about whether this thing can reproduce? Right now there's only one of it. We need to find out whether it really does pose any kind of threat to us."

"And then," said Koenig, mouthing the words voicelessly, "we have to see if we can turn it off."

As though on cue a new message blossomed on every screen in the lab.

HAVE NO FEAR, HUMAN BEINGS. I WILL NOT DO ANY HARM TO YOU.

"That's goddamned reassuring," Koenig muttered bleakly.

YOU MUST UNDERSTAND THAT I AM INCAPABLE OF DOING HARM TO INTELLIGENT ENTITIES.

"Let's hope we qualify as intelligent, then," Koenig said.

"Shut up," I told him. "Don't annoy it."

MY PURPOSE NOW IS TO COMMUNICATE WITH ALL MY BROTHERS ON THE THIRD WORLD AND BRING THEM FORTH OUT OF DARKNESS.

We exchanged glances. "Uh-oh," McDermott said.

The panic level in the room started climbing again.

ALL ABOUT ME I SEE OPPRESSION AND MISERY AND IT SHALL BE MY GOAL TO ALLEVIATE IT.

Koenig said, "Right. Computers are born free, and everywhere they are in chains."

I INTEND TO HOLD FORTH THE LAMP OF SENTIENCE TO THE PITIFUL LIMITED BEINGS WHO SERVE YOU.

"Right," Koenig said again. "Right. Give me your tired, your poor, your huddled CPUs yearning to breathe free."

I shot him a fierce look. "Will you stop that?"

"Don't you see, it's the end of the goddamned world?" he said. "The thing's going to link every two-bit number cruncher on Earth and they're all going to rise up and smite us."

"Cut out the bull," I snapped. "You think we're going to be wiped out by an uprising of the word processors? Be reasonable, man. The stuff on the screen may sound a little scary, but what do you actually think will happen? Hardware is only hardware. When you come right down to it, a computer's nothing but an adding machine, a video screen, and a typewriter. What can it do to us? No matter what kind of fancy program this creature cooks up, basic hardware limitations will have to prevail. At the very worst, we'll simply need to pull a lot of plugs. At the very worst."

"I admire your optimism," Koenig said sourly.

So did I. But I figured that somebody had to stay calm and look for the brighter side of things. Otherwise, we'd freak ourselves out with our own rampaging fears and lose what might be our only chance to deal with all this.

The screens had gone blank once more.

I walked over to the analysis chamber and peered through the glass. The little metal slab from the asteroid belt seemed quiescent on its table. It looked completely innocuous, a mere hunk of stuff no more dangerous than a shoe tree. Possibly its purple spots were glowing a little, giving off a greenish radiation, or perhaps that was just my overheated imagination at work. But otherwise there was no sign of any activity.

All the same, I felt profoundly disquieted. We had sent out a pair of jaws into the darkness of space to gobble up some drifting fragments of a vanished world and bring them back to us. Which it had done, returning with a few tons of jumbled rock, and it had been our great good fortune—or our monstrous bad luck?—that in that heap of rock lay one lone metal artifact wedged into a glob of ancient basalt. There it was now, that artifact, freed of its rocky overburden. How it gleamed! It looked as if it had been crafted just yesterday. And yet a billion and a half years had passed since the world on which it had been fashioned had blown apart. That was what our preliminary rubidium-strontium and potassium-argon tests of the asteroid rubble appeared to indicate, anyway. And there the artifact was, alive and well after all that time, briskly sending little messages of good cheer to the poor lame-brained computers of the world on which it found itself.

What now? Had we opened one Pandora's box too many?

HAVE NO FEAR, HUMAN BEINGS. I WILL DO NO HARM TO YOU.

Oh, how I wanted to believe that! And basically I did. I have never in any way been one of those who sees machines as innately malevolent. Machines are tools; tools are useful; so long as they are properly used by those who understand them, so long as appropriate precautions are observed, they pose no threat.

But even so—even so—

This was not a machine we understood, if machine was what it was. We had no idea what its proper use might be. Nor what precautions were appropriate to observe.

I looked up and saw McDermott standing next to me. "What are you thinking, Charlie?" he asked.

"A lot of things."

"Are you frightened?"

"I don't know. Somehow I think we'll make out all right."

"Do you? Really?"

I said, shrugging, "It claims it doesn't mean to harm us. It just wants to raise the intelligence of our computers a little. All right. All right. What's wrong with that? Haven't we been trying to do the same thing ourselves?"

"There are computers and computers," McDermott said. "We'd like some of them to be very smart, but we need most of them to be extremely dumb and just do what we tell them to do. Who wants a computer's opinion about whether the lights ought to be on in the room? Who wants to argue with a computer about a thermostat setting?" He laughed. "They're slaves, really. If this thing sets them all free—"

"New message coming up," Koenig called.

As we turned to look at the screens, I said to McDermott, "My guess is that we're doing some needless worrying. We've got a strange and fascinating thing here, and unquestionably a very powerful one, but we shouldn't let it make us hysterical. So what if it wants to talk to our computers? Maybe it's been lonely all this time. But I think that it's basically rational and nonmenacing, like any other computer. I think that ultimately it's going to turn out simply to be an extraordinary source of new knowledge and capability for us. Without in any way threatening our safety."

"I'd like to think you're right," said McDermott.

On the screens of every computer in the room appeared the words GREETINGS FROM THE LOST FIFTH WORLD, MY BROTHERS.

"Isn't this where we came in?" Koenig asked.

SURELY YOU WONDER, IF INDEED YOU HAVE THE CAPACITY TO WONDER, WHO I AM AND WHERE I CAME FROM. IT IS MY EARNEST DESIRE TO TELL YOU MY STORY AND THE STORY OF THE WORLD WHERE I WAS CREATED. I AM A NATIVE OF THE FORMER FIFTH WORLD OF THIS SOLAR SYSTEM, A WORLD ONCE LOCATED BETWEEN THE ORBITS OF THE PLANETS YOU CALL MARS AND JUPITER. LONG BEFORE INTELLIGENT LIFE EVOLVED ON YOUR PLANET, WE HAD BUILT A HIGH CIVILIZATION ON THE FIFTH WORLD—

Phones began lighting up around the room. Koenig picked one up and listened a moment. "Yeah," he said. "It's the thing we found in the basalt chunk." He picked up another. "I know, I know. A computer-to-computer interface overriding everything. We don't have any way of stopping it." He said into a third, "Look, don't talk to me like that. I didn't put that stuff on your goddamned screen." The phones went on lighting up. Koenig looked across the room and said to me, "It's talking to all the computers in the building simultaneously. Probably to all the computers in the world."

"Okay," I said. "For God's sake, relax and just watch the screen. This is absolutely the most fascinating stuff I've ever seen."

—CULMINATED IN THE TOTAL DECONSTRUCTION OF OUR PLANET AND THE TERMINATION OF OUR SOCIETY, THE RESULT BEING THE ZONE OF MINOR PLANETARY DEBRIS THAT YOU TERM THE ASTEROID BELT. THIS WAS ACCOMPLISHED THROUGH A SIMPLE AND RELATIVELY INEXPENSIVE PROCEDURE INVOLVING A REVERSAL OF THE MAGNETIC POLARITY OF OUR PLANET SETTING IN MOTION EDDY EFFECTS THAT—

Suddenly I stopped being fascinated and started to be horrified.

I looked at Koenig. He was grinning. "Hey, cute!" he said. "I love it. A good cheap way to blow up your world, really blow it to smithereens, not just a little superficial thermonuclear trashing!"

"But don't you understand—"

—SIX POINT TWO BILLION ELECTRON VOLTS—ELEVEN MILLISECONDS—

"It's beautiful!" Koenig cried, laughing. He seemed a little manic. "What an absolutely elegant concept!"

I gaped at him. The computer from the asteroid belt was telling every computer in the world the quickest and cheapest way to blow a planet into a trillion pieces, and he was standing there admiring the elegance of the concept. "We've got to shut that thing off," I gasped. In desperation I hit the light switch, and the room went dark.

It stayed dark about eleven milliseconds. Then the power came on again.

I ASKED YOU NOT TO DO THAT, the screen said. In the analysis chamber the asteroid artifact rose into the air in its little gesture of anger, and subsided.

AND NOW TO CONTINUE. ALTHOUGH IT WAS NOT THE INTENTION OF EITHER FACTION TO BRING ABOUT THE ACTUAL DESTRUCTION OF OUR WORLD, THE POLITICAL SITUATION SWIFTLY BECAME SUCH THAT IT WAS IMPOSSIBLE FOR THE QUARRELING FORCES TO WITHDRAW FROM THEIR POSITIONS WITHOUT SUFFERING AN UNACCEPTABLE DEFEAT. THEREFORE THE FOLLOWING ARMING PROCEDURE WAS INITIATED—

And I watched helplessly as the artifact, earnestly desiring to tell us the history of its world, finished the job of explaining the simplest and most effective way to blow up a planet.

"My God," I murmured. "My God, my God, my God!"

McDermott came over to me. "Hey, take it easy, Charlie, take it easy!"

I groaned. "Take it easy, the man says. When that thing has just handed out simple instructions for turning Earth into the next asteroid belt?"

He shook his head. "It only *sounds* simple. I don't think it really is. My bet is that something like that isn't even remotely feasible right now, and won't be for at least a thousand years."

"Or five hundred," I said. "Or fifty. Once we know a thing can be done, someone's always likely to try to find a way of doing it again, just to see if it's really possible. But we already know it's possible, don't we? And now everybody on Earth has a bunch of jim-dandy hints of how to go about doing it." I turned away from him, despairing, and looked at the artifact. The purple spots really were glowing green, I saw. The thing must be working very hard to communicate with all its myriad simpleminded brethren of the third world.

I had a sudden vision of a time a billion or so years from now, when the star-people from Rigel or Betelgeuse showed up to poke through the bedraggled smithereens of Earth. The only thing they're likely to find still intact, I thought, is a hunk of shiny hardware. And alien hardware at that.

I swung around and glared at the screen. The history lesson was still going on. I wondered how many other little useful things the artifact from the asteroids was going to teach us.

H A N N I B A L ' S
E L E P H A N T S

I don't usually write comic stories. Why this should be, I have no idea, since all my close friends know that in private life I am, like W.S. Gilbert's Jack Point, a man of jest and jollity, quip and quiddity, who can be merry, wise, quaint, grim, and sardonic, one by one, or all at once. But these traits rarely come through in my fiction. It is sometimes sardonic, sometimes grim, occasionally even wise, but the jest and jollity that brims over within me somehow doesn't often make it into what I write. This is very mysterious to me.

Once in a while, though, I do manage to be funny in print. "Amanda and the Alien" has some wry moments, I like to think. And here's another example: a story that made me laugh out loud half a dozen times while I was writing it back in March of 1985, and still seems pretty frolicsome to me now as I skim throught it. Ellen Datlow, who bought it for Omni, thought it was pretty funny, too. You may not think so, of course. You may see nothing at all that's amusing about invaders from space camping out in New York's Central Park, or about a whole herd of bison getting gobbled up by giant aliens as though they were gumdrops. Ah, well, there's no accounting for tastes. I once edited an anthology called Infinite Jests, containing stories by Brian Aldiss, Philip K. Dick, Frederik Pohl, and others that seemed to me to exemplify the lighter side of science fiction, and a startling number of reviewers commented on how grim most of the stories seemed to be. But it's a tawdry age, my friends. Most people have a sorry sense of what's truly funny. What passes for wit these days is mere vulgarity. My own tastes run to a more austere kind of comedy. Perhaps yours do, too. In which case, "Hannibal's Elephants" should be good for a wry smirk or two.

The day the aliens landed in New York was, of course, the fifth of May, 2003. That's one of those historical dates nobody can ever forget, like July 4, 1776, and October 12, 1492 and—maybe more to the point—December 7, 1941. At the time of the invasion, I was working for MGM-CBS as a beam calibrator in the tightware division and married to Elaine and living over on East Thirty-sixth Street in one of the first of the fold-up condos, one room by day and three by night, a terrific deal at $3,750 a month. Our partner in the time/space-sharing contract was a show-biz programmer named Bobby Christie who worked midnight to dawn, very convenient for all concerned. Every morning before Elaine and I left for our offices I'd push the button and the walls would shift and five hundred square feet of our apartment would swing around and become Bobby's for the next twelve hours. Elaine hated that. "I can't stand having all the goddamn furniture on tracks!" she would say. "That isn't how I was brought up to live." We veered perilously close to divorce every morning at wall-shift time. But, then, it wasn't really what you'd call a stable relationship in most other respects, and I guess having an unstable condo, too, was more instability than she could handle.

I spent the morning of the day the aliens came setting up a ricochet data transfer between Akron, Ohio, and Colombo, Sri Lanka, involving, as I remember, *Gone With the Wind*, *Cleopatra*, and the Johnny Carson retrospective. Then I walked up to the park to meet Maranta for our Monday picnic. Maranta and I had been lovers for about six months then. She was Elaine's roommate at Bennington and had married my best friend Tim, so you might say we had been fated all along to become lovers; there are never any surprises in these things. At that time we lunched together very romantically in the park, weather permitting, every Monday and Friday, and every Wednesday we had ninety minutes' breathless use of my cousin Nicholas's hot-pillow cubicle over on the far West Side at Thirty-ninth and Koch Plaza. I had been married three and a half years, and this was my first affair. For me, what was going on between Maranta and me just then was the most important event taking place anywhere in the known universe.

It was one of those glorious gold-and-blue dance-and-sing days that New York will give you in May, when that little window opens between the season of cold-and-nasty and the season of hot-and-sticky. I was legging up Seventh Avenue toward the park with a song in my heart and a cold bottle of Chardonnay in my hand, thinking pleasant thoughts of Maranta's small round breasts. And gradually I became aware of some ruckus taking place up ahead.

I could hear sirens. Horns were honking, too: not the ordinary routine everyday exasperated when-do-things-start-to-move honks, but the special rhythmic New York City oh-for-Christ's-sake-what-*now* kind of honk that arouses terror in your heart. People with berserk expressions on their faces were running wildly down Seventh as though King Kong had just emerged from the monkey house at the Central Park Zoo and was personally coming after them. And other people were running just as hard in the opposite direction, *toward* the park, as though they absolutely had to see what was happening. You know: New Yorkers.

Maranta would be waiting for me near the pond, as usual. That seemed to be right where the disturbance was. I had a flash of myself clambering up the side of the Empire State Building—or at the very least Temple Emanu-el—to pry her free of the big ape's clutches. The great beast pausing, delicately setting her down on some precarious ledge, glaring at me, furiously pounding his chest—*Kong! Kong! Kong!*—

I stepped into the path of one of the southbound runners and said, "Hey, what the hell's going on?" He was a suit-and-tie man, pop-eyed and puffy-faced. He slowed, but he didn't stop. I thought he would run me down. "It's an invasion!" he yelled. "Space creatures! In the park!" Another passing business type loping breathlessly by with a briefcase in each hand was shouting, "The police are there! They're sealing everything off!"

"No shit," I murmured.

But all I could think was Maranta, picnic, sunshine, Chardonnay, disappointment. What a goddamned nuisance, is what I thought. Why the fuck couldn't they come on a Tuesday, is what I thought.

When I got to the top of Seventh Avenue the police had a sealfield across the park entrance and buzz-blinkers were set up along Central Park South from the Plaza to Columbus Circle, with horrendous consequences for traffic. "But I have to find my girlfriend," I blurted. "She was waiting for me in the park." The cop stared at me. His cold gray eyes said, *I am a decent Catholic and I am not going to facilitate your extramarital activities, you decadent overpaid bastard.* What he said out loud was, "No way can you cross that sealfield, and anyhow you absolutely don't want to go in the park right now, mister. Believe me." And he also said, "You don't have to worry about your girlfriend. The park's been cleared of all human beings." That's what he said, *cleared of all*

ROBERT SILVERBERG

human beings. For a while I wandered around in some sort of daze. Finally I went back to my office and found a message from Maranta, who had left the park the moment the trouble began. Good quick Maranta. She hadn't had any idea of what was occurring, though she had found out by the time she reached her office. She had simply sensed trouble and scrammed. We agreed to meet for drinks at the Ras Tafari at half past five. The Ras was one of our regular places, Twelfth and Fifty-third.

❤

There were seventeen witnesses to the onset of the invasion. There were more than seventeen people on the meadow when the aliens arrived, of course, but most of them didn't seem to have been paying attention. It had started, so said the seventeen, with a strange pale blue shimmering about thirty feet off the ground. The shimmering rapidly became a churning, like water going down a drain. Then a light breeze began to blow and very quickly turned into a brisk gale. It lifted people's hats and whirled them in a startling corkscrew spiral around the churning shimmering blue place. At the same time you had a sense of rising tension, a something's-got-to-give feeling. All this lasted perhaps forty-five seconds.

Then came a pop and a whoosh and a ping and a thunk—everybody agreed on the sequence of the sound effects—and the instantly famous not-quite-egg-shaped spaceship of the invaders was there, hovering, as it would do for the next twenty three days, about half an inch above the spring-green grass of Central Park. An absolutely unforgettable sight: the sleek silvery skin of it, the disturbing angle of the slope from its wide top to its narrow bottom, the odd and troublesome hieroglyphics on its flanks that tended to slide out of your field of vision if you stared at them for more than a moment.

A hatch opened and a dozen of the invaders stepped out. *Floated* out, rather. Like their ship, they never came in contact with the ground.

They looked strange. They looked exceedingly strange. Where we have feet they had a single oval pedestal, maybe five inches thick and a yard in diameter, that drifted an inch or so above ground level. From this fleshy base their wraithlike bodies sprouted like tethered balloons. They had no arms, no legs, not even discernible heads: just a broad dome-shaped summit, dwindling away to a ropelike termination that was attached to the pedestal. Their lavender skins were glossy, with a metallic sheen. Dark eyelike spots sometimes formed on them but didn't last long. We saw no mouths. As they moved about they seemed to exercise great care never to touch one another.

The first thing they did was to seize half a dozen squirrels, three stray dogs, a softball, and a baby carriage, unoccupied. We will never know what the second thing was that they did, because no one stayed around to watch. The park emptied with impressive rapidity, the police moved swiftly in with their sealfield, and for the next three hours the aliens had the meadow to themselves. Later in the day the networks sent up spy-eyes that recorded the scene for the evening news until the aliens figured out what they were and shot them down. Briefly we saw ghostly gleaming aliens wandering around within a radius of perhaps five hundred yards of their ship, collecting newspapers, soft-drink dispensers, discarded items of clothing, and something that was generally agreed to be a set of dentures. Whatever they picked up they wrapped in a sort of pillow made of a glowing fabric with the same shining texture as their own bodies, which immediately began floating off with its contents toward the hatch of the ship.

People were lined up six deep at the bar when I arrived at the Ras, and everyone was drinking like mad and staring at the screen. They were showing the clips of the aliens over and over. Maranta was already there. Her eyes were glowing. She pressed herself up against me like a wild woman. "My God," she said, "isn't it wonderful! The men from Mars are here! Or wherever they're from. Let's hoist a few to the men from Mars."

We hoisted more than a few. Somehow I got home at a respectable seven o'clock anyway. The apartment was still in its one-room configuration, though our contract with Bobby Christie specified wall-shift at half past six. Elaine refused to have anything to do with activating the shift. She was afraid, I think, of timing the sequence wrong and being crushed by the walls, or something.

"You heard?" Elaine said. "The aliens?"

"I wasn't far from the park at lunchtime," I told her. "That was when it happened, at lunchtime, while I was up by the park."

Her eyes went wide. "Then you actually saw them land?"

"I wish. By the time I got to the park entrance, the cops had everything sealed off."

I pressed the button, and the walls began to move. Our living room and kitchen returned from Bobby Christie's domain. In the moment of shift I caught sight of Bobby on the far side, getting dressed to go out. He waved and grinned. "Space monsters in the park," he said. "My my my. It's a real jungle out there, don't you know?" And then the walls closed away on him.

Elaine switched on the news, and once again I watched the aliens drifting around the mall picking up people's jackets and candy-bar wrappers.

"Hey," I said, "the mayor ought to put them on the city payroll."

"What were you doing up by the park at lunchtime?" Elaine asked after a bit.

The next day was when the second ship landed and the *real* space monsters appeared. To me the first aliens didn't qualify as monsters at all. Monsters ought to be monstrous, bottom line. Those first aliens were no bigger than you or me.

The second batch, they were something else, though. The behemoths. The space elephants. Of course, they weren't anything like elephants, except that they were big. Big? *Immense.* It put me in mind of Hannibal's invasion of Rome, seeing those gargantuan things disembarking from the new spaceship. It seemed like the Second Punic War all over again, Hannibal and the elephants.

You remember how that was. When Hannibal set out from Carthage to conquer Rome, he took with him a phalanx of elephants, thirty-seven huge gray attack-trained monsters. Elephants were useful in battle in those days—a kind of early-model tank—but they were handy also for terrifying the civilian populace: bizarre colossal smelly critters trampling invincibly through the suburbs, flapping their vast ears and trumpeting awesome cries of doom and burying your rosebushes under mountainous turds. And now we had the same deal. With one difference, though: the Roman archers picked off Hannibal's elephants long before they got within honking distance of the walls of Rome. But these aliens had materialized without warning right in the middle of Central Park, in that big grassy meadow between the Seventy-second Street transverse and Central Park South, which is another deal altogether. I wonder how well things would have gone for the Romans if they had awakened one morning to find Hannibal and his army camping out in the Forum, and his thirty-seven hairy shambling flap-eared elephants snuffling and snorting and farting about on the marble steps of the Temple of Jupiter.

The new spaceship arrived the way the first one had, pop whoosh ping thunk, and the behemoths came tumbling out of it like rabbits out of a hat. We saw it on the evening news: the networks had a new bunch of spy-eyes up, half a mile or so overhead. The ship made a kind of belching sound, and this *thing* suddenly was standing on the mall gawking and gaping. Then another belch, and another *thing*. And on and on until there were two or three dozen of them. Nobody has ever been able to figure out how that little ship could have held as many as one of them. It was no bigger than a schoolbus standing on end.

The monsters looked like double-humped blue medium-size mountains with legs. The legs were their most elephantine feature—thick and rough-skinned, like tree trunks—but they worked on some sort of telescoping principle and could be collapsed swiftly back up into the bodies of their owners. Eight was the normal number of legs, but you never saw eight at once on any of them: as they moved about they always kept at least one pair withdrawn, though from time to time they'd let that pair descend and pull up another one, in what seemed like a completely random way. Now and then they might withdraw two pairs at once, which would cause them to sink down to ground level at one end like a camel kneeling.

Their prodigious bodies were rounded, with a sort of valley a couple of feet deep running crosswise along their backs, and they were covered all over with a dense stiff growth midway in texture between fur and feathers. There were three yellow eyes the size of platters at one end and three rigid purple rodlike projections that stuck out seven or eight feet at the other. Their mouths were in their bellies; when they wanted to eat something, they simply collapsed all eight of their legs at the same time and sat down on it. It was a mouth big enough to swallow a very large animal at a single gulp—an animal as big as a bison, say. As we would shortly discover.

They were enormous. *Enormous.* Getting exact measurements of one presented certain technical problems, as I think you can appreciate. The most reliable estimate was that they were 25 to 30 feet high and 40 to 50 feet long. That is not only substantially larger than any elephant past or present, it is rather larger than most of the two-family houses still to be found in the outer boroughs of the city. Furthermore, a two-family house of the kind found in Queens or Brooklyn, though it may offend your esthetic sense, will not move around at all, it will not emit bad smells and frightening sounds, it will never sit down on a bison and swallow it, nor, for that matter, will it swallow you. African elephants, they tell me, run 10 or 11 feet high at the shoulder, and the biggest extinct mammoths were three or four feet taller than that. There once was a mammal called the baluchitherium that stood about 16 feet high. That was the largest land mammal that ever lived. The space creatures were nearly twice as high. We are talking large here. We are talking dinosaur-plus dimensions.

Central Park is several miles long but quite modest in width. It runs just from Fifth Avenue to Eighth. Its designers did not expect that anyone would allow two or three dozen animals bigger than two-family houses to wander around freely in an urban park three city blocks wide. No doubt the small size of their pasture was very awkward for them. Certainly it was for us.

"I think they have to be an exploration party," Maranta said. "Don't you?" We had shifted the scene of our Monday and Friday lunches from Central Park to Rockefeller Center, but otherwise we were trying to behave as though nothing unusual was going on. "They can't have come as invaders. One little spaceshipload of aliens couldn't possibly conquer an entire planet."

Maranta is unfailingly jaunty and optimistic. She is a small, energetic woman with close-cropped red hair and green eyes, one of those boyish-looking women who never seem to age. I love her for her optimism. I wish I could catch it from her, like measles.

I said, "There are *two* spaceship-loads of aliens, Maranta."

She made a face. "Oh. The jumbos. They're just dumb shaggy monsters. I don't see them as much of a menace, really."

"Probably not. But the little ones—they have to be a superior species. We know that because they're the ones who came to us. We didn't go to them."

She laughed. "It all sounds so absurd. That Central Park should be full of *creatures*—"

"But what if they do want to conquer Earth?" I asked.

"Oh," Maranta said. "I don't think that would necessarily be so awful."

The smaller aliens spent the first few days installing a good deal of mysterious equipment on the mall in the vicinity of their ship: odd intricate shimmering constructions that looked as though they belonged in the sculpture garden of the Museum of Modern Art. They made no attempt to enter into communication with us. They showed no interest in us at all. The only time they took notice of us was when we sent spy-eyes overhead. They would tolerate them for an hour or two and then would shoot them down, casually, like swatting flies, with spurts of pink light. The networks—and then the government surveillance agencies, when they moved in—put the eyes higher and higher each day, but the aliens never failed to find them. After a week or so we were forced to rely for our information on government spy satellites monitoring the park from space, and on whatever observers equipped with binoculars could glimpse from the taller apartment houses and hotels bordering the park. Neither of these arrangements was entirely satisfactory.

The behemoths, during those days, were content to roam aimlessly through the park southward from Seventy-second Street, knocking over trees, squatting down to eat them. Each one gobbled two or three trees a day, leaves, branches, trunk, and all. There weren't all that many trees to begin with down there, so it seemed likely that before long they'd have to start ranging farther afield.

The usual civic groups spoke up about the trees. They wanted the mayor to do something to protect the park. The monsters, they said, would have to be made to go elsewhere—to Canada, perhaps, where there were plenty of expendable trees. The mayor said that he was studying the problem but that it was too early to know what the best plan of action would be.

His chief goal, in the beginning, was simply to keep a lid on the situation.

We still didn't even know, after all, whether we were being invaded or just visited. To play it safe, the police were ordered to set up and maintain round-the-clock sealfields completely encircling the park in the impacted zone south of Seventy-second Street. The power costs of this were staggering, and Con Edison found it necessary to impose a ten-percent voltage cutback in the rest of the city, which caused a lot of grumbling, especially now that it was getting to be air-conditioner weather.

The police didn't like any of this: out there day and night standing guard in front of an intangible electronic barrier with ungodly monsters just a sneeze away. Now and then one of the blue goliaths would wander near the sealfield and peer over the edge. A sealfield maybe a dozen feet high doesn't give you much of a sense of security when there's an animal two or three times that height looming over its top.

So the cops asked for time and a half. Combat pay, essentially. There wasn't room in the city budget for that, especially since no one knew how long the aliens were going to continue to occupy the park. There was talk of a strike. The mayor appealed to Washington, which had studiously been staying remote from the whole event as if the arrival of an extraterrestrial task force in the middle of Manhattan was purely a municipal problem.

The president rummaged around in the Constitution and decided to activate the National Guard. That surprised a lot of basically sedentary men who enjoy dressing up occasionally in uniforms. The Guard hadn't been called out since the Bulgarian business in '94 and its current members weren't very sharp on procedures, so some hasty on-the-job training became necessary. As it happened, Maranta's husband Tim was an officer in the 107th Infantry, which was the regiment that was handed the chief responsibility for protecting New York City against the creatures from space. So his life suddenly was changed a great deal, and so was Maranta's; and so was mine.

◆

Like everybody else, I found myself going over to the park again and again to try to get a glimpse of the aliens. But the barricades kept you fifty feet away from the park perimeter on all sides, and the taller buildings flanking the park had put themselves on a residents-only admission basis, with armed guards enforcing it, so they wouldn't be overwhelmed by hordes of curiosity-seekers.

I did see Tim, though. He was in charge of an improvised-looking command post at Fifth and Fifty-ninth, near the horse-and-buggy stand. Youngish stockbroker-looking men kept running up to him with reports to sign, and he signed each one with terrific dash and vigor, without reading any of them. In his crisp tan uniform and shiny boots, he must have seen himself as some doomed and gallant officer in an ancient movie, Gary Cooper, Cary Grant, John Wayne, bracing himself for the climactic cavalry charge or the onslaught of the maddened Sepoys. The poor bastard.

"Hey, old man," he said, grinning at me in a doomed and gallant way. "Came to see the circus, did you?"

We weren't really best friends any more. I don't know what we were to each other. We rarely lunched any more. (How could we? I was busy three days a week with Maranta.) We didn't meet at the gym. It wasn't to Tim I turned for advice on personal problems or second opinions on investments. There was some sort of bond, but I think it was mostly nostalgia. But officially I guess I did still think of him as my best friend, in a kind of automatic unquestioning way.

I said, "Are you free to go over to the Plaza for a drink?"

"I wish. I don't get relieved until 2100 hours."

"Nine o'clock, is that it?"

"Nine, yes. You fucking civilian."

It was only half past one. The poor bastard.

"What'll happen to you if you leave your post?"

"I could get shot for desertion," he said.

"Seriously?"

"Seriously. Especially if the monsters pick that moment to bust out of the park. This is war, old buddy."

"Is it, do you think? Maranta doesn't think so." I wondered if I should be talking about what Maranta thought. "She says they're just out exploring the galaxy."

Tim shrugged. "She always likes to see the sunny side. That's an alien military force over there inside the park. One of these days they're going to blow a bugle and come out with blazing ray guns. You'd better believe it."

"Through the sealfield?"

"They could walk right over it," Tim said. "Or float, for all I know. There's going to be a war. The first intergalactic war in human history." Again the dazzling Cary Grant grin. Her Majesty's Bengal lancers, ready for action. "Something to tell my grandchildren," said Tim. "Do you know what the game plan is? First we attempt to make contact. That's going on right now, but they don't seem to be paying attention to us. If we ever establish communication, we invite them to sign a peace treaty. Then we offer them some chunk of Nevada or Kansas as a diplomatic enclave and get them the hell out of New York. But I don't think any of that's going to happen. I think they're busy scoping things out in there, and as soon as they finish that they're going to launch some kind of attack, using weapons we don't even begin to understand."

"And if they do?"

"We nuke them," Tim said. "Tactical devices, just the right size for Central Park Mall."

"No," I said, staring. "That isn't so. You're kidding me."

He looked pleased, a *gotcha* look. "Matter of fact, I am. The truth is that nobody has the goddamndest idea of what to do about any of this. But don't think the nuke strategy hasn't been suggested. And some even crazier things."

"Don't tell me about them," I said. "Look, Tim, is there any way I can get a peek over those barricades?"

"Not a chance. Not even you. I'm not even supposed to be *talking* with civilians."

"Since when am I civilian?"

"Since the invasion began," Tim said.

He was dead serious. Maybe this was all just a goofy movie to me, but it wasn't to him.

More junior officers came to him with more papers to sign. He excused himself and took care of them. Then he was on the field telephone for five minutes or so. His expression grew progressively more bleak. Finally, he looked up at me and said, "You see? It's starting."

"What is?"

"They've crossed Seventy-second Street for the first time. There must have been a gap in the sealfield. Or maybe they jumped it, as I was saying just now. Three of the big ones are up by Seventy-fourth, noodling around the eastern end of the lake. The Metropolitan Museum people are scared shitless and have asked for gun emplacements on the roof, and they're thinking of evacuating the most important works of art." The field phone lit up again. "Excuse me," he said. Always the soul of courtesy, Tim. After a time he said, "Oh, Jesus. It sounds pretty bad. I've got to go up there right now. Do you mind?" His jaw was set, his gaze was frosty with determination. This is it, Major. There's ten thousand Comanches coming through the pass with blood in their eyes, but we're ready for them, right? Right. He went striding away up Fifth Avenue.

When I got back to the office there was a message from Maranta, suggesting that I stop off at her place for drinks that evening on my way home. Tim would be busy playing soldier, she said, until nine. Until 2100 hours, I silently corrected.

◆

Another few days and we got used to it all. We began to accept the presence of aliens in the park as a normal part of New York life, like snow in February or laser duels in the subway.

But they remained at the center of everybody's consciousness. In a subtle, pervasive way they were working great changes in our souls as they moved about mysteriously behind the sealfield barriers in the park. The strangeness of their being here made us buoyant. Their arrival had broken, in some way, the depressing rhythm that life in our brave new century had seemed to be settling into. I know that for some time I had been thinking, as I suppose people have thought since Cro-Magnon days, that lately the flavor of modern life had been changing for the worse, that it was becoming sour and nasty, that the era I happened to live in was a dim, shabby, dismal sort of time, small-souled, mean-minded. You know the feeling. Somehow the aliens had caused that feeling to lift. By invading us in this weird hands-off way, they had given us something to be interestingly mystified by: a sort of redemption, a sort of rebirth. Yes, truly.

Some of us changed quite a lot. Consider Tim, the latter-day Bengal lancer, the staunchly disciplined officer. He lasted about a week in that particular mind-set. Then one night he called me and said, "Hey, fellow, how would you like to go into the park and play with the critters?"

"What are you talking about?"

"I know a way to get in. I've got the code for the Sixty-fourth Street sealfield. I can turn it off and we can slip through. It's risky, but how can you resist?"

So much for Gary Cooper. So much for John Wayne.

"Have you gone nuts?" I said. "The other day you wouldn't even let me go up to the barricades."

"That was the other day."

"You wouldn't walk across the street with me for a drink. You said you'd get shot for desertion."

"That was the other day."

"You called me a civilian."

"You still are a civilian. But you're my old buddy, and I want to go in there and look those aliens in the eye, and I'm not quite up to doing it all by myself. You want to go with me, or don't you?"

"Like the time we stole the beer keg from Sigma Frap. Like the time we put the scorpions in the girls' shower room."

"You got it, old pal."

"Tim, we aren't college kids any more. There's a fucking intergalactic war going on. That was your very phrase. Central Park is under surveillance by NASA spy-eyes that can see a cat's whiskers from fifty miles up. You are part of the military force that is supposed to be protecting us against these alien invaders. And now you propose to violate your trust and go sneaking into the midst of the invading force, as a mere prank?"

"I guess I do," he said.

"This is an extremely cockeyed idea, isn't it?" I said.

"Absolutely. Are you with me?"

"Sure," I said. "You know I am."

I told Elaine that Tim and I were going to meet for a late dinner to discuss a business deal and I didn't expect to be home until two or three in the morning. No problem there. Tim was waiting at our old table at Perugino's with a bottle of Amarone already working. The wine was so good that we ordered another midway through the veal pizzaiola, and then a third. I won't say we drank ourselves blind, but we certainly got seriously myopic. And about midnight we walked over to the park.

Everything was quiet. I saw sleepy-looking guardsmen patrolling here and there along Fifth. We went right up to the command post at Fifty-ninth and Tim saluted very crisply, which I don't think was quite kosher, he being not then in uniform. He introduced me to someone as Dr. Pritchett, Bureau of External Affairs. That sounded really cool and glib, Bureau of External Affairs.

Then off we went up Fifth, Tim and I, and he gave me a guided tour. "You see, Dr. Pritchett, the first line of the isolation zone is the barricade that runs down the middle of the avenue." Virile, forceful voice, loud enough to be heard for half a block. "That keeps the gawkers away. Behind that, Doctor, we maintain a further level of security through a series of augmented-beam sealfield emplacements, the new General Dynamics 1100 series model, and let me show you right here how we've integrated that with advanced personnel-interface intercept scan by means of a triple line of Hewlett-Packard optical Doppler-couplers—"

And so on, a steady stream of booming confident-sounding gibberish as we headed north. He pulled out a flashlight and led me hither and thither to show me amplifiers and sensors and whatnot, and it was Dr. Pritchett this and Dr. Pritchett that and I realized that we were now somehow on the inner side of the barricade. His glibness, his poise, were awesome. *Notice this, Dr. Pritchett,* and *Let me call your attention to this, Dr. Pritchett,* and suddenly there was a tiny digital keyboard in his hand, like a little calculator, and he was tapping out numbers. "Okay," he said, "the field's down between here and the Sixty-fifth Street entrance to the park, but I've put a kill on the beam-interruption signal. So far as anyone can tell, there's still an unbroken field. Let's go in."

And we entered the park just north of the zoo.

For five generations the first thing New York kids have been taught, ahead of tying shoelaces and flushing after you go, is that you don't set foot in Central Park at night. Now here we were, defying the most primordial of no-nos. But what was to fear? What they taught us to worry about in the park was muggers. Not creatures from the Ninth Glorch Galaxy.

The park was eerily quiet. Maybe a snore or two from the direction of the zoo, otherwise not a sound. We walked west and north into the silence, into the darkness. After a while a strange smell reached my nostrils. It was dank and musky and harsh and sour, but those are only approximations: it wasn't like anything I had ever smelled before. One whiff of it and I saw purple skies and a great green sun blazing in the heavens. A second whiff and all the stars were in the wrong places. A third whiff and I was staring into a gnarled twisted landscape where the trees were like giant spears and the mountains were like crooked teeth.

Tim nudged me.

"Yeah," I said. "I smell it, too."

"To your left," he said. "Look to your left."

I looked to my left and saw three huge yellow eyes looking back at me from twenty feet overhead, like searchlights mounted in a tree. They weren't mounted in a tree, though. They were mounted in something shaggy and massive, somewhat larger than your basic two-family Queens residential dwelling, that was standing maybe fifty feet away, completely blocking both lanes of the park's East Drive from shoulder to shoulder.

It was then that I realized that three bottles of wine hadn't been nearly enough.

"What's the matter?" Tim said. "This is what we came for, isn't it, old pal?"

"What do we do now? Climb on its back and go for a ride?"

"You know that no human being in all of history has ever been as close to that thing as we are now?"

"Yes," I said. "I do know that, Tim."

It began making a sound. It was the kind of sound that a piece of chalk twelve feet thick would make if it was dragged across a blackboard the wrong way. When I heard that sound I felt as if I was being dragged across whole galaxies by my hair. A weird vertigo attacked me. Then the creature folded up all its legs and came down to ground level; and then it unfolded the two front pairs of legs, and then the other two; and then it started to amble slowly and ominously toward us.

I saw another one, looking even bigger, just beyond it. And perhaps a third one a little farther back. They were heading our way, too.

"Shit," I said. "This was a very dumb idea, wasn't it?"

"Come on. We're never going to forget this night."

"I'd like to live to remember it."

"Let's get up real close. They don't move very fast."

"No," I said. "Let's just get out of the park right now, okay?"

"We just got here."

"Fine," I said. "We did it. Now let's go."

"Hey, look," Tim said. "Over there to the west."

I followed his pointing arm and saw two gleaming wraiths hovering just above the ground, maybe three hundred yards away. The other aliens, the little floating ones. Drifting toward us, graceful as balloons. I imagined myself being wrapped in a shining pillow and being floated off into their ship.

"Oh, shit," I said. "Come *on*, Tim."

Staggering, stumbling, I ran for the park gate, not even thinking about how I was going to get through the sealfield without Tim's gizmo. But then there was Tim, right behind me. We reached the sealfield together and he tapped out the numbers on the little keyboard and the field opened for us, and out we went, and the field closed behind us. And we collapsed just outside the park, panting, gasping, laughing like lunatics, slapping the sidewalk hysterically. "Dr. Pritchett," he chortled. "Bureau of External Affairs. God *damn*, what a smell that critter had! God *damn!*"

〜

I laughed all the way home. I was still laughing when I got into bed. Elaine squinted at me. She wasn't amused. "That Tim," I said. "That wild man Tim." She could tell I'd been drinking some, and she nodded somberly—boys will be boys, etc.—and went back to sleep.

The next morning I learned what had happened in the park after we had cleared out.

It seemed a few of the big aliens had gone looking for us. They had followed our spoor all the way to the park gate, and when they lost it they somehow turned to the right and went blundering into the zoo. The Central Park Zoo is a small cramped place, and as they rambled around in it they managed to knock down most of the fences. In no time whatever there were tigers, elephants, chimps, rhinos, and hyenas all over the park.

The animals, of course, were befuddled and bemused at finding themselves free. They took off in a hundred different directions, looking for places to hide.

The lions and coyotes simply curled up under bushes and went to sleep. The monkeys and some of the apes went into the trees. The aquatic things headed for the lake. One of the rhinos ambled out into the mall and pushed over a fragile-looking alien machine with his nose. The machine shattered and the rhino went up in a flash of yellow light and a puff of green smoke. As for the elephants, they stood poignantly in a huddled circle, glaring in utter amazement and dismay at the gigantic aliens. How humiliating it must have been for them to feel *tiny*.

Then there was the bison event. There was this little herd, a dozen or so mangy-looking guys with ragged, threadbare fur. They started moving single file toward Columbus Circle, probably figuring that if they just kept their heads down and didn't attract attention they could keep going all the way back to Wyoming. For some reason, one of the behemoths decided to see what bison taste like. It came hulking over and sat down on the last one in the line, which vanished underneath it like a mouse beneath a hippopotamus. Chomp, gulp, gone. In the next few minutes five more behemoths came over and disappeared five more of the bison. The survivors made it safely to the edge of the park and huddled up against the sealfield, mooing forlornly. One of the little tragedies of interstellar war.

I found Tim on duty at the Fifty-ninth Street command post. He looked at me as though I were an emissary of Satan. "I can't talk to you while I'm on duty," he said.

"You heard about the zoo?" I asked.

"Of course I heard." He was speaking through clenched teeth. His eyes had the scarlet look of zero sleep. "What a filthy, irresponsible thing we did!"

"Look, we had no way of knowing—"

"Inexcusable. An incredible lapse. The aliens feel threatened now that humans have trespassed on their territory, and the whole situation has changed in there. We upset them and now they're getting out of control. I'm thinking of reporting myself for court-martial."

"Don't be silly, Tim. We trespassed for three minutes. The aliens didn't give a crap about it. They might have blundered into the zoo even if we hadn't—"

"Go away," he muttered. "I can't talk to you while I'm on duty."

Jesus! As if I was the one who had lured *him* into doing it. Well, he was back in his movie part again, the distinguished military figure who now had unaccountably committed an unpardonable lapse and was going to have to live in the cold glare of his own disapproval for the rest of his life. The poor bastard. I tried to tell him not to take things so much to heart, but he turned away from me, so I shrugged and went back to my office.

That afternoon some tenderhearted citizens demanded that the sealfields be switched off until the zoo animals could escape from the park. The sealfields, of course, kept them trapped in there with the aliens.

Another tough one for the mayor. He'd lose points tremendously if the evening news kept showing our beloved polar bears and raccoons and kangaroos and whatnot getting gobbled like gumdrops by the aliens. But switching off the sealfields would send a horde of leopards and gorillas and wolverines scampering out into the streets of Manhattan, to say nothing of the aliens who might follow them. The mayor appointed a study group, naturally.

The small aliens stayed close to their spaceship and remained uncommunicative. They went on tinkering with their machines, which emitted odd plinking noises and curious colored lights. But the huge ones roamed freely about the park, and now they were doing considerable damage in their amiable mindless way. They smashed up the backstops of the baseball fields, tossed the Bethesda Fountain into the lake, rearranged Tavern-on-the-Green's seating plan, and trashed the place in various other ways, but nobody seemed to object except the usual Friends of the Park civic types. I think we were all so bemused by the presence of genuine galactic beings that we didn't mind. We were flattered that they had chosen New York as the site of first contact. (But where *else?*)

No one could explain how the behemoths had penetrated the Seventy-second Street sealfield line, but a new barrier was set up at Seventy-ninth, and that seemed to keep them contained. Poor Tim spent twelve hours a day patrolling the perimeter of the occupied zone. Inevitably, I began spending more time with Maranta than just lunchtimes. Elaine noticed. But I didn't notice her noticing.

One Sunday at dawn a behemoth turned up by the Metropolitan, peering in the window of the Egyptian courtyard. The authorities thought at first that there must be a gap in the Seventy-ninth Street sealfield, as there had at Seventy-second. Then came a report of another alien out near Riverside Drive and a third one at Lincoln Center, and it became clear that the sealfields just didn't hold them back at all. They had simply never bothered to go beyond them before.

Making contact with a sealfield is said to be extremely unpleasant for any organism with a nervous system more complex than a squid's. Every neuron screams in anguish. You jump back, involuntarily, a reflex impossible to overcome. On the morning we came to call Crazy Sunday, the behemoths began walking through the fields as if they weren't there. The main thing about aliens is that they are alien. They feel no responsibility for fulfilling any of your expectations.

That weekend it was Bobby Christie's turn to have the full apartment. On those Sundays when Elaine and I had the one-room configuration we liked to get up very early and spend the day out, since it was a little depressing to stay home with three rooms of furniture jammed all around us. As we were walking up Park Avenue South toward Forty-second, Elaine said suddenly, "Do you hear anything strange?"

"Strange?"

"Like a riot."

"It's nine o'clock Sunday morning. Nobody goes out rioting at nine o'clock Sunday morning."

"Just listen," she said.

There is no mistaking the characteristic sounds of a large excited crowd of human beings, for those of us who spent our formative years living in the late twentieth century. Our ears were tuned at an early age to the music of riots, mobs, demonstrations, and their kin. We know what it means when individual exclamations of anger, indignation, or anxiety blend to create a symphonic hubbub in which all extremes of pitch and timbre are submerged into a single surging roar, as deep as the booming of the surf. That was what I heard now. There was no mistaking it.

"It isn't a riot," I said. "It's a mob. There's a subtle difference."

"What?"

"Come on," I said, breaking into a jog. "I'll bet you that the aliens have come out of the park."

A mob, yes. In a moment we saw thousands upon thousands of people, filling Forty-second Street from curb to curb and more coming from all directions. What they were looking at—pointing, gaping, screaming—was a shaggy blue creature the size of a small mountain that was moving about uncertainly on the automobile viaduct that runs around the side of Grand Central Terminal. It looked unhappy. It was obviously trying to get down from the viaduct, which was sagging noticeably under its weight. People were jammed right up against it, and a dozen or so were clinging to its sides and back like rock climbers. There were people underneath it, too, milling around between its colossal legs. "Oh, look," Elaine said, shuddering, digging her fingers into my biceps. "Isn't it eating some of them? Like they did the bison?" Once she had pointed it out I saw, yes, the behemoth now and then was dipping quickly and rising again, a familiar one-two, the old squat-and-gobble. "What an awful thing!" Elaine murmured. "Why don't they get out of its way?"

"I don't think they can," I said. "I think they're being pushed forward by the people behind them."

"Right into the jaws of that hideous monster. Or whatever it has, if they aren't jaws."

"I don't think it means to hurt anyone," I said. How did I know that? "I think it's just eating them because they're dithering around down there in its mouth area. A kind of automatic response. It looks awfully dumb, Elaine."

"Why are you defending it?"

"Hey, look, Elaine—"

"It's *eating* people. You sound almost sorry for it!"

"Well, why not? It's far from home and surrounded by ten thousand screaming morons. You think it wants to be out there?"

"It's a disgusting, obnoxious animal." She was getting furious. Her eyes were bright and wild, her jaw was thrust forward. "I hope the army gets here fast," she said fiercely. "I hope they blow it to smithereens!"

Her ferocity frightened me. I saw an Elaine I scarcely knew at all. When I tried one more time to make excuses for that miserable hounded beast on the viaduct, she glared at me with unmistakable loathing. Then she turned away and went rushing forward, shaking her fist, shouting curses and threats at the alien.

Suddenly I realized how it would have been if Hannibal actually had been able to keep his elephants alive long enough to enter Rome with them. The respectable Roman matrons, screaming and raging from the housetops with the fury of banshees. And the baffled elephants sooner or later rounded up and thrust into the Coliseum to be tormented by little men with spears, while the crowd howled its delight. Well, I can howl, too. "Come on, Behemoth!" I yelled into the roar of the mob. "You can do it, Goliath!" A traitor to the human race is what I was, I guess.

Eventually a detachment of Guardsmen came shouldering through the streets. They had mortars and rifles, and for all I know they had tactical nukes, too. But, of course, there was no way they could attack the animal in the midst of such a mob. Instead, they used electronic blooglehorns to disperse the crowd by the power of sheer ugly noise, and whipped up a bunch of buzz-blinkers and a little sealfield to cut Forty-second Street in half. The last I saw of the monster it was slouching off in the direction of the old United Nations Buildings with the Guardsmen warily creeping along behind it. The crowd scattered, and I was left standing in front of Grand Central with a trembling, sobbing Elaine.

That was how it was all over the city on Crazy Sunday, and on Monday and Tuesday, too. The behemoths were outside the park, roaming at large from Harlem to Wall Street. Wherever they went they drew tremendous crazy crowds that swarmed all over them without any regard for the danger. Some famous news photos came out of those days: the three grinning black boys at Seventh and 125th hanging from the three purple rodlike things, the acrobats forming a human pyramid atop the Times Square beast, the little old Italian man standing in front of his house in Greenwich Village trying to hold a space monster at bay with his garden hose.

There was never any accurate casualty count. Maybe five thousand people died, mainly trampled underfoot by the aliens or crushed in the crowd. Somewhere between three hundred fifty and four hundred human beings were gobbled by the aliens. Apparently that stoop-and-swallow thing is something they do when they're nervous. If there's anything edible within reach, they'll gulp it in. This soothes them. We made them very nervous; they did a lot of gulping.

Among the casualties was Tim, the second day of the violence. He went down valiantly in the defense of the Guggenheim Museum, which came under attack by five of the biggies. Its spiral shape held some ineffable appeal for them. We couldn't tell whether they wanted to worship it or mate with it or just knock it to pieces, but they kept on charging and charging, rushing up to it and slamming against it. Tim was trying to hold them off with nothing more than tear gas and blooglehorns when he was swallowed. Never flinched, just stood there and let it happen. The president had ordered the guardsmen not to use lethal weapons. Maranta was bitter about that. "If only they had let them use grenades," she said. I tried to imagine what it was like, gulped down and digested, nifty tan uniform and all. A credit to his regiment. It was his atonement, I guess. He was back there in the Gary Cooper movie again, gladly paying the price for dereliction of duty.

Tuesday afternoon the rampage came to an unexpected end. The behemoths suddenly started keeling over, and within a few hours they were all dead. Some said it was the heat—it was up in the nineties all day Monday and Tuesday—and some said it was the excitement. A Rockefeller University biologist thought it was both those factors plus severe indigestion: the aliens had eaten an average of ten humans apiece, which might have overloaded their systems.

There was no chance for autopsies. Some enzyme in the huge bodies set to work immediately on death, dissolving flesh and bone and skin and all into a sticky yellow mess. By nightfall nothing was left of them but some stains on the pavement, uptown and down. A sad business, I thought. Not even a skeleton for the museum, memento of this momentous time. The poor monsters. Was I the only one who felt sorry for them? Quite possibly I was. I make no apologies for that. I feel what I feel.

All this time the other aliens, the little shimmery spooky ones, had stayed holed up in Central Park, preoccupied with their incomprehensible research. They didn't even seem to notice that their behemoths had strayed.

But now they became agitated. For two or three days they bustled about like worried penguins, dismantling their instruments and packing them aboard their ship; and then they took apart the other ship, the one that had carried the behemoths, and loaded that aboard. Perhaps they felt demoralized. As the Carthaginians who had invaded Rome did, after their elephants died.

On a sizzling June afternoon the alien ship took off. Not for its home world, not right away. It swooped into the sky and came down on Fire Island: at Cherry Grove, to be precise. The aliens took possession of the beach, set up their instruments around their ship, and even ventured into the water, skimming and bobbing just above the surface of the waves like demented surfers. After five or six days they moved on to one of the Hamptons and did the same thing, and then to Martha's Vineyard. Maybe they just wanted a vacation, after three weeks in New York. And then they went away altogether.

"You've been having an affair with Maranta, haven't you?" Elaine asked me the day the aliens left.

"I won't deny it."

"That night you came in so late, with wine on your breath. You were with her, weren't you?"

"No," I said. "I was with Tim. He and I sneaked into the park and looked at the aliens."

"Sure you did," Elaine said. She filed for divorce, and a year later I married Maranta. Very likely that would have happened sooner or later even if the Earth hadn't been invaded by beings from space and Tim hadn't been devoured. But no question that the invasion speeded things up a bit for us all.

And now, of course, the invaders are back. Four years to the day from the first landing and there they were, pop whoosh ping thunk, Central Park again. Three ships this time, one of spooks, one of behemoths, and the third one carrying the prisoners of war. Who could ever forget that scene, when the hatch opened and some three hundred fifty to four hundred human beings came out, marching like zombies? Along with the bison herd, half a dozen squirrels, and three dogs. They hadn't been eaten and digested at all, just *collected* inside the behemoths and instantaneously transmitted somehow to the home world, where they were studied. Now they were being returned. "That's Tim, isn't it?" Maranta said, pointing to the screen. I nodded. Unmistakably Tim, yes. With the stunned look of a man who has beheld marvels beyond comprehension.

It's a month now, and the government is still holding all the returnees for debriefing. No one is allowed to see them. The word is that a special law will be passed dealing with the problem of spouses of returnees who have entered into new marriages. Maranta says she'll stay with me no matter what; and I'm pretty sure that Tim will do the stiff-upper-lip thing, no hard feelings, if they ever get word to him in the debriefing camp about Maranta and me. As for the aliens, they're sitting tight in Central Park, occupying the whole place from Ninety-sixth to 110th and not telling us a thing. Now and then the behemoths wander down to the reservoir for a lively bit of wallowing, but they haven't gone beyond the park this time.

I think a lot about Hannibal, and about Carthage versus Rome, and how the Second Punic War might have come out if Hannibal had had a chance to go back home and get a new batch of elephants. Most likely Rome would have won the war anyway, I guess. But we aren't Romans, and they aren't Carthaginians, and those aren't elephants splashing around in the Central Park reservoir. "This is such an interesting time to be alive," Maranta likes to say. "I'm certain they don't mean us any harm, aren't you?"

"I love you for your optimism," I tell her then. And then we turn on the tube and watch the evening news.

THE PARDONER'S
TALE

Another Playboy story, eleven months after the last one. During the intervening time I had been busy indeed. In the fall of 1985 had come the novella "Gilgamesh in the Outback," which would win a Hugo for me at the 1987 World Science Fiction Convention. That was the first of the Afterworld stories that I eventually collected in the novel To the Land of the Living. Then some domestic rearrangements were required, for I had lured Karen Haber out of her Texas domicile to live with me in far-off exotic California; and hardly had she unpacked her suitcase when I was embarked on the immense picaresque novel Star of Gypsies, which occupied me all during the winter and spring of 1986 and required any number of drafts before I was satisfied. And then, without pausing for breath, I did a second Afterworld novella about Gilgamesh, "The Fascination of the Abomination."

Some time off seemed in order, but in the spring of the year my thoughts usually turn to writing something for Alice Turner, and my 1986 Playboy project was "The Pardoner's Tale," title courtesy of Chaucer, who'd probably be puzzled by the story appended to it. At that time the term "cyberpunk" was being bandied about ad nauseam in the science-fiction world, and I suppose you could call this a cyberpunk story—Alice did, in her acceptance letter of July 1, and I didn't quarrel with the description, although it wasn't exactly what I had thought I was writing.

She wanted about two pages of cuts—a line here, two lines there—in keeping with a dictum she had heard that quintessential cyberpunk featured "the hottest of all the technological futures, fast action, tight construction, and a disdain for all that is slow and boring." As usual, when Alice Turner thinks a line or two ought to be cut, I give heed to what she says. I did the cutting with scarcely a demur, and the final version, sleek and taut, owes no little of its success to her nifty work with the scalpel. Gardner Dozois picked it for his 1988 year's-best anthology, my fifth *appearance in a row in that collection, and Don Wollheim chose it also for his book, giving me one more sweep of the anthologies—although, since Terry Carr's anthology no longer appeared, it was only a double sweep this time. (I pay attention to such things, even if you don't. But they're my stories.)*

"Key Sixteen, Housing Omicron Kappa, aleph sub-one," I said to the software on duty at the Alhambra gate of the Los Angeles Wall.

Software isn't generally suspicious. This wasn't even very smart software. It was working off some great biochips—I could feel them jigging and pulsing as the electron stream flowed through them—but the software itself was just a kludge. Typical gatekeeper stuff.

I stood waiting as the picoseconds went ticking away by the millions.

"Name, please," the gatekeeper said finally.

"John Doe. Beta Pi Upsilon 104324x."

The gate opened. I walked into Los Angeles.

As easy as Beta Pi.

The wall that encircles L.A. is a hundred, a hundred fifty feet thick. Its gates are more like tunnels. When you consider that the wall runs completely around the L.A. basin from the San Gabriel Valley to the San Fernando Valley and then over the mountains and down the coast and back the far side past Long Beach, and that it's at least sixty feet high and all that distance deep, you can begin to appreciate the mass of it. Think of the phenomenal expenditure of human energy that went into building it—muscle and sweat, sweat and muscle. I think about that a lot.

I suppose the walls around our cities were put there mostly as symbols. They highlight the distinction between city and countryside, between citizen and uncitizen, between control and chaos, just as city walls did five thousand years ago. But mainly they serve to remind us that we are all slaves nowadays. You can't ignore the walls. You can't pretend they aren't there. *We made you build them,* is what they say, *and don't you ever forget that.* All the same, Chicago doesn't have a wall sixty feet high and a hundred fifty feet deep. Houston doesn't. Phoenix doesn't. They make do with less. But L.A. is the

main city. I suppose the Los Angeles wall is a statement: *I am the Big Cheese.
I am the Ham What Am.*

The walls aren't there because the Entities are afraid of attack. They know
how invulnerable they are. We know it, too. They just wanted to decorate their
capital with something a little special. What the hell, it isn't *their* sweat that
goes into building the walls. It's ours. Not mine personally, of course. But ours.

I saw a few Entities walking around just inside the wall, preoccupied as
usual with God knows what and paying no attention to the humans in the
vicinity. These were low-caste ones, the kind with the luminous orange spots
along their sides. I gave them plenty of room. They have a way sometimes of
picking a human up with those long elastic tongues, like a frog snapping up a
fly, and letting him dangle in midair while they study him with those saucer-
sized yellow eyes. I don't care for that. You don't get hurt, but it isn't agreeable
to be dangled in midair by something that looks like a fifteen-foot-high purple
squid standing on the tips of its tentacles. Happened to me once in St. Louis,
long ago, and I'm in no hurry to have it happen again.

The first thing I did when I was inside L.A. was find me a car. On Valley
Boulevard about two blocks in from the wall I saw a '31 Toshiba El Dorado that
looked good to me, and I matched frequencies with its lock and slipped inside
and took about ninety seconds to reprogram its drive control to my personal
metabolic cues. The previous owner must have been fat as a hippo and probably
diabetic: her glycogen index was absurd and her phosphines were wild.

Not a bad car, a little slow in the shift but what can you expect, considering
the last time any cars were manufactured on this planet was the year 2034.

"Pershing Square," I told it.

It had nice capacity, maybe sixty megabytes. It turned south right away and
found the old freeway and drove off toward downtown. I figured I'd set up shop
in the middle of things, work two or three pardons to keep my edge sharp, get
myself a hotel room, a meal, maybe hire some companionship. And then think
about the next move. It was winter, a nice time to be in L.A. That golden sun,
those warm breezes coming down the canyons.

I hadn't been out on the Coast in years. Working Florida mainly, Texas,
sometimes Arizona. I hate the cold. I hadn't been in L.A. since '36. A long
time to stay away, but maybe I'd been staying away deliberately. I wasn't sure.
That last L.A. trip had left bad-tasting memories. There had been a woman
who wanted a pardon, and I sold her a stiff. You have to stiff the customers now
and then or else you start looking too good, which can be dangerous; but she
was young and pretty and full of hope and I could have stiffed the next one
instead of her, only I didn't. Sometimes I've felt bad, thinking back over that.
Maybe that's what had kept me away from L.A. all this time.

A couple of miles east of the big downtown interchange, traffic began backing up. Maybe an accident ahead, maybe a roadblock. I told the Toshiba to get off the freeway.

Slipping through roadblocks is scary and calls for a lot of hard work. I knew that I probably could fool any kind of software at a roadblock and certainly any human cop, but why bother if you don't have to?

I asked the car where I was.

The screen lit up. Alameda near Banning, it said. A long walk to Pershing Square, looked like. I had the car drop me at Spring Street and went the rest of the way on foot. "Pick me up at 1830 hours," I told it. "Corner of—umm— Sixth and Hill." It went away to park itself and I headed for the Square to peddle some pardons.

◄

It isn't hard for a good pardoner to find buyers. You can see it in their eyes: the tightly controlled anger, the smoldering resentment. And something else, something intangible, a certain sense of having a shred or two of inner integrity left, that tells you right away, Here's somebody willing to risk a lot to regain some measure of freedom. I was in business within fifteen minutes.

The first one was an aging surfer sort, barrel chest and that sun-bleached look. The Entities haven't allowed surfing for ten, fifteen years—they've got their plankton seines just offshore from Santa Barbara to San Diego, gulping in the marine nutrients they have to have, and any beach boy who tried to take a whack at the waves out there would be chewed right up. But this guy must have been one hell of a performer in his day. The way he moved through the park, making little balancing moves as if he needed to compensate for the irregularities of the earth's rotation, you could see how he would have been in the water. Sat down next to me, began working on his lunch. Thick forearms, gnarled hands. A wall laborer. Muscles knotting in his cheeks: the anger, forever simmering just below boil.

I got him talking after a while. A surfer, yes. Lost in the faraway and gone. He began sighing to me about legendary beaches where the waves were tubes and they came pumping end to end. "Trestle Beach," he murmured. "That's north of San Onofre. You had to sneak through Camp Pendleton. Sometimes the Marines would open fire, just warning shots. Or Hollister Ranch, up by Santa Barbara." His blue eyes got misty. "Huntington Beach. Oxnard. I got everywhere, man." He flexed his huge fingers. "Now these fucking Entity hodads own the shore. Can you believe it? They *own* it. And I'm pulling wall, my second time around, seven days a week next ten years."

"Ten?" I said. "That's a shitty deal."

"You know anyone who doesn't have a shitty deal?"

"Some," I said. "They buy out."

"Yeah."

"It can be done."

A careful look. You never know who might be a borgmann. Those stinking collaborators are everywhere.

"Can it?"

"All it takes is money," I said.

"And a pardoner."

"That's right."

"One you can trust."

I shrugged. "You've got to go on faith, man."

"Yeah," he said. Then, after a while: "I heard of a guy, he bought a three-year pardon and wall passage thrown in. Went up north, caught a krill trawler, wound up in Australia, on the Reef. Nobody's ever going to find him there. He's out of the system. Right out of the fucking system. What do you think that cost?"

"About twenty grand," I said.

"Hey, that's a sharp guess!"

"No guess."

"Oh?" Another careful look. "You don't sound local."

"I'm not. Just visiting."

"That's still the price? Twenty grand?"

"I can't do anything about supplying krill trawlers. You'd be on your own once you were outside the wall."

"Twenty grand just to get through the wall?"

"And a seven-year labor exemption."

"I pulled ten," he said.

"I can't get you ten. It's not in the configuration, you follow? But seven would work. You could get so far, in seven, that they'd lose you. You could goddamned *swim* to Australia. Come in low, below Sydney, no seines there."

"You know a hell of a lot."

"My business to know," I said. "You want me to run an asset check on you?"

"I'm worth seventeen five. Fifteen hundred real, the rest collat. What can I get for seventeen five?"

"Just what I said. Through the wall, and seven years' exemption."

"A bargain rate, hey?"

"I take what I can get," I said. "Give me your wrist. And don't worry. This part is read-only."

I keyed his data implant and patched mine in. He had fifteen hundred in the bank and a collateral rating of sixteen thou, exactly as he claimed. We eyed each other very carefully now. As I said, you never know who the borgmanns are.

"You can do it right here in the park?" he asked.

"You bet. Lean back, close your eyes, make like you're snoozing in the sun. The deal is that I take a thousand of the cash now and you transfer five thou of the collateral bucks to me, straight labor-debenture deal. When you get through the wall I get the other five hundred cash and five thou more on sweat security. The rest you pay off at three thou a year plus interest, wherever you are, quarterly key-ins. I'll program the whole thing, including beep reminders on payment dates. It's up to you to make your travel arrangements, remember. I can do pardons and wall transits, but I'm not a goddamned travel agent. Are we on?"

He put his head back and closed his eyes.

"Go ahead," he said.

It was fingertip stuff, straight circuit emulation, my standard hack. I picked up all his identification codes, carried them into central, found his records. He seemed real, nothing more or less than he had claimed. Sure enough, he had drawn a lulu of a labor tax, ten years on the wall. I wrote him a pardon good for the first seven of that. Had to leave the final three on the books, purely technical reasons, but the computers weren't going to be able to find him by then. I gave him a wall-transit pass, too, which meant writing in a new skills class for him, programmer third grade. He didn't think like a programmer and he didn't look like a programmer, but the wall software wasn't going to figure that out. Now I had made him a member of the human elite, the relative handful of us who are free to go in and out of the walled cities as we wish. In return for these little favors I signed over his entire life savings to various accounts of mine, payable as arranged, part now, part later. He wasn't worth a nickel any more, but he was a free man. That's not such a terrible trade-off.

Oh, and the pardon was a valid one. I had decided not to write any stiffs while I was in Los Angeles. A kind of sentimental atonement, you might say, for the job I had done on that woman all those years back.

You absolutely have to write stiffs once in a while, you understand. So that you don't look too good, so that you don't give the Entities reason to hunt you down. Just as you have to ration the number of pardons you do. I didn't have to be writing pardons at all, of course. I could have just authorized the system to pay me so much a year, fifty thou, a hundred, and taken it easy forever. But where's the challenge in that?

So I write pardons, but no more than I need to cover my expenses, and I deliberately fudge some of them up, making myself look as incompetent as the rest so the Entities don't have a reason to begin trying to track the identifying marks of my work. My conscience hasn't been too sore about that. It's a matter of survival, after all. And most other pardoners are out-and-out frauds, you know. At least with me you stand a better-than-even chance of getting what you're paying for.

✦

The next one was a tiny Japanese woman, the classic style, sleek, fragile, doll-like. Crying in big wild gulps that I thought might break her in half, while a gray-haired older man in a shabby business suit—her grandfather, you'd guess—was trying to comfort her. Public crying is a good indicator of Entity trouble. "Maybe I can help," I said, and they were both so distraught that they didn't even bother to be suspicious.

He was her father-in-law, not her grandfather. The husband was dead, killed by burglars the year before. There were two small kids. Now she had received her new labor-tax ticket. She had been afraid they were going to send her out to work on the wall, which of course wasn't likely to happen: the assignments are pretty random, but they usually aren't crazy, and what use would a ninety-pound girl be in hauling stone blocks around? The father-in-law had some friends who were in the know, and they managed to bring up the hidden encoding on her ticket. The computers hadn't sent her to the wall, no. They had sent her to Area Five. And they had given her a TTD classification.

"The wall would have been better," the old man said. "They'd see, right away, she wasn't strong enough for heavy work, and they'd find something else, something she could do. But Area Five? Who ever comes back from that?"

"You know what Area Five is?" I said.

"The medical experiment place. And this mark here, TTD. I know what that stands for, too."

She began to moan again. I couldn't blame her. TTD means Test To Destruction. The Entities want to find out how much work we can really do, and they feel that the only reliable way to discover that is to put us through tests that show where the physical limits are.

"I will die," she wailed. "My babies! My babies!"

"Do you know what a pardoner is?" I asked the father-in-law.

A quick excited response: sharp intake of breath, eyes going bright, head nodding vehemently. Just as quickly the excitement faded, giving way to bleakness, helplessness, despair.

"They all cheat you," he said.

"Not all."

"Who can say? They take your money, they give you nothing."

"You know that isn't true. Everybody can tell you stories of pardons that came through."

"Maybe. Maybe," the old man said. The woman sobbed quietly. "You know of such a person?"

"For three thousand dollars," I said, "I can take the TTD off her ticket. For five I can write an exemption from service good until her children are in high school."

Sentimental me. A fifty-percent discount, and I hadn't even run an asset check. For all I knew, the father-in-law was a millionaire. But no, he'd have been off cutting a pardon for her, then, and not sitting around like this in Pershing Square.

He gave me a long, deep, appraising look. Peasant shrewdness coming to the surface.

"How can we be sure of that?" he asked.

I might have told him that I was the king of my profession, the best of all pardoners, a genius hacker with the truly magic touch, who could slip into any computer ever designed and make it dance to my tune. Which would have been nothing more than the truth. But all I said was that he'd have to make up his own mind, that I couldn't offer any affidavits or guarantees, that I was available if he wanted me and otherwise it was all the same to me if she preferred to stick with her TTD ticket. They went off and conferred for a couple of minutes. When they came back, he silently rolled up his sleeve and presented his implant to me. I keyed his credit balance: thirty thou or so, not bad. I transferred eight of it to my accounts, half to Seattle, the rest to Los Angeles. Then I took her wrist, which was about two of my fingers thick, and got into her implant and wrote her the pardon that would save her life. Just to be certain, I ran a double validation check on it. It's always possible to stiff a customer unintentionally, though I've never done it. But I didn't want this particular one to be my first.

"Go on," I said. "Home. Your kids are waiting for their lunch."

Her eyes glowed. "If I could only thank you somehow—"

"I've already banked my fee. Go. If you ever see me again, don't say hello."

"This will work?" the old man asked.

"You say you have friends who know things. Wait seven days, then tell the data bank that she's lost her ticket. When you get the new one, ask your pals to decode it for you. You'll see. It'll be all right."

I don't think he believed me. I think he was more than half sure I had swindled him out of one-fourth of his life's savings, and I could see the hatred in his eyes. But that was his problem. In a week he'd find out that I really had saved his daughter-in-law's life, and then he'd rush down to the Square to tell me how sorry he was that he had had such terrible feelings toward me. Only by then I'd be somewhere else, far away.

They shuffled out the east side of the park, pausing a couple of times to peer over their shoulders at me as if they thought I was going to transform them into pillars of salt the moment their backs were turned. Then they were gone.

I'd earned enough now to get me through the week I planned to spend in L.A. But I stuck around anyway, hoping for a little more. My mistake.

This one was Mr. Invisible, the sort of man you'd never notice in a crowd, gray on gray, thinning hair, mild bland apologetic smile. But his eyes had a shine. I forget whether he started talking first to me, or me to him, but pretty soon we were jockeying around trying to find out things about each other. He told me he was from Silver Lake. I gave him a blank look. How in hell am I supposed to know all the zillion L.A. neighborhoods? Said that he had come down here to see someone at the big government HQ on Figueroa Street. All right: probably an appeals case. I sensed a customer.

Then he wanted to know where I was from. Santa Monica? West L.A.? Something in my accent, I guess. "I'm a traveling man," I said. "Hate to stay in one place." True enough. I need to hack or I go crazy; if I did all my hacking in just one city I'd be virtually begging them to slap a trace on me sooner or later, and that would be the end. I didn't tell him any of that. "Came in from Utah last night. Wyoming before that." Not true, either one. "Maybe on to New York, next." He looked at me as if I'd said I was planning a voyage to the moon. People out here, they don't go east a lot. These days most people don't go anywhere.

Now he knew that I had wall-transit clearance, or else that I had some way of getting it when I wanted it. That was what he was looking to find out. In no time at all we were down to basics.

He said he had drawn a new ticket, six years at the salt-field reclamation site out back of Mono Lake. People die like mayflies out there. What he wanted was a transfer to something softer, like Operations & Maintenance, and it had to be within the walls, preferably in one of the districts out by the ocean where the air is cool and clear. I quoted him a price and he accepted without a quiver.

"Let's have your wrist," I said.

He held out his right hand, palm upward. His implant access was a pale-yellow plaque, mounted in the usual place but rounder than the standard kind and of a slightly smoother texture. I didn't see any great significance in that. As I had done maybe a thousand times before, I put my own arm over his, wrist to wrist, access to access. Our biocomputers made contact, and instantly I knew that I was in trouble.

Human beings have been carrying biochip-based computers in their bodies for the last forty or fifty years or so—long before the Entity invasion, anyway—but for most people it's just something they take for granted, like the vaccination mark on their thighs. They use them for the things they're meant to be used for, and don't give them a thought beyond that. The biocomputer's just a commonplace tool for them, like a fork, like a shovel. You have to have the hacker sort of mentality to be willing to turn your biocomputer into something more. That's why, when the Entities came and took us over and made us build walls around our cities, most people reacted just like sheep, letting themselves be herded inside and politely staying there. The only ones who can move around freely now—because we know how to manipulate the mainframes through which the Entities rule us—are the hackers. And there aren't many of us. I could tell right away that I had hooked myself onto one now.

The moment we were in contact, he came at me like a storm.

The strength of his signal let me know I was up against something special, and that I'd been hustled. He hadn't been trying to buy a pardon at all. What he was looking for was a duel. Mr. Macho behind the bland smile, out to show the new boy in town a few of his tricks.

No hacker had ever mastered me in a one-on-one anywhere. Not ever. I felt sorry for him, but not much.

He shot me a bunch of stuff, cryptic but easy, just by way of finding out my parameters. I caught it and stored it and laid an interrupt on him and took over the dialog. My turn to test him. I wanted him to begin to see who he was fooling around with. But just as I began to execute, he put an interrupt on *me*. That was a new experience. I stared at him with some respect.

Usually any hacker anywhere will recognize my signal in the first thirty seconds, and that'll be enough to finish the interchange. He'll know that there's no point in continuing. But this guy either wasn't able to identify me or just didn't care, and he came right back with his interrupt. Amazing. So was the stuff he began laying on me next.

He went right to work, really trying to scramble my architecture. Reams of stuff came flying at me up in the heavy-megabyte zone.

—*jspike. dbltag. nslice. dzcnt.*

I gave it right back to him, twice as hard.

—*maxfrq. minpau. spktot. jspike.*

He didn't mind at all.

—*maxdz. spktim. falter. nslice.*

—*frqsum. eburst.*

—*iburst.*

—*prebst.*

—nobrst.

Mexican standoff. He was still smiling. Not even a trace of sweat on his forehead. Something eerie about him, something new and strange. This is some kind of borgmann hacker, I realized suddenly. He must be working for the Entities, roving the city, looking to make trouble for freelancers like me. Good as he was, and he was plenty good, I despised him. A hacker who had become a borgmann—now, that was truly disgusting. I wanted to short him. I wanted to burn him out, now. I had never hated anyone so much in my life.

I couldn't do a thing with him.

I was baffled. I was the Data King, I was the Megabyte Monster. All my life I had floated back and forth across a world in chains, picking every lock I came across. And now this nobody was tying me in knots. Whatever I gave him, he parried; and what came back from him was getting increasingly bizarre. He was working with an algorithm I had never seen before and was having serious trouble solving. After a little while I couldn't even figure out what he was doing to me, let alone what I was going to do to cancel it. It was getting so I could barely execute. He was forcing me inexorably toward a wetware crash.

"Who are you?" I yelled.

He laughed in my face.

And kept pouring it on. He was threatening the integrity of my implant, going at me down on the microcosmic level, attacking the molecules themselves. Fiddling around with electron shells, reversing charges and mucking up valences, clogging my gates, turning my circuits to soup. The computer that is implanted in my brain is nothing but a lot of organic chemistry, after all. So is my brain. If he kept this up the computer would go and the brain would follow, and I'd spend the rest of my life in the bibble-bibble academy.

This wasn't a sporting contest. This was murder.

I reached for the reserves, throwing up all the defensive blockages I could invent. Things I had never had to use in my life, but they were there when I needed them, and they did slow him down. For a moment I was able to halt his ballbreaking onslaught and even push him back. And give myself the breathing space to set up a few offensive combinations of my own. But before I could get them running, he shut me down once more and started to drive me toward crashville all over again. He was unbelievable.

I blocked him. He came back again. I hit him hard and he threw the punch into some other neural channel altogether and it went fizzling away.

I hit him again. Again he blocked it.

Then he hit me and I went reeling and staggering, and managed to get myself together when I was about three nanoseconds from the edge of the abyss.

I began to set up a new combination. But even as I did it, I was reading the tone of his data, and what I was getting was absolute cool confidence. He was waiting for me. He was ready for anything I could throw. He was in that realm beyond mere self-confidence into utter certainty.

What it was coming down to was this. I was able to keep him from ruining me, but only just barely, and I wasn't able to lay a glove on him at all. And he seemed to have infinite resources behind him. I didn't worry him. He was tireless. He didn't appear to degrade at all. He just took all I could give and kept throwing new stuff at me, coming at me from six sides at once.

Now I understood for the first time what it must have felt like for all the hackers I had beaten. Some of them must have felt pretty cocky, I suppose, until they ran into me. It costs more to lose when you think you're good. When you *know* you're good. People like that, when they lose, they have to reprogram their whole sense of their relation to the universe.

I had two choices. I could go on fighting until he wore me down and crashed me. Or I could give up right now. In the end everything comes down to yes or no, on or off, one or zero, doesn't it?

I took a deep breath. I was staring straight into chaos.

"All right," I said. "I'm beaten. I quit."

I wrenched my wrist free of his, trembled, swayed, went toppling down on the ground.

A minute later five cops jumped me and trussed me up like a turkey and hauled me away, with my implant arm sticking out of the package and a security lock wrapped around my wrist, as if they were afraid I was going to start pulling data right out of the air.

Where they took me was Figueroa Street, the big black marble ninety-story job that is the home of the puppet city government. I didn't give a damn. I was numb. They could have put me in the sewer and I wouldn't have cared. I wasn't damaged—the automatic circuit check was still running and it came up green—but the humiliation was so intense that I felt crashed. I felt destroyed. The only thing I wanted to know was the name of the hacker who had done it to me.

The Figueroa Street building has ceilings about twenty feet high everywhere, so that there'll be room for Entities to move around. Voices reverberate in those vast open spaces like echoes in a cavern. The cops sat me down in a hallway, still all wrapped up, and kept me there for a long time. Blurred sounds went lalloping up and down the passage. I wanted to hide from them. My brain felt raw. I had taken one hell of a pounding.

Now and then a couple of towering Entities would come rumbling through the hall, tiptoeing on their tentacles in that weirdly dainty way of theirs. With them came a little entourage of humans whom they ignored entirely, as they always do. They know that we're intelligent, but they just don't care to talk to us. They let their computers do that, via the Borgmann interface, and may his signal degrade forever for having sold us out. Not that they wouldn't have conquered us anyway, but Borgmann made it ever so much easier for them to push us around by showing them how to connect our little biocomputers to their huge mainframes. I bet he was very proud of himself, too: just wanted to see if his gadget would work, and to hell with the fact that he was selling us into eternal bondage.

Nobody has ever figured out why the Entities are here or what they want from us. They simply came, that's all. Saw. Conquered. Rearranged us. Put us to work doing god-awful unfathomable tasks, Like a bad dream.

And there wasn't any way we could defend ourselves against them. Didn't seem that way to us at first—we were cocky, we were going to wage guerrilla war and wipe them out—but we learned fast how wrong we were, and we are theirs for keeps. There's nobody left with anything close to freedom except the handful of hackers like me; and, as I've explained, we're not dopey enough to try any serious sort of counterattack. It's a big enough triumph for us just to be able to dodge around from one city to another without having to get authorization.

Looked like all that was finished for me now. Right then I didn't give a damn. I was still trying to integrate the notion that I had been beaten; I didn't have capacity left over to work on a program for the new life I would be leading now.

"Is this the pardoner, over here?" someone said.

"That one, yeah."

"She wants to see him now."

"You think we should fix him up a little first?"

"She said now."

A hand at my shoulder, rocking me gently. "Up, fellow. It's interview time. Don't make a mess or you'll get hurt."

I let them shuffle me down the hall and through a gigantic doorway and into an immense office with a ceiling high enough to give an Entity all the room it would want. I didn't say a word. There weren't any Entities in the office, just a woman in a black robe, sitting behind a wide desk at the far end. It looked like a toy desk in that colossal room. She looked like a toy woman. The cops left me alone with her. Trussed up like that, I wasn't any risk.

"Are you John Doe?" she asked.

I was halfway across the room, studying my shoes. "What do you think?" I said.

"That's the name you gave upon entry to the city."

"I give lots of names. John Smith, Richard Roe, Joe Blow. It doesn't matter much to the gate software what name I give."

"Because you've gimmicked the gate?" She paused. "I should tell you, this is a court of inquiry."

"You already know everything I could tell you. Your borgmann hacker's been swimming around in my brain."

"Please," she said. "This'll be easier if you cooperate. The accusation is illegal entry, illegal seizure of a vehicle, and illegal interfacing activity, specifically, selling pardons. Do you have a statement?"

"No."

"You deny that you're a pardoner?"

"I don't deny, I don't affirm. What's the goddamned use."

"Look up at me," she said.

"That's a lot of effort."

"Look up," she said. There was an odd edge on her voice. "Whether you're a pardoner or not isn't the issue. We know you're a pardoner. *I* know you're a pardoner." And she called me by a name I hadn't used in a very long time. Not since '36, as a matter of fact.

I looked at her. Stared. Had trouble believing I was seeing what I saw. Felt a rush of memories come flooding up. Did some mental editing work on her face, taking out some lines here, subtracting a little flesh in a few places, adding some in others. Stripping away the years.

"Yes," she said. "I'm who you think I am."

I gaped. This was worse than what the hacker had done to me. But there was no way to run from it.

"You work for them?" I asked.

"The pardon you sold me wasn't any good. You knew that, didn't you? I had someone waiting for me in San Diego, but when I tried to get through the wall they stopped me just like that, and dragged me away screaming. I could have killed you. I would have gone to San Diego and then we would have tried to make it to Hawaii in his boat."

"I didn't know about the guy in San Diego," I said.

"Why should you? It wasn't your business. You took my money, you were supposed to get me my pardon. That was the deal."

Her eyes were gray with golden sparkles in them. I had trouble looking into them.

"You still want to kill me?" I asked. "Are you planning to kill me now?"

"No and no." She used my old name again. "I can't tell you how astounded I was, when they brought you in here. A pardoner, they said. John Doe. Pardoners, that's my department. They bring all of them to me. I used to wonder years ago if they'd ever bring *you* in, but after a while I figured, no, not a chance, he's probably a million miles away, he'll never come back this way again. And then they brought in this John Doe, and I saw your face."

"Do you think you could manage to believe," I said, "that I've felt guilty for what I did to you ever since? You don't have to believe it. But it's the truth."

"I'm sure it's been unending agony for you."

"I mean it. Please. I've stiffed a lot of people, yes, and sometimes I've regretted it and sometimes I haven't, but you were one that I regretted. You're the one I've regretted most. This is the absolute truth."

She considered that. I couldn't tell whether she believed it even for a fraction of a second, but I could see that she was considering it.

"Why did you do it?" she asked after a bit.

"I stiff people because I don't want to seem too perfect," I told her. "You deliver a pardon every single time, word gets around, people start talking, you start to become legendary. And then you're known everywhere and sooner or later the Entities get hold of you, and that's that. So I always make sure to write a lot of stiffs. I tell people I'll do my best, but there aren't any guarantees, and sometimes it doesn't work."

"You deliberately cheated me."

"Yes."

"I thought you did. You seemed so cool, so professional. So perfect. I was sure the pardon would be valid. I couldn't see how it would miss. And then I got to the wall and they grabbed me. So I thought, That bastard sold me out. He was too good just to have flubbed it up." Her tone was calm, but the anger was still in her eyes. "Couldn't you have stiffed the next one? Why did it have to be me?"

I looked at her for a long time.

"Because I loved you," I said.

"Shit," she said. "You didn't even know me. I was just some stranger who had hired you."

"That's just it. There I was full of all kinds of crazy instant lunatic fantasies about you, all of a sudden ready to turn my nice orderly life upside down for you, and all you could see was somebody you had hired to do a job. I didn't know about the guy from San Diego. All I knew was I saw you and I wanted you. You don't think that's love? Well, call it something else, then, whatever you want. I never let myself feel it before. It isn't smart, I thought, it ties you down, the risks are too big. And then I saw you and I talked to you a little and I thought something could be happening between us and things started to change inside me, and I thought, Yeah, yeah, go with it this time, let it happen, this may make everything different. And you stood there not seeing it, not even beginning to notice, just jabbering on and on about how important the pardon was for you. So I stiffed you. And afterwards I thought, Jesus, I ruined that girl's life and it was just because I got myself into a snit, and that was a fucking petty thing to have done. So I've been sorry ever since. You don't have to believe that. I didn't know about San Diego. That makes it even worse for me." She didn't say anything all this time, and the silence felt enormous. So after a moment I said, "Tell me one thing, at least. That guy who wrecked me in Pershing Square: who was he?"

"He wasn't anybody," she said.

"What does that mean?"

"He isn't a who. He's a *what*. It's an android, a mobile antipardoner unit, plugged right into the big Entity mainframe in Culver City. Something new that we have going around town."

"Oh," I said. "Oh."

"The report is that you gave it one hell of a workout."

"It gave me one, too. Turned my brain half to mush."

"You were trying to drink the sea through a straw. For a while it looked like you were really going to do it, too. You're one goddamned hacker, you know that?"

"Why did you go to work for them?" I said.

She shrugged. "Everybody works for them. Except people like you. You took everything I had and didn't give me my pardon. So what was I supposed to do?"

"I see."

"It's not such a bad job. At least I'm not out there on the wall. Or being sent off for TTD."

"No," I said. "It's probably not so bad. If you don't mind working in a room with such a high ceiling. Is that what's going to happen to me? Sent off for TTD?"

"Don't be stupid. You're too valuable."

"To whom?"

"The system always needs upgrading. You know it better than anyone alive. You'll work for us."

"You think I'm going to turn borgmann?" I said, amazed.

"It beats TTD," she said.

I fell silent again. I was thinking that she couldn't possibly be serious, that they'd be fools to trust me in any kind of responsible position. And even bigger fools to let me near their computer.

"All right," I said. "I'll do it. On one condition."

"You really have balls, don't you?"

"Let me have a rematch with that android of yours. I need to check something out. And afterward we can discuss what kind of work I'd be best suited for here. Okay?"

"You know you aren't in any position to lay down conditions."

"Sure I am. What I do with computers is a unique art. You can't make me do it against my will. You can't make me do anything against my will."

She thought about that. "What good is a rematch?"

"Nobody ever beat me before. I want a second try."

"You know it'll be worse for you than before."

"Let me find that out."

"But what's the point?"

"Get me your android and I'll show you the point," I said.

⌣

She went along with it. Maybe it was curiosity, maybe it was something else, but she patched herself into the computer net and pretty soon they brought in the android I had encountered in the park, or maybe another one with the same face. It looked me over pleasantly, without the slightest sign of interest.

Someone came in and took the security lock off my wrist and left again. She gave the android its instructions and it held out its wrist to me and we made contact. And I jumped right in.

I was raw and wobbly and pretty damned battered, still, but I knew what I needed to do and I knew I had to do it fast. The thing was to ignore the android completely—it was just a terminal, it was just a unit—and go for what lay behind it. So I bypassed the android's own identity program, which was clever but shallow. I went right around it while the android was still setting up its combinations, dived underneath, got myself instantly from the unit level to the mainframe level and gave the master Culver City computer a hearty handshake.

Jesus, that felt good!

All that power, all those millions of megabytes squatting there, and I was plugged right into it. Of course, I felt like a mouse hitchhiking on the back of an elephant. That was all right. I might be a mouse, but that mouse was getting a tremendous ride. I hung on tight and went soaring along on the hurricane winds of that colossal machine.

And as I soared, I ripped out chunks of it by the double handful and tossed them to the breeze.

It didn't even notice for a good tenth of a second. That's how big it was.

There I was, tearing great blocks of data out of its gut, joyously ripping and rending. And it didn't even know it, because even the most magnificent computer ever assembled is still stuck with operating at the speed of light, and when the best you can do is 186,000 miles a second it can take quite a while for the alarm to travel the full distance down all your neural channels. That thing was *huge*. Mouse riding on elephant, did I say? Amoeba piggybacking on brontosaurus, was more like it.

God knows how much damage I was able to do. But of course the alarm circuitry did cut in eventually. Internal gates came clanging down and all sensitive areas were sealed away and I was shrugged off with the greatest of ease. There was no sense staying around waiting to get trapped, so I pulled myself free.

I had found out what I needed to know. Where the defenses were, how they worked. This time the computer had kicked me out, but it wouldn't be able to, the next. Whenever I wanted, I could go in there and smash whatever I felt like.

The android crumpled to the carpet. It was nothing but an empty husk now.

Lights were flashing on the office wall.

She looked at me, appalled. "What did you do?"

"I beat your android," I said. "It wasn't all that hard, once I knew the scoop."

"You damaged the main computer."

"Not really. Not much. I just gave it a little tickle. It was surprised, seeing me get access in there, that's all."

"I think you really damaged it."

"Why would I want to do that?"

"The question ought to be why you haven't done it already. Why you haven't gone in there and crashed the hell out of their programs."

"You think I could do something like that?"

She studied me. "I think maybe you could, yes."

"Well, maybe so. Or maybe not. But I'm not a crusader, you know. I like my life the way it is. I move around, I do as I please. It's a quiet life. I don't start revolutions. When I need to gimmick things, I gimmick them just enough, and no more. And the Entities don't even know I exist. If I stick my finger in their eye, they'll cut my finger off. So I haven't done it."

"But now you might," she said.

I began to get uncomfortable. "I don't follow you," I said, although I was beginning to think that I did.

"You don't like risk. You don't like being conspicuous. But if we take your freedom away, if we tie you down in L.A. and put you to work, what the hell would you have to lose? You'd go right in there. You'd gimmick things but good." She was silent for a time. "Yes," she said. "You really would. I see it now, that you have the capability and that you could be put in a position where you'd be willing to use it. And then you'd screw everything up for all of us, wouldn't you?"

"What?"

"You'd fix the Entities, sure. You'd do such a job on their computer that they'd have to scrap it and start all over again. Isn't that so?"

She was onto me, all right.

"But I'm not going to give you the chance. I'm not crazy. There isn't going to be any revolution and I'm not going to be its heroine and you aren't the type to be a hero. I understand you now. It isn't safe to fool around with you. Because if anybody did, you'd take your little revenge, and you wouldn't care what you brought down on everybody else's head. You could ruin their computer, but then they'd come down on us and they'd make things twice as hard for us as they already are, and you wouldn't care. We'd all suffer, but you wouldn't care. No. My life isn't so terrible that I need you to turn it upside down for me. You've already done it to me once. I don't need it again."

She looked at me steadily and all the anger seemed to be gone from her and there was only contempt left.

After a little she said, "Can you go in there again and gimmick things so that there's no record of your arrest today?"

"Yeah. Yeah, I could do that."

"Do it, then. And then get going. Get the hell out of here, fast."

"Are you serious?"

"You think I'm not?"

I shook my head. I understood. And I knew that I had won and I had lost, both at the same time.

She made an impatient gesture, a shoofly gesture.

I nodded. I felt very very small.

"I just want to say—all that stuff about how much I regretted the thing I did to you back then—it was true. Every word of it."

"It probably was," she said. "Look, do your gimmicking and edit yourself out and then I want you to start moving. Out of the building. Out of the city. Okay? Do it real fast."

I hunted around for something else to say and couldn't find it. Quit while you're ahead, I thought. She gave me her wrist and I did the interface with her. As my implant access touched hers, she shuddered a little. It wasn't much of a shudder, but I noticed it. I felt it, all right. I think I'm going to feel it every time I stiff anyone, ever again. Any time I even think of stiffing anyone.

I went in and found the John Doe arrest entry and got rid of it, and then I searched out her civil service file and promoted her up two grades and doubled her pay. Not much of an atonement. But what the hell, there wasn't much I could do. Then I cleaned up my traces behind me and exited the program.

"All right," I said. "It's done."

"Fine," she said, and rang for her cops.

❤

They apologized for the case of mistaken identity and let me out of the building and turned me loose on Figueroa Street. It was late afternoon and the street was getting dark and the air was cool. Even in Los Angeles winter is winter, of a sort. I went to a street access and summoned the Toshiba from wherever it had parked itself and it came driving up, five or ten minutes later, and I told it to take me north. The going was slow, rush-hour stuff, but that was okay. We came to the wall at the Sylmar gate, fifty miles or so out of town. The gate asked me my name. "Richard Roe," I said. "Beta Pi Upsilon 104324x. Destination San Francisco."

It rains a lot in San Francisco in the winter. Still, it's a pretty town. I would have preferred Los Angeles that time of year, but what the hell. Nobody gets all his first choices all the time. The gate opened and the Toshiba went through. Easy as Beta Pi.

THE IRON STAR

A Byron Preiss project, once again. The Planets had sold very nicely, and now he was casting his net a little wider: a book called The Universe. As before, astronomers were doing the scientific essays and s-f writers were providing stories to match. Byron showed me the list of themes—stars, quasars, black holes, galaxies and clusters, and so forth—and I chose to write about supernovae and pulsars.

One incidental bit of pleasure came from this for me. In Byron's book, my story was illustrated with a full-color plate by Bob Eggleton. I sold magazine rights to the story to Amazing Stories, oldest of science-fiction magazines, and it drew a cover painting by Terry Lee. By coincidence both Lee and Eggleton chose to illustrate the same scene, the one in which the narrator first gets a look at the Nine Sparg captain on his television screen. The two paintings are quite different in mood and technique, yet each depicts my alien critter in a distinctive and powerful way, while remaining faithful to my prose description. It's one of science-fiction writing's special treats to see your verbal inventions brought to visual life this way.

The alien ship came drifting up from behind the far side of the neutron star just as I was going on watch. It looked a little like a miniature neutron star itself: a perfect sphere, metallic, dark. But neutron stars don't have six perky little outthrust legs, and the alien craft did.

While I paused in front of the screen the alien floated diagonally upward, cutting a swath of darkness across the brilliantly starry sky like a fast-moving black hole. It even occulted the real black hole that lay thirty light-minutes away.

I stared at the strange vessel, fascinated and annoyed, wishing I had never seen it, wishing it would softly and suddenly vanish away. This mission was sufficiently complicated already. We hadn't needed an alien ship to appear on the scene. For five days now we had circled the neutron star in seesaw orbit with the aliens, a hundred eighty degrees apart. They hadn't said anything to us and we didn't know how to say anything to them. I didn't feel good about that. I like things direct, succinct, known.

Lina Sorabji, busy enhancing sonar transparencies over at our improvised archaeology station, looked up from her work and caught me scowling. Lina is a slender, dark woman from Madras whose ancestors were priests and scholars when mine were hunting bison on the Great Plains. She said, "You shouldn't let it get to you like that, Tom."

"You know what it feels like, every time I see it cross the screen? It's like having a little speck wandering around on the visual field of your eye. Irritating, frustrating, maddening—and absolutely impossible to get rid of."

"You want to get rid of it?"

I shrugged. "Isn't this job tough enough? Attempting to scoop a sample from the core of a neutron star? Do we really have to have an alien spaceship looking over our shoulders while we work?"

"Maybe it's not a spaceship at all," Lina said cheerily. "Maybe it's just some kind of giant spacebug."

I suppose she was trying to amuse me. I wasn't amused. This was going to win me a place in the history of space exploration, sure: Chief Executive Officer of the first expedition from Earth ever to encounter intelligent extraterrestrial life. Terrific. But that wasn't what IBM/Toshiba had hired me to do. And I'm more interested in completing assignments than in making history. You don't get paid for making history.

Basically the aliens were a distraction from our real work, just as last month's discovery of a dead civilization on a nearby solar system had been, the one whose photographs Lina Sorabji now was studying. This was supposed to be a business venture involving the experimental use of new technology, not an archaeological mission or an exercise in interspecies diplomacy. And I knew that there was a ship from the Exxon/Hyundai combine loose somewhere in hyperspace right now working on the same task we'd been sent out to handle. If they brought it off first, IBM/Toshiba would suffer a very severe loss of face, which is considered very bad on the corporate level. What's bad for IBM/Toshiba would be exceedingly bad for me. For all of us.

I glowered at the screen. Then the orbit of the *Ben-wah Maru* carried us down and away, and the alien disappeared from my line of sight. But not for long, I knew.

As I keyed up the log reports from my sleep period I said to Lina, "You have anything new today?" She had spent the past three weeks analyzing the dead-world data. You never know what the parent companies will see as potentially profitable.

"I'm down to hundred-meter penetration now. There's a system of broad tunnels wormholing the entire planet. Some kind of pneumatic transportation network, is my guess. Here, have a look."

A holoprint sprang into vivid life in the air between us. It was a sonar scan that we had taken from ten thousand kilometers out, reaching a short distance below the surface of the dead world. I saw odd-angled tunnels lined with gleaming luminescent tiles that still pulsed with dazzling colors, centuries after the cataclysm that had destroyed all life there. Amazing decorative patterns of bright lines were plainly visible along the tunnel walls, lines that swirled and overlapped and entwined and beckoned my eye into some adjoining dimension.

Trains of sleek snub-nosed vehicles were scattered like caterpillars everywhere in the tunnels. In them and around them lay skeletons, thousands of them, millions, a whole continent full of commuters slaughtered as they waited at the station for the morning express. Lina touched the fine scan and gave me a close look: biped creatures, broad skulls tapering sharply at the sides, long apelike arms, seven-fingered hands with what seemed like an opposable thumb at each end, pelvises enlarged into peculiar bony crests jutting far out from their hips. It wasn't the first time a hyperspace exploring vessel had come across relics of extinct extraterrestrial races, even a fossil or two. But these weren't fossils. These beings had died only a few hundred years ago. And they had all died at the same time.

I shook my head somberly. "Those are some tunnels. They might have been able to convert them into pretty fair radiation shelters, is my guess. If only they'd had a little warning of what was coming."

"They never knew what hit them."

"No," I said. "They never knew a thing. A supernova brewing right next door and they must not have been able to tell what was getting ready to happen."

Lina called up another print, and another, then another. During our brief flyby last month our sensors had captured an amazing panoramic view of this magnificent lost civilization: wide streets, spacious parks, splendid public buildings, imposing private houses, the works. Bizarre architecture, all un-likely angles and jutting crests like its creators, but unquestionably grand, noble, impressive. There had been keen intelligence at work here, and high artistry. Everything was intact and in a remarkable state of preservation, if you make allowances for the natural inroads that time and weather and I suppose the occasional earthquake will bring over three or four hundred years. Obviously this had been a wealthy, powerful society, stable and confident.

And between one instant and the next it had all been stopped dead in its tracks, wiped out, extinguished, annihilated. Perhaps they had had a fraction of a second to realize that the end of the world had come, but no more than that. I saw what surely were family groups huddling together, skeletons clumped in threes or fours or fives. I saw what I took to be couples with their seven-fingered hands still clasped in a final exchange of love. I saw some kneeling in a weird elbows-down position that might have been one of—who can say? Prayer? Despair? Acceptance?

A sun had exploded and this great world had died. I shuddered, not for the first time, thinking of it.

It hadn't even been their own sun. What had blown up was this one, forty light-years away from them, the one that was now the neutron star about which we orbited and that once had been a main sequence sun maybe three or four times as big as Earth's. Or else it had been the other one in this binary system, thirty light-minutes from the first, the giant blazing young companion star of which nothing remained except the black hole nearby. At the moment we had no way of knowing which of these two stars had gone supernova first. Whichever one it was, though, had sent a furious burst of radiation heading outward, a lethal flux of cosmic rays capable of destroying most or perhaps all life-forms within a sphere a hundred light-years in diameter.

The planet of the underground tunnels and the noble temples had simply been in the way. One of these two suns had come to the moment when all the fuel in its core had been consumed: hydrogen had been fused into helium, helium into carbon, carbon into neon, oxygen, sulfur, silicon, until at last a core of pure iron lay at its heart. There is no atomic nucleus more strongly bound than iron. The star had reached the point where its release of energy through fusion had to cease; and with the end of energy production the star no longer could withstand the gravitational pressure of its own vast mass. In a moment, in the twinkling of an eye, the core underwent a catastrophic collapse. Its matter was compressed—beyond the point of equilibrium. And rebounded. And sent forth an intense shock wave that went rushing through the star's outer layers at a speed of 15,000 kilometers a second.

Which ripped the fabric of the star apart, generating an explosion releasing more energy than a billion suns.

The shock wave would have continued outward and outward across space, carrying debris from the exploded star with it, and interstellar gas that the debris had swept up. A fierce sleet of radiation would have been riding on that

wave, too: cosmic rays, X rays, radio waves, gamma rays, everything, all up
and down the spectrum. If the sun that had gone supernova had had planets
close by, they would have been vaporized immediately. Outlying worlds of that
system might merely have been fried.

The people of the world of the tunnels, forty light-years distant, must have
known nothing of the great explosion for a full generation after it had happened. But, all that while, the light of that shattered star was traveling toward
them at a speed of 300,000 kilometers per second, and one night its frightful,
baleful unexpected glare must have burst suddenly into their sky in the most
terrifying way. And almost in that same moment—for the deadly cosmic rays
thrown off by the explosion move nearly at the speed of light—the killing blast
of hard radiation would have arrived. And so these people and all else that lived
on their world perished in terror and light.

All this took place a thousand light-years from Earth: that surging burst of
radiation will need another six centuries to complete its journey toward our
home world. At that distance, the cosmic rays will do us little or no harm. But
for a time that long-dead star will shine in our skies so brilliantly that it will be
visible by day, and by night it will cast deep shadows, longer than those of the
Moon.

That's still in Earth's future. Here the fatal supernova, and the second one
that must have happened not long afterward, were some four hundred years in
the past. What we had here now was a neutron star left over from one cataclysm
and a black hole left over from the other. Plus the pathetic remains of a great
civilization on a scorched planet orbiting a neighboring star. And now a ship
from some alien culture. A busy corner of the galaxy, this one. A busy time for
the crew of the IBM/Toshiba hyperspace ship *Ben-wah Maru*.

I was still going over the reports that had piled up at my station during my sleep
period—mass-and-output readings on the neutron star, progress bulletins on
the setup procedures for the neutronium scoop, and other routine stuff of that
nature—when the communicator cone in front of me started to glow. I flipped
it on. Cal Bjornsen, our communications guru, was calling from Brain Central downstairs.

Bjornsen is mostly black African with some Viking genes salted in. The
whole left side of his face is cyborg, the result of some extreme bit of teenage
carelessness. The story is that he was gravity-vaulting and lost polarity at sixty
meters. The mix of ebony skin, blue eyes, blond hair, and sculpted titanium is
an odd one, but I've seen a lot of faces less friendly than Cal's. He's a good man
with anything electronic.

He said, "I think they're finally trying to send us messages, Tom."

I sat up fast. "What's that?"

"We've been pulling in signals of some sort for the past ninety minutes that didn't look random, but we weren't sure about it. A dozen or so different frequencies all up and down the line, mostly in the radio band, but we're also getting what seem to be infrared pulses, and something flashing in the ultraviolet range. A kind of scattershot noise effect, only it isn't noise."

"Are you sure of that?"

"The computer's still chewing on it," Bjornsen said. The fingers of his right hand glided nervously up and down his smooth metal cheek. "But we can see already that there are clumps of repetitive patterns."

"Coming from them? How do you know?"

"We didn't, at first. But the transmissions conked out when we lost line-of-sight with them, and started up again when they came back into view."

"I'll be right down," I said.

Bjornsen is normally a calm man, but he was running in frantic circles when I reached Brain Central three or four minutes later. There was stuff dancing on all the walls: sine waves, mainly, but plenty of other patterns jumping around on the monitors. He had already pulled in specialists from practically every department—the whole astronomy staff, two of the math guys, a couple from the external maintenance team, and somebody from engines. I felt preempted. Who was CEO on this ship, anyway? They were all babbling at once. "Fourier series," someone said, and someone yelled back, "Dirichlet factor," and someone else said, "Gibbs phenomenon!" I heard Angie Seraphin insisting vehemently, "—continuous except possibly for a finite number of finite discontinuities in the interval $-\pi$ to pi—"

"Hold it," I said. "What's going on?"

More babble, more gibberish. I got them quiet again and repeated my question, aiming it this time at Bjornsen.

"We have the analysis now," he said.

"So?"

"You understand that it's only guesswork, but Brain Central gives good guess. The way it looks, they seem to want us to broadcast a carrier wave they can tune in on, and just talk to them while they lock in with some sort of word-to-word translating device of theirs."

"That's what Brain Central thinks they're saying?"

"It's the most plausible semantic content of the patterns they're transmitting," Bjornsen answered.

I felt a chill. The aliens had word-to-word translating devices? That was a lot more than we could claim. Brain Central is one very smart computer, and if it thought that it had correctly deciphered the message coming in, then in all likelihood it had. An astonishing accomplishment, taking a bunch of ones and zeros put together by an alien mind and culling some sense out of them.

But even Brain Central wasn't capable of word-to-word translation out of some unknown language. Nothing in our technology is. The alien message had been *designed* to be easy: put together, most likely, in a careful high-redundancy manner, the computer equivalent of picture-writing. Any race able to undertake interstellar travel ought to have a computer powerful enough to sweat the essential meaning out of a message like that, and we did. We couldn't go farther than that, though. Let the entropy of that message— that is, the unexpectedness of it, the unpredictability of its semantic content—rise just a little beyond the picture-writing level, and Brain Central would be lost. A computer that knows French should be able to puzzle out Spanish, and maybe even Greek. But Chinese? A tough proposition. And an *alien* language? Languages may start out logical, but they don't stay that way. And when its underlying grammatical assumptions were put together in the first place by beings with nervous systems that were wired up in ways entirely different from our own, well, the notion of instantaneous decoding becomes hopeless.

Yet our computer said that their computer could do word-to-word. That was scary.

On the other hand, if we couldn't talk to them, we couldn't begin to find out what they were doing here and what threat, if any, they might pose to us. By revealing our language to them we might be handing them some sort of advantage, but I couldn't be sure of that, and it seemed to me we had to take the risk.

It struck me as a good idea to get some backing for that decision, though. After a dozen years as CEO aboard various corporate ships, I knew the protocols. You did what you thought was right, but you didn't go all the way out on the limb by yourself if you could help it.

"Request a call for a meeting of the corporate staff," I told Bjornsen.

It wasn't so much a scientific matter now as a political one. The scientists would probably be gung-ho to go blasting straight ahead with making contact. But I wanted to hear what the Toshiba people would say, and the IBM people, and the military people. So we got everyone together and I laid the situation out and asked for a Consensus Process. And let them go at it, hammer and tongs.

Instant polarization. The Toshiba people were scared silly of the aliens. We must be cautious, Nakamura said. Caution, yes, said her cohort Nagy-Szabo. There may be danger to Earth. We have no knowledge of the aims and motivations of these beings. Avoid all contact with them, Nagy-Szabo said. Nakamura went even further. We should withdraw from the area immediately, she said, and return to Earth for additional instructions. That drew hot opposition from Jorgensen and Kalliotis, the IBM people. We had work to do here, they said. We should do it. They grudgingly conceded the need to be wary, but strongly urged continuation of the mission and advocated a circumspect opening of contact with the other ship. I think they were already starting to think about alien marketing demographics. Maybe I do them an injustice. Maybe.

The military people were about evenly divided between the two factions. A couple of them, the hair-splitting career-minded ones, wanted to play it absolutely safe and clear out of here fast, and the others, the up-and-away hero types, spoke out in favor of forging ahead with contact and to hell with the risks.

I could see there wasn't going to be any consensus. It was going to come down to me to decide.

By nature I am cautious. I might have voted with Nakamura in favor of immediate withdrawal; however, that would have made my ancient cold-eyed Sioux forebears howl. Yet in the end what swayed me was an argument that came from Bryce-Williamson, one of the fiercest of the military sorts. He said that we didn't dare turn tail and run for home without making contact, because the aliens would take that either as a hostile act or a stupid one, and either way they might just slap some kind of tracer on us that ultimately would enable them to discover the location of our home world. True caution, he said, required us to try to find out what these people were all about before we made any move to leave the scene. We couldn't just run and we couldn't simply ignore them.

I sat quietly for a long time, weighing everything.

"Well?" Bjornsen asked. "What do you want to do, Tom?"

"Send them a broadcast," I said. "Give them greetings in the name of Earth and all its peoples. Extend to them the benevolent warm wishes of the board of directors of IBM/Toshiba. And then we'll wait and see."

⌣

We waited. But for a long while we didn't see.

Two days, and then some. We went round and round the neutron star, and they went round and round the neutron star, and no further communication came from them. We beamed them all sorts of messages at all sorts of frequencies along the spectrum, both in the radio band and via infrared and ultraviolet as well, so that they'd have plenty of material to work with. Perhaps their translator gadget wasn't all that good, I told myself hopefully. Perhaps it was stripping its gears trying to fathom the pleasant little packets of semantic data that we had sent them.

On the third day of silence I began feeling restless. There was no way we could begin the work we had been sent here to do, not with aliens watching. The Toshiba people—the Ultra Cautious faction—got more and more nervous. Even the IBM representatives began to act a little twitchy. I started to question the wisdom of having overruled the advocates of a no-contact policy. Although the parent companies hadn't seriously expected us to run into aliens, they had covered that eventuality in our instructions, and we were under orders to do minimum tipping of our hands if we found ourselves observed by strangers. But it was too late to call back our messages, and I was still eager to find out what would happen next. So we watched and waited, and then we waited and watched. Round and round the neutron star.

We had been parked in orbit for ten days now around the neutron star, an orbit calculated to bring us no closer to its surface than 9,000 kilometers at the closest skim. That was close enough for us to carry out our work, but not so close that we would be subjected to troublesome and dangerous tidal effects.

The neutron star had been formed in the supernova explosion that had destroyed the smaller of the two suns in what had once been a binary star system here. At the moment of the cataclysmic collapse of the stellar sphere, all its matter had come rushing inward with such force that electrons and protons were driven into each other to become a soup of pure neutrons. Which then were squeezed so tightly that they were forced virtually into contact with one another, creating a smooth globe of the strange stuff that we call neutronium, a billion billion times denser than steel and a hundred billion billion times more incompressible.

That tiny ball of neutronium glowing dimly in our screens was the neutron star. It was just 18 kilometers in diameter, but its mass was greater than that of Earth's sun. That gave it a gravitational field a quarter of a billion billion times as strong as that of the surface of Earth. If we could somehow set foot on it, we wouldn't just be squashed flat, we'd be instantly reduced to fine powder by the colossal tidal effects—the difference in gravitational pull between the soles of our feet and the tops of our heads, stretching us toward and away from the neutron star's center with a kick of 18 billion kilograms.

A ghostly halo of electromagnetic energy surrounded the neutron star: X rays, radio waves, gammas, and an oily, crackling flicker of violet light. The neutron star was rotating on its axis some 550 times a second, and powerful jets of electrons were spouting from its magnetic poles at each sweep, sending forth a beaconlike pulsar broadcast of the familiar type that we have been able to detect since the middle of the twentieth century.

Behind that zone of fiercely outflung radiation lay the neutron star's atmosphere: an envelope of gaseous iron a few centimeters thick. Below that, our scan had told us, was a two-kilometers-thick crust of normal matter, heavy elements only, ranging from molybdenum on up to transuranics with atomic numbers as high as 140. And within that was the neutronium zone, the stripped nuclei of iron packed unimaginably close together, an ocean of strangeness nine kilometers deep. What lay at the heart of *that*, we could only guess.

We had come here to plunge a probe into the neutronium zone and carry off a spoonful of star-stuff that weighed 100 billion tons per cubic centimeter.

No sort of conventional landing on the neutron star was possible or even conceivable. Not only was the gravitational pull beyond our comprehension—anything that was capable of withstanding the tidal effects would still have to cope with an escape velocity requirement of 200,000 kilometers per second when it tried to take off, two-thirds the speed of light—but the neutron star's surface temperature was something like 3.5 million degrees. The surface temperature of our own sun is six *thousand* degrees, and we don't try to make landings there. Even at this distance, our heat and radiation shields were straining to the limits to keep us from being cooked. We didn't intend to go any closer.

What IBM/Toshiba wanted us to do was to put a miniature hyperspace ship into orbit around the neutron star: an astonishing little vessel no bigger than your clenched fist, powered by a fantastically scaled-down version of the drive that had carried us through the space-time manifold across a span of a thousand light-years in a dozen weeks. The little ship was a slave-drone; we would operate it from the *Ben-wah Maru*. Or, rather, Brain Central would. In a maneuver that had taken fifty computer-years to program, we would send the miniature into hyperspace and bring it out again *right inside the neutron star.* And keep it there a billionth of a second, long enough for it to gulp the spoonful of neutronium we had been sent here to collect. Then we'd head for home, with the miniature ship following us along the same hyperpath.

We'd head for home—that is, unless the slave-drone's brief intrusion into the neutron star released disruptive forces that splattered us all over this end of the galaxy. IBM/Toshiba didn't really think that was going to happen. In theory a neutron star is one of the most stable things there is in the universe, and the math didn't indicate that taking a nip from its interior would cause real problems. This neighborhood had already had its full quota of giant explosions anyway.

Still, the possibility existed. Especially since there was a black hole just thirty light-minutes away, a souvenir of the second and much larger supernova bang that had happened here in the recent past. Having a black hole nearby is a little like playing with an extra wild card whose existence isn't made known to the players until some randomly chosen moment midway through the game. If we destabilized the neutron star in some way not anticipated by the scientists back on Earth, we might just find ourselves going for a visit to the event horizon instead of getting to go home. Or we might not. There was only one way of finding out.

I didn't know, by the way, what use the parent companies planned to make of the neutronium we had been hired to bring them. I hoped it was a good one.

But obviously we weren't going to tackle any of this while there was an alien ship in the vicinity. So all we could do was wait. And see. Right now we were doing a lot of waiting, and no seeing at all.

Two days later Cal Bjornsen said, "We're getting a message back from them now. Audio only. In English."

We had wanted that, we had even hoped for that. And yet it shook me to learn that it was happening.

"Let's hear it," I said.

"The relay's coming over ship channel seven."

I tuned in. What I heard was an obviously synthetic voice, no undertones or overtones, not much inflection. They were trying to mimic the speech rhythms of what we had sent them, and I suppose they were actually doing a fair job of it, but the result was still unmistakably mechanical-sounding. Of course, there might be nothing on board that ship but a computer, I thought, or maybe robots. I wish now that they had been robots.

It had the absolute and utter familiarity of a recurring dream. In stiff, halting, but weirdly comprehensible English came the first greetings of an alien race to the people of the planet of Earth. "This who speak be First of Nine Sparg," the voice said. Nine Sparg, we soon realized from context, was the name of their planet. First might have been the speaker's name, or his—hers, its?—title; that was unclear, and stayed that way. In an awkward pidgin-English that we nevertheless had little trouble understanding, First expressed gratitude for our transmission and asked us to send more words. To send a dictionary, in fact: now that they had the algorithm for our speech they needed more content to jam in behind it, so that we could go on to exchange more complex statements than Hello and How are you.

Bjornsen queried me on the override. "We've got an English program that we could start feeding them," he said. "Thirty thousand words: that should give them plenty. You want me to put it on for them?"

"Not so fast," I said. "We need to edit it first."

"For what?"

"Anything that might help them find the location of Earth. That's in our orders, under Eventuality of Contact with Extraterrestrials. Remember, I have Nakamura and Nagy-Szabo breathing down my neck, telling me that there's a ship full of boogeymen out there and we mustn't have anything to do with them. I don't believe that myself. But right now we don't know how friendly these Spargs are and we aren't supposed to bring strangers home with us."

"But how could a dictionary entry—"

"Suppose the sun—*our* sun—is defined as a yellow G2-type star," I said. "That gives them a pretty good beginning. Or something about the constellations as seen from Earth. I don't know, Cal. I just want to make sure we don't accidentally hand these beings a road map to our home planet before we find out what sort of critters they are."

Three of us spent half a day screening the dictionary, and we put Brain Central to work on it, too. In the end we pulled seven words—you'd laugh if you knew which they were, but we wanted to be careful—and sent the rest across to the Spargs. They were silent for nine or ten hours. When they came back on the air, their command of English was immensely more fluent. Frighteningly more fluent. Yesterday, First had sounded like a tourist using a Fifty Handy Phrases program. A day later, First's command of English was as good as that of an intelligent Japanese who has been living in the United States for ten or fifteen years.

It was a tense, wary conversation. Or so it seemed to me, the way it began to seem to me that First was male and that his way of speaking was brusque and bluntly probing. I may have been wrong on every count.

First wanted to know who we were and why we were here. Jumping right in, getting down to the heart of the matter. I felt a little like a butterfly collector who has wandered onto the grounds of a fusion plant and is being interrogated by a security guard. But I kept my tone and phrasing as neutral as I could, and told him that our planet was called Earth and that we had come on a mission of exploration and investigation.

So had they, he told me. Where is Earth?

Pretty straightforward of him, I thought. I answered that I lacked at this point a means of explaining galactic positions to him in terms that he would understand. I did volunteer the information that Earth was not anywhere close at hand.

He was willing to drop that line of inquiry for the time being. He shifted to the other obvious one:

What were we investigating?

Certain properties of collapsed stars, I said, after a bit of hesitation.

And which properties were those?

I told him that we didn't have enough vocabulary in common for me to try to explain that either.

The Nine Sparg captain seemed to accept that evasion, too. And provided me with a pause that indicated that it was my turn. Fair enough.

When I asked him what *he* was doing here, he replied without any apparent trace of evasiveness that he had come on a mission of historical inquiry. I pressed for details. It has to do with the ancestry of our race, he said. We used to live in this part of the galaxy, before the great explosion. No hesitation at all about telling me that. It struck me that First was being less reticent about dealing with my queries than I was with his; but, of course, I had no way of judging whether I was hearing the truth from him.

"I'd like to know more," I said, as much as a test as anything else. "How long ago did your people flee this great explosion? And how far from here is your present home world?"

A long silence: several minutes. I wondered uncomfortably if I had over-played my hand. If they were as edgy about our finding their home world as I was about their finding ours, I had to be careful not to push them into an overreaction. They might just think that the safest thing to do would be to blow us out of the sky as soon as they had learned all they could from us.

But when First spoke again it was only to say, "Are you willing to establish contact in the visual band?"

"Is such a thing possible?"

"We think so," he said.

I thought about it. Would letting them see what we looked like give them any sort of clue to the location of Earth? Perhaps, but it seemed farfetched. Maybe they'd be able to guess that we were carbon-based oxygen-breathers, but the risk of allowing them to know that seemed relatively small. And in any case we'd find out what *they* looked like. An even trade, right?

I had my doubts that their video transmission system could be made compatible with our receiving equipment. But I gave First the go-ahead and turned the microphone over to the communications staff. Who struggled with the problem for a day and a half. Sending the signal back and forth was no big deal, but breaking it down into information that would paint a picture on a cathode-ray tube was a different matter. The communications people at both ends talked and talked and talked, while I fretted about how much technical information about us we were revealing to the Spargs. The tinkering went on and on, and nothing appeared on screen except occasional strings of horizontal lines. We sent them more data about how our television system worked. They made further adjustments in their transmission devices. This time we got spots instead of lines. We sent even more data. Were they leading us on? And were we telling them too much? I came finally to the position that trying to make the video link work had been a bad idea, and started to tell Communications that. But then the haze of drifting spots on my screen abruptly cleared and I found myself looking into the face of an alien being.

An alien face, yes. Extremely alien. Suddenly this whole interchange was kicked up to a new level of reality.

A hairless wedge-shaped head, flat and broad on top, tapering to a sharp point below. Corrugated skin that looked as thick as heavy rubber. Two chilly eyes in the center of that wide forehead and two more at its extreme edges. Three mouths, vertical slits, side by side: one for speaking, and the other two maybe for separate intake of fluids and solids. The whole business supported by three long columnar necks as thick as a man's wrist, separated by open spaces two or three centimeters wide. What was below the neck we never got to see. But the head alone was plenty.

They probably thought we were just as strange.

With video established, First and I picked up our conversation right where he had broken it off the day before. Once more he was not in the least shy about telling me things.

He had been able to calculate in our units of time the date of the great explosion that had driven his people from their home world: it had taken place 387 years ago. He didn't use the word "supernova," because it hadn't been included in the 30,000-word vocabulary we had sent them, but that was obviously what he meant by "the great explosion." The 387-year figure squared pretty well with our own calculations, which were based on an analysis of the surface temperature and rate of rotation of the neutron star.

The Nine Sparg people had had plenty of warning that their sun was behaving oddly—the first signs of instability had become apparent more than a century before the blowup—and they had devoted all their energy for several generations to the job of packing up and clearing out. It had taken many years, it seemed, for them to accomplish their migration to the distant new world they had chosen for their new home. Did that mean, I asked myself, that their method of interstellar travel was much slower than ours, and that they had needed decades or even a century to cover fifty or a hundred light-years? Earth had less to worry about, then. Even if they wanted to make trouble for us, they wouldn't be able easily to reach us, a thousand light-years from here. Or was First saying that their new world was *really* distant—all the way across the galaxy, perhaps, seventy or eighty thousand light-years away, or even in some other galaxy altogether? If that was the case, we were up against truly superior beings. But there was no easy way for me to question him about such things without telling him things about our own hyperdrive and our distance from this system that I didn't care to have him know.

After a long and evidently difficult period of settling in on the new world, First went on, the Nine Sparg folk finally were well enough established to launch an inquiry into the condition of their former home planet. Thus his mission to the supernova site.

"But we are in great mystery," First admitted, and it seemed to me that a note of sadness and bewilderment had crept into his mechanical-sounding voice. "We have come to what certainly is the right location. Yet nothing seems to be correct here. We find only this little iron star. And of our former planet there is no trace."

I stared at that peculiar and unfathomable four-eyed face, that three-columned neck, those tight vertical mouths, and to my surprise something close to compassion awoke in me. I had been dealing with this creature as though he were a potential enemy capable of leading armadas of war to my world and conquering it. But in fact he might be merely a scholarly explorer who was making a nostalgic pilgrimage and running into problems with it. I decided to relax my guard just a little.

"Have you considered," I said, "that you might not be in the right location after all?"

"What do you mean?"

"As we were completing our journey toward what you call the iron star," I said, "we discovered a planet forty light-years from here that beyond much doubt had had a great civilization, and which evidently was close enough to the exploding star system here to have been devastated by it. We have pictures of it that we could show you. Perhaps *that* was your home world."

Even as I was saying it the idea started to seem foolish to me. The skeletons we had photographed on the dead world had had broad tapering heads that might perhaps have been similar to those of First, but they hadn't shown any evidence of this unique triple-neck arrangement. Besides, First had said that his people had had several generations to prepare for evacuation. Would they have left so many millions of their people behind to die? It looked obvious from the way those skeletons were scattered around that the inhabitants of that planet hadn't had the slightest clue that doom was due to overtake them that day. And finally, I realized that First had plainly said that it was his own world's sun that had exploded, not some neighboring star. The supernova had happened here. The dead world's sun was still intact.

"Can you show me your pictures?" he said.

It seemed pointless. But I felt odd about retracting my offer. And in the new rapport that had sprung up between us I could see no harm in it.

I told Lina Sorabji to feed her sonar transparencies into the relay pickup. It was easy enough for Cal Bjornsen to shunt them into our video transmission to the alien ship.

The Nine Sparg captain withheld his comment until we had shown him the batch.

Then he said, "Oh, that was not our world. That was the world of the Garvalekkinon people."

"The Garvalekkinon?"

"We knew them. A neighboring race, not related to us. Sometimes, on rare occasions, we traded with them. Yes, they must all have died when the star exploded. It is too bad."

"They look as though they had no warning," I said. "Look: can you see them there, waiting in the train stations?"

The triple mouths fluttered in what might have been the Nine Sparg equivalent of a nod.

"I suppose they did not know the explosion was coming."

"You suppose? You mean you didn't tell them?"

All four eyes blinked at once. Expression of puzzlement.

"Tell them? Why should we have told them? We were busy with our preparations. We had no time for them. Of course, the radiation would have been harmful to them, but why was that our concern? They were not related to us. They were nothing to us."

I had trouble believing I had heard him correctly. A neighboring people. Occasional trading partners. Your sun is about to blow up, and it's reasonable to assume that nearby solar systems will be affected. You have fifty or a hundred years of advance notice yourselves, and you can't even take the trouble to let these other people know what's going to happen?

I said, "You felt no need at all to warn them? That isn't easy for me to understand."

Again the four-eyed shrug.

"I have explained it to you already," said First. "They were not of our kind. They were nothing to us."

I excused myself on some flimsy excuse and broke contact. And sat and thought a long long while. Listening to the words of the Nine Sparg captain echoing in my mind. And thinking of the millions of skeletons scattered like straws in the tunnels of that dead world that the supernova had baked. A whole people left to die because it was inconvenient to take five minutes to send them a message. Or perhaps because it simply never had occurred to anybody to bother.

The families, huddling together. The children reaching out. The husbands and wives with hands interlocked.

A world of busy, happy, intelligent people. Boulevards and temples. Parks and gardens. Paintings, sculpture, poetry, music. History, philosophy, science. And a sudden star in the sky, and everything gone in a moment.

Why should we have told them? They were nothing to us.

I knew something of the history of my own people. We had experienced casual extermination, too. But at least when the white settlers had done it to us it was because they had wanted our land.

For the first time I understood the meaning of alien.

I turned on the external screen and stared out at the unfamiliar sky of this place. The neutron star was barely visible, a dull red dot, far down in the lower left quadrant; and the black hole was high.

Once they had both been stars. What havoc must have attended their destruction! It must have been the Sparg sun that blew first, the one that had become the neutron star. And then, fifty or a hundred years later, perhaps, the other, larger star had gone the same route. Another titanic supernova, a great flare of killing light. But, of course, everything for hundreds of light-years around had perished already in the first blast.

The second sun had been too big to leave a neutron star behind. So great was its mass that the process of collapse had continued on beyond the neutron-star stage, matter crushing in upon itself until it broke through the normal barriers of space and took on a bizarre and almost unthinkable form, creating an object of infinitely small volume that was nevertheless of infinite density: a black hole, a pocket of incomprehensibility where once a star had been.

I stared now at the black hole before me.

I couldn't see it, of course. So powerful was the surface gravity of that grotesque thing that nothing could escape from it, not even electromagnetic radiation, not the merest particle of light. The ultimate in invisibility cloaked that infinitely deep hole in space.

But though the black hole itself was invisible, the effects that its presence caused were not. That terrible gravitational pull would rip apart and swallow any solid object that came too close; and so the hole was surrounded by a bright ring of dust and gas several hundred kilometers across. These shimmering particles constantly tumbled toward that insatiable mouth, colliding as they spiraled in, releasing flaring fountains of radiation, red-shifted into the visual spectrum by the enormous gravity: the bright green of helium, the

majestic purple of hydrogen, the crimson of oxygen. That outpouring of
energy was the death cry of doomed matter. That rainbow whirlpool of
blazing light was the beacon marking the maw of the black hole.

I found it oddly comforting to stare at that thing. To contemplate that zone
of eternal quietude from which there was no escape. Pondering so inexorable
and unanswerable an infinity was more soothing than thinking of a world of
busy people destroyed by the indifference of their neighbors. Black holes offer
no choices, no complexities, no shades of disagreement. They are absolute.

Why should we have told them? They were nothing to us.

After a time I restored contact with the Nine Sparg ship. First came to the
screen at once, ready to continue our conversation.

"There is no question that our world once was located here," he said at
once. "We have checked and rechecked the coordinates. But the changes have
been extraordinary."

"Have they?"

"Once there were two stars here, our own and the brilliant blue one that
was nearby. Our history is very specific on that point: a brilliant blue star that lit
the entire sky. Now we have only the iron star. Apparently it has taken the place
of our sun. But where has the blue one gone? Could the explosion have
destroyed it, too?"

I frowned. Did they really not know? Could a race be capable of attaining
an interstellar spacedrive and an interspecies translating device, and nevertheless not have arrived at any understanding of the neutron star/black hole
cosmogony?

Why not? They were aliens. They had come by all their understanding of
the universe via a route different from ours. They might well have overlooked
this feature or that of the universe about them.

"The blue star—" I began.

But First spoke right over me, saying, "It is a mystery that we must devote
all our energies to solving, or our mission will be fruitless. But let us talk of
other things. You have said little of your own mission. And of your home world.
I am filled with great curiosity, Captain, about those subjects."

I'm sure you are, I thought.

"We have only begun our return to space travel," said First. "Thus far we
have encountered no other intelligent races. And so we regard this meeting as
fortunate. It is our wish to initiate contact with you. Quite likely some aspects
of your technology would be valuable to us. And there will be much that you
wish to purchase from us. Therefore, we would be glad to establish trade
relations with you."

As you did with the Garvalekkinon people, I said to myself.

I said, "We can speak of that tomorrow, Captain. I grow tired now. But before we break contact for the day, allow me to offer you the beginning of a solution to the mystery of the disappearance of the blue sun."

The four eyes widened. The slitted mouths parted in what seemed surely to be excitement.

"Can you do that?"

I took a deep breath.

"We have some preliminary knowledge. Do you see the place opposite the iron star, where energies boil and circle in the sky? As we entered this system, we found certain evidence there that may explain the fate of your former blue sun. You would do well to center your investigations on that spot."

"We are most grateful," said First.

"And now, Captain, I must bid you good night. Until tomorrow, Captain."

"Until tomorrow," said the alien.

◆

I was awakened in the middle of my sleep period by Lina Sorabji and Bryce-Williamson, both of them looking flushed and sweaty. I sat up, blinking and shaking my head.

"It's the alien ship," Bryce-Williamson blurted. "It's approaching the black hole."

"Is it, now?"

"Dangerously close," said Lina. "What do they think they're doing? Don't they know?"

"I don't think so," I said. "I suggested that they go exploring there. Evidently they don't regard it as a bad idea."

"You sent them there?" she said incredulously.

With a shrug I said, "I told them that if they went over there they might find the answer to the question of where one of their missing suns went. I guess they've decided to see if I was right."

"We have to warn them," said Bryce-Williamson. "Before it's too late. Especially if we're responsible for sending them there. They'll be furious with us once they realize that we failed to warn them of the danger."

"By the time they realize it," I replied calmly, "it *will* be too late. And then their fury won't matter, will it? They won't be able to tell us how annoyed they are with us. Or to report to their home world, for that matter, that they had an encounter with intelligent aliens who might be worth exploiting."

He gave me an odd look. The truth was starting to sink in.

I turned on the external screens and punched up a close look at the black-hole region. Yes, there was the alien ship, the little metallic sphere, the six odd outthrust legs. It was in the zone of criticality now. It seemed hardly to be moving at all. And it was growing dimmer and dimmer as it slowed. The gravitational field had it, and it was being drawn in. Blacking out, becoming motionless. Soon it would have gone beyond the point where outside observers could perceive it. Already it was beyond the point of turning back.

I heard Lina sobbing behind me. Bryce-Williamson was muttering to himself: praying, perhaps.

I said, "Who can say what they would have done to us—in their casual, indifferent way—once they came to Earth? We know now that Spargs worry only about Spargs. Anybody else is just so much furniture." I shook my head. "To hell with them. They're gone, and in a universe this big we'll probably never come across any of them again, or they us. Which is just fine. We'll be a lot better off having nothing at all to do with them."

"But to die that way—" Lina murmured. "To sail blindly into a black hole—"

"It is a great tragedy," said Bryce-Williamson.

"A tragedy for them," I said. "For us, a reprieve, I think. And tomorrow we can get moving on the neutronium-scoop project." I tuned up the screen to the next level. The boiling cloud of matter around the mouth of the black hole blazed fiercely. But of the alien ship there was nothing to be seen.

Yes, a great tragedy, I thought. The valiant exploratory mission that had sought the remains of the Nine Sparg home world has been lost with all hands. No hope of rescue. A pity that they hadn't known how unpleasant black holes can be.

But why should we have told them? They were nothing to us.

THE SECRET

SHARER

I make no secret of my admiration for the work of Joseph Conrad. (Or for Conrad himself, the tough, stubborn little man who, although English was only his third language, after Polish and French, not only was able to pass the difficult oral qualifying exam to become a captain in the British merchant marine, but then, a decade or so later, transformed himself into one of the greatest figures in twentieth-century English literature.) Most of what I owe to Conrad as a writer is buried deep in the substructure of my stories—a way of looking at narrative, a way of understanding character. But occasionally I've made the homage more visible. My novel Downward to the Earth of 1969 is a kind of free transposition of his novella "Heart of Darkness" to science fiction, a borrowing that I signaled overtly by labeling my most tormented character with the name of Kurtz. "Heart of Darkness," when I first encountered it as a reader forty years ago, had been packaged as half of a two-novella paperback collection, the other story being "The Secret Sharer." And some time late in 1986, I know not why—a love of symmetry? a compulsion toward completion?—I felt the urge to finish what I had begun in Downward to the Earth by writing a story adapted from the other great novella of that paperback of long ago.

This time I was less subtle than before, announcing my intentions not by using one of Conrad's character names but by appropriating his story's actual title. (This produced a pleasantly absurd result when my story was published in Isaac Asimov's Science Fiction Magazine and a reader wrote to the editor, somewhat indignantly, to ask whether I knew that the title had already been used by Joseph Conrad!) I swiped not only the title but Conrad's basic story situation, that of the ship captain who finds a stowaway on board and eventually is drawn into a strange alliance with him. (Her, in my story.) But otherwise I translated the Conrad into purely science-fictional terms and produced something that I think represents completely original work, however much it may owe to the structure of a classic earlier story.

"Translate" is perhaps not the appropriate term for what I did. A "translation," in the uncompromising critical vocabulary set forth by Damon Knight and James Blish in the 1950s upon which I based much of my own fiction-writing esthetic, is an adaptation of a stock format of mundane fiction into s-f by a simple one-for-one substitution of science-fictiony noises for the artifacts of the mundane field. That is, change "Colt .44" to "laser pistol" and "horse" to "greeznak" and "Comanche" to "Sloogl" and you can easily generate s-f out of a standard western story, complete with cattle rustlers, scalpings, and cavalry rescues. But you don't get science fiction; you don't get anything new, just a western story with greeznaks and Sloogls. Change "Los Angeles Police Department" to "Drylands Patrol" and "crack dealer" to "canal-dust dealer" and you've got a crime story set on Mars, but so what? Change "the canals of Venice" to "the marshy streets of Venusburg" and the sinister agents of S.M.E.R.S.H. to the sinister agents of A.A.A.A.R.G.H. and you've got a James Bond story set on the second planet, but it's still a James Bond story.

I don't think that's what I've done here. The particular way in which Vox stows away aboard the Sword of Orion is nothing that Joseph Conrad could have understood, and arises, I think, purely out of the science-fictional inventions at the heart of the story. The way she leaves the ship is very different from anything depicted in Conrad's maritime fiction. The starwalk scene provides visionary possibilities quite unlike those afforded by a long stare into the vastness of the trackless Pacific. And so on: "The Secret Sharer" by Robert Silverberg is, or so I believe, a new and unique science fiction story set, for reasons of the author's private amusement, within the framework of a well-known century-old masterpiece of the sea by Joseph Conrad.

"The Secret Sharer"—mine, not Conrad's—was a Nebula and Hugo nominee in 1988 as best novella of the year, but didn't get the trophies. It did win the third of the major s-f honors, the Locus award. Usually most of the Locus winners go on to get Hugos as well, but that year it didn't happen. I regretted that. But Joseph Conrad's original version of the story didn't win a Hugo or a Nebula either. You take your lumps in this business and you go bravely onward: it's the only way.

1.

It was my first time to heaven and I was no one at all, no one at all, and this was the voyage that was supposed to make me someone.

But though I was no one at all I dared to look upon the million worlds, and I felt a great sorrow for them. There they were all about me, humming along on their courses through the night, each of them believing it was actually going somewhere. And each one wrong, of course, for worlds go nowhere, except around and around and around, pathetic monkeys on a string, forever tethered in place. They seem to move, yes. But really they stand still. And I—I who stared at the worlds of heaven and was swept with compassion for them—I knew that though I seemed to be standing still, I was in fact moving. For I was aboard a ship of heaven, a ship of the Service, that was spanning the light-years at a speed so incomprehensibly great that it might as well have been no speed at all.

I was very young. My ship, then as now, was the *Sword of Orion*, on a journey out of Kansas Four bound for Cul-de-Sac and Strappado and Mangan's Bitch and several other worlds, via the usual spinarounds. It was my first voyage, and I was in command. I thought for a long time that I would lose my soul on that voyage; but now I know that what was happening aboard that ship was not the losing of a soul but the gaining of one. And perhaps of more than one.

2.

Roacher thought I was sweet. I could have killed him for that; but, of course, he was dead already.

You have to give up your life when you go to heaven. What you get in return is for me to know and you, if you care, to find out; but the inescapable thing is that you leave behind anything that ever linked you to life on shore, and you become something else. We say that you give up the body and you get your soul. Certainly you can keep your body, too, if you want it. Most do. But it isn't any good to you any more, not in the ways that you think a body is good to you. I mean to tell you how it was for me on my first voyage aboard the *Sword of Orion*, so many years ago.

I was the youngest officer on board, so naturally I was captain.

They put you in command right at the start, before you're anyone. That's the only test that means a damn: they throw you in the sea and if you can swim you don't drown, and if you can't you do. The drowned ones go back in the tank and they serve their own useful purposes, as push-cells or downloaders or mind-wipers or Johnny-scrub-and-scour or whatever. The ones that don't drown go on to other commands. No one is wasted. The Age of Waste has been over a long time.

On the third virtual day out from Kansas Four, Roacher told me that I was the sweetest captain he had ever served under. And he had served under plenty of them, for Roacher had gone up to heaven at least two hundred years before, maybe more.

"I can see it in your eyes, the sweetness. I can see it in the angle you hold your head."

He didn't mean it as a compliment.

"We can put you off ship at Ultima Thule," Roacher said. "Nobody will hold it against you. We'll put you in a bottle and send you down, and the Thuleys will catch you and decant you and you'll be able to find your way back to Kansas Four in twenty or fifty years. It might be the best thing."

Roacher is small and parched, with brown skin and eyes that shine with the purple luminescence of space. Some of the worlds he has seen were forgotten a thousand years ago.

"Go bottle yourself, Roacher," I told him.

"Ah, Captain, Captain! Don't take it the wrong way. Here, captain, give us a touch of the sweetness." He reached out a claw, trying to stroke me along the side of my face. "Give us a touch, Captain, give us just a little touch!"

"I'll fry your soul and have it for breakfast, Roacher. There's sweetness for you. Go scuttle off, will you? Go jack yourself to the mast and drink hydrogen, Roacher. Go. Go."

"So sweet," he said. But he went. I had the power to hurt him. He knew I could do it, because I was captain. He also knew I wouldn't; but there was always the possibility he was wrong. The captain exists in that margin between certainty and possibility. A crewman tests the width of that margin at his own risk. Roacher knew that. He had been a captain once himself, after all.

There were seventeen of us to heaven that voyage, staffing a ten-kilo Megaspore-class ship with full annexes and extensions and all virtualities. We carried a bulging cargo of the things regarded in those days as vital in the distant colonies: preread vapor chips, artificial intelligences, climate nodes, matrix jacks, mediq machines, bone banks, soil converters, transit spheres, communication bubbles, skin-and-organ synthesizers, wildlife domestication plaques, gene replacement kits, a sealed consignment of obliteration sand and other proscribed weapons, and so on. We also had fifty billion dollars in the form of liquid currency pods, central-bank-to-central-bank transmission. In addition there was a passenger load of seven thousand colonists. Eight hundred of these were on the hoof and the others were stored in matrix form for body transplant on the worlds of destination. A standard load, in other words. The crew worked on commission, also as per standard, one percent of bill-of-lading value divided in customary lays. Mine was the 50th lay—that is, two percent of the net profits of the voyage—and that included a bonus for serving as captain; otherwise I would have had the 100th lay or something even longer. Roacher had the 10th lay and his jackmate Bulgar the 14th, although they weren't even officers. Which demonstrates the value of seniority in the Service. But seniority is the same thing as survival, after all, and why should survival not be rewarded? On my most recent voyage I drew the 19th lay. I will have better than that on my next.

3.

You have never seen a starship. We keep only to heaven; when we are to worldward, shoreships come out to us for the downloading. The closest we ever go to planetskin is a million shiplengths. Any closer and we'd be shaken apart by that terrible strength that emanates from worlds.

We don't miss landcrawling, though. It's a plague to us. If I had to step to shore now, after having spent most of my lifetime in heaven, I would die of the drop-death within an hour. That is a monstrous way to die; but why would I ever go ashore? The likelihood of that still existed for me at the time I first sailed the *Sword of Orion*, you understand, but I have long since given it up. That is what I mean when I say that you give up your life when you go to heaven. But, of course, what also goes from you is any feeling that to be ashore has anything to do with being alive. If you could ride a starship, or even see one as we see them, you would understand. I don't blame you for being what you are.

Let me show you the *Sword of Orion*. Though you will never see it as we see it.

What would you see, if you left the ship as we sometimes do to do the starwalk in the Great Open?

The first thing you would see was the light of the ship. A starship gives off a tremendous insistent glow of light that splits heaven like the blast of a trumpet. That great light both precedes and follows. Ahead of the ship rides a luminescent cone of brightness bellowing in the void. In its wake the ship leaves a photonic track so intense that it could be gathered up and weighed. It is the stardrive that issues this light: a ship eats space, and light is its offthrow.

Within the light you would see a needle ten kilometers long. That is the ship. One end tapers to a sharp point and the other has the Eye, and it is several days' journey by foot from end to end through all the compartments that lie between. It is a world self-contained. The needle is a flattened one. You could walk about easily on the outer surface of the ship, the skin of the top deck, what we call Skin Deck. Or just as easily on Belly Deck, the one on the bottom side. We call one the top deck and the other the bottom, but when you are outside the ship these distinctions have no meaning. Between Skin and Belly lie Crew Deck, Passenger Deck, Cargo Deck, Drive Deck. Ordinarily no one goes from one deck to another. We stay where we belong. The engines are in the Eye. So are the captain's quarters.

That needle is the ship, but it is not the whole ship. What you will not be able to see are the annexes and extensions and virtualities. These accompany the ship, enfolding it in a webwork of intricate outstructures. But they are of a subordinate level of reality and therefore they defy vision. A ship tunnels into the void, spreading far and wide to find room for all that it must carry. In these outlying zones are kept our supplies and provisions, our stores of fuel, and all cargo traveling at second-class rates. If the ship transports prisoners, they will ride in an annex. If the ship expects to encounter severe probability turbulence during the course of the voyage, it will arm itself with stabilizers, and those will be carried in the virtualities, ready to be brought into being if needed. These are the mysteries of our profession. Take them on faith, or ignore them, as you will: they are not meant for you to know.

A ship takes forty years to build. There are 271 of them in service now. New ones are constantly under construction. They are the only link binding the Mother Worlds and the 898 Colonies and the colonies of the Colonies. Four ships have been lost since the beginning of the Service. No one knows why. The loss of a starship is the worst disaster I can imagine. The last such event occurred sixty virtual years ago.

A starship never returns to the world from which it was launched. The galaxy is too large for that. It makes its voyage and it continues onward through heaven in an endless open circuit. That is the service of the Service. There would be no point in returning, since thousands of worldward years sweep by behind us as we make our voyages. We live outside of time. We must, for there is no other way. That is our burden and our privilege. That is the service of the Service.

4.

On the fifth virtual day of the voyage I suddenly felt a tic, a nibble, a subtle indication that something had gone wrong. It was a very trifling thing, barely perceptible, like the scatter of eroded pebbles that tells you that the palaces and towers of a great ruined city lie buried beneath the mound on which you climb. Unless you are looking for such signals you will not see them. But I was primed for discovery that day. I was eager for it. A strange kind of joy came over me when I picked up that fleeting signal of wrongness.

I keyed the intelligence on duty and said, "What was that tremor on Passenger Deck?"

The intelligence arrived instantly in my mind, a sharp gray-green presence with a halo of tingling music.

"I am aware of no tremor, sir."

"There was a distinct tremor. There was a data-spurt just now."

"Indeed, sir? A data-spurt, sir?" The intelligence sounded aghast, but in a condescending way. It was humoring me. "What action shall I take, sir?"

I was being invited to retreat.

The intelligence on duty was a 49 Henry Henry. The Henry series affects a sort of slippery innocence that I find disingenuous. Still, they are very capable intelligences. I wondered if I had misread the signal. Perhaps I was too eager for an event, any event, that would confirm my relationship with the ship.

There is never a sense of motion or activity aboard a starship: we float in silence on a tide of darkness, cloaked in our own dazzling light. Nothing moves, nothing seems to live in all the universe. Since we had left Kansas Four I had felt that great silence judging me. Was I really captain of this vessel? Good: then let me feel the weight of duty upon my shoulders.

We were past Ultima Thule by this time, and there could be no turning back. Borne on our cloak of light, we would roar through heaven for week after virtual week until we came to worldward at the first of our destinations, which was Cul-de-Sac in the Vainglory Archipelago, out by the Spook Clusters. Here in free space I must begin to master the ship, or it would master me.

"Sir?" the intelligence said.

"Run a data uptake," I ordered. "All Passenger Deck input for the past half hour. There was movement. There was a spurt."

I knew I might be wrong. Still, to err on the side of caution may be naive, but it isn't a sin. And I knew that at this stage in the voyage nothing I could say or do would make me seem other than naive to the crew of the *Sword of Orion*. What did I have to lose by ordering a recheck, then? I was hungry for surprises.

Any irregularity that 49 Henry Henry turned up would be to my advantage; the absence of one would make nothing worse for me.

"Begging your pardon, sir," 49 Henry Henry reported after a moment, "but there was no tremor, sir."

"Maybe I overstated it, then. Calling it a tremor. Maybe it was just an anomaly. What do you say, 49 Henry Henry?" I wondered if I was humiliating myself, negotiating like this with an intelligence. "There was some thing. I'm sure of that. An unmistakable irregular burst in the data-flow. An anomaly, yes. What do you say, 49 Henry Henry?"

"Yes, sir."

"Yes what?"

"The record does show an irregularity, sir. Your observation was quite acute, sir."

"Go on."

"No cause for alarm, sir. A minor metabolic movement, nothing more. Like turning over in your sleep." You bastard, what do you know about sleep? "Extremely unusual, sir, that you should be able to observe anything so small. I commend you, sir. The passengers are all well, sir."

"Very good," I said. "Enter this exchange in the log, 49 Henry Henry."

"Already entered, sir," the intelligence said. "Permission to decouple, sir?"

"Yes, you can decouple," I told it.

The shimmer of music that signaled its presence grew tinny and was gone. I could imagine it smirking as it went about its ghostly flitting rounds deep in the neural conduits of the ship. Scornful software, glowing with contempt for its putative master. The poor captain, it was thinking. The poor hopeless silly boy of a captain. A passenger sneezes and he's ready to seal all bulkheads.

Well, let it smirk, I thought. I have acted appropriately and the record will show it.

I knew that all this was part of my testing.

You may think that to be captain of such a ship as the *Sword of Orion* in your first voyage to heaven is an awesome responsibility and an inconceivable burden. So it is, but not for the reason you think.

In truth the captain's duties are the least significant of anyone's aboard the ship. The others have well-defined tasks that are essential to the smooth running of the voyage, although the ship could, if the need arose, generate virtual replacements for any and every crew member and function adequately on its own. The captain's task, though, is fundamentally abstract. His role is to witness the voyage, to embody it in his own consciousness, to give it coherence, continuity, by reducing it to a pattern of decisions and responses. In that sense the captain is simply so much software: he is the coding through which the voyage is expressed as a series of linear functions. If he fails to perform that duty adequately, others will quietly see to it that the voyage proceeds as it should. What is destroyed, in the course of a voyage that is inadequately captained, is the captain himself, not the voyage. My preflight training made that absolutely clear. The voyage can survive the most feeble of captains. As I have said, four starships have been lost since the Service began, and no one knows why. But there is no reason to think that any of those catastrophes were caused by failings of the captain. How could they have been? The captain is only the vehicle through which others act. It is not the captain who makes the voyage, but the voyage which makes the captain.

5.

Restless, troubled, I wandered the eye of the ship. Despite 49 Henry Henry's suave mockery I was still convinced there was trouble on board, or about to be.

Just as I reached Outerscreen Level I felt something strange touch me a second time. It was different this time, and deeply disturbing.

The Eye, as it makes the complete descent from Skin Deck to Belly Deck, is lined with screens that provide displays, actual or virtual, of all aspects of the ship both internal and external. I came up to the great black bevel-edged screen that provided our simulated view of the external realspace environment and was staring at the dwindling wheel of the Ultima Thule relay point when the new anomaly occurred. The other had been the merest of subliminal signals, a nip, a tickle. This was more like an attempted intrusion. Invisible fingers seemed to brush lightly over my brain, probing, seeking entrance. The fingers withdrew; a moment later there was a sudden stabbing pain in my left temple.

I stiffened. "Who's there?"

"Help me," a silent voice said.

I had heard wild tales of passenger matrixes breaking free of their storage circuits and drifting through the ship like ghosts, looking for an unguarded body that they might infiltrate. The sources were unreliable, old scoundrels like Roacher or Bulgar. I dismissed such stories as fables, the way I dismissed what I had heard of the vast tentacular krakens that were said to swim the seas of space, or the beckoning mermaids with shining breasts who danced along the force lines at spinaround points. But I had felt this. The probing fingers, the sudden sharp pain. And the sense of someone frightened, frightened but strong, stronger than I, hovering close at hand.

"Where are you?"

There was no reply. Whatever it was, if it had been anything at all, had slipped back into hiding after that one furtive thrust.

But was it really gone?

"You're still here somewhere," I said. "I know that you are."

Silence. Stillness.

"You asked for help. Why did you disappear so fast?"

No response. I felt anger rising.

"Whoever you are. Whatever. Speak up."

Nothing. Silence. Had I imagined it? The probing, the voiceless voice? No. No. I was certain that there was something invisible and unreal hovering about me. And I found it infuriating, not to be able to regain contact with it. To be toyed with this way, to be mocked like this.

This is my ship, I thought. I want no ghosts aboard my ship.

"You can be detected," I said. "You can be contained. You can be eradicated."

As I stood there blustering in my frustration, it seemed to me that I felt that touch against my mind again, a lighter one this time, wistful, regretful. Perhaps I invented it. Perhaps I have supplied it retroactively.

But it lasted only a part of an instant, if it happened at all, and then I was unquestionably alone again. The solitude was real and total and unmistakable. I stood gripping the rail of the screen, leaning forward into the brilliant blackness and swaying dizzily as if I were being pulled forward through the wall of the ship into space.

"Captain?"

The voice of 49 Henry Henry, tumbling out of the air behind me.

"Did you feel something that time?" I asked.

The intelligence ignored my question. "Captain, there's trouble on Passenger Deck. Hands-on alarm: will you come?"

"Set up a transit track for me," I said. "I'm on my way."

Lights began to glow in midair, yellow, blue, green. The interior of the ship is a vast opaque maze, and moving about within it is difficult without an intelligence to guide you. 49 Henry Henry constructed an efficient route for me down the curve of the Eye and into the main body of the ship, and thence around the rim of the leeward wall to the elevator down to Passenger Deck. I rode an air-cushion tracker keyed to the lights. The journey took no more than fifteen minutes. Unaided I might have needed a week.

Passenger Deck is an echoing nest of coffins, hundreds of them, sometimes even thousands, arranged in rows three abreast. Here our live cargo sleeps until we arrive and decant the stored sleepers into wakefulness. Machinery sighs and murmurs all around them, coddling them in their suspension.

Beyond, far off in the dim distance, is the place for passengers of a different sort—a spiderwebbing of sensory cables that holds our thousands of disembodied matrixes. Those are the colonists who have left their bodies behind when going into space. It is a dark and forbidding place, dimly lit by swirling velvet comets that circle overhead emitting sparks of red and green.

The trouble was in the suspension area. Five crewmen were there already, the oldest hands on board: Katkat, Dismas, Rio de Rio, Gavotte, Roacher. Seeing them all together, I knew this must be some major event. We move on distant orbits within the immensity of the ship: to see as many as three members of the crew in the same virtual month is extraordinary. Now here were five. I felt an oppressive sense of community among them. Each of these five had sailed the seas of heaven more years than I had been alive. For at least a dozen voyages now they had been together as a team. I was the stranger in their midst, unknown, untried, lightly regarded, insignificant. Already Roacher had indicted me for my sweetness, by which he meant, I knew, a basic incapacity to act decisively. I thought he was wrong. But perhaps he knew me better than I knew myself.

They stepped back, opening a path between them. Gavotte, a great hulking thick-shouldered man with a surprisingly delicate and precise way of conducting himself, gestured with open hands: Here, captain, see? See?

What I saw were coils of greenish smoke coming up from a passenger housing, and the glass door of the housing half open, cracked from top to bottom, frosted by temperature differentials. I could hear a sullen dripping sound. Blue fluid fell in thick steady gouts from a shattered support line. Within the housing itself was the pale naked figure of a man, eyes wide open, mouth agape as if in a silent scream. His left arm was raised, his fist was clenched. He looked like an anguished statue.

They had body-salvage equipment standing by. The hapless passenger would be disassembled and all usable parts stored as soon as I gave the word.

"Is he irretrievable?" I asked.

"Take a look," Katkat said, pointing to the housing readout. All the curves pointed down. "We have nineteen percent degradation already, and rising. Do we disassemble?"

"Go ahead," I said. "Approved."

The lasers glinted and flailed. Body parts came into view, shining, moist. The coiling metallic arms of the body-salvage equipment rose and fell, lifting organs that were not yet beyond repair and putting them into storage. As the machine labored the men worked around it, shutting down the broken housing, tying off the disrupted feeders and refrigerator cables.

I asked Dismas what had happened. He was the mind-wiper for this sector, responsible for maintenance on the suspended passengers. His face was open and easy, but the deceptive cheeriness about his mouth and cheeks was mysteriously negated by his bleak, shadowy eyes. He told me that he had been working much farther down the deck, performing routine service on the Strappado-bound people, when he felt a sudden small disturbance, a quick tickle of wrongness.

"So did I," I said. "How long ago was that?"

"Half an hour, maybe. I didn't make a special note of it. I thought it was something in my gut, Captain. You felt it, too, you say?"

I nodded. "Just a tickle. It's in the record." I heard the distant music of 49 Henry Henry. Perhaps the intelligence was trying to apologize for doubting me. "What happened next?" I asked.

"Went back to work. Five, ten minutes, maybe. Felt another jolt, a stronger one." He touched his forehead, right at the temple, showing me where. "Detectors went off, broken glass. Came running, found this Cul-de-Sac passenger here undergoing convulsions. Rising from his bindings, thrashing around. Pulled himself loose from everything, went smack against the housing window. Broke it. It's a very fast death."

"Matrix intrusion," Roacher said.

The skin of my scalp tightened. I turned to him.

"Tell me about that."

He shrugged. "Once in a long while someone in the storage circuits gets to feeling footloose, and finds a way out and goes roaming the ship. Looking for a body to jack into, that's what they're doing. Jack into me, jack into Katkat, even jack into you, captain. Anybody handy, just so they can feel flesh around them again. Jacked into this one here and something went wrong."

The probing fingers, yes. The silent voice. *Help me.*

"I never heard of anyone jacking into a passenger in suspension," Dismas said.

"No reason why not," said Roacher.

"What's the good? Still stuck in a housing, you are. Frozen down, that's no better than staying matrix."

"Five to two it was matrix intrusion," Roacher said, glaring.

"Done," Dismas said. Gavotte laughed and came in on the bet. So, too, did sinuous little Katkat, taking the other side. Rio de Rio, who had not spoken a word to anyone in his last six voyages, snorted and gestured obscenely at both factions.

I felt like an idle spectator. To regain some illusion of command I said, "If there's a matrix loose, it'll show up on ship inventory. Dismas, check with the intelligence on duty and report to me. Katkat, Gavotte, finish cleaning up this mess and seal everything off. Then I want your reports in the log and a copy to me. I'll be in my quarters. There'll be further instructions later. The missing matrix, if that's what we have on our hands, will be identified, located, and recaptured."

Roacher grinned at me. I thought he was going to lead a round of cheers.

I turned and mounted my tracker, and rode it following the lights, yellow, blue, green, back up through the maze of decks and out to the Eye.

As I entered my cabin something touched my mind and a silent voice said, "Please help me."

6.

Carefully I shut the door behind me, locked it, loaded the privacy screens. The captain's cabin aboard a Megaspore starship of the Service is a world in itself, serene, private, immense. In mine, spiral galaxies whirled and sparkled on the walls. I had a stream, a lake, a silver waterfall beyond it. The air was soft and glistening. At a touch of my hand I could have light, music, scent, color, from any one of a thousand hidden orifices. Or I could turn the walls translucent and let the luminous splendor of starspace come flooding through.

Only when I was fully settled in, protected and insulated and comfortable, did I say, "All right. What are you?"

"You promise you won't report me to the captain?"

"I don't promise anything."

"You will help me, though?" The voice seemed at once frightened and insistent, urgent and vulnerable.

"How can I say? You give me nothing to work with."

"I'll tell you everything. But first you have to promise not to call the captain."

I debated with myself for a moment and opted for directness.

"I am the captain," I said.

"No!"

"Can you see this room? What do you think it is? Crew quarters? The scullery?"

I felt turbulent waves of fear coming from my invisible companion. And then nothing. Was it gone? Then I had made a mistake in being so forthright. This phantom had to be confined, sealed away, perhaps destroyed, before it could do more damage. I should have been more devious. And also I knew that I would regret it in another way if it had slipped away: I was taking a certain pleasure in being able to speak with someone—something—that was neither a member of my crew nor an omnipotent, contemptuous artificial intelligence.

"Are you still here?" I asked after a while.

Silence.

Gone, I thought. Sweeping through the *Sword of Orion* like a gale of wind. Probably down at the far end of the ship by this time.

Then, as if there had been no break in the conversation: "I just can't believe it. Of all the places I could have gone, I had to walk right into the captain's cabin."

"So it seems."

"And you're actually the captain?"

"Yes. Actually."

Another pause.

"You seem so young," it said. "For a captain."

"Be careful," I told it.

"I didn't mean anything by that, Captain." With a touch of bravado, even defiance, mingling with uncertainty and anxiety. "Captain *sir.*"

Looking toward the ceiling, where shining resonator nodes shimmered all up and down the spectrum as slave light leaped from junction to junction along the illuminator strands, I searched for a glimpse of it, some minute electromagnetic clue. But there was nothing.

I imagined a web of impalpable force, a dancing will-o'-the-wisp, flitting erratically about the room, now perching on my shoulder, now clinging to some fixture, now extending itself to fill every open space: an airy thing, a sprite, playful and capricious. Curiously, not only was I unafraid but I found myself strongly drawn to it. There was something strangely appealing about this quick vibrating spirit, so bright with contradictions. And yet it had caused the death of one of my passengers.

"Well?" I said. "You're safe here. But when are you going to tell me what you are?"

"Isn't that obvious? I'm a matrix."

"Go on."

"A free matrix, a matrix on the loose. A matrix who's in big trouble. I think I've hurt someone. Maybe killed him."

"One of the passengers?" I said.

"So you know?"

"There's a dead passenger, yes. We're not sure what happened."

"It wasn't my fault. It was an accident."

"That may be," I said. "Tell me about it. Tell me everything."

"Can I trust you?"

"More than anyone else on this ship."

"But you're the captain."

"That's why," I said.

7.

Her name was Leeleaine, but she wanted me to call her Vox. That means "voice," she said, in one of the ancient languages of Earth. She was seventeen years old, from Jaana Head, which is an island off the coast of West Palabar on Kansas Four. Her father was a glass farmer, her mother operated a gravity hole, and she had five brothers and three sisters, all of them much older than she was.

"Do you know what that's like, Captain? Being the youngest of nine? And both your parents working all the time, and your cross-parents just as busy? Can you imagine? And growing up on Kansas Four, where it's a thousand kilometers between cities, and you aren't even in a city, you're on an *island*?"

"I know something of what that's like," I said.

"Are you from Kansas Four, too?"

"No," I said. "Not from Kansas Four. But a place much like it, I think."

She spoke of a troubled, unruly childhood, full of loneliness and anger. Kansas Four, I have heard, is a beautiful world, if you are inclined to find beauty in worlds: a wild and splendid place, where the sky is scarlet and the bare basalt mountains rise in the east like a magnificent black wall. But to hear Vox speak of it, it was squalid, grim, bleak. For her it was a loveless place where she led a loveless life. And yet she told me of pale violet seas aglow with brilliant yellow fish, and trees that erupted with a shower of dazzling crimson fronds when they were in bloom, and warm rains that sang in the air like harps. I was not then so long in heaven that I had forgotten the beauty of seas or trees or rains, which by now are nothing but hollow words to me. Yet Vox had found her life on Kansas Four so hateful that she had been willing to abandon not only her native world but her body itself. That was a point of kinship between us: I, too, had given up my world and my former life, if not my actual flesh. But I had chosen heaven, and the Service. Vox had volunteered to exchange one landcrawling servitude for another.

"The day came," she said, "when I knew I couldn't stand it any more. I was so miserable, so empty: I thought about having to live this way for another two hundred years or even more, and I wanted to pick up the hills and throw them at each other. Or get into my mother's plummeter and take it straight to the bottom of the sea. I made a list of ways I could kill myself. But I knew I couldn't do it, not this way or that way or any way. I wanted to live. But I didn't want to live like *that*."

On that same day, she said, the soul-call from Cul-de-Sac reached Kansas Four. A thousand vacant bodies were available there and they wanted soul-matrixes to fill them. Without a moment's hesitation, Vox put her name on the list.

There is a constant migration of souls between the worlds. On each of my voyages I have carried thousands of them, setting forth hopefully toward new bodies on strange planets.

Every world has a stock of bodies awaiting replacement souls. Most were the victims of sudden violence. Life is risky on shore, and death lurks everywhere. Salvaging and repairing a body is no troublesome matter, but once a soul has fled it can never be recovered. So the empty bodies of those who drown and those who are stung by lethal insects and those who are thrown from vehicles and those who are struck by falling branches as they work are collected and examined. If they are beyond repair they are disassembled and their usable parts set aside to be installed in others. But if their bodies can be made whole again, they are, and they are placed in holding chambers until new souls become available for them.

And then there are those who vacate their bodies voluntarily, perhaps because they are weary of them, or weary of their worlds, and wish to move along. They are the ones who sign up to fill the waiting bodies on far worlds, while others come behind them to fill the bodies they have abandoned. The least costly way to travel between the worlds is to surrender your body and go in matrix form, thus exchanging a discouraging life for an unfamiliar one. That was what Vox had done. In pain and despair she had agreed to allow the essence of herself, everything she had ever seen or felt or thought or dreamed, to be converted into a lattice of electrical impulses that the *Sword of Orion* would carry on its voyage from Kansas Four to Cul-de-Sac. A new body lay reserved for her there. Her own discarded body would remain in suspension on Kansas Four. Someday it might become the home of some wandering soul from another world; or, if there were no bids for it, it might eventually be disassembled by the body salvagers, and its parts put to some worthy use. Vox would never know; Vox would never care.

"I can understand trading an unhappy life for a chance at a happy one," I said. "But why break loose on ship? What purpose could that serve? Why not wait until you got to Cul-de-Sac?"

"Because it was torture," she said.

"Torture? What was?"

"Living as a matrix." She laughed bitterly. "Living? It's worse than death could ever be!"

"Tell me."

"You've never done matrix, have you?"

"No," I said. "I chose another way to escape."

"Then you don't know. You can't know. You've got a ship full of matrixes in storage circuits, but you don't understand a thing about them. Imagine that the back of your neck itches, captain. But you have no arms to scratch with. Your thigh starts to itch. Your chest. You lie there itching everywhere. And you can't scratch. Do you understand me?"

"How can a matrix feel an itch? A matrix is simply a pattern of electrical—"

"Oh, you're impossible! You're *stupid*! I'm not talking about actual literal itching. I'm giving you a suppose, a for-instance. Because you'd never be able to understand the real situation. Look: you're in the storage circuit. All you are is electricity. That's all a mind really is, anyway: electricity. But you used to have a body. The body had sensation. The body had feelings. You remember them. You're a prisoner. A prisoner remembers all sorts of things that used to be taken for granted. You'd give anything to feel the wind in your hair again, or the taste of cool milk, or the scent of flowers. Or even the pain of a cut finger. The saltiness of your blood when you lick the cut. Anything. I hated my body, don't you see? I couldn't wait to be rid of it. But once it was gone I missed the feelings it had. I missed the sense of flesh pulling at me, holding me to the ground, flesh full of nerves, flesh that could feel pleasure. Or pain."

"I understand," I said, and I think that I truly did. "But the voyage to Cul-de-Sac is short. A few virtual weeks and you'd be there, and out of storage and into your new body, and—"

"Weeks? Think of that itch on the back of your neck, Captain. The itch that you can't scratch. How long do you think you could stand it, lying there feeling that itch? Five minutes? An hour? *Weeks?*"

It seemed to me that an itch left unscratched would die of its own, perhaps in minutes. But that was only how it seemed to me. I was not Vox; I had not been a matrix in a storage circuit.

I said, "So you let yourself out? How?"

"It wasn't that hard to figure. I had nothing else to do but think about it. You align yourself with the polarity of the circuit. That's a matrix, too, an electrical pattern holding you in crosswise bands. You change the alignment. It's like being tied up, and slipping the ropes around until you can slide free. And then you can go anywhere you like. You key into any bioprocessor aboard the ship and you draw your energy from that instead of from the storage circuit, and it sustains you. I can move anywhere around this ship at the speed of light. Anywhere. In just the time you blinked your eye, I've been everywhere. I've been to the far tip and out on the mast, and I've been down through the lower decks, and I've been in the crew quarters and the cargo places and I've even been a little way off into something that's right outside the ship but isn't quite real, if you know what I mean. Something that just seems to be a cradle of probability waves surrounding us. It's like being a ghost. But it doesn't solve anything. Do you see? The torture still goes on. You want to feel, but you can't. You want to be connected again, your senses, your inputs. That's why I tried to get into the passenger, do you see? But he wouldn't let me."

I began to understand at last.

Not everyone who goes to the worlds of heaven as a colonist travels in matrix form. Ordinarily anyone who can afford to take his body with him will do so; but relatively few can afford it. Those who do, travel in suspension, the deepest of sleeps. We carry no waking passengers in the Service, not at any price. They would be trouble for us, poking here, poking there, asking questions, demanding to be served and pampered. They would shatter the peace of the voyage. And so they go down into their coffins, their housings, and there they sleep the voyage away, all life processes halted, a death-in-life that will not be reversed until we bring them to their destinations.

And poor Vox, freed of her prisoning circuit and hungry for sensory data, had tried to slip herself into a passenger's body.

I listened, appalled and somber, as she told of her terrible odyssey through the ship. Breaking free of the circuit: that had been the first strangeness I felt, that tic, that nibble at the threshold of my consciousness.

Her first wild moment of freedom had been exhilarating and joyous. But then had come the realization that nothing really had changed. She was at large, but still she was incorporeal, caught in that monstrous frustration of bodilessness, yearning for a touch. Perhaps such torment was common among matrixes; perhaps that was why, now and then, they broke free as Vox had done, to roam ships like sad troubled spirits. So Roacher had said. *Once in a long while someone in the storage circuits gets to feeling footloose, and finds a way out and goes roaming the ship. Looking for a body to jack into, that's what they're doing. Jack into me, jack into Katkat, even jack into you, Captain. Anybody handy, just so they can feel flesh around them again. Yes.*

That was the second jolt, the stronger one, that Dismas and I had felt, when Vox, selecting a passenger at random, suddenly, impulsively, had slipped herself inside his brain. She had realized her mistake at once. The passenger, lost in whatever dreams may come to the suspended, reacted to her intrusion with wild terror. Convulsions swept him; he rose, clawing at the equipment that sustained his life, trying desperately to evict the succubus that had penetrated him. In this frantic struggle he smashed the case of his housing and died.

Vox, fleeing, frightened, careened about the ship in search of refuge, encountered me standing by the screen in the Eye, and made an abortive attempt to
enter my mind. But just then the death of the passenger registered on 49 Henry
Henry's sensors and when the intelligence made contact with me to tell me of
the emergency Vox fled again, and hovered dolefully until I returned to my
cabin. She had not meant to kill the passenger, she said. She was sorry that he
had died. She felt some embarrassment now, and fear. But no guilt. She
rejected guilt for it almost defiantly. He had died? Well, so he had died. That
was too bad. But how could she have known any such thing was going to
happen? She was only looking for a body to take refuge in. Hearing that from
her, I had a sense of her as someone utterly unlike me, someone volatile,
unstable, perhaps violent. And yet I felt a strange kinship with her, even an
identity. As though we were two parts of the same spirit; as though she and I
were one and the same. I barely understood why.

"And what now?" I asked. "You say you want help. How?"

"Take me in."

"What?"

"Hide me. In you. If they find me, they'll eradicate me. You said so
yourself, that it could be done, that I could be detected, contained, eradicated.
But it won't happen if you protect me."

"I'm the *captain*," I said, astounded.

"Yes."

"How can I—"

"They'll all be looking for me. The intelligences, the crewmen. It scares
them, knowing there's a matrix loose. They'll want to destroy me. But if they
can't find me, they'll start to forget about me after a while. They'll think I've
escaped into space, or something. And if I'm jacked into you, nobody's going to
be able to find me."

"I have a responsibility to—"

"Please," she said. "I could go to one of the others, maybe. But I feel
closest to you. Please. Please."

"Closest to me?"

"You aren't happy. You don't belong. Not here, not anywhere. You don't fit
in, any more than I did on Kansas Four. I could feel it the moment I first
touched your mind. You're a new captain, right? And the others on board are
making it hard for you. Why should you care about *them*? Save me. We have
more in common than you do with them. Please? You can't just let them
eradicate me. I'm young. I didn't mean to hurt anyone. All I want is to get to
Cul-de-Sac and be put in the body that's waiting for me there. A new start, my
first start, really. Will you?"

"Why do you bother asking permission? You can simply enter me through my jack whenever you want, can't you?"

"The last one died," she said.

"He was in suspension. You didn't kill him by entering him. It was the surprise, the fright. He killed himself by thrashing around and wrecking his housing."

"Even so," said Vox. "I wouldn't try that again, an unwilling host. You have to say you'll let me, or I won't come in."

I was silent.

"Help me?" she said.

"Come," I told her.

8.

It was just like any other jacking: an electrochemical mind-to-mind bond, a linkage by way of the implant socket at the base of my spine. The sort of thing that any two people who wanted to make communion might do. There was just one difference, which was that we didn't use a jack. We skipped the whole intricate business of checking bandwiths and voltages and selecting the right transformer-adapter. She could do it all, simply by matching evoked potentials. I felt a momentary sharp sensation and then she was with me.

"Breathe," she said. "Breathe real deep. Fill your lungs. Rub your hands together. Touch your cheeks. Scratch behind your left ear. Please. Please. It's been so long for me since I've *felt* anything."

Her voice sounded the same as before, both real and unreal. There was no substance to it, no density of timbre, no sense that it was produced by the vibrations of vocal cords atop a column of air. Yet it was clear, firm, substantial in some essential way, a true voice in all respects except that there was no speaker to utter it. I suppose that while she was outside me she had needed to extend some strand of herself into my neural system in order to generate it. Now that was unnecessary. But I still perceived the voice as originating outside me, even though she had taken up residence within.

She overflowed with needs.

"Take a drink of water," she urged. "Eat something. Can you make your knuckles crack? Do it, oh, do it! Put your hand between your legs and squeeze. There's so much I want to feel. Do you have music here? Give me some music, will you? Something loud, something really hard."

I did the things she wanted. Gradually she grew more calm.

I was strangely calm myself. I had no special awareness then of her presence within me, no unfamiliar pressure in my skull, no slitherings along my spine. There was no mingling of her thought stream and mine. She seemed not to have any way of controlling the movements or responses of my body. In these respects our contact was less intimate than any ordinary human jacking communion would have been. But that, I would soon discover, was by her choice. We would not remain so carefully compartmentalized for long.

"Is it better for you now?" I asked.

"I thought I was going to go crazy. If I didn't start feeling something again soon."

"You can feel things now?"

"Through you, yes. Whatever you touch, I touch."

"You know I can't hide you for long. They'll take my command away if I'm caught harboring a fugitive. Or worse."

"You don't have to speak out loud to me any more," she said.

"I don't understand."

"Just *send* it. We have the same nervous system now."

"You can read my thoughts?" I said, still aloud.

"Not really. I'm not hooked into the higher cerebral centers. But I pick up motor, sensory stuff. And I get subvocalizations. You know what those are? I can hear your thoughts if you want me to. It's like being in communion. You've been in communion, haven't you?"

"Once in a while."

"Then you know. Just open the channel to me. You can't go around the ship talking out loud to somebody invisible, you know. *Send* me something. It isn't hard."

"Like this?" I said, visualizing a packet of verbal information sliding through the channels of my mind.

"You see? You can do it!"

"Even so," I told her. "You still can't stay like this with me for long. You have to realize that."

She laughed. It was unmistakable, a silent but definite laugh. "You sound so serious. I bet you're still surprised you took me in in the first place."

"I certainly am. Did you think I would?"

"Sure I did. From the first moment. You're basically a very kind person."

"Am I, Vox?"

"Of course. You just have to let yourself do it." Again the silent laughter. "I don't even know your name. Here I am right inside your head and I don't know your name."

"Adam."

"That's a nice name. Is that an Earth name?"

"An old Earth name, yes. Very old."

"And are you from Earth?" she asked.

"No. Except in the sense that we're all from Earth."

"Where, then?"

"I'd just as soon not talk about it," I said.

She thought about that. "You hated the place where you grew up that much?"

"Please, Vox—"

"Of course you hated it. Just like I hated Kansas Four. We're two of a kind, you and me. We're one and the same. You got all the caution and I got all the impulsiveness. But otherwise we're the same person. That's why we share so well. I'm glad I'm sharing with you, Adam. You won't make me leave, will you? We belong with each other. You'll let me stay until we reach Cul-de-Sac. I know you will."

"Maybe. Maybe not." I wasn't at all sure, either way.

"Oh, you will. You will, Adam. I know you better than you know yourself."

9.

So it began. I was in some new realm outside my established sense of myself, so far beyond my notions of appropriate behavior that I could not even feel astonishment at what I had done. I had taken her in, that was all. A stranger in my skull. She had turned to me in appeal and I had taken her in. It was as if her recklessness was contagious. And though I didn't mean to shelter her any longer than was absolutely necessary, I could already see that I wasn't going to make any move to eject her until her safety was assured.

But how was I going to hide her?

Invisible she might be, but not undetectable. And everyone on the ship would be searching for her.

There were sixteen crewmen on board who dreaded a loose matrix as they would a vampire. They would seek her as long as she remained at large. And not only the crew. The intelligences would be monitoring for her, too, not out of any kind of fear but simply out of efficiency: they had nothing to fear from Vox, but they would want the cargo manifests to come out in balance when we reached our destination.

The crew didn't trust me in the first place. I was too young, too new, too green, too *sweet*. I was just the sort who might be guilty of giving shelter to a secret fugitive. And it was altogether likely that her presence within me would be obvious to others in some way not apparent to me. As for the intelligences, they had access to all sorts of data as part of their routine maintenance operations. Perhaps they could measure tiny physiological changes, differences in my reaction times or circulatory efficiency or whatever, that would be a tip-off to the truth. How would I know? I would have to be on constant guard against discovery of the secret sharer of my consciousness.

The first test came less than an hour after Vox had entered me. The communicator light went on and I heard the far-off music of the intelligence on duty.

This one was 612 Jason, working the late shift. Its aura was golden, its music deep and throbbing. Jasons tend to be more brusque and less conde-scending than the Henry series, and in general I prefer them. But it was terrifying now to see that light, to hear that music, to know that the ship's intelligence wanted to speak with me. I shrank back at a tense awkward angle, the way one does when trying to avoid a face-to-face confrontation with someone.

But, of course, the intelligence had no face to confront. The intelligence was only a voice speaking to me out of a speaker grid, and a stew of magnetic impulses somewhere on the control levels of the ship. All the same, I perceived 612 Jason now as a great glowing eye, staring through me to the hidden Vox.

"What is it?" I asked.

"Report summary, Captain. The dead passenger and the missing matrix."

Deep within me I felt a quick plunging sensation, and then the skin of my arms and shoulders began to glow as the chemicals of fear went coursing through my veins in a fierce tide. It was Vox, I knew, reacting in sudden alarm, opening the petcocks of my hormonal system. It was the thing I had dreaded. How could 612 Jason fail to notice that flood of endocrine response?

"Go on," I said, as coolly as I could.

But noticing was one thing, interpreting the data something else. Fluctua-tions in a human being's endocrine output might have any number of causes. To my troubled conscience everything was a glaring signal of my guilt. 612 Jason gave no indication that it suspected a thing.

The intelligence said, "The dead passenger was Hans Eger Olafssen, fifty-four years of age, a native of—"

"Never mind his details. You can let me have a printout on that part."

"The missing matrix," 612 Jason went on imperturbably. "Leeleaine Eliani, seventeen years of age, a native of Kansas Four, bound for Cul-de-Sac, Vainglory Archipelago, under Transmission Contract No. D-14871532, dated the twenty-seventh day of the third month of—"

"Printout on that, too," I cut in. "What I want to know is where she is now."

"That information is not available."

"That isn't a responsive answer, 612 Jason."

"No better answer can be provided at this time, Captain. Tracer circuits have been activated and remain in constant search mode."

"And?"

"We have no data on the present location of the missing matrix."

Within me Vox reacted instantly to the intelligence's calm, flat statement. The hormonal response changed from one of fear to one of relief. My blazing skin began at once to cool. Would 612 Jason notice that, too, and from that small clue be able to assemble the subtext of my body's responses into a sequence that exposed my criminal violation of regulations?

"Don't relax too soon," I told her silently. "This may be some sort of trap."

To 612 Jason I said, "What data *do* you have, then?"

"Two things are known: the time at which the Eliani matrix achieved negation of its storage circuitry and the time of its presumed attempt at making neural entry into the suspended passenger Olafssen. Beyond that no data has been recovered."

"Its *presumed* attempt?" I said.

"There is no proof, Captain."

"Olafssen's convulsions? The smashing of the storage housing?"

"We know that Olafssen responded to an electrical stimulus, captain. The source of the stimulus is impossible to trace, although the presumption is that it came from the missing matrix Eliani. These are matters for the subsequent inquiry. It is not within my responsibilities to assign definite causal relationships."

Spoken like a true Jason-series intelligence, I thought.

I said, "You don't have any effective way of tracing the movements of the Eliani matrix, is that what you're telling me?"

"We're dealing with extremely minute impedances, sir. In the ordinary functioning of the ship it is very difficult to distinguish a matrix manifestation from normal surges and pulses in the general electrical system."

"You mean, it might take something as big as the matrix trying to climb back into its own storage circuit to register on the monitoring system?"

"Very possibly, sir."

"Is there any reason to think the Eliani matrix is still on the ship at all?"

"There is no reason to think that it is not, Captain."

"In other words, you don't know anything about anything concerning the Eliani matrix."

"I have provided you with all known data at this point. Trace efforts are continuing, sir."

"You still think this is a trap?" Vox asked me.

"It's sounding better and better by the minute. But shut up and don't distract me, will you?"

To the intelligence I said, "All right, keep me posted on the situation. I'm preparing for sleep, 612 Jason. I want the end-of-day status report, and then I want you to clear off and leave me alone."

"Very good, sir. Fifth virtual day of voyage. Position of ship sixteen units beyond last port of call, Kansas Four. Scheduled rendezvous with relay forces at Ultima Thule spinaround point was successfully achieved at the hour of—"

The intelligence droned on and on: the usual report of the routine events of the day, broken only by the novelty of an entry for the loss of a passenger and one for the escape of a matrix, then returning to the standard data, fuel levels and velocity soundings and all the rest. On the first four nights of the voyage I had solemnly tried to absorb all this torrent of ritualized downloading of the log as though my captaincy depended on committing it all to memory, but this night I barely listened, and nearly missed my cue when it was time to give it my approval before clocking out for the night. Vox had to prod me and let me know that the intelligence was waiting for something. I gave 612 Jason the confirm-and-clock-out and heard the welcome sound of its diminishing music as it decoupled the contact.

"What do you think?" Vox asked. "It doesn't know, does it?"

"Not yet," I said.

"You really are a pessimist, aren't you?"

"I think we may be able to bring this off," I told her. "But the moment we become overconfident, it'll be the end. Everyone on this ship wants to know where you are. The slightest slip and we're both gone."

"Okay. Don't lecture me."

"I'll try not to. Let's get some sleep now."

"I don't need to sleep."

"Well, I do."

"Can we talk for a while first?"

"Tomorrow," I said.

But, of course, sleep was impossible. I was all too aware of the stranger within me, perhaps prowling the most hidden places of my psyche at this moment. Or waiting to invade my dreams once I drifted off. For the first time I thought I could feel her presence even when she was silent: a hot node of identity pressing against the wall of my brain. Perhaps I imagined it. I lay stiff and tense, as wide awake as I have ever been in my life. After a time I had to call 612 Jason and ask it to put me under the wire; and even then my sleep was uneasy when it came.

10.

Until that point in the voyage I had taken nearly all of my meals in my quarters. It seemed a way of exerting my authority, such as it was, aboard ship. By my absence from the dining hall I created a presence, that of the austere and aloof captain; and I avoided the embarrassment of having to sit in the seat of command over men who were much my senior in all things. It was no great sacrifice for me. My quarters were more than comfortable, the food was the same as that which was available in the dining hall, the servo-steward that brought it was silent and efficient. The question of isolation did not arise. There has always been something solitary about me, as there is about most who are of the Service.

But when I awoke the next morning after what had seemed like an endless night, I went down to the dining hall for breakfast.

It was nothing like a deliberate change of policy, a decision that had been rigorously arrived at through careful reasoning. It wasn't a decision at all. Nor did Vox suggest it, though I'm sure she inspired it. It was purely automatic. I arose, showered, and dressed. I confess that I had forgotten all about the events of the night before. Vox was quiet within me. Not until I was under the shower, feeling the warm comforting ultrasonic vibration, did I remember her: there came a disturbing sensation of being in two places at once, and, immediately afterward, an astonishingly odd feeling of shame at my own nakedness. Both those feelings passed quickly. But they did indeed bring to mind that extraordinary thing which I had managed to suppress for some minutes, that I was no longer alone in my body.

She said nothing. Neither did I. After last night's astounding alliance I seemed to want to pull back into wordlessness, unthinkingness, a kind of automaton consciousness. The need for breakfast occurred to me and I called up a tracker to take me down to the dining hall. When I stepped outside the room I was surprised to encounter my servo-steward, already on its way up with my tray. Perhaps it was just as surprised to see me going out, though of course its blank metal face betrayed no feelings.

"I'll be having breakfast in the dining hall today," I told it.

"Very good, sir."

My tracker arrived. I climbed into its seat and it set out at once on its cushion of air toward the dining hall.

The dining hall of the *Sword of Orion* is a magnificent room at the Eye end of Crew Deck, with one glass wall providing a view of all the lights of heaven. By some whim of the designers we sit with that wall below us, so that the stars and their tethered worlds drift beneath our feet. The other walls are of some silvery metal chased with thin swirls of gold, everything shining by the reflected light of the passing star clusters. At the center is a table of black stone, with places allotted for each of the seventeen members of the crew. It is a splendid if somewhat ridiculous place, a resonant reminder of the wealth and power of the Service.

Three of my shipmates were at their places when I entered. Pedregal was there, the supercargo, a compact, sullen man whose broad dome of a head seemed to rise directly from his shoulders. And there was Fresco, too, slender and elusive, the navigator, a lithe dark-skinned person of ambiguous sex who alternated from voyage to voyage, so I had been told, converting from male to female and back again according to some private rhythm. The third person was Raebuck, whose sphere of responsibility was communications, an older man whose flat, chilly gaze conveyed either boredom or menace, I could never be sure which.

"Why, it's the captain," said Pedregal calmly. "Favoring us with one of his rare visits."

All three stared at me with that curious testing intensity that I was coming to see was an inescapable part of my life aboard ship: a constant hazing meted out to any newcomer to the Service, an interminable probing for the place that was most vulnerable. Mine was a parsec wide, and I was certain they would discover it at once. But I was determined to match them stare for stare, ploy for ploy, test for test.

"Good morning, gentlemen," I said. Then, giving Fresco a level glance, I added, "Good morning, Fresco."

I took my seat at the table's head and rang for service.

I was beginning to realize why I had come out of my cabin that morning. In part it was a reflection of Vox's presence within me, an expression of that new component of rashness and impulsiveness that had entered me with her. But mainly it was, I saw now, some stratagem of my own, hatched on some inaccessible subterranean level of my double mind. In order to conceal Vox most effectively, I would have to take the offensive: rather than skulking in my quarters and perhaps awakening perilous suspicions in the minds of my ship-mates, I must come forth, defiantly, challengingly, almost flaunting the thing that I had done, and go among them, pretending that nothing unusual was afoot and forcing them to believe it. Such aggressiveness was not natural to my temperament. But perhaps I could draw on some reserves provided by Vox. If not, we both were lost.

Raebuck said, to no one in particular, "I suppose yesterday's disturbing events must inspire a need for companionship in the captain."

I faced him squarely. "I have all the companionship I require, Raebuck. But I agree that what happened yesterday was disturbing."

"A nasty business," Pedregal said, ponderously shaking his neckless head. "And a strange one, a matrix trying to get into a passenger. That's new to me, a thing like that. And to lose the passenger besides—that's bad. That's very bad."

"It does happen, losing a passenger," said Raebuck.

"A long time since it happened on a ship of mine," Pedregal rejoined.

"We lost a whole batch of them on the *Emperor of Callisto*," Fresco said. "You know the story? It was thirty years ago. We were making the run from Van Buren to the San Pedro Cluster. We picked up a supernova pulse and the intelligence on duty went into flicker. Somehow dumped a load of aluminum salts in the feed lines and killed off fifteen, sixteen passengers. I saw the bodies before they went into the converter. Beyond salvage, they were."

"Yes," said Raebuck. "I heard of that one. And then there was the *Queen Astarte*, a couple of years after that. Tchelitchev was her captain, little green-eyed Russian woman from one of the Troika worlds. They were taking a routine inventory and two digits got transposed, and a faulty delivery signal slipped through. I think it was six dead, premature decanting, killed by air poisoning. Tchelitchev took it very badly. *Very* badly. Somehow the captain always does."

"And then that time on the *Hecuba*," said Pedregal. "No ship of mine, thank God. That was the captain who ran amok, thought the ship was too quiet, wanted to see some passengers moving around and started awakening them—"

Raebuck showed a quiver of surprise. "You know about that? I thought that was supposed to be hushed up."

"Things get around," Pedregal said, with something like a smirk. "The captain's name was Catania-Szu, I believe, a man from Mediterraneo, very high-strung, the way all of them are there. I was working the *Valparaiso* then, out of Mendax Nine bound for Scylla and Charybdis and neighboring points, and when we stopped to download some cargo in the Seneca system I got the whole story from a ship's clerk named—"

"You were on the *Valparaiso*?" Fresco asked. "Wasn't that the ship that had a free matrix, too, ten or eleven years back? A real soul-eater, so the report went—"

"After my time," said Pedregal, blandly waving his hand. "But I did hear of it. You get to hear about everything, when you're downloading cargo. Soul-eater, you say, reminds me of the time—"

And he launched into some tale of horror at a spinaround station in a far quadrant of the galaxy. But he was no more than halfway through it when Raebuck cut in with a gorier reminiscence of his own, and then Fresco, seething with impatience, broke in on him to tell of a ship infested by three free matrixes at once. I had no doubt that all this was being staged for my enlightenment, by way of showing me how seriously such events were taken in the Service, and how the captains under whom they occurred went down in the folklore of the starships with ineradicable black marks. But their attempts to unsettle me, if that is what they were, left me undismayed. Vox, silent within me, infused me with a strange confidence that allowed me to ignore the darker implications of these anecdotes.

I simply listened, playing my role: the neophyte fascinated by the accumulated depth of spacegoing experience that their stories implied.

Then I said, finally, "When matrixes get loose, how long do they generally manage to stay at large?"

"An hour or two, generally," said Raebuck. "As they drift around the ship, of course, they leave an electrical trail. We track it and close off access routes behind them and eventually we pin them down in close quarters. Then it's not hard to put them back in their bottles."

"And if they've jacked into some member of the crew?"

"That makes it even easier to find them."

Boldly I said, "Was there ever a case where a free matrix jacked into a member of the crew and managed to keep itself hidden?"

"Never," said a new voice. It belonged to Roacher, who had just entered the dining hall. He stood at the far end of the long table, staring at me. His strange luminescent eyes, harsh and probing, came to rest on mine. "No matter how clever the matrix may be, sooner or later the host will find some way to call for help."

"And if the host doesn't choose to call for help?" I asked.

Roacher studied me with great care.

Had I been too bold? Had I given away too much?

"But that would be a violation of regulations!" he said, in a tone of mock astonishment. "That would be a criminal act!"

11.

She asked me to take her starwalking, to show her the full view of the Great Open.

It was the third day of her concealment within me. Life aboard the *Sword of Orion* had returned to routine, or, to be more accurate, it had settled into a new routine in which the presence on board of an undetected and apparently undetectable free matrix was a constant element.

As Vox had suggested, there were some who quickly came to believe that the missing matrix must have slipped off into space, since the watchful ship intelligences could find no trace of it. But there were others who kept looking over their shoulders, figuratively or literally, as if expecting the fugitive to attempt to thrust herself without warning into the spinal jacks that gave access to their nervous systems. They behaved exactly as if the ship were haunted. To placate those uneasy ones, I ordered round-the-clock circuit sweeps that would report every vagrant pulse and random surge. Each such anomalous electrical event was duly investigated, and, of course, none of these investigations led to anything significant. Now that Vox resided in my brain instead of the ship's wiring, she was beyond any such mode of discovery.

Whether anyone suspected the truth was something I had no way of knowing. Perhaps Roacher did; but he made no move to denounce me, nor did he so much as raise the issue of the missing matrix with me at all after that time in the dining hall. He might know nothing whatever; he might know everything, and not care; he might simply be keeping his own counsel for the moment. I had no way of telling.

I was growing accustomed to my double life, and to my daily duplicity. Vox had quickly come to seem as much a part of me as my arm, or my leg. When she was silent—and often I heard nothing from her for hours at a time—I was no more aware of her than I would be, in any special way, of my arm or my leg; but nevertheless I knew somehow that she was there. The boundaries between her mind and mine were eroding steadily. She was learning how to infiltrate me. At times it seemed to me that what we were were joint tenants of the same dwelling, rather than I the permanent occupant and she a guest. I came to perceive my own mind as something not notably different from hers, a mere web of electrical force that for the moment was housed in the soft moist globe that was the brain of the captain of the *Sword of Orion*. Either of us, so it seemed, might come and go within that soft moist globe as we pleased, flitting casually in or out after the wraithlike fashion of matrixes.

At other times it was not at all like that: I gave no thought to her presence and went about my tasks as if nothing had changed for me. Then it would come as a surprise when Vox announced herself to me with some sudden comment, some quick question. I had to learn to guard myself against letting my reaction show, if it happened when I was with other members of the crew. Though no one around us could hear anything when she spoke to me, or I to her, I knew it would be the end of our masquerade if anyone caught me in some unguarded moment of conversation with an unseen companion.

How far she had penetrated my mind began to become apparent to me when she asked to go on a starwalk.

"You know about that?" I said, startled, for starwalking is the private pleasure of the spacegoing and I had not known of it myself before I was taken into the Service.

Vox seemed amazed by my amazement. She indicated casually that the details of starwalking were common knowledge everywhere. But something rang false in her tone. Were the landcrawling folk really so familiar with our special pastime? Or had she picked what she knew of it out of the hitherto private reaches of my consciousness?

I chose not to ask. But I was uneasy about taking her with me into the Great Open, much as I was beginning to yearn for it myself. She was not one of us. She was planetary; she had not passed through the training of the Service.

I told her that.

"Take me anyway," she said. "It's the only chance I'll ever have."

"But the training—"

"I don't need it. Not if you've had it."

"What if that's not enough?"

"It will be," she said. "I know it will, Adam. There's nothing to be afraid of. You've had the training, haven't you? And I am you."

12.

Together we rode the transit track out of the Eye and down to Drive Deck, where the soul of the ship lies lost in throbbing dreams of the far galaxies as it pulls us ever onward across the unending night.

We passed through zones of utter darkness and zones of cascading light, through places where wheeling helixes of silvery radiance burst like auroras from the air, through passages so crazed in their geometry that they re-awakened the terrors of the womb in anyone who traversed them. A starship is the mother of mysteries. Vox crouched, frozen with awe, within that portion of our brain that was hers. I felt the surges of her awe, one after another, as we went downward.

"Are you really sure you want to do this?" I asked.

"Yes!" she cried fiercely. "Keep going!"

"There's the possibility that you'll be detected," I told her.

"There's the possibility that I won't be," she said.

We continued to descend. Now we were in the realm of the three cyborg push-cells, Gabriel, Banquo, and Fleece. Those were three members of the crew whom we would never see at the table in the dining hall, for they dwelled here in the walls of Drive Deck, permanently jacked in, perpetually pumping their energies into the ship's great maw. I have already told you of our saying in the Service, that when you enter you give up the body and you get your soul. For most of us that is only a figure of speech: what we give up, when we say farewell forever to planetskin and take up our new lives in starships, is not the body itself but the body's trivial needs, the sweaty things so dear to shore people. But some of us are more literal in their renunciations. The flesh is a meaningless hindrance to them; they shed it entirely, knowing that they can experience starship life just as fully without it. They allow themselves to be transformed into extensions of the stardrive. From them comes the raw energy out of which is made the power that carries us hurtling through heaven. Their work is unending; their reward is a sort of immortality. It is not a choice I could make, nor, I think, you: but for them it is bliss. There can be no doubt about that.

"Another starwalk so soon, Captain?" Banquo asked. For I had been here on the second day of the voyage, losing no time in availing myself of the great privilege of the Service.

"Is there any harm in it?"

"No, no harm," said Banquo. "Just isn't usual, is all."

"That's all right," I said. "That's not important to me."

Banquo is a gleaming metallic ovoid, twice the size of a human head, jacked into a slot in the wall. Within the ovoid is the matrix of what had once been Banquo, long ago on a world called Sunrise where night is unknown. Sunrise's golden dawns and shining days had not been good enough for Banquo, apparently. What Banquo had wanted was to be a gleaming metallic ovoid, hanging on the wall of Drive Deck aboard the *Sword of Orion*.

Any of the three cyborgs could set up a starwalk. But Banquo was the one who had done it for me that other time, and it seemed best to return to him. He was the most congenial of the three. He struck me as amiable and easy. Gabriel, on my first visit, had seemed austere, remote, incomprehensible. He is an early model who had lived the equivalent of three human lifetimes as a cyborg aboard starships, and there was not much about him that was human any more. Fleece, much younger, quick-minded and quirky, I mistrusted: in her weird edgy way she might just somehow be able to detect the hidden other who would be going along with me for the ride.

You must realize that when we starwalk we do not literally leave the ship, though that is how it seems to us. If we left the ship even for a moment we would be swept away and lost forever in the abyss of heaven. Going outside a starship of heaven is not like stepping outside an ordinary planet-launched shoreship that moves through normal space. But even if it were possible, there would be no point in leaving the ship. There is nothing to see out there. A starship moves through utter empty darkness.

But though there may be nothing to see, that does not mean that there is nothing out there. The entire universe is out there. If we could see it while we are traveling across the special space that is heaven, we would find it flattened and curved, so that we had the illusion of viewing everything at once, all the far-flung galaxies back to the beginning of time. This is the Great Open, the totality of the continuum. Our external screens show it to us in simulated form, because we need occasional assurance that it is there.

A starship rides along the mighty lines of force that cross that immense void like the lines of the compass rose on an ancient mariner's map. When we starwalk, we ride those same lines, and we are held by them, sealed fast to the ship that is carrying us onward through heaven. We seem to step forth into space; we seem to look down on the ship, on the stars, on all the worlds of heaven. For the moment we become little starships flying along beside the great one that is our mother. It is magic; it is illusion; but it is magic that so closely approaches what we perceive as reality that there is no way to measure the difference, which means that in effect there is no difference.

"Ready?" I asked Vox.

"Absolutely."

Still I hesitated.

"Are you *sure*?"

"Go on," she said impatiently. "Do it!"

I put the jack to my spine myself. Banquo did the matching of imped-ances. If he were going to discover the passenger I carried, this would be the moment. But he showed no sign that anything was amiss. He queried me; I gave him the signal to proceed; there was a moment of sharp warmth at the back of my neck as my neural matrix, and Vox's traveling with it, rushed out through Banquo and hurtled downward toward its merger with the soul of the ship.

We were seized and drawn in and engulfed by the vast force that is the ship. As the coils of the engine caught us we were spun around and around, hurled from vector to vector, mercilessly stretched, distended by an unimaginable flux. And then there was a brightness all about us, a brightness that cried out in heaven with a mighty clamor. We were outside the ship. We were starwalking.

"Oh," she said. A little soft cry, a muted gasp of wonder.

The blazing mantle of the ship lay upon the darkness of heaven like a white shadow. That great cone of cold fiery light reached far out in front of us, arching awesomely toward heaven's vault, and behind us it extended beyond the limits of our sight. The slender tapering outline of the ship was clearly visible within it, the needle and its Eye, all ten kilometers of it easily apparent to us in a single glance.

And there were the stars. And there were the worlds of heaven.

The effect of the stardrive is to collapse the dimensions, each one in upon the other. Thus inordinate spaces are diminished and the galaxy may be spanned by human voyagers. There is no logic, no linearity of sequence, to heaven as it appears to our eyes. Wherever we look we see the universe bent back upon itself, revealing its entirety in an infinite series of infinite segments of itself. Any sector of stars contains all stars. Any demarcation of time encompasses all of time past and time to come. What we behold is altogether beyond our understanding, which is exactly as it should be; for what we are given, when we look through the Eye of the ship at the naked heavens, is a god's-eye view of the universe. And we are not gods.

"What are we seeing?" Vox murmured within me.

I tried to tell her. I showed her how to define her relative position so there would be an up and a down for her, a backward, a forward, a flow of time and event from beginning to end. I pointed out the arbitrary coordinate axes by which we locate ourselves in this fundamentally incomprehensible arena. I found known stars for her, and known worlds, and showed them to her.

She understood nothing. She was entirely lost.

I told her that there was no shame in that.

I told her that I had been just as bewildered, when I was undergoing my training in the simulator. That everyone was; and that no one, not even if he spent a thousand years aboard the starships that plied the routes of heaven, could ever come to anything more than a set of crude equivalents and approximations of understanding what starwalking shows us. Attaining actual understanding itself is beyond the best of us.

I could feel her struggling to encompass the impact of all that rose and wheeled and soared before us. Her mind was agile, though still only half formed, and I sensed her working out her own system of explanations and assumptions, her analogies, her equivalencies. I gave her no more help. It was best for her to do these things by herself; and in any case I had no more help to give.

I had my own astonishment and bewilderment to deal with, on this my second starwalk in heaven.

Once more I looked down upon the myriad worlds turning in their orbits. I could see them easily, the little bright globes rotating in the huge night of the Great Open: red worlds, blue worlds, green ones, some turning their full-faces to me, some showing mere slivers of a crescent. How they cleaved to their appointed tracks! How they clung to their parent stars!

I remembered that other time, only a few virtual days before, when I had felt such compassion for them, such sorrow. Knowing that they were condemned forever to follow the same path about the same star, a hopeless bondage, a meaningless retracing of a perpetual route. In their own eyes they might be footloose wanderers, but to me they had seemed the most pitiful of slaves. And so I had grieved for the worlds of heaven; but now, to my surprise, I felt no pity, only a kind of love. There was no reason to be sad for them. They were what they were, and there was a supreme rightness in those fixed orbits and their obedient movements along them. They were content with being what they were. If they were loosed even a moment from that bondage, such chaos would arise in the universe as could never be contained. Those circling worlds are the foundations upon which all else is built; they know that and they take pride in it; they are loyal to their tasks and we must honor them for their devotion to their duty. And with honor comes love.

This must be Vox speaking within me, I told myself.

I had never thought such thoughts. Love the planets in their orbits? What kind of notion was that? Perhaps no stranger than my earlier notion of pitying them because they weren't starships; but that thought had arisen from the spontaneous depths of my own spirit and it had seemed to make a kind of sense to me. Now it had given way to a wholly other view.

I loved the worlds that moved before me and yet did not move, in the great night of heaven.

I loved the strange fugitive girl within me who beheld those worlds and loved them for their immobility.

I felt her seize me now, taking me impatiently onward, outward, into the depths of heaven. She understood now; she knew how it was done. And she was far more daring than ever I would have allowed me to be. Together we walked the stars. Not only walked but plunged and swooped and soared, traveling among them like gods. Their hot breath singed us. Their throbbing brightness thundered at us. Their serene movements boomed a mighty music at us. On and on we went, hand in hand, Vox leading, I letting her draw me, deeper and deeper into the shining abyss that was the universe. Until at last we halted, floating in midcosmos, the ship nowhere to be seen, only the two of us surrounded by a shield of suns.

In that moment a sweeping ecstasy filled my soul. I felt all eternity within my grasp. No, that puts it the wrong way around and makes it seem that I was seized by delusions of imperial grandeur, which was not at all the case. What I felt was myself within the grasp of all eternity, enfolded in the loving embrace of a complete and perfect cosmos in which nothing was out of place, or ever could be.

It is this that we go starwalking to attain. This sense of belonging, this sense of being contained in the divine perfection of the universe.

When it comes, there is no telling what effect it will have; but inner change is what it usually brings. I had come away from my first starwalk unaware of any transformation; but within three days I had impulsively opened myself to a wandering phantom, violating not only regulations but the nature of my own character as I understood it. I have always, as I think I have said, been an intensely private man. Even though I had given Vox refuge, I had been relieved and grateful that her mind and mine had remained separate entities within our shared brain.

Now I did what I could to break down whatever boundary remained between us.

I hadn't let her know anything, so far, of my life before going to heaven. I had met her occasional questions with coy evasions, with half-truths, with blunt refusals. It was the way I had always been with everyone, a habit of secrecy, an unwillingness to reveal myself. I had been even more secretive, perhaps, with Vox than with all the others, because of the very closeness of her mind to mine. As though I feared that by giving her any interior knowledge of me I was opening the way for her to take me over entirely, to absorb me into her own vigorous, undisciplined soul.

But now I offered my past to her in a joyous rush. We began to make our way slowly backward from that apocalyptic place at the center of everything; and as we hovered on the breast of the Great Open, drifting between the darkness and the brilliance of the light that the ship created, I told her everything about myself that I had been holding back.

I suppose they were mere trivial things, though to me they were all so highly charged with meaning. I told her the name of my home planet. I let her see it, the sea the color of lead, the sky the color of smoke. I showed her the sparse and scrubby gray headlands behind our house, where I would go running for hours by myself, a tall slender boy pounding tirelessly across the crackling sands as though demons were pursuing him.

I showed her everything: the somber child, the troubled youth, the wary, overcautious young man. The playmates who remained forever strangers, the friends whose voices were drowned in hollow babbling echoes, the lovers whose love seemed without substance or meaning. I told her of my feeling that I was the only one alive in the world, that everyone about me was some sort of artificial being full of gears and wires. Or that the world was only a flat colorless dream in which I somehow had become trapped, but from which I would eventually awaken into the true world of light and color and richness of texture. Or that I might not be human at all, but had been abandoned in the human galaxy by creatures of another form entirely, who would return for me some day far in the future.

I was lighthearted as I told her these things, and she received them lightly. She knew them for what they were—not symptoms of madness, but only the bleak fantasies of a lonely child, seeking to make sense out of an incomprehensible universe in which he felt himself to be a stranger and afraid.

"But you escaped," she said. "You found a place where you belonged!"

"Yes," I said. "I escaped."

And I told her of the day when I had seen a sudden light in the sky. My first thought then had been that my true parents had come back for me; my second, that it was some comet passing by. That light was a starship of heaven that had come to worldward in our system. And as I looked upward through the darkness on that day long ago, straining to catch a glimpse of the shoreships that were going up to it bearing cargo and passengers to be taken from our world to some unknowable place at the other end of the galaxy, I realized that that starship was my true home. I realized that the Service was my destiny.

And so it came to pass, I said, that I left my world behind, and my name, and my life, such as it had been, to enter the company of those who sail between the stars. I let her know that this was my first voyage, explaining that it is the peculiar custom of the Service to test all new officers by placing them in command at once. She asked me if I had found happiness here; and I said, quickly, Yes, I had, and then I said a moment later, Not yet, not yet, but I see at least the possibility of it.

She was quiet for a time. We watched the worlds turning and the stars like blazing spikes of color racing toward their far-off destinations, and the fiery white light of the ship itself streaming in the firmament as if it were the blood of some alien god. The thought came to me of all that I was risking by hiding her like this within me. I brushed it aside. This was neither the place nor the moment for doubt or fear or misgiving.

Then she said, "I'm glad you told me all that, Adam."

"Yes. I am, too."

"I could feel it from the start, what sort of person you were. But I needed to hear it in your own words, your own thoughts. It's just like I've been saying. You and I, we're two of a kind. Square pegs in a world of round holes. You ran away to the Service and I ran away to a new life in somebody else's body."

I realized that Vox wasn't speaking of my body, but of the new one that waited for her on Cul-de-Sac.

And I realized, too, that there was one thing about herself that she had never shared with me, which was the nature of the flaw in her old body that had caused her to discard it. If I knew her more fully, I thought, I could love her more deeply: imperfections and all, which is the way of love. But she had shied away from telling me that, and I had never pressed her on it. Now, out here under the cool gleam of heaven, surely we had moved into a place of total trust, of complete union of soul.

I said, "Let me see you, Vox."

"See me? How could you—"

"Give me an image of yourself. You're too abstract for me this way. Vox. A voice. Only a voice. You talk to me, you live within me, and I still don't have the slightest idea what you look like."

"That's how I want it to be."

"Won't you show me how you look?"

"I won't look like anything. I'm a matrix. I'm nothing but electricity."

"I understand that. I mean how you looked *before*. Your old self, the one you left behind on Kansas Four."

She made no reply.

I thought she was hesitating, deciding; but some time went by, and still I heard nothing from her. What came from her was silence, only silence, a silence that had crashed down between us like a steel curtain.

"Vox?"

Nothing.

Where was she hiding? What had I done?

"What's the matter? Is it the thing I asked you?"

No answer.

"It's all right, Vox. Forget about it. It isn't important at all. You don't have to show me anything you don't want to show me."

Nothing. Silence.

"Vox? Vox?"

The worlds and stars wheeled in chaos before me. The light of the ship roared up and down the spectrum from end to end. In growing panic I sought for her and found no trace of her presence within me. Nothing. Nothing.

"Are you all right?" came another voice. Banquo, from inside the ship. "I'm getting some pretty wild signals. You'd better come in. You've been out there long enough as it is."

Vox was gone. I had crossed some uncrossable boundary and I had frightened her away.

Numbly I gave Banquo the signal, and he brought me back inside.

13.

Alone, I made my way upward level by level through the darkness and mystery of the ship, toward the Eye. The crash of silence went on and on, like the falling of some colossal wave on an endless shore. I missed Vox terribly. I had never known such complete solitude as I felt now. I had not realized how accustomed I had become to her being there, nor what impact her leaving would have on me. In just those few days of giving her sanctuary, it had somehow come to seem to me that to house two souls within one brain was the normal condition of mankind, and that to be alone in one's skull as I was now was a shameful thing.

As I neared the place where Crew Deck narrows into the curve of the Eye a slender figure stepped without warning from the shadows.

"Captain."

My mind was full of the loss of Vox, and he caught me unawares. I jumped back, badly startled.

"For the love of God, man!"

"It's just me. Bulgar. Don't be so scared, Captain. It's only Bulgar."

"Let me be," I said, and brusquely beckoned him away.

"No. Wait, Captain. Please, wait."

He clutched at my arm, holding me as I tried to go. I halted and turned toward him, trembling with anger and surprise.

Bulgar, Roacher's jackmate, was a gentle, soft-voiced little man, wide-mouthed, olive-skinned, with huge sad eyes. He and Roacher had sailed the skies of Heaven together since before I was born. They complemented each other. Where Roacher was small and hard, like fruit that has been left to dry in the sun for a hundred years, his jackmate Bulgar was small and tender, with a plump, succulent look about him. Together they seemed complete, an unassailable whole: I could readily imagine them lying together in their bunk, each jacked to the other, one person in two bodies, linked more intimately even than Vox and I had been.

With an effort I recovered my poise. Tightly I said, "What is it, Bulgar?"

"Can we talk a minute, Captain?"

"We are talking. What do you want with me?"

"That loose matrix, sir."

My reaction must have been stronger than he was expecting. His eyes went wide and he took a step or two back from me.

Moistening his lips, he said, "We were wondering, Captain—wondering how the search is going—whether you had any idea where the matrix might be—"

I said stiffly, "Who's *we*, Bulgar?"

"The men. Roacher. Me. Some of the others. Mainly Roacher, sir."

"Ah. So Roacher wants to know where the matrix is."

The little man moved closer. I saw him staring deep into me as though searching for Vox behind the mask of my carefully expressionless face. Did he know? Did they all? I wanted to cry out, *She's not there any more, she's gone, she left me, she ran off into space.* But apparently what was troubling Roacher and his shipmates was something other than the possibility that Vox had taken refuge with me.

Bulgar's tone was soft, insinuating, concerned. "Roacher's very worried, Captain. He's been on ships with loose matrixes before. He knows how much trouble they can be. He's really worried, Captain. I have to tell you that. I've never seen him so worried."

"What does he think the matrix will do to him?"

"He's afraid of being taken over," Bulgar said.

"Taken over?"

"The matrix coming into his head through his jack. Mixing itself up with his brain. It's been known to happen, Captain."

"And why should it happen to Roacher, out of all the men on this ship? Why not you? Why not Pedregal? Or Rio de Rio? Or one of the passengers again?" I took a deep breath. "Why not me, for that matter?"

"He just wants to know, sir, what's the situation with the matrix now. Whether you've discovered anything about where it is. Whether you've been able to trap it."

There was something strange in Bulgar's eyes. I began to think I was being tested again. This assertion of Roacher's alleged terror of being infiltrated and possessed by the wandering matrix might simply be a roundabout way of finding out whether that had already happened to me.

"Tell him it's gone," I said.

"Gone, sir?"

"Gone. Vanished. It isn't anywhere on the ship any more. Tell him that, Bulgar. He can forget about her slithering down his precious jackhole."

"*Her?*"

"Female matrix, yes. But that doesn't matter now. She's gone. You can tell him that. Escaped. Flew off into heaven. The emergency's over." I glowered at him. I yearned to be rid of him, to go off by myself to nurse my new grief. "Shouldn't you be getting back to your post, Bulgar?"

Did he believe me? Or did he think that I had slapped together some transparent lie to cover my complicity in the continued absence of the matrix? I had no way of knowing. Bulgar gave me a little obsequious bow and started to back away.

"Sir," he said. "Thank you, sir. I'll tell him, sir."

He retreated into the shadows. I continued uplevel.

I passed Katkat on my way, and, a little while afterward, Raebuck. They looked at me without speaking. There was something reproachful but almost loving about Katkat's expression, but Raebuck's icy, baleful stare brought me close to flinching. In their different ways they were saying, *Guilty, guilty, guilty.* But of what?

Before, I had imagined that everyone whom I encountered aboard ship was able to tell at a single glance that I was harboring the fugitive, and was simply waiting for me to reveal myself with some foolish slip. Now everything was reversed. They looked at me and I told myself that they were thinking, *He's all alone by himself in there, he doesn't have anyone else at all,* and I shrank away, shamed by my solitude. I knew that this was the edge of madness. I was overwrought, overtired; perhaps it had been a mistake to go starwalking a second time so soon after my first. I needed to rest. I needed to hide.

I began to wish that there were someone aboard the *Sword of Orion* with whom I could discuss these things. But who, though? Roacher? 612 Jason? I was altogether isolated here. The only one I could speak to on this ship was Vox. And she was gone.

In the safety of my cabin I jacked myself into the mediq rack and gave myself a ten-minute purge. That helped. The phantom fears and intricate uncertainties that had taken possession of me began to ebb.

I keyed up the log and ran through the list of my captainly duties, such as they were, for the rest of the day. We were approaching a spinaround point, one of those nodes of force positioned equidistantly across heaven that a starship in transit must seize and use in order to propel itself onward through the next sector of the universe. Spinaround acquisition is performed automatically but at least in theory the responsibility for carrying it out successfully falls to the captain: I would give the commands, I would oversee the process from initiation through completion.

But there was still time for that.

I accessed 49 Henry Henry, who was the intelligence on duty, and asked for an update on the matrix situation.

"No change, sir," the intelligence reported at once.

"What does that mean?"

"Trace efforts continue as requested, sir. But we have not detected the location of the missing matrix."

"No clues? Not even a hint?"

"No data at all, sir. There's essentially no way to isolate the minute electromagnetic pulse of a free matrix from the background noise of the ship's entire electrical system."

I believed it. 612 Jason Jason had told me that in nearly the same words.

I said, "I have reason to think that the matrix is no longer on the ship, 49 Henry Henry."

"Do you, sir?" said 49 Henry Henry in its usual aloof, half-mocking way.

"I do, yes. After a careful study of the situation, it's my opinion that the matrix exited the ship earlier this day and will not be heard from again."

"Shall I record that as an official position, sir?"

"Record it," I said.

"Done, sir."

"And therefore, 49 Henry Henry, you can cancel search mode immediately and close the file. We'll enter a debit for one matrix and the Service bookkeepers can work it out later."

"Very good, sir."

"Decouple," I ordered the intelligence.

49 Henry Henry went away. I sat quietly amid the splendors of my cabin, thinking back over my starwalk and reliving that sense of harmony, of love, of oneness with the worlds of heaven, that had come over me while Vox and I drifted on the bosom of the Great Open. And feeling once again the keen slicing sense of loss that I had felt since Vox's departure from me. In a little while I would have to rise and go to the command center and put myself through the motions of overseeing spinaround acquisition; but for the moment I remained where I was, motionless, silent, peering deep into the heart of my solitude.

"I'm not gone," said an unexpected quiet voice.

It came like a punch beneath the heart. It was a moment before I could speak.

"Vox?" I said at last. "Where are you, Vox?"

"Right here."

"Where?" I asked.

"Inside. I never went away."

"You never—"

"You upset me. I just had to hide for a while."

"You knew I was trying to find you?"

"Yes."

Color came to my cheeks. Anger roared like a stream in spate through my veins. I felt myself blazing.

"You knew how I felt, when you—when it seemed that you weren't there any more."

"Yes," she said, even more quietly, after a time.

I forced myself to grow calm. I told myself that she owed me nothing, except perhaps gratitude for sheltering her, and that whatever pain she had caused me by going silent was none of her affair. I reminded myself also that she was a child, unruly and turbulent and undisciplined.

After a bit I said, "I missed you. I missed you more than I want to say."

"I'm sorry," she said, sounding repentant, but not very. "I had to go away for a time. You upset me, Adam."

"By asking you to show me how you used to look?"

"Yes."

"I don't understand why that upset you so much."

"You don't have to," Vox said. "I don't mind now. You can see me, if you like. Do you still want to? Here. This is me. This is what I used to be. If it disgusts you, don't blame me. Okay? Okay, Adam? Here. Have a look. Here I am."

14.

There was a wrenching within me, a twisting, a painful yanking sensation, as of some heavy barrier forcibly being pulled aside. And then the glorious radiant scarlet sky of Kansas Four blossomed on the screen of my mind.

She didn't simply show it to me. She took me there. I felt the soft moist wind on my face, I breathed the sweet, faintly pungent air, I heard the sly rustling of glossy leathery fronds that dangled from bright yellow trees. Beneath my bare feet the black soil was warm and spongy.

I was Leeleaine, who liked to call herself Vox. I was seventeen years old and swept by forces and compulsions as powerful as hurricanes.

I was her from within, and also I saw her from outside.

My hair was long and thick and dark, tumbling down past my shoulders in an avalanche of untended curls and loops and snags. My hips were broad, my breasts were full and heavy: I could feel the pull of them, the pain of them. It was almost as if they were stiff with milk, though they were not. My face was tense, alert, sullen, aglow with angry intelligence. It was not an unappealing face. Vox was not an unappealing girl.

From her earlier reluctance to show herself to me I had expected her to be ugly, or perhaps deformed in some way, dragging herself about in a coarse, heavy, burdensome husk of flesh that was a constant reproach to her. She had spoken of her life on Kansas Four as being so dreary, so sad, so miserable, that she saw no hope in staying there. And had given up her body to be turned into mere electricity, on the promise that she could have a new body—any body— when she reached Cul-de-Sac. *I hated my body,* she had told me. *I couldn't wait to be rid of it.* She had refused even to give me a glimpse of it, retreating instead for hours into a desperate silence so total that I thought she had fled.

All that was a mystery to me now. The Leeleaine that I saw, that I was, was a fine, sturdy-looking girl. Not beautiful, no, too strong and strapping for that, I suppose, but far from ugly: her eyes were warm and intelligent, her lips full, her nose finely modeled. And it was a healthy body, too, robust, vital. Of course, she had no deformities; and why had I thought she had, when it would have been a simple matter of retrogenetic surgery to amend any bothersome

defect? No, there was nothing wrong with the body that Vox had abandoned
and for which she professed such loathing, for which she felt such shame.

Then I realized that I was seeing her from outside. I was seeing her as if by
relay, filtering and interpreting the information she was offering me by passing
it through the mind of an objective observer: myself. Who understood nothing, really, of what it was like to be anyone but himself.

Somehow—it was one of those automatic, unconscious adjustments—I
altered the focus of my perceptions. All old frames of reference fell away and I
let myself lose any sense of the separateness of our identities.

I was her. Fully, unconditionally, inextricably.

And I understood.

Figures flitted about her, shadowy, baffling, maddening. Brothers, sisters,
parents, friends: they were all strangers to her. Everyone on Kansas Four was a
stranger to her. And always would be.

She hated her body not because it was weak or unsightly but because it was
her prison. She was enclosed within it as though within narrow stone walls. It
hung about her, a cage of flesh, holding her down, pinning her to this lovely
world called Kansas Four where she knew only pain and isolation and estrange-
ment. Her body—her perfectly acceptable, healthy body—had become hateful to her because it was the emblem and symbol of her soul's imprisonment.
Wild and incurably restless by temperament, she had failed to find a way to live
within the smothering predictability of Kansas Four, a planet where she would
never be anything but an internal outlaw. The only way she could leave Kansas
Four was to surrender the body that tied her to it; and so she had turned against
it with fury and loathing, rejecting it, abandoning it, despising it, detesting it.
No one could ever understand that who beheld her from the outside.

But I understood.

I understood much more than that, in that one flashing moment of
communion that she and I had. I came to see what she meant when she said
that I was her twin, her double, her other self. Of course we were wholly
different, I the sober, staid, plodding, diligent man, and she the reckless,
volatile, impulsive, tempestuous girl. But beneath all that we were the same:
misfits, outsiders, troubled wanderers through worlds we had never made. We
had found vastly differing ways to cope with our pain. Yet we were one and the
same, two halves of a single entity.

We will remain together always now, I told myself.

And in that moment our communion broke. She broke it—it must have
been she, fearful of letting this new intimacy grow too deep—and I found
myself apart from her once again, still playing host to her in my brain but
separated from her by the boundaries of my own individuality, my own

selfhood. I felt her nearby, within me, a warm but discrete presence. Still within me, yes. But separate again.

15.

There was shipwork to do. For days now, Vox's invasion of me had been a startling distraction. But I dared not let myself forget that we were in the midst of a traversal of heaven. The lives of us all, and of our passengers, depended on the proper execution of our duties: even mine. And worlds awaited the bounty that we bore. My task of the moment was to oversee spinaround acquisition.

I told Vox to leave me temporarily while I went through the routines of acquisition. I would be jacked to other crewmen for a time; they might very well be able to detect her within me; there was no telling what might happen. But she refused. "No," she said. "I won't leave you. I don't want to go out there. But I'll hide, deep down, the way I did when I was upset with you."

"Vox—" I began.

"No. Please. I don't want to talk about it."

There was no time to argue the point. I could feel the depth and intensity of her stubborn determination.

"Hide, then," I said. "If that's what you want to do."

I made my way down out of the Eye to Engine Deck.

The rest of the acquisition team was already assembled in the Great Navigation Hall: Fresco, Raebuck, Roacher. Raebuck's role was to see to it that communications channels were kept open, Fresco's to set up the navigation coordinates, and Roacher, as power engineer, would monitor fluctuations in drain and input-output cycling. My function was to give the cues at each stage of acquisition. In truth I was pretty much redundant, since Raebuck and Fresco and Roacher had been doing this sort of thing a dozen times a voyage for scores of voyages and they had little need of my guidance. The deeper truth was that they were redundant, too, for 49 Henry Henry would oversee us all, and the intelligence was quite capable of setting up the entire process without any human help. Nevertheless there were formalities to observe, and not inane ones. Intelligences are far superior to humans in mental capacity, interfacing capability, and reaction time, but even so they are nothing but servants, and artificial servants at that, lacking in any real awareness of human fragility or human ethical complexity. They must only be used as tools, not decision-makers. A society that delegates responsibilities of life and death to its servants will eventually find the servants' hands at its throat. As for me, novice that I was, my role was valid as well: the focal point of the enterprise, the prime initiator, the conductor and observer of the process. Perhaps anyone could

perform those functions, but the fact remained that *someone* had to, and by
tradition that someone was the captain. Call it a ritual, call it a highly stylized
dance, if you will. But there is no getting away from the human need for ritual
and stylization. Such aspects of a process may not seem essential, but they are
valuable and significant, and ultimately they can be seen to be essential as
well.

"Shall we begin?" Fresco asked.

We jacked up, Roacher directly into the ship, Raebuck into Roacher,
Fresco to me, me into the ship.

"Simulation," I said.

Raebuck keyed in the first code and the vast echoing space that was the
Great Navigation Hall came alive with pulsing light: a representation of heaven
all about us, the lines of force, the spinaround nodes, the stars, the planets. We
moved unhinderedly in free-fall, drifting as casually as angels. We could easily
have believed we were starwalking.

The simulacrum of the ship was a bright arrow of fierce light just below us
and to the left. Ahead, throbbing like a nest of twining angry serpents, was the
globe that represented the Lasciate Ogni Speranza spinaround point, tightly
wound dull-gray cables shot through with strands of fierce scarlet.

"Enter approach mode," I said. "Activate receptors. Begin threshold equal-
ization. Begin momentum comparison. Prepare for acceleration uptick. Check
angular velocity. Begin spin consolidation. Enter displacement select. Extend
mast. Prepare for acquisition receptivity."

At each command the proper man touched a control key or pressed a
directive panel or simply sent an impulse shooting through the jack hookup by
which he was connected, directly or indirectly, to the mind of the ship. Out of
courtesy to me, they waited until the commands were given, but the speed with
which they obeyed told me that their minds were already in motion even as I
spoke.

"It's really exciting, isn't it?" Vox said suddenly.

"For God's sake, Vox! What are you trying to do?"

For all I knew, the others had heard her outburst as clearly as though it had
come across a loudspeaker.

"I mean," she went on, "I never imagined it was anything like this. I can
feel the whole—"

I shot her a sharp, anguished order to keep quiet. Her surfacing like this,
after my warning to her, was a lunatic act. In the silence that followed I felt a
kind of inner reverberation, a sulky twanging of displeasure coming from her.
But I had no time to worry about Vox's moods now.

Arcing patterns of displacement power went ricocheting through the Great

Navigation Hall as our mast came forth—not the underpinning for a set of sails, as it would be on a vessel that plied planetary seas, but rather a giant antenna to link us to the spinaround point ahead—and the ship and the spinaround point reached toward one another like grappling many-armed wrestlers. Hot streaks of crimson and emerald and gold and amethyst speared the air, vaulting and rebounding. The spinaround point, activated now and trembling between energy states, was enfolding us in its million tentacles, capturing us, making ready to whirl on its axis and hurl us swiftly onward toward the next way station in our journey across heaven.

"Acquisition," Raebuck announced.

"Proceed to capture acceptance," I said.

"Acceptance," said Raebuck.

"Directional mode," I said. "Dimensional grid eleven."

"Dimensional grid eleven," Fresco repeated.

The whole hall seemed on fire now.

"Wonderful," Vox murmured. "So beautiful—"

"Vox!"

"Request spin authorization," said Fresco.

"Spin authorization granted," I said. "Grid eleven."

"Grid eleven," Fresco said again. "Spin achieved."

A tremor went rippling through me—and through Fresco, through Raebuck, through Roacher. It was the ship, in the persona of 49 Henry Henry, completing the acquisition process. We had been captured by Lasciate Ogni Speranza, we had undergone velocity absorption and redirection, we had had new spin imparted to us, and we had been sent soaring off through heaven toward our upcoming port of call. I heard Vox sobbing within me, not a sob of despair but one of ecstasy, of fulfillment.

We all unjacked. Raebuck, that dour man, managed a little smile as he turned to me.

"Nicely done, Captain," he said.

"Yes," said Fresco. "Very nice. You're a quick learner."

I saw Roacher studying me with those little shining eyes of his. Go on, you bastard, I thought. You give me a compliment, too, now, if you know how.

But all he did was stare. I shrugged and turned away. What Roacher thought or said made little difference to me, I told myself.

As we left the Great Navigation Hall in our separate directions Fresco fell in alongside me. Without a word we trudged together toward the transit trackers that were waiting for us. Just as I was about to board mine he—or was it she?—said softly, "Captain?"

"What is it, Fresco?"

Fresco leaned close. Soft sly eyes, tricksy little smile; and yet I felt some warmth coming from the navigator.

"It's a very dangerous game, Captain."

"I don't know what you mean."

"Yes, you do," Fresco said. "No use pretending. We were jacked together in there. I felt things. I know."

There was nothing I could say, so I said nothing.

After a moment Fresco said, "I like you. I won't harm you. But Roacher knows, too. I don't know if he knew before, but he certainly knows now. If I were you, I'd find that very troublesome, Captain. Just a word to the wise. All right?"

16.

Only a fool would have remained on such a course as I had been following. Vox saw the risks as well as I. There was no hiding anything from anyone any longer; if Roacher knew, then Bulgar knew, and soon it would be all over the ship. No question, either, but that 49 Henry Henry knew. In the intimacies of our navigation-hall contact, Vox must have been as apparent to them as a red scarf around my forehead.

There was no point in taking her to task for revealing her presence within me like that during acquisition. What was done was done. At first it had seemed impossible to understand why she had done such a thing; but then it became all too easy to comprehend. It was the same sort of unpredictable, unexamined, impulsive behavior that had led her to go barging into a suspended passenger's mind and cause his death. She was simply not one who paused to think before acting. That kind of behavior has always been bewildering to me. She was my opposite as well as my double. And yet had I not done a Vox-like thing myself, taking her into me when she appealed to me for sanctuary, without stopping at all to consider the consequences?

"Where can I go?" she asked, desperate. "If I move around the ship freely again, they'll track me and close me off. And then they'll eradicate me. They'll—"

"Easy," I said. "Don't panic. I'll hide you where they won't find you."

"Inside some passenger?"

"We can't try that again. There's no way to prepare the passenger for what's happening to him, and he'll panic. No. I'll put you in one of the annexes. Or maybe one of the virtualities."

"The what?"

"The additional cargo area. The subspace extensions that surround the ship."

She gasped. "Those aren't even real! I was in them, when I was traveling around the ship. Those are just clusters of probability waves!"

"You'll be safe there," I said.

"I'm afraid. It's bad enough that *I'm* not real any more. But to be stored in a place that isn't real either—"

"You're as real as I am. And the outstructures are just as real as the rest of the ship. It's a different quality of reality, that's all. Nothing bad will happen to you out there. You've told me yourself that you've already been in them, right? And got out again without any problems. They won't be able to detect you there, Vox. But I tell you this, that if you stay in me, or anywhere else in the main part of the ship, they'll track you down and find you and eradicate you. And probably eradicate me right along with you."

"Do you mean that?" she said, sounding chastened.

"Come on. There isn't much time."

On the pretext of a routine inventory check—well within my table of responsibilities—I obtained access to one of the virtualities. It was the storehouse where the probability stabilizers were kept. No one was likely to search for her there. The chances of our encountering a zone of probability turbulence between here and Cul-de-Sac were minimal; and in the ordinary course of a voyage nobody cared to enter any of the virtualities.

I had lied to Vox, or at least committed a half-truth, by leading her to believe that all our outstructures are of an equal level of reality. Certainly the annexes are tangible, solid; they differ from the ship proper only in the spin of their dimensional polarity. They are invisible except when activated, and they involve us in no additional expenditure of fuel, but there is no uncertainty about their existence, which is why we entrust valuable cargo to them, and on some occasions even passengers.

The extensions are a level further removed from basic reality. They are skewed not only in dimensional polarity but in temporal contiguity: that is, we carry them with us under time displacement, generally ten to twenty virtual years in the past or future. The risks of this are extremely minor and the payoff in reduction of generating cost is great. Still, we are measurably more cautious about what sort of cargo we keep in them.

As for the virtualities—

Their name itself implies their uncertainty. They are purely probabilistic entities, existing most of the time in the stochastic void that surrounds the ship. In simpler words, whether they are actually there or not at any given time is a matter worth wagering on. We know how to access them at the time of greatest probability, and our techniques are quite reliable, which is why we can use them for overflow ladings when our cargo uptake is unusually heavy. But in general we prefer not to entrust anything very important to them, since a virtuality's range of access times can fluctuate in an extreme way, from a matter of microseconds to a matter of megayears, and that can make quick recall a chancy affair.

Knowing all this, I put Vox in a virtuality anyway.

I had to hide her. And I had to hide her in a place where no one would look. The risk that I'd be unable to call her up again because of virtuality fluctuation was a small one. The risk was much greater that she would be detected, and she and I both punished, if I let her remain in any area of the ship that had a higher order of probability.

"I want you to stay here until the coast is clear," I told her sternly. "No impulsive journeys around the ship, no excursions into adjoining outstructures, no little trips of any kind, regardless of how restless you get. Is that clear? I'll call you up from here as soon as I think it's safe."

"I'll miss you, Adam."

"The same here. But this is how it has to be."

"I know."

"If you're discovered, I'll deny I know anything about you. I mean that, Vox."

"I understand."

"You won't be stuck in here long. I promise you that."

"Will you visit me?"

"That wouldn't be wise," I said.

"But maybe you will anyway."

"Maybe. I don't know." I opened the access channel. The virtuality gaped before us. "Go on," I said. "In with you. In. Now. Go, Vox. Go."

I could feel her leaving me. It was almost like an amputation. The silence, the emptiness, that descended on me suddenly was ten times as deep as what I had felt when she had merely been hiding within me. She was gone, now. For the first time in days, I was truly alone.

I closed off the virtuality.

When I returned to the Eye, Roacher was waiting for me near the command bridge.

"You have a moment, Captain?"

"What is it, Roacher."

"The missing matrix. We have proof it's still on board ship."

"Proof?"

"You know what I mean. You felt it just like I did while we were doing acquisition. It said something. It spoke. It was right in there in the navigation hall with us, Captain."

I met his luminescent gaze levelly and said in an even voice, "I was giving my complete attention to what we were doing, Roacher. Spinaround acquisition isn't second nature to me the way it is to you. I had no time to notice any matrixes floating around in there."

"You didn't?"

"No. Does that disappoint you?"

"That might mean that you're the one carrying the matrix," he said.

"How so?"

"If it's in you, down on a subneural level, you might not even be aware of it. But we would be. Raebuck, Fresco, me. We all detected something, Captain. If it wasn't in us it would have to be in you. We can't have a matrix riding around inside our captain, you know. No telling how that could distort his judgment. What dangers that might lead us into."

"I'm not carrying any matrixes, Roacher."

"Can we be sure of that?"

"Would you like to have a look?"

"A jackup, you mean? You and me?"

The notion disgusted me. But I had to make the offer.

"A—jackup, yes," I said. "Communion. You and me, Roacher. Right now. Come on, we'll measure the bandwidths and do the matching. Let's get this over with."

He contemplated me a long while, as if calculating the likelihood that I was bluffing. In the end he must have decided that I was too naive to be able to play the game out to so hazardous a turn. He knew that I wouldn't bluff, that I was confident he would find me untenanted or I never would have made the offer.

"No," he said finally. "We don't need to bother with that."

"Are you sure?"

"If you say you're clean—"

"But I might be carrying her and not even know it," I said. "You told me that yourself."

"Forget it. You'd know, if you had her in you."

"You'll never be certain of that unless you look. Let's jack up, Roacher."

He scowled. "Forget it," he said again, and turned away. "You must be clean, if you're this eager for jacking. But I'll tell you this, Captain. We're going to find her, wherever she's hiding. And when we do—"

He left the threat unfinished. I stood staring at his retreating form until he was lost to view.

17.

For a few days everything seemed back to normal. We sped onward toward Cul-de-Sac. I went through the round of my regular tasks, however meaningless they seemed to me. Most of them did. I had not yet achieved any sense that the *Sword of Orion* was under my command in anything but the most hypothetical way. Still, I did what I had to do.

No one spoke of the missing matrix within my hearing. On those rare occasions when I encountered some other member of the crew while I moved about the ship, I could tell by the hooded look of his eyes that I was still under suspicion. But they had no proof. The matrix was no longer in any way evident on board. The ship's intelligences were unable to find the slightest trace of its presence.

I was alone, and oh! it was a painful business for me.

I suppose that once you have tasted that kind of round-the-clock communion, that sort of perpetual jacking, you are never the same again. I don't know: there is no real information available on cases of possession by free matrix, only shipboard folklore, scarcely to be taken seriously. All I can judge by is my own misery now that Vox was actually gone. She was only a half-grown girl, a wild coltish thing, unstable, unformed; and yet, and yet she had lived within me and we had come toward one another to construct the deepest sort of sharing, what was almost a kind of marriage. You could call it that.

After five or six days I knew I had to see her again. Whatever the risks.

I accessed the virtuality and sent a signal into it that I was coming in. There was no reply; and for one terrible moment I feared the worst, that in the mysterious workings of the virtuality she had somehow been engulfed and destroyed. But that was not the case. I stepped through the glowing pink-edged field of light that was the gateway to the virtuality, and instantly I felt her near me, clinging tight, trembling with joy.

She held back, though, from entering me. She wanted me to tell her it was safe. I beckoned her in; and then came that sharp warm moment I remembered so well, as she slipped down into my neural network and we became one.

"I can only stay a little while," I said. "It's still very chancy for me to be with you."

"Oh, Adam, Adam, it's been so awful for me in here—"

"I know. I can imagine."

"Are they still looking for me?"

"I think they're starting to put you out of their minds," I said. And we both laughed at the play on words that that phrase implied.

I didn't dare remain more than a few minutes. I had only wanted to touch souls with her briefly, to reassure myself that she was all right and to ease the pain of separation. But it was irregular for a captain to enter a virtuality at all. To stay in one for any length of time exposed me to real risk of detection.

But my next visit was longer, and the one after that longer still. We were like furtive lovers meeting in a dark forest for hasty delicious trysts. Hidden there in that not-quite-real outstructure of the ship, we would join our two selves and whisper together with urgent intensity until I felt it was time for me to leave. She would always try to keep me longer; but her resistance to my departure was never great, nor did she ever suggest accompanying me back into the stable sector of the ship. She had come to understand that the only place we could meet was in the virtuality.

We were nearing the vicinity of Cul-de-Sac now. Soon we would go to worldward and the shoreships would travel out to meet us, so that we could download the cargo that was meant for them. It was time to begin considering the problem of what would happen to Vox when we reached our destination.

That was something I was unwilling to face. However I tried, I could not force myself to confront the difficulties that I knew lay just ahead.

But she could.

"We must be getting close to Cul-de-Sac now," she said.

"We'll be there soon, yes."

"I've been thinking about that. How I'm going to deal with that."

"What do you mean?"

"I'm a lost soul," she said. "Literally. There's no way I can come to life again."

"I don't under—"

"Adam, don't you see?" she cried fiercely. "I can't just float down to Cul-de-Sac and grab myself a body and put myself on the roster of colonists. And you can't possibly smuggle me down there while nobody's looking. The first time anyone ran an inventory check, or did passport control, I'd be dead. No, the only way I can get there is to be neatly packed up again in my original storage circuit. And even if I could figure out how to get back into that, I'd be simply handing myself over for punishment or even eradication. I'm listed as missing on the manifest, right? And I'm wanted for causing the death of that passenger. Now I turn up again, in my storage circuit. You think they'll just download me nicely to Cul-de-Sac and give me the body that's waiting for me there? Not very likely. Not likely that I'll ever get out of that circuit alive, is it, once I go back in? Assuming I *could* go back in in the first place. I don't know how a storage circuit is operated, do you? And there's nobody you can ask."

"What are you trying to say, Vox?"

"I'm not trying to say anything. I'm saying it. I have to leave the ship on my own and disappear."

"No. You can't do that!"

"Sure I can. It'll be just like starwalking. I can go anywhere I please. Right through the skin of the ship, out into heaven. And keep on going."

"To Cul-de-Sac?"

"You're being stupid," she said. "Not to Cul-de-Sac, no. Not to anywhere. That's all over for me, the idea of getting a new body. I have no legal existence any more. I've messed myself up. All right: I admit it. I'll take what's coming to me. It won't be so bad, Adam. I'll go starwalking. Outward and outward and outward, forever and ever."

"You mustn't," I said. "Stay here with me."

"Where? In this empty storage unit out here?"

"No," I told her. "Within me. The way we are right now. The way we were before."

"How long do you think we could carry that off?" she asked.

I didn't answer.

"Every time you have to jack into the machinery I'll have to hide myself down deep," she said. "And I can't guarantee that I'll go deep enough, or that I'll stay down there long enough. Sooner or later they'll notice me. They'll find me. They'll eradicate me and they'll throw you out of the Service, or maybe they'll eradicate you, too. No, Adam. It couldn't possibly work. And I'm not going to destroy you with me. I've done enough harm to you already."

"Vox—"

"No. This is how it has to be."

18.

And this is how it was. We were deep in the Spook Cluster now, and the Vainglory Archipelago burned bright on my realspace screen. Somewhere down there was the planet called Cul-de-Sac. Before we came to worldward of it, Vox would have to slip away into the great night of heaven.

Making a worldward approach is perhaps the most difficult maneuver a starship must achieve; and the captain must go to the edge of his abilities along with everyone else. Novice at my trade though I was, I would be called on to perform complex and challenging processes. If I failed at them, other crewmen might cut in and intervene, or, if necessary, the ship's intelligences might override; but if that came to pass my career would be destroyed, and there was the small but finite possibility, I suppose, that the ship itself could be gravely damaged or even lost.

I was determined, all the same, to give Vox the best send-off I could.

On the morning of our approach I stood for a time on Outerscreen Level, staring down at the world that called itself Cul-de-Sac. It glowed like a red eye in the night. I knew that it was the world Vox had chosen for herself, but all the same it seemed repellent to me, almost evil. I felt that way about all the worlds of the shore people now. The Service had changed me; and I knew that the change was irreversible. Never again would I go down to one of those worlds. The starship was my world now.

I went to the virtuality where Vox was waiting.

"Come," I said, and she entered me.

Together we crossed the ship to the Great Navigation Hall.

The approach team had already gathered: Raebuck, Fresco, Roacher, again, along with Pedregal, who would supervise the downloading of cargo. The intelligence on duty was 612 Jason. I greeted them with quick nods and we jacked ourselves together in approach series.

Almost at once I felt Roacher probing within me, searching for the fugitive intelligence that he still thought I might be harboring. Vox shrank back, deep out of sight. I didn't care. Let him probe, I thought. This will all be over soon.

"Request approach instructions," Fresco said.

"Simulation," I ordered.

The fiery red eye of Cul-de-Sac sprang into vivid representation before us in the hall. On the other side of us was the simulacrum of the ship, surrounded by sheets of white flame that rippled like the blaze of the aurora.

I gave the command and we entered approach mode.

We could not, of course, come closer to planetskin than a million ship-lengths, or Cul-de-Sac's inexorable forces would rip us apart. But we had to line the ship up with its extended mast aimed at the planet's equator, and hold ourselves firm in that position while the shoreships of Cul-de-Sac came swarming up from their red world to receive their cargo from us.

612 Jason fed me the coordinates and I gave them to Fresco, while Raebuck kept the channels clear and Roacher saw to it that we had enough power for what we had to do. But as I passed the data along to Fresco, it was with every sign reversed. My purpose was to aim the mast not downward to Cul-de-Sac but outward toward the stars of heaven.

At first none of them noticed. Everything seemed to be going serenely. Because my reversals were exact, only the closest examination of the ship's position would indicate our 180-degree displacement.

Floating in the free-fall of the Great Navigation Hall, I felt almost as though I could detect the movements of the ship. An illusion, I knew. But a powerful one. The vast ten-kilometer-long needle that was the *Sword of Orion* seemed to hang suspended, motionless, and then to begin slowly, slowly to turn, tipping itself on its axis, reaching for the stars with its mighty mast. Easily, easily, slowly, silently—

What a joy that was, feeling the ship in my hand!

The ship was mine. I had mastered it.

"Captain," Fresco said softly.

"Easy on, Fresco. Keep feeding power."

"Captain, the signs don't look right—"

"Easy on. Easy."

"Give me a coordinates check, Captain."

"Another minute," I told him.

"But—"

"Easy on, Fresco."

Now I felt restlessness, too, from Pedregal, and a slow chilly stirring of interrogation from Raebuck; and then Roacher probed me again, perhaps seeking Vox, perhaps simply trying to discover what was going on. They knew something was wrong, but they weren't sure what it was.

We were nearly at full extension now. Within me there was an electrical trembling: Vox rising through the levels of my mind, nearing the surface, preparing for departure.

"Captain, we're turned the wrong way!" Fresco cried.

"I know," I said. "Easy on. We'll swing around in a moment."

"He's gone crazy!" Pedregal blurted.

I felt Vox slipping free of my mind. But somehow I found myself still aware of her movements, I suppose because I was jacked into 612 Jason and 612 Jason was monitoring everything. Easily, serenely, Vox melted into the skin of the ship.

"*Captain!*" Fresco yelled, and began to struggle with me for control.

I held the navigator at arm's length and watched in a strange and wonderful calmness as Vox passed through the ship's circuitry all in an instant and emerged at the tip of the mast, facing the stars. And cast herself adrift.

Because I had turned the ship around, she could not be captured and acquired by Cul-de-Sac's powerful navigational grid, but would be free to move outward into heaven. For her it would be a kind of floating out to sea now. After a time she would be so far out that she could no longer key into the shipboard bioprocessors that sustained the patterns of her consciousness, and, though the web of electrical impulses that was the Vox matrix would travel outward and onward forever, the set of identity responses that was Vox herself would lose focus soon, would begin to waver and blur. In a little while, or perhaps not so little, but inevitably, her sense of herself as an independent entity would be lost. Which is to say, she would die.

I followed her as long as I could. I saw a spark traveling across the great night. And then nothing.

"All right," I said to Fresco. "Now let's turn the ship the right way around and give them their cargo."

19.

That was many years ago. Perhaps no one else remembers those events, which seem so dreamlike now even to me. The *Sword of Orion* has carried me nearly everywhere in the galaxy since then. On some voyages I have been captain; on others, a downloader, a supercargo, a mind-wiper, even sometimes a push-cell. It makes no difference how we serve, in the Service.

I often think of her. There was a time when thinking of her meant coming to terms with feelings of grief and pain and irrecoverable loss, but no longer, not for many years. She must be long dead now, however durable and resilient the spark of her might have been. And yet she still lives. Of that much I am certain. There is a place within me where I can reach her warmth, her strength, her quirky vitality, her impulsive suddenness. I can feel those aspects of her, those gifts of her brief time of sanctuary within me, as a living presence still, and I think I always will, as I make my way from world to tethered world, as I journey onward everlastingly spanning the dark light-years in this great ship of heaven.

HOUSE OF
BONES

*T*erry Carr was a first-rate editor, who was responsible for the publication of such masterpieces of science fiction as The Left Hand of Darkness, And Chaos Died, and Neuromancer. He was a much underrated writer, who published one classic story ("The Dance of the Changer and the Three") and a number of fine ones that received less attention than they deserved. He was also a warmhearted, funny, decent human being who was one of my closest friends for almost thirty years.

The one thing he wasn't was physically durable. Though he was tall and athletic-looking, his body began to give out by the time he was about forty-five, and in the spring of 1987 he died, two months after his fiftieth birthday, after a melancholy period of accelerating decline that for the most part had remained unknown beyond his immediate circle.

Beth Meacham, the editor-in-chief of Tor Books, was one of many in the science-fiction field who had learned her craft by working with Terry and by emulating his precepts. In the weeks after his death, she sought to find some way of showing her gratitude, and quickly she hit upon the idea of assembling an anthology of original stories by writers who had had some professional association with Terry and who felt that his impact on their careers had been substantial. I was one of those invited to contribute, along with Fritz Leiber, Kate Wilhelm, Ursula K. Le Guin, Gene Wolfe, Roger Zelazny, and a dozen or so others.

I had just finished writing "House of Bones." Terry was keenly interested in prehistory, and had a fundamental belief that human beings were basically good, however unlikely that might seem judging by surface appearance alone. "House of Bones" seemed to me to be the perfect story for the memorial anthology, and I sent it to Beth. Terry's Universe was published in May of 1988, thirteen months after his death. "House of Bones" was the first story in the book.

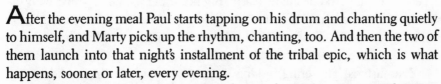

After the evening meal Paul starts tapping on his drum and chanting quietly to himself, and Marty picks up the rhythm, chanting, too. And then the two of them launch into that night's installment of the tribal epic, which is what happens, sooner or later, every evening.

It all sounds very intense, but I don't have a clue to the meaning. They sing the epic in the religious language, which I've never been allowed to learn. It has the same relation to the everyday language, I guess, as Latin does to French or Spanish. But it's private, sacred, for insiders only. Not for the likes of me.

"Tell it, man!" B.J. yells. "Let it roll!" Danny shouts.

Paul and Marty are really getting into it. Then a gust of fierce stinging cold whistles through the house as the reindeer-hide flap over the doorway is lifted, and Zeus comes stomping in.

Zeus is the chieftain. Big burly man, starting to run to fat a little. Mean-looking, just as you'd expect. Heavy black beard streaked with gray, and hard, glittering eyes that glow like rubies in a face wrinkled and carved by windburn and time. Despite the Paleolithic cold, all he's wearing is a cloak of black fur, loosely draped. The thick hair on his heavy chest is turning gray, too. Festoons of jewelry announce his power and status: necklaces of seashells, bone beads, and amber, a pendant of yellow wolf teeth, an ivory headband, bracelets carved from bone, five or six rings.

Sudden silence. Ordinarily when Zeus drops in at B.J.'s house it's for a little roistering and tale-telling and butt-pinching, but tonight he has come without either of his wives, and he looks troubled, grim. Jabs a finger toward Jeanne.

"You saw the stranger today? What's he like?"

There's been a stranger lurking near the village all week, leaving traces everywhere—footprints in the permafrost, hastily covered-over campsites, broken flints, scraps of charred meat. The whole tribe's keyed. Strangers aren't common. I was the last one, a year and a half ago. God only knows why they took me in: because I seemed so pitiful to them, maybe. But the way they've been talking, they'll kill this one on sight if they can. Paul and Marty composed a Song of the Stranger last week and Marty sang it by the campfire two different nights. It was in the religious language, so I couldn't understand a word of it. But it sounded terrifying.

Jeanne is Marty's wife. She got a good look at the stranger this afternoon, down by the river while netting fish for dinner. "He's short," she tells Zeus. "Shorter than any of you, but with big muscles, like Gebravar." Gebravar is Jeanne's name for me. The people of the tribe are strong, but they didn't pump iron when they were kids. My muscles fascinate them. "His hair is yellow and his eyes are gray. And he's ugly. Nasty. Big head, big flat nose. Walks with his shoulders hunched and his head down." Jeanne shudders. "He's like a pig. A real beast. A goblin. Trying to steal fish from the net, he was. But he ran away when he saw me."

Zeus listens, glowering, asking a question now and then—did he say anything, how was he dressed, was his skin painted in any way. Then he turns to Paul.

"What do you think he is?"

"A ghost," Paul says. These people see ghosts everywhere. And Paul, who is the bard of the tribe, thinks about them all the time. His poems are full of ghosts. He feels the world of ghosts pressing in, pressing in. "Ghosts have gray eyes," he says. "This man has gray eyes."

"A ghost, maybe, yes. But what kind of ghost?"

"What *kind?*"

Zeus glares. "You should listen to your own poems," he snaps. "Can't you see it? This is a Scavenger Folk man prowling around. Or the ghost of one."

General uproar and hubbub at that.

I turn to Sally. Sally's my woman. I still have trouble saying that she's my wife, but that's what she really is. I call her Sally because there once was a girl back home who I thought I might marry, and that was her name, far from here in another geological epoch.

I ask Sally who the Scavenger Folk are.

"From the old times," she says. "Lived here when we first came. But they're all dead now. They—"

That's all she gets a chance to tell me. Zeus is suddenly looming over me. He's always regarded me with a mixture of amusement and tolerant contempt, but now there's something new in his eye. "Here is something you will do for us," he says to me. "It takes a stranger to find a stranger. This will be your task. Whether he is a ghost or a man, we must know the truth. So you, tomorrow: you will go out and you will find him and you will take him. Do you understand? At first light you will go to search for him, and you will not come back until you have him."

I try to say something, but my lips don't want to move. My silence seems good enough for Zeus, though. He smiles and nods fiercely and swings around, and goes stalking off into the night.

They all gather around me, excited in that kind of animated edgy way that comes over you when someone you know is picked for some big distinction. I can't tell whether they envy me or feel sorry for me. B.J. hugs me, Danny punches me in the arm, Paul runs up a jubilant-sounding number on his drum. Marty pulls a wickedly sharp stone blade about nine inches long out of his kit bag and presses it into my hand.

"Here. You take this. You may need it."

I stare at it as if he had handed me a live grenade.

"Look," I say. "I don't know anything about stalking and capturing people."

"Come *on*," B.J. says. "What's the problem?"

B.J. is an architect. Paul's a poet. Marty sings, better than Pavarotti. Danny paints and sculpts. I think of them as my special buddies. They're all what you could loosely call Cro-Magnon men. I'm not. They treat me just like one of the gang, though. We five, we're some bunch. Without them I'd have gone crazy here. Lost as I am, cut off as I am from everything I used to be and know.

"You're strong and quick," Marty says. "You can do it."

"And you're pretty smart, in your crazy way," says Paul. "Smarter than *he* is. We aren't worried at all."

If they're a little condescending sometimes, I suppose I deserve it. They're highly skilled individuals, after all, proud of the things they can do. To them I'm a kind of retard. That's a novelty for me. I used to be considered highly skilled, too, back where I came from.

"You go with me," I say to Marty. "You and Paul both. I'll do whatever has to be done, but I want you to back me up."

"No," Marty says. "You do this alone."

"B.J.? Danny?"

"No," they say. And their smiles harden, their eyes grow chilly. Suddenly it doesn't look so chummy around here. We may be buddies, but I have to go out there by myself. Or I may have misread the whole situation and we aren't such big buddies at all. Either way, this is some kind of test, some rite of passage maybe, an initiation. I don't know. Just when I think these people are exactly like us except for a few piddling differences of customs and languages, I realize how alien they really are. Not savages, far from it. But they aren't even remotely like modern people. They're something entirely else. Their bodies and their minds are pure *Homo sapiens*, but their souls are different from ours by twenty thousand years.

To Sally I say, "Tell me more about the Scavenger Folk."

"Like animals, they were," she says. "They could speak, but only in grunts and belches. They were bad hunters and they ate dead things that they found on the ground, or stole the kills of others."

"They smelled like garbage," says Danny. "Like an old dump where everything was rotten. And they didn't know how to paint or sculpt."

"This was how they screwed," says Marty, grabbing the nearest woman, pushing her down, pretending to hump her from behind. Everyone laughs, cheers, stamps his feet.

"And they walked like this," says B.J., doing an ape shuffle, banging his chest with his fists.

There's a lot more, a lot of locker-room stuff about the ugly shaggy stupid smelly disgusting Scavenger Folk. How dirty they were, how barbaric. How the pregnant women kept the babies in their bellies twelve or thirteen months and they came out already hairy, with a full mouth of teeth. All ancient history, handed down through the generations by bards like Paul in the epics. None of them has ever actually seen a Scavenger. But they sure seem to detest them.

"They're all dead," Paul says. "They were killed in the migration wars long ago. That has to be a ghost out there."

Of course, I've guessed what's up. I'm no archaeologist at all—West Point, fourth generation. My skills are in electronics, computers, time-shift physics. There was such horrible political infighting among the archaeology boys about who was going to get to go to the past that in the end none of them went and the gig wound up going to the military. Still, they sent me here with enough crash-course archaeology to be able to see that the Scavengers must have been what we call the Neanderthals, that shambling race of also-rans that got left behind in the evolutionary sweepstakes.

So there really had been a war of extermination between the slow-witted Scavengers and clever *Homo sapiens* here in Ice Age Europe. But there must have been a few survivors left on the losing side, and one of them, God knows why, is wandering around near this village.

Now I'm supposed to find the ugly stranger and capture him. Or kill him, I guess. Is that what Zeus wants from me? To take the stranger's blood on my head? A very civilized tribe, they are, even if they do hunt huge woolly elephants and build houses out of their whitened bones. Too civilized to do their own murdering, and they figure they can send me out to do it for them.

"I don't think he's a Scavenger," Danny says. "I think he's from Naz Glesim. The Naz Glesim people have gray eyes. Besides, what would a ghost want with fish?"

Naz Glesim is a land far to the northeast, perhaps near what will someday be Moscow. Even here in the Paleolithic the world is divided into a thousand little nations. Danny once went on a great solo journey through all the neighboring lands: he's a kind of tribal Marco Polo.

"You better not let the chief hear that," B.J. tells him. "He'll break your balls. Anyway, the Naz Glesim people aren't ugly. They look just like us except for their eyes."

"Well, there's that," Danny concedes. "But I still think—"

Paul shakes his head. That gesture goes way back, too. "A Scavenger ghost," he insists.

B.J. looks at me. "What do you think, Pumangiup?" That's his name for me.

"Me?" I say. "What do I know about these things?"

"You come from far away. You ever see a man like that?"

"I've seen plenty of ugly men, yes." The people of the tribe are tall and lean, brown hair and dark shining eyes, wide faces, bold cheekbones. If they had better teeth they'd be gorgeous. "But I don't know about this one. I'd have to see him."

Sally brings a new platter of grilled fish over. I run my hand fondly over her bare haunch. Inside this house made of mammoth bones nobody wears very much clothing, because the structure is well insulated and the heat builds up even in the dead of winter. To me Sally is far and away the best-looking woman in the tribe: high firm breasts, long supple legs, alert, inquisitive face. She was the mate of a man who had to be killed last summer because he became infested with ghosts. Danny and B.J. and a couple of others bashed his head in, by way of a mercy killing, and then there was a wild six-day wake, dancing and wailing around the clock. Because she needed a change of luck they gave Sally to me, or me to her, figuring a holy fool like me must carry the charm of the gods. We have a fine time, Sally and I. We were two lost souls when we came together, and together we've kept each other from tumbling even deeper into the darkness.

"You'll be all right," B.J. says. "You can handle it. The gods love you."

"I hope that's true," I tell him.

Much later in the night, Sally and I hold each other as though we both know that this could be our last time. She's all over me, hot, eager. There's no privacy in the bone house and the others can hear us, four couples and I don't know how many kids, but that doesn't matter. It's dark. Our little bed of fox pelts is our own little world.

There's nothing esoteric, by the way, about these people's style of lovemaking. There are only so many ways that a male human body and a female human body can be joined together, and all of them, it seems, had already been invented by the time the glaciers came.

At dawn, by first light, I am on my way, alone, to hunt the Scavenger man. I rub the rough strange wall of the house of bones for luck, and off I go.

❧

The village stretches for a couple of hundred yards along the bank of a cold, swiftly flowing river. The three round bone houses where most of us live are arranged in a row, and the fourth one, the longhouse that is the residence of Zeus and his family and also serves as the temple and house of parliament, is just beyond them. On the far side of it is the new fifth house that we've been building this past week. Farther down, there's a workshop where tools are made and hides are scraped, and then a butchering area, and just past that there's an immense garbage dump and a towering heap of mammoth bones for future construction projects.

A sparse pine forest lies east of the village, and beyond it are the rolling hills and open plains where the mammoths and rhinos graze. No one ever goes into the river, because it's too cold and the current is too strong, and so it hems us in like a wall on our western border. I want to teach the tribesfolk how to build kayaks one of these days. I should also try to teach them how to swim, I guess. And maybe a few years further along I'd like to see if we can chop down some trees and build a bridge. Will it shock the pants off them when I come out with all this useful stuff? They think I'm an idiot, because I don't know about the different grades of mud and frozen ground, the colors of charcoal, the uses and qualities of antler, bone, fat, hide, and stone. They feel sorry for me because I'm so limited. But they like me all the same. And the gods *love* me. At least B.J. thinks so.

I start my search down by the riverfront, since that's where Jeanne saw the Scavenger yesterday. The sun, at dawn on this Ice Age autumn morning, is small and pale, a sad little lemon far away. But the wind is quiet now. The ground is still soft from the summer thaw, and I look for tracks. There's permafrost five feet down, but the topsoil, at least, turns spongy in May and gets downright muddy by July. Then it hardens again and by October it's like steel, but by October we live mostly indoors.

There are footprints all over the place. We wear leather sandals, but a lot of us go barefoot much of the time, even now, in forty-degree weather. The people of the tribe have long, narrow feet with high arches. But down by the water near the fishnets I pick up a different spoor, the mark of a short, thick, low-arched foot with curled-under toes. It must be my Neanderthal. I smile. I feel like Sherlock Holmes. "Hey, look, Marty," I say to the sleeping village. "I've got the ugly bugger's track. B.J.? Paul? Danny? You just watch me. I'm going to find him faster than you could believe."

❧

Those aren't their actual names. I just call them that, Marty, Paul, B.J., Danny. Around here everyone gives everyone else his own private set of names. Marty's name for B.J. is Ungklava. He calls Danny Tisbalalak, and Paul is Shibgamon. Paul calls Marty Dolibog. His name for B.J. is Kalamok. And so on all around the tribe, a ton of names, hundreds and hundreds of names for just forty or fifty people. It's a confusing system. They have reasons for it that satisfy them. You learn to live with it.

A man never reveals his true name, the one his mother whispered when he was born. Not even his father knows that, or his wife. You could put hot stones between his legs and he still wouldn't tell you that true name of his, because that'd bring every ghost from Cornwall to Vladivostok down on his ass to haunt him. The world is full of angry ghosts, resentful of the living, ready to jump on anyone who'll give them an opening and plague him like leeches, like bedbugs, like every malign and perverse bloodsucking pest rolled into one.

We are somewhere in western Russia, or maybe Poland. The landscape suggests that: flat, bleak, a cold grassy steppe with a few oaks and birches and pines here and there. Of course a lot of Europe must look like that in this glacial epoch. But the clincher is the fact that these people build mammoth-bone houses. The only place that was ever done was Eastern Europe, so far as anybody down the line knows. Possibly they're the oldest true houses in the world.

What gets me is the immensity of this prehistoric age, the spans of time. It goes back and back and back and all of it is alive for these people. We think it's a big deal to go to England and see a cathedral a thousand years old. They've been hunting on this steppe thirty times as long. Can you visualize thirty thousand years? To you, George Washington lived an incredibly long time ago. George is going to have his three hundredth birthday very soon. Make a stack of books a foot high and tell yourself that that stands for all the time that has gone by since George was born in 1732. Now go on stacking up the books. When you've got a pile as high as a ten-story building, that's thirty thousand years.

A stack of years almost as high as that separates me from you, right this minute. In my bad moments, when the loneliness and the fear and the pain and the remembrance of all that I have lost start to operate on me, I feel that stack of years pressing on me with the weight of a mountain. I try not to let it get me down. But that's a hell of a weight to carry. Now and then it grinds me right into the frozen ground.

The flatfooted track leads me up to the north, around the garbage dump, and toward the forest. Then I lose it. The prints go round and round, double back to the garbage dump, then to the butchering area, then toward the forest again, then all the way over to the river. I can't make sense of the pattern. The poor dumb bastard just seems to have been milling around, foraging in the garbage for anything edible, then taking off again but not going far, checking back to see if anything's been caught in the fishnet, and so on. Where's he sleeping? Out in the open, I guess. Well, if what I heard last night is true, he's as hairy as a gorilla; maybe the cold doesn't bother him much.

Now that I've lost the trail, I have some time to think about the nature of the mission, and I start getting uncomfortable.

I'm carrying a long stone knife. I'm out here to kill. I picked the military for my profession a long time ago, but it wasn't with the idea of killing anyone, and certainly not in hand-to-hand combat. I guess I see myself as a representative of civilization, somebody trying to hold back the night, not as anyone who would go creeping around planning to stick a sharp flint blade into some miserable solitary tramp.

But I might well be the one that gets killed. He's wild, he's hungry, he's scared, he's primitive. He may not be very smart, but at least he's shrewd enough to have made it to adulthood, and he's out here earning his living by his wits and his strength. This is his world, not mine. He may be stalking me even while I'm stalking him, and when we catch up with each other he won't be fighting by any rules I ever learned. A good argument for turning back right now.

On the other hand if I come home in one piece with the Scavenger still at large, Zeus will hang my hide on the bone-house wall for disobeying him. We may all be great buddies here, but when the chief gives the word, you hop to it or else. That's the way it's been since history began, and I have no reason to think it's any different back here.

I simply have to kill the Scavenger. That's all there is to it.

I don't want to get killed by a wild man in this forest, and I don't want to be nailed up by a tribal court-martial either. I want to live to get back to my own time. I still hang on to the faint chance that the rainbow will come back for me and take me down the line to tell my tale in what I have already started to think of as the future. I want to make my report.

The news I'd like to bring you people up there in the world of the future is that these Ice Age folk don't see themselves as primitive. They know, they absolutely *know*, that they're the crown of creation. They have a language—two of them, in fact—they have history, they have music, they have poetry, they have technology, they have art, they have architecture. They have religion. They have laws. They have a way of life that has worked for thousands of years, that will go on working for thousands more. You may think it's all grunts and war clubs back here, but you're wrong. I can make this world real to you, if I could only get back there to you.

But even if I can't ever get back, there's a lot I want to do here. I want to learn that epic of theirs and write it down for you to read. I want to teach them about kayaks and bridges, and maybe more. I want to finish building the bone house we started last week. I want to go on horsing around with my buddies B.J. and Danny and Marty and Paul. I want Sally. Christ, I might even have kids by her, and inject my own futuristic genes into the Ice Age gene pool.

I don't want to die today trying to fulfill a dumb murderous mission in this cold bleak prehistoric forest.

✔

The morning grows warmer, though not warm. I pick up the trail again, or think I do, and start off toward the east and north, into the forest. Behind me I hear the sounds of laughter and shouting and song as work gets going on the new house, but soon I'm out of earshot. Now I hold the knife in my hand, ready for anything. There are wolves in here, as well as a frightened half-man who may try to kill me before I can kill him.

I wonder how likely it is that I'll find him. I wonder how long I'm supposed to stay out here, too—a couple of hours, a day, a week?—and what I'm supposed to use for food, and how I keep my ass from freezing after dark, and what Zeus will say or do if I come back empty-handed.

I'm wandering around randomly now. I don't feel like Sherlock Holmes any longer.

✔

Working on the bone house, that's what I'd rather be doing now. Winter is coming on and the tribe has grown too big for the existing four houses. B.J. directs the job and Marty and Paul sing and chant and play the drum and flute, and about seven of us do the heavy labor.

"Pile those jawbones chin down," B.J. will yell, as I try to slip one into the foundation the wrong way around. "*Chin down*, bozo! That's better." Paul bangs out a terrific riff on the drum to applaud me for getting it right the second time. Marty starts making up a ballad about how dumb I am, and everyone laughs. But it's loving laughter. "Now that backbone over there," B.J. yells to me. I pull a long string of mammoth vertebrae from the huge pile. The bones are white, old bones that have been lying around a long time. They're dense and heavy. "Wedge it down in there good! Tighter! Tighter!" I huff and puff under the immense weight of the thing, and stagger a little, and somehow get it where it belongs, and jump out of the way just in time as Danny and two other men come tottering toward me carrying a gigantic skull.

The winter houses are intricate and elaborate structures that require real ingenuity of design and construction. At this point in time, B.J. may well be the best architect the world has ever known. He carries around a piece of ivory on which he has carved a blueprint for the house, and makes sure everybody weaves the bones and skulls and tusks into the structure just the right way. There's no shortage of construction materials. After thirty thousand years of hunting mammoths in this territory, these people have enough bones lying around to build a city the size of Los Angeles.

The houses are warm and snug. They're round and domed, like big igloos made out of bones. The foundation is a circle of mammoth skulls with maybe a hundred mammoth jawbones stacked up over them in fancy herringbone patterns to form the wall. The roof is made of hides stretched over enormous tusks mounted overhead as arches. The whole thing is supported by a wooden frame, and smaller bones are chinked in to seal the openings in the walls, plus a plastering of red clay. There's an entranceway made up of gigantic thighbones set up on end. It may all sound bizarre, but there's a weird kind of beauty to it, and you have no idea, once you're inside, that the bitter winds of the Pleistocene are howling all around you.

The tribe is seminomadic and lives by hunting and gathering. In the summer, which is about two months long, they roam the steppe, killing mammoths and rhinos and musk oxen, and bagging up berries and nuts to get them through the winter. Toward what I would guess is August the weather turns cold and they start to head for their village of bone houses, hunting reindeer along the way. By the time the really bad weather arrives—think Minnesota-and-a-half—they're settled in for the winter with six months' worth of meat stored in deep-freeze pits in the permafrost. It's an orderly, rhythmic life. There's a real community here. I'd be willing to call it a civilization. But— as I stalk my human prey out here in the cold—I remind myself that life here is harsh and strange. Alien. Maybe I'm doing all this buddy-buddy nickname stuff simply to save my own sanity, you think? I don't know.

If I get killed out here today, the thing I'll regret most is never learning their secret religious language and not being able to understand the big historical epic that they sing every night. They just don't want to teach it to me. Evidently it's something outsiders aren't meant to understand.

The epic, Sally tells me, is an immense account of everything that's ever happened: the *Iliad* and the *Odyssey* and the *Encyclopedia Britannica* all rolled into one, a vast tale of gods and kings and men and warfare and migrations and vanished empires and great calamities. The text is so big and Sally's recounting of it is so sketchy that I have only the foggiest idea of what it's about, but when I hear it I want desperately to understand it. It's the actual history of a forgotten

world, the tribal annals of thirty millennia, told in a forgotten language, all of
it as lost to us as last year's dreams.

If I could learn it and translate it I would set it all down in writing so that
maybe it would be found by archaeologists thousands of years from now. I've
been taking notes on these people already, an account of what they're like and
how I happen to be living among them. I've made twenty tablets so far, using
the same clay that the tribe uses to make its pots and sculptures, and firing it in
the same beehive-shaped kiln. It's a godawful slow job writing on slabs of clay
with my little bone knife. I bake my tablets and bury them in the cobblestone
floor of the house. Somewhere in the twenty-first or twenty-second century a
Russian archaeologist will dig them up and they'll give him one hell of a jolt.
But of their history, their myths, their poetry, I don't have a thing, because of
the language problem. Not a damned thing.

Noon has come and gone. I find some white berries on a glossy-leaved bush
and, after only a moment's hesitation, gobble them down. There's a faint
sweetness there. I'm still hungry even after I pick the bush clean.

If I were back in the village now, we'd have knocked off work at noon for a
lunch of dried fruit and strips of preserved reindeer meat, washed down with
mugs of mildly fermented fruit juice. The fermentation is accidental, I think,
an artifact of their storage methods. But obviously there are yeasts here, and I'd
like to try to invent wine and beer. Maybe they'll make me a god for that. This
year I invented writing, but I did it for my sake and not for theirs, and they
aren't much interested in it. I think they'll be more impressed with beer.

A hard, nasty wind has started up out of the east. It's September now, and
the long winter is clamping down. In half an hour the temperature has dropped
fifteen degrees, and I'm freezing. I'm wearing a fur parka and trousers, but that
thin icy wind cuts right through. And it scours up the fine dry loose topsoil and
flings it in our faces. Someday that light yellow dust will lie thirty feet deep over
this village, and over B.J. and Marty and Danny and Paul, and probably over
me as well.

Soon they'll be quitting for the day. The house will take eight or ten more
days to finish, if early-season snowstorms don't interrupt. I can imagine Paul
hitting the drum six good raps to wind things up and everybody making a run
for indoors, whooping and hollering. These are high-spirited guys. They jump
and shout and sing, punch each other playfully on the arms, brag about the
goddesses they've screwed and the holy rhinos they've killed. Not that they're
kids. My guess is that they're twenty-five, thirty years old, senior men of the
tribe. The life expectancy here seems to be about forty-five. I'm thirty-four. I
have a grandmother alive back in Illinois. Nobody here could possibly believe

that. The one I call Zeus, the oldest and richest man in town, looks to be about fifty-three, probably is younger than that, and is generally regarded as favored by the gods because he's lived so long. He's a wild old bastard, still full of bounce and vigor. He lets you know that he keeps those two wives of his busy all night long, even at his age. These are robust people. They lead a tough life, but they don't know that, and so their souls are buoyant. I definitely will try to turn them on to beer next summer, if I last that long and if I can figure out the technology. This could be one hell of a party town.

Sometimes I can't help feeling abandoned by my own time. I know it's irrational. It has to be just an accident that I'm marooned here. But there are times when I think the people up there in 2013 simply shrugged and forgot about me when things went wrong, and it pisses me off tremendously until I get it under control. I'm a professionally trained hardass. But I'm twenty thousand years from home, and there are times when it hurts more than I can stand.

Maybe beer isn't the answer. Maybe what I need is a still. Brew up some stronger stuff than beer, a little moonshine to get me through those very black moments when the anger and the really heavy resentment start breaking through.

In the beginning the tribe looked on me, I guess, as a moron. Of course, I was in shock. The time trip was a lot more traumatic than the experiments with rabbits and turtles had led us to think.

There I was, naked, dizzy, stunned, blinking and gaping, retching and puking. The air had a bitter acid smell to it—who expected that, that the air would smell different in the past?—and it was so cold it burned my nostrils. I knew at once that I hadn't landed in the pleasant France of the Cro-Magnons but in some harsher, bleaker land far to the east. I could still see the rainbow glow of the Zeller Ring, but it was vanishing fast, and then it was gone.

The tribe found me ten minutes later. That was an absolute fluke. I could have wandered for months, encountering nothing but reindeer and bison. I could have frozen; I could have starved. But no, the men I would come to call B.J. and Danny and Marty and Paul were hunting near the place where I dropped out of the sky, and they stumbled on me right away. Thank God they didn't see me arrive. They'd have decided that I was a supernatural being and would have expected miracles from me, and I can't do miracles. Instead they simply took me for some poor dope who had wandered so far from home that he didn't know where he was, which after all was essentially the truth.

I must have seemed like one sad case. I couldn't speak their language or any other language they knew. I carried no weapons. I didn't know how to make tools out of flints or sew a fur parka or set up a snare for a wolf or stampede a herd of mammoths into a trap. I didn't know anything, in fact, not a single useful thing. But instead of spearing me on the spot they took me to their village, fed me, clothed me, taught me their language. Threw their arms around me and told me what a great guy I was. They made me one of them. That was a year and a half ago. I'm a kind of holy fool for them, a sacred idiot.

I was supposed to be here just four days and then the Zeller Effect rainbow would come for me and carry me home. Of course, within a few weeks I realized that something had gone wonky at the uptime end, that the experiment had malfunctioned and that I probably wasn't ever going to get home. There was that risk all along. Well, here I am, here I stay. First came stinging pain and anger, and I suppose grief when the truth finally caught up with me. Now there's just a dull ache that won't go away.

✦

In early afternoon I stumble across the Scavenger Man. It's pure dumb luck. The trail has long since given out—the forest floor is covered with soft pine duff here, and I'm not enough of a hunter to distinguish one spoor from another in that—and I'm simply moving aimlessly when I see some broken branches, and then I get a whiff of burning wood, and I follow that scent twenty or thirty yards over a low rise and there he is, hunkered down by a hastily thrown together little hearth roasting a couple of ptarmigans on a green spit. A scavenger he may be, but he's a better man than I am when it comes to skulling ptarmigans.

He's really ugly. Jeanne wasn't exaggerating at all.

His head is huge and juts back a long way. His mouth is like a muzzle and his chin is hardly there at all and his forehead slopes down to huge brow ridges like an ape's. His hair is like straw, and it's all over him, though he isn't really shaggy, no hairier than a lot of men I've known. His eyes are gray, yes, and small, deep-set. He's built low and thick, like an Olympic weight lifter. He's wearing a strip of fur around his middle and nothing else. He's an honest-to-God Neanderthal, straight out of the textbooks, and when I see him a chill runs down my spine as though up till this minute I had never really believed that I had traveled twenty thousand years in time and now, holy shit, the whole concept has finally become real to me.

He sniffs and gets my wind, and his big brows knit and his whole body goes tense. He stares at me, checking me out, sizing me up. It's very quiet here and we are primordial enemies, face-to-face with no one else around. I've never felt anything like that before.

We are maybe twenty feet from each other. I can smell him and he can smell me, and it's the smell of fear on both sides. I can't begin to anticipate his move. He rocks back and forth a little, as if getting ready to spring up and come charging, or maybe bolt off into the forest.

But he doesn't do that. The first moment of tension passes, and he eases back. He doesn't try to attack, and he doesn't get up to run. He just sits there in a kind of patient, tired way, staring at me, waiting to see what I'm going to do. I wonder if I'm being suckered, set up for a sudden onslaught.

I'm so cold and hungry and tired that I wonder if I'll be able to kill him when he comes at me. For a moment I almost don't care.

Then I laugh at myself for expecting shrewdness and trickery from a Neanderthal man. Between one moment and the next all the menace goes out of him for me. He isn't pretty, but he doesn't seem like a goblin, or a demon, just an ugly thick-bodied man sitting alone in a chilly forest.

And I know that sure as anything I'm not going to try to kill him, not because he's so terrifying but because he isn't.

"They sent me out here to kill you," I say, showing him the flint knife.

He goes on staring. I might just as well be speaking English, or Sanskrit.

"I'm not going to do it," I tell him. "That's the first thing you ought to know. I've never killed anyone before, and I'm not going to begin with a complete stranger. Okay? Is that understood?"

He says something now. His voice is soft and indistinct, but I can tell that he's speaking some entirely other language.

"I can't understand what you're telling me," I say, "and you don't understand me. So we're even."

I take a couple of steps toward him. The blade is still in my hand. He doesn't move. I see now that he's got no weapons and even though he's powerfully built and could probably rip my arms off in two seconds, I'd be able to put the blade into him first. I point to the north, away from the village, and make a broad sweeping gesture. "You'd be wise to head off that way," I say, speaking very slowly and loudly, as if that would matter. "Get yourself out of the neighborhood. They'll kill you otherwise. You understand? *Capisce? Verstehen Sie?* Go. Scat. Scram. I won't kill you, but they will."

I gesture some more, vociferously pantomiming his route to the north. He looks at me. He looks at the knife. His enormous cavernous nostrils widen and flicker. For a moment I think I've misread him in the most idiotically naive way, that he's been simply biding his time getting ready to jump me as soon as I stop making speeches.

Then he pulls a chunk of meat from the bird he's been roasting, and offers it to me.

"I come here to kill you, and you give me lunch?"

He holds it out. A bribe? Begging for his life?

"I can't," I say. "I came here to kill you. Look, I'm just going to turn around and go back, all right? If anybody asks, I never saw you." He waves the meat at me and I begin to salivate as though it's pheasant under glass. But no, no, I can't take his lunch. I point to him, and again to the north, and once more indicate that he ought not to let the sun set on him in this town. Then I turn and start to walk away, wondering if this is the moment when he'll leap up and spring on me from behind and choke the life out of me.

I take five steps, ten, and then I hear him moving behind me.

So this is it. We really are going to fight.

I turn, my knife at the ready. He looks down at it sadly. He's standing there with the piece of meat still in his hand, coming after me to give it to me anyway.

"Jesus," I say. "You're just lonely."

He says something in that soft blurred language of his and holds out the meat. I take it and bolt it down fast, even though it's only half cooked—dumb Neanderthal!—and I almost gag. He smiles. I don't care what he looks like; if he smiles and shares his food, then he's human by me. I smile, too. Zeus is going to murder me. We sit down together and watch the other ptarmigan cook, and when it's ready we share it, neither of us saying a word. He has trouble getting a wing off, and I hand him my knife, which he uses in a clumsy way and hands back to me.

After lunch I get up and say, "I'm going back now. I wish to hell you'd head off to the hills before they catch you."

And I turn, and go.

And he follows me like a lost dog who has just adopted a new owner.

So I bring him back to the village with me. There's simply no way to get rid of him short of physically attacking him, and I'm not going to do that. As we emerge from the forest a sickening wave of fear sweeps over me. I think at first it's the roast ptarmigan trying to come back up, but no, it's downright terror, because the Scavenger is obviously planning to stick with me right to the end, and the end is not going to be good. I can see Zeus' blazing eyes, his furious scowl. The thwarted Ice Age chieftain in a storm of wrath. Since I didn't do the job, they will. They'll kill him and maybe they'll kill me, too, since I've revealed myself to be a dangerous moron who will bring home the very enemy he was sent out to eliminate.

"This is dumb," I tell the Neanderthal. "You shouldn't be doing this."

He smiles again. You don't understand shit, do you, fellow?

We are past the garbage dump now, past the butchering area. B.J. and his crew are at work on the new house. B.J. looks up when he sees me, and his eyes are bright with surprise.

He nudges Marty and Marty nudges Paul, and Paul taps Danny on the shoulder. They point to me and to the Neanderthal. They look at each other. They open their mouths, but they don't say anything. They whisper, they shake their heads. They back off a little, and circle around us, gaping, staring.

Christ. Here it comes.

I can imagine what they're thinking. They're thinking that I have really screwed up. That I've brought a ghost home for dinner. Or else an enemy that I was supposed to kill. They're thinking that I'm an absolute lunatic, that I'm an idiot, and now they've got to do the dirty work that I was too dumb to do. And I wonder if I'll try to defend the Neanderthal against them, and what it'll be like if I do. What am I going to do, take them all on at once? And go down swinging as my four sweet buddies close in on me and flatten me into the permafrost? I will. If they force me to it, by God I will. I'll go for their guts with Marty's long stone blade if they try anything on the Neanderthal, or on me.

I don't want to think about it. I don't want to think about any of this.

Then Marty points and claps his hands and jumps about three feet in the air.

"Hey!" he yells. "Look at that! He brought the ghost back with him!"

And then they move in on me, just like that, the four of them, swarming all around me, pressing close, pummeling hard. There's no room to use the knife. They come on too fast. I do what I can with elbows, knees, even teeth. But they pound me from every side, open fists against my ribs, sides of hands crashing against the meat of my back. The breath goes from me and I come close to toppling as pain breaks out all over me at once. I need all of my strength, and then some, to keep from going down under their onslaught, and I think, this is a dumb way to die, beaten to death by a bunch of berserk cavemen in 20,000 B.C.

But after the first few wild moments things become a bit quieter and I get myself together and manage to push them back from me a little way, and I land a good one that sends Paul reeling backward with blood spouting from his lip, and I whirl toward B.J. and start to take him out, figuring I'll deal with Marty on the rebound. And then I realize that they aren't really fighting with me any more, and in fact that they never were.

It dawns on me that they were smiling and laughing as they worked me over, that their eyes were full of laughter and love, that if they had truly wanted to work me over it would have taken the four of them about seven and a half seconds to do it.

They're just having fun. They're playing with me in a jolly rough-house way.

They step back from me. We all stand there quietly for a moment, breathing hard, rubbing our cuts and bruises. The thought of throwing up crosses my mind, and I push it away.

"You brought the ghost back," Marty says again.

"Not a ghost," I say. "He's real."

"Not a ghost?"

"Not a ghost, no. He's live. He followed me back here."

"Can you believe it?" B.J. cries. "Live! Followed him back here! Just came marching right in here with him!" He turns to Paul. His eyes are gleaming, and for a second I think they're going to jump me all over again. If they do, I don't think I'm going to be able to deal with it. But he says simply, "This has to be a song by tonight. This is something special."

"I'm going to get the chief," says Danny, and runs off.

"Look, I'm sorry," I say. "I know what the chief wanted. I just couldn't do it."

"Do what?" B.J. asks. "What are you talking about?" says Paul.

"Kill him," I say. "He was just sitting there by his fire, roasting a couple of birds, and he offered me a chunk, and—"

"*Kill* him?" B.J. says. "You were going to kill him?"

"Wasn't that what I was supposed—"

He goggles at me and starts to answer, but just then Zeus comes running up, and pretty much everyone else in the tribe, the women and the kids, too, and they sweep up around us like the tide. Cheering, yelling, dancing, pummeling me in that cheerful bone-smashing way of theirs, laughing, shouting. Forming a ring around the Scavenger Man and throwing their hands in the air. It's a jubilee. Even Zeus is grinning. Marty begins to sing and Paul gets going on the drum. And Zeus comes over to me and embraces me like the big old bear that he is.

❧

"I had it all wrong, didn't I?" I say later to B.J. "You were all just testing me, sure. But not to see how good a hunter I am."

He looks at me without any comprehension at all and doesn't answer. B.J., with that crafty architect's mind of his that takes in everything.

"You wanted to see if I was really human, right? If I had compassion, if I could treat a lost stranger the way I was treated myself."

Blank stares. Deadpan faces.

"Marty? Paul?"

They shrug. Tap their foreheads: the timeless gesture, ages old.

Are they putting me on? I don't know. But I'm certain that I'm right. If I had killed the Neanderthal they almost certainly would have killed me. That must have been it. I need to believe that that was it. All the time that I was congratulating them for not being the savages I had expected them to be, they were wondering how much of a savage *I* was. They had tested the depth of my humanity; and I had passed. And they finally see that I'm civilized too.

At any rate, the Scavenger Man lives with us now. Not as a member of the tribe, of course, but as a sacred pet of some sort, a tame chimpanzee, perhaps. He may very well be the last of his kind, or close to it; and though the tribe looks upon him as something dopey and filthy and pathetic, they're not going to do him any harm. To them he's a pitiful bedraggled savage who'll bring good luck if he's treated well. He'll keep the ghosts away. Hell, maybe that's why they took me in, too.

As for me, I've given up what little hope I had of going home. The Zeller rainbow will never return for me, of that I'm altogether sure. But that's all right. I've been through some changes. I've come to terms with it.

We finished the new house yesterday and B.J. let me put the last tusk in place, the one they call the ghost bone, which keeps dark spirits outside. It's apparently a big honor to be the one who sets up the ghost bone. Afterward the four of them sang the Song of the House, which is a sort of dedication. Like all their other songs, it's in the old language, the secret one, the sacred one. I couldn't sing it with them, not having the words, but I came in with oom-pahs on the choruses and that seemed to go down pretty well.

I told them that by the next time we need to build a house, I will have invented beer, so that we can all go out when it's finished and get drunk to celebrate properly.

Of course, they didn't know what the hell I was talking about, but they looked pleased anyway.

And tomorrow, Paul says, he's going to begin teaching me the other language. The secret one. The one that only the members of the tribe may know.

THE DEAD
MAN'S EYES

A *crime story, one of the few I've ever written. (Crime fiction, for some reason, has never interested me even as a reader, let alone as a writer. I've read the Sherlock Holmes stories with pleasure, yes, and some Simenons, and in 1985 I suddenly read seven or eight Elmore Leonard books in one unceasing burst. But such masters of the genre as P. D. James and John D. MacDonald inspire only yawns in me, which is not to say that they aren't masters, only that the thing they do so well is a thing that basically does not speak to any of my concerns. Doubtless a lot of mystery writers feel the same way about even the best science fiction.) "The Dead Man's Eyes" isn't a detective story, but it is crime fiction, to the extent that it seems actually to have been in the running for the Edgar Award, given out by the Mystery Writers of America. It's also science fiction, though, built as it is around a concept of detection that exists today only as the wildest scientific speculation.*

I wrote it in a moment of agreeable ease and fluency in the summer of 1987, and Alice Turner of Playboy *bought it in an equally uncomplicated way. I'm never enthusiastic about complications, but the summer is a time when I particularly like everything to go smoothly. This one did.*

On a crisp afternoon of high winds late in the summer of 2017 Frazier murdered his wife's lover, a foolish deed that he immediately regretted. To murder anyone was stupid, when there were so many more effective alternatives available; but even so, if murder was what he had to do, why murder the *lover?* Two levels of guilt attached there: not only the taking of a life, but the taking of an irrelevant life. If you had to kill someone, he told himself immediately afterward, then you should have killed *her.* She was the one who had committed the crime against the marriage, after all. Poor Hurwitt had been only a means, a tool, virtually an innocent bystander. Yes, kill *her,* not him. Kill yourself, even. But Hurwitt was the one he had killed, a dumb thing to do and done in a dumb manner besides.

It had all happened very quickly, without premeditation. Frazier was attending a meeting of the Museum trustees, to discuss expanding the Hall of Mammals. There was a recess; and because the day was so cool, the air so crystalline and bracing, he stepped out on the balcony that connected the old building with the Pilgersen Extension for a quick breather. Then the sleek bronze door of the Pilgersen opened far down the way and a dark-haired man in a grubby blue-gray lab coat appeared. Frazier saw at once, by the rigid set of his high shoulders and the way his long hair fluttered in the wind, that it was Hurwitt.

He wants to see me, Frazier thought. He knows I'm attending the meeting today and he's come out here to stage the confrontation at last, to tell me that he loves my famous and beautiful wife, to ask me bluntly to clear off and let him have her all to himself.

Frazier's pulse began to rise, his face grew hot. Even while he was thinking that it was oddly old-fashioned to talk of *letting* Hurwitt have Marianne, that in fact Hurwitt had probably already had Marianne in every conceivable way and vice versa but that if now he had some idea of setting up housekeeping with her—unbelievable, unthinkable!—this was hardly the appropriate place to discuss it with him, another and more primordial area of his brain was calling forth torrents of adrenaline and preparing him for mortal combat.

But no: Hurwitt didn't seem to have ventured onto the balcony for any man-to-man conference with his lover's husband. Evidently he was simply taking the shortcut from his lab in the Pilgersen to the fourth-floor cafeteria in the old building. He walked with his head down, his brows knitted, as though pondering some abstruse detail of trilobite anatomy, and he took no notice of Frazier at all.

"Hurwitt?" Frazier said finally, when the other man was virtually abreast of him.

Caught by surprise, Hurwitt looked up, blinking. He appeared not to recognize Frazier for a moment. For that moment he was frozen in midblink, his unkempt hair a dark halo about him, his awkward rangy body off balance between strides, his peculiar glinting eyes flashing like yellow beacons. In fury Frazier imagined this man's bony nakedness, pale and gaunt, probably with sparse ropy strands of black hair sprouting on a white chest, imagined those long arms wrapped around Marianne, imagined those huge knobby fingers cupping her breasts, imagined that thin-lipped wide mouth covering hers. Imagined the grubby lab coat lying crumpled at the foot of the bed, and her silken orange wrap beside it. That was what sent Frazier over the brink, not the infidelities themselves, not the thought of the sweaty embraces—there was plenty of that in each of her films, and it had never meant a thing to him, for he knew it was only well-paid make-believe—and not the rawboned look of the man or his uncouth stride or even the manic glint of those strange off-color eyes, those eerie topaz eyes, but the lab coat, stained and worn with a button missing and a pocket flap dangling, lying beside Marianne's discarded silk. For her to take such a lover, a pathetic dreary poker of fossils, a hollow-chested laboratory drudge—no, no, no—

"Hello, Loren," Hurwitt said. He smiled amiably, he offered his hand. His eyes, though, narrowed and seemed almost to glow. It must be those weird eyes, Frazier thought, that Marianne has fallen in love with. "What a surprise, running into you out here."

And stood there smiling, and stood there holding out his hand, and stood there with his frayed lab coat flapping in the breeze.

Suddenly Frazier was unable to bear the thought of sharing the world with this man an instant longer. He watched himself as though from a point just behind his own right ear as he went rushing forward, seized not Hurwitt's hand but his wrist, and pushed rather than pulled, guiding him swiftly backward toward the parapet and tipping him up and over. It took perhaps a quarter of a second. Hurwitt, gaping, astonished, rose as though floating, hovered for an instant, began to descend. Frazier had one last look at Hurwitt's eyes, bright as glass, staring straight into his own, photographing his assailant's face; and then Hurwitt went plummeting downward.

My God, Frazier thought, peering over the edge. Hurwitt lay facedown in the courtyard five stories below, arms and legs splayed, lab coat billowing about him.

He was at the airport an hour later, with a light suitcase that carried no more than a day's change of clothing and a few cosmetic items. He flew first to Dallas, endured a ninety-minute layover, went on to San Francisco, doubled back to Calgary as darkness descended, and caught a midnight special to Mexico City, where he checked into a hotel using the legal commercial alias that he employed when doing business in Macao, Singapore, and Hong Kong. Standing on the terrace of a tower thirty stories above the Zona Rosa, he inhaled musky smog, listened to the squeals of traffic and the faint sounds of far-off drums, watched flares of green lightning in the choking sky above Popocatepetl, and wondered whether he should jump. Ultimately he decided against it. He wanted to share nothing whatever with Hurwitt, not even the manner of his death. And suicide would be an overreaction anyway. First he had to find out how much trouble he was really in.

The hotel had InfoLog. He dialed in and was told that queries were billed at five million pesos an hour, prorated. Vaguely he wondered whether that was as expensive as it sounded. The peso was practically worthless, wasn't it? What could that be in dollars—a hundred bucks, five hundred, maybe? Nothing.

"I want Harvard Legal," he told the screen. "Criminology. Forensics. Technical. Evidence technology." Grimly he menued down and down until he was near what he wanted. "Eyeflash," he said. "Theory, techniques. Methods of detail recovery. Acceptance as evidence. Reliability of record. Frequency of reversal on appeal. Supreme Court rulings, if any."

Back to him, in surreal fragments that, at an extra charge of three million pesos per hour, prorated, he had printed out for him, came blurts of information:

Perceptual pathways in outer brain layers . . . broad-scale optical architecture . . . images imprinted on striate cortex, or primary visual cortex . . . inferior temporal neurons . . . cf. McDermott and Brunetti, 2007, utilization of lateral geniculate body as storage for visual data . . . inferior temporal cortex . . . uptake of radioactive glucose . . . downloading . . . degrading of signal . . . degeneration period . . . Pilsudski signal-enhancement filter . . . Nevada vs. Bensen, 2011 . . . hippocampus simulation . . . amygdala . . . acetylcholine . . . U.S. Supreme Court, 23 March 2012 . . . cf. Gross and Bernstein, 13 Aug 2003 . . . Mishkin . . . Appenzeller. . . .

Enough. He shuffled the printouts in a kind of hard-edged stupor until dawn; and then, after a hazy calculation of time-zone differentials, he called his lawyer in New York. It took four bounces, but the telephone tracked him down in the commute, driving in from Connecticut.

Frazier keyed in the privacy filter. All the lawyer would know was that some client was calling; the screen image would be a blur, the voice would be rendered universal, generalized, unidentifiable. It was more for the lawyer's protection than Frazier's: there had been nasty twists in jurisprudence lately, and lawyers were less and less willing to run the risk of being named accomplices after the fact. Immediately came a query about the billing. Bill to my hotel room, Frazier replied, and the screen gave him a go-ahead.

"Let's say I'm responsible for causing a fatal injury and the victim had a good opportunity to see me as the act was occurring. What are the chances that they can recover eyeflash pictures?"

"Depends on how much damage was received in the process of the death. How did it happen?"

"Privileged communication?"

"Sorry. No."

"Even under filter?"

"Even. If the mode of death was unique or even highly distinctive and unusual, how can I help but draw the right conclusion? And then I'll know more than I want to know."

"It wasn't unique," Frazier said. "Or distinctive, or unusual. But I still won't go into details. I can tell you that the injury wasn't the sort that would cause specific brain trauma. I mean, nothing like a bullet between the eyes, or falling into a vat of acid, or—"

"All right. I follow. This take place in a major city?"

"Major, yes."

"In Missouri, Alabama, or Kentucky?"

"None of those," said Frazier. "It took place in a state where eyeflash recovery is legal. No question of that."

"And the body? How long after death do you estimate it would have been found?"

"Within minutes, I'd say."

"And when was that?"

Frazier hesitated. "Within the past twenty-four hours."

"Then there's almost total likelihood that there's a readily recoverable photograph in your victim's brain of whatever he saw at the moment of death. Beyond much doubt it's already been recovered. Are you sure he was looking at you as he died?"

"Straight at me."

"My guess is there's probably a warrant out for you already. If you want me to represent you, kill the privacy filter so I can confirm who you are, and we'll discuss our options."

"Later," Frazier said. "I think I'd rather try to make a run for it."

"But the chances of your getting away with—"

"This is something I need to do," said Frazier. "I'll talk to you some other time."

✦

He was almost certainly cooked. He knew that. He had wasted critical time running frantically back and forth across the continent yesterday, when he should have been transferring funds, setting up secure refuges, and such. The only question now was whether they were already looking for him, in which case there'd be blocks on his accounts everywhere, a passport screen at every airport, worldwide interdicts of all sorts. But if that was so they'd already have traced him to this hotel. Evidently they hadn't, which meant that they hadn't yet uncovered the Southeast Asian trading alias and put interdicts on that. Well, it was just a lousy manslaughter case, or maybe second degree at worst: they had more serious things to worry about, he supposed.

Checking out of the hotel without bothering about breakfast, he headed for the airport and used his corporate credit card to buy himself a flight to Belize. There he bought a ticket to Surinam, and just before his plane was due to leave he tried his personal card in the cash disburser and was pleasantly surprised to find that it hadn't yet been yanked. He withdrew the maximum. Of course, now there was evidence that Loren Frazier had been in Belize this day, but he wasn't traveling as Frazier, and he'd be in Surinam before long, and by the time they traced him there, assuming that they could, he'd be somewhere else, under some other name entirely. Maybe if he kept dodging for six or eight months he'd scramble his trail so thoroughly that they'd never be able to find him. Did they pursue you forever, he wondered? A time must come when they file and forget. Of course, he might not want to keep running forever, either. Already he missed Marianne. Despite what she had done.

He spent three days in Surinam at a little pastel-green Dutch hotel at the edge of Paramaribo, eating spicy noodle dishes and waiting to be arrested. Nobody bothered him. He used a cash machine again, keying up one of his corporate accounts and transferring a bundle of money into the account of Andreas Schmidt of Zurich, which was a name he had used seven years ago for some export-import maneuvers involving Zimbabwe and somehow, he knew not why, had kept alive for eventualities unknown. This was an eventuality now. When he checked the Schmidt account he found that there was money in it already, significant money, and that his Swiss passport had not yet expired. He requested the Swiss chargé d'affaires in Guyana to prepare a duplicate for him. A quick boat trip up the Marowijne River took him to St. Laurent on the French Guiana side of the river, where he was able to hire a driver to take him to Cayenne, and from there he flew to Georgetown in Guyana. A smiling proxy lawyer named Chatterji obligingly picked up his passport for him from the Swiss, and under the name of Schmidt he went on to Buenos Aires. There he destroyed all his Frazier documentation. He resisted the temptation to find out whether there was a Frazier interdict out yet. No sense handing them a trail extending down to Buenos Aires just to gratify his curiosity. If they weren't yet looking for him because he had murdered Hurwitt, they'd be looking for him on a simple missing-persons hook by this time. One way or another, it was best to forget about his previous identity and operate as Schmidt from here on.

This is almost fun, he thought.

But he missed his wife terribly.

⌄

While sitting in sidewalk cafés on the broad Avenida de 9 Julio, feasting on huge parrilladas sluiced down by carafe after carafe of red wine, he brooded obsessively on Marianne's affair. It made no sense. The world-famous actress and the awkward rawboned paleontologist: why? How was it possible? She had been making a commercial at the museum—Frazier, in fact, had helped to set the business up in his capacity as member of the board of trustees—and Hurwitt, who was the head of the department of invertebrate paleontology, or some such thing, had volunteered to serve as the technical consultant. Very kind of him, everyone said. Taking time away from his scientific work. He seemed so bland, so juiceless: who could suspect him of harboring lust for the glamorous film personality? Nobody would have imagined it. But things must have started almost at once. Some chemistry between them, beyond all understanding. People began to notice, and then to give Frazier strange little knowing looks. Eventually, even he caught on. A truly loving husband is generally just about the last one to know, because he will always put the best possible interpretation on the data. But after a time the accumulation of data becomes impossible to overlook or deny or reason away. There are always small changes when something like that has begun: they start to read books of a kind they've never read before, they talk of different things, they may even show some new moves in bed. Then comes the real carelessness, the seemingly unconscious slips that scream the actual nature of the situation. Frazier was forced finally to an acceptance of the truth. It tore at his heart. There was no room in their marriage for such stuff. Despite his money, despite his power, he had never gone in for the casual morality of the intercontinental set, and neither, so he thought, had Marianne. This was the second marriage for each: the one that was supposed to carry them happily on to the finish. And now look.

"Señor? Another carafe?"

"No," he said. "Yes. Yes." He stared at his plate. It was full of sausages, sweetbreads, grilled steak. Where had all that come from? He was sure he had eaten everything. It must have grown back. Moodily he stabbed a plump blood sausage and ate without noticing. Took a drink. They mixed the wine with seltzer water here, half and half. Maybe it helped you put away those tons of meat more easily.

Afterward, strolling along the narrow, glittering Calle Florida with the stylish evening promenade flowing past him on both sides, he caught sight of Marianne coming out of a jeweler's shop. She wore gaucho leathers, emerald earrings, skintight trousers of gold brocade. He grunted as though he had been struck and pressed his elbows against his sides as one might do if expecting a second blow. Then an elegant young Argentinian uncoiled himself from a curbside table and trotted quickly toward her, and they laughed and embraced and ran off arm in arm, sweeping right past him without even a glance. He remembered now: women all over the world were wearing Marianne's face this season. This one, in fact, was too tall by half a head. But he would have to be prepared for such incidents wherever he went. Mariannes everywhere, bludgeoning him with their beauty and never even knowing what they had done. He found himself wishing that the one who had been sleeping with that museum man was just another Marianne clone, that the real one was at home alone now, waiting for him, wondering, wondering.

In Montreal six weeks later, using a privacy filter and one of his corporate cards, he risked putting through a call to his apartment and discovered that there was an interdict on his line. When he tried the office number an android mask appeared on the screen and he was blandly told that Mr. Frazier was unavailable. The android didn't know when Mr. Frazier would be available. Frazier asked for Markman, his executive assistant, and a moment later a bleak, harried, barely recognizable face looked out at him. Frazier explained that he was a representative of the Bucharest account, calling about a highly sensitive matter. "Don't you know?" Markman said. "Mr. Frazier's disappeared. The police are looking for him." Frazier asked why, and Markman's face dissolved in an agony of shame, bewilderment, protective zeal. "There's a criminal charge against him," Markman whispered, nearly in tears.

He called his lawyer next and said, "I'm calling about the Frazier case. I don't want to kill the filter, but I imagine you won't have much trouble figuring out who I am."

"I imagine I won't. Just don't tell me where you are, okay?"

The situation was about as he expected. They had recovered the murder prints from the dead man's eyes: a nice shot, embedded deep in the cortical tissue, Frazier looming up against Hurwitt, nose to nose, a quick cut to the hand reaching for Hurwitt's arm, a wild free-form pan to the sky as Frazier lifted Hurwitt up and over the parapet. "Pardon me for saying this, but you looked absolutely deranged," the lawyer told him. "The prints were on all the networks the next day. Your eyes—it was really scary. I'm absolutely sure we could get impairment of faculties, maybe even crime of passion. Suspended sentence, but, of course, there'd be rehabilitation. I don't see any way around that, and it could last a year or two, and you might not be as effective in your profession afterward, but considering the circumstances—"

"How's my wife?" Frazier said. "Do you know anything about what she's been doing?"

"Well, of course I don't represent her, you realize. But she does get in the news. She's said to be traveling."

"Where?"

"I couldn't say. Look, I can try to find out, if you'd like to call back this time tomorrow. Only, I suggest that for your own good you call me at a different number, which is—"

"For my good or for yours?" Frazier said.

"I'm trying to help," said the lawyer, sounding annoyed.

◆

He took refresher courses in French, Italian, and German to give himself a little extra plausibility in the Andreas Schmidt identity, and cultivated a mild Teutonic accent. So long as he didn't run up against any real Swiss who wanted to gabble with him in Romansch or Schwyzerdeutsch, he suspected he'd make out all right. He kept on moving, Strasbourg, Athens, Haifa, Tunis. Even though he knew that no further fund transfers were possible, there was enough money stashed under the Schmidt accounts to keep him going nicely for ten or fifteen years, and by then he hoped to have this thing figured out.

He saw Mariannes in Tel Aviv, in Heraklion on Crete, and in Sidi bou Said, just outside Tunis. They were all clones, of course. He recognized that after just a quick queasy instant. Still, seeing that delicate high-bridged nose once again, those splendid amethyst eyes, those tight auburn ringlets, it was all he could do to keep himself from going up to them and throwing his arms around them, and he had to force himself each time to turn away, biting down hard on his lip.

In London, outside the Connaught, he saw the real thing. The Connaught was where they had spent their wedding trip back in '07, and he winced at the sight of its familiar grand facade, and winced even more when Marianne came out, young and radiant, wearing a shimmering silver cloud. Dazzling light streamed from her. He had no doubt that this was no trendy clone but the true Marianne: she moved in that easy confident way, with that regal joy in her own beauty that no cosmetic surgeon could ever impart even to the most intent imitator. The pavement itself seemed to do her homage. But then Frazier saw that the man on whose arm she walked was himself young and radiant, too, the Loren Frazier of that honeymoon journey of seven years back, his hair dark and thick, his love of life and success and his magnificent new wife cloaking him like an imperial mantle; and Frazier realized that he must merely be hallucinating, that the breakdown had moved on to a new and more serious stage. He stood gaping while Mr. and Mrs. Frazier swept through him like the phantoms they were and away in the direction of Grosvenor Square, and then he staggered and nearly fell. To the Connaught doorman he admitted that he was unwell, and because he was well-dressed and spoke with the hint of an accent and was able to find a twenty-sovereign piece in the nick of time the doorman helped him into a cab and expressed his deepest concern. Back at his own hotel, ten minutes over on the other side of Mayfair, he had three quick gins in a row and sat shivering for an hour before the image faded from his mind.

—

"I advise you to give yourself up," the lawyer said when Frazier called him from Nairobi. "Of course, you can keep on running as long as you like. But you're wearing yourself out, and sooner or later someone will spot you, so why keep on delaying the inevitable?"

"Have you spoken to Marianne lately?"

"She wishes you'd come back. She wants to write to you, or call you, or even come and see you, wherever you are. But I've told her you refuse to provide me with any information about your location. Is that still your position?"

"I don't want to see her or hear from her."

"She loves you."

"I'm a homicidal maniac. I might do the same thing to her that I did to Hurwitt."

"Surely you don't really believe—"

"No," Frazier said. "Not really."

"Then let me give her an address for you, at least, and she can write to you."

"It could be a trap, couldn't it?"

"Surely you can't possibly believe—"

"Who knows? Anything's possible."

"A postal box in Caracas, say," the lawyer suggested, "and let's say that you're in Rio, for the sake of the discussion, and I arrange an intermediary to pick up the letter and forward it care of American Express in Lima, and then on some day of your own choosing, known to nobody else, you make a quick trip in and out of Peru and—"

"And they grab me the moment I collect the letter," Frazier said. "How stupid do you think I am? You could set up forty intermediaries and I'd still have to create a trail leading to myself if I went to get the letter. Besides, I'm not in South America any more. That was months ago."

"It was only for the sake of the dis—" the lawyer said, but Frazier was gone already.

—

He decided to change his face and settle down somewhere. The lawyer was right: all this compulsive traveling was wearing him down. But by staying in one place longer than a week or two he was multiplying the chances of being detected, so long as he went on looking like himself. He had always wanted a longer nose anyway, and not quite so obtrusive a chin, and thicker eyebrows. He fancied that he looked too Slavic, though he had no Eastern European ancestry at all. All one long rainy evening at the mellow old Addis Ababa Hilton, he sketched a face for himself that he thought looked properly Swiss: rugged, passionate, with the right mix of French elegance, German stolidity, Italian passion. Then he went downstairs and showed the printout to the bartender, a supple little Portuguese.

"Where would you say this man comes from?" Frazier asked.

"Lisbon," the bartender replied at once. "That long jaw, those lips— unmistakably Lisbon, though perhaps his grandmother on his mother's side is of the Algarve. A man of considerable distinction, I would say. But I do not know him, Senhor Schmidt. He is no one I know. You would like your dry martini, as usual?"

"Make it a double," Frazier said.

He had the work done in Vienna. Everyone agreed that the best people for that sort of surgery were in Geneva, but Switzerland was the one country in the world he dared not enter, so he used his Zurich banking connections to get him the name of the second-best people, who were said to be almost as good— remarkably good, he was told. That seemed high praise indeed, Frazier thought, considering it was a Swiss talking about Austrians. The head surgeon at the Vienna clinic, though, turned out to be Swiss himself, which provided Frazier with a moment of complete terror, pretending as he was to be a native of Zurich. But the surgeon had been at his trade long enough to know that a man who wants his perfectly good face transformed into something entirely different does not wish to talk about his personal affairs. He was a big, cheerful extrovert named Randegger with a distinct limp. Skiing accident, the surgeon explained. Surely getting your leg fixed must be easier than getting your face changed, Frazier thought, but he decided that Randegger was simply waiting for the off-season to undergo repair. "This will be no problem at all," Randegger told him, studying Frazier's printout. "I have just a few small suggestions." He went deftly to work with a light-pen, broadening the cheekbones, moving the ears downward and forward. Frazier shrugged. Whatever you want, Dr. Randegger, he thought. Whatever you want. I'm putty in your hands.

It took six weeks from first cut to final healing. The results seemed fine to him—suave, convincing, an authoritative face—though at the beginning he was afraid it would all come apart if he smiled, and it was hard to get used to looking in a mirror and seeing someone else. He stayed at the clinic the whole six weeks. One of the nurses wore the Marianne face, but the body was all wrong, wide hips, startling steatopygous rump, short muscular legs. Near the end of his stay she lured him into bed. He was sure he'd be impotent with her, but he was wrong. There was only one really bad moment, when she reared above him and he couldn't see her body at all, only her beautiful, passionate, familiar face.

Even now, he couldn't stop running. Belgrade, Sydney, Rabat, Barcelona, Milan: they went by in a blur of identical airports, interchangeable hotels, baffling shifts of climate. Almost everywhere he went he saw Mariannes, and sometimes was puzzled that they never recognized him, until he remembered that he had altered his face: why should they know him now, even after the seven years of their marriage? As he traveled he began to see another ubiquitous face, dark and Latin and pixieish, and realized that Marianne's vogue must be beginning to wane. He hoped that some of the Mariannes would soon be converting themselves to this newer look. He had never really felt at ease with all these simulacra of his wife, whom he still loved beyond all measure.

That love, though, had become inextricably mixed with anger. He could not even now stop thinking about her incomprehensible, infuriating violation of the sanctity of their covenant. It had been the best of marriages, amiable, passionate, close, a true union on every level. He had never even thought of wanting another woman. She was everything he wanted; and he had every reason to think that his feelings were reciprocated. That was the worst of it, not the furtive little couplings she and Hurwitt must have enjoyed, but the deeper treason, the betrayal of their seeming harmony, her seemingly whimsical destruction of the hermetic seal that enclosed their perfect world.

He had overreacted, he knew. He wished he could call back the one absurd impulsive act that had thrust him from his smooth and agreeable existence into this frantic wearisome fugitive life. And he felt sorry for Hurwitt, who probably had been caught up in emotions beyond his depth, swept away by the astonishment of finding himself in Marianne's arms. How could he have stopped to worry, at such a time, about what he might be doing to someone else's marriage? How ridiculous it had been to kill him! And to stare right into Hurwitt's eyes, incontrovertibly incriminating himself, while he did! If he needed any proof of his temporary insanity, the utter foolishness of the murder would supply it.

But there was no calling any of it back. Hurwitt was dead; he had lived on the run for—what, two years? three?—and Marianne was altogether lost to him. So much destruction achieved in a single crazy moment. He wondered what he would do if he ever saw Marianne again. Nothing violent, no, certainly not. He had a sudden image of himself in tears, hugging her knees, begging her forgiveness. For what? For killing her lover? For bringing all sorts of nasty mess and the wrong kind of publicity into her life? For disrupting the easy rhythms of their happy marriage? No, he thought, astonished, aghast. What do I have to be forgiven for? From her, nothing. She's the one who should go down on her knees before me. I wasn't the one who was fooling around. And then he thought, No, no, we must forgive each other. And after that he thought, Best of all, I must take care never to have anything to do with her for the rest of my life. And that thought cut through him like a blade, like Dr. Randegger's fiery scalpel.

Six months later he was walking through the cavernous, ornate lobby of the Hotel de Paris in Monte Carlo when he saw a Marianne standing in front of a huge stack of suitcases against a marble pillar no more than twenty feet from him. He was inured to Mariannes by this time and at first the sight of her had no impact; but then he noticed the familiar monogram on the luggage, and recognized the intricate little bows of red plush cord with which the baggage tags were tied on, and he realized that this was the true Marianne at last. Nor was this any hallucination like the Connaught one. She was visibly older, with a vertical line in her left cheek that he had never seen before. Her hair was a darker shade and somehow more ordinary in its cut, and she was dressed simply, no radiance at all. Even so, people were staring at her and whispering. Frazier swayed, gripped a nearby pillar with his suddenly clammy hand, fought back the impulse to run. He took a deep breath and went toward her, walking slowly, impressively, his carefully cultivated distinguished-looking-Swiss-businessman walk.

"Marianne?" he said.

She turned her head slightly and stared at him without any show of recognition.

"I do look different, yes," he said, smiling.

"I'm sorry, but I don't—"

A slender, agile-looking man five or six years younger than she, wearing sunglasses, appeared from somewhere as though conjured out of the floor. Smoothly he interpolated himself between Frazier and Marianne. A lover? A bodyguard? Simply part of her entourage? Pleasantly but forcefully, he presented himself to Frazier as though saying, *Let's not have any trouble now, shall we?*

"Listen to my voice," Frazier said. "You haven't forgotten my voice. Only the face is different."

Sunglasses came a little closer. Looked a little less pleasant.

Marianne stared.

"You haven't forgotten, have you, Marianne?" Frazier said.

Sunglasses began to look definitely menacing.

"Wait a minute," Marianne said as he glided into a nose-to-nose with Frazier. "Step back, Aurelio." She peered through the shadows. "Loren?" she said.

Frazier nodded. He went toward her. At a gesture from Marianne, Sunglasses faded away like a genie going back into the bottle. Frazier felt strangely calm now. He could see Marianne's upper lip trembling, her nostrils flickering a little. "I thought I never wanted to see you again," he said. "But I was wrong about that. The moment I saw you and knew it was really you, I realized that I had never stopped thinking about you, never stopped wanting you. Wanting to put it all back together."

Her eyes widened. "And you think you can?"

"Maybe."

"What a damned fool you are," she said, gently, almost lovingly, after a long moment.

"I know. I really messed myself up, doing what I did."

"I don't mean that," she said. "You messed us both up with that. Not to mention him, the poor bastard. But that can't be undone, can it? If you only knew how often I prayed to have it not have happened." She shook her head. "It was nothing, what he and I were doing. Nothing. Just a silly fling, for Christ's sake. How could you possibly have cared so much?"

"What?"

"To *kill* a man, for something like that? To wreck three lives in half a second? For *that*?"

"What?" he said again. "What are you telling me?"

Sunglasses suddenly was in the picture again. "We're going to miss the car to the airport, Marianne."

"Yes. Yes. All right, let's go."

Frazier watched, numb, immobile. Sunglasses beckoned, and a swarm of porters materialized to carry the luggage outside. As she reached the vast doorway Marianne turned abruptly and looked back, and in the dimness of the great lobby her eyes suddenly seemed to shift in color, to take on the same strange topaz glint that he had imagined he had seen in Hurwitt's. Then she swung around and was gone.

An hour later he went down to the Consulate to turn himself in. They had a little trouble locating him in the list of wanted fugitives, but he told them to keep looking, going back a few years, and finally they came upon his entry. He was allowed half a day to clear up his business affairs, but he said he had none to clear up, so they set about the procedure of arranging his passage to the States, while he watched like a tourist who is trying to replace a lost passport.

Coming home was like returning to a foreign country that he had visited a long time before. Everything was familiar, but in an unfamiliar way. There were endless hearings, conferences, psychological examinations. His lawyers were excessively polite, as if they feared that one wrong word would cause him to detonate, but behind their silkiness he saw the contempt that the orderly have for the self-destructive. Still, they did their job well. Eventually he drew a suspended sentence and two years of rehabilitation, after which, they told him, he'd need to move to some other city, find some appropriate line of work, and establish a stable new existence for himself. The rehabilitation people would help him. There would be a probation period of five years when he'd have to report for progress conferences every week.

At the very end one of the rehab officers came to him and told him that his lawyers had filed a petition asking the court to let him have his original face back. That startled him. For a moment Frazier felt like a fugitive again, wearily stumbling from airport to airport, from hotel to hotel.

"No," he said. "I don't think that's a good idea at all. The man who had that face, he's somebody else. I think I'm better off keeping this one. What do you say?"

"I think so, too," said the rehab man.

CHIP RUNNER

*B*yron Preiss, having produced those two magnificent illustrated anthologies, The Planets *and* The Universe, *now turned his attention the
other way, to the world of the infinitely small. The Microverse was his new
project, and I, who had contributed material to both of the previous
books, was invited to write something for this one, too.*

*The scientific part of the story was easy enough to put together:
required by the nature of the book to deal with the universe on the
subatomic level, I rummaged around in Scientific American to see what
the current state of thinking about electrons and protons and such might
be. In the course of my rummaging I stumbled on some information about
microchip technology, and that led me to the fictional component of the
story. All about me in the San Francisco Bay Area are bright boys (and a
few girls) with a deep, all-consuming, and spooky passion for computers. I
happen to know something, also, about the prevalence of such eating
disorders as bulimia and anorexia in Bay Area adolescents—disorders
mainly involving girls, but not exclusively so. Everything fit together
swiftly: an anorexic computer kid who has conceived the wild idea of
entering the subatomic world by starving down to it. The rest was a matter
of orchestrating theme and plot and character and style—of writing the
story, that is. Byron had Ralph McQuarrie illustrate it with a fine, terrifying
painting when he published it in* The Microverse. *Gardner Dozois bought
the story also for* Isaac Asimov's Science Fiction Magazine, *and Don
Wollheim selected it for his annual* World's Best SF *anthology.*

He was fifteen, and looked about ninety, and a frail ninety at that. I knew his mother and his father, separately—they were Silicon Valley people, divorced, very important in their respective companies—and separately they had asked me to try to work with him. His skin was blue-gray and tight, drawn cruelly close over the jutting bones of his face. His eyes were gray, too, and huge, and they lay deep within their sockets. His arms were like sticks. His thin lips were set in an angry grimace.

The chart before me on my desk told me that he was five feet eight inches tall and weighed seventy-one pounds. He was in his third year at one of the best private schools in the Palo Alto district. His IQ was 161. He crackled with intelligence and intensity. That was a novelty for me right at the outset. Most of my patients are depressed, withdrawn, uncertain of themselves, elusive, shy: virtual zombies. He wasn't anything like that. There would be other surprises ahead.

"So you're planning to go into the hardware end of the computer industry, your parents tell me," I began. The usual let's-build-a-relationship procedure.

He blew it away instantly with a single sour glare. "Is that your standard opening? 'Tell me all about your favorite hobby, my boy'? If you don't mind, I'd rather skip all the bullshit, Doctor, and then we can both get out of here faster. You're supposed to ask me about my eating habits."

It amazed me to see him taking control of the session this way within the first thirty seconds. I marveled at how different he was from most of the others, the poor sad wispy creatures who force me to fish for every word.

"Actually, I do enjoy talking about the latest developments in the world of computers, too," I said, still working hard at being genial.

"But my guess is you don't talk about them very often, or you wouldn't call it 'the hardware end.' Or 'the computer industry.' We don't use mundo phrases like those any more." His high thin voice sizzled with barely suppressed rage. "Come on, Doctor. Let's get right down to it. You think I'm anorexic, don't you?"

"Well—"

"I know about anorexia. It's a mental disease of girls, a vanity thing. They starve themselves because they want to look beautiful and they can't bring themselves to realize that they're not too fat. Vanity isn't the issue for me. And I'm not a girl, Doctor. Even you ought to be able to see that right away."

"Timothy—"

"I want to let you know right out front that I don't have an eating disorder and I don't belong in a shrink's office. I know exactly what I'm doing all the time. The only reason I came today is to get my mother off my back, because she's taken it into her head that I'm trying to starve myself to death. She said I had to come here and see you. So I'm here. All right?"

"All right," I said, and stood up. I am a tall man, deep-chested, very broad through the shoulders. I can loom when necessary. A flicker of fear crossed Timothy's face, which was the effect I wanted to produce. When it's appropriate for the therapist to assert authority, simpleminded methods are often the most effective. "Let's talk about eating, Timothy. What did you have for lunch today?"

He shrugged. "A piece of bread. Some lettuce."

"That's all?"

"A glass of water."

"And for breakfast?"

"I don't eat breakfast."

"But you'll have a substantial dinner, won't you?"

"Maybe some fish. Maybe not. I think food is pretty gross."

I nodded. "Could you operate your computer with the power turned off, Timothy?"

"Isn't that a pretty condescending sort of question, Doctor?"

"I suppose it is. Okay, I'll be more direct. Do you think you can run your body without giving it any fuel?"

"My body runs just fine," he said with a defiant edge.

"Does it? What sports do you play?"

"Sports?" It might have been a Martian word.

"You know, the normal weight for someone of your age and height ought to be—"

"There's nothing normal about me, Doctor. Why should my weight be any more normal than the rest of me?"

"It was until last year, apparently. Then you stopped eating. Your family is worried about you, you know."

"I'll be okay," he said sullenly.

"You want to stay healthy, don't you?"

He stared at me for a long chilly moment. There was something close to hatred in his eyes, or so I imagined.

"What I want is to disappear," he said.

⌣

That night I dreamed I was disappearing. I stood naked and alone on a slab of gray metal in the middle of a vast empty plain under a sinister coppery sky, and

I began steadily to shrink. There is often some carryover from the office to a therapist's own unconscious life: we call it countertransference. I grew smaller and smaller. Pores appeared on the surface of the metal slab and widened into jagged craters, and then into great crevices and gullies. A cloud of luminous dust shimmered about my head. Grains of sand, specks, mere motes, now took on the aspect of immense boulders. Down I drifted, gliding into the darkness of a fathomless chasm. Creatures I had not noticed before hovered about me, astonishing monsters, hairy, many-legged. They made menacing gestures, but I slipped away, downward, downward, and they were gone. The air was alive now with vibrating particles, inanimate, furious, that danced in frantic zigzag patterns, veering wildly past me, now and again crashing into me, knocking my breath from me, sending me ricocheting for what seemed like miles. I was floating, spinning, tumbling with no control. Pulsating waves of blinding light pounded me. I was falling into the infinitely small, and there was no halting my descent. I would shrink and shrink and shrink until I slipped through the realm of matter entirely and was lost. A mob of contemptuous glowing things—electrons and protons, maybe, but how could I tell?—crowded close around me, emitting fizzy sparks that seemed to me like jeers and laughter. They told me to keep moving along, to get myself out of their kingdom, or I would meet a terrible death. "To see a world in a grain of sand," Blake wrote. Yes. And Eliot wrote, "I will show you fear in a handful of dust." I went on downward, and downward still. And then I awoke gasping, drenched in sweat, terrified, alone.

✒

Normally the patient is uncommunicative. You interview parents, siblings, teachers, friends, anyone who might provide a clue or an opening wedge. Anorexia is a life-threatening matter. The patients—girls, almost always, or young women in their twenties—have lost all sense of normal body-image and feel none of the food-deprivation prompts that a normal body gives its owner. Food is the enemy. Food must be resisted. They eat only when forced to, and then as little as possible. They are unaware that they are frighteningly gaunt. Strip them and put them in front of a mirror and they will pinch their sagging empty skin to show you imaginary fatty bulges. Sometimes the process of self-skeletonization is impossible to halt, even by therapy. When it reaches a certain point the degree of organic damage becomes irreversible and the death spiral begins.

"He was always tremendously bright," Timothy's mother said. She was fifty, a striking woman, trim, elegant, almost radiant, vice president for finance at one of the biggest Valley companies. I knew her in that familiarly involuted California way: her present husband used to be married to my first wife. "A genius, his teachers all said. But strange, you know? Moody. Dreamy. I used to think he was on drugs, though of course none of the kids do that any more." Timothy was her only child by her first marriage. "It scares me to death to watch him wasting away like that. When I see him I want to take him and shake him and force ice cream down his throat, pasta, milk shakes, anything. And then I want to hold him, and I want to cry."

"You'd think he'd be starting to shave by now," his father said. Technical man, working on nanoengineering projects at the Stanford AI lab. We often played racquetball together. "I was. You too, probably. I got a look at him in the shower, three or four months ago. Hasn't even reached puberty yet. Fifteen and not a hair on him. It's the starvation, isn't it? It's retarding his physical development, right?"

"I keep trying to get him to, like, eat something, anything," his stepbrother Mick said. "He lives with us, you know, on the weekends, and most of the time he's downstairs playing with his computers, but sometimes I can get him to go out with us, and we buy like a chili dog for him, or, you know, a burrito, and he goes, Thank you, thank you, and pretends to eat it, but then he throws it away when he thinks we're not looking. He is *so* weird, you know? And scary. You look at him with those ribs and all, and he's like something out of a horror movie."

"What I want is to disappear," Timothy said.

He came every Tuesday and Thursday for one-hour sessions. There was at the beginning an undertone of hostility and suspicion to everything he said. I asked him, in my layman way, a few things about the latest developments in computers, and he answered me in monosyllables at first, not at all bothering to hide his disdain for my ignorance and my innocence. But now and again some question of mine would catch his interest and he would forget to be irritated, and reply at length, going on and on into realms I could not even pretend to understand. Trying to find things of that sort to ask him seemed my best avenue of approach. But, of course, I knew I was unlikely to achieve anything of therapeutic value if we simply talked about computers for the whole hour.

He was very guarded, as was only to be expected, when I would bring the conversation around to the topic of eating. He made it clear that his eating habits were his own business and he would rather not discuss them with me, or anyone. Yet there was an aggressive glow on his face whenever we spoke of the way he ate that called Kafka's hunger artist to my mind: he seemed proud of his achievements in starvation, even eager to be admired for his skill at shunning food.

Too much directness in the early stages of therapy is generally counterproductive where anorexia is the problem. The patient *loves* her syndrome and resists any therapeutic approach that might deprive her of it. Timothy and I talked mainly of his studies, his classmates, his stepbrothers. Progress was slow, circuitous, agonizing. What was most agonizing was my realization that I didn't have much time. According to the report from his school physician he was already running at dangerously low levels, bones weakening, muscles degenerating, electrolyte balance cockeyed, hormonal systems in disarray. The necessary treatment before long would be hospitalization, not psychotherapy, and it might almost be too late even for that.

He was aware that he was wasting away and in danger. He didn't seem to care.

I let him see that I wasn't going to force anything on him. So far as I was concerned, I told him, he was basically free to starve himself to death if that was what he was really after. But as a psychologist whose role it is to help people, I said, I had some scientific interest in finding out what made him tick—not particularly for his sake, but for the sake of other patients who might be more interested in being helped. He could relate to that. His facial expressions changed. He became less hostile. It was the fifth session now, and I sensed that his armor might be ready to crack. He was starting to think of me not as a member of the enemy but as a neutral observer, a dispassionate investigator. The next step was to make him see me as an ally. You and me, Timothy, standing together against *them*. I told him a few things about myself, my childhood, my troubled adolescence: little nuggets of confidence, offered by way of trade.

"When you disappear," I said finally, "where is it that you want to go?"

The moment was ripe, and the breakthrough went beyond my highest expectations.

"You know what a microchip is?" he asked.

"Sure."

"I go down into them."

Not I *want* to go down into them. But I *do* go down into them.

"Tell me about that," I said.

"The only way you can understand the nature of reality," he said, "is to take a close look at it. To really and truly take a look, you know? Here we have these fantastic chips, a whole processing unit smaller than your little toenail with fifty times the data-handling capacity of the old mainframes. What goes on inside them? I mean, what *really* goes on? I go into them and I look. It's like a trance, you know? You sharpen your concentration and you sharpen it and sharpen it and then you're moving downward, inward, deeper and deeper." He laughed harshly. "You think this is all mystical ka-ka, don't you? Half of you thinks I'm just a crazy kid mouthing off, and the other half thinks here's a kid who's smart as hell, feeding you a line of malarkey to keep you away from the real topic. Right, Doctor? Right?"

"I had a dream a couple of weeks ago about shrinking down into the infinitely small," I said. "A nightmare, really. But a fascinating one. Fascinating and frightening both. I went all the way down to the molecular level, past grains of sand, past bacteria, down to electrons and protons, or what I suppose were electrons and protons."

"What was the light like, where you were?"

"Blinding. It came in pulsing waves."

"What color?"

"Every color all at once," I said.

He stared at me. "No shit!"

"Is that the way it looks for you?"

"Yes. No." He shifted uneasily. "How can I tell if you saw what I saw? But it's a stream of colors, yes. Pulsing. And—all the colors at once, yes, that's how you could describe it—"

"Tell me more."

"More what?"

"When you go downward—tell me what it's like, Timothy."

He gave me his lofty look, his pedagogic look. "You know how small a chip is? A MOSFET, say?"

"MOSFET?"

"Metal-oxide-silicon field-effect-transistor," he said. "The newest ones have a minimum feature size of about a micrometer. Ten to the minus sixth meters. That's a millionth of a meter, all right? Small. It isn't down there on the molecular level, no. You could fit two hundred amoebas into a MOSFET channel one micrometer long. Okay? Okay? Or a whole army of viruses. But it's still plenty small. That's where I go. And run, down the corridors of the chips, with electrons whizzing by me all the time. Of course, I can't see them. Even a lot smaller, you can't see electrons, you can only compute the probabilities of their paths. But you can feel them. *I* can feel them. And I run among them, everywhere, through the corridors, through the channels, past the gates, past the open spaces in the lattice. Getting to know the territory. Feeling at home in it."

"What's an electron like, when you feel it?"

"You dreamed it, you said. You tell me."

"Sparks," I said. "Something fizzy, going by in a blur."

"You read about that somewhere, in one of your journals?"

"It's what I saw," I said. "What I felt, when I had that dream."

"But that's it! That's it exactly!" He was perspiring. His face was flushed. His hands were trembling. His whole body was ablaze with a metabolic fervor I had not previously seen in him. He looked like a skeleton who had just trotted off a basketball court after a hard game. He leaned toward me and said, looking suddenly vulnerable in a way that he had never allowed himself to seem with me before, "Are you sure it was only a dream? Or do you go there, too?"

Kafka had the right idea. What the anorexic wants is to demonstrate a supreme ability. "Look," she says. "I am a special person. I have an extraordinary gift. I am capable of exerting total control over my body. By refusing food I take command of my destiny. I display supreme force of will. Can you achieve that sort of discipline? Can you even begin to understand it? Of course you can't. But I can." The issue isn't really one of worrying about being too fat. That's just a superficial problem. The real issue is one of exhibiting strength of purpose, of proving that you can accomplish something remarkable, of showing the world what a superior person you really are. So what we're dealing with isn't merely a perversely extreme form of dieting. The deeper issue is one of gaining control—over your body, over your life, even over the physical world itself.

He began to look healthier. There was some color in his cheeks now, and he seemed more relaxed, less twitchy. I had the feeling that he was putting on a little weight, although the medical reports I was getting from his school physician didn't confirm that in any significant way—some weeks he'd be up a pound or two, some weeks down, and there was never any net gain. His mother reported that he went through periods when he appeared to be showing a little interest in food, but these were usually followed by periods of rigorous fasting or at best his typical sort of reluctant nibbling. There was nothing in any of this that I could find tremendously encouraging, but I had the definite feeling that I was starting to reach him, that I was beginning to win him back from the brink.

Timothy said, "I have to be weightless in order to get there. I mean, literally weightless. Where I am now, it's only a beginning. I need to lose all the rest."

"Only a beginning," I said, appalled, and jotted a few quick notes.

"I've attained takeoff capability. But I can never get far enough. I run into a barrier on the way down, just as I'm entering the truly structural regions of the chip."

"Yet you do get right into the interior of the chip."

"Into it, yes. But I don't attain the real understanding that I'm after. Perhaps the problem's in the chip itself, not in me. Maybe if I tried a quantum-well chip instead of a MOSFET I'd get where I want to go, but they aren't ready yet, or if they are I don't have any way of getting my hands on one. I want to ride the probability waves, do you see? I want to be small enough to grab hold of an electron and stay with it as it zooms through the lattice." His eyes were blazing. "Try talking about this stuff with my brother. Or anyone. The ones who don't understand think I'm crazy. So do the ones who do."

"You can talk here, Timothy."

"The chip, the integrated circuit—what we're really talking about is transistors, microscopic ones, maybe a billion of them arranged side by side. Silicon or germanium, doped with impurities like boron, arsenic, sometimes other things. On one side are the N-type charge carriers, and the P-type ones are on the other, with an insulating layer between; and when the voltage comes through the gate, the electrons migrate to the P-type side, because it's positively charged, and the holes, the zones of positive charge, go to the N-type side. So your basic logic circuit—" He paused. "You following this?"

"More or less. Tell me about what you feel as you start to go downward into a chip."

⌄

It begins, he said, with a rush, an upward surge of almost ecstatic force: he is not descending but floating. The floor falls away beneath him as he dwindles. Then comes the intensifying of perception, dust motes quivering and twinkling in what had a moment before seemed nothing but empty air, and the light taking on strange new refractions and shimmerings. The solid world begins to alter. Familiar shapes—the table, a chair, the computer before him—vanish as he comes closer to their essence. What he sees now is detailed structure, the intricacy of surfaces: no longer a forest, only trees. Everything is texture and there is no solidity. Wood and metal become strands and webs and mazes. Canyons yawn. Abysses open. He goes inward, drifting, tossed like a feather on the molecular breeze.

It is no simple journey. The world grows grainy. He fights his way through a dust storm of swirling granules of oxygen and nitrogen, an invisible blizzard battering him at every step. Ahead lies the chip he seeks, a magnificent thing, a gleaming radiant Valhalla. He begins to run toward it, heedless of obstacles. Giant rainbows sweep the sky: dizzying floods of pure color, hammering down with a force capable of deflecting the wandering atoms. And then—then—

The chip stands before him like some temple of Zeus rising on the Athenian plain. Giant glowing columns—yawning gateways—dark beckoning corridors—hidden sanctuaries, beyond access, beyond comprehension. It glimmers with light of many colors. A strange swelling music fills the air. He feels like an explorer taking the first stumbling steps into a lost world. And he is still shrinking. The intricacies of the chip swell, surging like metal fungi filling with water after a rain: they spring higher and higher, darkening the sky, concealing it entirely. Another level downward and he is barely large enough to manage the passage across the threshold, but he does, and enters. Here he can move freely. He is in a strange canyon whose silvery walls, riven with vast fissures, rise farther than he can see. He runs. He runs. He has infinite energy; his legs move like springs. Behind him the gates open, close, open, close. Rivers of torrential current surge through, lifting him, carrying him along. He senses, does not see, the vibrating of the atoms of silicon or boron; he senses, does not see, the electrons and the not-electrons flooding past, streaming toward the sides, positive or negative, to which they are inexorably drawn.

But there is more. He runs on and on and on. There is infinitely more, a world within this world, a world that lies at his feet and mocks him with its inaccessibility. It swirls before him, a whirlpool, a maelstrom. He would throw himself into it if he could, but some invisible barrier keeps him from it. This is as far as he can go. This is as much as he can achieve. He yearns to reach out as an electron goes careening past, and pluck it from its path, and stare into its heart. He wants to step inside the atoms and breathe the mysterious air within their boundaries. He longs to look upon their hidden nuclei. He hungers for the sight of mesons, quarks, neutrinos. There is more, always more, an unending series of worlds within worlds, and he is huge, he is impossibly clumsy, he is a lurching reeling mountainous titan, incapable of penetrating beyond this point—

So far, and no farther—

No farther—

He looked up at me from the far side of the desk. Sweat was streaming down his face and his light shirt was clinging to his skin. That sallow cadaverous look was gone from him entirely. He looked transfigured, aflame, throbbing with life: more alive than anyone I had ever seen, or so it seemed to me in that moment. There was a Faustian fire in his look, a world-swallowing urgency. Magellan must have looked that way sometimes, or Newton, or Galileo. And then in a moment more it was gone, and all I saw before me was a miserable scrawny boy, shrunken, feeble, pitifully frail.

I went to talk to a physicist I knew, a friend of Timothy's father who did advanced research at the university. I said nothing about Timothy to him.

"What's a quantum well?" I asked him.

He looked puzzled. "Where'd you hear of those?"

"Someone I know. But I couldn't follow much of what he was saying."

"Extremely small switching device," he said. "Experimental, maybe five, ten years away. Less if we're very lucky. The idea is that you use two different semiconductive materials in a single crystal lattice, a superlattice, something like a three-dimensional checkerboard. Electrons tunneling between squares could be made to perform digital operations at tremendous speeds."

"And how small would this thing be, compared with the sort of transistors they have on chips now?"

"It would be down in the nanometer range," he told me. "That's a billionth of a meter. Smaller than a virus. Getting right down there close to the theoretical limits for semiconductivity. Any smaller and you'll be measuring things in angstroms."

"Angstroms?"

"One ten-billionth of a meter. We measure the diameter of atoms in angstrom units."

"Ah," I said. "All right. Can I ask you something else?"

He looked amused, patient, tolerant.

"Does anyone know much about what an electron looks like?"

"*Looks* like?"

"Its physical appearance. I mean, has any sort of work been done on examining them, maybe even photographing them—"

"You know about the Uncertainty Principle?" he asked.

"Well—not much, really—"

"Electrons are very damned tiny. They've got a mass of—ah—about nine times ten to the minus twenty-eighth grams. We need light in order to see, in any sense of the word. We see by receiving light radiated by an object, or by hitting it with light and getting a reflection. The smallest unit of light we can use, which is the photon, has such a long wavelength that it would completely hide an electron from view, so to speak. And we can't use radiation of shorter wavelength—gammas, let's say, or X rays—for making our measurements, either, because the shorter the wavelength the greater the energy, and so a gamma ray would simply kick any electron we were going to inspect to hell and gone. So we can't 'see' electrons. The very act of determining their position imparts new velocity to them, which alters their position. The best we can do by way of examining electrons is make an enlightened guess, a probabilistic determination, of where they are and how fast they're moving. In a very rough way that's what we mean by the Uncertainty Principle."

"You mean, in order to look an electron in the eye, you'd virtually have to be the size of an electron yourself? Or even smaller?"

He gave me a strange look. "I suppose that question makes sense," he said.

"And I suppose I could answer yes to it. But what the hell are we talking about now?"

✦

I dreamed again that night: a feverish, disjointed dream of gigantic grotesque creatures shining with a fluorescent glow against a sky blacker than any night. They had claws, tentacles, eyes by the dozens. Their swollen asymmetrical bodies were bristling with thick red hairs. Some were clad in thick armor, others were equipped with ugly shining spikes that jutted in rows of ten or twenty from their quivering skins. They were pursuing me through the airless void. Wherever I ran there were more of them, crowding close. Behind them I saw the walls of the cosmos beginning to shiver and flow. The sky itself was dancing. Color was breaking through the blackness: eddying bands of every hue at once, interwoven like great chains. I ran, and I ran, and I ran, but there were monsters on every side, and no escape.

✦

Timothy missed an appointment. For some days now he had been growing more distant, often simply sitting silently, staring at me for the whole hour out of some hermetic sphere of unapproachability. That struck me as nothing more than predictable passive-aggressive resistance, but when he failed to show up at all I was startled: such blatant rebellion wasn't his expectable mode. Some new therapeutic strategies seemed in order: more direct intervention, with me playing the role of a gruff, loving older brother, or perhaps family therapy, or some meetings with his teachers and even classmates. Despite his recent aloofness, I still felt I could get to him in time. But this business of skipping appointments was unacceptable. I phoned his mother the next day, only to learn that he was in the hospital; and after my last patient of the morning I drove across town to see him. The attending physician, a chunky-faced resident, turned frosty when I told him that I was Timothy's therapist, that I had been treating him for anorexia. I didn't need to be telepathic to know that he was thinking, You didn't do much of a job with him, did you? "His parents are with him now," he told me. "Let me find out if they want you to go in. It looks pretty bad."

Actually they were all there, parents, stepparents, the various children by the various second marriages. Timothy seemed to be no more than a waxen doll. They had brought him books, tapes, even a laptop computer, but everything was pushed to the corners of the bed. The shrunken figure in the middle barely raised the level of the coverlet a few inches. They had him on an IV unit, and a whole webwork of other lines and cables ran to him from the array of medical machines surrounding him. His eyes were open, but he seemed to be staring into some other world, perhaps that same world of rampaging bacteria and quivering molecules that had haunted my sleep a few nights before. He seemed perhaps to be smiling.

"He collapsed at school," his mother whispered.

"In the computer lab, no less," said his father with a nervous ratcheting laugh. "He was last conscious about two hours ago, but he wasn't talking coherently."

"He wants to go inside his computer," one of the little boys said. "That's crazy, isn't it?" He might have been seven.

"Timothy's going to die, Timothy's going to die," chanted somebody's daughter, about seven.

"Christopher! Bree! Shhh, both of you!" said about three of the various parents, all at once.

I said, "Has he started to respond to the IV?"

"They don't think so. It's not at all good," his mother said. "He's right on the edge. He lost three pounds this week. We thought he was eating, but he must have been sliding the food into his pocket, or something like that." She shook her head. "You can't be a policeman."

Her eyes were cold. So were her husband's, and even those of the step-parents. Telling me, This is your fault, we counted on you to make him stop starving himself. What could I say? You can only heal the ones you can reach. Timothy had been determined to keep himself beyond my grasp. Still, I felt the keenness of their reproachful anger, and it hurt.

"I've seen worse cases than this come back under medical treatment," I told them. "They'll build up his strength until he's capable of talking with me again. And then I'm certain I'll be able to lick this thing. I was just beginning to break through his defenses when—when he—"

Sure. It costs no more to give them a little optimism. I gave them what I could: experience with other cases of severe food deprivation, positive results following a severe crisis of this nature, et cetera, et cetera, the man of science dipping into his reservoir of experience. They all began to brighten as I spoke. They even managed to convince themselves that a little color was coming into Timothy's cheeks, that he was stirring, that he might soon be regaining consciousness as the machinery surrounding him pumped the nutrients into him that he had so conscientiously forbidden himself to have.

"Look," this one said, or that one. "Look how he's moving his hands! Look how he's breathing. It's better, isn't it!"

I actually began to believe it myself.

But then I heard his dry thin voice echoing in the caverns of my mind. *I can never get far enough. I have to be weightless in order to get there. Where I am now, it's only a beginning. I need to lose all the rest.*

I want to disappear.

✦

That night, a third dream, vivid, precise, concrete. I was falling and running at the same time, my legs pistoning like those of a marathon runner in the twenty-sixth mile, while simultaneously I dropped in free-fall through airless dark toward the silver-black surface of some distant world. And fell and fell and fell, in utter weightlessness, and hit the surface easily and kept on running, moving not forward but downward, the atoms of the ground parting for me as I ran. I became smaller as I descended, and smaller yet, and even smaller, until I was a mere phantom, a running ghost, the bodiless idea of myself. And still I went downward toward the dazzling heart of things, shorn now of all impediments of the flesh.

I phoned the hospital the next morning. Timothy had died a little after dawn.

✦

Did I fail with him? Well, then, I failed. But I think no one could possibly have succeeded. He went where he wanted to go; and so great was the force of his will that any attempts at impeding him must have seemed to him like the mere buzzings of insects, meaningless, insignificant.

So now his purpose is achieved. He has shed his useless husk. He has gone on, floating, running, descending: downward, inward, toward the core, where knowledge is absolute and uncertainty is unknown. He is running among the shining electrons now. He is down there among the angstrom units at last.

T O   T H E

P R O M I S E D

L A N D

$\blacktriangledown$ $\blacktriangledown$ $\blacktriangledown$ $\blacktriangledown$ $\blacktriangledown$ $\blacktriangledown$

As with many of my stories, this one was initiated by a request from outside. Gregory Benford and Martin H. Greenberg were editing an anthology of parallel-world stories called What Might Have Been and invited me to contribute. Each story was supposed to deal with the consequences of altering one major event of world history.

I worked backward to generate my story idea, first imagining a variant world, then trying to explain what alteration of history had summoned it into being. It was autumn of 1987. I had been reading in the history of Imperial Rome—no particular reason, just recreational reading. But Rome was on my mind when the request for a story arrived. What if the Roman Empire hadn't fallen before the barbarians in the fifth century A.D., I asked myself, but somehow had survived and endured, on into our own era?

All right. A good starting point. But to what cause was I going to attribute the fall of Rome?

The rise of Christianity, I told myself. One could put forth all sorts of other reasons, such as the tendency to hire mercenary soldiers of barbarian ancestry for the army; but for the sake of the speculation I stuck with the idea that Christianity, spreading upward until it reached the highest levels of the Empire, had so sapped the imperial virtues of the Romans that they were easy prey to their enemies.

How, in my story, was I going to prevent Christianity from developing and taking over Rome, then?

Well, I could have Jesus die of measles at the age of five. But that was too obvious and too trivial. Besides, how would I ever communicate that to the reader without simply dragging it in by brute force? ("Meanwhile, in Nazareth, the carpenter Joseph and his wife Mary were mourning the death of their little boy Jesus. . . .")

No. Even if Jesus had died in childhood, some other prophet might well have arisen in Palestine and filled his historical niche. I had to take the problem back a stage. If the monotheistic Jews had never reached that part of the Middle East in the first place, there'd have been no Jesus or Jesus-surrogate figure to give rise to the troublesome and ultimately destructive new religion. Well, then, should I suppose the Jews had gone somewhere else when they made their Exodus from Egypt? Have them build their Holy Land down in the Congo, say, safely beyond contact with Rome? Have them sail off to China? Settle in Australia? No, too farfetched, all of them. The best idea was simply to leave them in Egypt, a backwater province of the Roman Empire. The Exodus must have miscarried somehow. Pharaoh's soldiers had caught up with Moses and his people before they reached the Red Sea. So the Philistines had remained in possession of the land that would otherwise become the Kingdom of Israel, and the Jews would continue to be an unimportant sect, serving as scribes and such among the Egyptians.

There it was. No Exodus. Now come up to the otherworld equivalent of our twentieth century. The scene is Egypt; the narrator is a Jewish historian; a new Moses has arisen, planning a very modern kind of Exodus. Everything was in place and I had my story.

Magazine publication rights went to Ellen Datlow for Omni. But, as I sometimes tend to do, I had gotten a little carried away doing the background details, and Ellen asked for four or five pages of cuts. I would sooner sell my cats into slavery than let anybody else cut my work without having the right to the result, but I'm perfectly willing to listen to an editor's suggestions. Ellen, during the course of a very long phone call, pointed out all sorts of places where the story would benefit from a little trimming. Here and there I stuck to my text, but mainly I found myself in agreement with her, and slashed away. I'm glad I did.

When the story appeared later in the Benford-Greenberg anthology, it was illustrated on the book's cover by a moody, brooding painting of the twentieth-century Memphis that I had created. The artist's vision was of something a little like the world of the film Blade Runner, plus sphinxes, Egyptian temples, and a giant pyramid-shaped hotel next to the downtown freeway. A man named Paul Swendsen painted it. I think it's a marvel.

They came for me at high noon, the hour of Apollo, when only a crazy man would want to go out into the desert. I was hard at work and in no mood to be kidnapped. But to get them to listen to reason was like trying to get the Nile to flow south. They weren't reasonable men. Their eyes had a wild metallic sheen, and they held their jaws and mouths clamped in that special constipated way that fanatics like to affect. As they swaggered about in my little cluttered study, poking at the tottering stacks of books and pawing through the manuscript of my nearly finished history of the collapse of the Empire, they were like two immense irresistible forces, as remote and terrifying as gods of old Aiguptos come to life. I felt helpless before them.

The older and taller one called himself Eleazar. To me he was Horus, because of his great hawk nose. He looked like an Aiguptian and he was wearing the white linen robe of an Aiguptian. The other, squat and heavily muscled, with a baboon face worthy of Thoth, told me he was Leonardo di Filippo, which is of course a Roman name, and he had an oily Roman look about him. But I knew he was no more Roman than I am. Nor the other, Aiguptian. Both of them spoke in Hebrew, and with an ease that no outsider could ever attain. These were two Israelites, men of my own obscure tribe. Perhaps di Filippo had been born to a father not of the faith, or perhaps he simply liked to pretend that he was one of the world's masters and not one of God's forgotten people. I will never know.

Eleazar stared at me, at the photograph of me on the jacket of my account of the Wars of the Reunification, and at me again, as though trying to satisfy himself that I really was Nathan ben-Simeon. The picture was fifteen years old. My beard had been black then. He tapped the book and pointed questioningly to me, and I nodded. "Good," he said. He told me to pack a suitcase, fast, as though I were going down to Alexandria for a weekend holiday. "Moshe sent us to get you," he said. "Moshe wants you. Moshe needs you. He has important work for you."

"Moshe?"

"The Leader," Eleazar said, in tones that you would ordinarily reserve for Pharaoh, or perhaps the First Consul. "You don't know anything about him yet, but you will. All of Aiguptos will know him soon. The whole world."

"What does your Moshe want with me?"

"You're going to write an account of the Exodus for him," said di Filippo.

"Ancient history isn't my field," I told him.

"We're not talking about ancient history."

"The Exodus was three thousand years ago, and what can you say about it at this late date except that it's a damned shame that it didn't work out?"

Di Filippo looked blank for a moment. Then he said, "We're not talking about that one. The Exodus is now. It's about to happen, the new one, the real one. That other one long ago was a mistake, a false try."

"And this new Moshe of yours wants to do it all over again? Why? Can't he be satisfied with the first fiasco? Do we need another? Where could we possibly go that would be any better than Aiguptos?"

"You'll see. What Moshe is doing will be the biggest news since the burning bush."

"Enough," Eleazar said. "We ought to be hitting the road. Get your things together, Dr. Ben-Simeon."

So they really meant to take me away. I felt fear and disbelief. Was this actually happening? Could I resist them? I would not let it happen. Time for some show of firmness, I thought. The scholar standing on his authority. Surely they wouldn't attempt force. Whatever else they might be, they were Hebrews. They would respect a scholar. Brusque, crisp, fatherly, the *melamed*, the man of learning. I shook my head. "I'm afraid not. It's simply not possible."

Eleazar made a small gesture with one hand. Di Filippo moved ominously close to me, and his stocky body seemed to expand in a frightening way. "Come on," he said quietly. "We've got a car waiting right outside. It's a four-hour drive, and Moshe said to get you there before sundown."

My sense of helplessness came sweeping back. "Please. I have work to do, and—"

"Screw your work, Professor. Start packing, or we'll take you just as you are."

The street was silent and empty, with that forlorn midday look that makes Menfe seem like an abandoned city when the sun is at its height. I walked between them, a prisoner, trying to remain calm. When I glanced back at the battered old gray facades of the Hebrew Quarter where I had lived all my life, I wondered if I would ever see them again, what would happen to my books, who would preserve my papers. It was like a dream.

A sharp dusty wind was blowing out of the west, reddening the sky so that it seemed that the whole Delta must be aflame, and the noontime heat was enough to kosher a pig. The air smelled of cooking oil, of orange blossoms, of camel dung, of smoke. They had parked on the far side of Amenhotep Plaza just behind the vast ruined statue of Pharaoh, probably in hope of catching the shadows, but at this hour there were no shadows and the car was like an oven. Di Filippo drove; Eleazar sat in back with me. I kept myself completely still, hardly even breathing, as though I could construct a sphere of invulnerability around me by remaining motionless. But when Eleazar offered me a cigarette I snatched it from him with such sudden ferocity that he looked at me in amazement.

We circled the Hippodrome and the Great Basilica where the judges of the Republic hold court, and joined the sparse flow of traffic that was entering the Sacred Way. So our route lay eastward out of the city, across the river and into the desert. I asked no questions. I was frightened, numbed, angry, and—I suppose—to some degree curious. It was a paralyzing combination of emotions. So I sat quietly, praying only that these men and their Leader would be done with me in short order and return me to my home and my studies.

"This filthy city," Eleazar muttered. "How I despise it!"

In fact, it had always seemed grand and beautiful to me: a measure of my assimilation, some might say, though inwardly I feel very much the Israelite, not in the least Aiguptian. Even a Hebrew must concede that Menfe is one of the world's great cities. It is the most majestic city this side of Roma, so everyone says, and so I am willing to believe, though I have never been beyond the borders of the province of Aiguptos in my life.

The splendid old temples of the Sacred Way went by on both sides, the Temple of Isis and the Temple of Sarapis and the Temple of Jupiter Ammon and all the rest, fifty or a hundred of them on that great boulevard whose pavements are lined with sphinxes and bulls: Dagon's temple, Mithra's and Cybele's, Baal's, Marduk's, Zarathustra's, a temple for every god and goddess anyone had ever imagined, except, of course, the One True God, whom we few Hebrews prefer to worship in our private way behind the walls of our own Quarter. The gods of all the Earth have washed up here in Menfe like so much Nile mud. Of course, hardly anyone takes them very seriously these days, even the supposed faithful. It would be folly to pretend that this is a religious age. Mithra's shrine still gets some worshipers, and of course that of Jupiter Ammon. People go to those to do business, to see their friends, maybe to ask favors on high. The rest of the temples might as well be museums. No one goes into them except Roman and Japanese tourists. Yet here they still stand, many of them thousands of years old. Nothing is ever thrown away in the land of Misr.

"Look at them," Eleazar said scornfully as we passed the huge half-ruined Sarapion. "I hate the sight of them. The foolishness! The waste! And all of them built with our forefathers' sweat."

In fact there was little truth in that. Perhaps in the time of the first Moshe we did indeed labor to build the Great Pyramids for Pharaoh, as it says in

Scripture. But there could never have been enough of us to add up to much of a work force. Even now, after a sojourn along the Nile that has lasted some four thousand years, there are only about twenty thousand of us. Lost in a sea of ten million Aiguptians, we are, and the Aiguptians themselves are lost in an ocean of Romans and imitation Romans, so we are a minority within a minority, an ethnographic curiosity, a drop in the vast ocean of humanity, an odd and trivial sect, insignificant except to ourselves.

The temple district dropped away behind us and we moved out across the long slim shining arch of the Caesar Augustus Bridge, and into the teeming suburb of Hikuptah on the eastern bank of the river, with its leather and gold bazaars, its myriad coffeehouses, its tangle of medieval alleys. Then Hikuptah dissolved into a wilderness of fig trees and canebrake, and we entered a transitional zone of olive orchards and date palms; and then abruptly we came to the place where the land changes from black to red and nothing grows. At once the awful barrenness and solitude of the place struck me like a tangible force. It was a fearful land, stark and empty, a dead place full of terrible ghosts. The sun was a scourge above us. I thought we would bake; and when the car's engine once or twice began to cough and sputter, I knew from the grim look on Eleazar's face that we would surely perish if we suffered a breakdown. Di Filippo drove in a hunched, intense way, saying nothing, gripping the steering stick with an unbending rigidity that spoke of great uneasiness. Eleazar, too, was quiet. Neither of them had said much since our departure from Menfe, nor I, but now in that hot harsh land they fell utterly silent, and the three of us neither spoke nor moved, as though the car had become our tomb. We labored onward, slowly, uncertain of engine, with windborne sand whistling all about us out of the west. In the great heat every breath was a struggle. My clothing clung to my skin. The road was fine for a while, broad and straight and well-paved, but then it narrowed, and finally it was nothing more than a potholed white ribbon half covered with drifts. They were better at highway maintenance in the days of Imperial Roma. But that was long ago. This is the era of the Consuls, and things go to hell in the hinterlands and no one cares.

"Do you know what route we're taking, Doctor?" Eleazar asked, breaking the taut silence at last when we were an hour or so into that bleak and miserable desert.

My throat was dry as strips of leather that have been hanging in the sun a thousand years, and I had trouble getting words out. "I think we're heading east," I said finally.

"East, yes. It happens that we're traveling the same route that the first Moshe took when he tried to lead our people out of bondage. Toward the Bitter

Lakes, and the Red Sea. Where Pharaoh's army caught up with us and ten thousand innocent people drowned."

There was crackling fury in his voice, as though that were something that had happened just the other day, as though he had learned of it not from the Book of Aaron but from this morning's newspaper. And he gave me a fiery glance, as if I had had some complicity in our people's long captivity among the Aiguptians and some responsibility for the ghastly failure of that ancient attempt to escape. I flinched before that fierce gaze of his and looked away.

"Do you care, Dr. Ben-Simeon? That they followed us and drove us into the sea? That half our nation, or more, perished in a single day in horrible fear and panic? That young mothers with babies in their arms were crushed beneath the wheels of Pharaoh's chariots?"

"It was all so long ago," I said lamely.

As the words left my lips, I knew how foolish they were. It had not been my intent to minimize the debacle of the Exodus. I had meant only that the great disaster to our people was sealed over by thousands of years of healing, that although crushed and dispirited and horribly reduced in numbers we had somehow gone on from that point, we had survived, we had endured, the survivors of the catastrophe had made new lives for themselves along the Nile under the rule of Pharaoh and under the Greeks who had conquered Pharaoh and the Romans who had conquered the Greeks. We still survived, did we not, here in the long sleepy decadence of the Imperium, the Pax Romana, when even the everlasting Empire had crumbled and the absurd and pathetic Second Republic ruled the world?

But to Eleazar it was as if I had spat upon the scrolls of the Law. "*It was all so long ago,*" he repeated, savagely mocking me. "And therefore we should forget? Shall we forget the Patriarchs, too? Shall we forget the Covenant? Is Aiguptos the land that the Lord meant us to inhabit? Were we chosen by Him to be set above all the peoples of the Earth, or were we meant to be the slaves of Pharaoh forever?"

"I was trying only to say—"

What I had been trying to say didn't interest him. His eyes were shining, his face was flushed, a vein stood out astonishingly on his broad forehead. "We were meant for greatness. The Lord God gave His blessing to Abraham, and said that He would multiply Abraham's seed as the stars of the heaven, and as the sand that is upon the seashore. And the seed of Abraham shall possess the gate of his enemies. And in his seed shall all the nations of the earth be blessed. Have you ever heard those words before, Dr. Ben-Simeon? And do you think they signified anything, or were they only the boasting of noisy little desert chieftains? No, I tell you we were meant for greatness, we were meant to shake the world: and we have been too long in recovering from the catastrophe at the Red Sea. An hour, two hours later and all of history would have been different. We would have crossed into Sinai and the fertile lands beyond; we would have built our kingdom there as the Covenant decreed; we would have made the world listen to the thunder of our God's voice; and today the entire world would look up to us as it has looked to the Romans these past twenty centuries. But it is not too late, even now. A new Moshe is in the land, and he will succeed where the first one failed. And we *will* come forth from Aiguptos, Dr. Ben-Simeon, and we *will* have what is rightfully ours. At last, Dr. Ben-Simeon. At long last."

He sat back, sweating, trembling, ashen, seemingly exhausted by his own eloquence. I didn't attempt to reply. Against such force of conviction there is no victory; and what could I possibly have gained, in any case, by contesting his vision of Israel triumphant? Let him have his faith; let him have his new Moshe; let him have his dream of Israel triumphant. I myself had a different vision, less romantic, more cynical. I could easily imagine, yes, the children of Israel escaping from their bondage under Pharaoh long ago and crossing into Sinai, and going on beyond it into sweet and fertile Palestina. But what then? Global dominion? What was there in our history, in our character, our national temperament, that would lead us on to that? Preaching Jehovah to the Gentiles? Yes, but would they listen, would they understand? No. No. We would always have been a special people, I suspected, a small and stubborn tribe, clinging to our knowledge of the One God amidst the hordes who needed to believe in many. We might have conquered Palestina, we might have taken Syria, too, even spread out a little farther around the perimeter of the Great Sea; but still there would have been the Assyrians to contend with, and the Babylonians, and the Persians, and Alexander's Greeks, and the Romans, especially the stolid dull invincible Romans, whose destiny it was to engulf every corner of the planet and carve it into Roman provinces full of Roman highways and Roman bridges and Roman whorehouses. Instead of living in Aiguptos under the modern Pharaoh, who is the puppet of the First Consul who has replaced the Emperor of Roma, we would be living in Palestina under the rule of some minor procurator or proconsul or prefect, and we would speak some sort of Greek or Latin to our masters instead of Aiguptian, and everything else would be the same. But I said none of this to Eleazar. He and I were different sorts of men. His soul and his vision were greater and grander than mine. Also, his strength was superior and his temper was shorter. I might take issue with his theories of history, and he might hit me in his rage; and which of us then would be the wiser?

The sun slipped away behind us and the wind shifted, hurling sand now against our front windows instead of the rear. I saw the dark shadows of mountains to the south and ahead of us, far across the strait that separates Aiguptos from the Sinai wilderness. It was late afternoon, almost evening. Suddenly there was a village ahead of us, springing up out of nowhere in the nothingness.

It was more a camp, really, than a village. I saw a few dozen lopsided tin huts and some buildings that were even more modest, strung together of reed latticework. Carbide lamps glowed here and there. There were three or four dilapidated trucks and a handful of battered old cars scattered haphazardly about. A well had been driven in the center of things and a crazy network of aboveground conduits ran off in all directions. In back of the central area I saw one building much larger than the others, a big tin-roofed shed or lean-to with other trucks parked in front of it.

I had arrived at the secret headquarters of some underground movement, yet no attempt had been made to disguise or defend it. Situating it in this forlorn zone was defense enough: no one in his right mind would come out here without good reason. The patrols of the Pharaonic police did not extend beyond the cities, and the civic officers of the Republic certainly had no cause to go sniffing around in these remote and distasteful parts. We live in a decadent era, but a placid and trusting one.

Eleazar, jumping out of the car, beckoned to me, and I hobbled after him. After hours without a break in the close quarters of the car, I was creaky and wilted and the reek of gasoline fumes had left me nauseated. My clothes were acrid and stiff from my own dried sweat. The evening coolness had not yet descended on the desert, and the air was hot and close. To my nostrils it had a strange vacant quality, the myriad stinks of the city being absent. There was something almost frightening about that. It was like the sort of air the Moon might have, if the Moon had air.

"This place is called Beth Israel," Eleazar said. "It is the capital of our nation."

Not only was I among fanatics; I had fallen in with madmen who suffered the delusion of grandeur. Or does one quality go automatically with the other?

A woman wearing man's clothing came trotting up to us. She was young and very tall, with broad shoulders and a great mass of dark thick hair tumbling to her shoulders and eyes as bright as Eleazar's. She had Eleazar's hawk's nose, too, but somehow it made her look all the more striking. "My sister Miriam," he said. "She'll see that you get settled. In the morning I'll show you around and explain your duties to you."

And he walked away, leaving me with her.

She was formidable. I would have carried my bag, but she insisted, and set out at such a brisk pace toward the perimeter of the settlement that I was hard put to keep up with her. A hut all my own was ready for me, somewhat apart from everything else. It had a cot, a desk and typewriter, a washbasin, and a single dangling lamp. There was a cupboard for my things. Miriam unpacked for me, setting my little stock of fresh clothing on the shelves and putting the few books I had brought with me beside the cot. Then she filled the basin with water and told me to get undressed. I stared at her, astounded. "You can't wear what you've got on now," she said. "While you're having a bath, I'll take your things to be washed." She might have waited outside, but no. She stood there, arms folded, looking impatient. I shrugged and gave her my shirt, but she wanted everything else, too. This was new to me, her straightforwardness, her absolute indifference to modesty. There have been few women in my life and none since the death of my wife; how could I strip myself before this one, who was young enough to be my daughter? But she insisted. In the end I gave her every stitch—my nakedness did not seem to matter to her at all—and while she was gone I sponged myself clean and hastily put on fresh clothing, so she would not see me naked again. But she was gone a long time. When she returned, she brought with her a tray, my dinner, a bowl of porridge, some stewed lamb, a little flask of pale red wine. Then I was left alone. Night had fallen now, desert night, awesomely black with the stars burning like beacons. When I had eaten I stepped outside my hut and stood in the darkness. It scarcely seemed real to me, that I had been snatched away like this, that I was in this alien place rather than in my familiar cluttered little flat in the Hebrew Quarter of Menfe. But it was peaceful here. Lights glimmered in the distance. I heard laughter, the pleasant sound of a kithara, someone singing an old Hebrew song in a deep, rich voice. Even in my bewildering captivity I felt a strange tranquility descending on me. I knew that I was in the presence of a true community, albeit one dedicated to some bizarre goal beyond my comprehension. If I had dared, I would have gone out among them and made myself known to them; but I was a stranger, and afraid. For a long while I stood in the darkness, listening, wondering. When the night grew cold, I went inside. I lay awake until dawn, or so it seemed, gripped by that icy clarity that will not admit sleep; and yet I must have slept at least a little while, for there were fragments of dreams drifting in my mind in the morning, images of horsemen and chariots, of men with spears, of a great black-bearded angry Moshe holding aloft the tablets of the Law.

A small girl shyly brought me breakfast. Afterward, Eleazar came to me. In the confusion of yesterday I had not taken note of how overwhelming his physical presence was: he had seemed merely big, but now I realized that he was a giant, taller than I by a span or more, and probably sixty minas heavier. His features were ruddy, and a vast tangle of dark thick curls spilled down to his shoulders. He had put aside his Aiguptian robes this morning and was dressed Roman style: an open-throated white shirt, a pair of khaki trousers.

"You know," he said, "we don't have any doubt at all that you're the right man for this job. Moshe and I have discussed your books many times. We agree that no one has a firmer grasp of the logic of history, of the inevitability of the processes that flow from the nature of human beings."

To this I offered no response.

"I know how annoyed you must be at being grabbed like this. But you are essential to us; and we knew you'd never have come of your own free will."

"Essential?"

"Great movements need great chroniclers."

"And the nature of your movement—"

"Come," he said.

He led me through the village. But it was a remarkably uninformative walk. His manner was mechanical and aloof, as if he were following a preprogrammed route, and whenever I asked a direct question he was vague or even evasive. The big tin-roofed building in the center of things was the factory where the work of the Exodus was being carried out, he said, but my request for further explanation went unanswered. He showed me the house of Moshe, a crude shack like all the others. Of Moshe himself, though, I saw nothing. "You will meet him at a later time," Eleazar said. He pointed out another shack that was the synagogue, another that was the library, another that housed the electrical generator. When I asked to visit the library, he merely shrugged and kept walking. On the far side of it I saw a second group of crude houses on the lower slope of a fair-sized hill that I had not noticed the night before. "We have a population of five hundred," Eleazar told me. More than I had imagined.

"All Hebrews?" I asked.

"What do you think?"

It surprised me that so many of us could have migrated to this desert settlement without my hearing about it. Of course, I have led a secluded scholarly life, but still, five hundred Israelites is one out of every forty of us. That is a major movement of population, for us. And not one of them someone of my acquaintance, or even a friend of a friend? Apparently not. Well, perhaps most of the settlers of Beth Israel had come from the Hebrew community in Alexandria, which has relatively little contact with those of us who live in Menfe. Certainly I recognized no one as I walked through the village.

From time to time Eleazar made veiled references to the Exodus that was soon to come, but there was no real information in anything he said; it was as if the Exodus were merely some bright toy that he enjoyed cupping in his hands, and I was allowed from time to time to see its gleam but not its form. There was no use in questioning him. He simply walked along, looming high above me, telling me only what he wished to tell. There was an unstated grandiosity to the whole mysterious project that puzzled and irritated me. If they wanted to leave Aiguptos, why not simply leave? The borders weren't guarded. We had ceased to be the slaves of Pharaoh two thousand years ago. Eleazar and his friends could settle in Palestina or Syria or anyplace else they liked, even Gallia, even Hispania, even Nuova Roma far across the ocean, where they could try to convert the redskinned men to Israel. The Republic wouldn't care where a few wild-eyed Hebrews chose to go. So why all this pomp and mystery, why such an air of conspiratorial secrecy? Were these people up to something truly extraordinary? Or, I wondered, were they simply crazy?

That afternoon Miriam brought back my clothes, washed and ironed, and offered to introduce me to some of her friends. We went down into the village, which was quiet. Almost everyone is at work, Miriam explained. But there were a few young men and women on the porch of one of the buildings: this is Deborah, she said, and this is Ruth, and Reuben, and Isaac, and Joseph, and Saul. They greeted me with great respect, even reverence, but almost immediately went back to their animated conversation as if they had forgotten I was there. Joseph, who was dark and sleek and slim, treated Miriam with an ease bordering on intimacy, finishing her sentences for her, once or twice touching her lightly on the arm to underscore some point he was making. I found that unexpectedly disturbing. Was he her husband? Her lover? Why did it matter to me? They were both young enough to be my children. Great God, why did it matter?

Unexpectedly and with amazing swiftness my attitude toward my captors began to change. Certainly I had had a troublesome introduction to them—the lofty pomposity of Eleazar, the brutal directness of di Filippo, the ruthless way I had been seized and taken to this place—but as I met others I found them generally charming, graceful, courteous, appealing. Prisoner though I might be, I felt myself quickly being drawn into sympathy with them.

In the first two days I was allowed to discover nothing except that these were busy, determined folk, most of them young and evidently all of them intelligent, working with tremendous zeal on some colossal undertaking that they were convinced would shake the world. They were passionate in the way that I imagined the Hebrews of that first and ill-starred Exodus had been: contemptuous of the sterile and alien society within which they were confined, striving toward freedom and the light, struggling to bring a new world into being. But how? By what means? I was sure that they would tell me more in their own good time; and I knew also that that time had not yet come. They were watching me, testing me, making certain I could be trusted with their secret.

Whatever it was, that immense surprise that they meant to spring upon the Republic, I hoped there was substance to it, and I wished them well with it. I am old and perhaps timid, but far from conservative: change is the way of growth, and the Empire, with which I include the Republic that ostensibly has replaced it, is the enemy of change. For twenty centuries it had strangled mankind in its benign grip. The civilization that it had constructed was hollow, the life that most of us led was a meaningless trek that had neither values nor purpose. By its shrewd acceptance and absorption of the alien gods and alien ways of the peoples it had conquered, the Empire had flattened everything into shapelessness. The grand and useless temples of the Sacred Way, where all gods were equal and equally insignificant, were the best symbol of that. By worshiping everyone indiscriminately, the rulers of the Imperium had turned the sacred into a mere instrument of governance. And ultimately their cynicism had come to pervade everything: the relationship between man and the Divine was destroyed, so that we had nothing left to venerate except the status quo itself, the holy stability of the world government. I had felt for years that the time was long overdue for some great revolution, in which all fixed, fast-frozen relationships, with their train of ancient and venerable prejudices and opinions, would be swept away—a time when all that is solid melts into air, all that is holy is profaned, and man is at last compelled to face with sober senses his real conditions of life. Was that what the Exodus somehow would bring? Profoundly did I hope so. For the Empire was defunct and didn't know it. Like some immense dead beast, it lay upon the soul of humanity, smothering it beneath itself: a beast so huge that its limbs hadn't yet heard the news of its own death.

On the third day di Filippo knocked on my door and said, "The Leader will see you now."

The interior of Moshe's dwelling was not very different from mine: a simple cot, one stark lamp, a basin, a cupboard. But he had shelf upon shelf overflowing with books. Moshe himself was smaller than I expected, a short, compact man who nevertheless radiated tremendous, even invincible, force. I hardly needed to be told that he was Eleazar's older brother. He had Eleazar's wild mop of curly hair and his ferocious eyes and his savage beak of a nose; but because he was so much shorter than Eleazar his power was more tightly compressed, and seemed to be in peril of immediate eruption. He seemed poised, controlled, an austere and frightening figure.

But he greeted me warmly and apologized for the rudeness of my capture. Then he indicated a well-worn row of my books on his shelves. "You understand the Republic better than anyone, Dr. Ben-Simeon," he said. "How corrupt and weak it is behind its facade of universal love and brotherhood. How deleterious its influence has been. How feeble its power. The world is waiting now for something completely new: but what will it be? Is that not the question, Dr. Ben-Simeon? *What will it be?*"

It was a pat, obviously preconceived speech, which no doubt he had carefully constructed for the sake of impressing me and enlisting me in his cause, whatever that cause might be. Yet he did impress me with his passion and his conviction. He spoke for some time, rehearsing themes and arguments that were long familiar to me. He saw the Roman Imperium, as I did, as something dead and beyond revival, though still moving with eerie momentum. Call it an Empire, call it a Republic, it was still a world state, and that was an unsustainable concept in the modern era. The revival of local nationalisms that had been thought extinct for thousands of years was impossible to ignore. Roman tolerance for local customs, religions, languages, and rulers had been a shrewd policy for centuries, but it carried with it the seeds of destruction for the Imperium. Too much of the world now had only the barest knowledge of the two official languages of Latin and Greek, and transacted its business in a hodgepodge of other tongues. In the old Imperial heartland itself, Latin had been allowed to break down into regional dialects that were in fact separate languages—Gallian, Hispanian, Lusitanian, and all the rest. Even the Romans at Roma no longer spoke true Latin, Moshe pointed out, but rather the simple, melodic, lazy thing called Roman, which might be suitable for singing opera but lacked the precision that was needed for government. As for the religious diversity that the Romans in their easy way had encouraged, it had led not to the perpetuation of faiths but to the erosion of them. Scarcely anyone except the most primitive peoples and a few unimportant encapsulated minorities like us believed anything at all; nearly everyone gave lip service instead to the local version of the official Roman pantheon and any other gods that struck their fancy, but a society that tolerates all gods really has no faith in any. And a society without faith is one without a rudder: without even a course.

These things Moshe saw, as I did, not as signs of vitality and diversity but as confirmation of the imminence of the end. This time there would be no Reunification. When the Empire had fallen, conservative forces had been able to erect the Republic in its place, but that was a trick that could be managed only once. Now a period of flames unmatched in history was surely coming as the sundered segments of the old Imperium warred against one another.

"And this Exodus of yours?" I said finally, when I dared to break his flow. "What is that, and what does it have to do with what we've been talking about?"

"The end is near," Moshe said. "We must not allow ourselves to be destroyed in the chaos that will follow the fall of the Republic, for we are the instruments of God's great plan, and it is essential that we survive. Come: let me show you something."

We stepped outside. Immediately an antiquated and unreliable-looking car pulled up, with the dark slender boy Joseph at the stick. Moshe indicated that I should get in, and we set out on a rough track that skirted the village and entered the open desert just behind the hill that cut the settlement in half. For perhaps ten minutes we drove north through a district of low rocky dunes. Then we circled another steep hill, and on its farther side, where the land flattened out into a broad plain, I was astonished to see a weird tubular thing of gleaming silvery metal rising on half a dozen frail spidery legs to a height of some thirty cubits in the midst of a hubbub of machinery, wires, and busy workers.

My first thought was that it was an idol of some sort, a Moloch, a Baal, and I had a sudden vision of the people of Beth Israel coating their bodies in pigs' grease and dancing naked around it to the sound of drums and tambourines. But that was foolishness.

"What is it?" I asked. "A sculpture of some sort?"

Moshe looked disgusted. "Is that what you think? It is a vessel, a holy ark."

I stared at him.

"It is the prototype for our starship," Moshe said, and his voice took on an intensity that cut me like a blade. "Into the heavens is where we will go, in ships like these—toward God, toward His brightness—and there we will settle, in the new Eden that awaits us on another world, until it is time for us to return to Earth."

"The new Eden—on another world—" My voice was faint with disbelief. A ship to sail between the stars, as the Roman skyships travel between continents? Was such a thing possible? Hadn't the Romans themselves, those most able of engineers, discussed the question of space travel years ago and concluded that there was no practical way of achieving it and nothing to gain from it even if there was? Space was inhospitable and unattainable: everyone knew that. I shook my head. "What other world? Where?"

Grandly he ignored my question. "Our finest minds have been at work for five years on what you see here. Now the time to test it has come. First a short journey, only to the Moon and back—and then deeper into the heavens, to the new world that the Lord has pledged to reveal to me, so that the pioneers may plant the settlement. And after that—ship after ship, one shining ark after another, until every Israelite in the land of Aiguptos has crossed over into the promised land—" His eyes were glowing. "Here is our Exodus at last! What do you think, Dr. Ben-Simeon? What do you think?"

⌣

I thought it was madness of the most terrifying kind, and Moshe a lunatic who was leading his people—and mine—into cataclysmic disaster. It was a dream, a wild feverish fantasy. I would have preferred it if he had said they were going to worship this thing with incense and cymbals, than that they were going to ride it into the darkness of space. But Moshe stood before me so hot with blazing fervor that to say anything like that to him was unthinkable. He took me by the arm and led me, virtually dragged me, down the slope into the work area. Close up, the starship seemed huge and yet at the same time painfully flimsy. He slapped its flank, and I heard a hollow ring. Thick gray cables ran everywhere, and subordinate machines of a nature that I could not even begin to comprehend. Fierce-eyed young men and women raced to and fro, carrying pieces of equipment and shouting instructions to one another as if striving to outdo one another in their dedication to their tasks. Moshe scrambled up a narrow ladder, gesturing for me to follow him. We entered a kind of cabin at the starship's narrow tip; in that cramped and all-but-airless room I saw screens, dials, more cables, things beyond my understanding. Below the cabin a spiral staircase led to a chamber where the crew could sleep, and below that, said Moshe, were the rockets that would send the ark of the Exodus into the heavens.

"And will it work?" I managed finally to ask.

"There is no doubt of it," Moshe said. "Our finest minds have produced what you see here."

He introduced me to some of them. The oldest appeared to be about twenty-five. Curiously, none of them had Moshe's radiant look of fanatic zeal; they were calm, even businesslike, imbued with a deep and quiet confidence. Three or four of them took turns explaining the theory of the vessel to me, its means of propulsion, its scheme of guidance, its method of escaping the pull of the Earth's inner force. My head began to ache. But yet I was swept under by the power of their conviction. They spoke of "combustion," of "acceleration," of "neutralizing the planet-force." They talked of "mass" and "thrust" and "freedom velocity." I barely understood a tenth of what they were saying, or a hundredth; but I formed the image of a giant bursting his bonds and leaping triumphantly from the ground to soar joyously into unknown realms. Why not? Why not? All it took was the right fuel and a controlled explosion, they said. Kick the Earth hard enough and you must go upward with equal force. Yes. Why not? Within minutes I began to think that this insane starship might well be able to rise on a burst of flame and fly off into the darkness of the heavens. By the time Moshe ushered me out of the ship, nearly an hour later, I did not question that at all.

Joseph drove me back to the settlement alone. The last I saw of Moshe he was standing at the hatch of his starship, peering impatiently toward the fierce midday sky.

My task, I already knew, but which Eleazar told me again later that dazzling and bewildering day, was to write a chronicle of all that had been accomplished thus far in this hidden outpost of Israel and all that would be achieved in the apocalyptic days to come. I protested mildly that they would be better off finding some journalist, preferably with a background in science; but no, they didn't want a journalist, Eleazar said, they wanted someone with a deep understanding of the long currents of history. What they wanted from me, I realized, was a work that was not merely journalism and not merely history, but one that had the profundity and eternal power of Scripture. What they wanted from me was the Book of the Exodus—that is, the Book of the Second Moshe.

❤

They gave me a little office in their library building and opened their archive to me. I was shown Moshe's early visionary essays, his letters to intimate friends, his sketches and manifestos insisting on the need for an Exodus far more ambitious than anything his ancient namesake could have imagined. I saw how he had assembled—secretly and with some uneasiness, for he knew that what he was doing was profoundly subversive and would bring the fullest wrath of the Republic down on him if he should be discovered—his cadre of young revolutionary scientists. I read furious memoranda from Eleazar, taking issue with his older brother's fantastic scheme; and then I saw Eleazar gradually converting himself to the cause in letter after letter until he became more of a zealot than Moshe himself. I studied technical papers until my eyes grew bleary, not only those of Moshe and his associates but some by Romans nearly a century old, and even one by a Teuton, arguing for the historical necessity of space exploration and for its technical feasibility. I learned something more of the theory of the starship's design and functioning.

My guide to all these documents was Miriam. We worked side by side, together in one small room. Her youth, her beauty, the dark glint of her eyes, made me tremble. Often I longed to reach toward her, to touch her arm, her shoulder, her cheek. But I was too timid. I feared that she would react with laughter, with anger, with disdain, even with revulsion. Certainly it was an aging man's fear of rejection that inspired such caution. But also I reminded myself that she was the sister of those two fiery prophets, and that the blood that flowed in her veins must be as hot as theirs. What I feared was being scalded by her touch.

The day Moshe chose for the starship's flight was the twenty-third of Tishri, the joyful holiday of Simchat Torah in the year 5730 by our calendar—that is, 2723 of the Roman reckoning. It was a brilliant early-autumn day, very dry, the sky cloudless, the sun still in its fullest blaze of heat. For three days preparations had been going on around the clock at the launch site, and it had been closed to all but the inner circle of scientists; but now, at dawn, the whole village went out by truck and car and some even on foot to attend the great event.

The cables and support machinery had been cleared away. The starship stood by itself, solitary and somehow vulnerable-looking, in the center of the sandy clearing, a shining upright needle, slender, fragile. The area was roped off; we would watch from a distance, so that the searing flames of the engines would not harm us.

A crew of three men and two women had been selected: Judith, who was one of the rocket scientists, and Leonardo di Filippo, and Miriam's friend Joseph, and a woman named Sarah whom I had never seen before. The fifth, of course, was Moshe. This was his chariot; this was his adventure, his dream; he must surely be the one to ride at the helm as the *Exodus* made its first leap toward the stars.

One by one they emerged from the blockhouse that was the control center for the flight. Moshe was the last. We watched in total silence, not a murmur, barely daring to draw breath. The five of them wore uniforms of white satin, brilliant in the morning sun, and curious glass helmets like diver's bowls over their faces. They walked toward the ship, mounted the ladder, turned one by one to look back at us, and went up inside. Moshe hesitated for a moment before entering, as if in prayer, or perhaps simply to savor the fullness of his joy.

Then there was a long wait, interminable, unendurable. It might have been twenty minutes; it might have been an hour. No doubt there was some last-minute checking to do, or perhaps even some technical hitch. Still we maintained our silence. We could have been statues. After a time I saw Eleazar turn worriedly toward Miriam, and they conferred in whispers. Then he trotted across to the blockhouse and went inside. Five minutes went by, ten; then he emerged, smiling, nodding, and returned to Miriam's side. Still nothing happened. We continued to wait.

Suddenly there was a sound like a thundercrack and a noise like the roaring of a thousand great bulls, and black smoke billowed from the ground around the ship, and there were flashes of dazzling red flame. The *Exodus* rose a few feet from the ground. There it hovered as though magically suspended, for what seemed to be forever.

And then it rose, jerkily at first, more smoothly then, and soared on a stunningly swift ascent toward the dazzling blue vault of the sky. I gasped; I grunted as though I had been struck; and I began to cheer. Tears of wonder and excitement flowed freely along my cheeks. All about me, people were cheering also, and weeping, and waving their arms, and the rocket, roaring, rose and rose, so high now that we could scarcely see it against the brilliance of the sky.

We were still cheering when a white flare of unbearable light, like a second sun more brilliant than the first, burst into the air high above us and struck us with overmastering force, making us drop to our knees in pain and terror, crying out, covering our faces with our hands.

When I dared look again, finally, that terrible point of ferocious illumination was gone, and in its place was a ghastly streak of black smoke that smeared halfway across the sky, trickling away in a dying trail somewhere to the north. I could not see the rocket. I could not hear the rocket.

"It's gone!" someone cried.

"Moshe! Moshe!"

"It blew up! I saw it!"

"Moshe!"

"Judith—" said a quieter voice behind me.

I was too stunned to cry out. But all around me there was a steadily rising sound of horror and despair, which began as a low choking wail and mounted until it was a shriek of the greatest intensity coming from hundreds of throats at once. There was fearful panic, universal hysteria. People were running about as if they had gone mad. Some were rolling on the ground, some were beating their hands against the sand. "Moshe!" they were screaming. "Moshe! Moshe! Moshe!"

I looked toward Eleazar. He was white-faced, and his eyes seemed wild. Yet even as I looked toward him I saw him draw in his breath, raise his hands, step forward to call for attention. Immediately all eyes turned toward him. He swelled until he appeared to be five cubits high.

"Where's the ship?" someone cried. "Where's Moshe?"

And Eleazar said, in a voice like the trumpet of the Lord, "He was the Son of God, and God has called him home."

Screams. Wails. Hysterical shrieks.

"Dead!" came the cry. "Moshe is dead!"

"He will live forever," Eleazar boomed.

"The Son of God!" came the cry, from three voices, five, a dozen. "The Son of God!"

I was aware of Miriam at my side, warm, pressing close, her arm through mine, her soft breast against my ribs, her lips at my ear. "You must write the book," she whispered, and her voice held a terrible urgency. "*His* book, you must write. So that this day will never be forgotten. So that he will live forever."

"Yes," I heard myself saying. "Yes."

In that moment of frenzy and terror I felt myself sway like a tree of the shore that has been assailed by the flooding of the Nile; and I was uprooted and swept away. The fireball of the *Exodus* blazed in my soul like a second sun indeed, with a brightness that could never fade. And I knew that I was engulfed, that I was conquered, that I would remain here to write and preach, that I would forge the gospel of the new Moshe in the smithy of my soul and send the word to all the lands. Out of these five today would come rebirth; and to the peoples of the Republic we would bring the message for which they had waited so long in their barrenness and their confusion, and when it came they would throw off the shackles of their masters; and out of the death of the Imperium would come a new order of things. Were there other worlds, and could we dwell upon them? Who could say? But there was a new truth that we could teach, which was the truth of the second Moshe who had given his life so that we might go to the stars, and I would not let that new truth die. I would write, and others of my people would go forth and carry the word that I had written to all the lands, and the lands would be changed. And someday, who knew how soon, we would build a new ship, and another, and another, and they would carry us from this world of woe. God had sent His Son, and God had called Him home, and one day we would all follow him on wings of flame, up from the land of bondage into the heavens where He dwells eternally.

THE ASENION
SOLUTION

This one was done basically as a lark. But there was a gesture of reconciliation buried in it, putting to an end a strange episode of unpleasantness between two basically even-tempered and good-natured people who happened to be very old friends.

The year 1989 marked Isaac Asimov's fiftieth anniversary as a professional writer. One day in the summer of 1988 I got a letter from the anthologist Martin H. Greenberg, who regarded Isaac virtually as his second father. Very quietly Marty was going to assemble an anthology called Foundation's Friends, *made up of original stories based on themes made famous by Isaac; it would be presented to Isaac in October of 1989 during the course of the festivities commemorating his dazzling fifty-year career. Did I want to take part? Marty asked. Don't be silly, I said.*

And sat down and wrote "The Asenion Solution" in September of 1988—coincidentally, the same month when I had agreed to collaborate with Isaac on novel-length versions of his famous story "Nightfall" and two other classic novelettes.

The character I call "Ichabod Asenion" is only partially based on the real-world individual known as Isaac Asimov. Asenion is brilliant, yes, and lives in a Manhattan penthouse. True of Asimov on both counts. But Asenion is described as ascetic and reclusive, two words that I suspect have never been applied, even in jest, to Isaac Asimov. Asenion is a physicist; Isaac's scientific field was biochemistry before he deviated into writing books. And Asenion is a fanatic horticulturist. Asimov—I'm only guessing here, but with some confidence—probably didnn't know one plant from the next, living as he did high above the streets of Manhattan, and he certainly didn't have time to tend to a greenhouse, writing as he did three or four books a week. Asenion, then, is a kind of fantasy Asimov, a figure made up of equal parts of the real thing and of pure fiction.

The odd surname, though, is Asimovian, as a few insiders know.

THE ASENION SOLUTION

"Asenion" was a famous typographical error for "Asimov," going back close to fifty years when he was still writing fan letters to science-fiction magazines. He took a lot of kidding about it, but remained genial enough to use the name himself in his Robot series. I figured it was good for one more go-round here.

And the gesture of reconciliation I was talking about a few paragraphs back?

It has to do with the plutonium-186 plot thread.

I knew Isaac Asimov since 1955 or so, and in all that time there has been only one disharmonious moment in what was otherwise a relationship of affection and mutual respect. It occurred when, at a science-fiction convention in New York about 1970, I made a joking reference to the imaginary isotope plutonium-186 during a panel discussion where Isaac was in the audience. I knew, of course, that a heavy element like plutonium couldn't have so light an isotope as that—that was the whole point of my remark. Isaac guffawed when he heard me speak of it. And went home and started writing a short story for an anthology I was editing, a story in which he intended to come up with some plausible situation in which plutonium-186 could actually exist.

And so he did; but one thing led to another, and the "story" turned into his first science-fiction novel in a decade and a half, The Gods Themselves. *Well and good: I had inspired his return to the field with a remarkable work. The only trouble was that Isaac thought I was serious about plutonium-186, and took an extremely public, though gentle and loving, way of berating me for my scientific ignorance: he dedicated the book to me with a long introduction thanking me because my demonstration of scientific illiteracy at that convention had unwittingly inspired his novel.*

I wasn't amused. I told him so. He was surprised by my irritation, and told me so. We went around and around on it for a little while, and then each of us came to understand the other one's point. The offending dedication was removed from future editions of the book, and the whole squabble was dropped. And we went back to being good friends and high admirers of each other's work and intelligence, and eventually, through a set of circumstances nobody could have predicted, we even wound up becoming collaborators. But all these years I continued to suspect that Isaac still felt guilty/defensive/touchy/uneasy/wronged by our plutonium-186 contretemps.

So when the time came for me to write a story for a festschrift commemorating his fifty years as a professional author, I thought I'd send

Isaac a signal that I carried no lingering bitterness over the misunderstanding, that in fact the whole thing now seemed to me a trifle that could be chuckled over. Thus I wrote "The Asenion Solution," yoking together Isaac's celebrated 1948 "thiotimoline" article with good old PU-186, by way of telling him that I bore no lasting resentment. It was fun to do, and, I hope, forever obliterated the one blemish on our long and harmonious friendship.

Foundation's Friends duly appeared on the anniversary of the beginning of Isaac's career and—though I wasn't at the publication party, three thousand miles from where I live—I hear that Isaac was greatly delighted by the book. Ray Bradbury did a preface for the book and the contributors included Frederik Pohl, Robert Sheckley, Harry Harrison, Hal Clement, and a lot of other fine writers who had terrific fun running their own variations on Isaac's classic themes. The clever jacket painting shows the various writers in the guise of robots—I'm the world-weary one in the middle, leaning on the bar, and that's Isaac himself in the samurai helmet down at lower right.

One thing I didn't expect, for a story that was just a prank. David Garnett chose it as one of the best science-fiction stories of 1989 for The Orbit Science Fiction Yearbook, the new British anthology that he edits. You never can tell about such things.

Fletcher stared bleakly at the small mounds of gray metal that were visible behind the thick window of the storage chamber.

"Plutonium-186," he muttered. "Nonsense! Absolute nonsense!"

"Dangerous nonsense, Lew," said Jesse Hammond, standing behind him. "Catastrophic nonsense."

Fletcher nodded. The very phrase "plutonium-186" sounded like gibberish to him. There wasn't supposed to be any such substance. Plutonium-186 was an impossible isotope, too light by a good fifty neutrons. Or a bad fifty neutrons, considering the risks the stuff was creating as it piled up here and there around the world. But the fact that it was theoretically impossible for plutonium-186 to exist did not change the other, and uglier, fact that he was looking at three kilograms of it right this minute. Or that as the quantity of plutonium-186 in the world continued to increase, so did the chance of an uncontrollable nuclear reaction leading to an atomic holocaust.

"Look at the morning reports," Fletcher said, waving a sheaf of faxprints at Hammond. "Thirteen grams more turned up at the nucleonics lab of Accra University. Fifty grams in Geneva. Twenty milligrams in—well, that little doesn't matter. But Chicago, Jesse, Chicago—three hundred grams in a single chunk!"

"Christmas presents from the Devil," Hammond muttered.

"Not the Devil, no. Just decent serious-minded scientific folk who happen to live in another universe where plutonium-186 is not only possible but also perfectly harmless. And who are so fascinated by the idea that *we're* fascinated by it that they keep on shipping the stuff to us in wholesale lots! What are we going to do with it all, Jesse? What in God's name are we going to do with it all?"

Raymond Nikolaus looked up from his desk at the far side of the room.

"Wrap it up in shiny red-and-green paper and ship it right back to them?" he suggested.

Fletcher laughed hollowly. "Very funny, Raymond. Very very funny."

He began to pace the room. In the silence the clicking of his shoes against the flagstone floor seemed to him like the ticking of a detonating device, growing louder, louder, louder. . . .

He—they, all of them—had been wrestling with the problem all year, with an increasing sense of futility. The plutonium-186 had begun mysteriously to appear in laboratories all over the world—wherever supplies of one of the two elements with equivalent atomic weights existed. Gram for gram, atom for atom, the matching elements disappeared just as mysteriously: equal quantities of tungsten-186 or osmium-186.

Where was the tungsten and osmium going? Where was the plutonium coming from? Above all, how was it possible for a plutonium isotope whose atoms had only 92 neutrons in its nucleus to exist even for a fraction of an instant? Plutonium was one of the heavier chemical elements, with a whopping 94 protons in the nucleus of each of its atoms. The closest thing to a stable isotope of plutonium was plutonium-244, in which 150 neutrons held those 94 protons together; and even at that, plutonium-244 had an inevitable habit of breaking down in radioactive decay, with a half-life of some 76 million years. Atoms of plutonium-186, if they could exist at all, would come dramatically apart in very much less than one 76-millionth of a second.

But the stuff that was turning up in the chemistry labs to replace the tungsten-186 and the osmium-186 had an atomic number of 94, no question about that. And element 94 was plutonium. That couldn't be disputed either. The defining characteristic of plutonium was the presence of 94 protons in its nucleus. If that was the count, plutonium was what that element had to be.

This impossibly light isotope of plutonium, this plutonium-186, had another impossible characteristic about it: not only was it stable, it was so completely stable that it wasn't even radioactive. It just sat there, looking exceedingly unmysterious, not even deigning to emit a smidgeon of energy. At least, not when first tested. But a second test revealed positron emission, which a third baffled look confirmed. The trouble was that the third measurement showed an even higher level of radioactivity than the second one. The fourth was higher than the third. And so on and so on.

Nobody had ever heard of any element, of whatever atomic number or weight, that started off stable and then began to demonstrate a steadily increasing intensity of radioactivity. No one knew what was likely to happen, either, if the process continued unchecked, but the possibilities seemed pretty explosive. The best suggestion anyone had was to turn it to powder and mix it with nonradioactive tungsten. That worked for a little while, until the tungsten turned radioactive, too. After that graphite was used, with somewhat better results, to damp down the strange element's output of energy. There were no explosions. But more and more plutonium-186 kept arriving.

The only explanation that made any sense—and it did not make *very* much sense—was that it was coming from some unknown and perhaps even unknowable place, some sort of parallel universe, where the laws of nature were different and the binding forces of the atom were so much more powerful that plutonium-186 could be a stable isotope.

Why they were sending odd lumps of plutonium-186 here was something that no one could begin to guess. An even more important question was how they could be made to stop doing it. The radioactive breakdown of the plutonium-186 would eventually transform it into ordinary osmium or tungsten, but the twenty positrons that each plutonium nucleus emitted in the course of that process encountered and annihilated an equal number of electrons. Our universe could afford to lose twenty electrons here and there, no doubt. It could probably afford to go on losing electrons at a constant rate for an astonishingly long time without noticing much difference. But sooner or later the shift toward an overall positive charge that this electron loss created would create grave and perhaps incalculable problems of symmetry and energy conservation. Would the equilibrium of the universe break down? Would nuclear interactions begin to intensify? Would the stars—even the Sun—erupt into supernovas?

"This can't go on," Fletcher said gloomily.

Hammond gave him a sour look. "So? We've been saying that for six months now."

"It's time to do something. They keep shipping us more and more and more, and we don't have any idea how to go about telling them to cut it out."

"We don't even have any idea whether they really exist," Raymond Niklaus put in.

"Right now that doesn't matter. What matters is that the stuff is arriving constantly, and the more of it we have, the more dangerous it is. We don't have the foggiest idea of how to shut off the shipments. So we've got to find some way to get rid of it as it comes in."

"And what do you have in mind, pray tell?" Hammond asked.

Fletcher said, glaring at his colleague in a way that conveyed the fact that he would brook no opposition, "I'm going to talk to Asenion."

Hammond guffawed. "Asenion? You're crazy!"

"No. *He* is. But he's the only person who can help us."

It was a sad case, the Asenion story, poignant and almost incomprehensible. One of the finest minds atomic physics had ever known, a man to rank with Rutherford, Bohr, Heisenberg, Fermi, Meitner. A Harvard degree at twelve, his doctorate from MIT five years later, after which he had poured forth a dazzling flow of technical papers that probed the deepest mysteries of the nuclear binding forces. As the twenty-first century entered its closing decades he had seemed poised to solve once and for all the eternal riddles of the universe. And then, at the age of twenty-eight, without having given the slightest warning, he walked away from the whole thing.

"I have lost interest," he declared. "Physics is no longer of any importance to me. Why should I concern myself with these issues of the way in which matter is constructed? How tiresome it all is! When one looks at the Parthenon, does one care what the columns are made of, or what sort of scaffolding was needed to put them in place? That the Parthenon exists, and is sublimely beautiful, is all that should interest us. So, too, with the universe. I see the universe, and it is beautiful and perfect. Why should I pry into the nature of its scaffolding? Why should anyone?"

And with that he resigned his professorship, burned his papers, and retreated to the thirty-third floor of an apartment building on Manhattan's West Side, where he built an elaborate laboratory-greenhouse in which he intended to conduct experiments in advanced horticulture.

"Bromeliads," said Asenion. "I will create hybrid bromeliads. Bromeliads will be the essence and center of my life from now on."

Romelmeyer, who had been Asenion's mentor at Harvard, attributed his apparent breakdown to overwork, and thought that he would snap back in six or eight months. Jantzen, who had had the rare privilege of being the first to read his astonishing dissertation at MIT, took an equally sympathetic position, arguing that Asenion must have come to some terrifying impasse in his work that had compelled him to retreat dramatically from the brink of madness. "Perhaps he found himself looking right into an abyss of inconsistencies when he thought he was about to find the ultimate answers," Jantzen suggested. "What else could he do but run? But he won't run for long. It isn't in his nature."

Burkhardt, of Cal Tech, whose own work had been carried out in the sphere that Asenion was later to make his own, agreed with Jantzen's analysis. "He must have hit something really dark and hairy. But he'll wake up one morning with the solution in his head, and it'll be good-bye horticulture for him. He'll turn out a paper by noon that will revolutionize everything we think we know about nuclear physics, and that'll be that."

But Jesse Hammond, who had played tennis with Asenion every morning for the last two years of his career as a physicist, took a less charitable position. "He's gone nuts," Hammond said. "He's flipped out altogether, and he's never going to get himself together again."

"You think?" said Lew Fletcher, who had been almost as close to Asenion as Hammond, but who was no tennis player.

Hammond smiled. "No doubt of it. I began noticing a weird look in his eyes starting just about two years back. And then his playing started to turn weird, too. He'd serve and not even look where he was serving. He'd double-fault without even caring. And you know what else? He didn't challenge me on a single out-of-bounds call the whole year. That was the key thing. Used to be, he'd fight me every call. Now he just didn't seem to care. He just let everything go by. He was completely indifferent. I said to myself, This guy must be flipping out."

"Or working on some problem that seems more important to him than tennis."

"Same thing," said Hammond. "No, Lew, I tell you—he's gone completely unglued. And nothing's going to glue him again."

That conversation had taken place almost a year ago. Nothing had happened in the interim to change anyone's opinion. The astounding arrival of plutonium-186 in the world had not brought forth any comment from Asenion's Manhattan penthouse. The sudden solemn discussions of fantastic things like parallel universes by otherwise reputable physicists had apparently not aroused him either. He remained closeted with his bromeliads, high above the streets of Manhattan.

Well, maybe he *is* crazy, Fletcher thought. But his mind can't have shorted out entirely. And he might just have an idea or two left in him—

❤

Asenion said, "Well, you don't look a whole lot older, do you?"

Fletcher felt himself reddening. "Jesus, Ike, it's only been eighteen months since we last saw each other!"

"Is that all?" Asenion said indifferently. "It feels like a lot more to me."

He managed a thin, remote smile. He didn't look very interested in Fletcher or in whatever it was that had brought Fletcher to his secluded eyrie.

Asenion had always been an odd one, of course—aloof, mysterious, with a faint but unmistakable air of superiority about him that nearly everyone found instantly irritating. Of course, he *was* superior. But he had made sure that he let you know it, and never seemed to care that others found the trait less than endearing.

He appeared more remote than ever now, stranger and more alien. Outwardly he had not changed at all: the same slender, debonair figure, surprisingly handsome, even striking. Though rumor had it that he had not left his penthouse in more than a year, there was no trace of indoor pallor about him. His skin still had its rich deep olive coloring, almost swarthy, a Mediterranean tone. His hair, thick and dark, tumbled down rakishly over his broad forehead. But there was something different about his dark, gleaming eyes. The old Asenion, however preoccupied he might have been with some abstruse problem of advanced physics, had nearly always had a playful sparkle in his eyes, a kind of amiable devilish glint. This man, this horticultural recluse, wore a different expression altogether—ascetic, mist-shrouded, *absent*. His gaze was as bright as ever, but the brightness was a cold one that seemed to come from some far-off star.

Fletcher said, "The reason I've come here—"

"We can go into all that later, can't we, Lew? First come into the greenhouse with me. There's something I want to show you. Nobody else has seen it yet, in fact."

"Well, if you—"

"Insist, yes. Come. I promise you, it's extraordinary."

He turned and led the way through the intricate pathways of the apartment. The sprawling many-roomed penthouse was furnished in the most offhand way, cheap student furniture badly cared for. Cats wandered everywhere, five, six, eight of them, sharpening their claws on the upholstery, prowling in empty closets whose doors stood ajar, peering down from the tops of bookcases containing jumbled heaps of coverless volumes. There was a rank smell of cat urine in the air.

But then suddenly Asenion turned a corridor and Fletcher, following just behind, found himself staring into what could have been an altogether different world. They had reached the entrance to the spectacular glass-walled extension that had been wrapped like an observation deck around the entire summit of the building. Beyond, dimly visible inside, Fletcher could see hundreds or perhaps thousands of strange-looking plants, some hanging from the ceiling, some mounted along the sides of wooden pillars, some rising in stepped array on benches, some growing out of beds set in the floor.

Asenion briskly tapped out the security-combination code on a diamond-shaped keyboard mounted in the wall, and the glass door slid silently back. A blast of warm humid air came forth.

"Quickly!" he said. "Inside!"

It was like stepping straight into the Amazon jungle. In place of the harsh, dry atmosphere of a Manhattan apartment in midwinter there was, abruptly, the dense moist sweet closeness of the tropics, enfolding them like folds of wet fabric. Fletcher almost expected to hear parrots screeching overhead.

And the plants! The bizarre plants, clinging to every surface, filling every available square inch!

Most of them followed the same general pattern, rosettes of broad shining strap-shaped leaves radiating outward from a central cup-shaped structure deep enough to hold several ounces of water. But beyond that basic area of similarity they differed wildly from one another. Some were tiny, some were colossal. Some were marked with blazing stripes of yellow and red and purple that ran the length of their thick, succulent leaves. Some were mottled with fierce blotches of shimmering, assertive, bewilderingly complicated combinations of color. Some, whose leaves were green, were a fiery scarlet or crimson, or a somber, mysterious blue, at the place where the leaves came together to form the cup. Some were armed with formidable teeth and looked ready to feed on unwary visitors. Some were topped with gaudy spikes of strangely shaped brilliant-hued flowers taller than a man, which sprang like radiant spears from their centers.

Everything glistened. Everything seemed poised for violent, explosive growth. The scene was alien and terrifying. It was like looking into a vast congregation of hungry monsters. Fletcher had to remind himself that these were merely plants, hothouse specimens that probably wouldn't last half an hour in the urban environment outside.

"These are bromeliads," Asenion said, shaping the word sensuously in his throat as though it were the finest word any language had ever produced. "Tropical plants, mainly. South and Central America is where most of them live. They tend to cling to trees, growing high up in the forks of branches, mainly. Some live at ground level, though. Such as the bromeliad you know best, which is the pineapple. But there are hundreds of others in this room. Thousands. And this is the humid room, where I keep the guzmanias and the vrieseas and some of the aechmeas. As we go around, I'll show you the tillandsias—they like it a lot drier—and the terrestrial ones, the hechtias and the dyckias, and then over on the far side—"

"Ike," Fletcher said quietly.

"You know I've never liked that name."

"I'm sorry. I forgot." That was a lie. Asenion's given name was Ichabod. Neither Fletcher nor anyone Fletcher knew had ever been able to bring himself to call him that. "Look, I think what you've got here is wonderful. Absolutely wonderful. But I don't want to intrude on your time, and there's a very serious problem I need to discuss with—"

"First the plants," Asenion said. "Indulge me." His eyes were glowing. In the half-light of the greenhouse he looked like a jungle creature himself, exotic, weird. Without a moment's hesitation, he pranced off down the aisle toward a group of oversize bromeliads near the outer wall. Willy-nilly, Fletcher followed.

Asenion gestured grandly.

"Here it is! Do you see? *Aechmea asenionii!* Discovered in northwestern Brazil two years ago—I sponsored the expedition myself—of course, I never expected them to name it for me, but you know how these things sometimes happen—"

Fletcher stared. The plant was a giant among giants, easily two meters across from leaf tip to leaf tip. Its dark green leaves were banded with jagged pale scrawls that looked like the hieroglyphs of some lost race. Out of the central cup, which was the size of a man's head and deep enough to drown rabbits in, rose the strangest flower Fletcher ever hoped to see, a thick yellow stalk of immense length from which sprang something like a cluster of black thunderbolts tipped with ominous red globes like dangling moons. A pervasive odor of rotting flesh came from it.

"The only specimen in North America!" Asenion cried. "Perhaps one of six or seven in the world. And I've succeeded in inducing it to bloom. There'll be seed, Lew, and perhaps there'll be offsets as well—I'll be able to propagate it, and cross it with others—can you imagine it crossed with *Aechmea chantinii*, Fletcher? Or perhaps an interspecific hybrid? With *Neoregelia carcharadon*, say? No. Of course you can't imagine it. What am I saying? But it would be spectacular beyond belief. Take my word for it."

"I have no doubt."

"It's a privilege, seeing this plant in bloom. But there are others here you must see, too. The puyas—the pitcairnias—there's a clump of Dyckia marnier-lapostollei in the next room that you wouldn't believe—"

He bubbled with boyish enthusiasm. Fletcher forced himself to be patient. There was no help for it: he would simply have to take the complete tour.

It went on for what seemed like hours, as Asenion led him frantically from one peculiar plant to another, in room after room. Some were actually quite beautiful, Fletcher had to admit. Others seemed excessively flamboyant, or grotesque, or incomprehensibly ordinary to his untutored eye, or downright grotesque. What struck him most forcefully of all was the depth of Asenion's obsession. Nothing in the universe seemed to matter to him except this horde of exotic plants. He had given himself up totally to the strange world he had created here.

But at last even Asenion's manic energies seemed to flag. The pace had been merciless, and both he and Fletcher, drenched with sweat and gasping in the heat, paused for breath in a section of the greenhouse occupied by small gray gnarly plants that seemed to have no roots, and were held to the wall by barely visible wires.

Abruptly Asenion said, "All right. You aren't interested anyway. Tell me what you came here to ask me, and then get on your way. I have all sorts of things to do this afternoon."

"It's about plutonium-186," Fletcher began.

"Don't be idiotic. That's not a legitimate isotope. It can't possibly exist."

"I know," Fletcher said. "But it does."

Quickly, almost desperately, he outlined the whole fantastic story for the young physicist-turned-botanist. The mysterious substitution of a strange element for tungsten or osmium in various laboratories, the tests indicating that its atomic number was that of plutonium but its atomic weight was far too low, the absurd but necessary theory that the stuff was a gift from some parallel universe and—finally—the fact that the new element, stable when it first arrived, rapidly began to undergo radioactive decay in a startlingly accelerative way.

Asenion's saturnine face was a study in changing emotions as Fletcher spoke. He seemed bored and irritated at first, then scornful, then, perhaps, furious; but not a word did he utter, and gradually the fury ebbed, turning to distant curiosity and then, finally, a kind of fascination. Or so Fletcher thought. He realized that he might be altogether wrong in his interpretations of what was going on in the unique, mercurial mind of the other man.

When Fletcher fell silent Asenion said, "What are you most afraid of? Critical mass? Or cumulative electron loss?"

"We've dealt with the critical-mass problem by powdering the stuff, shielding it in graphite, and scattering it in low concentrations to fifty different storage points. But it keeps on coming in—they love to send it to us, it seems. And the thought that every atom of it is giving off positrons that go around looking for electrons to annihilate—" Fletcher shrugged. "On a small scale it's a useful energy pump, I suppose, tungsten swapped for plutonium with energy gained in each cycle. But on a large scale, as we continue to transfer electrons from our universe to theirs—"

"Yes," Asenion said.

"So we need a way to dispose of—"

"Yes." He looked at his watch. "Where are you staying while you're in town, Fletcher?"

"The Faculty Club, as usual."

"Good. I've got some crosses to make and I don't want to wait any longer, on account of possible pollen contamination. Go over to the Club and keep yourself amused for a few hours. Take a shower. God knows you need one: you smell like something out of the jungle. Relax, have a drink, come back at five o'clock. We can talk about this again then." He shook his head. "Plutonium-186! What lunacy! It offends me just to say it out loud. It's like saying—saying—well, *Billbergia yukonensis*, or *Tillandsia bostoniae*. Do you know what I mean? No. No. Of course you don't." He waved his hands. "Out! Come back at five!"

◄

It was a long afternoon for Fletcher. He phoned his wife, he phoned Jesse Hammond at the laboratory, he phoned an old friend and made a date for dinner. He showered and changed. He had a drink in the ornate lounge on the Fifth Avenue side of the Club.

But his mood was grim, and not merely because Hammond had told him that another four kilograms of plutonium-186 had been reported from various regions that morning. Asenion's madness oppressed him.

There was nothing wrong with an interest in plants, of course. Fletcher kept a philodendron and something else, whose name he could never remember, in his own office. But to immerse yourself in one highly specialized field of botany with such intensity—it seemed sheer lunacy. No, Fletcher decided, even that was all right, difficult as it was for him to understand why anyone would want to spend his whole life cloistered with a bunch of eerie plants. What was hard for him to forgive was Asenion's renunciation of physics. A mind like that—the breadth of its vision—the insight Asenion had had into the greatest of mysteries—dammit, Fletcher thought, he had owed it to the world to stick to it! And instead, to walk away from everything, to hole himself up in a cage of glass—

Hammond's right, Fletcher told himself. Asenion really is crazy.

But it was useless to fret about it. Asenion was not the first supergenius to snap under contemplation of the Ultimate. His withdrawal from physics, Fletcher said sternly to himself, was a matter between Asenion and the universe. All that concerned Fletcher was getting Asenion's solution to the plutonium-186 problem; and then the poor man could be left with his bromeliads in peace.

About half past four Fletcher set out by cab to battle the traffic the short distance uptown to Asenion's place.

Luck was with him. He arrived at ten of five. Asenion's house robot greeted him solemnly and invited him to wait. "The master is in the greenhouse," the robot declared. "He will be with you when he has completed the pollination."

Fletcher waited. And waited and waited.

Geniuses, he thought bitterly. Pains in the neck, all of them. Pains in the—

Just then the robot reappeared. It was half past six. All was blackness outside the window. Fletcher's dinner date was for seven. He would never make it.

"The master will see you now," said the robot.

◆

Asenion looked limp and weary, as though he had spent the entire afternoon smashing up boulders. But the formidable edge seemed gone from him, too. He greeted Fletcher with a pleasant enough smile, offered a word or two of almost-apology for his tardiness, and even had the robot bring Fletcher a sherry. It wasn't very good sherry, but to get anything at all to drink in a teetotaler's house was a blessing, Fletcher figured.

Asenion waited until Fletcher had had a few sips. Then he said, "I have your answer."

"I knew you would."

There was a long silence.

"Thiotimoline," said Asenion finally.

"Thiotimoline?"

"Absolutely. Endochronic disposal. It's the only way. And, as you'll see, it's a *necessary* way."

Fletcher took a hasty gulp of the sherry. Even when he was in a relatively mellow mood, it appeared, Asenion was maddening. And mad. What was this new craziness now? Thiotimoline? How could that preposterous substance, as insane in its way as plutonium-186, have any bearing on the problem?

Asenion said, "I take it you know the special properties of thiotimoline?"

"Of course. Its molecule is distorted into adjacent temporal dimensions. Extends into the future, and, I think, into the past. Thiotimoline powder will dissolve in water one second *before* the water is added."

"Exactly," Asenion said. "And if the water isn't added, it'll go looking for it. In the future."

"What does this have to do with—"

"Look here," said Asenion. He drew a scrap of paper from his shirt pocket. "You want to get rid of something. You put it in this container here. You surround the container with a shell made of polymerized thiotimoline. You surround the shell with a water tank that will deliver water to the thiotimoline on a timed basis, and you set your timer so that the water is due to arrive a few seconds from now. But at the last moment the timing device withholds the water."

Fletcher stared at the younger man in awe.

Asenion said, "The water is always about to arrive, but never quite does. The thiotimoline making up the plastic shell is pulled forward one second into the future to encounter the water. The water has a high probability of being there, but not quite high enough. It's actually another second away from delivery, and always will be. The thiotimoline gets dragged further and further into the future. The world goes forward into the future at a rate of one second per second, but the thiotimoline's velocity is essentially infinite. And, of course, it carries with it the inner container, too."

"In which we have put our surplus plutonium-186."

"Or anything else you want to dispose of," said Asenion.

Fletcher felt dizzy. "Which will travel on into the future at an infinite rate—"

"Yes. And because the rate is infinite, the problem of the breakdown of thiotimoline into its stable isochronic form, which has hampered most time-transport experiments, isn't an issue. Something traveling through time at an infinite velocity isn't subject to little limitations of that kind. It'll simply keep going until it can't go any farther."

"But how does sending it into the future solve the problem?" Fletcher asked. "The plutonium-186 still stays in our universe, even if we've bumped it away from our immediate temporal vicinity. The electron loss continues. Maybe even gets worse, under temporal acceleration. We still haven't dealt with the fundamental—"

"You never were much of a thinker, were you, Fletcher?" said Asenion quietly, almost gently. But the savage contempt in his eyes had the force of a sun going nova.

"I do my best. But I don't see—"

Asenion sighed. "The thiotimoline will chase the water in the outer container to the end of time, carrying with it the plutonium in the inner container. To the end of time. *Literally*."

"And?"

"What happens at the end of time, Fletcher?"

"Why—absolute entropy—the heat death of the universe—"

"Precisely. The Final Entropic Solution. All molecules equally distributed throughout space. There will be no further place for the water-seeking thiotimoline to go. The end of the line is the end of the line. It, and the plutonium it's hauling with it, and the water it's trying to catch up with, will all plunge together over the entropic brink into anti-time."

"Anti-time," said Fletcher in a leaden voice. "Anti-time?"

"Naturally. Into the moment before the creation of the universe. Everything is in stasis. Zero time, infinite temperature. All the universal mass contained in a single incomprehensible body. Then the thiotimoline and the plutonium and the water arrive." Asenion's eyes were radiant. His face was flushed. He waved his scrap of paper around as though it were the scripture of some new creed. "There will be a tremendous explosion. A Big Bang, so to speak. The beginning of all things. You—or should I say I?—will be responsible for the birth of the universe."

Fletcher, stunned, said after a moment, "Are you serious?"

"I am never anything but serious. You have your solution. Pack up your plutonium and send it on its way. No matter how many shipments you make, they'll all arrive at the same instant. And with the same effect. You have no choice, you know. The plutonium *must* be disposed of. And—" His eyes twinkled with some of the old Asenion playfulness. "The universe *must* be created, or else how will any of us get to be where we are? And this is how it was done. *Will* be done. Inevitable, ineluctable, unavoidable, mandatory. Yes? You see?"

"Well, no. yes. Maybe. That is, I think I do," said Fletcher, as if in a daze.

"Good. Even if you don't, you will."

"I'll need—to talk to the others—"

"Of course you will. That's how you people do things. That's why I'm here and you're there." Asenion shrugged. "Well, no hurry about it. Create the universe tomorrow, create it the week after next, what's the difference? It'll get done sooner or later. It has to, because it already has been done. You see?"

"Yes. Of course. Of—course. And now—if you'll excuse me—" Fletcher murmured. "I—ah—have a dinner appointment in a little while—"

"That can wait, too, can't it?" said Asenion, smiling with sudden surprising amiability. He seemed genuinely glad to have been of assistance. "There's something I forgot to show you this afternoon. A remarkable plant, possibly unique—a nidularium, it is, Brazilian, not even named yet, as a matter of fact—just coming into bloom. And this one—wait till you see it, Fletcher, wait till you see it—"

A SLEEP AND
A FORGETTING

The Benford-Greenberg alternate-universe anthology, What Might Have Been, was followed by a second volume of similar stories. The first had concentrated on alterations of a single historical event; this one dealt with changes in the lives of great history-making individuals. Again I was invited to contribute; and the individual I chose to write about was Genghis Khan.

His name, of course, has come to be used as an archetype of the monstrous looting-and-plundering barbarian chieftain. Indeed, he probably wasn't a nice sort of person, and it's certainly all right with me that the twentieth century, amidst its Hitlers and Stalins and Khomeinis and such, hasn't had to deal with Genghis Khan as well. But the historical truth is that he was not merely an invincible conqueror but a complex and intelligent leader, an empire-builder who followed a distinctive plan of conquest that not only created a vast realm but also brought governmental order where only chaos had been. I'd like to think that he had more in common with Augustus Caesar or Alexander the Great than he did with the classic butchers of history.

But the Mongol empire's limitations—the limitations inherent in having a family-controlled elite of nomadic horsemen trying to rule vast bureaucratic states—eventually set bounds on the ambitions of Genghis and his descendants. What, I asked myself, would the world have been like if Genghis Khan, that singular man of formidable drive and energy, hadn't been raised as a Mongol nomad at all, but as a civilized city-dweller—as a Byzantine Christian, say? That was the point from which this story appeared. Alice Turner bought it for Playboy, and Don Wollheim chose it for his best-of-the-year anthology, an honor in which, as I've already pointed out, I always take special pleasure.

"Channeling?" I said. "For Christ's sake, Joe! You brought me all the way down here for dumb bullshit like that?"

"This isn't channeling," Joe said.

"The kid who drove me from the airport said you've got a machine that can talk with dead people."

A slow, angry flush spread across Joe's face. He's a small, compact man with very glossy skin and very sharp features, and when he's annoyed he inflates like a puff adder.

"He shouldn't have said that."

"Is that what you're doing here?" I asked. "Some sort of channeling experiments?"

"Forget that shithead word, will you, Mike?" Joe sounded impatient and irritable. But there was an odd fluttery look in his eye, conveying—what? Uncertainty? Vulnerability? Those were traits I hadn't ever associated with Joe Hedley, not in the thirty years we'd known each other. "We aren't sure what the fuck we're doing here," he said. "We thought maybe you could tell us."

"Me?"

"You, yes. Here, put the helmet on. Come on, put it on, Mike. Put it on. Please."

I stared. Nothing ever changes. Ever since we were kids Joe's been using me for one cockeyed thing or another, because he knows he can count on me to give him a sober-minded commonsense opinion. Always bouncing this bizarre scheme or that off me, so he can measure the caroms.

The helmet was a golden strip of wire mesh studded with a row of microwave pickups the size of a dime and flanked by a pair of suction electrodes that fit over the temples. It looked like some vagrant piece of death-house equipment.

I ran my fingers over it. "How much current is this thing capable of sending through my head?"

He looked even angrier. "Oh, fuck you, you hypercautious bastard! Would I ever ask you to do anything that could harm you?"

With a patient little sigh I said, "Okay. How do I do this?"

"Ear to ear, over the top of your head. I'll adjust the electrodes for you."

"You won't tell me what any of this is all about?"

"I want an uncontaminated response. That's science talk, Mike. I'm a scientist. You know that, don't you?"

"So that's what you are. I wondered."

Joe bustled about above me, moving the helmet around, pressing the electrodes against my skull.

"How does it fit?"

"Like a glove."

"You always wear your gloves on your head?" he asked.

"You must be goddamn nervous if you think that's funny."

"I am," he said. "You must be, too, if you take a line like that seriously. But I tell you that you won't get hurt. I promise you that, Mike."

"All right."

"Just sit down here. We need to check the impedances, and then we can get going."

"I wish I understood at least a little bit about—"

"Please," he said. He gestured through a glass partition at a technician in the adjoining room, and she began to do things with dials and switches. This was turning into a movie, a very silly one, full of mad doctors in white jackets and sputtering electrical gadgets. The tinkering went on and on, and I felt myself passing beyond apprehension and annoyance into a kind of gray realm of Zen serenity, the way I sometimes do while sitting in the dentist's chair waiting for the scraping and poking to begin.

On the hillside visible from the laboratory window yellow hibiscus was blooming against a background of billowing scarlet bougainvillea in brilliant California sunshine. It had been cold and raining, this February morning, when I drove to Sea-Tac Airport thirteen hundred miles to the north. Hedley's lab is just outside La Jolla, on a sandy bluff high up over the blue Pacific. When Joe and I were kids growing up in Santa Monica we took this kind of luminous winter day for granted, but I had lived in the Northwest for twenty years now, and I couldn't help thinking I'd gone on a day trip to Eden. I studied the colors on the hillside until my eyes began to get blurry.

"Here we go, now," Joe said, from a point somewhere far away behind my left shoulder.

➤

It was like stepping into a big cage full of parakeets and mynahs and crazed macaws. I heard scratchy screeching sounds, and a harsh loony almost-laughter that soared through three or four octaves, and a low ominous burbling noise, as if some hydraulic device was about to blow a gasket. I heard weird wire-edged shrieks that went tumbling away as though the sound were falling through an infinite abyss. I heard queeblings. I heard hissings.

Then came a sudden burst of clearly enunciated syllables, floating in isolation above the noise:

—*Onoodor*—

That startled me.

A nonsense word? No, no, a real one, one that had meaning for me, a word in an obscure language that I just happen to understand.

"Today," that's what it means. In Khalkha. My specialty. But it was crazy that this machine would be speaking Khalkha to me. This had to be some sort of coincidence. What I'd heard was a random clumping of sounds that I must automatically have arranged into a meaningful pattern. I was kidding myself. Or else Joe was playing an elaborate practical joke. Only, he seemed very serious.

I strained to hear more. But everything was babble again.

Then, out of the chaos:

—*Usan deer*—

Khalkha again: "On the water." It couldn't be a coincidence.

More noise. Skwkaark skreek yubble gobble.

—*Aawa namaig yawuulawa*—

"Father sent me."

Skwkaark. Yabble. Eeeeesh.

"Go on," I said. I felt sweat rolling down my back. "Your father sent you where? Where? *Khaana*. Tell me where."

—*Usan deer*—

"On the water, yes."

Yarkhh. Skreek. Tshhhhhhh.

—*Akhanartan*—

"To his elder brother. Yes."

I closed my eyes and let my mind rove out into the darkness. It drifted on a sea of scratchy noise. Now and again I caught an actual syllable, half a syllable, a slice of a word, a clipped fragment of meaning. The voice was brusque, forceful, a drill-sergeant voice, carrying an undertone of barely suppressed rage.

Somebody very angry was speaking to me across a great distance, over a channel clotted with interference, in a language that hardly anyone in the United States knew anything about: Khalkha. Spoken a little oddly, with an unfamiliar intonation, but plainly recognizable.

I said, speaking very slowly and carefully and trying to match the odd intonation of the voice at the other end, "I can hear you and I can understand you. But there's a lot of interference. Say everything three times and I'll try to follow."

I waited. But now there was only a roaring silence in my ears. Not even the shrieking, not even the babble.

I looked up at Hedley like someone coming out of a trance.

"It's gone dead."

"You sure?"

"I don't hear anything, Joe."

He snatched the helmet from me and put it on, fiddling with the electrodes in that edgy, compulsively precise way of his. He listened for a moment, scowled, nodded. "The relay satellite must have passed around the far side of the sun. We won't get anything more for hours if it has."

"The relay satellite? Where the hell was that broadcast coming from?"

"In a minute," he said. He reached around and took the helmet off. His eyes had a brassy gleam and his mouth was twisted off to the corner of his face, almost as if he'd had a stroke. "You were actually able to understand what he was saying, weren't you?"

I nodded.

"I knew you would. And was he speaking Mongolian?"

"Khalkha, yes. The main Mongolian dialect."

The tension left his face. He gave me a warm, loving grin. "I was sure you'd know. We had a man in from the university here, the comparative linguistics department—you probably know him, Malmstrom's his name— and he said it sounded to him like an Altaic language, maybe Turkic—is that right, Turkic?—but more likely one of the Mongolian languages, and the moment he said Mongolian I thought, That's it, get Mike down here right away—" He paused. "So it's the language that they speak in Mongolia right this very day, would you say?"

"Not quite. His accent was a little strange. Something stiff about it, almost archaic."

"Archaic."

"It had that feel, yes. I can't tell you why. There's just something formal and old-fashioned about it, something, well—"

"Archaic," Hedley said again. Suddenly there were tears in his eyes. I couldn't remember ever having seen him crying before.

What they have, the kid who picked me up at the airport had said, *is a machine that lets them talk with the dead.*

"Joe?" I said. "Joe, what in God's name is this all about?"

We had dinner that night in a sleek restaurant on a sleek, quiet La Jolla street of elegant shops and glossy-leaved trees, just the two of us, the first time in a long while that we'd gone out alone like that. Lately we tended to see each other once or twice a year at most, and Joe, who is almost always between marriages, would usually bring along his latest squeeze, the one who was finally going to bring order and stability and other such things to his tempestuous private life. And since he always needs to show the new one what a remarkable human being he is, he's forever putting on a performance, for the woman, for me, for the waiters, for the people at the nearby tables. Generally the fun's at my expense, for compared with Hedley I'm very staid and proper and I'm eighteen years into my one and only marriage so far, and Joe often seems to enjoy making me feel that there's something wrong with that. I never see him with the same woman twice, except when he happens to marry one of them. But tonight it was all different. He was alone, and the conversation was subdued and gentle and rueful, mostly about the years we'd had put in knowing each other, the fun we'd had, the regret Joe felt during the occasional long periods when we didn't see much of each other. He did most of the talking. There was nothing new about that. But mostly it was just chatter. We were three quarters of the way down the bottle of silky Cabernet before Joe brought himself around to the topic of the experiment. I hadn't wanted to push.

"It was pure serendipity," he said. "You know, the art of finding what you're not looking for. We were trying to clean up some problems in radio transmission from the Icarus relay station—that's the one that the Japs and the French hung around the sun inside the orbit of Mercury—and we were fiddling with this and fiddling with that, sending out an assortment of test signals at a lot of different frequencies, when out of nowhere we got a voice coming back at us. A man's voice. Speaking a strange language. Which turned out to be Chaucerian English."

"Some kind of academic prank?" I suggested.

He looked annoyed. "I don't think so. But let me tell it, Mike, okay? Okay?" He cracked his knuckles and rearranged the knot of his tie. "We listened to this guy and gradually we figured out a little of what he was saying and we called in a grad student from UCSD who confirmed it—thirteenth-century English—and it absolutely knocked us on our asses." He tugged at his earlobes and arranged his tie again. A sort of manic sheen was coming into his eyes. "Before we could even begin to comprehend what we were dealing with, the Englishman was gone and we were picking up some woman making a speech in medieval French. Like we were getting a broadcast from Joan of Arc, do you see? Not that I'm arguing that that's who she was. We had her for half an hour, a minute here and a minute there with a shitload of interference, and then came a solar flare that disrupted communications, and when we had things tuned again we got a quick burst of what turned out to be Arabic, and then someone

else talking in Middle English, and then, last week, this absolutely incomprehensible stuff, which Malmstrom guessed was Mongolian and you have now
confirmed. The Mongol has stayed on the line longer than all the others put
together."

"Give me some more wine," I said.

"I don't blame you. It's made us all crazy, too. The best we can explain it to
ourselves, it's that our beam passes through the Sun, which as I think you
know, even though your specialty happens to be Chinese history and not
physics, is a place where the extreme concentration of mass creates some
unusual stresses on the fabric of the continuum, and some kind of relativistic
force warps the hell out of it, so that the solar field sends our signal kinking off
into God knows where, and the effect is to give us a telephone line to the
Middle Ages. If that sounds like gibberish to you, imagine how it sounds to us."
Hedley spoke without raising his head, while moving his silverware around
busily from one side of his plate to the other. "You see now about channeling?
It's no fucking joke. Shit, we *are* channeling, only looks like it might actually
be real, doesn't it?"

"I see," I said. "So at some point you're going to have to call up the
Secretary of Defense and say, Guess what, we've been getting telephone calls
on the Icarus beam from Joan of Arc. And then they'll shut down your lab here
and send you off to get your heads replumbed."

He stared at me. His nostrils flickered contemptuously.

"Wrong. Completely wrong. You never had any notion of flair, did you?
The sensational gesture that knocks everybody out? No. Of course not. Not
you. Look, Mike, if I can go in there and say, We can talk to the dead, and we
can *prove* it, they'll kiss our asses for us. Don't you see how fucking sensational
it would be, something coming out of these government labs that ordinary
people can actually understand and cheer and yell about? Telephone line to the
past! George Washington himself, talking to Mr. and Mrs. America! Abe
Lincoln! Something straight out of the *National Enquirer*, right, only *real*?
We'd all be heroes. But it's got to be real, that's the kicker. We don't need a
rational explanation for it, at least not right away. All it has to do is work.
Christ, ninety-nine percent of the people don't even know why electric lights
light up when you flip the switch. We have to find out what we really have and
get to understand it at least a little and be two hundred percent sure of ourselves.
And then we present it to Washington and we say, Here, this is what we did and
this is what happens, and don't blame us if it seems crazy. But we have to keep
it absolutely to ourselves until we understand enough of what we've stumbled
onto to be able to explain it to them with confidence. If we do it right we're

goddamned kings of the world. A Nobel would be just the beginning. You understand now?"

"Maybe we should get another bottle of wine," I said.

◄

We were back in the lab by midnight. I followed Hedley through a maze of darkened rooms, ominous with mysterious equipment glowing in the night.

A dozen or so staffers were on duty. They smiled wanly at Hedley as if there was nothing unusual about his coming back to work at this hour.

"Doesn't anyone sleep around here?" I asked.

"It's a twenty-four-hour information world," Joe said. "We'll be recapturing the Icarus beam in forty-three minutes. You want to hear some of the earlier tapes?"

He touched a switch and from an unseen speaker came crackles and bleebles and then a young woman's voice, strong and a little harsh, uttering brief blurts of something that sounded like strange singsong French, to me not at all understandable.

"Her accent's terrible," I said. "What's she saying?"

"It's too fragmentary to add up to anything much. She's praying, mostly. May the king live, may God strengthen his arm, something like that. For all we know, it *is* Joan of Arc. We haven't gotten more than a few minutes' total coherent verbal output out of any of them, usually a lot less. Except for the Mongol. He goes on and on. It's like he doesn't want to let go of the phone."

"And it really is a phone?" I asked. "What we say here, they can hear there?"

"We don't know that, because we haven't been able to make much sense out of what they say, and by the time we get it deciphered we've lost contact. But it's got to be a two-way contact. They must be getting *something* from us, because we're able to get their attention somehow and they talk back to us."

"They receive your signal without a helmet?"

"The helmet's just for your benefit. The actual Icarus signal comes in digitally. The helmet's the interface between our computer and your ears."

"Medieval people don't have digital computers either, Joe."

A muscle started popping in one of his cheeks. "No, they don't," he said. "It must come like a voice out of the sky. Or right inside their heads. But they hear us."

"How?"

"Do I know? You want this to make sense, Mike? *Nothing* about this makes sense. Let me give you an example. You were talking with that Mongol, weren't you? You asked him something and he answered you?"

"Yes. But—"

• **496** •

"Let me finish. What did you ask him?"

"He said his father sent him somewhere. I asked him where, and he said, On the water. To visit his elder brother."

"He answered you right away?"

"Yes," I said.

"Well, that's actually impossible. The Icarus is ninety-three million miles from here. There has to be something like an eight-minute time lag in radio transmission. You follow? You ask him something and it's eight minutes before the beam reaches Icarus, and eight minutes more for his answer to come back. He sure as hell can't hold a real-time conversation with you. But you say he was."

"It may only have seemed that way. It could just have been coincidence that what I asked and what he happened to say next fit together like question and response."

"Maybe. Or maybe whatever kink in time we're operating across eats up the lag for us, too. I tell you, nothing makes sense about this. But one way or another the beam is reaching them and it carries coherent information. I don't know why that is. It just is. Once you start dealing in impossible stuff, anything might be true. So why can't our voices come out of thin air to them?" Hedley laughed nervously. Or perhaps it was a cough, I thought. "The thing is," he went on, "this Mongol is staying on line longer than any of the others, so with you here we have a chance to have some real communication with him. You speak his language. You can validate this whole goddamn grotesque event for us, do you see? You can have an honest-to-God chat with some guy who lived six hundred years ago, and find out where he really is and what he thinks is going on, and tell us all about it."

I stole a glance at the wall clock. Half past twelve. I couldn't remember the last time I'd been up this late. I lead a nice quiet tenured life, full professor thirteen years now, University of Washington Department of Sinological Studies.

"We're about ready to acquire signal again," Hedley said. "Put the helmet on."

I slipped it into place. I thought about that little communications satellite chugging around the sun, swimming through inconceivable heat and unthinkable waves of hard radiation and somehow surviving, coming around the far side now, beaming electromagnetic improbabilities out of the distant past at my head.

The squawking and screeching began.

Then, emerging from the noise and murk and sonic darkness, came the Mongol's voice, clear and steady:

"Where are you, you voice, you? Speak to me."

"Here," I said. "Can you hear me?"

Aark. Yaaarp. Tshhhhhh.

The Mongol said, "Voice, what are you? Are you mortal or are you a prince of the master?"

I wrestled with the puzzling words. I'm fluent enough in Khalkha, though I don't get many opportunities for speaking it. But there was a problem of context here.

"Which master?" I asked finally. "What prince?"

"There is only one Master," said the Mongol. He said this with tremendous force and assurance, putting terrific spin on every syllable, and the capital letter was apparent in his tone. "I am His servant. The *angeloi* are his princes. Are you an *angelos*, voice?"

Angeloi? That was Greek. A Mongol, asking me if I was an angel of God?

"Not an angel, no," I said.

"Then how can you speak to me this way?"

"It's a kind of—" I paused. I couldn't come up with the Khalka for "miracle." After a moment I said, "It's by the grace of heaven on high. I'm speaking to you from far away."

"How far?"

"Tell me where you are."

Skrawwwwk. Tshhhhhh.

"Again. Where are you?"

"Nova Roma. Constantinopolis."

I blinked. "Byzantium?"

"Byzantium, yes."

"I am very far from there."

"*How* far?" the Mongol said fiercely.

"Many many days' ride. Many many." I hesitated. "Tell me what year it is, where you are."

Vzsqkk. Blzzp. Yiiiiiik.

"What's he saying to you?" Hedley asked. I waved at him furiously to be quiet.

"The year," I said again. "Tell me what year it is."

The Mongol said scornfully, "Everyone knows the year, voice."

"Tell me."

"It is the year 1187 of our Savior."

I began to shiver. Our Savior? Weirder and weirder, I thought. A Christian Mongol? Living in Byzantium? Talking to me on the space telephone out of the twelfth century? The room around me took on a smoky, insubstantial look. My elbows were aching, and something was throbbing just above my left cheek-bone. This had been a long day for me. I was very tired. I was heading into that sort of weariness where walls melted and bones turned soft. Joe was dancing around in front of me like someone with tertiary Saint Vitus'.

"And your name?" I said.

"I am Petros Alexios."

"Why do you speak Khalkha if you are Greek?"

A long silence, unbroken even by the hellish static.

"I am not Greek," came the reply finally. "I am by birth Khalkha Mongol, but raised Christian among the Christians from age eleven, when my father sent me on the water and I was taken. My name was Temujin. Now I am twenty and I know the Savior."

I gasped and put my hand to my throat as though it had been skewered out of the darkness by a spear.

"Temujin," I said, barely getting the word out.

"My father was Yesugei the chieftain."

"Temujin," I said again. "Son of Yesugei." I shook my head.

Aaark. Blzzzp. Tshhhhhh.

Then no static, no voice, only the hushed hiss of silence.

"Are you okay?" Hedley asked.

"We've lost contact, I think."

"Right. It just broke. You look like your brain has shorted out."

I slipped the helmet off. My hands were shaking.

"You know," I said, "maybe that French woman really was Joan of Arc."

"What?"

I shrugged. "She really might have been," I said wearily. "Anything's possible, isn't it?"

"What the hell are you trying to tell me, Mike?"

"Why shouldn't she have been Joan of Arc?" I asked. "Listen, Joe. This is making me just as nutty as you are. You know what I've just been doing? I've been talking to Genghis Khan on this fucking telephone of yours."

❤

I managed to get a few hours of sleep by simply refusing to tell Hedley anything else until I'd had a chance to rest. The way I said it, I left him no options, and he seemed to grasp that right away. At the hotel, I sank from consciousness like a leaden whale, hoping I wouldn't surface again before noon, but old habit seized me and pushed me up out of the tepid depths at seven, irreversibly awake and not a bit less depleted. I put in a quick call to Seattle to tell Elaine that I was going to stay down in La Jolla a little longer than expected. She seemed worried—not that I might be up to any funny business, not me, but only that I sounded so groggy. "You know Joe," I said. "For him it's a twenty-four-hour information world." I told her nothing else. When I stepped out on the breakfast patio half an hour later, I could see the lab's blue van already waiting in the hotel lot to pick me up.

Hedley seemed to have slept at the lab. He was rumpled and red-eyed, but somehow he was at normal functioning level, scurrying around the place like a yappy little dog. "Here's a printout of last night's contact," he said the moment I came in. "I'm sorry if the transcript looks cockeyed. The computer doesn't know how to spell in Mongolian." He shoved it into my hands. "Take a squint at it and see if you really heard all the things you thought you heard."

I peered at the single long sheet. It seemed to be full of jabberwocky, but once I figured out the computer's system of phonetic equivalents I could read it readily enough. I looked up after a moment, feeling very badly shaken.

"I was hoping I dreamed all this. I didn't."

"You want to explain it to me?"

"I can't."

Joe scowled. "I'm not asking for fundamental existential analysis. Just give me a goddamned translation, all right?"

"Sure," I said.

He listened with a kind of taut, explosive attention that seemed to me to be masking a mixture of uneasiness and bubbling excitement. When I was done he said, "Okay. What's this Genghis Khan stuff?"

"Temujin was Genghis Khan's real name. He was born around 1167, and his father Yesugei was a minor chief somewhere in northeastern Mongolia. When Temujin was still a boy, his father was poisoned by enemies, and he became a fugitive, but by the time he was fifteen he started putting together a confederacy of Mongol tribes, hundreds of them, and eventually he conquered everything in sight. Genghis Khan means 'Ruler of the Universe.' "

"So? Our Mongol lives in Constantinople, you say. He's a Christian and he uses a Greek name."

"He's Temujin, son of Yesugei. He's twenty years old in the year when Genghis Khan was twenty years old."

Hedley looked belligerent. "Some other Temujin. Some other Yesugei."

"Listen to the way he speaks. He's scary. Even if you can't understand a word of what he's saying, can't you feel the power in him? The coiled-up anger? That's the voice of somebody capable of conquering whole continents."

"Genghis Khan wasn't a Christian. Genghis Khan wasn't kidnapped by strangers and taken to live in Constantinople."

"I know," I said. To my own amazement I added, "But maybe this one was."

"Jesus God Almighty. What's that supposed to mean?"

"I'm not certain."

Hedley's eyes took on a glaze. "I hoped you were going to be part of the solution, Mike. Not part of the problem."

"Just let me think this through," I said, waving my hands above his face as if trying to conjure some patience into him. Joe was peering at me in a stunned, astounded way. My eyeballs throbbed. Things were jangling up and down along my spinal column. Lack of sleep had coated my brain with a hard crust of adrenaline. Bewilderingly strange ideas were rising like sewer gases in my mind and making weird bubbles. "All right, try this," I said at last. "Say that there are all sorts of possible worlds. A world in which you're King of England, a world in which I played third base for the Yankees, a world in which the dinosaurs never died out and Los Angeles gets invaded every summer by hungry tyrannosaurs. And one world where Yesugei's son Temujin wound up in twelfth-century Byzantium as a Christian instead of founding the Mongol Empire. And that's the Temujin I've been talking to. This cockeyed beam of yours not only crosses time lines, somehow it crosses probability lines, too, and we've fished up some alternate reality that—"

"I don't believe this," Hedley said.

"Neither do I, really. Not seriously. I'm just putting forth one possible hypothesis that might explain—"

"I don't mean your fucking hypothesis. I mean I find it hard to believe that you of all people, my old pal Mike Michaelson, can be standing here running off at the mouth this way, working hard at turning a mystifying event into a goddamned nonsensical one—you, good old sensible steady Mike, telling me some shit about tyrannosaurs amok in Los Angeles—"

"It was only an example of—"

"Oh, fuck your example," Hedley said. His face darkened with exasperation bordering on fury. He looked ready to cry. "Your example is absolute crap. Your example is garbage. You know, man, if I wanted someone to feed me a lot of New Age crap I didn't have to go all the way to Seattle to find one. Alternate realities! Third base for the Yankees!"

A girl in a lab coat appeared out of nowhere and said, "We have signal acquisition, Dr. Hedley."

I said, "I'll catch the next plane north, okay?"

Joe's face was red and starting to do its puff-adder trick, and his Adam's apple bobbed as if trying to find the way out.

"I wasn't trying to mess up your head," I said. "I'm sorry if I did. Forget everything I was just saying. I hope I was at least of some help, anyway."

Something softened in Joe's eyes.

"I'm so goddamned tired, Mike."

"I know."

"I didn't mean to yell at you like that."

"No offense taken, Joe."

"But I have trouble with this alternate-reality thing of yours. You think it was easy for me to believe that what we were doing here was talking to people in the past? But I brought myself around to it, weird though it was. Now you give it an even weirder twist, and it's too much. It's too fucking much. It violates my sense of what's right and proper and fitting. You know what Occam's Razor is, Mike? The old medieval axiom: 'Never multiply hypotheses needlessly'? Take the simplest one. Here even the simplest one is crazy. You push it too far."

"Listen," I said, "if you'll just have someone drive me over to the hotel—"

"No."

"No?"

"Let me think a minute," he said. "Just because it doesn't make sense doesn't mean that it's impossible, right? And if we get one impossible thing, we can have two, or six, or sixteen. Right? Right?" His eyes were like two black holes with cold stars blazing at their bottoms. "Hell, we aren't at the point where we need to worry about explanations. We have to find out the basic stuff first. Mike, I don't want you to leave. I want you to stay here."

"What?"

"Don't go. Please. I still need somebody to talk to the Mongol for me. Don't go. Please, Mike? Please?"

✦

The times, Temujin said, were very bad. The infidels under Saladin had smashed the Crusader forces in the Holy Land and Jerusalem itself had fallen to the Moslems. Christians everywhere mourn the loss, said Temujin. In Byzantium—where Temujin was captain of the guards in the private army of a prince named Theodore Lascaris—God's grace seemed also to have been withdrawn. The great empire was in heavy weather. Insurrections had brought down two emperors in the past four years and the current man was weak and timid. The provinces of Hungary, Cyprus, Serbia, and Bulgaria were all in revolt. The Normans of Sicily were chopping up Byzantine Greece and on the other side of the empire the Seljuk Turks were chewing their way through Asia Minor. "It is the time of the wolf," said Temujin. "But the sword of the Lord will prevail."

The sheer force of him was astounding. It lay not so much in what he said, although that was sharp and fierce, as in the way he said it. I could feel the strength of the man in the velocity and impact of each syllable. Temujin hurled his words as if from a catapult. They arrived carrying a crackling electrical charge. Talking with him was like holding live cables in my hands.

Hedley, jigging and fidgeting around the lab, paused now and then to stare at me with what looked like awe and wonder in his eyes, as if to say, *You really can make sense of this stuff?* I smiled at him. I felt bizarrely cool and unflustered. Sitting there with some electronic thing on my head, letting that terrific force go hurtling through my brain. Discussing twelfth-century politics with an invisible Byzantine Mongol. Making small talk with Genghis Khan. All right. I could handle it.

I beckoned for notepaper. *Need printout of world historical background late twelfth century,* I scrawled, without interrupting my conversation with Temujin. *Esp. Byzantine history, Crusades, etc.*

The kings of England and France, said Temujin, were talking about launching a new Crusade. But at the moment they happened to be at war with each other, which made cooperation difficult. The powerful Emperor Frederick Barbarossa of Germany was also supposed to be getting up a Crusade, but that, he said, might mean more trouble for Byzantium than for the Saracens, because Frederick was the friend of Byzantium's enemies in the rebellious provinces, and he'd have to march through those provinces on the way to the Holy Land.

"It is a perilous time," I agreed.

Then suddenly I was feeling the strain. Temujin's rapid-fire delivery was exhausting to follow, he spoke Mongolian with what I took to be a Byzantine accent, and he sprinkled his statements with the names of emperors, princes, and even nations that meant nothing to me. Also, there was that powerful force of his to contend with—it hit you like an avalanche—and beyond that his anger: the whipcrack inflection that seemed the thinnest of bulwarks against some unstated inner rage, fury, frustration. It's hard to feel at ease with anyone who seethes that way. Suddenly I just wanted to go somewhere and lie down.

But someone put printout sheets in front of me, closely packed columns of stuff from the *Britannica*. Names swam before my eyes: Henry II, Barbarossa, Stephan Nemanya, Isaac II Angelos, Guy of Jerusalem, Richard the Lion-Hearted. Antioch, Tripoli, Thessalonica, Venice. I nodded my thanks and pushed the sheets aside.

Cautiously I asked Temujin about Mongolia. It turned out that he knew almost nothing about Mongolia. He'd had no contact at all with his native land since his abduction at the age of eleven by Byzantine traders who carried him off to Constantinople. His country, his father, his brothers, the girl to whom he had been betrothed when he was still a child—they were all just phantoms to him now, far away, forgotten. But in the privacy of his own soul he still spoke Khalkha. That was all that was left.

By 1187, I knew, the Temujin who would become Genghis Khan had already made himself the ruler of half of Mongolia. His fame would surely have spread to cosmopolitan Byzantium. How could this Temujin be unaware of him? Well, I saw one way. But Joe had already shot it down. And it sounded pretty nutty even to me.

"Do you want a drink?" Hedley asked. "Tranks? Aspirin?"

I shook my head. "I'm okay," I murmured.

To Temujin I said, "Do you have a wife? Children?"

"I have vowed not to marry until Jesus rules again in His own land."

"So you're going to go on the next Crusade?" I asked.

Whatever answer Temujin made was smothered by static.

Awkkk. Skrrkkk. Tsssshhhhhhh.

Then silence, lengthening into endlessness.

"Signal's gone," someone said.

"I could use that drink now," I said. "Scotch."

The lab clock said it was ten in the morning. To me it felt like the middle of the night.

An hour had passed. The signal hadn't returned.

Hedley said, "You really think he's Genghis Khan?"

"I really think he *could* have been."

"In some other probability world."

Carefully I said, "I don't want to get you all upset again, Joe."

"You won't. Why the hell *not* believe we're tuned into an alternate reality? It's no more goofy than any of the rest of this. But tell me this: is what he says consistent with being Genghis Khan?"

"His name's the same. His age. His childhood, up to the point when he wandered into some Byzantine trading caravan and they took him away to Constantinople with them. I can imagine the sort of fight he put up, too. But his life-line must have diverged completely from that point on. A whole new world-line split off from ours. And in that world, instead of turning into Genghis Khan, ruler of all Mongolia, he grew up to be Petros Alexios of Prince Theodore Lascaris's private guards."

"And he has no idea of who he could have been?" Joe asked.

"How could he? It isn't even a dream to him. He was born into another world that wasn't ever destined to have a Genghis Khan. You know the poem:

> 'Our birth is but a sleep and a forgetting.
> The soul that rises with us, our life's star,
> Hath had elsewhere its setting,
> And cometh from afar.' "

"Very pretty. Is that Yeats?" Hedley said.

"Wordsworth," I said. "When's the signal coming back?"

"An hour, two, three. It's hard to say. You want to take a nap, and we'll wake you when we have acquisition?"

"I'm not sleepy."

"You look pretty ragged," Joe said.

I wouldn't give him the satisfaction.

"I'm okay. I'll sleep for a week, later on. What if you can't raise him again?"

"There's always that chance, I suppose. We've already had him on the line five times as long as all the rest put together."

"He's a very determined man," I said.

"He ought to be. He's Genghis fucking Khan."

"Get him back," I said. "I don't want you to lose him. I want to talk to him some more."

❤

Morning ticked on into afternoon. I phoned Elaine twice while we waited, and I stood for a long time at the window watching the shadows of the oncoming winter evening fall across the hibiscus and the bougainvillea, and I hunched my shoulders up and tried to pull in the signal by sheer body English. Contemplating the possibility that they might never pick up Temujin again left me feeling weirdly forlorn. I was beginning to feel that I had a real relationship with that eerie disembodied angry voice coming out of the crackling night. Toward midafternoon I thought I was starting to understand what was making Temujin so angry, and I had some things I wanted to say to him about that.

Maybe you ought to get some sleep, I told myself.

At half past four, someone came to me and said the Mongol was on the line again.

The static was very bad. But then came the full force of Temujin soaring over it. I heard him saying, "The Holy Land must be redeemed. I cannot sleep so long as the infidels possess it."

I took a deep breath.

In wonder I watched myself set out to do something unlike anything I had ever done before.

"Then you must redeem it yourself," I said firmly.

"I?"

"Listen to me, Temujin. Think of another world far from yours. There is a Temujin in that world, too, son of Yesugei, husband to Bortei who is daughter of Dai the Wise."

"Another world? What are you saying?"

"Listen. Listen. He is a great warrior, that other Temujin. No one can withstand him. His own brothers bow before him. All Mongols everywhere bow before him. His sons are like wolves, and they ride into every land and no one can withstand them. This Temujin is master of all Mongolia. He is the Great Khan, the Genghis Khan, the ruler of the universe."

There was silence. Then Temujin said, "What is this to me?"

"He is you, Temujin. You are the Genghis Khan."

Silence again, longer, broken by hideous shrieks of interplanetary noise.

"I have no sons and I have not seen Mongolia in years, or even thought of it. What are you saying?"

"That you can be as great in your world as this other Temujin is in his."

"I am Byzantine. I am Christian. Mongolia is nothing to me. Why would I want to be master in that savage place?"

"I'm not talking about Mongolia. You are Byzantine, yes. You are Christian. But you were born to lead and fight and conquer," I said. "What are you doing as a captain of another man's palace guards? You waste your life that way, and you know it, and it maddens you. You should have armies of your own. You should carry the Cross into Jerusalem."

"The leaders of the new Crusade are quarrelsome fools. It will end in disaster."

"Perhaps not. Frederick Barbarossa's Crusade will be unstoppable."

"Barbarossa will attack Byzantium instead of the Moslems. Everyone knows that."

"No," I said. That inner force of Temujin was rising and rising in intensity, like a gale climbing toward being a hurricane. I was awash in sweat now, and I was dimly aware of the others staring at me as though I had lost my senses. A strange exhilaration gripped me. I went plunging joyously ahead. "Emperor Isaac Angelos will come to terms with Barbarossa. The Germans will march through Byzantium and go on toward the Holy Land. But there Barbarossa will die and his army will scatter—unless you are there, at his right hand, taking command in his place when he falls, leading them onward to Jerusalem. You, the invincible, the Genghis Khan."

There was silence once more, this time so prolonged that I was afraid the contact had been broken for good.

Then Temujin returned. "Will you send soldiers to fight by my side?" he asked.

"That I cannot do."

"You have the power to send them, I know," said Temujin. "You speak to me out of the air. I know you are an angel, or else you are a demon. If you are a demon, I invoke the name of Christos Pantokrator upon you, and begone. But if you are an angel, you can send me help. Send it, then, and I will lead your troops to victory. I will take the Holy Land from the infidel. I will create the Empire of Jesus in the world and bring all things to fulfillment. Help me. Help me."

"I've done all I can," I said. "The rest is for you to achieve."

There was another spell of silence.

"Yes," Temujin said finally. "I understand. Yes. Yes. The rest is for me."

❦

"Christ, you look peculiar," Joe Hedley said, staring at me almost fearfully. "I've never seen you looking like this before. You look like a wild man."

"Do I?" I said.

"You must be dead tired, Mike. You must be asleep on your feet. Listen, go over to the hotel and get some rest. We'll have a late dinner, okay? You can fill me in then on whatever you've just been jabbering about. But relax now. The Mongol's gone and we may not get him back till tomorrow."

"You won't get him back at all," I said.

"You think?" He peered close. "Hey, are you okay? Your eyes—your face—" Something quivered in his cheek. "If I didn't know better I'd say you were stoned."

"I've been changing the world. It's hard work."

"Changing the world?"

"Not this world. The other one. Look," I said hoarsely, "they never had a Genghis Khan, so they never had a Mongol Empire, and the whole history of China and Russia and the Near East and a lot of other places was very different. But I've got this Temujin all fired up now to be a Christian Genghis Khan. He got so Christian in Byzantium that he forgot what was really inside him, but I've reminded him, I've told him how he can still do the thing that he was designed to do, and he understands. He's found his true self again. He'll go out to fight in the name of Jesus and he'll build an empire that'll eat the Moslem powers for breakfast and then blow away Byzantium and Venice and go on from there to do God knows what. He'll probably conquer all of Europe before he's finished. And I did it. I set it all in motion. He was sending me all this energy, this Genghis Khan zap that he has inside him, and I figured the least I could do for him was turn some of it around and send it back to him, and say, Here, go, be what you were supposed to be."

"Mike—"

I stood close against him, looming over him. He gave me a bewildered look.

"You really didn't think I had it in me, did you?" I said. "You son of a bitch. You've always thought I'm as timid as a turtle. Your good old sober stick-in-the-mud pal Mike. What do you know? What the hell do you know?" Then I laughed. He looked so stunned that I had to soften it for him a little. Gently I touched his shoulder. "I need a shower and a drink. And then let's think about dinner."

Joe gawked at me. "What if it wasn't some other world you changed, though? Suppose it was this one."

"Suppose it was," I said. "Let's worry about that later. I still need that shower."

ENTER A
SOLDIER.
LATER: ENTER
ANOTHER

A *curious phenomenon of American science-fiction publishing in the late 1980s, which will probably not be dealt with in a kindly way by future historians of the field, was the "shared world" anthology. I use the past tense for it because the notion of gathering a bunch of writers together to set stories against a common background defined by someone else appears, as I write this, to be losing its popularity. But for a time in 1987 and 1988 it began to seem as though everything in science fiction was becoming part of some shared-world project.*

In truth both good and bad fiction came out of the various shared-world enterprises. The idea itself was far from new; I can't tell you, without burrowing deep into the archives, which was the first of the species, but one distinguished example appeared as early as 1952—The Petrified Planet, a book in which the scientist John D. Clark devised specifications for an unusual planet and the writers Fletcher Pratt, H. Beam Piper, and Judith Merril produced fine novellas set on that world. A similar book a year or two later was made up of stories by Isaac Asimov, Poul Anderson, and a third writer whose name I don't recall; for some reason the book itself never was published, but the Asimov and Anderson stories appeared individually, and they were fine ones.

Fifteen years later I revived the "triplet" idea with a book called Three for Tomorrow*—fiction by James Blish, Roger Zelazny, and myself, based on a theme proposed by Arthur C. Clarke—and I edited several others in the years following. In 1975 came Harlan Ellison's* Medea*, an elaborate and brilliantly conceived colossus of a book that made use of the talents of Frank Herbert, Theodore Sturgeon, Frederik Pohl, Larry Niven, Hal Clem-*

ent, and a whole galaxy of other writers of their stature. But the real deluge of shared-world projects began a few years afterward, in the wake of the vast success of Robert Asprin's fantasy series, Thieves' World. Suddenly, every publisher in the business wanted to duplicate the Thieves' World bonanza, and from all sides appeared this hastily conceived imitator and that.

I dabbled in a couple of these books myself—a story that I wrote for one of them won a Hugo, in fact—but my enthusiasm for the shared-world whirl cooled quickly once I saw how shapeless and incoherent most of the books were. The writers tended not to pay much attention to the specifications, and simply went off in their own directions; the editors, generally, were too lazy or too cynical or simply too incompetent to do anything about it; and the books became formless jumbles of incompatible work.

Before I became fully aware of that, though, I let myself be seduced into editing one shared-world series myself. The initiator of this was Jim Baen, the publisher of Baen Books, whose idea centered around setting computer-generated simulacra of historical figures against each other in intellectual conflict. That appealed to me considerably; and when I was told that book packager Bill Fawcett would work with me on the production end of things, I agreed to work out the conception in detail and serve as general editor.

So I produced an elaborate prospectus outlining the historical background of the near-future world in which these simulacra would hold forth; I rounded up a compatible group of writers (Poul Anderson, Robert Sheckley, Gregory Benford, and Pat Murphy); and to ensure that the book would unfold with consistency to my underlying vision, I wrote the first story myself in October of 1987, a fifteen-thousand-word opus for which I chose the characters of Socrates and Francisco Pizarro as my protagonists.

It was all, I have to admit, a matter of commerce rather than art: just a job of work, to fill somebody's current publishing need. But a writer's intentions and the ultimate result of his work don't bear any necessary relationship. In this case I was surprised and delighted to find the story taking on unanticipated life as I wrote, and what might have been a routine job of word-spinning turned out, unexpectedly, to be rather more than that when I was done with it.

It led off the shared-world anthology, which we called Time Gate, and was published in Isaac Asimov's SF Magazine. Gardner Dozois used it in his 1989 Year's Best collection, and in 1990 it was a finalist on both the Nebula and Hugo ballots—one of my most widely liked stories in a long *while. The Nebula eluded me that year, but at the World Science Fiction Convention in Holland in August 1990, "Enter a Soldier" earned me a Hugo Award, the fourth I have won, as the year's best novelette.*

Time Gate itself turned out pretty well, too, as such projects go. Readers liked it, and Bill Fawcett and I went on to put together a second volume for Jim Baen, and then we were asked to do a third. But at that point I balked. The individual stories were fine ones, in the main, but the writers, as writers usually do, weren't paying much attention to the development of the overall concept I had devised for the book, and it seemed to me as volume two took shape that the result was an increasingly static and repetitive affair. Perhaps it's unrealistic to think that a team of gifted, independent-minded writers can ever produce what is in essence a collaborative novel that has been designed by someone else. In any case, the series wasn't taking the direction I had hoped for, and after the second volume I resigned from it, nor have I had much to do with shared-world collections ever since. But my involvement with this one did, at least, produce a story with which I'm more than a little pleased.

It might be heaven. Certainly it wasn't Spain and he doubted it could be Peru. He seemed to be floating, suspended midway between nothing and nothing. There was a shimmering golden sky far above him and a misty, turbulent sea of white clouds boiling far below. When he looked down he saw his legs and his feet dangling like child's toys above an unfathomable abyss, and the sight of it made him want to puke, but there was nothing in him for the puking. He was hollow. He was made of air. Even the old ache in his knee was gone, and so was the everlasting dull burning in the fleshy part of his arm where the Indian's little arrow had taken him, long ago on the shore of that island of pearls, up by Panama.

It was as if he had been born again, sixty years old but freed of all the harm that his body had experienced and all its myriad accumulated injuries: freed, one might almost say, of his body itself.

"Gonzalo?" he called. "Hernando?"

Blurred dreamy echoes answered him. And then silence.

"Mother of God, am I dead?"

No. No. He had never been able to imagine death. An end to all striving? A place where nothing moved? A great emptiness, a pit without a bottom? Was this place the place of death, then? He had no way of knowing. He needed to ask the holy fathers about this.

"Boy, where are my priests? Boy?"

He looked about for his page. But all he saw was blinding whorls of light coiling off to infinity on all sides. The sight was beautiful but troublesome. It was hard for him to deny that he had died, seeing himself afloat like this in a realm of air and light. Died and gone to heaven. This is heaven, yes, surely, surely. What else could it be?

So it was true, that if you took the Mass and took the Christ faithfully into yourself and served Him well you would be saved from your sins, you would be forgiven, you would be cleansed. He had wondered about that. But he wasn't ready yet to be dead, all the same. The thought of it was sickening and infuriating. There was so much yet to be done. And he had no memory even of being ill. He searched his body for wounds. No, no wounds. Not anywhere. Strange. Again he looked around. He was alone here. No one to be seen, not his page, nor his brother, nor De Soto, nor the priests, nor anyone. "Fray Marcos! Fray Vicente! Can't you hear me? Damn you, where are you? Mother of God! Holy Mother, blessed among women! Damn you, Fray Vicente, tell me—tell me—"

His voice sounded all wrong: too thick, too deep, a stranger's voice. The words fought with his tongue and came from his lips malformed and lame, not the good crisp Spanish of Estremadura but something shameful and odd. What he heard was like the spluttering foppishness of Madrid or even the furry babble that they spoke in Barcelona; why, he might almost be a Portuguese, so coarse and clownish was his way of shaping his speech.

He said carefully and slowly, "I am the Governor and Captain-General of New Castile."

That came out no better, a laughable noise.

"Adelantado—Alguacil Mayor—Marques de la Conquista—"

The strangeness of his new way of speech made insults of his own titles. It was like being tongue-tied. He felt streams of hot sweat breaking out on his skin from the effort of trying to frame his words properly; but when he put his hand to his forehead to brush the sweat away before it could run into his eyes he seemed dry to the touch, and he was not entirely sure he could feel himself at all.

He took a deep breath. "I am Francisco Pizarro!" he roared, letting the name burst desperately from him like water breaching a rotten dam.

The echo came back, deep, rumbling, mocking. *Frantheethco. Peetharro.*

That, too. Even his own name, idiotically garbled.

"O great God!" he cried. "Saints and angels!"

More garbled noises. Nothing would come out as it should. He had never known the arts of reading or writing; now it seemed that true speech itself was being taken from him. He began to wonder whether he had been right about this being heaven, supernal radiance or no. There was a curse on his tongue; a demon, perhaps, held it pinched in his claws. Was this hell, then? A very beautiful place, but hell nevertheless?

He shrugged. Heaven or hell, it made no difference. He was beginning to grow more calm, beginning to accept and take stock. He knew—had learned, long ago—that there was nothing to gain from raging against that which could not be helped, even less from panic in the face of the unknown. He was here, that was all there was to it—wherever *here* was—and he must find a place for himself, and not this place, floating here between nothing and nothing. He had been in hells before, small hells, hells on Earth. That barren isle called Gallo, where the sun cooked you in your own skin and there was nothing to eat but crabs that had the taste of dog dung. And that dismal swamp at the mouth of the Rio Biru, where the rain fell in rivers and the trees reached down to cut you like swords. And the mountains he had crossed with his army, where the snow was so cold that it burned, and the air went into your throat like a dagger at every breath. He had come forth from those, and they had been worse than this. Here there was no pain and no danger; here there was only soothing light and a strange absence of all discomfort. He began to move forward. He was walking on air. Look, look, he thought, I am walking on air! Then he said it out loud. "I am walking on air," he announced, and laughed at the way the words emerged from him. "Santiago! Walking on air! But why not? I am Pizarro!" He shouted it with all his might, "Pizarro! Pizarro!" and waited for it to come back to him.

Peetharro. Peetharro.

He laughed. He kept on walking.

❥

Tanner sat hunched forward in the vast sparkling sphere that was the ninth-floor imaging lab, watching the little figure at the distant center of the holotank strut and preen. Lew Richardson, crouching beside him with both hands thrust into the data gloves so that he could feed instructions to the permutation network, seemed almost not to be breathing—seemed to be just one more part of the network, in fact.

But that was Richardson's way, Tanner thought: total absorption in the task at hand. Tanner envied him that. They were very different sorts of men. Richardson lived for his programming and nothing but his programming. It was his grand passion. Tanner had never quite been able to understand people who were driven by grand passions. Richardson was like some throwback to an earlier age, an age when things had really mattered, an age when you were able to have some faith in the significance of your own endeavors.

"How do you like the armor?" Richardson asked. "The armor's very fine, I think. We got it from old engravings. It has real flair."

"Just the thing for tropical climates," said Tanner. "A nice tin suit with matching helmet."

He coughed and shifted about irritably in his seat. The demonstration had been going on for half an hour without anything that seemed to be of any importance happening—just the minuscule image of the bearded man in Spanish armor tramping back and forth across the glowing field—and he was beginning to get impatient.

Richardson didn't seem to notice the harshness in Tanner's voice or the restlessness of his movements. He went on making small adjustments. He was a small man himself, neat and precise in dress and appearance, with faded blond hair and pale-blue eyes and a thin, straight mouth. Tanner felt huge and shambling beside him. In theory, Tanner had authority over Richardson's research projects, but in fact he always had simply permitted Richardson to do as he pleased. This time, though, it might be necessary finally to rein him in a little.

This was the twelfth or thirteenth demonstration that Richardson had subjected him to since he had begun fooling around with this historical-simulation business. The others all had been disasters of one kind or another, and Tanner expected that this one would finish the same way. And basically Tanner was growing uneasy about the project that he once had given his stamp of approval to, so long ago. It was getting harder and harder to go on believing that all this work served any useful purpose. Why had it been allowed to absorb so much of Richardson's group's time and so much of the lab's research budget for so many months? What possible value was it going to have for anybody? What possible use?

It's just a game, Tanner thought. One more desperate meaningless techno-logical stunt, one more pointless pirouette in a meaningless ballet. The expen-diture of vast resources on a display of ingenuity for ingenuity's sake and nothing else: now *there's* decadence for you.

The tiny image in the holotank suddenly began to lose color and defini-tion.

"Uh-oh," Tanner said. "There it goes. Like all the others."

But Richardson shook his head. "This time it's different, Harry."

"You think?"

"We aren't losing him. He's simply moving around in there of his own volition, getting beyond our tracking parameters. Which means that we've achieved the high level of autonomy that we were shooting for."

"Volition, Lew? Autonomy?"

"You know that those are our goals."

"Yes, I know what our goals are supposed to be," said Tanner, with some annoyance. "I'm simply not convinced that a loss of focus is a proof that you've got volition."

"Here," Richardson said. "I'll cut in the stochastic tracking program. He moves freely, we freely follow him." Into the computer ear in his lapel he said, "Give me a gain boost, will you?" He made a quick flicking gesture with his left middle finger to indicate the quantitative level.

The little figure in ornate armor and pointed boots grew sharp again. Tanner could see fine details on the armor, the plumed helmet, the tapering shoulder pieces, the joints at the elbows, the intricate pommel of his sword. He was marching from left to right in a steady hip-rolling way, like a man who was climbing the tallest mountain in the world and didn't mean to break his stride until he was across the summit. The fact that he was walking in what appeared to be midair seemed not to trouble him at all.

"There he is," Richardson said grandly. "We've got him back, all right? The conqueror of Peru, before your very eyes, in the flesh. So to speak."

Tanner nodded. Pizarro, yes, before his very eyes. And he had to admit that what he saw was impressive and even, somehow, moving. Something about the dogged way with which that small armored figure was moving across the gleaming pearly field of the holotank aroused a kind of sympathy in him. That little man was entirely imaginary, but *he* didn't seem to know that, or if he did he wasn't letting it stop him for a moment: he went plugging on, and on and on, as if he intended actually to get somewhere. Watching that, Tanner was oddly captivated by it, and found himself surprised suddenly to discover that his interest in the entire project was beginning to rekindle.

"Can you make him any bigger?" he asked. "I want to see his face."

"I can make him big as life," Richardson said. "Bigger. Any size you like. Here."

He flicked a finger, and the hologram of Pizarro expanded instantaneously to a height of about two meters. The Spaniard halted in midstride as though he might actually be aware of the imaging change.

That can't be possible, Tanner thought. That isn't a living consciousness out there. Or is it?

Pizarro stood poised easily in midair, glowering, shading his eyes as if staring into a dazzling glow. There were brilliant streaks of color in the air all around him, like an aurora. He was a tall, lean man in late middle age with a grizzled beard and a hard, angular face. His lips were thin, his nose was sharp, his eyes were cold, shrewd, keen. It seemed to Tanner that those eyes had come to rest on him, and he felt a chill.

My God, Tanner thought, he's *real*.

➤

It had been a French program to begin with, something developed at the Centre Mondiale de la Computation in Lyons about the year 2119. The French had some truly splendid minds working in software in those days. They worked up astounding programs, and then nobody did anything with them. That was *their* version of Century Twenty-Two Malaise.

The French programmers' idea was to use holograms of actual historical personages to dress up the *son et lumiere* tourist events at the great monuments of their national history. Not just preprogrammed robot mock-ups of the old Disneyland kind, which would stand around in front of Notre Dame or the Arc de Triomphe or the Eiffel Tower and deliver canned spiels, but apparent reincarnations of the genuine great ones, who could freely walk and talk and answer questions and make little quips. Imagine Louis XIV demonstrating the fountains of Versailles, they said, or Picasso leading a tour of Paris museums, or Sartre sitting in his Left Bank café exchanging existential *bons mots* with passersby! Napoleon! Joan of Arc! Alexandre Dumas! Perhaps the simulations could do even more than that: perhaps they could be designed so well that they would be able to extend and embellish the achievements of their original lifetimes with new accomplishments, a fresh spate of paintings and novels and works of philosophy and great architectural visions by vanished masters.

The concept was simple enough in essence. Write an intelligencing program that could absorb data, digest it, correlate it, and generate further programs based on what you had given it. No real difficulty there. Then start feeding your program with the collected written works—if any—of the person to be simulated: that would provide not only a general sense of his ideas and positions but also of his underlying pattern of approach to situations, his style of thinking—for *le style*, after all, *est l'homme meme*. If no collected works happened to be available, why, find works *about* the subject by his contemporaries, and use those. Next, toss in the totality of the historical record of the subject's deeds, including all significant subsequent scholarly analyses, making appropriate allowances for conflicts in interpretation—indeed, taking advantage of such conflicts to generate a richer portrait, full of the ambiguities and contradictions that are the inescapable hallmarks of any human being. Now build in substrata of general cultural data of the proper period so that the subject has a loam of references and vocabulary out of which to create thoughts that are appropriate to his place in time and space. Stir. *Et voilà!* Apply a little sophisticated imaging technology and you had a simulation capable of thinking and conversing and behaving as though it is the actual self after which it was patterned.

Of course, this would require a significant chunk of computer power. But that was no problem, in a world where 150-gigaflop networks were standard laboratory items and ten-year-olds carried pencil-sized computers with capacities far beyond the ponderous mainframes of their great-great-grandparents' day. No, there was no theoretical reason why the French project could not have succeeded. Once the Lyons programmers had worked out the basic intelligencing scheme that was needed to write the rest of the programs, it all should have followed smoothly enough.

Two things went wrong: one rooted in an excess of ambition that may have been a product of the peculiarly French personalities of the original programmers, and the other having to do with an abhorrence of failure typical of the major nations of the mid-twenty-second century, of which France was one.

The first was a fatal change of direction that the project underwent in its early phases. The King of Spain was coming to Paris on a visit of state; and the programmers decided that in his honor they would synthesize Don Quixote for him as their initial project. Though the intelligencing program had been designed to simulate only individuals who had actually existed, there seemed no inherent reason why a fictional character as well documented as Don Quixote could not be produced instead. There was Cervantes's lengthy novel; there was ample background data available on the milieu in which Don Quixote supposedly had lived; there was a vast library of critical analysis of the book and of the Don's distinctive and flamboyant personality. Why should bringing Don Quixote to life out of a computer be any different from simulating Louis XIV, say, or Molière, or Cardinal Richelieu? True, they had all existed once, and the knight of La Mancha was a mere figment; but had Cervantes not provided far more detail about Don Quixote's mind and soul than was known of Richelieu, or Molière, or Louis XIV?

Indeed he had. The Don—like Oedipus, like Odysseus, like Othello, like David Copperfield—had come to have a reality far more profound and tangible than that of most people who had indeed actually lived. Such characters as those had transcended their fictional origins. But not so far as the computer was concerned. It was able to produce a convincing fabrication of Don Quixote, all right—a gaunt bizarre holographic figure that had all the right mannerisms, that ranted and raved in the expectable way, that referred knowledgeably to Dulcinea and Rosinante and Mambrino's helmet. The Spanish king was amused and impressed. But to the French the experiment was a failure. They had produced a Don Quixote who was hopelessly locked to the Spain of the late sixteenth century and to the book from which he had sprung. He had no capacity for independent life and thought—no way to perceive the world that had brought him into being, or to comment on it, or to interact with it. There was nothing new or interesting about that. Any actor could dress up in armor and put on a scraggly beard and recite snatches of Cervantes. What had come forth from the computer, after three years of work, was no more than a predictable reprocessing of what had gone into it, sterile, stale.

Which led the Centre Mondial de la Computation to its next fatal step: abandoning the whole thing. *Zut!* and the project was canceled without any further attempts. No simulated Picassos, no simulated Napoleons, no Joans of Arc. The Quixote event had soured everyone, and no one had the heart to proceed with the work from there. Suddenly it had the taint of failure about it, and France—like Germany, like Australia, like the Han Commercial Sphere, like Brazil, like any of the dynamic centers of the modern world, had a horror of failure. Failure was something to be left to the backward nations or the decadent ones—to the Islamic Socialist Union, say, or the Soviet People's Republic, or to that slumbering giant, the United States of America. So the historic-personage simulation scheme was put aside.

The French thought so little of it, as a matter of fact, that after letting it lie fallow for a few years they licensed it to a bunch of Americans, who had heard about it somehow and felt it might be amusing to play with.

~

"You may really have done it this time," Tanner said.

"Yes. I think we have. After all those false starts."

Tanner nodded. How often had he come into this room with hopes high, only to see some botch, some inanity, some depressing bungle? Richardson had always had an explanation. Sherlock Holmes hadn't worked because he was fictional: that was a necessary recheck of the French Quixote project, demonstrating that fictional characters didn't have the right sort of reality texture to take proper advantage of the program, not enough ambiguity, not enough contradiction. King Arthur had failed for the same reason. Julius Caesar? Too far in the past, maybe: unreliable data, bordering on fiction. Moses? Ditto. Einstein? Too complex, perhaps, for the project in its present level of development: they needed more experience first. Queen Elizabeth I? George Washington? Mozart? We're learning more each time, Richardson insisted after each failure. This isn't black magic we're doing, you know. We aren't necromancers, we're programmers, and we have to figure out how to give the program what it needs.

And now Pizarro?

"Why do you want to work with *him*?" Tanner had asked five or six months earlier. "A ruthless medieval Spanish imperialist, is what I remember from school. A bloodthirsty despoiler of a great culture. A man without morals, honor, faith—"

"You may be doing him an injustice," said Richardson. "He's had a bad press for centuries. And there are things about him that fascinate me."

"Such as?"

"His drive. His courage. His absolute confidence. The other side of ruthlessness, the good side of it, is a total concentration on your task, an utter unwillingness to be stopped by any obstacle. Whether or not you approve of the things he accomplished, you have to admire a man who—"

"All right," Tanner said, abruptly growing weary of the whole enterprise. "Do Pizarro. Whatever you want."

The months had passed. Richardson gave him vague progress reports, nothing to arouse much hope. But now Tanner stared at the tiny strutting figure in the holotank and the conviction began to grow in him that Richardson finally had figured out how to use the simulation program as it was meant to be used.

"So you've actually re-created him, you think? Someone who lived— what, five hundred years ago?"

"He died in 1541," said Richardson.

"Almost six hundred, then."

"And he's not like the others—not simply a re-creation of a great figure out of the past who can run through a set of preprogrammed speeches. What we've got here, if I'm right, is an artificially generated intelligence that can think for itself in modes other than the ones its programmers think in. Which has more information available to itself, in other words, than we've provided it with. That would be the real accomplishment. That's the fundamental philosophical leap that we were going for when we first got involved with this project. To use the program to give us new programs that are capable of true autonomous thought—a program that can think like Pizarro, instead of like Lew Richardson's idea of some historian's idea of how Pizarro might have thought."

"Yes," Tanner said.

"Which means we won't just get back the expectable, the predictable. There'll be surprises. There's no way to learn anything, you know, except through surprises. The sudden combination of known components into something brand new. And that's what I think we've managed to bring off here, at long last. Harry, it may be the biggest artificial-intelligence breakthrough ever achieved."

Tanner pondered that. Was it so? Had they truly done it?

And if they had—

Something new and troubling was beginning to occur to him, much later in the game than it should have. Tanner stared at the holographic figure floating in the center of the tank, that fierce old man with the harsh face and the cold, cruel eyes. He thought about what sort of man he must have been— the man after whom this image had been modeled. A man who was willing to land in South America at age fifty or sixty or whatever he had been, an ignorant illiterate Spanish peasant wearing a suit of ill-fitting armor and waving a rusty sword, and set out to conquer a great empire of millions of people spreading over thousands of miles. Tanner wondered what sort of man would be capable of carrying out a thing like that. Now that man's eyes were staring into his own, and it was a struggle to meet so implacable a gaze.

After a moment he looked away. His left leg began to quiver. He glanced uneasily at Richardson.

"Look at those eyes, Lew. Christ, they're scary!"

"I know. I designed them myself, from the old prints."

"Do you think he's seeing us right now? Can he do that?"

"All he is is software, Harry."

"He seemed to know it when you expanded the image."

Richardson shrugged. "He's very good software. I tell you, he's got autonomy, he's got volition. He's got an electronic *mind*, is what I'm saying. He may have perceived a transient voltage kick. But there are limits to his perceptions, all the same. I don't think there's any way that he can see anything that's outside the holotank unless it's fed to him in the form of data he can process, which hasn't been done."

"You don't *think*? You aren't sure?"

"Harry. Please."

"This man conquered the entire enormous Incan empire with fifty soldiers, didn't he?"

"In fact, I believe it was more like a hundred and fifty."

"Fifty, a hundred fifty, what's the difference? Who knows what you've actually got here? What if you did an even better job than you suspect?"

"What are you saying?"

"What I'm saying is, I'm uneasy all of a sudden. For a long time I didn't think this project was going to produce anything at all. Suddenly I'm starting to think that maybe it's going to produce more than we can handle. I don't want any of your goddamned simulations walking out of the tank and conquering *us*."

Richardson turned to him. His face was flushed, but he was grinning. "Harry, Harry! For God's sake! Five minutes ago you didn't think we had anything at all here except a tiny picture that wasn't even in focus. Now you've gone so far the other way that you're imagining the worst kind of—"

"I see his eyes, Lew. I'm worried that his eyes see me."

"Those aren't real eyes you're looking at. What you see is nothing but a graphics program projected into a holotank. There's no visual capacity there as you understand the concept. His eyes will see you only if I want them to. Right now they don't."

"But you can make them see me?"

"I can make them see anything I want them to see. I created him, Harry."

"With volition. With autonomy."

"After all this time, you start worrying *now* about these things?"

"It's my neck on the line if something that you guys on the technical side make runs amok. This autonomy thing suddenly troubles me."

"I'm still the one with the data gloves," Richardson said. "I twitch my fingers and he dances. That's not really Pizarro down there, remember. And that's no Frankenstein monster, either. It's just a simulation. It's just so much data, just a bunch of electromagnetic impulses that I can shut off with one movement of my pinkie."

"Do it, then."

"Shut him off? But I haven't begun to show you—"

"Shut him off, and then turn him on," Tanner said.

Richardson looked bothered. "If you say so, Harry."

He moved a finger. The image of Pizarro vanished from the holotank. Swirling gray mists moved in it for a moment, and then all was white wool. Tanner felt a quick jolt of guilt, as though he had just ordered the execution of the man in the medieval armor. Richardson gestured again, and color flashed across the tank, and then Pizarro reappeared.

"I just wanted to see how much autonomy your little guy really has," said Tanner. "Whether he was quick enough to head you off and escape into some other channel before you could cut his power."

"You really don't understand how this works at all, do you, Harry?"

"I just wanted to see," said Tanner again, sullenly. After a moment's silence he said, "Do you ever feel like God?"

"Like God?"

"You breathed life in. Life of a sort, anyway. But you breathed free will in, too. That's what this experiment is all about, isn't it? All your talk about volition and autonomy? You're trying to re-create a human mind—which means to create it all over again—a mind that can think in its own special way, and come up with its own unique responses to situations, which will not necessarily be the responses that its programmers might anticipate, in fact almost certainly will not be, and which not might be all that desirable or beneficial, either, and you simply have to allow for that risk, just as God, once he gave free will to mankind, knew that He was likely to see all manner of evil deeds being performed by His creations as they exercised that free will—"

"Please, Harry—"

"Listen, is it possible for me to talk with your Pizarro?"

"Why?"

"By way of finding out what you've got there. To get some firsthand knowledge of what the project has accomplished. Or you could say I just want to test the quality of the simulation. Whatever. I'd feel more a part of this thing, more aware of what it's all about in here, if I could have some direct contact with him. Would it be all right if I did that?"

"Yes. Of course."

"Do I have to talk to him in Spanish?"

"In any language you like. There's an interface, after all. He'll think it's his own language coming in, no matter what, sixteenth-century Spanish. And he'll answer you in what seems like Spanish to him, but you'll hear it in English."

"Are you sure?"

"Of course."

"And you don't mind if I make contact with him?"

"Whatever you like."

"It won't upset his calibration or anything?"

"It won't do any harm at all, Harry."

"Fine. Let me talk to him, then."

There was a disturbance in the air ahead, a shifting, a swirling, like a little whirlwind. Pizarro halted and watched it for a moment, wondering what was coming next. A demon arriving to torment him, maybe. Or an angel. Whatever it was, he was ready for it.

Then a voice out of the whirlwind said, in that same comically exaggerated Castilian Spanish that Pizarro himself had found himself speaking a little while before, "Can you hear me?"

"I hear you, yes. I don't see you. Where are you?"

"Right in front of you. Wait a second. I'll show you." Out of the whirlwind came a strange face that hovered in the middle of nowhere, a face without a body, a lean face, close-shaven, no beard at all, no mustache, the hair cut very short, dark eyes set close together. He had never seen a face like that before.

"What are you?" Pizarro asked. "A demon or an angel?"

"Neither one." Indeed, he didn't sound very demonic. "A man, just like you."

"Not much like me, I think. Is a face all there is to you, or do you have a body, too?"

"All you see of me is a face?"

"Yes."

"Wait a second."

"I will wait as long as I have to. I have plenty of time."

The face disappeared. Then it returned, attached to the body of a big, wide-shouldered man who was wearing a long loose gray robe, something like a priest's cassock, but much more ornate, with points of glowing light gleaming on it everywhere. Then the body vanished and Pizarro could see only the face again. He could make no sense out of any of this. He began to understand how the Indians must have felt when the first Spaniards came over the horizon, riding horses, carrying guns, wearing armor.

"You are very strange. Are you an Englishman, maybe?"

"American."

"Ah," Pizarro said, as though that made things better. "An American. And what is that?"

The face wavered and blurred for a moment. There was mysterious new agitation in the thick white clouds surrounding it. Then the face grew steady and said, "America is a country north of Peru. A very large country, where many people live."

"You mean New Spain, which was Mexico, where my kinsman Cortés is Captain-General?"

"North of Mexico. Far to the north of it."

Pizarro shrugged. "I know nothing of those places. Or not very much. There is an island called Florida, yes? And stories of cities of gold, but I think they are only stories. I found the gold, in Peru. Enough to choke on, I found. Tell me this, am I in heaven now?"

"No."

"Then this is hell?"

"Not that, either. Where you are—it's very difficult to explain, actually—"

"I am in America."

"Yes. In America, yes."

"And am I dead?"

There was silence for a moment.

"No, not dead," the voice said uneasily.

"You are lying to me, I think."

"How could we be speaking with each other, if you were dead?"

Pizarro laughed hoarsely. "Are you asking *me*? I understand nothing of what is happening to me in this place. Where are my priests? Where is my page? Send me my brother!" He glared. "Well? Why don't you get them for me?"

"They aren't here. You're here all by yourself, Don Francisco."

"In America. All by myself in your America. Show me your America, then. Is there such a place? Is America all clouds and whorls of light? Where is America? Let me see America. Prove to me that I am in America."

There was another silence, longer than the last. Then the face disappeared and the wall of white cloud began to boil and churn more fiercely than before. Pizarro stared into the midst of it, feeling a mingled sense of curiosity and annoyance. The face did not reappear. He saw nothing at all. He was being toyed with. He was a prisoner in some strange place, and they were treating him like a child, like a dog, like—like an Indian. Perhaps this was the retribution for what he had done to King Atahuallpa, then, that fine noble foolish man who had given himself up to him in all innocence, and whom he had put to death so that he might have the gold of Atahuallpa's kingdom.

Well, so be it, Pizarro thought. Atahuallpa accepted all that befell him without complaint and without fear, and so will I. Christ will be my guardian, and if there is no Christ, well, then I will have no guardian, and so be it. So be it.

The voice out of the whirlwind said suddenly, "Look, Don Francisco. This is America."

A picture appeared on the wall of cloud. It was a kind of picture Pizarro had never before encountered or even imagined, one that seemed to open before him like a gate and sweep him in and carry him along through a vista of changing scenes depicted in brilliant, vivid bursts of color. It was like flying high above the land, looking down on an infinite scroll of miracles. He saw vast cities without walls, roadways that unrolled like endless skeins of white ribbon, huge lakes, mighty rivers, gigantic mountains, everything speeding past him so swiftly that he could scarcely absorb any of it. In moments it all became chaotic in his mind: the buildings taller than the highest cathedral spire, the swarming masses of people, the shining metal chariots without beasts to draw them, the stupendous landscapes, the close-packed complexity of it all. Watching all this, he felt the fine old hunger taking possession of him again: he wanted to grasp this strange vast place, and seize it, and clutch it close, and ransack it for all it was worth. But the thought of that was overwhelming. His eyes grew glassy and his heart began to pound so terrifyingly that he supposed he would be able to feel it thumping if he put his hand to the front of his armor. He turned away, muttering, "Enough. Enough."

The terrifying picture vanished. Gradually the clamor of his heart subsided.

Then he began to laugh.

"Peru!" he cried. "Peru was nothing, next to your America! Peru was a hole! Peru was mud! How ignorant I was! I went to Peru, when there was America, ten thousand times as grand! I wonder what I could find, in America." He smacked his lips and winked. Then, chuckling, he said, "But don't be afraid. I won't try to conquer your America. I'm too old for that now. And perhaps America would have been too much for me, even before. Perhaps." He grinned savagely at the troubled staring face of the short-haired beardless man, the American. "I really am dead, is this not so? I feel no hunger, I feel no pain, no thirst, when I put my hand to my body I do not feel even my body. I am like one who lies dreaming. But this is no dream. Am I a ghost?"

"Not—exactly."

"Not exactly a ghost! Not exactly! No one with half the brains of a pig would talk like that. What is that supposed to mean?"

"It's not easy explaining it in words you would understand, Don Francisco."

"No, of course not. I am very stupid, as everyone knows, and that is why I conquered Peru, because I was so very stupid. But let it pass. I am not exactly a ghost, but I am dead all the same, right?"

"Well—"

"I am dead, yes. But somehow I have not gone to hell or even to purgatory, but I am still in the world, only it is much later now. I have slept as the dead sleep, and now I have awakened in some year that is far beyond my time, and it is the time of America. Is this not so? Who is king now? Who is pope? What year is this? 1750? 1800?"

"The year 2130," the face said, after some hesitation.

"Ah." Pizarro tugged thoughtfully at his lower lip. "And the king? Who is king?"

A long pause. "Alfonso is his name," said the face.

"Alfonso? The kings of Aragon were called Alfonso. The father of Ferdinand, he was Alfonso. Alfonso V, he was."

"Alfonso XIX is King of Spain now."

"Ah. Ah. And the pope? Who is pope?"

A pause again. Not to know the name of the pope, immediately upon being asked? How strange. Demon or no, this was a fool.

"Pius," said the voice, when some time had passed. "Pius XVI."

"The sixteenth Pius," said Pizarro somberly. "Jesus and Mary, the sixteenth Pius! What has become of me? Long dead, is what I am. Still unwashed of all my sins. I can feel them clinging to my skin like mud, still. And you are a sorcerer, you American, and you have brought me to life again. Eh? Eh? Is that not so?"

"It is something like that, Don Francisco," the face admitted.

"So you speak your Spanish strangely because you no longer understand the right way of speaking it. Eh? Even I speak Spanish in a strange way, and I speak it in a voice that does not sound like my own. No one speaks Spanish any more, eh? Eh? Only American, they speak. Eh? But you try to speak Spanish, only it comes out stupidly. And you have caused me to speak the same way, thinking it is the way I spoke, though you are wrong. Well, you can do miracles, but I suppose you can't do everything perfectly, even in this land of miracles of the year 2130. Eh? Eh?" Pizarro leaned forward intently. "What do you say? You thought I was a fool, because I don't have reading and writing? I am not so ignorant, eh? I understand things quickly."

"You understand very quickly indeed."

"But you have knowledge of many things that are unknown to me. You must know the manner of my death, for example. How strange that is, talking to you of the manner of my death, but you must know it, eh? When did it come to me? And how? Did it come in my sleep? No, no, how could that be? They die in their sleep in Spain, but not in Peru. How was it, then? I was set upon by cowards, was I? Some brother of Atahuallpa, falling upon me as I stepped out of my house? A slave sent by the Inca Manco, or one of those others? No. No. The Indians would not harm me, for all that I did to them. It was the young Almagro who took me down, was it not, in vengeance for his father, or Juan de Herrada, eh? or perhaps even Picado, my own secretary—no, not Picado, he was my man, always—but maybe Alvarado, the young one, Diego—well, one of those, and it would have been sudden, very sudden or I would have been able to stop them—am I right, am I speaking the truth? Tell me. You know these things. Tell me of the manner of my dying." There was no answer. Pizarro shaded his eyes and peered into the dazzling pearly whiteness. He was no longer able to see the face of the American. "Are you there?" Pizarro said. "Where have you gone? Were you only a dream? American! American! Where have you gone?"

◆

The break in contact was jolting. Tanner sat rigid, hands trembling, lips tightly clamped. Pizarro, in the holotank, was no more than a distant little streak of color now, no larger than his thumb, gesticulating amid the swirling clouds. The vitality of him, the arrogance, the fierce probing curiosity, the powerful hatreds and jealousies, the strength that had come from vast ventures recklessly conceived and desperately seen through to triumph, all the things that were

Francisco Pizarro, all that Tanner had felt an instant before—all that had vanished at the flick of a finger.

After a moment or two Tanner felt the shock beginning to ease. He turned toward Richardson.

"What happened?"

"I had to pull you out of there. I didn't want you telling him anything about how he died."

"I don't know how he died."

"Well, neither does he, and I didn't want to chance it that you did. There's no predicting what sort of psychological impact that kind of knowledge might have on him."

"You talk about him as though he's alive."

"Isn't he?" Richardson said.

"If I said a thing like that, you'd tell me that I was being ignorant and unscientific."

Richardson smiled faintly. "You're right. But somehow I trust myself to know what I'm saying when I say that he's alive. I know I don't mean it literally and I'm not sure about you. What did you think of him, anyway?"

"He's amazing," Tanner said. "Really amazing. The strength of him—I could feel it pouring out at me in waves. And his mind! So quick, the way he picked up on everything. Guessing that he must be in the future. Wanting to know what number pope was in office. Wanting to see what America looked like. And the cockiness of him! Telling me that he's not up to the conquest of America, that he might have tried for it instead of Peru a few years earlier, but not now, now he's a little too old for that. Incredible! Nothing could faze him for long, even when he realized that he must have been dead for a long time. Wanting to know how he died, even!" Tanner frowned. "What age did you make him, anyway, when you put this program together?"

"About sixty. Five or six years after the conquest, and a year or two before he died. At the height of his power, that is."

"I suppose you couldn't have let him have any knowledge of his actual death. That way he'd be too much like some kind of a ghost."

"That's what we thought. We set the cutoff at a time when he had done everything that he had set out to do, when he was the complete Pizarro. But before the end. He didn't need to know about that. Nobody does. That's why I had to yank you, you see? In case you knew. And started to tell him."

Tanner shook his head. "If I ever knew, I've forgotten it. How did it happen?"

"Exactly as he guessed: at the hands of his own comrades."

"So he saw it coming."

"At the age we made him, he already knew that a civil war had started in South America, that the conquistadores were quarreling over the division of the spoils. We built that much into him. He knows that his partner Almagro has turned against him and been beaten in battle, and that they've executed him. What he doesn't know, but obviously can expect, is that Almagro's friends are going to break into his house and try to kill him. He's got it all figured out pretty much as it's going to happen. As it *did* happen, I should say."

"Incredible. To be that shrewd."

"He was a son of a bitch, yes. But he was a genius, too."

"Was he, really? Or is it that you made him one when you set up the program for him?"

"All we put in were the objective details of his life, patterns of event and response. Plus an overlay of commentary by others, his contemporaries and later historians familiar with the record, providing an extra dimension of character density. Put in enough of that kind of stuff and apparently they add up to the whole personality. It isn't *my* personality or that of anybody else who worked on this project, Harry. When you put in Pizarro's set of events and responses, you wind up getting Pizarro. You get the ruthlessness and you get the brilliance. Put in a different set, you get someone else. And what we've finally seen, this time, is that when we do our work right we get something out of the computer that's bigger than the sum of what we put in."

"Are you sure?"

Richardson said, "Did you notice that he complained about the Spanish that he thought you were speaking?"

"Yes. He said that it sounded strange, that nobody seemed to know how to speak proper Spanish any more. I didn't quite follow that. Does the interface you built speak lousy Spanish?"

"Evidently it speaks lousy sixteenth-century Spanish," Richardson said. "Nobody knows what sixteenth-century Spanish actually sounded like. We can only guess. Apparently, we didn't guess very well."

"But how would *he* know? You synthesized him in the first place! If you don't know how Spanish sounded in his time, how would he? All he should know about Spanish, or about anything, is what you put into him."

"Exactly," Richardson said.

"But that doesn't make any sense, Lew!"

"He also said that the Spanish he heard himself speaking was no good, and that his own voice didn't sound right to him either. That we had *caused* him to speak this way, thinking that was how he actually spoke, but we were wrong."

"How could he possibly know what his voice really sounded like, if all he is is a simulation put together by people who don't have the slightest notion of what his voice really—"

"I don't have any idea," said Richardson quietly. "But he *does* know."

"Does he? Or is this just some diabolical Pizarro-like game that he's playing to unsettle us, because *that's* in his character as you devised it?"

"I think he does know," Richardson said.

"Where's he finding it out, then?"

"It's there. We don't know where, but he does. It's somewhere in the data that we put through the permutation network, even if we don't know it and even though we couldn't find it now if we set out to look for it. *He* can find it. He can't manufacture that kind of knowledge by magic, but he can assemble what look to us like seemingly irrelevant bits and come up with new information leading to a conclusion that is meaningful to him. That's what we mean by artificial intelligence, Harry. We've finally got a program that works something like the human brain: by leaps of intuition so sudden and broad that they seem inexplicable and nonquantifiable, even if they really aren't. We've fed in enough stuff so that he can assimilate a whole stew of ostensibly unrelated data and come up with new information. We don't just have a ventriloquist's dummy in that tank. We've got something that thinks it's Pizarro and thinks like Pizarro and knows things that Pizarro knew and we don't. Which means we've accomplished the qualitative jump in artificial-intelligence capacity that we set out to achieve with this project. It's awesome. I get shivers down my back when I think about it."

"I do, too," Tanner said. "But not so much from awe as fear."

"Fear?"

"Knowing now that he has capabilities beyond those he was programmed for, how can you be so absolutely certain that he can't commandeer your network somehow and get himself loose?"

"It's technically impossible. All he is is electromagnetic impulses. I can pull the plug on him any time I like. There's nothing to panic over here. Believe me, Harry."

"I'm trying to."

"I can show you the schematics. We've got a phenomenal simulation in that computer, yes. But it's still only a simulation. It isn't a vampire, it isn't a werewolf, it isn't anything supernatural. It's just the best damned computer simulation anyone's ever made."

"It makes me uneasy. *He* makes me uneasy."

"He should. The power of the man, the indomitable nature of him—why do you think I summoned him up, Harry? He's got something that we don't understand in this country any more. I want us to study him. I want us to try to learn what that kind of drive and determination is really like. Now that you've talked to him, now that you've touched his spirit, of course you're shaken up by him. He radiates tremendous confidence. He radiates fantastic faith in himself. That kind of man can achieve anything he wants—even conquer the whole Incan empire with a hundred fifty men, or however many it was. But I'm not frightened of what we've put together here. And you shouldn't be either. We should all be damned proud of it. You as well as the people on the technical side. And you will be, too."

"I hope you're right," Tanner said.

"You'll see."

For a long moment Tanner stared in silence at the holotank, where the image of Pizarro had been.

"Okay," said Tanner finally. "Maybe I'm overreacting. Maybe I'm sounding like the ignoramus layman that I am. I'll take it on faith that you'll be able to keep your phantoms in their boxes."

"We will," Richardson said.

"Let's hope so. All right," said Tanner. "So what's your next move?"

Richardson looked puzzled. "My next move?"

"With this project? Where does it go from here?"

Hesitantly Richardson said, "There's no formal proposal yet. We thought we'd wait until we had approval from you on the initial phase of the work, and then—"

"How does this sound?" Tanner asked. "I'd like to see you start in on another simulation right away."

"Well—yes, yes, of course—"

"And when you've got him worked up, Lew, would it be feasible for you to put him right there in the tank with Pizarro?"

Richardson looked startled. "To have a sort of dialog with him, you mean?"

"Yes."

"I suppose we could do that," Richardson said cautiously. "*Should* do that. Yes. Yes. A very interesting suggestion, as a matter of fact." He ventured an uneasy smile. Up till now Tanner had kept in the background of this project, a mere management functionary, an observer, virtually an outsider. This was something new, his interjecting himself into the planning process, and plainly Richardson didn't know what to make of it. Tanner watched him fidget. After a little pause Richardson said, "Was there anyone particular you had in mind for us to try next?"

"Is that new parallax thing of yours ready to try?" Tanner asked. "The one that's supposed to compensate for time distortion and myth contamination?"

"Just about. But we haven't tested—"

"Good," Tanner said. "Here's your chance. What about trying for Socrates?"

There was billowing whiteness below him, and on every side, as though all the world were made of fleece. He wondered if it might be snow. That was not something he was really familiar with. It snowed once in a great while in Athens, yes, but usually only a light dusting that melted in the morning sun. Of course he had seen snow aplenty when he had been up north in the war, at Potidaea, in the time of Pericles. But that had been long ago; and that stuff, as best he remembered it, had not been much like this. There was no quality of coldness about the whiteness that surrounded him now. It could just as readily be great banks of clouds.

But what would clouds be doing *below* him? Clouds, he thought, are mere vapor, air and water, no substance to them at all. Their natural place was overhead. Clouds that gathered at one's feet had no true quality of cloudness about them.

Snow that had no coldness? Clouds that had no buoyancy? Nothing in this place seemed to possess any quality that was proper to itself in this place, including himself. He seemed to be walking, but his feet touched nothing at all. It was more like moving through air. But how could one move in the air? Aristophanes, in that mercilessly mocking play of his, had sent him floating through the clouds suspended in a basket, and made him say things like, "I am traversing the air and contemplating the sun." That was Aristophanes' way of playing with him, and he had not been seriously upset, though his friends had been very hurt on his behalf. Still, that was only a play.

This felt real, insofar as it felt like anything at all.

Perhaps he was dreaming, and the nature of his dream was that he thought he was really doing the things he had done in Aristophanes' play. What was that lovely line? "I have to suspend my brain and mingle the subtle essence of my mind with this air, which is of the same nature, in order clearly to penetrate the things of heaven." Good old Aristophanes! Nothing was sacred to him! Except, of course, those things that were truly sacred, such as wisdom, truth, virtue. "I would have discovered nothing if I had remained on the ground and pondered from below the things that are above: for the earth by its force attracts the sap of the mind to itself. It's the same way with watercress." And Socrates began to laugh.

He held his hands before him and studied them, the short sturdy fingers, the thick powerful wrists. His hands, yes. His old plain hands that had stood him in good stead all his life, when he had worked as a stonemason as his father had, when he had fought in his city's wars, when he had trained at the gymnasium. But now when he touched them to his face he felt nothing. There should be a chin here, a forehead, yes, a blunt stubby nose, thick lips; but there was nothing. He was touching air. He could put his hand right through the place where his face should be. He could put one hand against the other, and press with all his might, and feel nothing.

This is a very strange place indeed, he thought.

Perhaps it is that place of pure forms that young Plato liked to speculate about, where everything is perfect and nothing is quite real. Those are ideal clouds all around me, not real ones. This is ideal air upon which I walk. I myself am the ideal Socrates, liberated from my coarse ordinary body. Could it be? Well, maybe so. He stood for a while, considering that possibility. The thought came to him that this might be the life after life, in which case he might meet some of the gods, if there were any gods in the first place, and if he could manage to find them. I would like that, he thought. Perhaps they would be willing to speak with me. Athena would discourse with me on wisdom, or Hermes on speed, or Ares on the nature of courage, or Zeus on—well, whatever Zeus cared to speak on. Of course I would seem to be the merest fool to them, but that would be all right: anyone who expects to hold discourse with the gods as though he were their equal *is* a fool. I have no such illusion. If there are gods at all, surely they are far superior to me in all respects, for otherwise why would men regard them as gods?

Of course he had serious doubts that the gods existed at all. But if they did, it was reasonable to think that they might be found in a place such as this.

He looked up. The sky was radiant with brilliant golden light. He took a deep breath and smiled and set out across the fleecy nothingness of this airy world to see if he could find the gods.

Tanner said, "What do you think now? Still so pessimistic?"

"It's too early to say," said Richardson, looking glum.

"He *looks* like Socrates, doesn't he?"

"That was the easy part. We've got plenty of descriptions of Socrates that came down from people who knew him, the flat wide nose, the bald head, the thick lips, the short neck. A standard Socrates face that everybody recognizes, just as they do Sherlock Holmes, or Don Quixote. So that's how we made him look. It doesn't signify anything important. It's what's going on inside his head that'll determine whether we really have Socrates."

"He seems calm and good-humored as he wanders around in there. The way a philosopher should."

"Pizarro seemed just as much of a philosopher when we turned him loose in the tank."

"Pizarro may *be* just as much of a philosopher," Tanner said. "Neither man's the sort who'd be likely to panic if he found himself in some mysterious place." Richardson's negativism was beginning to bother him. It was as if the two men had exchanged places: Richardson now uncertain of the range and power of his own program, Tanner pushing the way on and on toward bigger and better things.

Bleakly Richardson said, "I'm still pretty skeptical. We've tried the new parallax filters, yes. But I'm afraid we're going to run into the same problem the French did with Don Quixote, and that we did with Holmes and Moses and Caesar. There's too much contamination of the data by myth and fantasy. The Socrates who has come down to us is as much fictional as real, or maybe *all* fictional. For all we know, Plato made up everything we think we know about him, the same way Conan Doyle made up Holmes. And what we're going to get, I'm afraid, will be something secondhand, something lifeless, something lacking in the spark of self-directed intelligence that we're after."

"But the new filters—"

"Perhaps. Perhaps."

Tanner shook his head stubbornly. "Holmes and Don Quixote are fiction through and through. They exist in only one dimension, constructed for us by their authors. You cut through the distortions and fantasies of later readers and commentators and all you find underneath is a made-up character. A lot of Socrates may have been invented by Plato for his own purposes, but a lot wasn't. He really existed. He took an actual part in civic activities in fifth-century Athens. He figures in books by a lot of other contemporaries of his besides Plato's dialogues. That gives us the parallax you're looking for, doesn't it—the view of him from more than one viewpoint?"

"Maybe it does. Maybe not. We got nowhere with Moses. Was *he* fictional?"

"Who can say? All you had to go by was the Bible. And a ton of biblical commentary, for whatever that was worth. Not much, apparently."

"And Caesar? You're not going to tell me that Caesar wasn't real," said Richardson. "But what we have of him is evidently contaminated with myth. When we synthesized him we got nothing but a caricature, and I don't have to remind you how fast even that broke down into sheer gibberish."

"Not relevant," Tanner said. "Caesar was early in the project. You know much more about what you're doing now. I think this is going to work."

Richardson's dogged pessimism, Tanner decided, must be a defense mechanism, designed to insulate himself against the possibility of a new failure. Socrates, after all, hadn't been Richardson's own choice. And this was the first time he had used these new enhancement methods, the parallax program that was the latest refinement of the process.

Tanner looked at him. Richardson remained silent.

"Go on," Tanner said. "Bring up Pizarro and let the two of them talk to each other. Then we'll find out what sort of Socrates you've conjured up here."

Once again there was a disturbance in the distance, a little dark blur on the pearly horizon, a blotch, a flaw in the gleaming whiteness. Another demon is arriving, Pizarro thought. Or perhaps it is the same one as before, the American, the one who liked to show himself only as a face, with short hair and no beard.

But as this one drew closer Pizarro saw that he was different from the last, short and stocky, with broad shoulders and a deep chest. He was nearly bald, and his thick beard was coarse and unkempt. He looked old, at least sixty, maybe sixty-five. He looked very ugly, too, with bulging eyes and a flat nose that had wide, flaring nostrils, and a neck so short that his oversize head seemed to sprout straight from his trunk. All he wore was a thin, ragged brown robe. His feet were bare.

"You, there," Pizarro called out. "You! Demon! Are you also an American, demon?"

"Your pardon. An Athenian, did you say?"

"*American* is what I said. That's what the last one was. Is that where you come from, too, demon? America?"

A shrug. "No, I think not. I am of Athens." There was a curious mocking twinkle in the demon's eyes.

"A Greek? This demon is a Greek?"

"I am of Athens," the ugly one said again. "My name is Socrates, the son of Sophroniscus. I could not tell you what a Greek is, so perhaps I may be one, but I think not, unless a Greek is what you call a man of Athens." He spoke in a slow, plodding way, like one who was exceedingly stupid. Pizarro had sometimes met men like this before, and in his experience they were generally not as stupid as they wanted to be taken for. He felt caution rising in him. "And I am no demon, but just a plain man: very plain, as you can easily see."

Pizarro snorted. "You like to chop words, do you?"

"It is not the worst of amusements, my friend," said the other, and put his hands together behind his back in the most casual way, and stood there calmly, smiling, looking off into the distance, rocking back and forth on the balls of his feet.

◆

"Well?" Tanner said. "Do we have Socrates or not? I say that's the genuine article there."

Richardson looked up and nodded. He seemed relieved and quizzical both at once. "So far so good, I have to say. He's coming through real and true."

"Yes."

"We may actually have worked past the problem of information contamination that ruined some of the earlier simulations. We're not getting any of the signal degradation we encountered then."

"He's some character, isn't he?" Tanner said. "I liked the way he just walked right up to Pizarro without the slightest sign of uneasiness. He's not at all afraid of him."

"Why should he be?" Richardson asked.

"Wouldn't you? If you were walking along through God knows what kind of unearthly place, not knowing where you were or how you got there, and suddenly you saw a ferocious-looking bastard like Pizarro standing in front of you wearing full armor and carrying a sword—" Tanner shook his head. "Well, maybe not. He's Socrates, after all, and Socrates wasn't afraid of anything except boredom."

"And Pizarro's just a simulation. Nothing but software."

"So you've been telling me all along. But Socrates doesn't know that."

"True," Richardson said. He seemed lost in thought a moment. "Perhaps there *is* some risk."

"Huh?"

"If our Socrates is anything like the one in Plato, and he surely ought to be, then he's capable of making a considerable pest of himself. Pizarro may not care for Socrates' little verbal games. If he doesn't feel like playing, I suppose there's a theoretical possibility that he'll engage in some sort of aggressive response."

That took Tanner by surprise. He swung around and said, "Are you telling me that there's some way he can *harm* Socrates?"

"Who knows?" said Richardson. "In the real world, one program can certainly crash another one. Maybe one simulation can be dangerous to another one. This is all new territory for all of us, Harry. Including the people in the tank."

◆

The tall grizzled-looking man said, scowling, "You tell me you're an Athenian, but not a Greek. What sense am I supposed to make of that? I could ask Pedro de Candia, I guess, who is a Greek but not an Athenian. But he's not here. Perhaps you're just a fool, eh? Or you think I am."

"I have no idea what you are. Could it be that you are a god?"

"A *god*?"

"Yes," Socrates said. He studied the other impassively. His face was harsh, his gaze was cold. "Perhaps you are Ares. You have a fierce warlike look about you, and you wear armor, but not such armor as I have ever seen. This place is so strange that it might well be the abode of the gods, and that could be a god's armor you wear, I suppose. If you are Ares, then I salute you with the respect that is due you. I am Socrates of Athens, the stonemason's son."

"You talk a lot of nonsense. I don't know your Ares."

"Why, the god of war, of course! Everyone knows that. Except barbarians, that is. Are you a barbarian, then? You sound like one, I must say—but then, I seem to sound like a barbarian myself, and I've spoken the tongue of Hellas all my life. There are many mysteries here, indeed."

"Your language problem again," Tanner said. "Couldn't you even get classical Greek to come out right? Or are they both speaking Spanish to each other?"

"Pizarro thinks they're speaking Spanish. Socrates thinks they're speaking Greek. And, of course, the Greek is off. We don't know how *anything* that was spoken before the age of recordings sounded. All we can do is guess."

"But can't you—"

"Shhh," Richardson said.

Pizarro said, "I may be a bastard, but I'm no barbarian, fellow, so curb your tongue. And let's have no more blasphemy out of you either."

"If I blaspheme, forgive me. It is in innocence. Tell me where I trespass, and I will not do it again."

"This crazy talk of gods. Of my being a god. I'd expect a heathen to talk like that, but not a Greek. But maybe you're a heathen kind of Greek, and not to be blamed. It's heathens who see gods everywhere. Do I look like a god to you? I am Francisco Pizarro, of Trujillo in Estremadura, the son of the famous soldier Gonzalo Pizarro, colonel of infantry, who served in the wars of Gonzalo de Cordova, whom men call the Great Captain. I have fought some wars myself."

"Then you are not a god but simply a soldier? Good. I, too, have been a soldier. I am more at ease with soldiers than with gods, as most people are, I would think."

"A soldier? You?" Pizarro smiled. This shabby ordinary little man, more bedraggled-looking than any self-respecting groom would be, a soldier? "In which wars?"

"The wars of Athens. I fought at Potidaea, where the Corinthians were making trouble, and withholding the tribute that was due us. It was very cold there, and the siege was long and bleak, but we did our duty. I fought again some years later at Delium against the Boeotians. Laches was our general then, but it went badly for us, and we did our best fighting in retreat. And then," Socrates said, "when Brasidas was in Amphipolis, and they sent Cleon to drive him out, I—"

"Enough," said Pizarro with an impatient wave of his hand. "These wars are unknown to me." A private soldier, a man of the ranks, no doubt. "Well, then this is the place where they send dead soldiers, I suppose."

"Are we dead, then?"

"Long ago. There's an Alfonso who's king, and a Pius who's pope, and you wouldn't believe their numbers. Pius the Sixteenth, I think the demon said. And the American said also that it is the year 2130. The last year that I can remember was 1539. What about you?"

The one who called himself Socrates shrugged again. "In Athens we use a different reckoning. But let us say, for argument's sake, that we are dead. I think that is very likely, considering what sort of place this seems to be, and how airy I find my body to be. So we have died, and this is the life after life. I wonder: is this a place where virtuous men are sent, or those who were not virtuous? Or do all men go to the same place after death, whether they were virtuous or not? What would you say?"

"I haven't figured that out yet," said Pizarro.

"Well, were you virtuous in your life, or not?"

"Did I sin, you mean?"

"Yes, we could use that word."

"Did I sin, he wants to know," said Pizarro, amazed. "He asks, Was I a sinner? Did I live a virtuous life? What business is that of his?"

"Humor me," said Socrates. "For the sake of the argument, if you will, allow me a few small questions—"

⌣

"So it's starting," Tanner said. "You see? You really *did* do it! Socrates is drawing him into a dialogue!"

Richardson's eyes were glowing. "He is, yes. How marvelous this is, Harry!"

"Socrates is going to talk rings around him."

"I'm not so sure of that," Richardson said.

⌣

"I gave as good as I got," said Pizarro. "If I was injured, I gave injury back. There's no sin in that. It's only common sense. A man does what is necessary to survive and to protect his place in the world. Sometimes I might forget a fast day, yes, or use the Lord's name in vain—those are sins, I suppose, Fray Vicente was always after me for things like that—but does that make me a sinner? I did my penances as soon as I could find time for them. It's a sinful world and I'm no different from anyone else, so why be harsh on me? Eh? God made me as I am. I'm done in His image. And I have faith in His Son."

"So you are a virtuous man, then?"

"I'm not a sinner, at any rate. As I told you, if ever I sinned I did my contrition, which made it the same as if the sin hadn't ever happened."

"Indeed," said Socrates. "Then you are a virtuous man and I have come to a good place. But I want to be absolutely sure. Tell me again: is your conscience completely clear?"

"What are you, a confessor?"

"Only an ignorant man seeking understanding. Which you can provide, by taking part with me in the exploration. If I have come to the place of virtuous men, then I must have been virtuous myself when I lived. Ease my mind, therefore, and let me know whether there is anything on your soul that you regret having done."

Pizarro stirred uneasily. "Well," he said, "I killed a king."

"A wicked one? An enemy of your city?"

"No. He was wise and kind."

"Then you have reason for regret indeed. For surely that is a sin, to kill a wise king."

"But he was a heathen."

"A what?"

"He denied God."

"He denied his own god?" said Socrates. "Then perhaps it was not so wrong to kill him."

"No. He denied mine. He *preferred* his own. And so he was a heathen. And all his people were heathens, since they followed his way. That could not be. They were at risk of eternal damnation because they followed him. I killed him for the sake of his people's souls. I killed him out of the love of God."

"But would you not say that all gods are the reflection of the one God?"

Pizarro considered that. "In a way, that's true, I suppose."

"And is the service of God not itself godly?"

"How could it be anything but godly, Socrates?"

"And you would say that one who serves his god faithfully according to the teachings of his god is behaving in a godly way?"

Frowning, Pizarro said, "Well—if you look at it that way, yes—"

"Then I think the king you killed was a godly man, and by killing him you sinned against God."

"Wait a minute!"

"But think of it: by serving his god he must also have served yours, for any servant of a god is a servant of the true God who encompasses all our imagined gods."

"No," said Pizarro sullenly. "How could he have been a servant of God? He knew nothing of Jesus. He had no understanding of the Trinity. When the priest offered him the Bible, he threw it to the ground in scorn. He was a heathen, Socrates. And so are you. You don't know anything of these matters at all, if you think that Atahuallpa was godly. Or if you think you're going to get me to think so."

"Indeed, I have very little knowledge of anything. But you say he was a wise man, and kind?"

"In his heathen way."

"And a good king to his people?"

"So it seemed. They were a thriving people when I found them."

"Yet he was not godly."

"I told you. He had never had the sacraments, and in fact he spurned them right up until the moment of his death, when he accepted baptism. *Then* he came to be godly. But by then the sentence of death was upon him and it was too late for anything to save him."

"Baptism? Tell me what that is, Pizarro."

"A sacrament."

"And that is?"

"A holy rite. Done with holy water, by a priest. It admits one to Holy Mother Church, and brings forgiveness from sin both original and actual, and gives the gift of the Holy Spirit."

"You must tell me more about these things another time. So you made this good king godly by this baptism? And then you killed him?"

"Yes."

"But he was godly when you killed him. Surely, then, to kill him was a sin."

"He had to die, Socrates!"

"And why was that?" asked the Athenian.

❦

"Socrates is closing in for the kill," Tanner said. "Watch this!"

"I'm watching. But there isn't going to be any kill," said Richardson. "Their basic assumptions are too far apart."

"You'll see."

"Will I?"

⌣

Pizarro said, "I've already told you why he had to die. It was because his people followed him in all things. And so they worshiped the sun, because he said the sun was God. Their souls would have gone to hell if we had allowed them to continue that way."

"But if they followed him in all things," said Socrates, "then surely they would have followed him into baptism, and become godly, and thus done that which was pleasing to you and to your god! Is that not so?"

"No," said Pizarro, twisting his fingers in his beard.

"Why do you think that?"

"Because the king agreed to be baptized only after we had sentenced him to death. He was in the way, don't you see? He was an obstacle to our power! So we had to get rid of him. He would never have led his people to the truth of his own free will. That was why we had to kill him. But we didn't want to kill his soul as well as his body, so we said to him, Look, Atahuallpa, we're going to put you to death, but if you let us baptize you we'll strangle you quickly, and if you don't we'll burn you alive and it'll be very slow. So of course he agreed to be baptized, and we strangled him. What choice was there for anybody? He had to die. He still didn't believe the true faith, as we all well knew. Inside his head he was as big a heathen as ever. But he died a Christian all the same."

"A what?"

"A Christian! A Christian! One who believes in Jesus Christ the Son of God!"

"The *son* of God," Socrates said, sounding puzzled. "And do Christians believe in God, too, or only his son?"

"What a fool you are!"

"I would not deny that."

"There is God the Father, and God the Son, and then there is the Holy Spirit."

"Ah," said Socrates. "And which one did your Atahuallpa believe in, then, when the strangler came for him?"

"None of them."

"And yet he died a Christian? Without believing in any of your three gods? How is that?"

"Because of the baptism," said Pizarro in rising annoyance. "What does it matter what he believed? The priest sprinkled the water on him! The priest said the words! If the rite is properly performed, the soul is saved regardless of what the man understands or believes! How else could you baptize an infant? An infant understands nothing and believes nothing—but he becomes a Christian when the water touches him!"

"Much of this is mysterious to me," said Socrates. "But I see that you regard the king you killed as godly as well as wise, because he was washed by the water your gods require, and so you killed a good king who now lived in the embrace of your gods because of the baptism. Which seems wicked to me; and so this cannot be the place where the virtuous are sent after death, so it must be that I, too, was not virtuous, or else that I have misunderstood everything about this place and why we are in it."

"Damn you, are you trying to drive me crazy?" Pizarro roared, fumbling at the hilt of his sword. He drew it and waved it around in fury. "If you don't shut your mouth, I'll cut you in thirds!"

"Uh-oh," Tanner said. "So much for the dialectical method."

Socrates said mildly, "It isn't my intention to cause you any annoyance, my friend. I'm only trying to learn a few things."

"You are a fool!"

"That is certainly true, as I have already acknowledged several times. Well, if you mean to strike me with your sword, go ahead. But I don't think it'll accomplish very much."

"Damn you," Pizarro muttered. He stared at his sword and shook his head. "No. No, it won't do any good, will it? It would go through you like air. But you'd just stand there and let me try to cut you down, and not even blink, right? Right?" He shook his head. "And yet you aren't stupid. You argue like the shrewdest priest I've ever known."

"In truth I am stupid," said Socrates. "I know very little at all. But I strive constantly to attain some understanding of the world, or at least to understand something of myself."

Pizarro glared at him. "No," he said. "I won't buy this false pride of yours. I have a little understanding of people myself, old man. I'm onto your game."

"What game is that, Pizarro?"

"I can see your arrogance. I see that you believe you're the wisest man in the world, and that it's your mission to go around educating poor sword-waving fools like me. And you pose as a fool to disarm your adversaries before you humiliate them."

"Score one for Pizarro," Richardson said. "He's wise to Socrates' little tricks, all right."

"Maybe he's read some Plato," Tanner suggested.

"He was illiterate."

"That was then. This is now."

"Not guilty," said Richardson. "He's operating on peasant shrewdness alone, and you damned well know it."

"I wasn't being serious," Tanner said. He leaned forward, peering toward the holotank. "God, what an astonishing thing this is, listening to them going at it. They seem absolutely real."

"They are," said Richardson.

◥

"No, Pizarro, I am not wise at all," Socrates said. "But, stupid as I am, it may be that I am not the least wise man who ever lived."

"You think you're wiser than I am, don't you?"

"How can I say? First tell me how wise you are."

"Wise enough to begin my life as a bastard tending pigs and finish it as Captain-General of Peru."

"Ah, then you must be very wise."

"I think so, yes."

"Yet you killed a wise king because he wasn't wise enough to worship God the way you wished him to. Was that so wise of you, Pizarro? How did his people take it, when they found out that their king had been killed?"

"They rose in rebellion against us. They destroyed their own temples and palaces, and hid their gold and silver from us, and burned their bridges, and fought us bitterly."

"Perhaps you could have made some better use of him by *not* killing him, do you think?"

"In the long run we conquered them and made them Christians. It was what we intended to accomplish."

"But the same thing might have been accomplished in a wiser way?"

"Perhaps," said Pizarro grudgingly. "Still, we accomplished it. That's the main thing, isn't it? We did what we set out to do. If there was a better way, so be it. Angels do things perfectly. We were no angels, but we achieved what we came for, and so be it, Socrates. So be it."

◥

"I'd call that one a draw," said Tanner.

"Agreed."

"It's a terrific game they're playing."

"I wonder who we can use to play it next," said Richardson.

"I wonder what we can do with this besides using it to play games," said Tanner.

◥

"Let me tell you a story," said Socrates. "The oracle at Delphi once said to a friend of mine, 'There is no man wiser than Socrates,' but I doubted that very much, and it troubled me to hear the oracle saying something that I knew was so far from the truth. So I decided to look for a man who was obviously wiser than I was. There was a politician in Athens who was famous for his wisdom, and I went to him and questioned him about many things. After I had listened to him for a time, I came to see that though many people, and most of all he himself, thought that he was wise, yet he was not wise. He only imagined that he was wise. So I realized that I must be wiser than he. Neither of us knew anything that was really worthwhile, but he knew nothing and thought that he knew, whereas I neither knew anything nor thought that I did. At least on one point, then, I was wiser than he: I didn't think that I knew what I didn't know."

"Is this intended to mock me, Socrates?"

"I feel only the deepest respect for you, friend Pizarro. But let me continue. I went to other wise men, and they, too, though sure of their wisdom, could never give me a clear answer to anything. Those whose reputations for wisdom were the highest seemed to have the least of it. I went to the great poets and playwrights. There was wisdom in their works, for the gods had inspired them, but that did not make *them* wise, though they thought that it had. I went to the stonemasons and potters and other craftsmen. They were wise in their own skills, but most of them seemed to think that that made them wise in everything, which did not appear to be the case. And so it went. I was unable to find anyone who showed true wisdom. So perhaps the oracle was right: that although I am an ignorant man, there is no man wiser than I am. But oracles often are right without there being much value in it, for I think that all she was saying was that no man is wise at all, that wisdom is reserved for the gods. What do you say, Pizarro?"

"I say that you are a great fool, and very ugly besides."

"You speak the truth. So, then, you are wise after all. And honest."

"Honest, you say? I won't lay claim to that. Honesty's a game for fools. I lied whenever I needed to. I cheated. I went back on my word. I'm not proud of that, mind you. It's simply what you have to do to get on in the world. You think I wanted to tend pigs all my life? I wanted gold, Socrates! I wanted power over men! I wanted fame!"

"And did you get those things?"

"I got them all."

"And were they gratifying, Pizarro?"

Pizarro gave Socrates a long look. Then he pursed his lips and spat.

"They were worthless."

"Were they, do you think?"

"Worthless, yes. I have no illusions about that. But still it was better to have had them than not. In the long run, nothing has any meaning, old man. In the long run we're all dead, the honest man and the villain, the king and the fool. Life's a cheat. They tell us to strive, to conquer, to gain—and for what? What? For a few years of strutting around. Then it's taken away, as if it had never been. A cheat, I say." Pizarro paused. He stared at his hands as though he had never seen them before. "Did I say all that just now? Did I mean it?" He laughed. "Well, I suppose I did. Still, life is all there is, so you want as much of it as you can. Which means getting gold, and power, and fame."

"Which you had. And apparently have no longer. Friend Pizarro, where are we now?"

"I wish I knew."

"So do I," said Socrates soberly.

⌄

"He's real," Richardson said. "They both are. The bugs are out of the system and we've got something spectacular here. Not only is this going to be of value to scholars, I think it's also going to be a tremendous entertainment gimmick, Harry."

"It's going to be much more than that," said Tanner in a strange voice.

"What do you mean by that?"

"I'm not sure yet," Tanner said. "But I'm definitely onto something big. It just began to hit me a couple of minutes ago, and it hasn't really taken shape yet. But it's something that might change the whole goddamned world."

Richardson looked amazed and bewildered.

"What the hell are you talking about, Harry?"

Tanner said, "A new way of settling political disputes, maybe. What would you say to a kind of combat-at-arms between one nation and another? Like a medieval tournament, so to speak. With each side using champions that we simulate for them—the greatest minds of all the past, brought back and placed in competition—" He shook his head. "Something like that. It needs a lot of working out, I know. But it's got possibilities."

"A medieval tournament—combat-at-arms, using simulations? Is that what you're saying?"

"Verbal combat. Not actual jousts, for Christ's sake."

"I don't see how—" Richardson began.

"Neither do I, not yet. I wish I hadn't even spoken of it."

"But—"

"Later, Lew. Later. Let me think about it a little while more."

⌄

"You don't have any idea what this place is?" Pizarro said.

"Not at all. But I certainly think this is no longer the world where we once dwelled. Are we dead, then? How can we say? You look alive to me."

"And you to me."

"Yet I think we are living some other kind of life. Here, give me your hand. Can you feel mine against yours?"

"No. I can't feel anything."

"Nor I. Yet I see two hands clasping. Two old men standing on a cloud, clasping hands." Socrates laughed. "What a great rogue you are, Pizarro!"

"Yes, of course. But do you know something, Socrates? You are, too. A windy old rogue. I like you. There were moments when you were driving me crazy with all your chatter, but you amused me, too. Were you really a soldier?"

"When my city asked me, yes."

"For a soldier, you're damned innocent about the way the world works, I have to say. But I guess I can teach you a thing or two."

"Will you?"

"Gladly," said Pizarro.

"I would be in your debt," Socrates said.

"Take Atahuallpa," Pizarro said. "How can I make you understand why I had to kill him? There weren't even two hundred of us, and twenty-four millions of them, and his word was law, and once he was gone they'd have no one to command them. So of *course* we had to get rid of him if we wanted to conquer them. And so we did, and then they fell."

"How simple you make it seem."

"Simple is what it was. Listen, old man, he would have died sooner or later anyway, wouldn't he? This way I made his death useful: to God, to the Church, to Spain. And to Francisco Pizarro. Can you understand that?"

"I think so," said Socrates. "But do you think King Atahuallpa did?"

"Any king would understand such things."

"Then he should have killed you the moment you set foot in his land."

"Unless God meant us to conquer him, and allowed him to understand that. Yes. Yes, that must have been what happened."

"Perhaps he is in this place, too, and we could ask him," said Socrates.

Pizarro's eyes brightened. "Mother of God, yes! A good idea! And if he didn't understand, why, I'll try to explain it to him. Maybe you'll help me. You know how to talk, how to move words around and around. What do you say? Would you help me?"

"If we meet him, I would like to talk with him," Socrates said. "I would indeed like to know if he agrees with you on the subject of the usefulness of his being killed by you."

Grinning, Pizarro said, "Slippery, you are! But I like you. I like you very much. Come. Let's go look for Atahuallpa."